JACOB'S ROOM
MRS DALLOWAY
TO THE LIGHTHOUSE
THE WAVES

VIRGINIA WOOLF was born Adeline Virginia Stephen on 25 January 1882 at 22 Hyde Park Gate, Kensington, London. Her parents, Leslie Stephen and Julia Duckworth, had strong literary associations, and Virginia had the run of her father's library, although, like other girls of her class, she did not go to school. In 1895 her mother died, and her first breakdown followed. Her father fell ill in 1902 and died two years later; Virginia suffered another breakdown. On her recovery she moved, with her brothers and sister, to Bloomsbury, where the now famous Bloomsbury Group was to congregate.

In 1905 she began to write for publication in the *Times Literary Supplement*. She was often ill, but managed to write, travel, do some adult-education teaching, work for female suffrage, and conduct a busy social life. In 1912 she married Leonard Woolf. By now *The Voyage Out* was in preparation, and was published in 1915 by her half-brother Gerald Duckworth. In 1917 she and Leonard installed a printing press and began to publish books under the imprint of the Hogarth Press. Duckworth published *Night and Day* in 1919, the year the Woolfs moved to Monk's House at Rodmell in Sussex, and in 1922 the Hogarth Press published *Jacob's Room*. The next years were very productive, and *Mrs Dalloway*, *To the Lighthouse*, *Orlando*, and *The Waves* appeared in quick succession.

Woolf had also written and published many shorter works of non-fiction during this time, including *The Common Reader* and *A Room of One's Own*. She struggled with *The Years* during the 1930s, eventually publishing it in 1937, followed by *Three Guineas* in 1938. Leaving war-torn London, she worked on *Between the Acts* at Monk's House, and finished it in February 1941. After that her health rapidly deteriorated, and on 28 March she drowned herself in the River Ouse near Rodmell.

Woolf's output was remarkable—nine novels, including some of the great masterpieces of the century—along with other writings and numerous journals and letters. Her refusal to compromise in her art has changed the way we view both narrative and the novel itself, and has made her one of the most influential writers in English.

VIRGINIA WOOLF

Jacob's Room

Mrs Dalloway

To the Lighthouse

The Waves

Oxford   New York
OXFORD UNIVERSITY PRESS

Oxford University Press, Walton Street, Oxford OX2 6DP

Oxford New York
Athens Auckland Bangkok Bombay
Calcutta Cape Town Dar es Salaam Delhi
Florence Hong Kong Istanbul Karachi
Kuala Lumpur Madras Madrid Melbourne
Mexico City Nairobi Paris Singapore
Taipei Tokyo Toronto

and associated companies in
Berlin Ibadan

Oxford is a trade mark of Oxford University Press

British Library Cataloguing in Publication Data
Data available
ISBN 0-19-282287-X

3 5 7 9 10 8 6 4

Printed in Great Britain by
Biddles Ltd
Guildford and King's Lynn

CONTENTS

A CHRONOLOGY OF
VIRGINIA WOOLF

1882   (25 Jan.) Born Adeline Virginia Stephen.

1895   (5 May) Death of mother, Julia Stephen. VW's first breakdown.

1896   Travels in France with sister Vanessa.

1897   (19 July) Death of half-sister Stella. VW learning Greek.

1899   VW's brother Thoby goes to Trinity College, Cambridge, where he forms friendships with Lytton Strachey, Leonard Woolf, Clive Bell, and others of the future Bloomsbury Group. (The other brother Adrian followed him to Trinity in 1902.)

1904   Death of father, Sir Leslie Stephen. In spring VW travels in Italy with Vanessa and friend Violet Dickinson. (May) VW has another serious collapse. Moves to Gordon Square.

1905   Travels in Spain and Portugal. Writes reviews and teaches at Morley College.

1906   Travels in Greece. (20 Nov.) Death of Thoby Stephen.

1907   Marriage of Vanessa to Clive Bell. VW moves with Adrian to Fitzroy Square. Works on a novel, *Melymbrosia* (working title for *The Voyage Out*).

1908   Visits Italy with the Bells.

1909   (17 Feb.) Lytton Strachey proposes marriage.

      First meets Lady Ottoline Morrell. Visits Florence and later Bayreuth.

1910   Roger Fry's first Post-Impressionist Exhibition.

1911   Travels to Turkey, where Vanessa is ill. Moves to Brunswick Square, sharing house with Adrian, Keynes, Duncan Grant, and Leonard Woolf.

1912   (10 Aug.) Marriage to Leonard Woolf; travels in Provence, Spain, and Italy. Moves to Clifford's Inn.

1913   Unwell most of summer. (9 Sept.) Suicide attempt.

1914   Moves to Richmond.

1915   Purchase of Hogarth House, Richmond. *The Voyage Out* published. Bout of violent madness.

1917   Hogarth Press commences publication with *The Mark on the Wall*. Begins work on *Night and Day*.

1918   Writes reviews and *Night and Day*; also sets type for the Press. (15 Nov.) First meets T. S. Eliot.

1919   Purchase of Monk's House, Rodmell. *Night and Day* published.

1920   Works on journalism and *Jacob's Room*.

1921   Ill for summer months. Finishes *Jacob's Room*.

1922   (14 Dec.) First meets V. Sackville-West. *Jacob's Room* published.

1923   Visits Spain. Works on first version of *Mrs Dalloway*.

1924   Purchase of lease on house in Tavistock Square. Gives lecture that became 'Mr Bennett and Mrs Brown'. Finishes *Mrs Dalloway*.

1925   *The Common Reader* published. *Mrs Dalloway* published. Ill during summer.

1926   Writes *To the Lighthouse*.

1927   *To the Lighthouse* published. Travels to Sicily. Begins *Orlando*.

1928   *Orlando* published.

1929   Travels to Berlin. *A Room of One's Own* published.

1930   Writes and rewrites *The Waves*.

1931   Tours in France. *The Waves* published. Writes *Flush*.

1932   Death of Lytton Strachey. *The Common Reader*, 2nd series, published. Begins *The Years*.

1933   *Flush* published.

1934   Works on *The Years*. Death of Roger Fry.

1935   Rewrites *The Years*. Reads for Fry biography.

1936   (May–Oct.) Ill. Finishes *The Years*. Begins *Three Guineas*.

1937   *The Years* published. Begins *Roger Fry*. Death in Spanish Civil War of Julian Bell, son of Vanessa.

1938   *Three Guineas* published. Works on *Roger Fry*, and thinks about *Between the Acts*.

1939   Woolfs move to Mecklenburgh Square, but live mostly at Monk's House. Works on *Between the Acts*.

1940   *Roger Fry* published. Mecklenburgh Square house damaged, house in Tavistock Square destroyed. (23 Nov.) Finishes *Between the Acts*.

1941   (26 Feb.) Revises *Between the Acts*. Becomes ill. (28 Mar.) Drowns herself in River Ouse. *Between the Acts* published.

Jacob's Room

'So of course,' wrote Betty Flanders, pressing her heels rather deeper in the sand, 'there was nothing for it but to leave.'

Slowly welling from the point of her gold nib, pale blue ink dissolved the full stop; for there her pen stuck; her eyes fixed, and tears slowly filled them. The entire bay quivered; the lighthouse wobbled; and she had the illusion that the mast of Mr Connor's little yacht was bending like a wax candle in the sun. She winked quickly. Accidents were awful things. She winked again. The mast was straight; the waves were regular; the lighthouse was upright; but the blot had spread.

'. . . nothing for it but to leave,' she read.

'Well, if Jacob doesn't want to play' (the shadow of Archer, her eldest son, fell across the notepaper and looked blue on the sand, and she felt chilly—it was the third of September already), 'if Jacob doesn't want to play'—what a horrid blot! It must be getting late.

'Where *is* that tiresome little boy?' she said. 'I don't see him. Run and find him. Tell him to come at once.' '. . . but mercifully,' she scribbled, ignoring the full stop, 'everything seems satisfactorily arranged, packed though we are like herrings in a barrel, and forced to stand the perambulator which the landlady quite naturally won't allow . . .'

Such were Betty Flanders's letters to Captain Barfoot—many-paged, tear-stained. Scarborough is seven hundred miles from Cornwall: Captain Barfoot is in Scarborough: Seabrook is dead. Tears made all the dahlias in her garden undulate in red waves and flashed the glass house in her eyes, and spangled the kitchen with bright knives, and made Mrs Jarvis, the rector's wife, think at church, while the hymn-tune played and Mrs Flanders bent low over her little boys' heads, that marriage is a fortress and widows stray solitary in the open fields, picking up stones, gleaning a few golden straws, lonely, unprotected, poor creatures. Mrs Flanders had been a widow these two years.

'Ja—cob! Ja—cob!' Archer shouted.

'Scarborough,' Mrs Flanders wrote on the envelope, and dashed a bold line beneath; it was her native town; the hub of the universe. But a stamp? She ferreted in her bag; then held it up mouth downwards; then fumbled in her lap, all so vigorously that Charles Steele in the Panama hat suspended his paint-brush.

Like the antennae of some irritable insect it positively trembled. Here was that woman moving—actually going to get up—confound her! He struck the canvas a hasty violet-black dab. For the landscape needed it. It was too pale—greys flowing into lavenders, and one star or a white gull suspended just so—too pale as usual. The critics would say it was too pale, for he was an unknown man exhibiting obscurely, a favourite with his landladies' children, wearing a cross on his watch chain, and much gratified if his landladies liked his pictures—which they often did.

'Ja—cob! Ja—cob!' Archer shouted.

Exasperated by the noise, yet loving children, Steele picked nervously at the dark little coils on his palette.

'I saw your brother—I saw your brother,' he said, nodding his head, as Archer lagged past him, trailing his spade, and scowling at the old gentleman in spectacles.

'Over there—by the rock,' Steele muttered, with his brush between his teeth, squeezing out raw sienna, and keeping his eyes fixed on Betty Flanders's back.

'Ja—cob! Ja—cob!' shouted Archer, lagging on after a second.

The voice had an extraordinary sadness. Pure from all body, pure from all passion, going out into the world, solitary, unanswered, breaking against rocks—so it sounded.

Steele frowned; but was pleased by the effect of the black—it was just *that* note which brought the rest together. 'Ah, one may learn to paint at fifty! There's Titian . . .' and so, having found the right tint, up he looked and saw to his horror a cloud over the bay.

Mrs Flanders rose, slapped her coat this side and that to get the sand off, and picked up her black parasol.

The rock was one of those tremendously solid brown, or rather black, rocks which emerge from the sand like something primitive. Rough with crinkled limpet shells and sparsely strewn with locks of dry seaweed, a small boy has to stretch his legs far apart, and indeed to feel rather heroic, before he gets to the top.

But there, on the very top, is a hollow full of water, with a sandy bottom; with a blob of jelly stuck to the side, and some mussels. A fish darts across. The fringe of yellow-brown seaweed flutters, and out pushes an opal-shelled crab——

'Oh, a huge crab,' Jacob murmured——
and begins his journey on weakly legs on the sandy bottom. Now! Jacob plunged his hand. The crab was cool and very light. But the water was thick with sand, and so, scrambling down, Jacob was about to jump, holding his bucket in front of him, when he saw, stretched entirely rigid, side by side, their faces very red, an enormous man and woman.

An enormous man and woman (it was early-closing day) were stretched motionless, with their heads on pocket-handkerchiefs, side by side, within a few feet of the sea, while two or three gulls gracefully skirted the incoming waves, and settled near their boots.

The large red faces lying on the bandanna handkerchiefs stared up at Jacob. Jacob stared down at them. Holding his bucket very carefully, Jacob then jumped deliberately and trotted away very nonchalantly at first, but faster and faster as the waves came creaming up to him and he had to swerve to avoid them, and the gulls rose in front of him and floated out and settled again a little farther on. A large black woman was sitting on the sand. He ran towards her.

'Nanny! Nanny!' he cried, sobbing the words out on the crest of each gasping breath.

The waves came round her. She was a rock. She was covered with the seaweed which pops when it is pressed. He was lost.

There he stood. His face composed itself. He was about to roar when, lying among the black sticks and straw under the cliff, he saw a whole skull—perhaps a cow's skull, a skull, perhaps, with the teeth in it. Sobbing, but absent-mindedly, he ran farther and farther away until he held the skull in his arms.

'There he is!' cried Mrs Flanders, coming round the rock and covering the whole space of the beach in a few seconds. 'What has he got hold of? Put it down, Jacob! Drop it this moment! Something horrid, I know. Why didn't you stay with us? Naughty little boy! Now put it down. Now come along both of you,' and she swept round, holding Archer by one hand and fumbling for Jacob's arm with the other. But he ducked down and picked up the sheep's jaw, which was loose.

Swinging her bag, clutching her parasol, holding Archer's hand, and telling the story of the gunpowder explosion in which poor Mr Curnow had lost his eye, Mrs Flanders hurried up the steep lane, aware all the time in the depths of her mind of some buried discomfort.

There on the sand not far from the lovers lay the old sheep's skull without its jaw. Clean, white, wind-swept, sand-rubbed, a more unpolluted piece of bone existed nowhere on the coast of Cornwall. The

sea holly would grow through the eye-sockets; it would turn to powder,
or some golfer, hitting his ball one fine day, would disperse a little
dust.—No, but not in lodgings, thought Mrs Flanders. It's a great
experiment coming so far with young children. There's no man to help
with the perambulator. And Jacob is such a handful; so obstinate
already.

'Throw it away, dear, do,' she said, as they got into the road; but
Jacob squirmed away from her; and the wind rising, she took out her
bonnet-pin, looked at the sea, and stuck it in afresh. The wind was
rising. The waves showed that uneasiness, like something alive, restive,
expecting the whip, of waves before a storm. The fishing-boats were
leaning to the water's brim. A pale yellow light shot across the purple
sea; and shut. The lighthouse was lit. 'Come along,' said Betty Flanders.
The sun blazed in their faces and gilded the great blackberries trembling
out from the hedge which Archer tried to strip as they passed.

'Don't lag, boys. You've got nothing to change into,' said Betty,
pulling them along, and looking with uneasy emotion at the earth
displayed so luridly, with sudden sparks of light from greenhouses in
gardens, with a sort of yellow and black mutability, against this blazing
sunset, this astonishing agitation and vitality of colour, which stirred
Betty Flanders and made her think of responsibility and danger. She
gripped Archer's hand. On she plodded up the hill.

'What did I ask you to remember?' she said.

'I don't know,' said Archer.

'Well, I don't know either,' said Betty, humorously and simply, and
who shall deny that this blankness of mind, when combined with
profusion, mother wit, old wives' tales, haphazard ways, moments of
astonishing daring, humour, and sentimentality—who shall deny that
in these respects every woman is nicer than any man?

Well, Betty Flanders, to begin with.

She had her hand upon the garden gate.

'The meat!' she exclaimed, striking the latch down.

She had forgotten the meat.

There was Rebecca at the window.

The bareness of Mrs Pearce's front room was fully displayed at ten
o'clock at night when a powerful oil lamp stood on the middle of the
table. The harsh light fell on the garden; cut straight across the lawn; lit
up a child's bucket and a purple aster and reached the hedge. Mrs
Flanders had left her sewing on the table. There were her large reels of

white cotton and her steel spectacles; her needle-case; her brown wool wound round an old postcard. There were the bulrushes and the *Strand* magazines; and the linoleum sandy from the boys' boots. A daddy-long-legs shot from corner to corner and hit the lamp globe. The wind blew straight dashes of rain across the window, which flashed silver as they passed through the light. A single leaf tapped hurriedly, persistently, upon the glass. There was a hurricane out at sea.

Archer could not sleep.

Mrs Flanders stooped over him. 'Think of the fairies,' said Betty Flanders. 'Think of the lovely, lovely birds settling down on their nests. Now shut your eyes and see the old mother bird with a worm in her beak. Now turn and shut your eyes,' she murmured, 'and shut your eyes.'

The lodging-house seemed full of gurgling and rushing; the cistern overflowing; water bubbling and squeaking and running along the pipes and streaming down the windows.

'What's all that water rushing in?' murmured Archer.

'It's only the bath water running away,' said Mrs Flanders.

Something snapped out of doors.

'I say, won't that steamer sink?' said Archer, opening his eyes.

'Of course it won't,' said Mrs Flanders. 'The Captain's in bed long ago. Shut your eyes, and think of the fairies, fast asleep, under the flowers.'

'I thought he'd never get off—such a hurricane,' she whispered to Rebecca, who was bending over a spirit-lamp in the small room next door. The wind rushed outside, but the small flame of the spirit-lamp burnt quietly, shaded from the cot by a book stood on edge.

'Did he take his bottle well?' Mrs Flanders whispered, and Rebecca nodded and went to the cot and turned down the quilt, and Mrs Flanders bent over and looked anxiously at the baby, asleep, but frowning. The window shook, and Rebecca stole like a cat and wedged it. The two women murmured over the spirit-lamp, plotting the eternal conspiracy of hush and clean bottles while the wind raged and gave a sudden wrench at the cheap fastenings.

Both looked round at the cot. Their lips were pursed. Mrs Flanders crossed over to the cot.

'Asleep?' whispered Rebecca, looking at the cot.

Mrs Flanders nodded.

'Good-night, Rebecca,' Mrs Flanders murmured, and Rebecca called her ma'am, though they were conspirators plotting the eternal conspiracy of hush and clean bottles.

Mrs Flanders had left the lamp burning in the front room. There were her spectacles, her sewing; and a letter with the Scarborough postmark. She had not drawn the curtains either.

The light blazed out across the patch of grass; fell on the child's green bucket with the gold line round it, and upon the aster which trembled violently beside it. For the wind was tearing across the coast, hurling itself at the hills, and leaping, in sudden gusts, on top of its own back. How it spread over the town in the hollow! How the lights seemed to wink and quiver in its fury, lights in the harbour, lights in bedroom windows high up! And rolling dark waves before it, it raced over the Atlantic, jerking the stars above the ships this way and that.

There was a click in the front sitting-room. Mr Pearce had extinguished the lamp. The garden went out. It was but a dark patch. Every inch was rained upon. Every blade of grass was bent by rain. Eyelids would have been fastened down by the rain. Lying on one's back one would have seen nothing but muddle and confusion—clouds turning and turning, and something yellow-tinted and sulphurous in the darkness.

The little boys in the front bedroom had thrown off their blankets and lay under the sheets. It was hot; rather sticky and steamy. Archer lay spread out, with one arm striking across the pillow. He was flushed; and when the heavy curtain blew out a little he turned and half-opened his eyes. The wind actually stirred the cloth on the chest of drawers, and let in a little light, so that the sharp edge of the chest of drawers was visible, running straight up, until a white shape bulged out; and a silver streak showed in the looking-glass.

In the other bed by the door Jacob lay asleep, fast asleep, profoundly unconscious. The sheep's jaw with the big yellow teeth in it lay at his feet. He had kicked it against the iron bed-rail.

Outside the rain poured down more directly and powerfully as the wind fell in the early hours of the morning. The aster was beaten to the earth. The child's bucket was half-full of rainwater; and the opal-shelled crab slowly circled round the bottom, trying with its weakly legs to climb the steep side; trying again and falling back, and trying again and again.

II

'Mrs Flanders'—'Poor Betty Flanders'—'Dear Betty'—'She's very attractive still'—'Odd she don't marry again!' 'There's Captain Barfoot to be sure—calls every Wednesday as regular as clockwork, and never brings his wife.'

'But that's Ellen Barfoot's fault,' the ladies of Scarborough said. 'She don't put herself out for no one.'

'A man likes to have a son—that we know.'

'Some tumours have to be cut; but the sort my mother had you bear with for years and years, and never even have a cup of tea brought up to you in bed.'

(Mrs Barfoot was an invalid.)

Elizabeth Flanders, of whom this and much more than this had been said and would be said, was, of course, a widow in her prime. She was half-way between forty and fifty. Years and sorrow between them; the death of Seabrook, her husband; three boys; poverty; a house on the outskirts of Scarborough; her brother, poor Morty's, downfall and possible demise—for where was he? what was he? Shading her eyes, she looked along the road for Captain Barfoot—yes, there he was, punctual as ever; the attentions of the Captain—all ripened Betty Flanders, enlarged her figure, tinged her face with jollity, and flooded her eyes for no reason that any one could see perhaps three times a day.

True, there's no harm in crying for one's husband, and the tombstone, though plain, was a solid piece of work, and on summer's days when the widow brought her boys to stand there one felt kindly towards her. Hats were raised higher than usual; wives tugged their husbands' arms. Seabrook lay six foot beneath, dead these many years; enclosed in three shells; the crevices sealed with lead, so that, had earth and wood been glass, doubtless his very face lay visible beneath, the face of a young man whiskered, shapely, who had gone out duck-shooting and refused to change his boots.

'Merchant of this city,' the tombstone said; though why Betty Flanders had chosen so to call him when, as many still remembered, he had only sat behind an office window for three months, and before that had broken horses, ridden to hounds, farmed a few fields, and run a little wild—well, she had to call him something. An example for the boys.

Had he, then, been nothing? An unanswerable question, since even if it weren't the habit of the undertaker to close the eyes, the light so soon goes out of them. At first, part of herself; now one of a company, he had merged in the grass, the sloping hillside, the thousand white stones, some slanting, others upright, the decayed wreaths, the crosses of green tin, the narrow yellow paths, and the lilacs that drooped in April, with a scent like that of an invalid's bedroom, over the churchyard wall. Seabrook was now all that; and when, with her skirt hitched up, feeding the chickens, she heard the bell for service or funeral, that was Seabrook's voice—the voice of the dead.

The rooster had been known to fly on her shoulder and peck her neck, so that now she carried a stick or took one of the children with her when she went to feed the fowls.

'Wouldn't you like my knife, mother?' said Archer.

Sounding at the same moment as the bell, her son's voice mixed life and death inextricably, exhilaratingly.

'What a big knife for a small boy!' she said. She took it to please him. Then the rooster flew out of the hen-house, and, shouting to Archer to shut the door into the kitchen garden, Mrs Flanders set her meal down, clucked for the hens, went bustling about the orchard, and was seen from over the way by Mrs Cranch, who, beating her mat against the wall, held it for a moment suspended while she observed to Mrs Page next door that Mrs Flanders was in the orchard with the chickens.

Mrs Page, Mrs Cranch, and Mrs Garfit could see Mrs Flanders in the orchard because the orchard was a piece of Dods Hill enclosed; and Dods Hill dominated the village. No words can exaggerate the importance of Dods Hill. It was the earth; the world against the sky; the horizon of how many glances can best be computed by those who have lived all their lives in the same village, only leaving it once to fight in the Crimea, like old George Garfit, leaning over his garden gate smoking his pipe. The progress of the sun was measured by it; the tint of the day laid against it to be judged.

'Now she's going up the hill with little John,' said Mrs Cranch to Mrs Garfit, shaking her mat for the last time, and bustling indoors.

Opening the orchard gate, Mrs Flanders walked to the top of Dods Hill, holding John by the hand. Archer and Jacob ran in front or lagged behind; but they were in the Roman fortress when she came there, and shouting out what ships were to be seen in the bay. For there was a magnificent view—moors behind, sea in front, and the whole of Scarborough from one end to the other laid out flat like a puzzle. Mrs Flanders, who was growing stout, sat down in the fortress and looked about her.

The entire gamut of the view's changes should have been known to her; its winter aspect, spring, summer, and autumn; how storms came up from the sea; how the moors shuddered and brightened as the clouds went over; she should have noted the red spot where the villas were building; and the criss-cross of lines where the allotments were cut; and the diamond flash of little glass houses in the sun. Or, if details like these escaped her, she might have let her fancy play upon the gold tint of the sea at sunset, and thought how it lapped in coins of gold upon the shingle. Little pleasure boats shoved out into it; the black arm of the pier hoarded it up. The whole city was pink and gold; domed; mist-wreathed; resonant; strident. Banjoes strummed; the parade smelt of tar which stuck to the heels; goats suddenly cantered their carriages through crowds. It was observed how well the Corporation had laid out the flower-beds. Sometimes a straw hat was blown away. Tulips burnt in the sun. Numbers of sponge-bag trousers were stretched in rows. Purple bonnets fringed soft, pink, querulous faces on pillows in bath chairs. Triangular hoardings were wheeled along by men in white coats. Captain George Boase had caught a monster shark. One side of the triangular hoarding said so in red, blue, and yellow letters; each line ended with three differently coloured notes of exclamation.

So that was a reason for going down into the Aquarium, where the sallow blinds, the stale smell of spirits of salt, the bamboo chairs, the tables with ash-trays, the revolving fish, the attendant knitting behind six or seven chocolate boxes (often she was quite alone with the fish for hours at a time) remained in the mind as part of the monster shark, he himself being only a flabby yellow receptacle, like an empty Gladstone bag in a tank. No one had ever been cheered by the Aquarium; but the faces of those emerging quickly lost their dim, chilled expression when they perceived that it was only by standing in a queue that one could be admitted to the pier. Once through the turnstiles, everyone walked for a yard or two very briskly; some flagged at this stall; others at that. But it was the band that drew them all to it finally; even the fishermen on the lower pier taking up their pitch within its range.

The band played in the Moorish kiosk. Number nine went up on the board. It was a waltz tune. The pale girls, the old widow lady, the three Jews lodging in the same boarding-house, the dandy, the major, the horse-dealer, and the gentleman of independent means, all wore the same blurred, drugged expression, and through the chinks in the planks at their feet they could see the green summer waves, peacefully, amiably, swaying round the iron pillars of the pier.

But there was a time when none of this had any existence (thought the young man leaning against the railings). Fix your eyes upon the lady's skirt; the grey one will do—above the pink silk stockings. It changes; drapes her ankles—the nineties; then it amplifies—the seventies; now it's burnished red and stretched above a crinoline—the sixties;

a tiny black foot wearing a white cotton stocking peeps out. Still sitting there? Yes—she's still on the pier. The silk now is sprigged with roses, but somehow one no longer sees so clearly. There's no pier beneath us. The heavy chariot may swing along the turnpike road, but there's no pier for it to stop at, and how grey and turbulent the sea is in the seventeenth century! Let's to the museum. Cannon-balls; arrow-heads; Roman glass and a forceps green with verdigris. The Rev. Jaspar Floyd dug them up at his own expense early in the forties in the Roman camp on Dods Hill—see the little ticket with the faded writing on it.

And now, what's the next thing to see in Scarborough?

Mrs Flanders sat on the raised circle of the Roman camp, patching Jacob's breeches; only looking up as she sucked the end of her cotton, or when some insect dashed at her, boomed in her ear, and was gone.

John kept trotting up and slapping down in her lap grass or dead leaves which he called 'tea', and she arranged them methodically but absent-mindedly, laying the flowery heads of the grasses together, thinking how Archer had been awake again last night; the church clock was ten or thirteen minutes fast; she wished she could buy Garfit's acre.

'That's an orchid leaf, Johnny. Look at the little brown spots. Come, my dear. We must go home. Ar—cher! Ja—cob!'

'Ar—cher—Ja—cob!' Johnny piped after her, pivoting round on his heel, and strewing the grass and leaves in his hands as if he were sowing seed. Archer and Jacob jumped up from behind the mound where they had been crouching with the intention of springing upon their mother unexpectedly, and they all began to walk slowly home.

'Who is that?' said Mrs Flanders, shading her eyes.

'That old man in the road?' said Archer, looking below.

'He's not an old man,' said Mrs Flanders. 'He's—no, he's not—I thought it was the Captain, but it's Mr Floyd. Come along, boys.'

'Oh, bother Mr Floyd!' said Jacob, switching off a thistle's head, for he knew already that Mr Floyd was going to teach them Latin, as indeed he did for three years in his spare time, out of kindness, for there was no other gentleman in the neighbourhood whom Mrs Flanders could have asked to do such a thing, and the elder boys were getting beyond her, and must be got ready for school, and it was more than most clergymen would have done, coming round after tea, or having them in his own room—as he could fit it in—for the parish was a very large one, and Mr Floyd, like his father before him, visited cottages miles away on the moors, and, like old Mr Floyd, was a great scholar, which made it so unlikely—she had never dreamt of such a thing. Ought she to have guessed? But let alone being a scholar he was eight years younger than she was. She knew his mother—old Mrs Floyd. She had tea there. And it was that very evening when she came back from having tea with old Mrs Floyd that she found the note in the hall and took it into the kitchen with her when she went to give Rebecca the fish, thinking it must be something about the boys.

'Mr Floyd brought it himself, did he?—I think the cheese must be in the parcel in the hall—oh, in the hall——' for she was reading. No, it was not about the boys.

'Yes, enough for fish-cakes tomorrow certainly—Perhaps Captain Barfoot——' she had come to the word 'love'. She went into the garden and read, leaning against the walnut tree to steady herself. Up and down went her breast. Seabrook came so vividly before her. She shook her head and was looking through her tears at the little shifting leaves against the yellow sky when three geese, half-running, half-flying, scuttled across the lawn with Johnny behind them, brandishing a stick.

Mrs Flanders flushed with anger.

'How many times have I told you?' she cried, and seized him and snatched his stick away from him.

'But they'd escaped!' he cried, struggling to get free.

'You're a very naughty boy. If I've told you once, I've told you a thousand times. I won't *have* you chasing the geese!' she said, and crumpling Mr Floyd's letter in her hand, she held Johnny fast and herded the geese back into the orchard.

'How could I think of marriage!' she said to herself bitterly, as she fastened the gate with a piece of wire. She had always disliked red hair in men, she thought, thinking of Mr Floyd's appearance, that night when the boys had gone to bed. And pushing her work-box away, she drew the blotting-paper towards her, and read Mr Floyd's letter again, and her breast went up and down when she came to the word 'love', but not so fast this time, for she saw Johnny chasing the geese, and knew that it was impossible for her to marry anyone—let alone Mr Floyd, who was so much younger than she was, but what a nice man—and such a scholar too.

'Dear Mr Floyd,' she wrote.—'Did I forget about the cheese?' she wondered, laying down her pen. No, she had told Rebecca that the cheese was in the hall. 'I am much surprised . . .' she wrote.

But the letter which Mr Floyd found on the table when he got up early next morning did not begin 'I am much surprised,' and it was such a motherly, respectful, inconsequent, regretful letter that he kept it for many years; long after his marriage with Miss Wimbush, of Andover; long after he had left the village. For he asked for a parish in Sheffield, which was given him; and, sending for Archer, Jacob, and John to say good-bye, he told them to choose whatever they liked in his study to remember him by. Archer chose a paper-knife, because he did not like to choose anything too good; Jacob chose the works of Byron in one volume; John, who was still too young to make a proper choice, chose Mr Floyd's kitten, which his brothers thought an absurd choice, but Mr Floyd upheld him when he said: 'It has fur like you.' Then Mr Floyd spoke about the King's Navy (to which Archer was going); and about Rugby (to which Jacob was going); and next day he received a silver salver and went—first to Sheffield, where he met Miss Wimbush, who was on a visit to her uncle, then to Hackney—then to Maresfield House, of which he became the principal, and finally, becoming editor of a well-known series of Ecclesiastical Biographies, he retired to Hampstead with his wife and daughter, and is often to be seen feeding the ducks on Leg of Mutton Pond. As for Mrs Flanders's letter—when he looked for it the other day he could not find it, and did not like to ask his wife whether she had put it away. Meeting Jacob in Piccadilly lately, he recognized him after three seconds. But Jacob had grown such a fine young man that Mr Floyd did not like to stop him in the street.

'Dear me,' said Mrs Flanders, when she read in the *Scarborough and Harrogate Courier* that the Rev. Andrew Floyd, etc., etc., had been made Principal of Maresfield House, 'that must be our Mr Floyd'.

A slight gloom fell upon the table. Jacob was helping himself to jam; the postman was talking to Rebecca in the kitchen; there was a bee humming at the yellow flower which nodded at the open window. They were all alive, that is to say, while poor Mr Floyd was becoming Principal of Maresfield House.

Mrs Flanders got up and went over to the fender and stroked Topaz on the neck behind the ears.

'Poor Topaz,' she said (for Mr Floyd's kitten was now a very old cat, a little mangy behind the ears, and one of these days would have to be killed).

'Poor old Topaz,' said Mrs Flanders, as he stretched himself out in the sun, and she smiled, thinking how she had had him gelded, and how she did not like red hair in men. Smiling, she went into the kitchen.

Jacob drew rather a dirty pocket-handkerchief across his face. He went upstairs to his room.

The stag-beetle dies slowly (it was John who collected the beetles). Even on the second day its legs were supple. But the butterflies were dead. A whiff of rotten eggs had vanquished the pale clouded yellows which came pelting across the orchard and up Dods Hill and away on to the moor, now lost behind a furze bush, then off again helter skelter in a broiling sun. A fritillary basked on a white stone in the Roman camp. From the valley came the sound of church bells. They were all eating roast beef in Scarborough; for it was Sunday when Jacob caught the pale clouded yellows in the clover field, eight miles from home.

Rebecca had caught the death's-head moth in the kitchen.

A strong smell of camphor came from the butterfly boxes.

Mixed with the smell of camphor was the unmistakable smell of seaweed. Tawny ribbons hung on the door. The sun beat straight upon them.

The upper wings of the moth which Jacob held were undoubtedly marked with kidney-shaped spots of a fulvous hue. But there was no crescent upon the underwing. The tree had fallen the night he caught it. There had been a volley of pistol-shots suddenly in the depths of the wood. And his mother had taken him for a burglar when he came home late. The only one of her sons who never obeyed her, she said.

Morris called it 'an extremely local insect found in damp or marshy places'. But Morris is sometimes wrong. Sometimes Jacob, choosing a very fine pen, made a correction in the margin.

The tree had fallen, though it was a windless night, and the lantern, stood upon the ground, had lit up the still green leaves and the dead beech leaves. It was a dry place. A toad was there. And the red underwing had circled round the light and flashed and gone. The red underwing had never come back, though Jacob had waited. It was after twelve when he crossed the lawn and saw his mother in the bright room, playing patience, sitting up.

'How you frightened me!' she had cried. She thought something dreadful had happened. And he woke Rebecca, who had to be up so early.

There he stood pale, come out of the depths of darkness, in the hot room, blinking at the light.

No, it could not be a straw-bordered underwing.

The mowing-machine always wanted oiling. Barnet turned it under Jacob's window, and it creaked—creaked, and rattled across the lawn and creaked again.

Now it was clouding over.

Back came the sun, dazzlingly.

It fell like an eye upon the stirrups, and then suddenly and yet very gently rested upon the bed, upon the alarum clock, and upon the butterfly box stood open. The pale clouded yellows had pelted over the moor; they had zigzagged across the purple clover. The fritillaries flaunted along the hedgerows. The blues settled on little bones lying on the turf with the sun beating on them, and the painted ladies and the peacocks feasted upon bloody entrails dropped by a hawk. Miles away from home, in a hollow among teasles beneath a ruin, he had found the commas. He had seen a white admiral circling higher and higher round an oak tree, but he had never caught it. An old cottage woman living alone, high up, had told him of a purple butterfly which came every summer to her garden. The fox cubs played in the gorse in the early morning, she told him. And if you looked out at dawn you could always see two badgers. Sometimes they knocked each other over like two boys fighting, she said.

'You won't go far this afternoon, Jacob,' said his mother, popping her head in at the door, 'for the Captain's coming to say good-bye.' It was the last day of the Easter holidays.

Wednesday was Captain Barfoot's day. He dressed himself very neatly in blue serge, took his rubber-shod stick—for he was lame and wanted two fingers on the left hand, having served his country—and set out from the house with the flagstaff precisely at four o'clock in the afternoon.

At three Mr Dickens, the bath-chair man, had called for Mrs Barfoot.

'Move me,' she would say to Mr Dickens, after sitting on the esplanade for fifteen minutes. And again, 'That'll do, thank you, Mr Dickens.' At the first command he would seek the sun; at the second he would stay the chair there in the bright strip.

An old inhabitant himself, he had much in common with Mrs Barfoot—James Coppard's daughter. The drinking-fountain, where West Street joins Broad Street, is the gift of James Coppard, who was mayor at the time of Queen Victoria's jubilee, and Coppard is painted upon municipal watering-carts and over shop windows, and upon the zinc blinds of solicitors' consulting-room windows. But Ellen Barfoot never visited the Aquarium (though she had known Captain Boase who had caught the shark quite well), and when the men came by with the posters she eyed them superciliously, for she knew that she would never see the Pierrots, or the brothers Zeno, or Daisy Budd and her troupe of performing seals. For Ellen Barfoot in her bath-chair on the esplanade was a prisoner—civilization's prisoner—all the bars of her cage falling across the esplanade on sunny days when the town hall, the drapery stores, the swimming-bath, and the memorial hall striped the ground with shadow.

An old inhabitant himself, Mr Dickens would stand a little behind her, smoking his pipe. She would ask him questions—who people were—who now kept Mr Jones's shop—then about the season—and had Mrs Dickens tried, whatever it might be—the words issuing from her lips like crumbs of dry biscuit.

She closed her eyes. Mr Dickens took a turn. The feelings of a man had not altogether deserted him, though as you saw him coming towards you, you noticed how one knobbed black boot swung tremulously in front of the other; how there was a shadow between his waistcoat and his trousers; how he leant forward unsteadily, like an old horse who finds himself suddenly out of the shafts drawing no cart. But as Mr Dickens sucked in the smoke and puffed it out again, the feelings of a man were perceptible in his eyes. He was thinking how Captain Barfoot was now on his way to Mount Pleasant; Captain Barfoot, his master. For at home in the little sitting-room above the mews, with the canary in the window, and the girls at the sewing-machine, and Mrs Dickens huddled up with the rheumatics—at home where he was made little of, the thought of being in the employ of Captain Barfoot supported him. He liked to think that while he chatted with Mrs Barfoot on the front, he helped the Captain on his way to Mrs Flanders. He, a man, was in charge of Mrs Barfoot, a woman.

Turning, he saw that she was chatting with Mrs Rogers. Turning again, he saw that Mrs Rogers had moved on. So he came back to the bath-chair, and Mrs Barfoot asked him the time, and he took out his great silver watch and told her the time very obligingly, as if he knew a great deal more about the time and everything than she did. But Mrs Barfoot knew that Captain Barfoot was on his way to Mrs Flanders.

Indeed he was well on his way there, having left the tram, and seeing Dods Hill to the south-east, green against a blue sky that was suffused with dust colour on the horizon. He was marching up the hill. In spite of his lameness there was something military in his approach. Mrs Jarvis, as she came out of the Rectory gate, saw him coming, and her Newfoundland dog, Nero, slowly swept his tail from side to side.

'Oh, Captain Barfoot!' Mrs Jarvis exclaimed.

'Good-day, Mrs Jarvis,' said the Captain.

They walked on together, and when they reached Mrs Flanders's gate Captain Barfoot took off his tweed cap, and said, bowing very courteously:

'Good-day to you, Mrs Jarvis.'

And Mrs Jarvis walked on alone.

She was going to walk on the moor. Had she again been pacing her
lawn late at night? Had she again tapped on the study window and
cried: 'Look at the moon, look at the moon, Herbert!'

And Herbert looked at the moon.

Mrs Jarvis walked on the moor when she was unhappy, going as far
as a certain saucer-shaped hollow, though she always meant to go to a
more distant ridge; and there she sat down, and took out the little book
hidden beneath her cloak and read a few lines of poetry, and looked
about her. She was not very unhappy, and, seeing that she was forty-
five, never perhaps would be very unhappy, desperately unhappy that
is, and leave her husband, and ruin a good man's career, as she
sometimes threatened.

Still there is no need to say what risks a clergyman's wife runs when
she walks on the moor. Short, dark, with kindling eyes, a pheasant's
feather in her hat, Mrs Jarvis was just the sort of woman to lose her
faith upon the moors—to confound her God with the universal that is—
but she did not lose her faith, did not leave her husband, never read her
poem through, and went on walking the moors, looking at the moon
behind the elm trees, and feeling as she sat on the grass high above
Scarborough . . . Yes, yes, when the lark soars; when the sheep, moving
a step or two onwards, crop the turf, and at the same time set their bells
tinkling; when the breeze first blows, then dies down, leaving the cheek
kissed; when the ships on the sea below seem to cross each other and
pass on as if drawn by an invisible hand; when there are distant
concussions in the air and phantom horsemen galloping, ceasing; when
the horizon swims blue, green, emotional—then Mrs Jarvis, heaving a
sigh, thinks to herself, 'If only some one could give me . . . if I could give
some one . . .' But she does not know what she wants to give, nor who
could give it her.

'Mrs Flanders stepped out only five minutes ago, Captain,' said
Rebecca. Captain Barfoot sat him down in the arm-chair to wait.
Resting his elbows on the arms, putting one hand over the other, sticking
his lame leg straight out, and placing the stick with the rubber ferrule
beside it, he sat perfectly still. There was something rigid about him.
Did he think? Probably the same thoughts again and again. But were
they 'nice' thoughts, interesting thoughts? He was a man with a temper;
tenacious; faithful. Women would have felt, 'Here is law. Here is order.
Therefore we must cherish this man. He is on the Bridge at night,' and,
handing him his cup, or whatever it might be, would run on to visions

of shipwreck and disaster, in which all the passengers come tumbling from their cabins, and there is the captain, buttoned in his pea-jacket, matched with the storm, vanquished by it but by none other. 'Yet I have a soul,' Mrs Jarvis would bethink her, as Captain Barfoot suddenly blew his nose in a great red bandanna handkerchief, 'and it's the man's stupidity that's the cause of this, and the storm's my storm as well as his' . . . so Mrs Jarvis would bethink her when the Captain dropped in to see them and found Herbert out, and spent two or three hours, almost silent, sitting in the arm-chair. But Betty Flanders thought nothing of the kind.

'Oh, Captain,' said Mrs Flanders, bursting into the drawing-room, 'I had to run after Barker's man . . . I hope Rebecca . . . I hope Jacob . . .'

She was very much out of breath, yet not at all upset, and as she put down the hearth-brush which she had bought of the oil-man, she said it was hot, flung the window further open, straightened a cover, picked up a book, as if she were very confident, very fond of the Captain, and a great many years younger than he was. Indeed, in her blue apron she did not look more than thirty-five. He was well over fifty.

She moved her hands about the table; the Captain moved his head from side to side, and made little sounds, as Betty went on chattering, completely at his ease—after twenty years.

'Well,' he said at length. 'I've heard from Mr Polegate.'

He had heard from Mr Polegate that he could advise nothing better than to send a boy to one of the universities.

'Mr Floyd was at Cambridge . . . no, at Oxford . . . well, at one or the other,' said Mrs Flanders.

She looked out of the window. Little windows, and the lilac and green of the garden were reflected in her eyes.

'Archer is doing very well,' she said. 'I have a very nice report from Captain Maxwell.'

'I will leave you the letter to show Jacob,' said the Captain, putting it clumsily back in its envelope.

'Jacob is after his butterflies as usual,' said Mrs Flanders irritably, but was surprised by a sudden afterthought, 'Cricket begins this week, of course.'

'Edward Jenkinson has handed in his resignation,' said Captain Barfoot.

'Then you will stand for the Council?' Mrs Flanders exclaimed, looking the Captain full in the face.

'Well, about that,' Captain Barfoot began, settling himself rather deeper in his chair.

Jacob Flanders, therefore, went up to Cambridge in October, 1906.

III

'This is not a smoking-carriage,' Mrs Norman protested, nervously but very feebly, as the door swung open and a powerfully built young man jumped in. He seemed not to hear her. The train did not stop before it reached Cambridge, and here she was shut up alone, in a railway carriage, with a young man.

She touched the spring of her dressing-case, and ascertained that the scent-bottle and a novel from Mudie's were both handy (the young man was standing up with his back to her; putting his bag in the rack). She would throw the scent-bottle with her right hand, she decided, and tug the communication cord with her left. She was fifty years of age, and had a son at college. Nevertheless, it is a fact that men are dangerous. She read half a column of her newspaper; then stealthily looked over the edge to decide the question of safety by the infallible test of appearance . . . She would like to offer him her paper. But do young men read the *Morning Post*? She looked to see what he was reading—the *Daily Telegraph*.

Taking note of socks (loose), of tie (shabby), she once more reached his face. She dwelt upon his mouth. The lips were shut. The eyes bent down, since he was reading. All was firm, yet youthful, indifferent, unconscious—as for knocking one down! No, no, no! She looked out of the window, smiling slightly now, and then came back again, for he didn't notice her. Grave, unconscious . . . now he looked up, past her . . . he seemed so out of place, somehow, alone with an elderly lady . . . then he fixed his eyes—which were blue—on the landscape. He had not realized her presence, she thought. Yet it was none of *her* fault that this was not a smoking-carriage—if that was what he meant.

Nobody sees any one as he is, let alone an elderly lady sitting opposite a strange young man in a railway carriage. They see a whole—they see all sorts of things—they see themselves . . . Mrs Norman now read three pages of one of Mr Norris's novels. Should she say to the young man (and after all he was just the same age as her own boy): 'If you want to smoke, don't mind me'? No: he seemed absolutely indifferent to her presence . . . she did not wish to interrupt.

But since, even at her age, she noted his indifference, presumably he was in some way or other—to her at least—nice, handsome, interesting, distinguished, well built, like her own boy? One must do the best one can with her report. Anyhow, this was Jacob Flanders, aged nineteen. It is no use trying to sum people up. One must follow hints, not exactly what is said, nor yet entirely what is done—for instance, when the train drew into the station, Mr Flanders burst open the door, and put the lady's dressing-case out for her, saying, or rather mumbling: 'Let me' very shyly; indeed he was rather clumsy about it.

'Who . . .' said the lady, meeting her son: but as there was a great crowd on the platform and Jacob had already gone, she did not finish her sentence. As this was Cambridge, as she was staying there for the weekend, as she saw nothing but young men all day long, in streets and round tables, this sight of her fellow-traveller was completely lost in her mind, as the crooked pin dropped by a child into the wishing-well twirls in the water and disappears for ever.

They say the sky is the same everywhere. Travellers, the shipwrecked, exiles, and the dying draw comfort from the thought, and no doubt if you are of a mystical tendency, consolation, and even explanation, shower down from the unbroken surface. But above Cambridge— anyhow above the roof of King's College Chapel—there is a difference. Out at sea a great city will cast brightness into the night. Is it fanciful to suppose the sky, washed into the crevices of King's College Chapel, lighter, thinner, more sparkling than the sky elsewhere? Does Cambridge burn not only into the night, but into the day?

Look, as they pass into service, how airily the gowns blow out, as though nothing dense and corporeal were within. What sculptured faces, what certainty, authority controlled by piety, although great boots march under the gowns. In what orderly procession they advance. Thick wax candles stand upright; young men rise in white gowns; while the subservient eagle bears up for inspection the great white book.

An inclined plane of light comes accurately through each window, purple and yellow even in its most diffused dust, while, where it breaks upon stone, that stone is softly chalked red, yellow, and purple. Neither snow nor greenery, winter nor summer, has power over the old stained glass. As the sides of a lantern protect the flame so that it burns steady even in the wildest night—burns steady and gravely illumines the tree-trunks—so inside the Chapel all was orderly. Gravely sounded the voices; wisely the organ replied, as if buttressing human faith with the assent of the elements. The white-robed figures crossed from side to side; now mounted steps, now descended, all very orderly.

. . . If you stand a lantern under a tree every insect in the forest creeps up to it—a curious assembly, since though they scramble and swing and knock their heads against the glass, they seem to have no purpose— something senseless inspires them. One gets tired of watching them, as they amble round the lantern and blindly tap as if for admittance, one large toad being the most besotted of any and shouldering his way through the rest. Ah, but what's that? A terrifying volley of pistol-shots rings out—cracks sharply; ripples spread—silence laps smooth over sound. A tree—a tree has fallen, a sort of death in the forest. After that, the wind in the trees sounds melancholy.

But this service in King's College Chapel—why allow women to take part in it? Surely, if the mind wanders (and Jacob looked extraordinarily vacant, his head thrown back, his hymn-book open at the wrong place), if the mind wanders it is because several hat shops and cupboards upon cupboards of coloured dresses are displayed upon rush-bottomed chairs. Though heads and bodies may be devout enough, one has a sense of individuals—some like blue, others brown; some feathers, others pansies and forget-me-nots. No one would think of bringing a dog into church. For though a dog is all very well on a gravel path, and shows no disrespect to flowers, the way he wanders down an aisle, looking, lifting a paw, and approaching a pillar with a purpose that makes the blood run cold with horror (should you be one of a congregation—alone, shyness is out of the question), a dog destroys the service completely. So do these women—though separately devout, distinguished, and vouched for by the theology, mathematics, Latin, and Greek of their husbands. Heaven knows why it is. For one thing, thought Jacob, they're as ugly as sin.

Now there was a scraping and murmuring. He caught Timmy Durrant's eye; looked very sternly at him; and then, very solemnly, winked.

'Waverley', the villa on the road to Girton was called, not that Mr Plumer admired Scott or would have chosen any name at all, but names are useful when you have to entertain undergraduates, and as they sat waiting for the fourth undergraduate, on Sunday at lunch-time, there was talk of names upon gates.

'How tiresome,' Mrs Plumer interrupted impulsively. 'Does anybody know Mr Flanders?'

Mr Durrant knew him; and therefore blushed slightly, and said, awkwardly, something about being sure—looking at Mr Plumer and hitching the right leg of his trouser as he spoke. Mr Plumer got up and stood in front of the fireplace. Mrs Plumer laughed like a straightforward friendly fellow. In short, anything more horrible than the scene, the setting, the prospect, even the May garden being afflicted with chill sterility and a cloud choosing that moment to cross the sun, cannot be imagined. There was the garden, of course. Everyone at the same moment looked at it. Owing to the cloud, the leaves ruffled grey, and the sparrows—there were two sparrows.

'I think,' said Mrs Plumer, taking advantage of the momentary respite, while the young men stared at the garden, to look at her husband, and he, not accepting full responsibility for the act, nevertheless touched the bell.

There can be no excuse for this outrage upon one hour of human life, save the reflection which occurred to Mr Plumer as he carved the mutton, that if no don ever gave a luncheon party, if Sunday after Sunday passed, if men went down, became lawyers, doctors, members of Parliament, business men—if no don ever gave a luncheon party——

'Now, does lamb make the mint sauce, or mint sauce make the lamb?' he asked the young man next him, to break a silence which had already lasted five minutes and a half.

'I don't know, sir,' said the young man, blushing very vividly.

At this moment in came Mr Flanders. He had mistaken the time.

Now, though they had finished their meat, Mrs Plumer took a second helping of cabbage. Jacob determined, of course, that he would eat his meat in the time it took her to finish her cabbage, looking once or twice to measure his speed—only he was infernally hungry. Seeing this, Mrs Plumer said that she was sure Mr Flanders would not mind—and the tart was brought in. Nodding in a peculiar way, she directed the maid to give Mr Flanders a second helping of mutton. She glanced at the mutton. Not much of the leg would be left for luncheon.

It was none of her fault—since how could she control her father begetting her forty years ago in the suburbs of Manchester? and once begotten, how could she do other than grow up cheese-paring, ambitious, with an instinctively accurate notion of the rungs of the ladder and an ant-like assiduity in pushing George Plumer ahead of her to the top of the ladder? What was at the top of the ladder? A sense that all the rungs were beneath one apparently; since by the time that George Plumer became Professor of Physics, or whatever it might be, Mrs

Plumer could only be in a condition to cling tight to her eminence, peer down at the ground, and goad her two plain daughters to climb the rungs of the ladder.

'I was down at the races yesterday,' she said, 'with my two little girls.'

It was none of *their* fault either. In they came to the drawing-room, in white frocks and blue sashes. They handed the cigarettes. Rhoda had inherited her father's cold grey eyes. Cold grey eyes George Plumer had, but in them was an abstract light. He could talk about Persia and the Trade winds, the Reform Bill and the cycle of the harvests. Books were on his shelves by Wells and Shaw; on the table serious sixpenny weeklies written by pale men in muddy boots—the weekly creak and screech of brains rinsed in cold water and wrung dry—melancholy papers.

'I don't feel that I know the truth about anything till I've read them both!' said Mrs Plumer brightly, tapping the table of contents with her bare red hand, upon which the ring looked so incongruous.

'Oh God, oh God, oh God!' exclaimed Jacob, as the four undergraduates left the house. 'Oh, my God!'

'Bloody beastly!' he said, scanning the street for lilac or bicycle—anything to restore his sense of freedom.

'Bloody beastly,' he said to Timmy Durrant, summing up his discomfort at the world shown him at lunch-time, a world capable of existing—there was no doubt about that—but so unnecessary, such a thing to believe in—Shaw and Wells and the serious sixpenny weeklies! What were they after, scrubbing and demolishing, these elderly people? Had they never read Homer, Shakespeare, the Elizabethans? He saw it clearly outlined against the feelings he drew from youth and natural inclination. The poor devils had rigged up this meagre object. Yet something of pity was in him. Those wretched little girls——

The extent to which he was disturbed proves that he was already agog. Insolent he was and inexperienced, but sure enough the cities which the elderly of the race have built upon the skyline showed like brick suburbs, barracks, and places of discipline against a red and yellow flame. He was impressionable; but the word is contradicted by the composure with which he hollowed his hand to screen a match. He was a young man of substance.

Anyhow, whether undergraduate or shop boy, man or woman, it must come as a shock about the age of twenty—the world of the elderly—

thrown up in such black outline upon what we are; upon the reality; the moors and Byron; the sea and the lighthouse; the sheep's jaw with the yellow teeth in it; upon the obstinate irrepressible conviction which makes youth so intolerably disagreeable—'I am what I am, and intend to be it,' for which there will be no form in the world unless Jacob makes one for himself. The Plumers will try to prevent him from making it. Wells and Shaw and the serious sixpenny weeklies will sit on its head. Every time he lunches out on Sunday—at dinner parties and tea parties—there will be this same shock—horror—discomfort—then pleasure, for he draws into him at every step as he walks by the river such steady certainty, such reassurance from all sides, the trees bowing, the grey spires soft in the blue, voices blowing and seeming suspended in the air, the springy air of May, the elastic air with its particles— chestnut bloom, pollen, whatever it is that gives the May air its potency, blurring the trees, gumming the buds, daubing the green. And the river too runs past, not at flood, nor swiftly, but cloying the oar that dips in it and drops white drops from the blade, swimming green and deep over the bowed rushes, as if lavishly caressing them.

Where they moored their boat the trees showered down, so that their topmost leaves trailed in the ripples and the green wedge that lay in the water being made of leaves shifted in leaf-breadths as the real leaves shifted. Now there was a shiver of wind—instantly an edge of sky; and as Durrant ate cherries he dropped the stunted yellow cherries through the green wedge of leaves, their stalks twinkling as they wriggled in and out, and sometimes one half-bitten cherry would go down red into the green. The meadow was on a level with Jacob's eyes as he lay back; gilt with buttercups, but the grass did not run like the thin green water of the graveyard grass about to overflow the tombstones, but stood juicy and thick. Looking up, backwards, he saw the legs of children deep in the grass, and the legs of cows. Munch, munch, he heard; then a short step through the grass; then again munch, munch, munch, as they tore the grass short at the roots. In front of him two white butterflies circled higher and higher round the elm tree.

'Jacob's off,' thought Durrant, looking up from his novel. He kept reading a few pages and then looking up in a curiously methodical manner, and each time he looked up he took a few cherries out of the bag and ate them abstractedly. Other boats passed them, crossing the backwater from side to side to avoid each other, for many were now moored, and there were now white dresses and a flaw in the column of air between two trees, round which curled a thread of blue—Lady Miller's picnic party. Still more boats kept coming, and Durrant, without getting up, shoved their boat closer to the bank.

'Oh-h-h-h,' groaned Jacob, as the boat rocked, and the trees rocked, and the white dresses and the white flannel trousers drew out long and wavering up the bank.

'Oh-h-h-h!' He sat up, and felt as if a piece of elastic had snapped in his face.

'They're friends of my mother's,' said Durrant. 'So old Bow took no end of trouble about the boat.'

And this boat had gone from Falmouth to St Ives Bay, all round the coast. A larger boat, a ten-ton yacht, about the twentieth of June, properly fitted out, Durrant said . . .

'There's the cash difficulty,' said Jacob.

'My people'll see to that,' said Durrant (the son of a banker, deceased).

'I intend to preserve my economic independence,' said Jacob stiffly. (He was getting excited.)

'My mother said something about going to Harrogate,' he said with a little annoyance, feeling the pocket where he kept his letters.

'Was that true about your uncle becoming a Mohammedan?' asked Timmy Durrant.

Jacob had told the story of his Uncle Morty in Durrant's room the night before.

'I expect he's feeding the sharks, if the truth were known,' said Jacob. 'I say, Durrant, there's none left!' he exclaimed, crumpling the bag which had held the cherries, and throwing it into the river. He saw Lady Miller's picnic party on the island as he threw the bag into the river.

A sort of awkwardness, grumpiness, gloom came into his eyes.

'Shall we move on . . . this beastly crowd . . .' he said.

So up they went, past the island.

The feathery white moon never let the sky grow dark; all night the chestnut blossoms were white in the green; dim was the cow-parsley in the meadows.

The waiters at Trinity must have been shuffling china plates like cards, from the clatter that could be heard in the Great Court. Jacob's rooms, however, were in Nevile's Court; at the top; so that reaching his door one went in a little out of breath; but he wasn't there. Dining in Hall, presumably. It will be quite dark in Nevile's Court long before midnight, only the pillars opposite will always be white, and the fountains. A curious effect the gate has, like lace upon pale green. Even in the window you hear the plates; a hum of talk, too, from the diners; the Hall lit up, and the swing-doors opening and shutting with a soft thud. Some are late.

Jacob's room had a round table and two low chairs. There were yellow flags in a jar on the mantelpiece; a photograph of his mother; cards from societies with little raised crescents, coats of arms, and initials; notes and pipes; on the table lay paper ruled with a red margin—an essay, no doubt—'Does History consist of the Biographies of Great Men?' There were books enough; very few French books, but then anyone who's worth anything reads just what he likes, as the mood takes him, with extravagant enthusiasm. Lives of the Duke of Wellington, for example; Spinoza; the works of Dickens; the *Faery Queen*; a Greek dictionary with the petals of poppies pressed to silk between the pages; all the Elizabethans. His slippers were incredibly shabby, like boats burnt to the water's rim. Then there were photographs from the Greeks, and a mezzotint from Sir Joshua—all very English. The works of Jane Austen, too, in deference, perhaps, to someone else's standard. Carlyle was a prize. There were books upon the Italian painters of the Renaissance, a *Manual of the Diseases of the Horse*, and all the usual textbooks. Listless is the air in an empty room, just swelling the curtain; the flowers in the jar shift. One fibre in the wicker armchair creaks, though no one sits there.

Coming down the steps a little sideways [Jacob sat on the window-seat talking to Durrant; he smoked, and Durrant looked at the map], the old man, with his hands locked behind him, his gown floating black, lurched, unsteadily, near the wall; then, upstairs he went into his room. Then another, who raised his hand and praised the columns, the gate, the sky; another, tripping and smug. Each went up a staircase; three lights were lit in the dark windows.

If any light burns above Cambridge, it must be from three such rooms; Greek burns here; science there; philosophy on the ground floor. Poor old Huxtable can't walk straight;—Sopwith, too, has praised the sky any night these twenty years; and Cowan still chuckles at the same stories. It is not simple, or pure, or wholly splendid, the lamp of learning, since if you see them there under its light (whether Rossetti's on the wall, or Van Gogh reproduced, whether there are lilacs in the bowl or rusty pipes), how priestly they look! How like a suburb where you go to see a view and eat a special cake! 'We are the sole purveyors of this cake.' Back you go to London; for the treat is over.

Old Professor Huxtable, performing with the method of a clock his change of dress, let himself down into his chair; filled his pipe; chose his paper; crossed his feet; and extracted his glasses. The whole flesh of his face then fell into folds as if props were removed. Yet strip a whole seat of an underground railway carriage of its heads and old Huxtable's head will hold them all. Now, as his eye goes down the print, what a procession tramps through the corridors of his brain, orderly, quick-stepping, and reinforced, as the march goes on, by fresh runnels, till the whole hall, dome, whatever one calls it, is populous with ideas. Such a muster takes place in no other brain. Yet sometimes there he'll sit for hours together, gripping the arm of the chair, like a man holding fast because stranded, and then, just because his corn twinges, or it may be the gout, what execrations, and, dear me, to hear him talk of money, taking out his leather purse and grudging even the smallest silver coin, secretive and suspicious as an old peasant woman with all her lies. Strange paralysis and constriction—marvellous illumination. Serene over it all rides the great full brow, and sometimes asleep or in the quiet spaces of the night you might fancy that on a pillow of stone he lay triumphant.

Sopwith, meanwhile, advancing with a curious trip from the fireplace, cut the chocolate cake into segments. Until midnight or later there would be undergraduates in his room, sometimes as many as twelve, sometimes three or four; but nobody got up when they went or when they came; Sopwith went on talking. Talking, talking, talking—as if everything could be talked—the soul itself slipped through the lips in thin silver disks which dissolve in young men's minds like silver, like moonlight. Oh, far away they'd remember it, and deep in dulness gaze back on it, and come to refresh themselves again.

'Well, I never. That's old Chucky. My dear boy, how's the world treating you?' And in came poor little Chucky, the unsuccessful provincial, Stenhouse his real name, but of course Sopwith brought back by using the other everything, everything, 'all I could never be'—yes, though next day, buying his newspaper and catching the early train, it all seemed to him childish, absurd; the chocolate cake, the young men; Sopwith summing things up; no, not all; he would send his son there. He would save every penny to send his son there. Sopwith went on talking; twining stiff fibres of awkward speech—things young men blurted out—plaiting them round his own smooth garland, making the bright side show, the vivid greens, the sharp thorns, manliness. He loved it. Indeed to Sopwith a man could say anything, until perhaps he'd grown old, or gone under, gone deep, when the silver disks would tinkle hollow, and the inscription read a little too simple, and the old stamp look too pure, and the impress always the same—a Greek boy's head. But he would respect still. A woman, divining the priest, would, involuntarily, despise.

Cowan, Erasmus Cowan, sipped his port alone, or with one rosy little man, whose memory held precisely the same span of time; sipped his port, and told his stories, and without book before him intoned Latin, Virgil, and Catullus, as if language were wine upon his lips. Only— sometimes it will come over one—what if the poet strode in? '*This* my image?' he might ask, pointing to the chubby man, whose brain is, after all, Virgil's representative among us, though the body gluttonize, and as for arms, bees, or even the plough, Cowan takes his trips abroad with a French novel in his pocket, a rug about his knees, and is thankful to be home again in his place, in his line, holding up in his snug little mirror the image of Virgil, all rayed round with good stories of the dons of Trinity and red beams of port. But language is wine upon his lips. Nowhere else would Virgil hear the like. And though, as she goes sauntering along the Backs, old Miss Umphelby sings him melodiously enough, accurately too, she is always brought up by this question as she reaches Clare Bridge: 'But if I met him, what should I wear?'—and then, taking her way up the avenue towards Newnham, she lets her fancy play upon other details of men's meeting with women which have never got into print. Her lectures, therefore, are not half so well attended as those of Cowan, and the thing she might have said in elucidation of the text for ever left out. In short, face a teacher with the image of the taught and the mirror breaks. But Cowan sipped his port, his exaltation over, no longer the representative of Virgil. No, the builder, assessor, surveyor, rather; ruling lines between names, hanging lists above doors. Such is the fabric through which the light must shine, if shine it can—the light of all these languages, Chinese and Russian, Persian and Arabic, of symbols and figures, of history, of things that are known and things that are about to be known. So that if at night, far out at sea over the tumbling waves, one saw a haze on the waters, a city illuminated, a whiteness even in the sky, such as that now over the Hall of Trinity where they're still dining, or washing up plates, that would be the light burning there— the light of Cambridge.

'Let's go round to Simeon's room,' said Jacob, and they rolled up the map, having got the whole thing settled.

All the lights were coming out round the court, and falling on the cobbles, picking out dark patches of grass and single daisies. The young men were now back in their rooms. Heaven knows what they were doing. What was it that could *drop* like that? And leaning down over a foaming window-box, one stopped another hurrying past, and upstairs they went and down they went, until a sort of fulness settled on the court, the hive full of bees, the bees home thick with gold, drowsy, humming, suddenly vocal; the Moonlight Sonata answered by a waltz.

The Moonlight Sonata tinkled away; the waltz crashed. Although young men still went in and out, they walked as if keeping engagements. Now and then there was a thud, as if some heavy piece of furniture had fallen, unexpectedly, of its own accord, not in the general stir of life after dinner. One supposed that young men raised their eyes from their books as the furniture fell. Were they reading? Certainly there was a sense of concentration in the air. Behind the grey walls sat so many young men, some undoubtedly reading, magazines, shilling shockers, no doubt; legs, perhaps, over the arms of chairs; smoking; sprawling over tables, and writing while their heads went round in a circle as the pen moved—simple young men, these, who would—but there is no need to think of them grown old; others eating sweets; here they boxed; and, well, Mr Hawkins must have been mad suddenly to throw up his window and bawl: 'Jo—seph! Jo—seph!' and then he ran as hard as ever he could across the court, while an elderly man, in a green apron, carrying an immense pile of tin covers, hesitated, balanced, and then went on. But this was a diversion. There were young men who read, lying in shallow armchairs, holding their books as if they had hold in their hands of something that would see them through; they being all in a torment, coming from midland towns, clergymen's sons. Others read Keats. And those long histories in many volumes—surely someone was now beginning at the beginning in order to understand the Holy Roman Empire, as one must. That was part of the concentration, though it would be dangerous on a hot spring night—dangerous, perhaps, to concentrate too much upon single books, actual chapters, when at any moment the door opened and Jacob appeared; or Richard Bonamy, reading Keats no longer, began making long pink spills from an old newspaper, bending forward, and looking eager and contented no more, but almost fierce. Why? Only perhaps that Keats died young—one wants to write poetry too and to love—oh, the brutes! It's damnably difficult. But, after all, not so difficult if on the next staircase, in the large room, there are two, three, five young men all convinced of this—of brutality, that is, and the clear division between right and wrong. There was a sofa, chairs, a square table, and the window being open, one could see how they sat—legs issuing here, one there crumpled in a corner of the sofa; and, presumably, for you could not see him, somebody stood by the fender, talking. Anyhow, Jacob, who sat astride a chair and ate dates from a long box, burst out laughing. The answer came from the sofa corner; for his pipe was held in the air, then replaced. Jacob wheeled round. He had something to say to *that*, though the sturdy red-haired boy at the table seemed to deny it, wagging his head slowly from side to side; and then, taking out his penknife, he dug the point of it again and again into a knot in the table, as if affirming that the voice from the fender spoke the truth—which Jacob could not deny. Possibly, when he had done arranging the date-stones, he might find something to say to it—indeed his lips opened—only then there broke out a roar of laughter.

The laughter died in the air. The sound of it could scarcely have reached anyone standing by the Chapel, which stretched along the opposite side of the court. The laughter died out, and only gestures of arms, movements of bodies, could be seen shaping something in the room. Was it an argument? A bet on the boat races? Was it nothing of the sort? What was shaped by the arms and bodies moving in the twilight room?

A step or two beyond the window there was nothing at all, except the enclosing buildings—chimneys upright, roofs horizontal; too much brick and building for a May night, perhaps. And then before one's eyes would come the bare hills of Turkey—sharp lines, dry earth, coloured flowers, and colour on the shoulders of the women, standing naked-legged in the stream to beat linen on the stones. The stream made loops of water round their ankles. But none of that could show clearly through the swaddlings and blanketings of the Cambridge night. The stroke of the clock even was muffled; as if intoned by somebody reverent from a pulpit; as if generations of learned men heard the last hour go rolling through their ranks and issued it, already smooth and time-worn, with their blessing, for the use of the living.

Was it to receive this gift from the past that the young man came to the window and stood there, looking out across the court? It was Jacob. He stood smoking his pipe while the last stroke of the clock purred softly round him. Perhaps there had been an argument. He looked satisfied; indeed masterly; which expression changed slightly as he stood there, the sound of the clock conveying to him (it may be) a sense of old buildings and time; and himself the inheritor; and then to-morrow; and friends; at the thought of whom, in sheer confidence and pleasure, it seemed, he yawned and stretched himself.

Meanwhile behind him the shape they had made, whether by argument or not, the spiritual shape, hard yet ephemeral, as of glass compared with the dark stone of the Chapel, was dashed to splinters, young men rising from chairs and sofa corners, buzzing and barging about the room, one driving another against the bedroom door, which giving way, in they fell. Then Jacob was left there, in the shallow armchair, alone with Masham? Anderson? Simeon? Oh, it was Simeon. The others had all gone.

'. . . Julian the Apostate. . . .' Which of them said that and the other words murmured round it? But about midnight there sometimes rises, like a veiled figure suddenly woken, a heavy wind; and this now flapping through Trinity lifted unseen leaves and blurred everything. 'Julian the Apostate'—and then the wind. Up go the elm branches, out blow the sails, the old schooners rear and plunge, the grey waves in the hot Indian Ocean tumble sultrily, and then all falls flat again.

So, if the veiled lady stepped through the Courts of Trinity, she now drowsed once more, all her draperies about her, her head against a pillar.

'Somehow it seems to matter.'

The low voice was Simeon's.

The voice was even lower that answered him. The sharp tap of a pipe on the mantelpiece cancelled the words. And perhaps Jacob only said 'hum', or said nothing at all. True, the words were inaudible. It was the intimacy, a sort of spiritual suppleness, when mind prints upon mind indelibly.

'Well, you seem to have studied the subject,' said Jacob, rising and standing over Simeon's chair. He balanced himself; he swayed a little. He appeared extraordinarily happy, as if his pleasure would brim and spill down the sides if Simeon spoke.

Simeon said nothing. Jacob remained standing. But intimacy—the room was full of it, still, deep, like a pool. Without need of movement or speech it rose softly and washed over everything, mollifying, kindling, and coating the mind with the lustre of pearl, so that if you talk of a light, of Cambridge burning, it's not languages only. It's Julian the Apostate.

But Jacob moved. He murmured goodnight. He went out into the court. He buttoned his jacket across his chest. He went back to his rooms, and being the only man who walked at that moment back to his rooms, his footsteps rang out, his figure loomed large. Back from the Chapel, back from the Hall, back from the Library, came the sound of his footsteps, as if the old stone echoed with magisterial authority: 'The young man—the young man—the young man—back to his rooms.'

IV

What's the use of trying to read Shakespeare, especially in one of those little thin paper editions whose pages get ruffled, or stuck together with sea-water? Although the plays of Shakespeare had frequently been praised, even quoted, and placed higher than the Greek, never since they started had Jacob managed to read one through. Yet what an opportunity!

For the Scilly Isles had been sighted by Timmy Durrant lying like mountain-tops almost a-wash in precisely the right place. His calculations had worked perfectly, and really the sight of him sitting there, with his hand on the tiller, rosy gilled, with a sprout of beard, looking sternly at the stars, then at a compass, spelling out quite correctly his page of the eternal lesson-book, would have moved a woman. Jacob, of course, was not a woman. The sight of Timmy Durrant was no sight for him, nothing to set against the sky and worship; far from it. They had quarrelled. Why the right way to open a tin of beef, with Shakespeare on board, under conditions of such splendour, should have turned them to sulky schoolboys, none can tell. Tinned beef is cold eating, though; and salt water spoils biscuits; and the waves tumble and lollop much the same hour after hour—tumble and lollop all across the horizon. Now a spray of seaweed floats past—now a log of wood. Ships have been wrecked here. One or two go past, keeping their own side of the road. Timmy knew where they were bound, what their cargoes were, and, by looking through his glass, could tell the name of the line, and even guess what dividends it paid its shareholders. Yet that was no reason for Jacob to turn sulky.

The Scilly Isles had the look of mountaintops almost a-wash . . . Unfortunately, Jacob broke the pin of the Primus stove.

The Scilly Isles might well be obliterated by a roller sweeping straight across.

But one must give young men the credit of admitting that, though breakfast eaten under these circumstances is grim, it is sincere enough. No need to make conversation. They got out their pipes.

Timmy wrote up some scientific observations; and—what was the question that broke the silence—the exact time or the day of the month? anyhow, it was spoken without the least awkwardness; in the most matter-of-fact way in the world; and then Jacob began to unbutton his clothes and sat naked, save for his shirt, intending, apparently, to bathe.

The Scilly Isles were turning bluish; and suddenly blue, purple, and green flushed the sea; left it grey; struck a stripe which vanished; but when Jacob had got his shirt over his head the whole floor of the waves was blue and white, rippling and crisp, though now and again a broad purple mark appeared, like a bruise; or there floated an entire emerald tinged with yellow. He plunged. He gulped in water, spat it out, struck with his right arm, struck with his left, was towed by a rope, gasped, splashed, and was hauled on board.

The seat in the boat was positively hot, and the sun warmed his back as he sat naked with a towel in his hand, looking at the Scilly Isles which—confound it! the sail flapped. Shakespeare was knocked overboard. There you could see him floating merrily away, with all his pages ruffling innumerably; and then he went under.

Strangely enough, you could smell violets, or if violets were impossible in July, they must grow something very pungent on the mainland then. The mainland, not so very far off—you could see clefts in the cliffs, white cottages, smoke going up—wore an extraordinary look of calm; of sunny peace, as if wisdom and piety had descended upon the dwellers there. Now a cry sounded, as of a man calling pilchards in a main street. It wore an extraordinary look of piety and peace, as if old men smoked by the door, and girls stood, hands on hips, at the well, and horses stood; as if the end of the world had come, and cabbage fields and stone walls, and coastguard stations, and, above all, the white sand bays with the waves breaking unseen by any one, rose to heaven in a kind of ecstasy.

But imperceptibly the cottage smoke droops, has the look of a mourning emblem, a flag floating its caress over a grave. The gulls, making their broad flight and then riding at peace, seem to mark the grave.

No doubt if this were Italy, Greece, or even the shores of Spain, sadness would be routed by strangeness and excitement and the nudge of a classical education. But the Cornish hills have stark chimneys standing on them; and, somehow or other, loveliness is infernally sad. Yes, the chimneys and the coastguard stations and the little bays with the waves breaking unseen by anyone make one remember the overpowering sorrow. And what can this sorrow be?

It is brewed by the earth itself. It comes from the houses on the coast. We start transparent, and then the cloud thickens. All history backs our pane of glass. To escape is vain.

But whether this is the right interpretation of Jacob's gloom as he sat naked, in the sun, looking at the Land's End, it is impossible to say; for he never spoke a word. Timmy sometimes wondered (only for a second) whether his people bothered him . . . No matter. There are things that can't be said. Let's shake it off. Let's dry ourselves, and take up the first thing that comes handy ... Timmy Durrant's notebook of scientific observations.

'Now . . .' said Jacob.

It is a tremendous argument.

Some people can follow every step of the way, and even take a little one, six inches long, by themselves at the end; others remain observant of the external signs.

The eyes fix themselves upon the poker; the right hand takes the poker and lifts it; turns it slowly round, and then, very accurately, replaces it. The left hand, which lies on the knee, plays some stately but intermittent piece of march music. A deep breath is taken; but allowed to evaporate unused. The cat marches across the hearth-rug. No one observes her.

'That's about as near as I can get to it,' Durrant wound up.

The next minute is quiet as the grave.

'It follows . . .' said Jacob.

Only half a sentence followed; but these half-sentences are like flags set on tops of buildings to the observer of external sights down below. What was the coast of Cornwall, with its violet scents, and mourning emblems, and tranquil piety, but a screen happening to hang straight behind as his mind marched up?

'It follows . . .' said Jacob.

'Yes,' said Timmy, after reflection. 'That is so.'

Now Jacob began plunging about, half to stretch himself, half in a kind of jollity, no doubt, for the strangest sound issued from his lips as he furled the sail, rubbed the plates—gruff, tuneless—a sort of pæan, for having grasped the argument, for being master of the situation, sunburnt, unshaven, capable into the bargain of sailing round the world in a ten-ton yacht, which, very likely, he would do one of these days instead of settling down in a lawyer's office, and wearing spats.

'Our friend Masham', said Timmy Durrant, 'would rather not be seen in our company as we are now.' His buttons had come off.

'D'you know Masham's aunt?' said Jacob.

'Never knew he had one,' said Timmy.

'Masham has millions of aunts,' said Jacob.

'Masham is mentioned in Domesday Book,' said Timmy.

'So are his aunts,' said Jacob.

'His sister', said Timmy, 'is a very pretty girl.'

'That's what'll happen to you, Timmy,' said Jacob.

'It'll happen to you first,' said Timmy.

'But this woman I was telling you about—Masham's aunt——'

'Oh, do get on,' said Timmy, for Jacob was laughing so much that he could not speak.

'Masham's aunt . . .'
Timmy laughed so much that he could not speak.
'Masham's aunt . . .'
'What is there about Masham that makes one laugh?' said Timmy.
'Hang it all—a man who swallows his tie-pin,' said Jacob.
'Lord Chancellor before he's fifty,' said Timmy.
'He's a gentleman,' said Jacob.
'The Duke of Wellington was a gentleman,' said Timmy.
'Keats wasn't.'
'Lord Salisbury was.'
'And what about God?' said Jacob.
    The Scilly Isles now appeared as if directly pointed at by a golden
finger issuing from a cloud; and everybody knows how portentous that
sight is, and how these broad rays, whether they light upon the Scilly
Isles or upon the tombs of crusaders in cathedrals, always shake the
very foundations of scepticism and lead to jokes about God.

> 'Abide with me:
> Fast falls the eventide;
> The shadows deepen;
> Lord, with me abide,'

sang Timmy Durrant.
    'At my place we used to have a hymn which began

> 'Great God, what do I see and hear?'

said Jacob.
    Gulls rode gently swaying in little companies of two or three quite
near the boat: the cormorant, as if following his long strained neck in
eternal pursuit, skimmed an inch above the water to the next rock; and
the drone of the tide in the caves came across the water, low, monotonous, like the voice of some one talking to himself.

> 'Rock of Ages, cleft for me,
> Let me hide myself in thee,'

sang Jacob.
    Like the blunt tooth of some monster, a rock broke the surface; brown;
overflown with perpetual waterfalls.

> 'Rock of Ages,'

Jacob sang, lying on his back, looking up into the sky at mid-day, from
which every shred of cloud had been withdrawn, so that it was like
something permanently displayed with the cover off.

By six o'clock a breeze blew in off an icefield; and by seven the water was more purple than blue; and by half-past seven there was a patch of rough gold-beater's skin round the Scilly Isles, and Durrant's face, as he sat steering, was of the colour of a red lacquer box polished for generations. By nine all the fire and confusion had gone out of the sky, leaving wedges of apple-green and plates of pale yellow; and by ten the lanterns on the boat were making twisted colours upon the waves, elongated or squab, as the waves stretched or humped themselves. The beam from the lighthouse strode rapidly across the water. Infinite millions of miles away powdered stars twinkled; but the waves slapped the boat, and crashed, with regular and appalling solemnity, against the rocks.

Although it would be possible to knock at the cottage door and ask for a glass of milk, it is only thirst that would compel the intrusion. Yet perhaps Mrs Pascoe would welcome it. The summer's day may be wearing heavy. Washing in her little scullery, she may hear the cheap clock on the mantelpiece tick, tick, tick . . . tick, tick, tick. She is alone in the house. Her husband is out helping Farmer Hosken; her daughter married and gone to America. Her elder son is married too, but she does not agree with his wife. The Wesleyan minister came along and took the younger boy. She is alone in the house. A steamer, probably bound for Cardiff, now crosses the horizon, while near at hand one bell of a foxglove swings to and fro with a bumble-bee for clapper.

These white Cornish cottages are built on the edge of the cliff; the garden grows gorse more readily than cabbages; and for hedge, some primeval man has piled granite boulders. In one of these, to hold, an historian conjectures, the victim's blood, a basin has been hollowed, but in our time it serves more tamely to seat those tourists who wish for an uninterrupted view of the Gurnard's Head. Not that anyone objects to a blue print dress and a white apron in a cottage garden.

'Look—she has to draw her water from a well in the garden.'

'Very lonely it must be in winter, with the wind sweeping over those hills, and the waves dashing on the rocks.'

Even on a summer's day you hear them murmuring.

Having drawn her water, Mrs Pascoe went in. The tourists regretted that they had brought no glasses, so that they might have read the name of the tramp steamer. Indeed, it was such a fine day that there was no saying what a pair of field-glasses might not have fetched into view. Two fishing luggers, presumably from St Ives Bay, were now sailing in an opposite direction from the steamer and the floor of the sea became alternately clear and opaque. As for the bee, having sucked its fill of honey, it visited the teasle and thence made a straight line to Mrs Pascoe's patch, once more directing the tourists' gaze to the old woman's print dress and white apron, for she had come to the door of the cottage and was standing there.

There she stood, shading her eyes and looking out to sea.

For the millionth time, perhaps, she looked at the sea. A peacock butterfly now spread himself upon the teasle, fresh and newly emerged, as the blue and chocolate down on his wings testified. Mrs Pascoe went indoors, fetched a cream pan, came out, and stood scouring it. Her face was assuredly not soft, sensual, or lecherous, but hard, wise, wholesome rather, signifying in a room full of sophisticated people the flesh and blood of life. She would tell a lie, though, as soon as the truth. Behind her on the wall hung a large dried skate. Shut up in the parlour she prized mats, china mugs, and photographs, though the mouldy little room was saved from the salt breeze only by the depth of a brick, and between lace curtains you saw the gannet drop like a stone, and on stormy days the gulls came shuddering through the air, and the steamers' lights were now high, now deep. Melancholy were the sounds on a winter's night.

The picture papers were delivered punctually on Sunday, and she pored long over Lady Cynthia's wedding at the Abbey. She, too, would have liked to ride in a carriage with springs. The soft, swift syllables of educated speech often shamed her few rude ones. And then all night to hear the grinding of the Atlantic upon the rocks instead of hansom cabs and footmen whistling for motor cars . . . So she may have dreamed, scouring her cream pan. But the talkative, nimble-witted people have taken themselves to towns. Like a miser, she has hoarded her feelings within her own breast. Not a penny piece has she changed all these years, and, watching her enviously, it seems as if all within must be pure gold.

The wise old woman, having fixed her eyes upon the sea, once more withdrew. The tourists decided that it was time to move on to the Gurnard's Head.

Three seconds later Mrs Durrant rapped upon the door.

'Mrs Pascoe?' she said.

Rather haughtily, she watched the tourists cross the field path. She came of a Highland race, famous for its chieftains.

Mrs Pascoe appeared.

'I envy you that bush, Mrs Pascoe,' said Mrs Durrant, pointing the parasol with which she had rapped on the door at the fine clump of St John's wort that grew beside it. Mrs Pascoe looked at the bush deprecatingly.

'I expect my son in a day or two,' said Mrs Durrant. 'Sailing from Falmouth with a friend in a little boat . . . Any news of Lizzie yet, Mrs Pascoe?'

Her long-tailed ponies stood twitching their ears on the road twenty yards away. The boy, Curnow, flicked flies off them occasionally. He saw his mistress go into the cottage; come out again; and pass, talking energetically to judge by the movements of her hands, round the vegetable plot in front of the cottage. Mrs Pascoe was his aunt. Both women surveyed a bush. Mrs Durrant stooped and picked a sprig from it. Next she pointed (her movements were peremptory; she held herself very upright) at the potatoes. They had the blight. All potatoes that year had the blight. Mrs Durrant showed Mrs Pascoe how bad the blight was on her potatoes. Mrs Durrant talked energetically; Mrs Pascoe listened submissively. The boy Curnow knew that Mrs Durrant was saying that it is perfectly simple; you mix the powder in a gallon of water; 'I have done it with my own hands in my own garden,' Mrs Durrant was saying.

'You won't have a potato left—you won't have a potato left,' Mrs Durrant was saying in her emphatic voice as they reached the gate. The boy Curnow became as immobile as stone.

Mrs Durrant took the reins in her hands and settled herself on the driver's seat.

'Take care of that leg, or I shall send the doctor to you,' she called back over her shoulder; touched the ponies; and the carriage started forward. The boy Curnow had only just time to swing himself up by the toe of his boot. The boy Curnow, sitting in the middle of the back seat, looked at his aunt.

Mrs Pascoe stood at the gate looking after them; stood at the gate till the trap was round the corner; stood at the gate, looking now to the right, now to the left; then went back to her cottage.

Soon the ponies attacked the swelling moor road with striving forelegs. Mrs Durrant let the reins fall slackly, and leant backwards. Her vivacity had left her. Her hawk nose was thin as a bleached bone through which you almost see the light. Her hands, lying on the reins in her lap, were firm even in repose. The upper lip was cut so short that it raised itself almost in a sneer from the front teeth. Her mind skimmed leagues where Mrs Pascoe's mind adhered to its solitary patch. Her mind skimmed leagues as the ponies climbed the hill road. Forwards and backwards she cast her mind, as if the roofless cottages, mounds of slag, and cottage gardens overgrown with foxglove and bramble cast shade upon her mind. Arrived at the summit, she stopped the carriage. The pale hills were round her, each scattered with ancient stones; beneath was the sea, variable as a southern sea; she herself sat there looking from hill to sea, upright, aquiline, equally poised between gloom and laughter. Suddenly she flicked the ponies so that the boy Curnow had to swing himself up by the toe of his boot.

The rooks settled; the rooks rose. The trees which they touched so capriciously seemed insufficient to lodge their numbers. The tree-tops sang with the breeze in them; the branches creaked audibly and dropped now and then, though the season was midsummer, husks or twigs. Up went the rooks and down again, rising in lesser numbers each time as the sager birds made ready to settle, for the evening was already spent enough to make the air inside the wood almost dark. The moss was soft; the tree-trunks spectral. Beyond them lay a silvery meadow. The pampas grass raised its feathery spears from mounds of green at the end of the meadow. A breadth of water gleamed. Already the convolvulus moth was spinning over the flowers. Orange and purple, nasturtium and cherry pie, were washed into the twilight, but the tobacco plant and the passion flower, over which the great moth spun, were white as china. The rooks creaked their wings together on the tree-tops, and were settling down for sleep when, far off, a familiar sound shook and trembled—increased—fairly dinned in their ears—scared sleepy wings into the air again—the dinner bell at the house.

After six days of salt wind, rain, and sun, Jacob Flanders had put on a dinner jacket. The discreet black object had made its appearance now and then in the boat among tins, pickles, preserved meats, and as the voyage went on had become more and more irrelevant, hardly to be believed in. And now, the world being stable, lit by candle-light, the dinner jacket alone preserved him. He could not be sufficiently thankful. Even so his neck, wrists, and face were exposed without cover, and his whole person, whether exposed or not, tingled and glowed so as to make even black cloth an imperfect screen. He drew back the great red hand that lay on the table-cloth. Surreptitiously it closed upon slim glasses and curved silver forks. The bones of the cutlets were decorated with pink frills—and yesterday he had gnawn ham from the bone! Opposite him were hazy, semi-transparent shapes of yellow and blue. Behind them, again, was the grey-green garden, and among the pear-shaped leaves of the escallonia fishing-boats seemed caught and suspended. A sailing ship slowly drew past the women's backs. Two or three figures crossed the terrace hastily in the dusk. The door opened and shut. Nothing settled or stayed unbroken. Like oars rowing now this side, now that, were the sentences that came now here, now there, from either side of the table.

'Oh, Clara, Clara!' exclaimed Mrs Durrant, and Timothy Durrant adding, 'Clara, Clara,' Jacob named the shape in yellow gauze Timothy's sister, Clara. The girl sat smiling and flushed. With her brother's dark eyes, she was vaguer and softer than he was. When the laugh died down she said: 'But, mother, it was true. He said so, didn't he? Miss Eliot agreed with us . . .'

But Miss Eliot, tall, grey-headed, was making room beside her for the old man who had come in from the terrace. The dinner would never end, Jacob thought, and he did not wish it to end, though the ship had sailed from one corner of the window-frame to the other, and a light marked the end of the pier. He saw Mrs Durrant gaze at the light. She turned to him.

'Did you take command, or Timothy?' she said. 'Forgive me if I call you Jacob. I've heard so much of you.' Then her eyes went back to the sea. Her eyes glazed as she looked at the view.

'A little village once,' she said, 'and now grown . . .' She rose, taking her napkin with her, and stood by the window.

'Did you quarrel with Timothy?' Clara asked shyly. 'I should have.'

Mrs Durrant came back from the window.

'It gets later and later,' she said, sitting upright, and looking down the table. 'You ought to be ashamed—all of you. Mr Clutterbuck, you ought to be ashamed.' She raised her voice, for Mr Clutterbuck was deaf.

'We *are* ashamed,' said a girl. But the old man with the beard went on eating plum tart. Mrs Durrant laughed and leant back in her chair, as if indulging him.

'We put it to you, Mrs Durrant,' said a young man with thick spectacles and a fiery moustache. 'I say the conditions were fulfilled. She owes me a sovereign.'

'Not *before* the fish—*with* it, Mrs Durrant,' said Charlotte Wilding.

'That was the bet; with the fish,' said Clara seriously. 'Begonias, mother. To eat them with his fish.'

'Oh dear,' said Mrs Durrant.

'Charlotte won't pay you,' said Timothy.

'How dare you . . .' said Charlotte.

'That privilege will be mine,' said the courtly Mr Wortley, producing a silver case primed with sovereigns and slipping one coin on to the table. Then Mrs Durrant got up and passed down the room, holding herself very straight, and the girls in yellow and blue and silver gauze followed her, and elderly Miss Eliot in her velvet; and a little rosy woman, hesitating at the door, clean, scrupulous, probably a governess. All passed out at the open door.

'When you are as old as I am, Charlotte,' said Mrs Durrant, drawing the girl's arm within hers as they paced up and down the terrace.

'Why are you so sad?' Charlotte asked impulsively.

'Do I seem to you sad? I hope not,' said Mrs Durrant.

'Well, just now. You're *not* old.'

'Old enough to be Timothy's mother.' They stopped.

Miss Eliot was looking through Mr Clutterbuck's telescope at the edge of the terrace. The deaf old man stood beside her, fondling his beard, and reciting the names of the constellations: 'Andromeda, Bootes, Sidonia, Cassiopeia . . .'

'Andromeda,' murmured Miss Eliot, shifting the telescope slightly.

Mrs Durrant and Charlotte looked along the barrel of the instrument pointed at the skies.

'There are *millions* of stars,' said Charlotte with conviction. Miss Eliot turned away from the telescope. The young men laughed suddenly in the dining-room.

'Let *me* look,' said Charlotte eagerly.

'The stars bore me,' said Mrs Durrant, walking down the terrace with Julia Eliot. 'I read a book once about the stars . . . What are they saying?' She stopped in front of the dining-room window. 'Timothy,' she noted.

'The silent young man,' said Miss Eliot.

'Yes, Jacob Flanders,' said Mrs Durrant.

'Oh, mother! I didn't recognize you!' exclaimed Clara Durrant, coming from the opposite direction with Elsbeth. 'How delicious,' she breathed, crushing a verbena leaf.

Mrs Durrant turned and walked away by herself.

'Clara!' she called. Clara went to her.

'How unlike they are!' said Miss Eliot.

Mr Wortley passed them, smoking a cigar.

'Every day I live I find myself agreeing . . .' he said as he passed them.

'It's so interesting to guess . . .' murmured Julia Eliot.

'When first we came out we could see the flowers in that bed,' said Elsbeth.

'We see very little now,' said Miss Eliot.

'She must have been so beautiful, and everybody loved her, of course,' said Charlotte. 'I suppose Mr Wortley . . .' she paused.

'Edward's death was a tragedy,' said Miss Eliot decidedly.

Here Mr Erskine joined them.

'There's no such thing as silence,' he said positively. 'I can hear twenty different sounds on a night like this without counting your voices.'

'Make a bet of it?' said Charlotte.

'Done,' said Mr Erskine. 'One, the sea; two, the wind; three, a dog; four . . .'

The others passed on.

'Poor Timothy,' said Elsbeth.

'A very fine night,' shouted Miss Eliot into Mr Clutterbuck's ear.

'Like to look at the stars?' said the old man, turning the telescope towards Elsbeth.

'Doesn't it make you melancholy—looking at the stars?' shouted Miss Eliot.

'Dear me no, dear me no,' Mr Clutterbuck chuckled when he understood her. 'Why should it make me melancholy? Not for a moment—dear me no.'

'Thank you, Timothy, but I'm coming in,' said Miss Eliot. 'Elsbeth, here's a shawl.'

'I'm coming in,' Elsbeth murmured with her eye to the telescope. 'Cassiopeia,' she murmured. 'Where are you all?' she asked, taking her eye away from the telescope. 'How dark it is!'

Mrs Durrant sat in the drawing-room by a lamp winding a ball of wool. Mr Clutterbuck read *The Times*. In the distance stood a second lamp, and round it sat the young ladies, flashing scissors over silver-spangled stuff for private theatricals. Mr Wortley read a book.

'Yes; he is perfectly right,' said Mrs Durrant, drawing herself up and ceasing to wind her wool. And while Mr Clutterbuck read the rest of Lord Lansdowne's speech she sat upright, without touching her ball.

'Ah, Mr Flanders,' she said, speaking proudly, as if to Lord Lansdowne himself. Then she sighed and began to wind her wool again.

'Sit *there*,' she said.

Jacob came out from the dark place by the window where he had hovered. The light poured over him, illuminating every cranny of his skin; but not a muscle of his face moved as he sat looking out into the garden.

'I want to hear about your voyage,' said Mrs Durrant.

'Yes,' he said.

'Twenty years ago we did the same thing.'

'Yes,' he said. She looked at him sharply.

'He is extraordinarily awkward,' she thought, noticing how he fingered his socks. 'Yet so distinguished-looking.'

'In those days . . .' she resumed, and told him how they had sailed . . . 'my husband, who knew a good deal about sailing, for he kept a yacht before we married' . . . and then how rashly they had defied the fishermen, 'almost paid for it with our lives, but so proud of ourselves!' She flung the hand out that held the ball of wool.

'Shall I hold your wool?' Jacob asked stiffly.

'You do that for your mother,' said Mrs Durrant, looking at him again keenly, as she transferred the skein. 'Yes, it goes much better.'

He smiled; but said nothing.

Elsbeth Siddons hovered behind them with something silver on her arm.

'We want,' she said . . . 'I've come . . .' she paused.

'Poor Jacob,' said Mrs Durrant, quietl/ as if she had known him all his life. 'They're going to make you act in their play.'

'How I love you!' said Elsbeth, kneeling beside Mrs Durrant's chair.

'Give me the wool,' said Mrs Durrant.

'He's come—he's come!' cried Charlotte Wilding. 'I've won my bet!'

'There's another bunch higher up,' murmured Clara Durrant, mounting another step of the ladder. Jacob held the ladder as she stretched out to reach the grapes high up on the vine.

'There!' she said, cutting through the stalk. She looked semi-transparent, pale, wonderfully beautiful up there among the vine leaves and the yellow and purple bunches, the lights swimming over her in coloured islands. Geraniums and begonias stood in pots along planks; tomatoes climbed the walls.

'The leaves really want thinning,' she considered, and one green one, spread like the palm of a hand, circled down past Jacob's head.

'I have more than I can eat already,' he said, looking up.

'It does seem absurd . . .' Clara began, 'going back to London . . .'

'Ridiculous,' said Jacob, firmly.

'Then . . .' said Clara, 'you must come next year, properly,' she said, snipping another vine leaf, rather at random.

'If . . . If . . .'

A child ran past the greenhouse shouting. Clara slowly descended the ladder with her basket of grapes.

'One bunch of white, and two of purple ' she said, and she placed two great leaves over them where they lay curled warm in the basket.

'I have enjoyed myself,' said Jacob, looking down the greenhouse.

'Yes, it's been delightful,' she said vaguely.

'Oh, Miss Durrant,' he said, taking the basket of grapes; but she walked past him towards the door of the greenhouse.

'You're too good—too good,' she thought, thinking of Jacob, thinking that he must not say that he loved her. No, no, no.

The children were whirling past the door, throwing things high into the air.

'Little demons!' she cried. 'What have they got?' she asked Jacob.

'Onions, I think,' said Jacob. He looked at them without moving.

'Next August, remember, Jacob,' said Mrs Durrant, shaking hands with him on the terrace where the fuchsia hung, like a scarlet ear-ring, behind her head. Mr Wortley came out of the window in yellow slippers, trailing *The Times* and holding out his hand very cordially.

'Good-bye,' said Jacob. 'Good-bye,' he repeated. 'Good-bye,' he said once more. Charlotte Wilding flung up her bedroom window and cried out: 'Good-bye, Mr Jacob!'

'Mr Flanders!' cried Mr Clutterbuck, trying to extricate himself from his beehive chair. 'Jacob Flanders!'

'Too late, Joseph,' said Mrs Durrant.

'Not to sit for me,' said Miss Eliot, planting her tripod upon the lawn.

v

'I rather think,' said Jacob, taking his pipe from his mouth, 'it's in Virgil,' and pushing back his chair, he went to the window.

The rashest drivers in the world are, certainly, the drivers of post-office vans. Swinging down Lamb's Conduit Street, the scarlet van rounded the corner by the pillar box in such a way as to graze the kerb and make the little girl who was standing on tiptoe to post a letter look up, half frightened, half curious. She paused with her hand in the mouth of the box; then dropped her letter and ran away. It is seldom only that we see a child on tiptoe with pity—more often a dim discomfort, a grain of sand in the shoe which it's scarcely worth while to remove—that's our feeling, and so—Jacob turned to the bookcase.

Long ago great people lived here, and coming back from Court past midnight stood, huddling their satin skirts, under the carved door-posts while the footman roused himself from his mattress on the floor, hurriedly fastened the lower buttons of his waistcoat, and let them in. The bitter eighteenth-century rain rushed down the kennel. South-ampton Row, however, is chiefly remarkable nowadays for the fact that you will always find a man there trying to sell a tortoise to a tailor. 'Showing off the tweed, sir; what the gentry wants is something singular to catch the eye, sir—and clean in their habits, sir!' So they display their tortoises.

At Mudie's corner in Oxford Street all the red and blue beads had run together on the string. The motor omnibuses were locked. Mr Spalding going to the city looked at Mr Charles Budgeon bound for Shepherd's Bush. The proximity of the omnibuses gave the outside passengers an opportunity to stare into each other's faces. Yet few took advantage of it. Each had his own business to think of. Each had his past shut in him like the leaves of a book known to him by heart; and his friends could only read the title, James Spalding, or Charles Budgeon, and the passengers going the opposite way could read nothing at all—save 'a man with a red moustache', 'a young man in grey smoking a pipe'. The October sunlight rested upon all these men and women sitting immobile; and little Johnnie Sturgeon took the chance to swing down the staircase, carrying his large mysterious parcel, and so dodging a zigzag course between the wheels he reached the pavement, started to whistle a tune and was soon out of sight—for ever. The omnibuses jerked on, and every single person felt relief at being a little nearer to his journey's end, though some cajoled themselves past the immediate engagement by promise of indulgence beyond—steak and kidney pudding, drink, or a game of dominoes in the smoky corner of a city restaurant. Oh yes, human life is very tolerable on the top of an omnibus in Holborn, when the policeman holds up his arm and the sun beats on your back, and if there is such a thing as a shell secreted by man to fit man himself here we find it, on the banks of the Thames, where the great streets join and St Paul's Cathedral, like the volute on the top of the snail shell, finishes it off. Jacob, getting off his omnibus, loitered up the steps, consulted his watch, and finally made up his mind to go in . . . Does it need an effort? Yes. These changes of mood wear us out.

Dim it is, haunted by ghosts of white marble, to whom the organ for ever chaunts. If a boot creaks, it's awful; then the order; the discipline.

The verger with his rod has life ironed out beneath him. Sweet and holy are the angelic choristers. And for ever round the marble shoulders, in and out of the folded fingers, go the thin high sounds of voice and organ. For ever requiem—repose. Tired with scrubbing the steps of the Prudential Society's office, which she did year in year out, Mrs Lidgett took her seat beneath the great Duke's tomb, folded her hands, and half closed her eyes. A magnificent place for an old woman to rest in, by the very side of the great Duke's bones, whose victories mean nothing to her, whose name she knows not, though she never fails to greet the little angels opposite, as she passes out, wishing the like on her own tomb, for the leathern curtain of the heart has flapped wide, and out steal on tiptoe thoughts of rest, sweet melodies . . . Old Spicer, jute merchant, thought nothing of the kind though. Strangely enough he'd never been in St Paul's these fifty years, though his office windows looked on the churchyard. 'So that's all? Well, a gloomy old place . . . Where's Nelson's tomb? No time now—come again—a coin to leave in the box . . . Rain or fine is it? Well, if it would only make up its mind!' Idly the children stray in—the verger dissuades them—and another and another . . . man, woman, man, woman, boy . . . casting their eyes up, pursing their lips, the same shadow brushing the same faces; the leathern curtain of the heart flaps wide.

Nothing could appear more certain from the steps of St Paul's than that each person is miraculously provided with coat, skirt, and boots; an income; an object. Only Jacob, carrying in his hand Finlay's *Byzantine Empire*, which he had bought in Ludgate Hill, looked a little different; for in his hand he carried a book, which book he would at nine-thirty precisely, by his own fireside, open and study, as no one else of all these multitudes would do. They have no houses. The streets belong to them; the shops; the churches; theirs the innumerable desks; the stretched office lights; the vans are theirs, and the railway slung high above the street. If you look closer you will see that three elderly men at a little distance from each other run spiders along the pavement as if the street were their parlour, and here, against the wall, a woman stares at nothing, boot-laces extended, which she does not ask you to buy. The posters are theirs too; and the news on them. A town destroyed; a race won. A homeless people, circling beneath the sky whose blue or white is held off by a ceiling cloth of steel filings and horse dung shredded to dust.

There, under the green shade, with his head bent over white paper, Mr Sibley transferred figures to folios, and upon each desk you observe, like provender, a bunch of papers, the day's nutriment, slowly consumed by the industrious pen. Innumerable overcoats of the quality prescribed hung empty all day in the corridors, but as the clock struck six each was exactly filled, and the little figures, split apart into trousers or moulded into a single thickness, jerked rapidly with angular forward motion along the pavement; then dropped into darkness. Beneath the pavement, sunk in the earth, hollow drains lined with yellow light for ever conveyed them this way and that, and large letters upon enamel plates represented in the underworld the parks, squares, and circuses of the upper. 'Marble Arch—Shepherd's Bush'—to the majority the Arch and the Bush are eternally white letters upon a blue ground. Only at one point—it may be Acton, Holloway, Kensal Rise, Caledonian Road—does the name mean shops where you buy things, and houses, in one of which, down to the right, where the pollard trees grow out of the paving stones, there is a square curtained window, and a bedroom.

Long past sunset an old blind woman sat on a camp-stool with her back to the stone wall of the Union of London and Smith's Bank, clasping a brown mongrel tight in her arms and singing out loud, not for coppers, no, from the depths of her gay wild heart—her sinful, tanned heart—for the child who fetches her is the fruit of sin, and should have been in bed, curtained, asleep, instead of hearing in the lamplight her mother's wild song, where she sits against the Bank, singing not for coppers, with her dog against her breast.

Home they went. The grey church spires received them; the hoary city, old, sinful, and majestic. One behind another, round or pointed, piercing the sky or massing themselves, like sailing ships, like granite cliffs, spires and offices, wharves and factories crowd the bank; eternally the pilgrims trudge; barges rest in mid stream heavy laden; as some believe, the city loves her prostitutes.

But few, it seems, are admitted to that degree. Of all the carriages that leave the arch of the Opera House, not one turns eastward, and when the little thief is caught in the empty market-place no one in black-and-white or rose-coloured evening dress blocks the way by pausing with a hand upon the carriage door to help or condemn—though Lady Charles, to do her justice, sighs sadly as she ascends her staircase, takes down Thomas à Kempis, and does not sleep till her mind has lost itself tunnelling into the complexity of things. 'Why? Why? Why?' she sighs. On the whole it's best to walk back from the Opera House. Fatigue is the safest sleeping draught.

The autumn season was in full swing. Tristan was twitching his rug up under his armpits twice a week; Isolde waved her scarf in miraculous sympathy with the conductor's baton. In all parts of the house were to be found pink faces and glittering breasts. When a Royal hand attached to an invisible body slipped out and withdrew the red and white bouquet reposing on the scarlet ledge, the Queen of England seemed a name worth dying for. Beauty, in its hothouse variety (which is none of the worst), flowered in box after box; and though nothing was said of profound importance, and though it is generally agreed that wit deserted beautiful lips about the time that Walpole died—at any rate when Victoria in her nightgown descended to meet her ministers, the lips (through an opera glass) remained red, adorable. Bald distinguished men with gold-headed canes strolled down the crimson avenues between the stalls, and only broke from intercourse with the boxes when the lights went down, and the conductor, first bowing to the Queen, next to the bald-headed men, swept round on his feet and raised his wand.

Then two thousand hearts in the semi-darkness remembered, anticipated, travelled dark labyrinths; and Clara Durrant said farewell to Jacob Flanders, and tasted the sweetness of death in effigy; and Mrs Durrant, sitting behind her in the dark of the box, sighed her sharp sigh; and Mr Wortley, shifting his position behind the Italian Ambassador's wife, thought that Brangaena was a trifle hoarse; and suspended in the gallery many feet above their heads, Edward Whittaker surreptitiously held a torch to his miniature score; and . . . and . . .

In short, the observer is choked with observations. Only to prevent us from being submerged by chaos, nature and society between them have arranged a system of classification which is simplicity itself; stalls, boxes, amphitheatre, gallery. The moulds are filled nightly. There is no need to distinguish details. But the difficulty remains—one has to choose. For though I have no wish to be Queen of England—or only for a moment—I would willingly sit beside her; I would hear the Prime Minister's gossip; the countess whisper, and share her memories of halls and gardens; the massive fronts of the respectable conceal after all their secret code; or why so impermeable? And then, doffing one's own headpiece, how strange to assume for a moment someone's—anyone's—to be a man of valour who has ruled the Empire; to refer while Brangaena sings to the fragments of Sophocles, or see in a flash, as the shepherd pipes his tune, bridges and aqueducts. But no—we must choose. Never was there a harsher necessity! or one which entails greater pain, more certain disaster; for wherever I seat myself, I die in exile: Whittaker in his lodging-house; Lady Charles at the Manor.

A young man with a Wellington nose, who had occupied a seven-and-sixpenny seat, made his way down the stone stairs when the opera ended, as if he were still set a little apart from his fellows by the influence of the music.

At midnight Jacob Flanders heard a rap on his door.

'By Jove!' he exclaimed. 'You're the very man I want!' and without more ado they discovered the lines which he had been seeking all day; only they come not in Virgil, but in Lucretius.

'Yes; that should make him sit up,' said Bonamy, as Jacob stopped reading. Jacob was excited. It was the first time he had read his essay aloud.

'Damned swine!' he said, rather too extravagantly; but the praise had gone to his head. Professor Bulteel, of Leeds, had issued an edition of Wycherley without stating that he had left out, disembowelled, or indicated only by asterisks, several indecent words and some indecent phrases. An outrage, Jacob said; a breach of faith; sheer prudery; token of a lewd mind and a disgusting nature. Aristophanes and Shakespeare were cited. Modern life was repudiated. Great play was made with the professorial title, and Leeds as a seat of learning was laughed to scorn. And the extraordinary thing was that these young men were perfectly right—extraordinary, because, even as Jacob copied his pages, he knew that no one would ever print them; and sure enough back they came from the *Fortnightly*, the *Contemporary*, the *Nineteenth Century*—when Jacob threw them into the black wooden box where he kept his mother's letters, his old flannel trousers, and a note or two with the Cornish postmark. The lid shut upon the truth.

This black wooden box, upon which his name was still legible in white paint, stood between the long windows of the sitting-room. The street ran beneath. No doubt the bedroom was behind. The furniture—three wicker chairs and a gate-legged table—came from Cambridge. These houses (Mrs Garfit's daughter, Mrs Whitehorn, was the landlady of this one) were built, say, a hundred and fifty years ago. The rooms are shapely, the ceilings high; over the doorway a rose, or a ram's skull, is carved in the wood. The eighteenth century has its distinction. Even the panels, painted in raspberry-coloured paint, have their distinction . . .

'Distinction'—Mrs Durrant said that Jacob Flanders was 'distinguished-looking'. 'Extremely awkward,' she said, 'but so distinguished-looking.' Seeing him for the first time that no doubt is the word for him. Lying back in his chair, taking his pipe from his lips, and saying to Bonamy: 'About this opera now' (for they had done with indecency). 'This fellow Wagner' . . . distinction was one of the words to use naturally, though, from looking at him, one would have found it difficult to say which seat in the opera house was his, stalls, gallery, or dress circle. A writer? He lacked self-consciousness. A painter? There was something in the shape of his hands (he was descended on his mother's side from a family of the greatest antiquity and deepest obscurity) which indicated taste. Then his mouth—but surely, of all futile occupations this of cataloguing features is the worst. One word is sufficient. But if one cannot find it?

'I like Jacob Flanders,' wrote Clara Durrant in her diary. 'He is so unworldly. He gives himself no airs, and one can say what one likes to him, though he's frightening because . . .' But Mr Letts allows little space in his shilling diaries. Clara was not the one to encroach upon Wednesday. Humblest, most candid of women! 'No, no, no,' she sighed, standing at the greenhouse door, 'don't break—don't spoil'—what? Something infinitely wonderful.

But then, this is only a young woman's language, one, too, who loves, or refrains from loving. She wished the moment to continue for ever precisely as it was that July morning. And moments don't. Now, for instance, Jacob was telling a story about some walking tour he'd taken, and the inn was called 'The Foaming Pot', which, considering the landlady's name . . . They shouted with laughter. The joke was indecent.

Then Julia Eliot said 'the silent young man', and as she dined with Prime Ministers, no doubt she meant: 'If he is going to get on in the world, he will have to find his tongue.'

Timothy Durrant never made any comment at all.

The housemaid found herself very liberally rewarded.

Mr Sopwith's opinion was as sentimental as Clara's, though far more skilfully expressed.

Betty Flanders was romantic about Archer and tender about John; she was unreasonably irritated by Jacob's clumsiness in the house.

Captain Barfoot liked him best of the boys; but as for saying why . . .

It seems then that men and women are equally at fault. It seems that a profound, impartial, and absolutely just opinion of our fellow-creatures is utterly unknown. Either we are men, or we are women. Either we are cold, or we are sentimental. Either we are young, or growing old. In any case life is but a procession of shadows, and God knows why it is that we embrace them so eagerly, and see them depart with such anguish, being shadows. And why, if this and much more than this is true, why are we yet surprised in the window corner by a sudden vision that the young man in the chair is of all things in the world the most real, the

most solid, the best known to us—why indeed? For the moment after
we know nothing about him.

Such is the manner of our seeing. Such the conditions of our love.

('I'm twenty-two. It's nearly the end of October. Life is thoroughly
pleasant, although unfortunately there are a great number of fools about.
One must apply oneself to something or other—God knows what.
Everything is really very jolly—except getting up in the morning and
wearing a tail coat.')

'I say, Bonamy, what about Beethoven?'

('Bonamy is an amazing fellow. He knows practically everything—
not more about English literature than I do—but then he's read all
those Frenchmen.')

'I rather suspect you're talking rot, Bonamy. In spite of what you say,
poor old Tennyson . . .'

('The truth is one ought to have been taught French. Now, I suppose,
old Barfoot is talking to my mother. That's an odd affair to be sure. But
I can't see Bonamy down there. Damn London!') for the market carts
were lumbering down the street.

'What about a walk on Saturday?'

('What's happening on Saturday?')

Then, taking out his pocket-book, he assured himself that the night of
the Durrants' party came next week.

But though all this may very well be true—so Jacob thought and
spoke—so he crossed his legs—filled his pipe—sipped his whisky, and
once looked at his pocket-book, rumpling his hair as he did so, there
remains over something which can never be conveyed to a second person
save by Jacob himself. Moreover, part of this is not Jacob but Richard
Bonamy—the room; the market carts; the hour; the very moment of
history. Then consider the effect of sex—how between man and woman
it hangs wavy, tremulous, so that here's a valley, there's a peak, when
in truth, perhaps, all's as flat as my hand. Even the exact words get the
wrong accent on them. But something is always impelling one to hum
vibrating, like the hawk moth, at the mouth of the cavern of mystery,
endowing Jacob Flanders with all sorts of qualities he had not at all—
for though, certainly, he sat talking to Bonamy, half of what he said was
too dull to repeat; much unintelligible (about unknown people and
Parliament); what remains is mostly a matter of guess work. Yet over
him we hang vibrating.

'Yes,' said Captain Barfoot, knocking out his pipe on Betty Flanders's hob, and buttoning his coat. 'It doubles the work, but I don't mind that.'

He was now town councillor. They looked at the night, which was the same as the London night, only a good deal more transparent. Church bells down in the town were striking eleven o'clock. The wind was off the sea. And all the bedroom windows were dark—the Pages were asleep; the Garfits were asleep; the Cranches were asleep—whereas in London at this hour they were burning Guy Fawkes on Parliament Hill.

VI

The flames had fairly caught.

'There's St Paul's!' someone cried.

As the wood caught the city of London was lit up for a second; on the other sides of the fire there were trees. Of the faces which came out fresh and vivid as though painted in yellow and red, the most prominent was a girl's face. By a trick of the firelight she seemed to have no body. The oval of the face and hair hung beside the fire with a dark vacuum for background. As if dazed by the glare, her green-blue eyes stared at the flames. Every muscle of her face was taut. There was something tragic in her thus staring—her age between twenty and twenty-five.

A hand descending from the chequered darkness thrust on her head the conical white hat of a pierrot. Shaking her head, she still stared. A whiskered face appeared above her. They dropped two legs of a table upon the fire and a scattering of twigs and leaves. All this blazed up and showed faces far back, round, pale, smooth, bearded, some with billycock hats on; all intent; showed too St Paul's floating on the uneven white mist, and two or three narrow, paper-white, extinguisher-shaped spires.

The flames were struggling through the wood and roaring up when, goodness knows where from, pails flung water in beautiful hollow shapes, as of polished tortoiseshell; flung again and again; until the hiss was like a swarm of bees; and all the faces went out.

'Oh Jacob,' said the girl, as they pounded up the hill in the dark, 'I'm so frightfully unhappy!'

Shouts of laughter came from the others—high, low; some before, others after.

The hotel dining-room was brightly lit. A stag's head in plaster was at one end of the table; at the other some Roman bust blackened and

reddened to represent Guy Fawkes, whose night it was. The diners were
linked together by lengths of paper roses, so that when it came to singing
'Auld Lang Syne' with their hands crossed a pink and yellow line rose
and fell the entire length of the table. There was an enormous tapping
of green wine-glasses. A young man stood up, and Florinda, taking one
of the purplish globes that lay on the table, flung it straight at his head.
It crushed to powder.

'I'm so frightfully unhappy!' she said, turning to Jacob, who sat
beside her.

The table ran, as if on invisible legs, to the side of the room, and a
barrel-organ decorated with a red cloth and two pots of paper flowers
reeled out waltz music.

Jacob could not dance. He stood against the wall smoking a pipe.

'We think', said two of the dancers, breaking off from the rest, and
bowing profoundly before him, 'that you are the most beautiful man we
have ever seen.'

So they wreathed his head with paper flowers. Then somebody
brought out a white and gilt chair and made him sit on it. As they
passed, people hung glass grapes on his shoulders, until he looked like
the figure-head of a wrecked ship. Then Florinda got upon his knee and
hid her face in his waistcoat. With one hand he held her; with the other,
his pipe.

'Now let us talk', said Jacob, as he walked down Haverstock Hill
between four and five o'clock in the morning of November the sixth
arm-in-arm with Timmy Durrant, 'about something sensible.'

The Greeks—yes, that was what they talked about—how when all's
said and done, when one's rinsed one's mouth with every literature in
the world, including Chinese and Russian (but these Slavs aren't
civilized), it's the flavour of Greek that remains. Durrant quoted
Aeschylus—Jacob Sophocles. It is true that no Greek could have
understood or professor refrained from pointing out—Never mind; what
is Greek for if not to be shouted on Haverstock Hill in the dawn?
Moreover, Durrant never listened to Sophocles, nor Jacob to Aeschylus.
They were boastful, triumphant; it seemed to both that they had read
every book in the world; known every sin, passion, and joy. Civilizations
stood round them like flowers ready for picking. Ages lapped at their

feet like waves fit for sailing. And surveying all this, looming through the fog, the lamplight, the shades of London, the two young men decided in favour of Greece.

'Probably,' said Jacob, 'we are the only people in the world who know what the Greeks meant.'

They drank coffee at a stall where the urns were burnished and little lamps burnt along the counter.

Taking Jacob for a military gentleman, the stall-keeper told him about his boy at Gibraltar, and Jacob cursed the British army and praised the Duke of Wellington. So on again they went down the hill talking about the Greeks.

A strange thing—when you come to think of it—this love of Greek, flourishing in such obscurity, distorted, discouraged, yet leaping out, all of a sudden, especially on leaving crowded rooms, or after a surfeit of print, or when the moon floats among the waves of the hills, or in hollow, sallow, fruitless London days, like a specific; a clean blade; always a miracle. Jacob knew no more Greek than served him to stumble through a play. Of ancient history he knew nothing. However, as he tramped into London it seemed to him that they were making the flagstones ring on the road to the Acropolis, and that if Socrates saw them coming he would bestir himself and say 'my fine fellows', for the whole sentiment of Athens was entirely after his heart; free, venturesome, high-spirited . . . She had called him Jacob without asking his leave. She had sat upon his knee. Thus did all good women in the days of the Greeks.

At this moment there shook out into the air a wavering, quavering, doleful lamentation which seemed to lack strength to unfold itself, and yet flagged on; at the sound of which doors in back streets burst sullenly open; workmen stumped forth.

Florinda was sick.

Mrs Durrant, sleepless as usual, scored a mark by the side of certain lines in the *Inferno*.

Clara slept buried in her pillows; on her dressing-table dishevelled roses and a pair of long white gloves.

Still wearing the conical white hat of a pierrot, Florinda was sick.

The bedroom seemed fit for these catastrophes—cheap, mustard-coloured, half attic, half studio, curiously ornamented with silver paper stars. Welshwomen's hats, and rosaries pendent from the gas brackets. As for Florinda's story, her name had been bestowed upon her by a painter who had wished to signify that the flower of her maidenhood was still unplucked. Be that as it may, she was without a surname, and for parents had only the photograph of a tombstone beneath which, she said, her father lay buried. Sometimes she would dwell upon the size of it, and rumour had it that Florinda's father had died from the growth of his bones which nothing could stop; just as her mother enjoyed the confidence of a Royal master, and now and again Florinda herself was a Princess, but chiefly when drunk. Thus deserted, pretty into the bargain, with tragic eyes and the lips of a child, she talked more about virginity than women mostly do; and had lost it only the night before, or cherished it beyond the heart in her breast, according to the man she talked to. But did she always talk to men? No, she had her confidante: Mother Stuart. Stuart, as the lady would point out, is the name of a Royal house; but what that signified, and what her business was, no one knew; only that Mrs Stuart got postal orders every Monday morning, kept a parrot, believed in the transmigration of souls, and could read the future in tea leaves. Dirty lodging-house wallpaper she was behind the chastity of Florinda.

Now Florinda wept, and spent the day wandering the steets; stood at Chelsea watching the river swim past; trailed along the shopping streets; opened her bag and powdered her cheeks in omnibuses; read love letters, propping them against the milk pot in the A.B.C. shop; detected glass in the sugar bowl; accused the waitress of wishing to poison her; declared that young men stared at her; and found herself towards evening slowly sauntering down Jacob's street, when it struck her that she liked that man Jacob better than dirty Jews, and sitting at his table (he was copying his essay upon the Ethics of Indecency), drew off her gloves and told him how Mother Stuart had banged her on the head with the tea-cosy.

Jacob took her word for it that she was chaste. She prattled, sitting by the fireside, of famous painters. The tomb of her father was mentioned. Wild and frail and beautiful she looked, and thus the women of the Greeks were, Jacob thought; and this was life; and himself a man and Florinda chaste.

She left with one of Shelley's poems beneath her arm. Mrs Stuart, she said, often talked of him.

Marvellous are the innocent. To believe that the girl herself transcends all lies (for Jacob was not such a fool as to believe implicitly), to wonder enviously at the unanchored life—his own seeming petted and even cloistered in comparison—to have at hand as sovereign specifics for all disorders of the soul Adonais and the plays of Shakespeare; to figure out a comradeship all spirited on her side, protective on his, yet equal on both, for women, thought Jacob, are just the same as men— innocence such as this is marvellous enough, and perhaps not so foolish after all.

For when Florinda got home that night she first washed her head; then ate chocolate creams; then opened Shelley. True, she was horribly bored. What on earth was it *about*? She had to wager with herself that she would turn the page before she ate another. In fact she slept. But then her day had been a long one, Mother Stuart had thrown the tea-cosy;—there are formidable sights in the streets, and though Florinda was ignorant as an owl, and would never learn to read even her love letters correctly, still she had her feelings, liked some men better than others, and was entirely at the beck and call of life. Whether or not she was a virgin seems a matter of no importance whatever. Unless, indeed, it is the only thing of any importance at all.

Jacob was restless when she left him.

All night men and women seethed up and down the well-known beats. Late home-comers could see shadows against the blinds even in the most respectable suburbs. Not a square in snow or fog lacked its amorous couple. All plays turned on the same subject. Bullets went through heads in hotel bedrooms almost nightly on that account. When the body escaped mutilation, seldom did the heart go to the grave unscarred. Little else was talked of in theatres and popular novels. Yet we say it is a matter of no importance at all.

What with Shakespeare and Adonais, Mozart and Bishop Berkeley— choose whom you like—the fact is concealed and the evenings for most of us pass reputably, or with only the sort of tremor that a snake makes sliding through the grass. But then concealment by itself distracts the mind from the print and the sound. If Florinda had had a mind, she might have read with clearer eyes than we can. She and her sort have solved the question by turning it to a trifle of washing the hands nightly before going to bed, the only difficulty being whether you prefer your water hot or cold, which being settled, the mind can go about its business unassailed.

But it did occur to Jacob, half-way through dinner, to wonder whether she had a mind.

They sat at a little table in the restaurant.

Florinda leant the points of her elbows on the table and held her chin in the cup of her hands. Her cloak had slipped behind her. Gold and white with bright beads on her she emerged, her face flowering from her body, innocent, scarcely tinted, the eyes gazing frankly about her, or slowly settling on Jacob and resting there. She talked:

'You know that big black box the Australian left in my room ever so long ago? . . . I do think furs make a woman look old . . . That's Bechstein come in now . . . I was wondering what you looked like when you were a little boy, Jacob.' She nibbled her roll and looked at him.

'Jacob. You're like one of those statues . . . I think there are lovely things in the British Museum, don't you? Lots of lovely things . . .' she spoke dreamily. The room was filling; the heat increasing. Talk in a restaurant is dazed sleep-walkers' talk, so many things to look at—so much noise—other people talking. Can one overhear? Oh, but they mustn't overhear *us*.

'That's like Ellen Nagle—that girl . . .' and so on.

'I'm awfully happy since I've known you, Jacob. You're such a *good* man.'

The room got fuller and fuller; talk louder; knives more clattering.

'Well, you see what makes her say things like that is . . .'

She stopped. So did everyone.

'Tomorrow . . . Sunday . . . a beastly . . . you tell me . . . go then!' Crash! And out she swept.

It was at the table next them that the voice spun higher and higher. Suddenly the woman dashed the plates to the floor. The man was left there. Everybody stared. Then—'Well, poor chap, we mustn't sit staring. What a go! Did you hear what she said? By God, he looks a fool! Didn't come up to the scratch, I suppose. All the mustard on the table-cloth. The waiters laughing.'

Jacob observed Florinda. In her face there seemed to him something horribly brainless—as she sat staring.

Out she swept, the black woman with the dancing feather in her hat.

Yet she had to go somewhere. The night is not a tumultuous black ocean in which you sink or sail as a star. As a matter of fact it was a wet November night. The lamps of Soho made large greasy spots of light upon the pavement. The by-streets were dark enough to shelter man or woman leaning against the doorways. One detached herself as Jacob and Florinda approached.

'She's dropped her glove,' said Florinda.

Jacob pressing forward, gave it her.

Effusively she thanked him; retraced her steps; dropped her glove again. But why? For whom?

Meanwhile, where had the other woman got to? And the man?

The street lamps do not carry far enough to tell us. The voices, angry, lustful, despairing, passionate, were scarcely more than the voices of caged beasts at night. Only they are not caged, nor beasts. Stop a man; ask him the way; he'll tell it you; but one's afraid to ask him the way. What does one fear?—the human eye. At once the pavement narrows, the chasm deepens. There! They've melted into it—both man and woman. Further on, blatantly advertising its meritorious solidity, a boarding-house exhibits behind uncurtained windows its testimony to the soundness of London. There they sit, plainly illuminated, dressed like ladies and gentlemen, in bamboo chairs. The widows of business men prove laboriously that they are related to judges. The wives of coal merchants instantly retort that their fathers kept coachmen. A servant brings coffee, and the crochet basket has to be moved. And so on again into the dark, passing a girl here for sale, or there an old woman with only matches to offer, passing the crowd from the Tube station, the women with veiled hair, passing at length no one but shut doors, carved door-posts, and a solitary policeman, Jacob, with Florinda on his arm, reached his room and, lighting the lamp, said nothing at all.

'I don't like you when you look like that,' said Florinda.

The problem is insoluble. The body is harnessed to a brain. Beauty goes hand in hand with stupidity. There she sat staring at the fire as she had stared at the broken mustard-pot. In spite of defending indecency, Jacob doubted whether he liked it in the raw. He had a violent reversion towards male society, cloistered rooms, and the works of the classics; and was ready to turn with wrath upon whoever it was who had fashioned life thus.

Then Florinda laid her hand upon his knee.

After all, it was none of her fault. But the thought saddened him. It's not catastrophes, murders, deaths, diseases, that age and kill us; it's the way people look and laugh, and run up the steps of omnibuses.

Any excuse, though, serves a stupid woman. He told her his head ached.

But when she looked at him, dumbly, half-guessing, half-understanding, apologizing perhaps, anyhow saying as he had said, 'It's none of my fault,' straight and beautiful in body, her face like a shell within its

cap, then he knew that cloisters and classics are no use whatever. The
problem is insoluble.

VII

About this time a firm of merchants having dealings with the East put
on the market little paper flowers which opened on touching water. As
it was the custom also to use finger-bowls at the end of dinner, the new
discovery was found of excellent service. In these sheltered lakes the
little coloured flowers swam and slid; surmounted smooth slippery
waves, and sometimes foundered and lay like pebbles on the glass floor.
Their fortunes were watched by eyes intent and lovely. It is surely a
great discovery that leads to the union of hearts and foundation of
homes. The paper flowers did no less.

It must not be thought, though, that they ousted the flowers of nature.
Roses, lilies, carnations in particular, looked over the rims of vases and
surveyed the bright lives and swift dooms of their artificial relations. Mr
Stuart Ormond made this very observation; and charming it was
thought; and Kitty Craster married him on the strength of it six months
later. But real flowers can never be dispensed with. If they could, human
life would be a different affair altogether. For flowers fade; chrysanthe-
mums are the worst; perfect over night; yellow and jaded next morning—not fit to be seen. On the whole, though the price is sinful,
carnations pay best;—it's a question, however, whether it's wise to have
them wired. Some shops advise it. Certainly it's the only way to keep
them at a dance; but whether it is necessary at dinner parties, unless the
rooms are very hot, remains in dispute. Old Mrs Temple used to
recommend an ivy leaf—just one—dropped in the bowl. She said it kept
the water pure for days and days. But there is some reason to think that
old Mrs Temple was mistaken.

The little cards, however, with names engraved on them, are a more
serious problem than the flowers. More horses' legs have been worn out,
more coachmen's lives consumed, more hours of sound afternoon time
vainly lavished than served to win us the battle of Waterloo, and pay for
it into the bargain. The little demons are the source of as many reprieves,
calamities, and anxieties as the battle itself. Sometimes Mrs Bonham
has just gone out, at others she is at home. But, even if the cards should
be superseded, which seems unlikely, there are unruly powers blowing
life into storms, disordering sedulous mornings, and uprooting the
stability of the afternoon—dressmakers, that is to say, and confectioners'
shops. Six yards of silk will cover one body; but if you have to devise six

hundred shapes for it, and twice as many colours?—in the middle of which there is the urgent question of the pudding with tufts of green cream and battlements of almond paste. It has not arrived.

The flamingo hours fluttered softly through the sky. But regularly they dipped their wings in pitch black; Notting Hill, for instance, or the purlieus of Clerkenwell. No wonder that Italian remained a hidden art, and the piano always played the same sonata. In order to buy one pair of elastic stockings for Mrs Page, widow, aged sixty-three, in receipt of five shillings out-door relief, and help from her only son employed in Messrs Mackie's dye-works, suffering in winter with his chest, letters must be written, columns filled up in the same round, simple hand that wrote in Mr Letts's diary how the weather was fine, the children demons, and Jacob Flanders unworldly. Clara Durrant procured the stockings, played the sonata, filled the vases, fetched the pudding, left the cards, and when the great invention of paper flowers to swim in finger bowls was discovered, was one of those who most marvelled at their brief lives.

Nor were there wanting poets to celebrate the theme. Edwin Mallett, for example, wrote his verses ending:

> And read their doom in Chloe's eyes,

which caused Clara to blush at the first reading, and to laugh at the second, saying that it was just like him to call her Chloe when her name was Clara. Ridiculous young man! But when, between ten and eleven on a rainy morning, Edwin Mallett laid his life at her feet she ran out of the room and hid herself in her bedroom, and Timothy below could not get on with his work all that morning on account of her sobs.

'Which is the result of enjoying yourself,' said Mrs Durrant severely, surveying the dance programme all scored with the same initials, or rather they were different ones this time—R. B. instead of E. M.; Richard Bonamy it was now, the young man with the Wellington nose.

'But I could never marry a man with a nose like that,' said Clara.

'Nonsense,' said Mrs Durrant.

'But I am too severe,' she thought to herself. For Clara, losing all vivacity, tore up her dance programme and threw it in the fender.

Such were the very serious consequences of the invention of paper flowers to swim in bowls.

'Please,' said Julia Eliot, taking up her position by the curtain almost opposite the door, 'don't introduce me. I like to look on. The amusing thing,' she went on, addressing Mr Salvin, who, owing to his lameness, was accommodated with a chair, 'the amusing thing about a party is to watch the people—coming and going, coming and going.'

'Last time we met', said Mr Salvin, 'was at the Farquhars. Poor lady! She has much to put up with.'

'Doesn't she look charming?' exclaimed Miss Eliot, as Clara Durrant passed them.

'And which of them . . .?' asked Mr Salvin, dropping his voice and speaking in quizzical tones.

'There are so many . . .' Miss Eliot replied. Three young men stood at the doorway looking about for their hostess.

'You don't remember Elizabeth as I do,' said Mr Salvin, 'dancing Highland reels at Banchorie. Clara lacks her mother's spirit. Clara is a little pale.'

'What different people one sees here!' said Miss Eliot.

'Happily we are not governed by the evening papers,' said Mr Salvin.

'I never read them,' said Miss Eliot. 'I know nothing about politics,' she added.

'The piano is in tune,' said Clara, passing them, 'but we may have to ask someone to move it for us.'

'Are they going to dance?' asked Mr Salvin.

'Nobody shall disturb you,' said Mrs Durrant peremptorily as she passed.

'Julia Eliot. It *is* Julia Eliot!' said old Lady Hibbert, holding out both her hands. 'And Mr Salvin. What is going to happen to us, Mr Salvin? With all my experience of English politics—My dear, I was thinking of your father last night—one of my oldest friends, Mr Salvin. Never tell me that girls of ten are incapable of love! I had all Shakespeare by heart before I was in my teens, Mr Salvin!'

'You don't say so,' said Mr Salvin.

'But I do,' said Lady Hibbert.

'Oh, Mr Salvin, I'm so sorry . . .'

'I will remove myself if you'll kindly lend me a hand,' said Mr Salvin.

'You shall sit by my mother,' said Clara. 'Everybody seems to come in here . . . Mr Calthorp, let me introduce you to Miss Edwards.'

'Are you going away for Christmas?' said Mr Calthorp.

'If my brother gets his leave,' said Miss Edwards.

'What regiment is he in?' said Mr Calthorp.

'The Twentieth Hussars,' said Miss Edwards.

'Perhaps he knows my brother?' said Mr Calthorp.

'I am afraid I did not catch your name,' said Miss Edwards.

'Calthorp,' said Mr Calthorp.

'But what proof was there that the marriage service was actually performed?' said Mr Crosby.

'There is no reason to doubt that Charles James Fox . . .' Mr Burley began; but here Mrs Stretton told him that she knew his sister well; had stayed with her not six weeks ago; and thought the house charming, but bleak in winter.

'Going about as girls do nowadays——' said Mrs Forster.

Mr Bowley looked round him, and catching sight of Rose Shaw moved towards her, threw out his hands, and exclaimed: 'Well!'

'Nothing!' she replied. 'Nothing at all—though I left them alone the entire afternoon on purpose.'

'Dear me, dear me,' said Mr Bowley. 'I will ask Jimmy to breakfast.'

'But who could resist her?' cried Rose Shaw. 'Dearest Clara—I know we mustn't try to stop you . . .'

'You and Mr Bowley are talking dreadful gossip, I know,' said Clara.

'Life is wicked—life is detestable!' cried Rose Shaw.

'There's not much to be said for this sort of thing, is there?' said Timothy Durrant to Jacob.

'Women like it.'

'Like what?' said Charlotte Wilding, coming up to them.

'Where have you come from?' said Timothy. 'Dining somewhere, I suppose.'

'I don't see why not,' said Charlotte.

'People must go downstairs,' said Clara, passing. 'Take Charlotte, Timothy. How d'you do, Mr Flanders.'

'How d'you do, Mr Flanders,' said Julia Eliot, holding out her hand. 'What's been happening to you?'

> 'Who is Silvia? what is she?
> That all our swains commend her?'

sang Elsbeth Siddons.

Every one stood where they were, or sat down if a chair was empty. 'Ah,' sighed Clara, who stood beside Jacob, half-way through.

> 'Then to Silvia let us sing,
>   That Silvia is excelling;
> She excels each mortal thing
>   Upon the dull earth dwelling.
> To her let us garlands bring,'

sang Elsbeth Siddons.

'Ah!' Clara exclaimed out loud, and clapped her gloved hands; and Jacob clapped his bare ones; and then she moved forward and directed people to come in from the doorway.

'You are living in London?' asked Miss Julia Eliot.

'Yes,' said Jacob.

'In rooms?'

'Yes.'

'There is Mr Clutterbuck. You always see Mr Clutterbuck here. He is not very happy at home, I am afraid. They say that Mrs Clutterbuck . . .' she dropped her voice. 'That's why he stays with the Durrants. Were you there when they acted Mr Wortley's play? Oh, no, of course not—at the last moment, did you hear—you had to go to join your mother, I remember, at Harrogate—At the last moment, as I was saying, just as everything was ready, the clothes finished and everything—Now Elsbeth is going to sing again. Clara is playing her accompaniment or turning over for Mr Carter, I think. No, Mr Carter is playing by himself—This is *Bach*,' she whispered, as Mr Carter played the first bars.

'Are you fond of music?' said Mrs Durrant.

'Yes. I like hearing it,' said Jacob. 'I know nothing about it.'

'Very few people do that,' said Mrs Durrant. 'I daresay you were never taught. Why is that, Sir Jasper?—Sir Jasper Bigham—Mr Flanders. Why is nobody taught anything that they ought to know, Sir Jasper?' She left them standing against the wall.

Neither of the gentlemen said anything for three minutes, though Jacob shifted perhaps five inches to the left, and then as many to the right. Then Jacob grunted, and suddenly crossed the room.

'Will you come and have something to eat?' he said to Clara Durrant.

'Yes, an ice. Quickly. Now,' she said.

Downstairs they went.

But half-way down they met Mr and Mrs Gresham, Herbert Turner, Sylvia Rashleigh, and a friend, whom they had dared to bring, from America, 'knowing that Mrs Durrant—wishing to show Mr Pilcher.—Mr Pilcher from New York—This is Miss Durrant.'

'Whom I have heard so much of,' said Mr Pilcher, bowing low.

So Clara left him.

VIII

About half-past nine Jacob left the house, his door slamming, other doors slamming, buying his paper, mounting his omnibus, or, weather permitting, walking his road as other people do. Head bent down, a desk, a telephone, books bound in green leather, electric light . . . 'Fresh coals, sir?' . . . 'Your tea, sir.' . . . Talk about football, the Hotspurs, the Harlequins; six-thirty *Star* brought in by the office boy; the rooks of Gray's Inn passing overhead; branches in the fog thin and brittle; and through the roar of traffic now and again a voice shouting: 'Verdict—verdict—winner—winner,' while letters accumulate in a basket, Jacob signs them, and each evening finds him, as he takes his coat down, with some muscle of the brain new stretched.

Then, sometimes a game of chess; or pictures in Bond Street, or a long way home to take the air with Bonamy on his arm, meditatively marching, head thrown back, the world a spectacle, the early moon above the steeples coming in for praise, the sea-gulls flying high, Nelson on his column surveying the horizon, and the world our ship.

Meanwhile, poor Betty Flanders's letter, having caught the second post, lay on the hall table—poor Betty Flanders writing her son's name, Jacob Alan Flanders, Esq., as mothers do, and the ink pale, profuse, suggesting how mothers down at Scarborough scribble over the fire with their feet on the fender, when tea's cleared away, and can never, never say, whatever it may be—probably this—Don't go with bad women, do be a good boy; wear your thick shirts; and come back, come back, come back to me.

But she said nothing of the kind. 'Do you remember old Miss Wargrave, who used to be so kind when you had the whooping-cough?' she wrote; 'she's dead at last, poor thing. They would like it if you wrote. Ellen came over and we spent a nice day shopping. Old Mouse gets very stiff, and we have to walk him up the smallest hill. Rebecca, at last, after I don't know how long, went into Mr Adamson's. Three teeth, he says, must come out. Such mild weather for the time of year, the little

buds actually on the pear trees. And Mrs Jarvis tells me——' Mrs
Flanders liked Mrs Jarvis, always said of her that she was too good for
such a quiet place, and, though she never listened to her discontent and
told her at the end of it (looking up, sucking her thread, or taking off her
spectacles) that a little peat wrapped round the iris roots keeps them
from the frost, and Parrot's great white sale is Tuesday next, 'do
remember,'—Mrs Flanders knew precisely how Mrs Jarvis felt; and
how interesting her letters were, about Mrs Jarvis, could one read them
year in, year out—the unpublished works of women, written by the
fireside in pale profusion, dried by the flame, for the blotting-paper's
worn to holes and the nib cleft and clotted. Then Captain Barfoot. Him
she called 'the Captain', spoke of frankly, yet never without reserve. The
Captain was enquiring for her about Garfit's acre; advised chickens;
could promise profit; or had the sciatica; or Mrs Barfoot had been
indoors for weeks; or the Captain says things look bad, politics that is,
for as Jacob knew, the Captain would sometimes talk, as the evening
waned, about Ireland or India; and then Mrs Flanders would fall
musing about Morty, her brother, lost all these years—had the natives
got him, was his ship sunk—would the Admiralty tell her?—the Captain
knocking his pipe out, as Jacob knew, rising to go, stiffly stretching to
pick up Mrs Flanders's wool which had rolled beneath the chair. Talk
of the chicken farm came back and back, the woman, even at fifty,
impulsive at heart, sketching on the cloudy future flocks of Leghorns,
Cochin Chinas, Orpingtons; like Jacob in the blur of her outline; but
powerful as he was; fresh and vigorous, running about the house,
scolding Rebecca.

The letter lay upon the hall table; Florinda coming in that night took
it up with her, put it on the table as she kissed Jacob, and Jacob seeing
the hand, left it there under the lamp, between the biscuit-tin and the
tobacco-box. They shut the bedroom door behind them.

The sitting-room neither knew nor cared. The door was shut; and to
suppose that wood, when it creaks, transmits anything save that rats are
busy and wood dry is childish. These old houses are only brick and
wood, soaked in human sweat, grained with human dirt. But if the pale
blue envelope lying by the biscuit-box had the feelings of a mother, the
heart was torn by the little creak, the sudden stir. Behind the door was
the obscene thing, the alarming presence, and terror would come over
her as at death, or the birth of a child. Better, perhaps, burst in and face
it than sit in the antechamber listening to the little creak, the sudden
stir, for her heart was swollen, and pain threaded it. My son, my son—
such would be her cry, uttered to hide her vision of him stretched with
Florinda, inexcusable, irrational, in a woman with three children living
at Scarborough. And the fault lay with Florinda. Indeed, when the door

opened and the couple came out, Mrs Flanders would have flounced upon her—only it was Jacob who came first, in his dressing-gown, amiable, authoritative, beautifully healthy, like a baby after an airing, with an eye clear as running water. Florinda followed, lazily stretching; yawning a little; arranging her hair at the looking-glass—while Jacob read his mother's letter.

Let us consider letters—how they come at breakfast, and at night, with their yellow stamps and their green stamps, immortalized by the postmark—for to see one's own envelope on another's table is to realize how soon deeds sever and become alien. Then at last the power of the mind to quit the body is manifest, and perhaps we fear or hate or wish annihilated this phantom of ourselves, lying on the table. Still, there are letters that merely say how dinner's at seven; others ordering coal; making appointments. The hand in them is scarcely perceptible, let alone the voice or the scowl. Ah, but when the post knocks and the letter comes always the miracle seems repeated—speech attempted. Venerable are letters, infinitely brave, forlorn, and lost.

Life would split asunder without them. 'Come to tea, come to dinner, what's the truth of the story? have you heard the news? life in the capital is gay; the Russian dancers . . .' These are our stays and props. These lace our days together and make of life a perfect globe. And yet, and yet . . . when we go to dinner, when pressing finger-tips we hope to meet somewhere soon, a doubt insinuates itself; is this the way to spend our days? the rare, the limited, so soon dealt out to us—drinking tea? dining out? And the notes accumulate. And the telephones ring. And everywhere we go wires and tubes surround us to carry the voices that try to penetrate before the last card is dealt and the days are over. 'Try to penetrate,' for as we lift the cup, shake the hand, express the hope, something whispers, Is this all? Can I never know, share, be certain? Am I doomed all my days to write letters, send voices, which fall upon the tea-table, fade upon the passage, making appointments, while life dwindles, to come and dine? Yet letters are venerable; and the telephone valiant, for the journey is a lonely one, and if bound together by notes and telephones we went in company, perhaps—who knows?—we might talk by the way.

Well, people have tried. Byron wrote letters. So did Cowper. For centuries the writing-desk has contained sheets fit precisely for the communications of friends. Masters of language, poets of long ages, have turned from the sheet that endures to the sheet that perishes, pushing aside the tea-tray, drawing close to the fire (for letters are written when the dark presses round a bright red cave), and addressed themselves to the task of reaching, touching, penetrating the individual heart. Were it possible! But words have been used too often; touched and turned, and left exposed to the dust of the street. The words we seek hang close to the tree. We come at dawn and find them sweet beneath the leaf.

Mrs Flanders wrote letters; Mrs Jarvis wrote them; Mrs Durrant too; Mother Stuart actually scented her pages, thereby adding a flavour which the English language fails to provide; Jacob had written in his day long letters about art, morality, and politics to young men at college. Clara Durrant's letters were those of a child. Florinda—the impediment between Florinda and her pen was something impassable. Fancy a butterfly, gnat, or other winged insect, attached to a twig which, clogged with mud, it rolls across a page. Her spelling was abominable. Her sentiments infantile. And for some reason when she wrote she declared her belief in God. Then there were crosses—tear stains; and the hand itself rambling and redeemed only by the fact—which always did redeem Florinda—by the fact that she cared. Yes, whether it was for chocolate creams, hot baths, the shape of her face in the looking-glass, Florinda could no more pretend a feeling than swallow whisky. Incontinent was her rejection. Great men are truthful, and these little prostitutes, staring in the fire, taking out a powder-puff, decorating lips at an inch of looking-glass, have (so Jacob thought) an inviolable fidelity.

Then he saw her turning up Greek Street upon another man's arm.

The light from the arc lamp drenched him from head to toe. He stood for a minute motionless beneath it. Shadows chequered the street. Other figures, single and together, poured out, wavered across, and obliterated Florinda and the man.

The light drenched Jacob from head to toe. You could see the pattern on his trousers; the old thorns on his stick; his shoe laces; bare hands; and face.

It was as if a stone were ground to dust; as if white sparks flew from a livid whetstone, which was his spine; as if the switchback railway, having swooped to the depths, fell, fell, fell. This was in his face.

Whether we know what was in his mind is another question. Granted ten years' seniority and a difference of sex, fear of him comes first; this is swallowed up by a desire to help—overwhelming sense, reason, and the time of night; anger would follow close on that—with Florinda, with destiny; and then up would bubble an irresponsible optimism. 'Surely there's enough light in the street at this moment to drown all our cares in gold!' Ah, what's the use of saying it? Even while you speak and look over your shoulder towards Shaftesbury Avenue, destiny is chipping a dent in him. He has turned to go. As for following him back to his rooms, no—that we won't do.

Yet that, of course, is precisely what one does. He let himself in and shut the door, though it was only striking ten on one of the city clocks. No one can go to bed at ten. Nobody was thinking of going to bed. It was January and dismal, but Mrs Wagg stood on her doorstep, as if expecting something to happen. A barrel-organ played like an obscene nightingale beneath wet leaves. Children ran across the road. Here and there one could see brown panelling inside the hall door . . . The march that the mind keeps beneath the windows of others is queer enough. Now distracted by brown panelling; now by a fern in a pot; here improvising a few phrases to dance with the barrel-organ; again snatching a detached gaiety from a drunken man; then altogether absorbed by words the poor shout across the street at each other (so outright, so lusty)—yet all the while having for centre, for magnet, a young man alone in his room.

'Life is wicked—life is detestable,' cried Rose Shaw.

The strange thing about life is that though the nature of it must have been apparent to every one for hundreds of years, no one has left any adequate account of it. The streets of London have their map; but our passions are uncharted. What are you going to meet if you turn this corner?

'Holborn straight ahead of you,' says the policeman. Ah, but where are you going if instead of brushing past the old man with the white beard, the silver medal, and the cheap violin, you let him go on with his story, which ends in an invitation to step somewhere, to his room, presumably, off Queen's Square, and there he shows you a collection of birds' eggs and a letter from the Prince of Wales's secretary, and this (skipping the intermediate stages) brings you one winter's day to the Essex coast, where the little boat makes off to the ship, and the ship sails and you behold on the skyline the Azores; and the flamingoes rise; and there you sit on the verge of the marsh drinking rum-punch, an outcast from civilization, for you have committed a crime, are infected with yellow fever as likely as not, and—fill in the sketch as you like.

As frequent as street corners in Holborn are these chasms in the continuity of our ways. Yet we keep straight on.

Rose Shaw, talking in rather an emotional manner to Mr Bowley at Mrs Durrant's evening party a few nights back, said that life was wicked because a man called Jimmy refused to marry a woman called (if memory serves) Helen Aitken.

Both were beautiful. Both were inanimate. The oval tea-table invariably separated them, and the plate of biscuits was all he ever gave her. He bowed; she inclined her head. They danced. He danced divinely. They sat in the alcove; never a word was said. Her pillow was wet with tears. Kind Mr Bowley and dear Rose Shaw marvelled and deplored. Bowley had rooms in the Albany. Rose was re-born every evening precisely as the clock struck eight. All four were civilization's triumphs, and if you persist that a command of the English language is part of our inheritance, one can only reply that beauty is almost always dumb. Male beauty in association with female beauty breeds in the onlooker a sense of fear. Often have I seen them—Helen and Jimmy—and likened them to ships adrift, and feared for my own little craft. Or again, have you ever watched fine collie dogs couchant at twenty yards' distance? As she passed him his cup there was that quiver in her flanks. Bowley saw what was up—asked Jimmy to breakfast. Helen must have confided in Rose. For my own part, I find it exceedingly difficult to interpret songs without words. And now Jimmy feeds crows in Flanders and Helen visits hospitals. Oh, life is damnable, life is wicked, as Rose Shaw said.

The lamps of London uphold the dark as upon the points of burning bayonets. The yellow canopy sinks and swells over the great four-poster. Passengers in the mail-coaches running into London in the eighteenth century looked through leafless branches and saw it flaring beneath them. The light burns behind yellow blinds and pink blinds, and above fanlights, and down in basement windows. The street market in Soho is fierce with light. Raw meat, china mugs, and silk stockings blaze in it. Raw voices wrap themselves round the flaring gas-jets. Arms akimbo, they stand on the pavement bawling—Messrs Kettle and Wilkinson; their wives sit in the shop, furs wrapped round their necks, arms folded, eyes contemptuous. Such faces as one sees. The little man fingering the meat must have squatted before the fire in innumerable lodging-houses, and heard and seen and known so much that it seems to utter itself even volubly from dark eyes, loose lips, as he fingers the meat silently, his face sad as a poet's, and never a song sung. Shawled women carry babies with purple eyelids; boys stand at street corners; girls look across the road—rude illustrations, pictures in a book whose pages we turn over and over as if we should at last find what we look for. Every face, every shop, bedroom window, public-house, and dark square is a picture feverishly turned—in search of what? It is the same with books. What do we seek through millions of pages? Still hopefully turning the pages— oh, here is Jacob's room.

He sat at the table reading the *Globe*. The pinkish sheet was spread flat before him. He propped his face in his hand, so that the skin of his cheek was wrinkled in deep folds. Terribly severe he looked, set, and defiant. (What people go through in half an hour! But nothing could save him. These events are features of our landscape. A foreigner coming to London could scarcely miss seeing St Paul's.) He judged life. These pinkish and greenish newspapers are thin sheets of gelatine pressed nightly over the brain and heart of the world. They take the impression of the whole. Jacob cast his eye over it. A strike, a murder, football, bodies found; vociferation from all parts of England simultaneously. How miserable it is that the *Globe* newspaper offers nothing better to Jacob Flanders! When a child begins to read history one marvels, sorrowfully, to hear him spell out in his new voice the ancient words.

The Prime Minister's speech was reported in something over five columns. Feeling in his pocket, Jacob took out a pipe and proceeded to fill it. Five minutes, ten minutes, fifteen minutes passed. Jacob took the paper over to the fire. The Prime Minister proposed a measure for giving Home Rule to Ireland. Jacob knocked out his pipe. He was certainly thinking about Home Rule in Ireland—a very difficult matter. A very cold night.

The snow, which had been falling all night, lay at three o'clock in the afternoon over the fields and the hill. Clumps of withered grass stood out upon the hill-top; the furze bushes were black, and now and then a black shiver crossed the snow as the wind drove flurries of frozen particles before it. The sound was that of a broom sweeping—sweeping.

The stream crept along by the road unseen by anyone. Sticks and leaves caught in the frozen grass. The sky was sullen grey and the trees of black iron. Uncompromising was the severity of the country. At four o'clock the snow was again falling. The day had gone out.

A window tinged yellow about two feet across alone combated the white fields and the black trees . . . At six o'clock a man's figure carrying a lantern crossed the field . . . A raft of twigs stayed upon a stone, suddenly detached itself, and floated towards the culvert . . . A load of snow slipped and fell from a fir branch . . . Later there was a mournful cry . . . A motor car came along the road shoving the dark before it . . . The dark shut down behind it . . .

Spaces of complete immobility separated each of these movements. The land seemed to lie dead . . . Then the old shepherd returned stiffly across the field. Stiffly and painfully the frozen earth was trodden under and gave beneath pressure like a treadmill. The worn voices of clocks repeated the fact of the hour all night long.

Jacob, too, heard them, and raked out the fire. He rose. He stretched himself. He went to bed.

IX

The Countess of Rocksbier sat at the head of the table alone with Jacob. Fed upon champagne and spices for at least two centuries (four, if you count the female line), the Countess Lucy looked well fed. A discriminating nose she had for scents, prolonged, as if in quest of them; her underlip protruded a narrow red shelf; her eyes were small, with sandy tufts for eyebrows, and her jowl was heavy. Behind her (the window looked on Grosvenor Square) stood Moll Pratt on the pavement, offering violets for sale; and Mrs Hilda Thomas, lifting her skirts, preparing to cross the road. One was from Walworth; the other from Putney. Both wore black stockings, but Mrs Thomas was coiled in furs. The comparison was much in Lady Rocksbier's favour. Moll had more humour, but was violent; stupid too. Hilda Thomas was mealy-mouthed, all her silver frames aslant; egg-cups in the drawing-room; and the windows shrouded. Lady Rocksbier, whatever the deficiencies of her profile, had been a great rider to hounds. She used her knife with authority, tore her chicken bones, asking Jacob's pardon, with her own hands.

'Who is that driving by?' she asked Boxall, the butler.

'Lady Fittlemere's carriage, my lady,' which reminded her to send a card to ask after his lordship's health. A rude old lady, Jacob thought. The wine was excellent. She called herself 'an old woman'—'so kind to lunch with an old woman'—which flattered him. She talked of Joseph Chamberlain, whom she had known. She said that Jacob must come and meet—one of our celebrities. And the Lady Alice came in with three dogs on a leash, and Jackie, who ran to kiss his grandmother, while Boxall brought in a telegram, and Jacob was given a good cigar.

A few moments before a horse jumps it slows, sidles, gathers itself together, goes up like a monster wave, and pitches down on the further side. Hedges and sky swoop in a semicircle. Then as if your own body ran into the horse's body and it was your own forelegs grown with his that sprang, rushing through the air you go, the ground resilient, bodies a mass of muscles, yet you have command too, upright stillness, eyes accurately judging. Then the curves cease, changing to downright hammer strokes, which jar; and you draw up with a jolt; sitting back a little, sparkling, tingling, glazed with ice over pounding arteries, gasping: 'Ah! ho! Hah!' the steam going up from the horses as they jostle together at the cross-roads, where the signpost is, and the woman in the apron stands and stares at the doorway. The man raises himself from the cabbages to stare too.

So Jacob galloped over the fields of Essex, flopped in the mud, lost the hunt, and rode by himself eating sandwiches, looking over the hedges, noticing the colours as if new scraped, cursing his luck.

He had tea at the Inn; and there they all were, slapping, stamping, saying, 'After you,' clipped, curt, jocose, red as the wattles of turkeys, using free speech until Mrs Horsefield and her friend Miss Dudding appeared at the doorway with their skirts hitched up, and hair looping down. Then Tom Dudding rapped at the window with his whip. A motor car throbbed in the courtyard. Gentlemen, feeling for matches, moved out, and Jacob went into the bar with Brandy Jones to smoke with the rustics. There was old Jevons with one eye gone, and his clothes the colour of mud, his bag over his back, and his brains laid feet down in earth among the violet roots and the nettle roots; Mary Sanders with her box of wood; and Tom sent for beer, the half-witted son of the sexton—all this within thirty miles of London.

Mrs Papworth, of Endell Street, Covent Garden, did for Mr Bonamy in New Square, Lincoln's Inn, and as she washed up the dinner things in the scullery she heard the young gentlemen talking in the room next door. Mr Sanders was there again; Flanders she meant; and where an inquisitive old woman gets a name wrong, what chance is there that she will faithfully report an argument? As she held the plates under water and then dealt them on the pile beneath the hissing gas, she listened: heard Sanders speaking in a loud rather overbearing tone of voice: 'good' he said, and 'absolute' and 'justice' and 'punishment', and 'the will of the majority'. Then her gentleman piped up; she backed him for argument against Sanders. Yet Sanders was a fine young fellow (here all the scraps went swirling round the sink, scoured after by her purple, almost nailless hands). 'Women'—she thought, and wondered what Sanders and her gentleman did in *that* line, one eyelid sinking perceptibly as she mused, for she was the mother of nine—three still-born and one deaf and dumb from birth. Putting the plates in the rack she heard once more Sanders at it again ('He don't give Bonamy a chance,' she thought). 'Objective something,' said Bonamy; and 'common ground' and something else—all very long words, she noted. 'Book learning does it,' she thought to herself, and, as she thrust her arms into her jacket, heard something—might be the little table by the fire—fall; and then stamp, stamp, stamp—as if they were having at each other—round the room, making the plates dance.

'Tomorrow's breakfast, sir,' she said, opening the door; and there were Sanders and Bonamy like two bulls of Bashan driving each other up and down, making such a racket, and all them chairs in the way. They never noticed her. She felt motherly towards them. 'Your breakfast, sir,' she said, as they came near. And Bonamy, all his hair touzled and his tie flying, broke off, and pushed Sanders into the armchair, and said Mr Sanders had smashed the coffee-pot and he was teaching Mr Sanders—

Sure enough, the coffee-pot lay broken on the hearthrug.

'Any day this week except Thursday,' wrote Miss Perry, and this was not the first invitation by any means. Were all Miss Perry's weeks blank with the exception of Thursday, and was her only desire to see her old friend's son? Time is issued to spinster ladies of wealth in long white ribbons. These they wind round and round, round and round, assisted by five female servants, a butler, a fine Mexican parrot, regular meals, Mudie's library, and friends dropping in. A little hurt she was already that Jacob had not called.

'Your mother', she said, 'is one of my oldest friends.'

Miss Rosseter, who was sitting by the fire, holding the *Spectator* between her cheek and the blaze, refused to have a fire screen, but finally accepted one. The weather was then discussed, for in deference to Parkes, who was opening little tables, graver matters were postponed. Miss Rosseter drew Jacob's attention to the beauty of the cabinet.

'So wonderfully clever in picking things up,' she said. Miss Perry had found it in Yorkshire. The North of England was discussed. When Jacob spoke they both listened. Miss Perry was bethinking her of something suitable and manly to say when the door opened and Mr Benson was announced. Now there were four people sitting in that room. Miss Perry aged 66; Miss Rosseter 42; Mr Benson 38; and Jacob 25.

'My old friend looks as well as ever,' said Mr Benson, tapping the bars of the parrot's cage; Miss Rosseter simultaneously praised the tea; Jacob handed the wrong plates; and Miss Perry signified her desire to approach more closely. 'Your brothers,' she began vaguely.

'Archer and John,' Jacob supplied her. Then to her pleasure she recovered Rebecca's name; and how one day 'when you were all little boys, playing in the drawing-room——'

'But Miss Perry has the kettle-holder,' said Miss Rosseter, and indeed Miss Perry was clasping it to her breast. (Had she, then, loved Jacob's father?)

'So clever'—'not so good as usual'—'I thought it most unfair,' said Mr Benson and Miss Rosseter, discussing the Saturday *Westminster*. Did they not compete regularly for prizes? Had not Mr Benson three times won a guinea, and Miss Rosseter once ten and sixpence? Of course Everard Benson had a weak heart, but still, to win prizes, remember parrots, toady Miss Perry, despise Miss Rosseter, give tea-parties in his rooms (which were in the style of Whistler, with pretty books on tables), all this, so Jacob felt without knowing him, made him a contemptible ass. As for Miss Rosseter, she had nursed cancer, and now painted water-colours.

'Running away so soon?' said Miss Perry vaguely. 'At home every afternoon, if you've nothing better to do—except Thursdays.'

'I've never known you desert your old ladies once,' Miss Rosseter was saying, and Mr Benson was stooping over the parrot's cage, and Miss Perry was moving towards the bell . . .

The fire burnt clear between two pillars of greenish marble, and on the mantelpiece there was a green clock guarded by Britannia leaning on her spear. As for pictures—a maiden in a large hat offered roses over the garden gate to a gentleman in eighteenth-century costume. A mastiff lay extended against a battered door. The lower panes of the windows were of ground glass, and the curtains, accurately looped, were of plush and green too.

Laurette and Jacob sat with their toes in the fender side by side, in two large chairs covered in green plush. Laurette's skirts were short, her legs long, thin, and transparently covered. Her fingers stroked her ankles.

'It's not exactly that I don't understand them,' she was saying thoughtfully. 'I must go and try again.'

'What time will you be there?' said Jacob.

She shrugged her shoulders.

'Tomorrow?'

No, not tomorrow.

'This weather makes me long for the country,' she said, looking over her shoulder at the back view of tall houses through the window.

'I wish you'd been with me on Saturday,' said Jacob.

'I used to ride,' she said. She got up gracefully, calmly. Jacob got up. She smiled at him. As she shut the door he put so many shillings on the mantelpiece.

Altogether a most reasonable conversation; a most respectable room; an intelligent girl. Only Madame herself seeing Jacob out had about her that leer, that lewdness, that quake of the surface (visible in the eyes chiefly), which threatens to spill the whole bag of ordure, with difficulty held together, over the pavement. In short, something was wrong.

Not so very long ago the workmen had gilt the final 'y' in Lord Macaulay's name, and the names stretched in unbroken file round the dome of the British Museum. At a considerable depth beneath, many hundreds of the living sat at the spokes of a cart-wheel copying from printed books into manuscript books; now and then rising to consult the catalogue; regaining their places stealthily, while from time to time a silent man replenished their compartments.

There was a little catastrophe. Miss Marchmont's pile overbalanced and fell into Jacob's compartment. Such things happened to Miss Marchmont. What was she seeking through millions of pages, in her old plush dress, and her wig of claret-coloured hair, with her gems and her chilblains? Sometimes one thing, sometimes another, to confirm her philosophy that colour is sound—or, perhaps, it has something to do with music. She could never quite say, though it was not for lack of trying. And she could not ask you back to her room, for it was 'not very clean, I'm afraid', so she must catch you in the passage, or take a chair in Hyde Park to explain her philosophy. The rhythm of the soul depends on it—('how rude the little boys are!' she would say), and Mr Asquith's Irish policy, and Shakespeare comes in, 'and Queen Alexandra most graciously once acknowledged a copy of my pamphlet,' she would say, waving the little boys magnificently away. But she needs funds to publish her book, for 'publishers are capitalists—publishers are cowards'. And so, digging her elbow into her pile of books it fell over.

Jacob remained quite unmoved.

But Fraser, the atheist, on the other side, detesting plush, more than once accosted with leaflets, shifted irritably. He abhorred vagueness—the Christian religion, for example, and old Dean Parker's pronouncements. Dean Parker wrote books and Fraser utterly destroyed them by force of logic and left his children unbaptized—his wife did it secretly in the washing basin—but Fraser ignored her, and went on supporting blasphemers, distributing leaflets, getting up his facts in the British Museum, always in the same check suit and fiery tie, but pale, spotted, irritable. Indeed, what a work—to destroy religion!

Jacob transcribed a whole passage from Marlowe.

Miss Julia Hedge, the feminist, waited for her books. They did not come. She wetted her pen. She looked about her. Her eye was caught by the final letters in Lord Macaulay's name. And she read them all round the dome—the names of great men which remind us——'Oh damn,' said Julia Hedge, 'why didn't they leave room for an Eliot or a Brontë?'

Unfortunate Julia! wetting her pen in bitterness, and leaving her shoe laces untied. When her books came she applied herself to her gigantic labours, but perceived through one of the nerves of her exasperated sensibility how composedly, unconcernedly, and with every consideration the male readers applied themselves to theirs. That young man for example. What had he got to do except copy out poetry? And she must study statistics. There are more women than men. Yes; but if you let women work as men work, they'll die off much quicker. They'll become

extinct. That was her argument. Death and gall and bitter dust were on
her pen-tip; and as the afternoon wore on, red had worked into her
cheek-bones and a light was in her eyes.

But what brought Jacob Flanders to read Marlowe in the British
Museum?

Youth, youth—something savage—something pedantic. For example,
there is Mr Masefield, there is Mr Bennett. Stuff them into the flame of
Marlowe and burn them to cinders. Let not a shred remain. Don't
palter with the second rate. Detest your own age. Build a better one.
And to set that on foot read incredibly dull essays upon Marlowe to
your friends. For which purpose one must collate editions in the British
Museum. One must do the thing oneself. Useless to trust to the
Victorians, who disembowel, or to the living, who are mere publicists.
The flesh and blood of the future depends entirely upon six young men.
And as Jacob was one of them, no doubt he looked a little regal and
pompous as he turned his page, and Julia Hedge disliked him naturally
enough.

But then a pudding-faced man pushed a note towards Jacob, and
Jacob, leaning back in his chair, began an uneasy murmured conversation, and they went off together (Julia Hedge watched them), and
laughed aloud (she thought) directly they were in the hall.

Nobody laughed in the reading-room. There were shiftings, murmur-
ings, apologetic sneezes, and sudden unashamed devastating coughs.
The lesson hour was almost over. Ushers were collecting exercises. Lazy
children wanted to stretch. Good ones scribbled assiduously—ah,
another day over and so little done! And now and then was to be heard
from the whole collection of human beings a heavy sigh, after which the
humiliating old man would cough shamelessly, and Miss Marchmont
hinnied like a horse.

Jacob came back only in time to return his books.

The books were now replaced. A few letters of the alphabet were
sprinkled round the dome. Closely stood together in a ring round the
dome were Plato, Aristotle, Sophocles, and Shakespeare; the literatures
of Rome, Greece, China, India, Persia. One leaf of poetry was pressed
flat against another leaf, one burnished letter laid smooth against
another in a density of meaning, a conglomeration of loveliness.

'One does want one's tea,' said Miss Marchmont, reclaiming her
shabby umbrella.

Miss Marchmont wanted her tea, but could never resist a last look at
the Elgin Marbles. She looked at them sideways, waving her hand and
muttering a word or two of salutation which made Jacob and the other
man turn round. She smiled at them amiably. It all came into her

philosophy—that colour is sound, or perhaps it has something to do with music. And having done her service, she hobbled off to tea. It was closing time. The public collected in the hall to receive their umbrellas.

For the most part the students wait their turn very patiently. To stand and wait while someone examines white discs is soothing. The umbrella will certainly be found. But the fact leads you on all day through Macaulay, Hobbes, Gibbon; through octavos, quartos, folios; sinks deeper and deeper through ivory pages and morocco bindings into this density of thought, this conglomeration of knowledge.

Jacob's walking-stick was like all the others; they had muddled the pigeon-holes perhaps.

There is in the British Museum an enormous mind. Consider that Plato is there cheek by jowl with Aristotle; and Shakespeare with Marlowe. This great mind is hoarded beyond the power of any single mind to possess it. Nevertheless (as they take so long finding one's walking-stick) one can't help thinking how one might come with a notebook, sit at a desk, and read it all through. A learned man is the most venerable of all—a man like Huxtable of Trinity, who writes all his letters in Greek, they say, and could have kept his end up with Bentley. And then there is science, pictures, architecture,—an enormous mind.

They pushed the walking-stick across the counter. Jacob stood beneath the porch of the British Museum. It was raining. Great Russell Street was glazed and shining—here yellow, here, outside the chemist's, red and pale blue. People scuttled quickly close to the wall; carriages rattled rather helter-skelter down the streets. Well, but a little rain hurts nobody. Jacob walked off much as if he had been in the country; and late that night there he was sitting at his table with his pipe and his book.

The rain poured down. The British Museum stood in one solid immense mound, very pale, very sleek in the rain, not a quarter of a mile from him. The vast mind was sheeted with stone; and each compartment in the depths of it was safe and dry. The night-watchmen, flashing their lanterns over the backs of Plato and Shakespeare, saw that on the twenty-second of February neither flame, rat, nor burglar was going to violate these treasures—poor, highly respectable men, with wives and families at Kentish Town, do their best for twenty years to protect Plato and Shakespeare, and then are buried at Highgate.

Stone lies solid over the British Museum, as bone lies cool over the visions and heat of the brain. Only here the brain is Plato's brain and Shakespeare's; the brain has made pots and statues, great bulls and little jewels, and crossed the river of death this way and that incessantly, seeking some landing, now wrapping the body well for its long sleep;

now laying a penny piece on the eyes; now turning the toes scrupulously to the East. Meanwhile, Plato continues his dialogue; in spite of the rain; in spite of the cab whistles; in spite of the woman in the mews behind Great Ormond Street who has come home drunk and cries all night long, 'Let me in! Let me in!'

In the street below Jacob's room voices were raised.

But he read on. For after all Plato continues imperturbably. And Hamlet utters his soliloquy. And there the Elgin Marbles lie, all night long, old Jones's lantern sometimes recalling Ulysses, or a horse's head; or sometimes a flash of gold, or a mummy's sunk yellow cheek. Plato and Shakespeare continue; and Jacob, who was reading the *Phaedrus*, heard people vociferating round the lamp-post, and the woman battering at the door and crying, 'Let me in!' as if a coal had dropped from the fire, or a fly, falling from the ceiling, had lain on its back, too weak to turn over.

The *Phaedrus* is very difficult. And so, when at length one reads straight ahead, falling into step, marching on, becoming (so it seems) momentarily part of this rolling, imperturbable energy, which has driven darkness before it since Plato walked the Acropolis, it is impossible to see to the fire.

The dialogue draws to its close. Plato's argument is done. Plato's argument is stowed away in Jacob's mind, and for five minutes Jacob's mind continues alone, onwards, into the darkness. Then, getting up, he parted the curtains, and saw, with astonishing clearness, how the Springetts opposite had gone to bed; how it rained; how the Jews and the foreign woman, at the end of the street, stood by the pillar-box, arguing.

Every time the door opened and fresh people came in, those already in the room shifted slightly; those who were standing looked over their shoulders; those who were sitting stopped in the middle of sentences. What with the light, the wine, the strumming of a guitar, something exciting happened each time the door opened. Who was coming in?

'That's Gibson.'

'The painter?'

'But go on with what you were saying.'

They were saying something that was far, far too intimate to be said outright. But the noise of the voices served like a clapper in little Mrs Withers's mind, scaring into the air flocks of small birds, and then they'd settle, and then she'd feel afraid, put one hand to her hair, bind both round her knees, and look up at Oliver Skelton nervously, and say:

'Promise, *promise*, you'll tell no one' . . . so considerate he was, so tender. It was her husband's character that she discussed. He was cold, she said.

Down upon them came the splendid Magdalen, brown, warm, voluminous, scarcely brushing the grass with her sandalled feet. Her hair flew; pins seemed scarcely to attach the flying silks. An actress of course, a line of light perpetually beneath her. It was only 'My dear' that she said, but her voice went jodelling between Alpine passes. And down she tumbled on the floor, and sang, since there was nothing to be said, round ah's and oh's. Mangin, the poet, coming up to her, stood looking down at her, drawing at his pipe. The dancing began.

Grey-haired Mrs Keymer asked Dick Graves to tell her who Mangin was, and said that she had seen too much of this sort of thing in Paris (Magdalen had got upon his knees; now his pipe was in her mouth) to be shocked. 'Who is that?' she said, staying her glasses when they came to Jacob, for indeed he looked quiet, not indifferent, but like someone on a beach, watching.

'Oh, my dear, let me lean on you,' gasped Helen Askew, hopping on one foot, for the silver cord round her ankle had worked loose. Mrs Keymer turned and looked at the picture on the wall.

'Look at Jacob,' said Helen (they were binding his eyes for some game).

And Dick Graves, being a little drunk, very faithful, and very simple-minded, told her that he thought Jacob the greatest man he had ever known. And down they sat cross-legged upon cushions and talked about Jacob, and Helen's voice trembled, for they both seemed heroes to her, and the friendship between them so much more beautiful than women's friendships. Anthony Pollett now asked her to dance, and as she danced she looked at them, over her shoulder, standing at the table, drinking together.

The magnificent world—the live, sane, vigorous world . . . These words refer to the stretch of wood pavement between Hammersmith and Holborn in January between two and three in the morning. That was the ground beneath Jacob's feet. It was healthy and magnificent because one room, above a mews, somewhere near the river, contained fifty excited, talkative, friendly people. And then to stride over the pavement (there was scarcely a cab or policeman in sight) is of itself exhilarating. The long loop of Piccadilly, diamond-stitched, shows to best advantage when it is empty. A young man has nothing to fear. On the contrary, though he may not have said anything brilliant, he feels pretty confident he can hold his own. He was pleased to have met Mangin; he admired the young woman on the floor; he liked them all; he liked that sort of thing. In short, all the drums and trumpets were sounding. The street scavengers were the only people about at the moment. It is scarcely necessary to say how well-disposed Jacob felt towards them; how it pleased him to let himself in with his latch-key at his own door; how he seemed to bring back with him into the empty room ten or eleven people whom he had not known when he set out; how he looked about for something to read, and found it, and never read it, and fell asleep.

Indeed, drums and trumpets is no phrase. Indeed, Piccadilly and Holborn, and the empty sitting-room and the sitting-room with fifty people in it are liable at any moment to blow music into the air. Women perhaps are more excitable than men. It is seldom that anyone says anything about it, and to see the hordes crossing Waterloo Bridge to catch the non-stop to Surbiton one might think that reason impelled them. No, no. It is the drums and trumpets. Only, should you turn aside into one of those little bays on Waterloo Bridge to think the matter over, it will probably seem to you all a muddle—all a mystery.

They cross the Bridge incessantly. Sometimes in the midst of carts and omnibuses a lorry will appear with great forest trees chained to it. Then, perhaps, a mason's van with newly lettered tombstones recording how someone loved someone who is buried at Putney. Then the motor car in front jerks forward, and the tombstones pass too quick for you to read more. All the time the stream of people never ceases passing from the Surrey side to the Strand; from the Strand to the Surrey side. It seems as if the poor had gone raiding the town, and now trapesed back to their own quarters, like beetles scurrying to their holes, for that old woman fairly hobbles towards Waterloo, grasping a shiny bag, as if she had been out into the light and now made off with some scraped chicken bones to her hovel underground. On the other hand, though the wind is rough and blowing in their faces, those girls there, striding hand in hand, shouting out a song, seem to feel neither cold nor shame. They are hatless. They triumph.

The wind has blown up the waves. The river races beneath us, and the men standing on the barges have to lean all their weight on the tiller. A black tarpaulin is tied down over a swelling load of gold. Avalanches of coal glitter blackly. As usual, painters are slung on planks across the great riverside hotels, and the hotel windows have already points of light in them. On the other side the city is white as if with age; St Paul's swells white above the fretted, pointed, or oblong buildings beside it. The cross alone shines rosy-gilt. But what century have we reached? Has this procession from the Surrey side to the Strand gone on for ever? That old man has been crossing the Bridge these six hundred years, with the rabble of little boys at his heels, for he is drunk, or blind with misery, and tied round with old clouts of clothing such as pilgrims might have worn. He shuffles on. No one stands still. It seems as if we marched to the sound of music; perhaps the wind and the river; perhaps these same drums and trumpets—the ecstasy and hubbub of the soul. Why, even the unhappy laugh, and the policeman, far from judging the drunk man, surveys him humorously, and the little boys scamper back again, and the clerk from Somerset House has nothing but tolerance for him, and the man who is reading half a page of *Lothair* at the bookstall muses charitably, with his eyes off the print, and the girl hesitates at the crossing and turns on him the bright yet vague glance of the young.

Bright yet vague. She is perhaps twenty-two. She is shabby. She crosses the road and looks at the daffodils and the red tulips in the florist's window. She hesitates, and makes off in the direction of Temple Bar. She walks fast, and yet anything distracts her. Now she seems to see, and now to notice nothing.

X

Through the disused graveyard in the parish of St Pancras, Fanny Elmer strayed between the white tombs which lean against the wall, crossing the grass to read a name, hurrying on when the grave-keeper approached, hurrying into the street, pausing now by a window with blue china, now quickly making up for lost time, abruptly entering a baker's shop, buying rolls, adding cakes, going on again so that anyone wishing to follow must fairly trot. She was not drably shabby, though. She wore silk stockings, and silver-buckled shoes, only the red feather in her hat drooped, and the clasp of her bag was weak, for out fell a copy of Madame Tussaud's programme as she walked. She had the ankles of a stag. Her face was hidden. Of course, in this dusk, rapid movements, quick glances, and soaring hopes come naturally enough. She passed right beneath Jacob's window.

The house was flat, dark, and silent. Jacob was at home engaged upon a chess problem, the board being on a stool between his knees. One hand was fingering the hair at the back of his head. He slowly brought it forward and raised the white queen from her square; then put her down again on the same spot. He filled his pipe; ruminated; moved two pawns; advanced the white knight; then ruminated with one finger upon the bishop. Now Fanny Elmer passed beneath the window.

She was on her way to sit to Nick Bramham the painter.

She sat in a flowered Spanish shawl, holding in her hand a yellow novel.

'A little lower, a little looser, so—better, that's right,' Bramham mumbled, who was drawing her, and smoking at the same time, and was naturally speechless. His head might have been the work of a sculptor, who had squared the forehead, stretched the mouth, and left marks of his thumbs and streaks from his fingers in the clay. But the eyes had never been shut. They were rather prominent, and rather bloodshot, as if from staring and staring, and when he spoke they looked for a second disturbed, but went on staring. An unshaded electric light hung above her head.

As for the beauty of women, it is like the light on the sea, never constant to a single wave. They all have it; they all lose it. Now she is dull and thick as bacon; now transparent as a hanging glass. The fixed faces are the dull ones. Here comes Lady Venice displayed like a monument for admiration, but carved in alabaster, to be set on the mantelpiece and never dusted. A dapper brunette complete from head to foot serves only as an illustration to lie upon the drawing-room table. The women in the streets have the faces of playing cards; . outlines accurately filled in with pink or yellow, and the line drawn tightly round them. Then, at a top-floor window, leaning out, looking down, you see beauty itself; or in the corner of an omnibus; or squatted in a ditch— beauty glowing, suddenly expressive, withdrawn the moment after. No one can count on it or seize it or have it wrapped in paper. Nothing is to be won from the shops, and Heaven knows it would be better to sit at home than haunt the plate-glass windows in the hope of lifting the shining green, the glowing ruby, out of them alive. Sea glass in a saucer loses its lustre no sooner than silks do. Thus if you talk of a beautiful woman you mean only something flying fast which for a second uses the eyes, lips, or cheeks of Fanny Elmer, for example, to glow through.

She was not beautiful, as she sat stiffly; her underlip too prominent; her nose too large; her eyes too near together. She was a thin girl, with brilliant cheeks and dark hair, sulky just now, or stiff with sitting. When Bramham snapped his stick of charcoal she started. Bramham was out of temper. He squatted before the gas fire warming his hands. Meanwhile she looked at his drawing. He grunted. Fanny threw on a dressing-gown and boiled a kettle.

'By God, it's bad,' said Bramham.

Fanny dropped on to the floor, clasped her hands round her knees, and looked at him, her beautiful eyes—yes, beauty, flying through the room, shone there for a second. Fanny's eyes seemed to question, to commiserate, to be, for a second, love itself. But she exaggerated. Bramham noticed nothing. And when the kettle boiled, up she scrambled, more like a colt or a puppy than a loving woman.

Now Jacob walked over to the window and stood with his hands in his pockets. Mr Springett opposite came out, looked at his shop window, and went in again. The children drifted past, eyeing the pink sticks of sweetstuff. Pickford's van swung down the street. A small boy twirled from a rope. Jacob turned away. Two minutes later he opened the front door, and walked off in the direction of Holborn.

Fanny Elmer took down her cloak from the hook. Nick Bramham unpinned his drawing and rolled it under his arm. They turned out the lights and set off down the street, holding on their way through all the people, motor cars, omnibuses, carts, until they reached Leicester Square, five minutes before Jacob reached it, for his way was slightly longer, and he had been stopped by a block in Holborn waiting to see the King drive by, so that Nick and Fanny were already leaning over the barrier in the promenade at the Empire when Jacob pushed through the swing doors and took his place beside them.

'Hullo, never noticed you,' said Nick, five minutes later.

'Bloody rot,' said Jacob.

'Miss Elmer,' said Nick.

Jacob took his pipe out of his mouth very awkwardly.

Very awkward he was. And when they sat upon a plush sofa and let the smoke go up between them and the stage, and heard far off the high-pitched voices and the jolly orchestra breaking in opportunely he was still awkward, only Fanny thought: 'What a beautiful voice!' She thought how little he said yet how firm it was. She thought how young men are dignified and aloof, and how unconscious they are, and how quietly one might sit beside Jacob and look at him. And how childlike he would be,

come in tired of an evening, she thought, and how majestic; a little
overbearing perhaps; 'But I wouldn't give way,' she thought. He got up
and leant over the barrier. The smoke hung about him.

And for ever the beauty of young men seems to be set in smoke,
however lustily they chase footballs, or drive cricket balls, dance, run,
or stride along roads. Possibly they are soon to lose it. Possibly they look
into the eyes of far-away heroes, and take their station among us half
contemptuously, she thought (vibrating like a fiddle-string, to be played
on and snapped). Anyhow, they love silence, and speak beautifully, each
word falling like a disc new cut, not a hubble-bubble of small smooth
coins such as girls use; and they move decidedly, as if they knew how
long to stay and when to go—oh, but Mr Flanders was only gone to get
a programme.

'The dancers come right at the end,' he said, coming back to them.

And isn't it pleasant, Fanny went on thinking, how young men bring
out lots of silver coins from their trouser pockets, and look at them,
instead of having just so many in a purse?

Then there she was herself, whirling across the stage in white flounces,
and the music was the dance and fling of her own soul, and the whole
machinery, rock and gear of the world was spun smoothly into those
swift eddies and falls, she felt, as she stood rigid leaning over the barrier
two feet from Jacob Flanders.

Her screwed-up black glove dropped to the floor. When Jacob gave it
her, she started angrily. For never was there a more irrational passion.
And Jacob was afraid of her for a moment—so violent, so dangerous is
it when young women stand rigid; grasp the barrier; fall in love.

It was the middle of February. The roofs of Hampstead Garden
Suburb lay in a tremulous haze. It was too hot to walk. A dog barked,
barked, barked down in the hollow. The liquid shadows went over the
plain.

The body after long illness is languid, passive, receptive of sweetness,
but too weak to contain it. The tears well and fall as the dog barks in
the hollow, the children skim after hoops, the country darkens and
brightens. Beyond a veil it seems. Ah, but draw the veil thicker lest I
faint with sweetness. Fanny Elmer sighed, as she sat on a bench in
Judges Walk looking at Hampstead Garden Suburb. But the dog went
on barking. The motor cars hooted on the road. She heard a far-away
rush and humming. Agitation was at her heart. Up she got and walked.
The grass was freshly green; the sun hot. All round the pond children

were stooping to launch little boats; or were drawn back screaming by their nurses.

At midday young women walk out into the air. All the men are busy in the town. They stand by the edge of the blue pond. The fresh wind scatters the children's voices all about. *My* children, thought Fanny Elmer. The women stand round the pond, beating off great prancing shaggy dogs. Gently the baby is rocked in the perambulator. The eyes of all the nurses, mothers, and wandering women are a little glazed, absorbed. They gently nod instead of answering when the little boys tug at their skirts, begging them to move on.

And Fanny moved, hearing some cry—a workman's whistle perhaps—high in mid air. Now, among the trees, it was the thrush trilling out into the warm air a flutter of jubilation, but fear seemed to spur him, Fanny thought; as if he too were anxious with such joy at his heart—as if he were watched as he sang, and pressed by tumult to sing. There! Restless, he flew to the next tree. She heard his song more faintly. Beyond it was the humming of the wheels and the wind rushing.

She spent tenpence on lunch.

'Dear, miss, she's left her umberella,' grumbled the mottled woman in the glass box near the door at the Express Dairy Company's shop.

'Perhaps I'll catch her,' answered Milly Edwards, the waitress with the pale plaits of hair; and she dashed through the door.

'No good,' she said, coming back a moment later with Fanny's cheap umbrella. She put her hand to her plaits.

'Oh, that door!' grumbled the cashier.

Her hands were cased in black mittens, and the finger-tips that drew in the paper slips were swollen as sausages.

'Pie and greens for one. Large coffee and crumpets. Eggs on toast. Two fruit cakes.'

Thus the sharp voices of the waitresses snapped. The lunchers heard their orders repeated with approval; saw the next table served with anticipation. Their own eggs on toast were at last delivered. Their eyes strayed no more.

Damp cubes of pastry fell into mouths opened like triangular bags.

Nelly Jenkinson, the typist, crumbled her cake indifferently enough. Every time the door opened she looked up. What did she expect to see?

The coal merchant read the *Telegraph* without stopping, missed the saucer, and, feeling abstractedly, put the cup down on the table-cloth.

'Did you ever hear the like of that for impertinence?' Mrs Parsons wound up, brushing the crumbs from her furs.

'Hot milk and scone for one. Pot of tea. Roll and butter,' cried the waitresses.

The door opened and shut.

Such is the life of the elderly.

It is curious, lying in a boat, to watch the waves. Here are three coming regularly one after another, all much of a size. Then, hurrying after them comes a fourth, very large and menacing; it lifts the boat; on it goes; somehow merges without accomplishing anything; flattens itself out with the rest.

What can be more violent than the fling of boughs in a gale, the tree yielding itself all up the trunk, to the very tip of the branch, streaming and shuddering the way the wind blows, yet never flying in dishevelment away?

The corn squirms and abases itself as if preparing to tug itself free from the roots, and yet is tied down.

Why, from the very windows, even in the dusk, you see a swelling run through the street, an aspiration, as with arms outstretched, eyes desiring, mouths agape. And then we peaceably subside. For if the exaltation lasted we should be blown like foam into the air. The stars would shine through us. We should go down the gale in salt drops—as sometimes happens. For the impetuous spirits will have none of this cradling. Never any swaying or aimlessly lolling for them. Never any making believe, or lying cosily, or genially supposing that one is much like another, fire warm, wine pleasant, extravagance a sin.

'People are so nice, once you know them.'

'I couldn't think ill of her. One must remember——' But Nick perhaps, or Fanny Elmer, believing implicitly in the truth of the moment, fling off, sting the cheek, are gone like sharp hail.

'Oh,' said Fanny, bursting into the studio three-quarters of an hour late because she had been hanging about the neighbourhood of the Found-ling Hospital merely for the chance of seeing Jacob walk down the street, take out his latch-key, and open the door, 'I'm afraid I'm late'; upon which Nick said nothing and Fanny grew defiant.

'I'll never come again!' she cried at length.

'Don't, then,' Nick replied, and off she ran without so much as good-night.

How exquisite it was—that dress in Evelina's shop off Shaftesbury Avenue! It was four o'clock on a fine day early in April, and was Fanny the one to spend four o'clock on a fine day indoors? Other girls in that very street sat over ledgers, or drew long threads wearily between silk and gauze; or, festooned with ribbons in Swan and Edgars, rapidly added up pence and farthings on the back of the bill and twisted the yard and three-quarters in tissue paper and asked 'Your pleasure?' of the next comer.

In Evelina's shop off Shaftesbury Avenue the parts of a woman were shown separate. In the left hand was her skirt. Twining round a pole in the middle was a feather boa. Ranged like the heads of malefactors on Temple Bar were hats—emerald and white, lightly wreathed or drooping beneath deep-dyed feathers. And on the carpet were her feet—pointed gold, or patent leather slashed with scarlet.

Feasted upon by the eyes of women, the clothes by four o'clock were flyblown like sugar cakes in a baker's window. Fanny eyed them too.

But coming along Gerrard Street was a tall man in a shabby coat A shadow fell across Evelina's window—Jacob's shadow, though it was not Jacob. And Fanny turned and walked along Gerrard Street and wished that she had read books. Nick never read books, never talked of Ireland, or the House of Lords; and as for his finger-nails! She would learn Latin and read Virgil. She had been a great reader. She had read Scott; she had read Dumas. At the Slade no one read. But no one knew Fanny at the Slade, or guessed how empty it seemed to her; the passion for ear-rings, for dances, for Tonks and Steer—when it was only the French who could paint, Jacob said. For the moderns were futile; painting the least respectable of the arts; and why read anything but Marlowe and Shakespeare, Jacob said, and Fielding if you must read novels?

'Fielding,' said Fanny, when the man in Charing Cross Road asked her what book she wanted.

She bought *Tom Jones*.

At ten o'clock in the morning, in a room which she shared with a school teacher, Fanny Elmer read *Tom Jones*—that mystic book. For this dull stuff (Fanny thought) about people with odd names is what Jacob likes. Good people like it. Dowdy women who don't mind how they cross their legs read *Tom Jones*—a mystic book; for there is something, Fanny thought, about books which if I had been educated I could have liked—much better than ear-rings and flowers, she sighed, thinking of the corridors at the Slade and the fancy-dress dance next week. She had nothing to wear.

They are real, thought Fanny Elmer, setting her feet on the mantel-piece. Some people are. Nick perhaps, only he was so stupid. And women never—except Miss Sargent, but she went off at lunch-time and gave herself airs. There they sat quietly of a night, reading, she thought. Not going to music-halls; not looking in at shop windows; not wearing each other's clothes, like Robertson who had worn her shawl, and she had worn his waistcoat, which Jacob could only do very awkwardly; for he liked *Tom Jones*.

There it lay on her lap, in double columns, price three and sixpence; the mystic book in which Henry Fielding ever so many years ago rebuked Fanny Elmer for feasting on scarlet, in perfect prose, Jacob said. For he never read modern novels. He liked *Tom Jones*.

'I do like *Tom Jones*,' said Fanny, at five-thirty that same day early in April when Jacob took out his pipe in the armchair opposite.

Alas, women lie! But not Clara Durrant. A flawless mind; a candid nature; a virgin chained to a rock (somewhere off Lowndes Square) eternally pouring out tea for old men in white waistcoats, blue-eyed, looking you straight in the face, playing Bach. Of all women, Jacob honoured her most. But to sit at a table with bread and butter, with dowagers in velvet, and never say more to Clara Durrant than Benson said to the parrot when old Miss Perry poured out tea, was an insufferable outrage upon the liberties and decencies of human nature—or words to that effect. For Jacob said nothing. Only he glared at the fire. Fanny laid down *Tom Jones*.

She stitched or knitted.

'What's that?' asked Jacob.

'For the dance at the Slade.'

And she fetched her head-dress; her trousers; her shoes with red tassels. What should she wear?

'I shall be in Paris,' said Jacob.

And what is the point of fancy-dress dances? thought Fanny. You meet the same people; you wear the same clothes; Mangin gets drunk; Florinda sits on his knee. She flirts outrageously—with Nick Bramham just now.

'In Paris?' said Fanny.

'On my way to Greece,' he replied.

For, he said, there is nothing so detestable as London in May.

He would forget her.

A sparrow flew past the window trailing a straw—a straw from a stack stood by a barn in a farmyard. The old brown spaniel snuffs at the base for a rat. Already the upper branches of the elm trees are blotted

with nests. The chestnuts have flirted their fans. And the butterflies are
flaunting across the rides in the Forest. Perhaps the Purple Emperor is
feasting, as Morris says, upon a mass of putrid carrion at the base of an
oak tree.

Fanny thought it all came from *Tom Jones*. He could go alone with a
book in his pocket and watch the badgers. He would take a train at
eight-thirty and walk all night. He saw fireflies, and brought back glow-
worms in pill-boxes. He would hunt with the New Forest Staghounds.
It all came from *Tom Jones*; and he would go to Greece with a book in
his pocket and forget her.

She fetched her hand-glass. There was her face. And suppose one
wreathed Jacob in a turban? There was his face. She lit the lamp. But
as the daylight came through the window only half was lit up by the
lamp. And though he looked terrible and magnificent and would chuck
the Forest, he said, and come to the Slade, and be a Turkish knight or a
Roman emperor (and he let her blacken his lips and clenched his teeth
and scowled in the glass), still—there lay *Tom Jones*.

XI

'Archer', said Mrs Flanders with that tenderness which mothers so often
display towards their eldest sons, 'will be at Gibraltar tomorrow.'

The post for which she was waiting (strolling up Dods Hill while the
random church bells swung a hymn tune about her head, the clock
striking four straight through the circling notes; the grass purpling under
a storm-cloud; and the two dozen houses of the village cowering,
infinitely humble, in company under a leaf of shadow), the post, with all
its variety of messages, envelopes addressed in bold hands, in slanting
hands, stamped now with English stamps, again with Colonial stamps,
or sometimes hastily dabbed with a yellow bar, the post was about to
scatter a myriad messages over the world. Whether we gain or not by
this habit of profuse communication it is not for us to say. But that
letter-writing is practised mendaciously nowadays, particularly by
young men travelling in foreign parts, seems likely enough.

For example, take this scene.

Here was Jacob Flanders gone abroad and staying to break his
journey in Paris. (Old Miss Birkbeck, his mother's cousin, had died last
June and left him a hundred pounds.)

'You needn't repeat the whole damned thing over again, Cruttendon,' said Mallinson, the little bald painter who was sitting at a marble table, splashed with coffee and ringed with wine, talking very fast, and undoubtedly more than a little drunk.

'Well, Flanders, finished writing to your lady?' said Cruttendon, as Jacob came and took his seat beside them, holding in his hand an envelope addressed to Mrs Flanders, near Scarborough, England.

'Do you uphold Velasquez?' said Cruttendon.

'By God, he does,' said Mallinson.

'He always gets like this,' said Cruttendon irritably.

Jacob looked at Mallinson with excessive composure.

'I'll tell you the three greatest things that were ever written in the whole of literature,' Cruttendon burst out. '"Hang there like fruit my soul,"' he began . . .

'Don't listen to a man who don't like Velasquez,' said Mallinson.

'Adolphe, don't give Mr Mallinson any more wine,' said Cruttendon.

'Fair play, fair play,' said Jacob judicially. 'Let a man get drunk if he likes. That's Shakespeare, Cruttendon. I'm with you there. Shakespeare had more guts than all these damned frogs put together. "Hang there like fruit my soul,"' he began quoting, in a musical rhetorical voice, flourishing his wine-glass. 'The devil damn you black, you cream-faced loon!' he exclaimed as the wine washed over the rim.

'"Hang there like fruit my soul,"' Cruttendon and Jacob both began at the same moment, and both burst out laughing.

'Curse these flies,' said Mallinson, flicking at his bald head. 'What do they take me for?'

'Something sweet-smelling,' said Cruttendon.

'Shut up, Cruttendon,' said Jacob. 'The fellow has no manners,' he explained to Mallinson very politely. 'Wants to cut people off their drink. Look here. I want grilled bone. What's the French for grilled bone? Grilled bone, Adolphe. Now you juggins, don't you understand?'

'And I'll tell you, Flanders, the second most beautiful thing in the whole of literature,' said Cruttendon, bringing his feet down on to the floor, and leaning right across the table, so that his face almost touched Jacob's face.

'"Hey diddle diddle, the cat and the fiddle,"' Mallinson interrupted, strumming his fingers on the table. 'The most ex-qui-sitely beautiful thing in the whole of literature . . . Cruttendon is a very good fellow,' he remarked confidentially. 'But he's a bit of a fool.' And he jerked his head forward.

Well, not a word of this was ever told to Mrs Flanders; nor what happened when they paid the bill and left the restaurant, and walked along the Boulevard Raspaille.

Then here is another scrap of conversation; the time about eleven in the morning; the scene a studio; and the day Sunday.

'I tell you, Flanders,' said Cruttendon, 'I'd as soon have one of Mallinson's little pictures as a Chardin. And when I say that . . .' he squeezed the tail of an emaciated tube . . . 'Chardin was a great swell . . . He sells 'em to pay his dinner now. But wait till the dealers get hold of him. A great swell—oh, a very great swell.'

'It's an awfully pleasant life,' said Jacob, 'messing away up here. Still, it's a stupid art, Cruttendon.' He wandered off across the room. 'There's this man, Pierre Louÿs now.' He took up a book.

'Now my good sir, are you going to settle down?' said Cruttendon.

'That's a solid piece of work,' said Jacob, standing a canvas on a chair.

'Oh, that I did ages ago,' said Cruttendon, looking over his shoulder.

'You're a pretty competent painter in my opinion,' said Jacob after a time.

'Now if you'd like to see what I'm after at the present moment,' said Cruttendon, putting a canvas before Jacob. 'There. That's it. That's more like it. That's . . .' he squirmed his thumb in a circle round a lamp globe painted white.

'A pretty solid piece of work,' said Jacob, straddling his legs in front of it. 'But what I wish you'd explain . . .'

Miss Jinny Carslake, pale, freckled, morbid, came into the room.

'Oh Jinny, here's a friend. Flanders. An Englishman. Wealthy. Highly connected. Go on, Flanders . . .'

Jacob said nothing.

'It's *that*—that's not right,' said Jinny Carslake.

'No,' said Cruttendon decidedly. 'Can't be done.'

He took the canvas off the chair and stood it on the floor with its back to them.

'Sit down, ladies and gentlemen. Miss Carslake comes from your part of the world, Flanders. From Devonshire. Oh, I thought you said Devonshire. Very well. She's a daughter of the church too. The black sheep of the family. Her mother writes her such letters. I say—have you one about you? It's generally Sundays they come. Sort of church-bell effect, you know.'

'Have you met all the painter men?' said Jinny. 'Was Mallinson drunk? If you go to his studio he'll give you one of his pictures. I say, Teddy . . .'

'Half a jiff,' said Cruttendon. 'What's the season of the year?' He looked out of the window.

'We take a day off on Sundays, Flanders.'

'Will he . . .' said Jinny, looking at Jacob. 'You . . .'

'Yes, he'll come with us,' said Cruttendon.

And then, here is Versailles.

Jinny stood on the stone rim and leant over the pond, clasped by Cruttendon's arms or she would have fallen in. 'There! There!' she cried. 'Right up to the top!' Some sluggish, sloping-shouldered fish had floated up from the depths to nip her crumbs. 'You look,' she said, jumping down. And then the dazzling white water, rough and throttled, shot up into the air. The fountain spread itself. Through it came the sound of military music far away. All the water was puckered with drops. A blue air-ball gently bumped the surface. How all the nurses and children and old men and young crowded to the edge, leant over and waved their sticks! The little girl ran stretching her arms towards her air-ball, but it sank beneath the fountain.

Edward Cruttendon, Jinny Carslake, and Jacob Flanders walked in a row along the yellow gravel path; got on to the grass; so passed under the trees; and came out at the summer-house where Marie Antoinette used to drink chocolate. In went Edward and Jinny, but Jacob waited outside, sitting on the handle of his walking-stick. Out they came again.

'Well?' said Cruttendon, smiling at Jacob.

Jinny waited; Edward waited; and both looked at Jacob.

'Well?' said Jacob, smiling and pressing both hands on his stick.

'Come along,' he decided; and started off. The others followed him, smiling.

And then they went to the little café in the by-street where people sit drinking coffee, watching the soldiers, meditatively knocking ashes into trays.

'But he's quite different,' said Jinny, folding her hands over the top of her glass. 'I don't suppose you know what Ted means when he says a thing like that,' she said, looking at Jacob. 'But I do. Sometimes I could kill myself. Sometimes he lies in bed all day long—just lies there . . . I don't want you right on the table'; she waved her hands. Swollen iridescent pigeons were waddling round their feet.

'Look at that woman's hat,' said Cruttendon. 'How do they come to think of it? . . . No, Flanders, I don't think I could live like you. When one walks down that street opposite the British Museum—what's it called?—that's what I mean. It's all like that. Those fat women—and the man standing in the middle of the road as if he were going to have a fit . . .'

'Everybody feeds them,' said Jinny, waving the pigeons away. 'They're stupid old things.'

'Well, I don't know,' said Jacob, smoking his cigarette. 'There's St Paul's.'

'I mean going to an office,' said Cruttendon.

'Hang it all,' Jacob expostulated.

'But you don't count,' said Jinny, looking at Cruttendon. 'You're mad. I mean, you just think of painting.'

'Yes, I know. I can't help it. I say, will King George give way about the peers?'

'He'll jolly well have to,' said Jacob.

'There!' said Jinny. 'He really knows.'

'You see, I would if I could,' said Cruttendon, 'but I simply can't.'

'I *think* I could,' said Jinny. 'Only, it's all the people one dislikes who do it. At home, I mean. They talk of nothing else. Even people like my mother.'

'Now if I came and lived here——' said Jacob. 'What's my share, Cruttendon? Oh, very well. Have it your own way. Those silly birds, directly one wants them—they've flown away.'

And finally under the arc lamps in the Gare des Invalides, with one of those queer movements which are so slight yet so definite, which may wound or pass unnoticed but generally inflict a good deal of discomfort, Jinny and Cruttendon drew together; Jacob stood apart. They had to separate. Something must be said. Nothing was said. A man wheeled a trolley past Jacob's legs so near that he almost grazed them. When Jacob recovered his balance the other two were turning away, though Jinny looked over her shoulder, and Cruttendon, waving his hand, disappeared like the very great genius that he was.

No—Mrs Flanders was told none of this, though Jacob felt, it is safe to say, that nothing in the world was of greater importance; and as for Cruttendon and Jinny, he thought them the most remarkable people he had ever met—being of course unable to foresee how it fell out in the course of time that Cruttendon took to painting orchards; had therefore to live in Kent; and must, one would think, see through apple blossom by this time, since his wife, for whose sake he did it, eloped with a novelist; but no; Cruttendon still paints orchards, savagely, in solitude. Then Jinny Carslake, after her affair with Lefanu the American painter, frequented Indian philosophers, and now you find her in pensions in Italy cherishing a little jeweller's box containing ordinary pebbles picked off the road. But if you look at them steadily, she says, multiplicity becomes unity, which is somehow the secret of life, though it does not prevent her from following the macaroni as it goes round the table, and sometimes, on spring nights, she makes the strangest confidences to shy young Englishmen.

Jacob had nothing to hide from his mother. It was only that he could make no sense himself of his extraordinary excitement, and as for writing it down——

'Jacob's letters are so like him,' said Mrs Jarvis, folding the sheet.

'Indeed he seems to be having . . .' said Mrs Flanders, and paused, for she was cutting out a dress and had to straighten the pattern, '. . . a very gay time.'

Mrs Jarvis thought of Paris. At her back the window was open, for it was a mild night; a calm night; when the moon seemed muffled and the apple trees stood perfectly still.

'I never pity the dead,' said Mrs Jarvis, shifting the cushion at her back, and clasping her hands behind her head. Betty Flanders did not hear, for her scissors made so much noise on the table.

'They are at rest,' said Mrs Jarvis. 'And we spend our days doing foolish unnecessary things without knowing why.'

Mrs Jarvis was not liked in the village.

'You never walk at this time of night?' she asked Mrs Flanders.

'It is certainly wonderfully mild,' said Mrs Flanders.

Yet it was years since she had opened the orchard gate and gone out on Dods Hill after dinner.

'It is perfectly dry,' said Mrs Jarvis, as they shut the orchard door and stepped on to the turf.

'I shan't go far,' said Betty Flanders. 'Yes, Jacob will leave Paris on Wednesday.'

'Jacob was always my friend of the three,' said Mrs Jarvis.

'Now, my dear, I am going no further,' said Mrs Flanders. They had climbed the dark hill and reached the Roman camp.

The rampart rose at their feet—the smooth circle surrounding the camp or the grave. How many needles Betty Flanders had lost there! and her garnet brooch.

'It is much clearer than this sometimes,' said Mrs Jarvis, standing upon the ridge. There were no clouds, and yet there was a haze over the sea, and over the moors. The lights of Scarborough flashed, as if a woman wearing a diamond necklace turned her head this way and that.

'How quiet it is!' said Mrs Jarvis.

Mrs Flanders rubbed the turf with her toe, thinking of her garnet brooch.

Mrs Jarvis found it difficult to think of herself tonight. It was so calm. There was no wind; nothing racing, flying, escaping. Black shadows stood still over the silver moors. The furze bushes stood perfectly still. Neither did Mrs Jarvis think of God. There was a church behind them, of course. The church clock struck ten. Did the strokes reach the furze bush, or did the thorn tree hear them?

Mrs Flanders was stooping down to pick up a pebble. Sometimes people do find things, Mrs Jarvis thought, and yet in this hazy moonlight it was impossible to see anything, except bones, and little pieces of chalk.

'Jacob bought it with his own money, and then I brought Mr Parker up to see the view, and it must have dropped——' Mrs Flanders murmured.

Did the bones stir, or the rusty swords? Was Mrs Flanders's two-penny-halfpenny brooch for ever part of the rich accumulation? and if all the ghosts flocked thick and rubbed shoulders with Mrs Flanders in the circle, would she not have seemed perfectly in her place, a live English matron, growing stout?

The clock struck the quarter.

The frail waves of sound broke among the stiff gorse and the hawthorn twigs as the church clock divided time into quarters.

Motionless and broad-backed the moors received the statement 'It is fifteen minutes past the hour,' but made no answer, unless a bramble stirred.

Yet even in this light the legends on the tombstones could be read, brief voices saying, 'I am Bertha Ruck', 'I am Tom Gage'. And they say which day of the year they died, and the New Testament says something for them, very proud, very emphatic, or consoling.

The moors accept all that too.

The moonlight falls like a pale page upon the church wall, and illumines the kneeling family in the niche, and the tablet set up in 1780 to the Squire of the parish who relieved the poor, and believed in God— so the measured voice goes on down the marble scroll, as though it could impose itself upon time and the open air.

Now a fox steals out from behind the gorse bushes.

Often, even at night, the church seems full of people. The pews are worn and greasy, and the cassocks in place, and the hymn-books on the ledges. It is a ship with all its crew aboard. The timbers strain to hold the dead and the living, the ploughmen, the carpenters, the fox-hunting gentlemen and the farmers smelling of mud and brandy. Their tongues join together in syllabling the sharp-cut words, which for ever slice asunder time and the broad-backed moors. Plaint and belief and elegy, despair and triumph, but for the most part good sense and jolly indifference, go trampling out of the windows any time these five hundred years.

Still, as Mrs Jarvis said, stepping out on to the moors, 'How quiet it is!' Quiet at midday, except when the hunt scatters across it; quiet in the afternoon, save for the drifting sheep; at night the moor is perfectly quiet.

A garnet brooch has dropped into its grass. A fox pads stealthily. A leaf turns on its edge. Mrs Jarvis, who is fifty years of age, reposes in the camp in the hazy moonlight.

'. . . and,' said Mrs Flanders, straightening her back, 'I never cared for Mr Parker.'

'Neither did I,' said Mrs Jarvis. They began to walk home.

But their voices floated for a little above the camp. The moonlight destroyed nothing. The moor accepted everything. Tom Gage cries aloud so long as his tombstone endures. The Roman skeletons are in safe keeping. Betty Flanders' darning needles are safe too and her garnet brooch. And sometimes at midday, in the sunshine, the moor seems to hoard these little treasures, like a nurse. But at midnight when no one speaks or gallops, and the thorn tree is perfectly still, it would be foolish to vex the moor with questions—what? and why?

The church clock, however, strikes twelve.

XII

The water fell off a ledge like lead—like a chain with thick white links. The train ran out into a steep green meadow, and Jacob saw striped tulips growing and heard a bird singing, in Italy.

A motor car full of Italian officers ran along the flat road and kept up with the train, raising dust behind it. There were trees laced together with vines—as Virgil said. Here was a station; and a tremendous leave-taking going on, with women in high yellow boots and odd pale boys in ringed socks. Virgil's bees had gone about the plains of Lombardy. It was the custom of the ancients to train vines between elms. Then at Milan there were sharp-winged hawks, of a bright brown, cutting figures over the roofs.

These Italian carriages get damnably hot with the afternoon sun on them, and the chances are that before the engine has pulled to the top of the gorge the clanking chain will have broken. Up, up, up, it goes, like a train on a scenic railway. Every peak is covered with sharp trees, and amazing white villages are crowded on ledges. There is always a white tower on the very summit, flat red-frilled roofs, and a sheer drop beneath. It is not a country in which one walks after tea. For one thing there is no grass. A whole hillside will be ruled with olive trees. Already in April the earth is clotted into dry dust between them. And there are neither stiles nor footpaths, nor lanes chequered with the shadows of leaves nor eighteenth-century inns with bow-windows, where one eats ham and eggs. Oh no, Italy is all fierceness, bareness, exposure, and black priests shuffling along the roads. It is strange, too, how you never get away from villas.

Still, to be travelling on one's own with a hundred pounds to spend is a fine affair. And if his money gave out, as it probably would, he would go on foot. He could live on bread and wine—the wine in straw bottles—for after doing Greece he was going to knock off Rome. The Roman civilization was a very inferior affair, no doubt. But Bonamy talked a lot of rot, all the same. 'You ought to have been in Athens,' he would say to Bonamy when he got back. 'Standing on the Parthenon,' he would say, or 'The ruins of the Coliseum suggest some fairly sublime reflections,' which he would write out at length in letters. It might turn to an essay upon civilization. A comparison between the ancients and moderns, with some pretty sharp hits at Mr Asquith—something in the style of Gibbon.

A stout gentleman laboriously hauled himself in, dusty, baggy, slung with gold chains, and Jacob, regretting that he did not come of the Latin race, looked out of the window.

It is a strange reflection that by travelling two days and nights you are in the heart of Italy. Accidental villas among olive trees appear; and men-servants watering the cactuses. Black victorias drive in between pompous pillars with plaster shields stuck to them. It is at once momentary and astonishingly intimate—to be displayed before the eyes of a foreigner. And there is a lonely hill-top where no one ever comes, and yet it is seen by me who was lately driving down Piccadilly on an omnibus. And what I should like would be to get out among the fields, sit down and hear the grasshoppers, and take up a handful of earth— Italian earth, as this is Italian dust upon my shoes.

Jacob heard them crying strange names at railway stations through the night. The train stopped and he heard frogs croaking close by, and he wrinkled back the blind cautiously and saw a vast strange marsh all white in the moonlight. The carriage was thick with cigar smoke, which floated round the globe with the green shade on it. The Italian gentleman lay snoring with his boots off and his waistcoat unbuttoned ... And all this business of going to Greece seemed to Jacob an intolerable weariness—sitting in hotels by oneself and looking at monuments—he'd have done better to go to Cornwall with Timmy Durrant ... 'O—h,' Jacob protested, as the darkness began breaking in front of him and the light showed through, but the man was reaching across him to get something—the fat Italian man in his dicky, unshaven, crumpled, obese, was opening the door and going off to have a wash.

So Jacob sat up, and saw a lean Italian sportsman with a gun walking down the road in the early morning light, and the whole idea of the Parthenon came upon him in a clap.

'By Jove!' he thought, 'we must be nearly there!' and he stuck his head out of the window and got the air full in his face.

It is highly exasperating that twenty-five people of your acquaintance should be able to say straight off something very much to the point about being in Greece, while for yourself there is a stopper upon all emotions whatsoever. For after washing at the hotel at Patras, Jacob had followed the tram lines a mile or so out; and followed them a mile or so back; he had met several droves of turkeys; several strings of donkeys; had got lost in back streets; had read advertisements of corsets and of Maggi's consommé; children had trodden on his toes; the place smelt of bad cheese; and he was glad to find himself suddenly come out opposite his hotel. There was an old copy of the *Daily Mail* lying among coffee-cups; which he read. But what could he do after dinner?

No doubt we should be, on the whole, much worse off than we are without our astonishing gift for illusion. At the age of twelve or so, having given up dolls and broken our steam engines, France, but much more probably Italy, and India almost for a certainty, draws the superfluous imagination. One's aunts have been to Rome; and everyone has an uncle who was last heard of—poor man—in Rangoon. He will never come back any more. But it is the governesses who start the Greek myth. Look at that for a head (they say)—nose, you see, straight as a dart, curls, eyebrows—everything appropriate to manly beauty; while his legs and arms have lines on them which indicate a perfect degree of development—the Greeks caring for the body as much as for the face. And the Greeks could paint fruit so that birds pecked at it. First you read Xenophon; then Euripides. One day—that was an occasion, by God—what people have said appears to have sense in it; 'the Greek spirit'; the Greek this, that, and the other; though it is absurd, by the way, to say that any Greek comes near Shakespeare. The point is, however, that we have been brought up in an illusion.

Jacob, no doubt, thought something in this fashion, the *Daily Mail* crumpled in his hand; his legs extended; the very picture of boredom.

'But it's the way we're brought up,' he went on.

And it all seemed to him very distasteful. Something ought to be done about it. And from being moderately depressed he became like a man about to be executed. Clara Durrant had left him at a party to talk to an American called Pilchard. And he had come all the way to Greece and left her. They wore evening-dresses, and talked nonsense—what damned nonsense—and he put out his hand for the *Globe Trotter*, an international magazine which is supplied free of charge to the proprietors of hotels.

In spite of its ramshackle condition modern Greece is highly advanced in the electric tramway system, so that while Jacob sat in the hotel sitting-room the trams clanked, chimed, rang, rang, rang imperiously to get the donkeys out of the way, and one old woman who refused to budge, beneath the windows. The whole of civilization was being condemned.

The waiter was quite indifferent to that too. Aristotle, a dirty man, carnivorously interested in the body of the only guest now occupying the only armchair, came into the room ostentatiously, put something down, put something straight, and saw that Jacob was still there.

'I shall want to be called early tomorrow,' said Jacob, over his shoulder. 'I am going to Olympia.'

This gloom, this surrender to the dark waters which lap us about, is a modern invention. Perhaps, as Cruttendon said, we do not believe enough. Our fathers at any rate had something to demolish. So have we for the matter of that, thought Jacob, crumpling the *Daily Mail* in his hand. He would go into Parliament and make fine speeches—but what use are fine speeches and Parliament, once you surrender an inch to the black waters? Indeed there has never been any explanation of the ebb and flow in our veins—of happiness and unhappiness. That respectability and evening parties where one has to dress, and wretched slums at the back of Gray's Inn—something solid, immovable, and grotesque—is at the back of it, Jacob thought probable. But then there was the British Empire which was beginning to puzzle him; nor was he altogether in favour of giving Home Rule to Ireland. What did the *Daily Mail* say about that?

For he had grown to be a man, and was about to be immersed in things—as indeed the chamber-maid, emptying his basin upstairs, fingering keys, studs, pencils, and bottles of tabloids strewn on the dressing-table, was aware.

That he had grown to be a man was a fact that Florinda knew, as she knew everything, by instinct.

And Betty Flanders even now suspected it, as she read his letter, posted at Milan, 'Telling me', she complained to Mrs Jarvis, 'really nothing that I want to know;' but she brooded over it.

Fanny Elmer felt it to desperation. For he would take his stick and his hat and would walk to the window, and look perfectly absent-minded and very stern too, she thought.

'I am going', he would say, 'to cadge a meal off Bonamy.'

'Anyhow, I can drown myself in the Thames,' Fanny cried, as she hurried past the Foundling Hospital.

'But the *Daily Mail* isn't to be trusted,' Jacob said to himself, looking about for something else to read. And he sighed again, being indeed so profoundly gloomy that doom must have been lodged in him to cloud him at any moment, which was odd in a man who enjoyed things so, was not much given to analysis, but was horribly romantic, of course, Bonamy thought, in his rooms in Lincoln's Inn.

'He will fall in love,' thought Bonamy. 'Some Greek woman with a straight nose.'

It was to Bonamy that Jacob wrote from Patras—to Bonamy who couldn't love a woman and never read a foolish book.

There are very few good books after all, for we can't count profuse histories, travels in mule carts to discover the sources of the Nile, or the volubility of fiction.

I like books whose virtue is all drawn together in a page or two. I like sentences that don't budge though armies cross them. I like words to be hard—such were Bonamy's views, and they won him the hostility of those whose taste is all for the fresh growths of the morning, who throw up the window, and find the poppies spread in the sun, and can't forbear a shout of jubilation at the astonishing fertility of English literature. That was not Bonamy's way at all. That his taste in literature affected his friendships, and made him silent, secretive, fastidious, and only quite at his ease with one or two young men of his own way of thinking, was the charge against him.

But then Jacob Flanders was not at all of his own way of thinking— far from it. Bonamy sighed, laying the thin sheets of notepaper on the table and falling into thought about Jacob's character, not for the first time.

The trouble was this romantic vein in him. 'But mixed with the stupidity which leads him into these absurd predicaments,' thought Bonamy, 'there is something—something'—he sighed, for he was fonder of Jacob than of anyone in the world.

Jacob went to the window and stood with his hands in his pockets. There he saw three Greeks in kilts; the masts of ships; idle or busy people of the lower classes strolling or stepping out briskly, or falling into groups and gesticulating with their hands. Their lack of concern for him was not the cause of his gloom; but some more profound conviction—it was not that he himself happened to be lonely, but that all people are.

Yet next day, as the train slowly rounded a hill on the way to Olympia, the Greek peasant women were out among the vines; the old Greek men were sitting at the stations, sipping sweet wine. And though Jacob remained gloomy he had never suspected how tremendously pleasant it is to be alone; out of England; on one's own; cut off from the whole thing. There are very sharp bare hills on the way to Olympia;

and between them blue sea in triangular spaces. A little like the Cornish coast. Well now, to go walking by oneself all day—to get on to that track and follow it up between the bushes—or are they small trees?—to the top of that mountain from which one can see half the nations of antiquity——

'Yes,' said Jacob, for his carriage was empty, 'let's look at the map.'

Blame it or praise it, there is no denying the wild horse in us. To gallop intemperately; fall on the sand tired out; to feel the earth spin; to have—positively—a rush of friendship for stones and grasses, as if humanity were over, and as for men and women, let them go hang— there is no getting over the fact that this desire seizes up pretty often.

The evening air slightly moved the dirty curtains in the hotel window at Olympia.

'I am full of love for everyone,' thought Mrs Wentworth Williams, '—for the poor most of all—for the peasants coming back in the evening with their burdens. And everything is soft and vague and very sad. It is sad, it is sad. But everything has meaning,' thought Sandra Wentworth Williams, raising her head a little and looking very beautiful, tragic, and exalted. 'One must love everything.'

She held in her hand a little book convenient for travelling—stories by Tchekov—as she stood, veiled, in white, in the window of the hotel at Olympia. How beautiful the evening was! and her beauty was its beauty. The tragedy of Greece was the tragedy of all high souls. The inevitable compromise. She seemed to have grasped something. She would write it down. And moving to the table where her husband sat reading she leant her chin in her hands and thought of the peasants, of suffering, of her own beauty, of the inevitable compromise, and of how she would write it down. Nor did Evan Williams say anything brutal, banal, or foolish when he shut his book and put it away to make room for the plates of soup which were now being placed before them. Only his drooping bloodhound eyes and his heavy sallow cheeks expressed his melancholy tolerance, his conviction that though forced to live with circumspection and deliberation he could never possibly achieve any of those objects which, as he knew, are the only ones worth pursuing. His consideration was flawless; his silence unbroken.

'Everything seems to mean so much,' said Sandra. But with the sound of her own voice the spell was broken. She forgot the peasants. Only there remained with her a sense of her own beauty, and in front, luckily, there was a looking-glass.

'I am very beautiful,' she thought.

She shifted her hat slightly. Her husband saw her looking in the glass; and agreed that beauty is important; it is an inheritance; one cannot ignore it. But it is a barrier; it is in fact rather a bore. So he drank his soup; and kept his eyes fixed upon the window.

'Quails,' said Mrs Wentworth Williams languidly. 'And then goat, I suppose; and then . . .'

'Caramel custard presumably,' said her husband in the same cadence, with his toothpick out already.

She laid her spoon upon her plate, and her soup was taken away half finished. Never did she do anything without dignity; for hers was the English type which is so Greek, save that villagers have touched their hats to it, the vicarage reveres it; and upper-gardeners and under-gardeners respectfully straighten their backs as she comes down the broad terrace on Sunday morning, dallying at the stone urns with the Prime Minister to pick a rose—which, perhaps, she was trying to forget, as her eye wandered round the dining-room of the inn at Olympia, seeking the window where her book lay, where a few minutes ago she had discovered something—something very profound it had been, about love and sadness and the peasants.

But it was Evan who sighed; not in despair nor indeed in rebellion. But, being the most ambitious of men and temperamentally the most sluggish, he had accomplished nothing; had the political history of England at his finger-ends, and living much in company with Chatham, Pitt, Burke, and Charles James Fox could not help contrasting himself and his age with them and theirs. 'Yet there never was a time when great men are more needed,' he was in the habit of saying to himself, with a sigh. Here he was picking his teeth in an inn at Olympia. He had done. But Sandra's eyes wandered.

'Those pink melons are sure to be dangerous,' he said gloomily. And as he spoke the door opened and in came a young man in a grey check suit.

'Beautiful but dangerous,' said Sandra, immediately talking to her husband in the presence of a third person. ('Ah, an English boy on tour,' she thought to herself.)

And Evan knew all that too.

Yes, he knew all that; and he admired her. Very pleasant, he thought, to have affairs. But for himself, what with his height (Napoleon was five feet four, he remembered), his bulk, his inability to impose his own personality (and yet great men are needed more than ever now, he sighed), it was useless. He threw away his cigar, went up to Jacob and asked him, with a simple sort of sincerity which Jacob liked, whether he had come straight out from England.

'How very English!' Sandra laughed when the waiter told them next morning that the young gentleman had left at five to climb the mountain. 'I am sure he asked you for a bath?' at which the waiter shook his head, and said that he would ask the manager.

'You do not understand,' laughed Sandra. 'Never mind.'

Stretched on the top of the mountain, quite alone, Jacob enjoyed himself immensely. Probably he had never been so happy in the whole of his life.

But at dinner that night Mr Williams asked him whether he would like to see the paper; then Mrs Williams asked him (as they strolled on the terrace smoking—and how could he refuse that man's cigar?) whether he'd seen the theatre by moonlight; whether he knew Everard Sherborn; whether he read Greek and whether (Evan rose silently and went in) if he had to sacrifice one it would be the French literature or the Russian?

'And now,' wrote Jacob in his letter to Bonamy, 'I shall have to read her cursed book'—her Tchekov, he meant, for she had lent it him.

Though the opinion is unpopular it seems likely enough that bare places, fields too thick with stones to be ploughed, tossing sea-meadows half-way between England and America, suit us better than cities.

There is something absolute in us which despises qualification. It is this which is teased and twisted in society. People come together in a room. 'So delighted', says somebody, 'to meet you,' and that is a lie. And then: 'I enjoy the spring more than the autumn now. One does, I think, as one gets older.' For women are always, always, always talking about what one feels, and if they say 'as one gets older', they mean you to reply with something quite off the point.

Jacob sat himself down in the quarry where the Greeks had cut marble for the theatre. It is hot work walking up Greek hills at midday. The wild red cyclamen was out; he had seen the little tortoises hobbling from clump to clump; the air smelt strong and suddenly sweet, and the sun, striking on jagged splinters of marble, was very dazzling to the eyes. Composed, commanding, contemptuous, a little melancholy, and bored with an august kind of boredom, there he sat smoking his pipe.

Bonamy would have said that this was the sort of thing that made him uneasy—when Jacob got into the doldrums, looked like a Margate fisherman out of a job, or a British Admiral. You couldn't make him understand a thing when he was in a mood like that. One had better leave him alone. He was dull. He was apt to be grumpy.

He was up very early, looking at the statues with his Baedeker.

Sandra Wentworth Williams, ranging the world before breakfast in quest of adventure or a point of view, all in white, not so very tall perhaps, but uncommonly upright—Sandra Williams got Jacob's head exactly on a level with the head of the Hermes of Praxiteles. The comparison was all in his favour. But before she could say a single word he had gone out of the Museum and left her.

Still, a lady of fashion travels with more than one dress, and if white suits the morning hour, perhaps sandy yellow with purple spots on it, a black hat, and a volume of Balzac, suit the evening. Thus she was arranged on the terrace when Jacob came in. Very beautiful she looked. With her hands folded she mused, seemed to listen to her husband, seemed to watch the peasants coming down with brushwood on their backs, seemed to notice how the hill changed from blue to black, seemed to discriminate between truth and falsehood, Jacob thought, and crossed his legs suddenly, observing the extreme shabbiness of his trousers.

'But he is very distinguished looking,' Sandra decided.

And Evan Williams, lying back in his chair with the paper on his knees, envied them. The best thing he could do would be to publish, with Macmillans, his monograph upon the foreign policy of Chatham. But confound this tumid, queasy feeling—this restlessness, swelling, and heat—it was jealousy! jealousy! jealousy! which he had sworn never to feel again.

'Come with us to Corinth, Flanders,' he said with more than his usual energy, stopping by Jacob's chair. He was relieved by Jacob's reply, or rather by the solid, direct, if shy manner in which he said that he would like very much to come with them to Corinth.

'Here is a fellow', thought Evan Williams, 'who might do very well in politics.'

'I intend to come to Greece every year so long as I live,' Jacob wrote to Bonamy. 'It is the only chance I can see of protecting oneself from civilization.'

'Goodness knows what he means by that,' Bonamy sighed. For as he never said a clumsy thing himself, these dark sayings of Jacob's made

him feel apprehensive, yet somehow impressed, his own turn being all
for the definite, the concrete, and the rational.

Nothing could be much simpler than what Sandra said as she descended
the Acro-Corinth, keeping to the little path, while Jacob strode over
rougher ground by her side. She had been left motherless at the age of
four; and the Park was vast.

'One never seemed able to get out of it,' she laughed. Of course there
was the library, and dear Mr Jones, and notions about things. 'I used to
stray into the kitchen and sit upon the butler's knees,' she laughed,
sadly though.

Jacob thought that if he had been there he would have saved her; for
she had been exposed to great dangers, he felt, and, he thought to
himself, 'People wouldn't understand a woman talking as she talks.'

She made little of the roughness of the hill; and wore breeches, he
saw, under her short skirts.

'Women like Fanny Elmer don't,' he thought. 'What's-her-name
Carslake didn't; yet they pretend . . .'

Mrs Williams said things straight out. He was surprised by his own
knowledge of the rules of behaviour; how much more can be said than
one thought; how open one can be with a woman; and how little he had
known himself before.

Evan joined them on the road; and as they drove along up hill and
down hill (for Greece is in a state of effervescence, yet astonishingly
clean-cut, a treeless land, where you see the ground between the blades,
each hill cut and shaped and outlined as often as not against sparkling
deep blue waters, islands white as sand floating on the horizon,
occasional groves of palm trees standing in the valleys, which are
scattered with black goats, spotted with little olive trees and sometimes
have white hollows, rayed and criss-crossed, in their flanks), as they
drove up hill and down he scowled in the corner of the carriage, with
his paw so tightly closed that the skin was stretched between the
knuckles and the little hairs stood upright. Sandra rode opposite,
dominant, like a Victory prepared to fling into the air.

'Heartless!' thought Evan (which was untrue).

'Brainless!' he suspected (and that was not true either). 'Still . . .!' He
envied her.

When bedtime came the difficulty was to write to Bonamy, Jacob
found. Yet he had seen Salamis, and Marathon in the distance. Poor old

Bonamy! No; there was something queer about it. He could not write to Bonamy.

'I shall go to Athens all the same,' he resolved, looking very set, with this hook dragging in his side.

The Williamses had already been to Athens.

Athens is still quite capable of striking a young man as the oddest combination, the most incongruous assortment. Now it is suburban; now immortal. Now cheap continental jewellery is laid upon plush trays. Now the stately woman stands naked, save for a wave of drapery above the knee. No form can he set on his sensations as he strolls, one blazing afternoon, along the Parisian boulevard and skips out of the way of the royal landau which, looking indescribably ramshackle, rattles along the pitted roadway, saluted by citizens of both sexes cheaply dressed in bowler hats and continental costumes; though a shepherd in kilt, cap, and gaiters very nearly drives his herd of goats between the royal wheels; and all the time the Acropolis surges into the air, raises itself above the town, like a large immobile wave with the yellow columns of the Parthenon firmly planted upon it.

The yellow columns of the Parthenon are to be seen at all hours of the day firmly planted upon the Acropolis; though at sunset, when the ships in the Piraeus fire their guns, a bell rings, a man in uniform (the waistcoat unbuttoned) appears; and the women roll up the black stockings which they are knitting in the shadow of the columns, call to the children, and troop off down the hill back to their houses.

There they are again, the pillars, the pediment, the Temple of Victory and the Erechtheum, set on a tawny rock cleft with shadows, directly you unlatch your shutters in the morning and, leaning out, hear the clatter, the clamour, the whip cracking in the street below. There they are.

The extreme definiteness with which they stand, now a brilliant white, again yellow, and in some lights red, imposes ideas of durability, of the emergence through the earth of some spiritual energy elsewhere dissipated in elegant trifles. But this durability exists quite independently of our admiration. Although the beauty is sufficiently humane to weaken us, to stir the deep deposit of mud—memories, abandonments, regrets, sentimental devotions—the Parthenon is separate from all that; and if you consider how it has stood out all night, for centuries, you begin to connect the blaze (at midday the glare is dazzling and the frieze almost invisible) with the idea that perhaps it is beauty alone that is immortal.

Added to this, compared with the blistered stucco, the new love songs rasped out to the strum of guitar and gramophone, and the mobile yet insignificant faces of the street, the Parthenon is really astonishing in its silent composure; which is so vigorous that, far from being decayed, the Parthenon appears, on the contrary, likely to outlast the entire world.

'And the Greeks, like sensible men, never bothered to finish the backs of their statues,' said Jacob, shading his eyes and observing that the side of the figure which is turned away from view is left in the rough.

He noted the slight irregularity in the line of the steps which 'the artistic sense of the Greeks preferred to mathematical accuracy', he read in his guidebook.

He stood on the exact spot where the great statue of Athena used to stand, and identified the more famous landmarks of the scene beneath.

In short he was accurate and diligent; but profoundly morose. Moreover he was pestered by guides. This was on Monday.

But on Wednesday he wrote a telegram to Bonamy, telling him to come at once. And then he crumpled it in his hand and threw it in the gutter.

'For one thing he wouldn't come,' he thought. 'And then I daresay this sort of thing wears off.' 'This sort of thing' being that uneasy, painful feeling, something like selfishness—one wishes almost that the thing would stop—it is getting more and more beyond what is possible— 'If it goes on much longer I shan't be able to cope with it—but if someone else were seeing it at the same time—Bonamy is stuffed in his room in Lincoln's Inn—oh, I say, damn it all, I say,'—the sight of Hymettus, Pentelicus, Lycabettus on one side, and the sea on the other, as one stands in the Parthenon at sunset, the sky pink feathered, the plain all colours, the marble tawny in one's eyes, is thus oppressive. Luckily Jacob had little sense of personal association; he seldom thought of Plato or Socrates in the flesh; on the other hand his feeling for architecture was very strong; he preferred statues to pictures; and he was beginning to think a great deal about the problems of civilization, which were solved, of course, so very remarkably by the ancient Greeks, though their solution is no help to us. Then the hook gave a great tug in his side as he lay in bed on Wednesday night; and he turned over with a desperate sort of tumble, remembering Sandra Wentworth Williams with whom he was in love.

Next day he climbed Pentelicus.

The day after he went up to the Acropolis. The hour was early: the place almost deserted; and possibly there was thunder in the air. But the sun struck full upon the Acropolis.

Jacob's intention was to sit down and read, and, finding a drum of marble conveniently placed, from which Marathon could be seen, and yet it was in the shade, while the Erechtheum blazed white in front of him, there he sat. And after reading a page he put his thumb in his book. Why not rule countries in the way they should be ruled? And he read again.

No doubt his position there overlooking Marathon somehow raised his spirits. Or it may have been that a slow capacious brain has these moments of flowering. Or he had, insensibly, while he was abroad, got into the way of thinking about politics.

And then looking up and seeing the sharp outline, his meditations were given an extraordinary edge; Greece was over; the Parthenon in ruins; yet there he was.

(Ladies with green and white umbrellas passed through the court-yard—French ladies on their way to join their husbands in Constantinople.)

Jacob read on again. And laying the book on the ground he began, as if inspired by what he had read, to write a note upon the importance of history—upon democracy—one of those scribbles upon which the work of a lifetime may be based; or again, it falls out of a book twenty years later, and one can't remember a word of it. It is a little painful. It had better be burnt.

Jacob wrote; began to draw a straight nose; when all the French ladies opening and shutting their umbrellas just beneath him exclaimed, looking at the sky, that one did not know what to expect—rain or fine weather?

Jacob got up and strolled across to the Erechtheum. There are still several women standing there holding the roof on their heads. Jacob straightened himself slightly; for stability and balance affect the body first. These statues annulled things so! He stared at them, then turned, and there was Madame Lucien Gravé perched on a block of marble with her kodak pointed at his head. Of course she jumped down, in spite of her age, her figure, and her tight boots—having, now that her daughter was married, lapsed with a luxurious abandonment, grand enough in its way, into the fleshy grotesque; she jumped down, but not before Jacob had seen her.

'Damn these women—damn these women!' he thought. And he went to fetch his book which he had left lying on the ground in the Parthenon.

'How they spoil things,' he murmured, leaning against one of the pillars, pressing his book tight between his arm and his side. (As for the weather, no doubt the storm would break soon; Athens was under cloud.)

'It is those damned women,' said Jacob, without any trace of bitterness, but rather with sadness and disappointment that what might have been should never be.

(This violent disillusionment is generally to be expected in young men in the prime of life, sound of wind and limb, who will soon become fathers of families and directors of banks.)

Then, making sure that the Frenchwomen had gone, and looking cautiously round him, Jacob strolled over to the Erechtheum and looked rather furtively at the goddess on the left-hand side holding the roof on her head. She reminded him of Sandra Wentworth Williams. He looked at her, then looked away. He looked at her, then looked away. He was extraordinarily moved, and with the battered Greek nose in his head, with Sandra in his head, with all sorts of things in his head, off he started to walk right up to the top of Mount Hymettus, alone, in the heat.

That very afternoon Bonamy went expressly to talk about Jacob to tea with Clara Durrant in the square behind Sloane Street where, on hot spring days, there are striped blinds over the front windows, single horses pawing the macadam outside the doors, and elderly gentlemen in yellow waistcoats ringing bells and stepping in very politely when the maid demurely replies that Mrs Durrant is at home.

Bonamy sat with Clara in the sunny front room with the barrel organ piping sweetly outside; the water-cart going slowly along spraying the pavement; the carriages jingling, and all the silver and chintz, brown and blue rugs and vases filled with green boughs, striped with trembling yellow bars.

The insipidity of what was said needs no illustration—Bonamy kept on gently returning quiet answers and accumulating amazement at an existence squeezed and emasculated within a white satin shoe (Mrs Durrant meanwhile enunciating strident politics with Sir Somebody in the back room) until the virginity of Clara's soul appeared to him candid; the depths unknown; and he would have brought out Jacob's name had he not begun to feel positively certain that Clara loved him—and could do nothing whatever.

'Nothing whatever!' he exclaimed, as the door shut, and, for a man of his temperament, got a very queer feeling, as he walked through the park, of carriages irresistibly driven; of flower-beds uncompromisingly geometrical; of force rushing round geometrical patterns in the most senseless way in the world. 'Was Clara', he thought, pausing to watch the boys bathing in the Serpentine, 'the silent woman?—would Jacob marry her?'

But in Athens in the sunshine, in Athens, where it is almost impossible to get afternoon tea, and elderly gentlemen who talk politics talk them all the other way round, in Athens sat Sandra Wentworth Williams, veiled, in white, her legs stretched in front of her, one elbow on the arm of the bamboo chair, blue clouds wavering and drifting from her cigarette.

The orange trees which flourish in the Square of the Constitution, the band, the dragging of feet, the sky, the houses, lemon and rose coloured—all this became so significant to Mrs Wentworth Williams after her second cup of coffee that she began dramatizing the story of the noble and impulsive Englishwoman who had offered a seat in her carriage to the old American lady at Mycenae (Mrs Duggan)—not altogether a false story, though it said nothing of Evan, standing first on one foot, then on the other, waiting for the women to stop chattering.

'I am putting the life of Father Damien into verse,' Mrs Duggan had said, for she had lost everything—everything in the world, husband and child and everything, but faith remained.

Sandra, floating from the particular to the universal, lay back in a trance.

The flight of time which hurries us so tragically along: the eternal drudge and drone, now bursting into fiery flame like those brief balls of yellow among green leaves (she was looking at orange trees); kisses on lips that are to die; the world turning, turning in mazes of heat and sound—though to be sure there is the quiet evening with its lovely pallor, 'For I am sensitive to every side of it,' Sandra thought, 'and Mrs Duggan will write to me for ever, and I shall answer her letters.' Now the royal band marching by with the national flag stirred wider rings of emotion, and life became something that the courageous mount and ride out to sea on—the hair blown back (so she envisaged it, and the breeze

stirred slightly among the orange trees) and she herself was emerging
from silver spray—when she saw Jacob. He was standing in the Square
with a book under his arm looking vacantly about him. That he was
heavily built and might become stout in time was a fact.

But she suspected him of being a mere bumpkin.

'There is that young man,' she said, peevishly, throwing away her
cigarette, 'that Mr Flanders.'

'Where?' said Evan. 'I don't see him.'

'Oh, walking away—behind the trees now. No, you can't see him.
But we are sure to run into him,' which, of course, they did.

But how far was he a mere bumpkin? How far was Jacob Flanders at
the age of twenty-six a stupid fellow? It is no use trying to sum people
up. One must follow hints, not exactly what is said, nor yet entirely
what is done. Some, it is true, take ineffaceable impressions of character
at once. Others dally, loiter, and get blown this way and that. Kind old
ladies assure us that cats are often the best judges of character. A cat
will always go to a good man, they say; but then, Mrs Whitehorn,
Jacob's landlady, loathed cats.

There is also the highly respectable opinion that character-mongering
is much overdone nowadays. After all, what does it matter—that Fanny
Elmer was all sentiment and sensation, and Mrs Durrant hard as iron?
that Clara, owing (so the character-mongers said) largely to her mother's
influence, never yet had the chance to do anything off her own bat, and
only to very observant eyes displayed deeps of feeling which were
positively alarming; and would certainly throw herself away upon
someone unworthy of her one of these days unless, so the character-
mongers said, she had a spark of her mother's spirit in her—was
somehow heroic. But what a term to apply to Clara Durrant! Simple to
a degree, others thought her. And that is the very reason, so they said,
why she attracts Dick Bonamy—the young man with the Wellington
nose. Now *he's* a dark horse if you like. And there these gossips would
suddenly pause. Obviously they meant to hint at his peculiar disposition—long rumoured among them.

'But sometimes it is precisely a woman like Clara that men of that
temperament need . . .' Miss Julia Eliot would hint.

'Well,' Mr Bowley would reply, 'it may be so.'

For however long these gossips sit, and however they stuff out their
victims' characters till they are swollen and tender as the livers of geese
exposed to a hot fire, they never come to a decision.

'That young man, Jacob Flanders,' they would say, 'so distinguished looking—and yet so awkward.' Then they would apply themselves to Jacob and vacillate eternally between the two extremes. He rode to hounds—after a fashion, for he hadn't a penny.

'Did you ever hear who his father was?' asked Julia Eliot.

'His mother, they say, is somehow connected with the Rocksbiers,' replied Mr Bowley.

'He doesn't overwork himself anyhow.'

'His friends are very fond of him.'

'Dick Bonamy, you mean?'

'No, I didn't mean that. It's evidently the other way with Jacob. He is precisely the young man to fall headlong in love and repent it for the rest of his life.'

'Oh, Mr Bowley,' said Mrs Durrant, sweeping down upon them in her imperious manner, 'you remember Mrs Adams? Well, that is her niece.' And Mr Bowley, getting up, bowed politely and fetched strawberries.

So we are driven back to see what the other side means—the men in clubs and Cabinets—when they say that character-drawing is a frivolous fireside art, a matter of pins and needles, exquisite outlines enclosing vacancy, flourishes, and mere scrawls.

The battleships ray out over the North Sea, keeping their stations accurately apart. At a given signal all the guns are trained on a target which (the master gunner counts the seconds, watch in hand—at the sixth he looks up) flames into splinters. With equal nonchalance a dozen young men in the prime of life descend with composed faces into the depths of the sea; and there impassively (though with perfect mastery of machinery) suffocate uncomplainingly together. Like blocks of tin soldiers the army covers the cornfield, moves up the hillside, stops, reels slightly this way and that, and falls flat, save that, through field-glasses, it can be seen that one or two pieces still agitate up and down like fragments of broken match-stick.

These actions, together with the incessant commerce of banks, laboratories, chancellories, and houses of business, are the strokes which oar the world forward, they say. And they are dealt by men as smoothly sculptured as the impassive policeman at Ludgate Circus. But you will observe that far from being padded to rotundity his face is stiff from force of will, and lean from the effort of keeping it so. When his right arm rises, all the force in his veins flows straight from shoulder to finger-tips; not an ounce is diverted into sudden impulses, sentimental regrets, wire-drawn distinctions. The buses punctually stop.

It is thus that we live, they say, driven by an unseizable force. They say that the novelists never catch it; that it goes hurtling through their nets and leaves them torn to ribbons. This, they say, is what we live by—this unseizable force.

'Where are the men?' said old General Gibbons, looking round the drawing-room, full as usual on Sunday afternoons of well-dressed people. 'Where are the guns?'

Mrs Durrant looked too.

Clara, thinking that her mother wanted her, came in; then went out again.

They were talking about Germany at the Durrants, and Jacob (driven by this unseizable force) walked rapidly down Hermes Street and ran straight into the Williamses.

'Oh!' cried Sandra, with a cordiality which she suddenly felt. And Evan added, 'What luck!'

The dinner which they gave him in the hotel which looks on to the Square of the Constitution was excellent. Plated baskets contained fresh rolls. There was real butter. And the meat scarcely needed the disguise of innumerable little red and green vegetables glazed in sauce.

It was strange, though. There were the little tables set out at intervals on the scarlet floor with the Greek King's monogram wrought in yellow. Sandra dined in her hat, veiled as usual. Evan looked this way and that over his shoulder; imperturbable yet supple; and sometimes sighed. It was strange. For they were English people come together in Athens on a May evening. Jacob, helping himself to this and that, answered intelligently, yet with a ring in his voice.

The Williamses were going to Constantinople early next morning, they said.

'Before you are up,' said Sandra.

They would leave Jacob alone, then. Turning very slightly, Evan ordered something—a bottle of wine—from which he helped Jacob, with a kind of solicitude, with a kind of paternal solicitude, if that were possible. To be left alone—that was good for a young fellow. Never was there a time when the country had more need of men. He sighed.

'And you have been to the Acropolis?' asked Sandra.

'Yes,' said Jacob. And they moved off to the window together, while Evan spoke to the head waiter about calling them early.

'It is astonishing,' said Jacob, in a gruff voice.

Sandra opened her eyes very slightly. Possibly her nostrils expanded a little too.

'At half-past six then,' said Evan, coming towards them, looking as if he faced something in facing his wife and Jacob standing with their backs to the window.

Sandra smiled at him.

And, as he went to the window and had nothing to say she added, in broken half-sentences:

'Well, but how lovely—wouldn't it be? The Acropolis, Evan—or are you too tired?'

At that Evan looked at them, or, since Jacob was staring ahead of him, at his wife, surlily, sullenly, yet with a kind of distress—not that she would pity him. Nor would the implacable spirit of love, for anything he could do, cease its tortures.

They left him and he sat in the smoking-room, which looks out on to the Square of the Constitution.

'Evan is happier alone,' said Sandra. 'We have been separated from the newspapers. Well, it is better that people should have what they want . . . You have seen all these wonderful things since we met . . . What impression . . . I think that you are changed.'

'You want to go to the Acropolis,' said Jacob. 'Up here then.'

'One will remember it all one's life,' said Sandra.

'Yes,' said Jacob. 'I wish you could have come in the day-time.'

'This is more wonderful,' said Sandra, waving her hand.

Jacob looked vaguely.

'But you should see the Parthenon in the day-time,' he said. 'You couldn't come tomorrow—it would be too early?'

'You have sat there for hours and hours by yourself?'

'There were some awful women this morning,' said Jacob.

'Awful women?' Sandra echoed.

'Frenchwomen.'

'But something very wonderful has happened,' said Sandra. Ten minutes, fifteen minutes, half an hour—that was all the time before her.

'Yes,' he said.

'When one is your age—when one is young. What will you do? You will fall in love—oh yes! But don't be in too great a hurry. I am so much older.'

She was brushed off the pavement by parading men.

'Shall we go on?' Jacob asked.

'Let us go on,' she insisted.

For she could not stop until she had told him—or heard him say—or was it some action on his part that she required? Far away on the horizon she discerned it and could not rest.

'You'd never get English people to sit out like this,' he said.

'Never—no. When you get back to England you won't forget this—or come with us to Constantinople!' she cried suddenly.

'But then . . .'

Sandra sighed.

'You must go to Delphi, of course,' she said. 'But,' she asked herself, 'what do I want from him? Perhaps it is something that I have missed . . .'

'You will get there about six in the evening,' she said. 'You will see the eagles.'

Jacob looked set and even desperate by the light at the street corner; and yet composed. He was suffering, perhaps. He was credulous. Yet there was something caustic about him. He had in him the seeds of extreme disillusionment, which would come to him from women in middle life. Perhaps if one strove hard enough to reach the top of the hill it need not come to him—this disillusionment from women in middle life.

'The hotel is awful,' she said. 'The last visitors had left their basins full of dirty water. There is always that,' she laughed.

'The people one meets *are* beastly,' Jacob said.

His excitement was clear enough.

'Write and tell me about it,' she said. 'And tell me what you feel and what you think. Tell me everything.'

The night was dark. The Acropolis was a jagged mound.

'I should like to, awfully,' he said.

'When we get back to London, we shall meet . . .'

'Yes.'

'I suppose they leave the gates open?' he asked.

'We could climb them!' she answered wildly.

Obscuring the moon and altogether darkening the Acropolis the clouds passed from east to west. The clouds solidified; the vapours thickened; the trailing veils stayed and accumulated.

It was dark now over Athens, except for gauzy red streaks where the streets ran; and the front of the Palace was cadaverous from electric light. At sea the piers stood out, marked by separate dots; the waves being invisible, and promontories and islands were dark humps with a few lights.

'I'd love to bring my brother, if I may,' Jacob murmured.

'And then when your mother comes to London——,' said Sandra.

The mainland of Greece was dark; and somewhere off Euboea a cloud must have touched the waves and spattered them—the dolphins circling deeper and deeper into the sea. Violent was the wind now rushing down the Sea of Marmara between Greece and the plains of Troy.

In Greece and the uplands of Albania and Turkey, the wind scours the sand and the dust, and sows itself thick with dry particles. And then it pelts the smooth domes of the mosques, and makes the cypresses, standing stiff by the turbaned tombstones of Mohammedans, creak and bristle.

Sandra's veils were swirled about her.

'I will give you my copy,' said Jacob. 'Here. Will you keep it?'

(The book was the poems of Donne.)

Now the agitation of the air uncovered a racing star. Now it was dark. Now one after another lights were extinguished. Now great towns—Paris—Constantinople—London—were black as strewn rocks. Waterways might be distinguished. In England the trees were heavy in leaf. Here perhaps in some southern wood an old man lit dry ferns and the birds were startled. The sheep coughed; one flower bent slightly towards another. The English sky is softer, milkier than the Eastern. Something gentle has passed into it from the grass-rounded hills, something damp. The salt gale blew in at Betty Flanders' bedroom window, and the widow lady, raising herself slightly on her elbow, sighed like one who realizes, but would fain ward off a little longer—oh, a little longer!—the oppression of eternity.

But to return to Jacob and Sandra.

They had vanished. There was the Acropolis; but had they reached it? The columns and the Temple remain; the emotion of the living breaks fresh on them year after year; and of that what remains?

As for reaching the Acropolis who shall say that we ever do it, or that when Jacob woke next morning he found anything hard and durable to keep for ever? Still, he went with them to Constantinople.

Sandra Wentworth Williams certainly woke to find a copy of Donne's poems upon her dressing-table. And the book would be stood on the shelf in the English country house where Sally Duggan's *Life of Father Damien* in verse would join it one of these days. There were ten or twelve little volumes already. Strolling in at dusk, Sandra would open the books and her eyes would brighten (but not at the print), and subsiding into the armchair she would suck back again the soul of the moment; or, for sometimes she was restless, would pull out book after book and swing across the whole space of her life like an acrobat from bar to bar. She had had her moments. Meanwhile, the great clock on the landing ticked and Sandra would hear time accumulating, and ask herself, 'What for? What for?'

'What for? What for?' Sandra would say, putting the book back, and strolling to the looking-glass and pressing her hair. And Miss Edwards would be startled at dinner, as she opened her mouth to admit roast mutton, by Sandra's sudden solicitude: 'Are you happy, Miss Edwards?'—a thing Cissy Edwards hadn't thought of for years.

'What for? What for?' Jacob never asked himself any such question, to judge by the way he laced his boots; shaved himself; to judge by the depth of his sleep that night, with the wind fidgeting at the shutters, and half-a-dozen mosquitoes singing in his ears. He was young—a man. And then Sandra was right when she judged him to be credulous as yet. At forty it might be a different matter. Already he had marked the things he liked in Donne, and they were savage enough. However, you might place beside them passages of the purest poetry in Shakespeare.

But the wind was rolling the darkness through the streets of Athens, rolling it, one might suppose, with a sort of trampling energy of mood which forbids too close an analysis of the feelings of any single person, or inspection of features. All faces—Greek, Levantine, Turkish, English—would have looked much the same in that darkness. At length the columns and the Temples whiten, yellow, turn rose; and the Pyramids and St Peter's arise, and at last sluggish St Paul's looms up.

The Christians have the right to rouse most cities with their interpretation of the day's meaning. Then, less melodiously, dissenters of different sects issue a cantankerous emendation. The steamers, resounding like gigantic tuning-forks, state the old old fact—how there is a sea coldly, greenly, swaying outside. But nowadays it is the thin voice of duty, piping in a white thread from the top of a funnel, that collects the largest multitudes, and night is nothing but a long-drawn sigh between hammer-strokes, a deep breath—you can hear it from an open window even in the heart of London.

But who, save the nerve-worn and sleepless, or thinkers standing with hands to the eyes on some crag above the multitude, see things thus in skeleton outline, bare of flesh? In Surbiton the skeleton is wrapped in flesh.

'The kettle never boils so well on a sunny morning,' says Mrs Grandage, glancing at the clock on the mantelpiece. Then the grey Persian cat stretches itself on the window-seat, and buffets a moth with soft round paws. And before breakfast is half over (they were late today), a baby is deposited in her lap, and she must guard the sugar basin while Tom Grandage reads the golfing article in *The Times*, sips his coffee, wipes his moustaches, and is off to the office, where he is the greatest authority upon the foreign exchanges and marked for promotion.

The skeleton is well wrapped in flesh. Even this dark night when the wind rolls the darkness through Lombard Street and Fetter Lane and Bedford Square it stirs (since it is summer-time and the height of the season), plane trees spangled with electric light, and curtains still preserving the room from the dawn. People still murmur over the last word said on the staircase, or strain, all through their dreams, for the voice of the alarum clock. So when the wind roams through a forest innumerable twigs stir; hives are brushed; insects sway on grass blades; the spider runs rapidly up a crease in the bark; and the whole air is tremulous with breathing; elastic with filaments.

Only here—in Lombard Street and Fetter Lane and Bedford Square—each insect carries a globe of the world in his head, and the webs of the forest are schemes evolved for the smooth conduct of business; and honey is treasure of one sort and another; and the stir in the air is the indescribable agitation of life.

But colour returns; runs up the stalks of the grass; blows out into tulips and crocuses; solidly stripes the tree trunks; and fills the gauze of the air and the grasses and pools.

The Bank of England emerges; and the Monument with its bristling head of golden hair; the dray horses crossing London Bridge show grey and strawberry and iron-coloured. There is a whir of wings as the suburban trains rush into the terminus. And the light mounts over the faces of all the tall blind houses, slides through a chink and paints the lustrous bellying crimson curtains; the green wine-glasses; the coffee-cups; and the chairs standing askew.

Sunlight strikes in upon shaving-glasses; and gleaming brass cans; upon all the jolly trappings of the day; the bright, inquisitive, armoured, resplendent, summer's day, which has long since vanquished chaos; which has dried the melancholy mediaeval mists; drained the swamp and stood glass and stone upon it; and equipped our brains and bodies with such an armoury of weapons that merely to see the flash and thrust of limbs engaged in the conduct of daily life is better than the old pageant of armies drawn out in battle array upon the plain.

XIII

'The height of the season,' said Bonamy.

The sun had already blistered the paint on the backs of the green chairs in Hyde Park; peeled the bark off the plane trees; and turned the earth to powder and to smooth yellow pebbles. Hyde Park was circled, incessantly, by turning wheels.

'The height of the season,' said Bonamy sarcastically.

He was sarcastic because of Clara Durrant; because Jacob had come back from Greece very brown and lean, with his pockets full of Greek notes, which he pulled out when the chair man came for pence; because Jacob was silent.

'He has not said a word to show that he is glad to see me,' thought Bonamy bitterly.

The motor-cars passed incessantly over the bridge of the Serpentine; the upper classes walked upright, or bent themselves gracefully over the palings; the lower classes lay with their knees cocked up, flat on their backs; the sheep grazed on pointed wooden legs; small children ran down the sloping grass, stretched their arms, and fell.

'Very urbane,' Jacob brought out.

'Urbane' on the lips of Jacob had mysteriously all the shapeliness of a character which Bonamy thought daily more sublime, devastating, terrific than ever, though he was still, and perhaps would be for ever, barbaric, obscure.

What superlatives! What adjectives! How acquit Bonamy of sentimentality of the grossest sort; of being tossed like a cork on the waves; of having no steady insight into character; of being unsupported by reason, and of drawing no comfort whatever from the works of the classics?

'The height of civilization,' said Jacob.

He was fond of using Latin words.

Magnanimity, virtue—such words when Jacob used them in talk with Bonamy meant that he took control of the situation; that Bonamy would play round him like an affectionate spaniel; and that (as likely as not) they would end by rolling on the floor.

'And Greece?' said Bonamy. 'The Parthenon and all that?'

'There's none of this European mysticism,' said Jacob.

'It's the atmosphere, I suppose,' said Bonamy. 'And you went to Constantinople?'

'Yes,' said Jacob.

Bonamy paused, moved a pebble; then darted in with the rapidity and certainty of a lizard's tongue.

'You are in love!' he exclaimed.

Jacob blushed.

The sharpest of knives never cut so deep.

As for responding, or taking the least account of it, Jacob stared straight ahead of him, fixed, monolithic—oh, very beautiful!—like a British Admiral, exclaimed Bonamy in a rage, rising from his seat and walking off; waiting for some sound; none came; too proud to look back; walking quicker and quicker until he found himself gazing into motor-

cars and cursing women. Where was the pretty woman's face? Clara's—
Fanny's—Florinda's? Who was the pretty little creature?

Not Clara Durrant.

The Aberdeen terrier must be exercised, and as Mr Bowley was going
that very moment—would like nothing better than a walk—they went
together, Clara and kind little Bowley—Bowley who had rooms in the
Albany, Bowley who wrote letters to *The Times* in a jocular vein about
foreign hotels and the Aurora Borealis—Bowley who liked young people
and walked down Piccadilly with his right arm resting on the boss of his
back.

'Little demon!' cried Clara, and attached Troy to his chain.

Bowley anticipated—hoped for—a confidence. Devoted to her
mother, Clara sometimes felt her a little, well, her mother was so sure of
herself that she could not understand other people being—being—'as
ludicrous as I am,' Clara jerked out (the dog tugging her forwards).
And Bowley thought she looked like a huntress and turned over in his
mind which it should be—some pale virgin with a slip of the moon in
her hair, which was a flight for Bowley.

The colour was in her cheeks. To have spoken outright about her
mother—still, it was only to Mr Bowley, who loved her, as everybody
must; but to speak was unnatural to her, yet it was awful to feel, as she
had done all day, that she *must* tell some one.

'Wait till we cross the road,' she said to the dog, bending down.

Happily she had recovered by that time.

'She thinks so much about England,' she said. 'She is so
anxious——'

Bowley was defrauded as usual. Clara never confided in any one.

'Why don't the young people settle it, eh?' he wanted to ask. 'What's
all this about England?'—a question poor Clara could not have
answered, since, as Mrs Durrant discussed with Sir Edgar the policy of
Sir Edward Grey, Clara only wondered why the cabinet looked dusty,
and Jacob had never come. Oh, here was Mrs Cowley Johnson . . .

And Clara would hand the pretty china teacups, and smile at the
compliment—that no one in London made tea so well as she did.

'We get it at Brocklebank's,' she said, 'in Cursitor Street.'

Ought she not to be grateful? Ought she not to be happy? Especially
since her mother looked so well and enjoyed so much talking to Sir
Edgar about Morocco, Venezuela, or some such place.

'Jacob! Jacob!' thought Clara; and kind Mr Bowley, who was ever so good with old ladies, looked; stopped; wondered whether Elizabeth wasn't too harsh with her daughter; wondered about Bonamy, Jacob—which young fellow was it?—and jumped up directly Clara said she must exercise Troy.

They had reached the site of the old Exhibition. They looked at the tulips. Stiff and curled, the little rods of waxy smoothness rose from the earth, nourished yet contained, suffused with scarlet and coral pink. Each had its shadow; each grew trimly in the diamond-shaped wedge as the gardener had planned it.

'Barnes never gets them to grow like that,' Clara mused; she sighed.

'You are neglecting your friends,' said Bowley, as someone, going the other way, lifted his hat. She started; acknowledged Mr Lionel Parry's bow; wasted on him what had sprung for Jacob.

('Jacob! Jacob!' she thought.)

'But you'll get run over if I let you go,' she said to the dog.

'England seems all right,' said Mr Bowley.

The loop of the railing beneath the statue of Achilles was full of parasols and waistcoats; chains and bangles; of ladies and gentlemen, lounging elegantly, lightly observant.

'"This statue was erected by the women of England . . ."' Clara read out with a foolish little laugh. 'Oh, Mr Bowley! Oh!' Gallop—gallop—gallop—a horse galloped past without a rider. The stirrups swung; the pebbles spurted.

'Oh, stop! Stop it, Mr Bowley!' she cried, white, trembling, gripping his arm, utterly unconscious, the tears coming.

'Tut-tut!' said Mr Bowley in his dressing-room an hour later. 'Tut-tut!'—a comment that was profound enough, though inarticulately expressed, since his valet was handing his shirt studs.

Julia Eliot, too, had seen the horse run away, and had risen from her seat to watch the end of the incident, which, since she came of a sporting family, seemed to her slightly ridiculous. Sure enough the little man came pounding behind with his breeches dusty; looked thoroughly annoyed; and was being helped to mount by a policeman when Julia Eliot, with a sardonic smile, turned towards the Marble Arch on her errand of mercy. It was only to visit a sick old lady who had known her mother and perhaps the Duke of Wellington; for Julia shared the love of her sex for the distressed; liked to visit deathbeds; threw slippers at weddings; received confidences by the dozen; knew more pedigrees than a scholar knows dates, and was one of the kindliest, most generous, least continent of women.

Yet five minutes after she had passed the statue of Achilles she had the rapt look of one brushing through crowds on a summer's afternoon, when the trees are rustling, the wheels churning yellow, and the tumult of the present seems like an elegy for past youth and past summers, and there rose in her mind a curious sadness, as if time and eternity showed through skirts and waistcoats, and she saw people passing tragically to destruction. Yet, Heaven knows, Julia was no fool. A sharper woman at a bargain did not exist. She was always punctual. The watch on her wrist gave her twelve minutes and a half in which to reach Bruton Street. Lady Congreve expected her at five.

The gilt clock at Verrey's was striking five.

Florinda looked at it with a dull expression, like an animal. She looked at the clock; looked at the door; looked at the long glass opposite; disposed her cloak; drew closer to the table, for she was pregnant—no doubt about it, Mother Stuart said, recommending remedies, consulting friends; sunk, caught by the heel, as she tripped so lightly over the surface.

Her tumbler of pinkish sweet stuff was set down by the waiter; and she sucked, through a straw, her eyes on the looking-glass, on the door, now soothed by the sweet taste. When Nick Bramham came in it was plain, even to the young Swiss waiter, that there was a bargain between them. Nick hitched his clothes together clumsily; ran his fingers through his hair; sat down, to an ordeal, nervously. She looked at him; and set off laughing; laughed—laughed—laughed. The young Swiss waiter, standing with crossed legs by the pillar, laughed too.

The door opened; in came the roar of Regent Street, the roar of traffic, impersonal, unpitying; and sunshine grained with dirt. The Swiss waiter must see to the newcomers. Bramham lifted his glass.

'He's like Jacob,' said Florinda, looking at the newcomer.
'The way he stares.' She stopped laughing.

Jacob, leaning forward, drew a plan of the Parthenon in the dust in
Hyde Park, a network of strokes at least, which may have been the
Parthenon, or again a mathematical diagram. And why was the pebble
so emphatically ground in at the corner? It was not to count his notes
that he took out a wad of papers and read a long flowing letter which
Sandra had written two days ago at Milton Dower House with his book
before her and in her mind the memory of something said or attempted,
some moment in the dark on the road to the Acropolis which (such was
her creed) mattered for ever.

'He is', she mused, 'like that man in Molière.'

She meant Alceste. She meant that he was severe. She meant that she
could deceive him.

'Or could I not?' she thought; putting the poems of Donne back in the
bookcase. 'Jacob,' she went on, going to the window and looking over
the spotted flower-beds across the grass where the piebald cows grazed
under beech trees, 'Jacob would be shocked.'

The perambulator was going through the little gate in the railing. She
kissed her hand; directed by the nurse, Jimmy waved his.

'*He's* a small boy,' she said, thinking of Jacob.

And yet—Alceste?

'What a nuisance you are!' Jacob grumbled, stretching out first one leg
and then the other and feeling in each trouser-pocket for his chair ticket.

'I expect the sheep have eaten it,' he said. 'Why do you keep sheep?'

'Sorry to disturb you, sir,' said the ticket-collector, his hand deep in
the enormous pouch of pence.

'Well, I hope they pay you for it,' said Jacob. 'There you are. No.
You can stick to it. Go and get drunk.'

He had parted with half-a-crown, tolerantly, compassionately, with
considerable contempt for his species.

Even now poor Fanny Elmer was dealing, as she walked along the Strand, in her incompetent way with this very careless, indifferent, sublime manner he had of talking to railway guards or porters; or Mrs Whitehorn, when she consulted him about her little boy who was beaten by the schoolmaster.

Sustained entirely upon picture postcards for the past two months, Fanny's idea of Jacob was more statuesque, noble, and eyeless than ever. To reinforce her vision she had taken to visiting the British Museum, where, keeping her eyes downcast until she was alongside of the battered Ulysses, she opened them and got a fresh shock of Jacob's presence, enough to last her half a day. But this was wearing thin. And she wrote now—poems, letters that were never posted, saw his face in advertisements on hoardings, and would cross the road to let the barrel-organ turn her musings to rhapsody. But at breakfast (she shared rooms with a teacher), when the butter was smeared about the plate, and the prongs of the forks were clotted with old egg yolk, she revised these visions violently; was, in truth, very cross; was losing her complexion, as Margery Jackson told her, bringing the whole thing down (as she laced her stout boots) to a level of mother-wit, vulgarity, and sentiment, for she had loved too; and been a fool.

'One's godmothers ought to have told one,' said Fanny, looking in at the window of Bacon, the mapseller, in the Strand—told one that it is no use making a fuss; this is life, they should have said, as Fanny said it now, looking at the large yellow globe marked with steamship lines.

'This is life. This is life,' said Fanny.

'A very hard face,' thought Miss Barrett, on the other side of the glass, buying maps of the Syrian desert and waiting impatiently to be served. 'Girls look old so soon nowadays.'

The equator swam behind tears.

'Piccadilly?' Fanny asked the conductor of the omnibus, and climbed to the top. After all, he would, he must, come back to her.

But Jacob might have been thinking of Rome; of architecture; of jurisprudence; as he sat under the plane tree in Hyde Park.

The omnibus stopped outside Charing Cross; and behind it were clogged omnibuses, vans, motor-cars, for a procession with banners was passing down Whitehall, and elderly people were stiffly descending from between the paws of the slippery lions, where they had been testifying to their faith, singing lustily, raising their eyes from their music to look into the sky, and still their eyes were on the sky as they marched behind the gold letters of their creed.

The traffic stopped, and the sun, no longer sprayed out by the breeze, became almost too hot. But the procession passed; the banners glittered far away down Whitehall; the traffic was released; lurched on; spun to a smooth continuous uproar; swerving round the curve of Cockspur Street; and sweeping past Government offices and equestrian statues down Whitehall to the prickly spires, the tethered grey fleet of masonry, and the large white clock of Westminster.

Five strokes Big Ben intoned; Nelson received the salute. The wires of the Admiralty shivered with some far-away communication. A voice kept remarking that Prime Ministers and Viceroys spoke in the Reichstag; entered Lahore; said that the Emperor travelled; in Milan they rioted; said there were rumours in Vienna; said that the Ambassador at Constantinople had audience with the Sultan; the fleet was at Gibraltar. The voice continued, imprinting on the faces of the clerks in Whitehall (Timothy Durrant was one of them) something of its own inexorable gravity, as they listened, deciphered, wrote down. Papers accumulated, inscribed with the utterances of Kaisers, the statistics of ricefields, the growling of hundreds of workpeople, plotting sedition in back streets, or gathering in the Calcutta bazaars, or mustering their forces in the uplands of Albania, where the hills are sand-coloured, and bones lie unburied.

The voice spoke plainly in the square quiet room with heavy tables, where one elderly man made notes on the margin of type-written sheets, his silver-topped umbrella leaning against the bookcase.

His head—bald, red-veined, hollow-looking—represented all the heads in the building. His head, with the amiable pale eyes, carried the burden of knowledge across the street; laid it before his colleagues, who came equally burdened; and then the sixteen gentlemen, lifting their pens or turning perhaps rather wearily in their chairs, decreed that the course of history should shape itself this way or that way, being manfully determined, as their faces showed, to impose some coherency upon Rajahs and Kaisers and the muttering in bazaars, the secret gatherings, plainly visible in Whitehall, of kilted peasants in Albanian uplands; to control the course of events.

Pitt and Chatham, Burke and Gladstone looked from side to side with fixed marble eyes and an air of immortal quiescence which perhaps the living may have envied, the air being full of whistling and concussions, as the procession with its banners passed down Whitehall. Moreover, some were troubled with dyspepsia; one had at that very moment cracked the glass of his spectacles; another spoke in Glasgow tomorrow;

altogether they looked too red, fat, pale or lean, to be dealing, as the marble heads had dealt, with the course of history.

Timmy Durrant in his little room in the Admiralty, going to consult a Blue book, stopped for a moment by the window, and observed the placard tied round the lamp-post.

Miss Thomas, one of the typists, said to her friend that if the Cabinet was going to sit much longer she should miss her boy outside the Gaiety.

Timmy Durrant, returning with his Blue book under his arm, noticed a little knot of people at the street corner; conglomerated as though one of them knew something; and the others, pressing round him, looked up, looked down, looked along the street. What was it that he knew?

Timothy, placing the Blue book before him, studied a paper sent round by the Treasury for information. Mr Crawley, his fellow-clerk, impaled a letter on a skewer.

Jacob rose from his chair in Hyde Park, tore his ticket to pieces, and walked away.

'Such a sunset,' wrote Mrs Flanders in her letter to Archer at Singapore. 'One couldn't make up one's mind to come indoors,' she wrote. 'It seemed wicked to waste even a moment.'

The long windows of Kensington Palace flushed fiery rose as Jacob walked away; a flock of wild duck flew over the Serpentine; and the trees were stood against the sky, blackly, magnificently.

'Jacob', wrote Mrs Flanders, with the red light on her page, 'is hard at work after his delightful journey . . .'

'The Kaiser', the far-away voice remarked in Whitehall, 'received me in audience.'

'Now I know that face—' said the Reverend Andrew Floyd, coming out of Carter's shop in Piccadilly, 'but who the dickens—?' and he watched Jacob, turned round to look at him, but could not be sure——

'Oh, Jacob Flanders!' he remembered in a flash.

But he was so tall; so unconscious; such a fine young fellow.

'I gave him Byron's works,' Andrew Floyd mused, and started forward, as Jacob crossed the road; but hesitated, and let the moment pass, and lost the opportunity.

Another procession, without banners, was blocking Long Acre. Carriages, with dowagers in amethyst and gentlemen spotted with carnations, intercepted cabs and motor-cars turned in the opposite direction, in which jaded men in white waistcoats lolled, on their way home to shrubberies and billiard-rooms in Putney and Wimbledon.

Two barrel-organs played by the kerb, and horses coming out of Aldridge's with white labels on their buttocks straddled across the road and were smartly jerked back.

Mrs Durrant, sitting with Mr Wortley in a motor-car, was impatient lest they should miss the overture.

But Mr Wortley, always urbane, always in time for the overture, buttoned his gloves, and admired Miss Clara.

'A shame to spend such a night in the theatre!' said Mrs Durrant, seeing all the windows of the coachmakers in Long Acre ablaze.

'Think of your moors!' said Mr Wortley to Clara.

'Ah! but Clara likes this better,' Mrs Durrant laughed.

'I don't know—really,' said Clara, looking at the blazing windows. She started.

She saw Jacob.

'Who?' asked Mrs Durrant sharply, leaning forward.

But she saw no one.

Under the arch of the Opera House large faces and lean ones, the powdered and the hairy, all alike were red in the sunset; and, quickened by the great hanging lamps with their repressed primrose lights, by the tramp, and the scarlet, and the pompous ceremony, some ladies looked for a moment into steaming bedrooms near by, where women with loose hair leaned out of windows, where girls—where children—(the long mirrors held the ladies suspended) but one must follow; one must not block the way.

Clara's moors were fine enough. The Phoenicians slept under their piled grey rocks; the chimneys of the old mines pointed starkly; early moths blurred the heather-bells; cartwheels could be heard grinding on the road far beneath; and the suck and sighing of the waves sounded gently, persistently, for ever.

Shading her eyes with her hand Mrs Pascoe stood in her cabbage-garden looking out to sea. Two steamers and a sailing-ship crossed each other; passed each other; and in the bay the gulls kept alighting on a log, rising high, returning again to the log, while some rode in upon the waves and stood on the rim of the water until the moon blanched all to whiteness.

Mrs Pascoe had gone indoors long ago.

But the red light was on the columns of the Parthenon, and the Greek women who were knitting their stockings and sometimes crying to a child to come and have the insects picked from its head were as jolly as sand-martins in the heat, quarrelling, scolding, suckling their babies, until the ships in the Piraeus fired their guns.

The sound spread itself flat, and then went tunnelling its way with fitful explosions among the channels of the islands.

Darkness drops like a knife over Greece.

'The guns?' said Betty Flanders, half asleep, getting out of bed and going to the window, which was decorated with a fringe of dark leaves.

'Not at this distance,' she thought. 'It is the sea.'

Again, far away, she heard the dull sound, as if nocturnal women were beating great carpets. There was Morty lost, and Seabrook dead; her sons fighting for their country. But were the chickens safe? Was that someone moving downstairs? Rebecca with the toothache? No. The nocturnal women were beating great carpets. Her hens shifted slightly on their perches.

XIV

'He left everything just as it was,' Bonamy marvelled. 'Nothing arranged. All his letters strewn about for anyone to read. What did he expect? Did he think he would come back?' he mused, standing in the middle of Jacob's room.

The eighteenth century has its distinction. These houses were built, say, a hundred and fifty years ago. The rooms are shapely, the ceilings high; over the doorways a rose or a ram's skull is carved in the wood. Even the panels, painted in raspberry-coloured paint, have their distinction.

Bonamy took up a bill for a hunting-crop.

'That seems to be paid,' he said.

There were Sandra's letters.

Mrs Durrant was taking a party to Greenwich.

Lady Rocksbier hoped for the pleasure . . .

Listless is the air in an empty room, just swelling the curtain; the flowers in the jar shift. One fibre in the wicker armchair creaks, though no one sits there.

Bonamy crossed to the window. Pickford's van swung down the street. The omnibuses were locked together at Mudie's corner. Engines throbbed, and carters, jamming the brakes down, pulled their horses sharp up. A harsh and unhappy voice cried something unintelligible. And then suddenly all the leaves seemed to raise themselves.

'Jacob! Jacob!' cried Bonamy, standing by the window. The leaves sank down again.

'Such confusion everywhere!' exclaimed Betty Flanders, bursting open the bedroom door.

Bonamy turned away from the window.

'What am I to do with these, Mr Bonamy?'

She held out a pair of Jacob's old shoes.

THE END

Mrs Dalloway

A Map of Mrs Dalloway's London

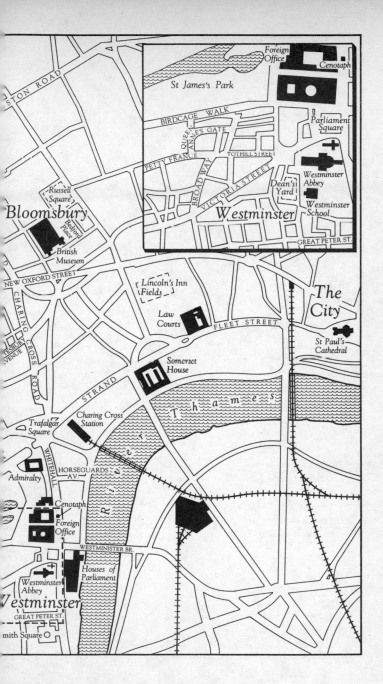

MRS DALLOWAY

Mrs Dalloway said she would buy the flowers herself.

For Lucy had her work cut out for her. The doors would be taken off their hinges; Rumpelmayer's men were coming. And then, thought Clarissa Dalloway, what a morning—fresh as if issued to children on a beach.

What a lark! What a plunge! For so it had always seemed to her when, with a little squeak of the hinges, which she could hear now, she had burst open the French windows and plunged at Bourton into the open air. How fresh, how calm, stiller than this of course, the air was in the early morning; like the flap of a wave; the kiss of a wave; chill and sharp and yet (for a girl of eighteen as she then was) solemn, feeling as she did, standing there at the open window, that something awful was about to happen; looking at the flowers, at the trees with the smoke winding off them and the rooks rising, falling; standing and looking until Peter Walsh said, 'Musing among the vegetables?'—was that it?—'I prefer men to cauliflowers'—was that it? He must have said it at breakfast one morning when she had gone out on to the terrace—Peter Walsh. He would be back from India one of these days, June or July, she forgot which, for his letters were awfully dull; it was his sayings one remembered; his eyes, his pocket-knife, his smile, his grumpiness and, when millions of things had utterly vanished—how strange it was!—a few sayings like this about cabbages.

She stiffened a little on the kerb, waiting for Durtnall's van to pass. A charming woman, Scrope Purvis thought her (knowing her as one does know people who live next door to one in Westminster); a touch of the bird about her, of the jay, blue-green, light, vivacious, though she was over fifty, and grown very white since her illness. There she perched, never seeing him, waiting to cross, very upright.

For having lived in Westminster—how many years now? over twenty,—one feels even in the midst of the traffic, or waking at night, Clarissa was positive, a particular hush, or solemnity; an indescribable pause; a suspense (but that might be her heart, affected, they said, by influenza) before Big Ben strikes. There! Out it boomed. First a warning, musical; then the hour, irrevocable. The leaden circles dissolved in the air. Such fools we are, she thought, crossing Victoria Street. For Heaven only knows why one loves it so, how one sees it so, making it up, building it round one, tumbling it, creating it every moment afresh; but the veriest frumps, the most dejected of miseries sitting on doorsteps (drink their downfall) do the same; can't be dealt with, she felt positive, by Acts of Parliament for that very reason: they love life. In people's eyes, in the swing, tramp, and trudge; in the bellow and the uproar; the carriages, motor cars, omnibuses, vans, sandwich men shuffling and swinging; brass bands; barrel organs; in the triumph and the jingle and the strange high singing of some aeroplane overhead was what she loved; life; London; this moment of June.

For it was the middle of June. The War was over, except for some one like Mrs Foxcroft at the Embassy last night eating her heart out because that nice boy was killed and now the old Manor House must go to a cousin; or Lady Bexborough who opened a bazaar, they said, with the telegram in her hand, John, her favourite, killed; but it was over; thank Heaven—over. It was June. The King and Queen were at the Palace. And everywhere, though it was still so early, there was a beating, a stirring of galloping ponies, tapping of cricket bats; Lords, Ascot, Ranelagh and all the rest of it; wrapped in the soft mesh of the grey-blue morning air, which, as the day wore on, would unwind them, and set down on their lawns and pitches the bouncing ponies, whose forefeet just struck the ground and up they sprung, the whirling young men, and laughing girls in their transparent muslins who, even now, after dancing all night, were taking their absurd woolly dogs for a run; and even now, at this hour, discreet old dowagers were shooting out in their motor cars on errands of mystery; and the shop-keepers were fidgeting in their windows with their paste and diamonds, their lovely old sea-green brooches in eighteenth-century settings to tempt Americans (but one must economize, not buy things rashly for Elizabeth), and she, too, loving it as she did with an absurd and faithful passion, being part of it, since her people were courtiers once in the time of the Georges, she, too, was going that very night to kindle and illuminate; to give her party. But how strange, on entering the Park, the silence; the mist; the hum; the slow-swimming happy ducks; the pouched birds waddling; and who should be coming along with his back against the Government buildings, most appropriately, carrying a despatch box stamped with the Royal Arms, who but Hugh Whitbread; her old friend Hugh—the admirable Hugh!

'Good-morning to you, Clarissa!' said Hugh, rather extravagantly, for they had known each other as children. 'Where are you off to?'

'I love walking in London,' said Mrs Dalloway. 'Really, it's better than walking in the country.'

They had just come up—unfortunately—to see doctors. Other people came to see pictures; go to the opera; take their daughters out; the Whitbreads came 'to see doctors'. Times without number Clarissa had visited Evelyn Whitbread in a nursing home. Was Evelyn ill again?

Evelyn was a good deal out of sorts, said Hugh, intimating by a kind of
pout or swell of his very well-covered, manly, extremely handsome,
perfectly upholstered body (he was almost too well dressed always, but
presumably had to be, with his little job at Court) that his wife had
some internal ailment, nothing serious, which, as an old friend, Clarissa
Dalloway would quite understand without requiring him to specify. Ah
yes, she did of course; what a nuisance; and felt very sisterly and oddly
conscious at the same time of her hat. Not the right hat for the early
morning, was that it? For Hugh always made her feel, as he bustled on,
raising his hat rather extravagantly and assuring her that she might be
a girl of eighteen, and of course he was coming to her party tonight,
Evelyn absolutely insisted, only a little late he might be after the party
at the Palace to which he had to take one of Jim's boys,—she always felt
a little skimpy beside Hugh; schoolgirlish; but attached to him, partly
from having known him always, but she did think him a good sort in his
own way, though Richard was nearly driven mad by him, and as for
Peter Walsh, he had never to this day forgiven her for liking him.

She could remember scene after scene at Bourton—Peter furious;
Hugh not, of course, his match in any way, but still not a positive
imbecile as Peter made out; not a mere barber's block. When his old
mother wanted him to give up shooting or to take her to Bath he did it,
without a word; he was really unselfish, and as for saying, as Peter did,
that he had no heart, no brain, nothing but the manners and breeding
of an English gentleman, that was only her dear Peter at his worst; and
he could be intolerable; he could be impossible; but adorable to walk
with on a morning like this.

(June had drawn out every leaf on the trees. The mothers of Pimlico
gave suck to their young. Messages were passing from the Fleet to the
Admiralty. Arlington Street and Piccadilly seemed to chafe the very air
in the Park and lift its leaves hotly, brilliantly, on waves of that divine
vitality which Clarissa loved. To dance, to ride, she had adored all
that.)

For they might be parted for hundreds of years, she and Peter; she
never wrote a letter and his were dry sticks; but suddenly it would come
over her, if he were with me now what would he say?—some days, some
sights bringing him back to her calmly, without the old bitterness; which
perhaps was the reward of having cared for people; they came back in
the middle of St James's Park on a fine morning—indeed they did. But
Peter—however beautiful the day might be, and the trees and the grass,
and the little girl in pink—Peter never saw a thing of all that. He would
put on his spectacles, if she told him to; he would look. It was the state
of the world that interested him; Wagner, Pope's poetry, people's
characters eternally, and the defects of her own soul. How he scolded

her! How they argued! She would marry a Prime Minister and stand at the top of a staircase; the perfect hostess he called her (she had cried over it in her bedroom), she had the makings of the perfect hostess, he said.

So she would still find herself arguing in St James's Park, still making out that she had been right—and she had too—not to marry him. For in marriage a little licence, a little independence there must be between people living together day in day out in the same house; which Richard gave her, and she him. (Where was he this morning, for instance? Some committee, she never asked what.) But with Peter everything had to be shared; everything gone into. And it was intolerable, and when it came to that scene in the little garden by the fountain, she had to break with him or they would have been destroyed, both of them ruined, she was convinced; though she had borne about her for years like an arrow sticking in her heart the grief, the anguish: and then the horror of the moment when someone told her at a concert that he had married a woman met on the boat going to India! Never should she forget all that. Cold, heartless, a prude, he called her. Never could she understand how he cared. But those Indian women did presumably—silly, pretty, flimsy nincompoops. And she wasted her pity. For he was quite happy, he assured her—perfectly happy, though he had never done a thing that they talked of; his whole life had been a failure. It made her angry still.

She had reached the Park gates. She stood for a moment, looking at the omnibuses in Piccadilly.

She would not say of anyone in the world now that they were this or were that. She felt very young; at the same time unspeakably aged. She sliced like a knife through everything; at the same time was outside, looking on. She had a perpetual sense, as she watched the taxicabs, of being out, out, far out to sea and alone; she always had the feeling that it was very, very dangerous to live even one day. Not that she thought herself clever, or much out of the ordinary. How she had got through life on the few twigs of knowledge Fräulein Daniels gave them she could not think. She knew nothing; no language, no history; she scarcely read a book now, except memoirs in bed; and yet to her it was absolutely absorbing; all this; the cabs passing; and she would not say of Peter, she would not say of herself, I am this, I am that.

Her only gift was knowing people almost by instinct, she thought, walking on. If you put her in a room with someone, up went her back like a cat's; or she purred. Devonshire House, Bath House, the house with the china cockatoo, she had seen them all lit up once; and remembered Sylvia, Fred, Sally Seton—such hosts of people; and dancing all night; and the waggons plodding past to market; and driving home across the Park. She remembered once throwing a shilling into the

Serpentine. But everyone remembered; what she loved was this, here, now, in front of her; the fat lady in the cab. Did it matter then, she asked herself, walking towards Bond Street, did it matter that she must inevitably cease completely; all this must go on without her; did she resent it; or did it not become consoling to believe that death ended absolutely? but that somehow in the streets of London, on the ebb and flow of things, here, there, she survived, Peter survived, lived in each other, she being part, she was positive, of the trees at home; of the house there, ugly, rambling all to bits and pieces as it was; part of people she had never met; being laid out like a mist between the people she knew best, who lifted her on their branches as she had seen the trees lift the mist, but it spread ever so far, her life, herself. But what was she dreaming as she looked into Hatchards' shop window? What was she trying to recover? What image of white dawn in the country, as she read in the book spread open:

> Fear no more the heat o' the sun
> Nor the furious winter's rages.

This late age of world's experience had bred in them all, all men and women, a well of tears. Tears and sorrows; courage and endurance; a perfectly upright and stoical bearing Think, for example, of the woman she admired most, Lady Bexborough, opening the bazaar.

There were Jorrocks' *Jaunts and Jollities*; there were *Soapy Sponge* and Mrs Asquith's *Memoirs* and *Big Game Shooting in Nigeria*, all spread open. Ever so many books there were; but none that seemed exactly right to take to Evelyn Whitbread in her nursing home. Nothing that would serve to amuse her and make that indescribably dried-up little woman look, as Clarissa came in, just for a moment cordial; before they settled down for the usual interminable talk of women's ailments. How much she wanted it—that people should look pleased as she came in, Clarissa thought and turned and walked back towards Bond Street, annoyed, because it was silly to have other reasons for doing things. Much rather would she have been one of those people like Richard who did things for themselves, whereas, she thought, waiting to cross, half the time she did things not simply, not for themselves; but to make people think this or that; perfect idiocy she knew (and now the policeman held up his hand) for no one was ever for a second taken in. Oh if she could have had her life over again! she thought, stepping on to the pavement, could have looked even differently!

She would have been, in the first place, dark like Lady Bexborough, with a skin of crumpled leather and beautiful eyes. She would have been, like Lady Bexborough, slow and stately; rather large; interested in politics like a man; with a country house; very dignified, very sincere.

Instead of which she had a narrow pea-stick figure; a ridiculous little face, beaked like a bird's. That she held herself well was true; and had nice hands and feet; and dressed well, considering that she spent little. But often now this body she wore (she stopped to look at a Dutch picture), this body, with all its capacities, seemed nothing—nothing at all. She had the oddest sense of being herself invisible; unseen; unknown; there being no more marrying, no more having of children now, but only this astonishing and rather solemn progress with the rest of them, up Bond Street, this being Mrs Dalloway; not even Clarissa any more; this being Mrs Richard Dalloway.

Bond Street fascinated her; Bond Street early in the morning in the season; its flags flying; its shops; no splash; no glitter; one roll of tweed in the shop where her father had bought his suits for fifty years; a few pearls; salmon on an iceblock.

'That is all,' she said, looking at the fishmonger's. 'That is all,' she repeated, pausing for a moment at the window of a glove shop where, before the War, you could buy almost perfect gloves. And her old Uncle William used to say a lady is known by her shoes and her gloves. He had turned on his bed one morning in the middle of the War. He had said, 'I have had enough.' Gloves and shoes; she had a passion for gloves; but her own daughter, her Elizabeth, cared not a straw for either of them.

Not a straw, she thought, going on up Bond Street to a shop where they kept flowers for her when she gave a party. Elizabeth really cared for her dog most of all. The whole house this morning smelt of tar. Still, better poor Grizzle than Miss Kilman; better distemper and tar and all the rest of it than sitting mewed in a stuffy bedroom with a prayer book! Better anything, she was inclined to say. But it might be only a phase, as Richard said, such as all girls go through. It might be falling in love. But why with Miss Kilman? who had been badly treated of course; one must make allowances for that, and Richard said she was very able, had a really historical mind. Anyhow they were inseparable, and Elizabeth, her own daughter, went to Communion; and how she dressed, how she treated people who came to lunch she did not care a bit, it being her experience that the religious ecstasy made people callous (so did causes); dulled their feelings, for Miss Kilman would do anything for the Russians, starve herself for the Austrians, but in private inflicted positive torture, so insensitive was she, dressed in a green mackintosh coat. Year in year out she wore that coat; she perspired; she was never in the room five minutes without making you feel her superiority, your inferiority; how poor she was; how rich you were; how she lived in a slum without a cushion or a bed or a rug or whatever it might be, all her soul rusted with that grievance sticking in it, her dismissal from school during the

War—poor, embittered, unfortunate creature! For it was not her one hated but the idea of her, which undoubtedly had gathered into itself a great deal that was not Miss Kilman; had become one of those spectres with which one battles in the night; one of those spectres who stand astride us and suck up half our life-blood, dominators and tyrants; for no doubt with another throw of the dice, had the black been uppermost and not the white, she would have loved Miss Kilman! But not in this world. No.

It rasped her, though, to have stirring about in her this brutal monster! to hear twigs cracking and feel hooves planted down in the depths of that leaf-encumbered forest, the soul; never to be content quite, or quite secure, for at any moment the brute would be stirring, this hatred, which, especially since her illness, had power to make her feel scraped, hurt in her spine; gave her physical pain, and made all pleasure in beauty, in friendship, in being well, in being loved and making her home delightful, rock, quiver, and bend as if indeed there were a monster grubbing at the roots, as if the whole panoply of content were nothing but self love! this hatred!

Nonsense, nonsense! she cried to herself, pushing through the swing doors of Mulberry's the florists.

She advanced, light, tall, very upright, to be greeted at once by button-faced Miss Pym, whose hands were always bright red, as if they had been stood in cold water with the flowers.

There were flowers: delphiniums, sweet peas, bunches of lilac; and carnations, masses of carnations. There were roses; there were irises. Ah yes—so she breathed in the earthy-garden sweet smell as she stood talking to Miss Pym who owed her help, and thought her kind, for kind she had been years ago; very kind, but she looked older, this year, turning her head from side to side among the irises and roses and nodding tufts of lilac with her eyes half closed, snuffing in, after the street uproar, the delicious scent, the exquisite coolness. And then, opening her eyes, how fresh, like frilled linen clean from a laundry laid in wicker trays, the roses looked; and dark and prim the red carnations, holding their heads up; and all the sweet peas spreading in their bowls, tinged violet, snow white, pale—as if it were the evening and girls in muslin frocks came out to pick sweet peas and roses after the superb summer's day, with its almost blue-black sky, its delphiniums, its carnations, its arum lilies, was over; and it was the moment between six and seven when every flower—roses, carnations, irises, lilac—glows; white, violet, red, deep orange; every flower seems to burn by itself, softly, purely in the misty beds; and how she loved the grey white moths spinning in and out, over the cherry pie, over the evening primroses!

And as she began to go with Miss Pym from jar to jar, choosing, nonsense, nonsense, she said to herself, more and more gently, as if this beauty, this scent, this colour, and Miss Pym liking her, trusting her, were a wave which she let flow over her and surmount that hatred, that monster, surmount it all; and it lifted her up and up when—oh! a pistol shot in the street outside!

'Dear, those motor cars,' said Miss Pym, going to the window to look, and coming back and smiling apologetically with her hands full of sweet peas, as if those motor cars, those tyres of motor cars, were all *her* fault.

The violent explosion which made Mrs Dalloway jump and Miss Pym go to the window and apologize came from a motor car which had drawn to the side of the pavement precisely opposite Mulberry's shop window. Passers-by, who, of course, stopped and stared, had just time to see a face of the very greatest importance against the dove-grey upholstery, before a male hand drew the blind and there was nothing to be seen except a square of dove grey.

Yet rumours were at once in circulation from the middle of Bond Street to Oxford Street on one side, to Atkinson's scent shop on the other, passing invisibly, inaudibly, like a cloud, swift, veil-like upon hills, falling indeed with something of a cloud's sudden sobriety and stillness upon faces which a second before had been utterly disorderly. But now mystery had brushed them with her wing; they had heard the voice of authority; the spirit of religion was abroad with her eyes bandaged tight and her lips gaping wide. But nobody knew whose face had been seen. Was it the Prince of Wales's, the Queen's, the Prime Minister's? Whose face was it? Nobody knew.

Edgar J. Watkiss, with his roll of lead piping round his arm, said audibly, humorously of course: 'The Proime Minister's kyar.'

Septimus Warren Smith, who found himself unable to pass, heard him.

Septimus Warren Smith, aged about thirty, pale-faced, beak-nosed, wearing brown shoes and a shabby overcoat, with hazel eyes which had that look of apprehension in them which makes complete strangers apprehensive too. The world has raised its whip; where will it descend?

Everything had come to a standstill. The throb of the motor engines sounded like a pulse irregularly drumming through an entire body. The sun became extraordinarily hot because the motor car had stopped outside Mulberry's shop window; old ladies on the tops of omnibuses spread their black parasols; here a green, here a red parasol opened with a little pop. Mrs Dalloway, coming to the window with her arms full of sweet peas, looked out with her little pink face pursed in inquiry. Everyone looked at the motor car. Septimus looked. Boys on bicycles sprang off. Traffic accumulated. And there the motor car stood, with drawn blinds, and upon them a curious pattern like a tree, Septimus thought, and this gradual drawing together of everything to one centre before his eyes, as if some horror had come almost to the surface and was about to burst into flames, terrified him. The world wavered and quivered and threatened to burst into flames. It is I who am blocking the way, he thought. Was he not being looked at and pointed at; was he not weighted there, rooted to the pavement, for a purpose? But for what purpose?

'Let us go on, Septimus,' said his wife, a little woman, with large eyes in a sallow pointed face; an Italian girl.

But Lucrezia herself could not help looking at the motor car and the tree pattern on the blinds. Was it the Queen in there—the Queen going shopping?

The chauffeur, who had been opening something, turning something, shutting something, got on to the box.

'Come on,' said Lucrezia.

But her husband, for they had been married four, five years now, jumped, started, and said, 'All right!' angrily, as if she had interrupted him.

People must notice; people must see. People, she thought, looking at the crowd staring at the motor car; the English people, with their children and their horses and their clothes, which she admired in a way; but they were 'people' now, because Septimus had said, 'I will kill myself'; an awful thing to say. Suppose they had heard him? She looked at the crowd. Help, help! she wanted to cry out to butchers' boys and women. Help! Only last autumn she and Septimus had stood on the Embankment wrapped in the same cloak and, Septimus reading a paper instead of talking, she had snatched it from him and laughed in the old man's face who saw them! But failure one conceals. She must take him away into some park.

'Now we will cross,' she said.

She had a right to his arm, though it was without feeling. He would give her, who was so simple, so impulsive, only twenty-four, without friends in England, who had left Italy for his sake, a piece of bone.

The motor car with its blinds drawn and an air of inscrutable reserve proceeded towards Piccadilly, still gazed at, still ruffling the faces on both sides of the street with the same dark breath of veneration whether for Queen, Prince, or Prime Minister nobody knew. The face itself had been seen only once by three people for a few seconds. Even the sex was now in dispute. But there could be no doubt that greatness was seated within; greatness was passing, hidden, down Bond Street, removed only by a hand's-breadth from ordinary people who might now, for the first time and last, be within speaking distance of the majesty of England, of

the enduring symbol of the state which will be known to curious
antiquaries, sifting the ruins of time, when London is a grass-grown
path and all those hurrying along the pavement this Wednesday
morning are but bones with a few wedding rings mixed up in their dust
and the gold stoppings of innumerable decayed teeth. The face in the
motor car will then be known.

It is probably the Queen, thought Mrs Dalloway, coming out of
Mulberry's with her flowers: the Queen. And for a second she wore a
look of extreme dignity standing by the flower shop in the sunlight while
the car passed at a foot's pace, with its blinds drawn. The Queen going
to some hospital; the Queen opening some bazaar, thought Clarissa.

The crush was terrific for the time of day. Lords, Ascot, Hurlingham,
what was it? she wondered, for the street was blocked. The British
middle classes sitting sideways on the tops of omnibuses with parcels
and umbrellas, yes, even furs on a day like this, were, she thought, more
ridiculous, more unlike anything there has ever been than one could
conceive; and the Queen herself held up; the Queen herself unable to
pass. Clarissa was suspended on one side of Brook Street; Sir John
Buckhurst, the old Judge, on the other, with the car between them (Sir
John had laid down the law for years and liked a well-dressed woman)
when the chauffeur, leaning ever so slightly, said or showed something
to the policeman, who saluted and raised his arm and jerked his head
and moved the omnibus to the side and the car passed through. Slowly
and very silently it took its way.

Clarissa guessed; Clarissa knew of course; she had seen something
white, magical, circular, in the footman's hand, a disc inscribed with a
name,—the Queen's, the Prince of Wales's, the Prime Minister's?—
which, by force of its own lustre, burnt its way through (Clarissa saw
the car diminishing, disappearing), to blaze among candelabras, glittering stars, breasts stiff with oak leaves, Hugh Whitbread and all his
colleagues, the gentlemen of England, that night in Buckingham Palace.
And Clarissa, too, gave a party. She stiffened a little; so she would stand
at the top of her stairs.

The car had gone, but it had left a slight ripple which flowed through
glove shops and hat shops and tailors' shops on both sides of Bond
Street. For thirty seconds all heads were inclined the same way—to the
window. Choosing a pair of gloves—should they be to the elbow or
above it, lemon or pale grey?—ladies stopped; when the sentence was
finished something had happened. Something so trifling in single
instances that no mathematical instrument, though capable of transmit-
ting shocks in China, could register the vibration; yet in its fullness
rather formidable and in its common appeal emotional; for in all the hat
shops and tailors' shops strangers looked at each other and thought of

the dead; of the flag; of Empire. In a public-house in a back street a Colonial insulted the House of Windsor, which led to words, broken beer glasses, and a general shindy, which echoed strangely across the way in the ears of girls buying white underlinen threaded with pure white ribbon for their weddings. For the surface agitation of the passing car as it sunk grazed something very profound.

Gliding across Piccadilly, the car turned down St James's Street. Tall men, men of robust physique, well-dressed men with their tail-coats and their white slips and their hair raked back, who, for reasons difficult to discriminate, were standing in the bow window of White's with their hands behind the tails of their coats, looking out, perceived instinctively that greatness was passing, and the pale light of the immortal presence fell upon them as it had fallen upon Clarissa Dalloway. At once they stood even straighter, and removed their hands, and seemed ready to attend their Sovereign, if need be, to the cannon's mouth, as their ancestors had done before them. The white busts and the little tables in the background covered with copies of the *Tatler* and bottles of soda water seemed to approve; seemed to indicate the flowing corn and the manor houses of England; and to return the frail hum of the motor wheels as the walls of a whispering gallery return a single voice expanded and made sonorous by the might of a whole cathedral. Shawled Moll Pratt with her flowers on the pavement wished the dear boy well (it was the Prince of Wales for certain) and would have tossed the price of a pot of beer—a bunch of roses—into St James's Street out of sheer light-heartedness and contempt of poverty had she not seen the constable's eye upon her, discouraging an old Irishwoman's loyalty. The sentries at St James's saluted; Queen Alexandra's policeman approved.

A small crowd, meanwhile, had gathered at the gates of Buckingham Palace. Listlessly, yet confidently, poor people all of them, they waited; looked at the Palace itself with the flag flying; at Victoria, billowing on her mound, admired her shelves of running water, her geraniums; singled out from the motor cars in the Mall first this one, then that; bestowed emotion, vainly, upon commoners out for a drive; recalled their tribute to keep it unspent while this car passed and that; and all the time let rumour accumulate in their veins and thrill the nerves in their thighs at the thought of Royalty looking at them; the Queen bowing; the Prince saluting; at the thought of the heavenly life divinely bestowed upon Kings; of the equerries and deep curtsies; of the Queen's old doll's house; of Princess Mary married to an Englishman, and the Prince—ah! the Prince! who took wonderfully, they said, after old King Edward, but was ever so much slimmer. The Prince lived at St James's; but he might come along in the morning to visit his mother.

So Sarah Bletchley said with her baby in her arms, tipping her foot up and down as though she were by her own fender in Pimlico, but keeping her eyes on the Mall, while Emily Coates ranged over the Palace windows and thought of the housemaids, the innumerable housemaids, the bedrooms, the innumerable bedrooms. Joined by an elderly gentleman with an Aberdeen terrier, by men without occupation, the crowd increased. Little Mr Bowley, who had rooms in the Albany and was sealed with wax over the deeper sources of life, but could be unsealed suddenly, inappropriately, sentimentally, by this sort of thing—poor women waiting to see the Queen go past—poor women, nice little children, orphans, widows, the War—tut-tut—actually had tears in his eyes. A breeze flaunting ever so warming down the Mall through the thin trees, past the bronze heroes, lifted some flag flying in the British breast of Mr Bowley and he raised his hat as the car turned into the Mall and held it high as the car approached and let the poor mothers of Pimlico press close to him, and stood very upright. The car came on.

Suddenly Mrs Coates looked up into the sky. The sound of an aeroplane bored ominously into the ears of the crowd. There it was coming over the trees, letting out white smoke from behind, which curled and twisted, actually writing something! making letters in the sky! Everyone looked up.

Dropping dead down, the aeroplane soared straight up, curved in a loop, raced, sank, rose, and whatever it did, wherever it went, out fluttered behind it a thick ruffled bar of white smoke which curled and wreathed upon the sky in letters. But what letters? A C was it? an E, then an L? Only for a moment did they lie still; then they moved and melted and were rubbed out up in the sky, and the aeroplane shot further away and again, in a fresh space of sky, began writing a K, and E, a Y perhaps?

'Blaxo,' said Mrs Coates in a strained, awestricken voice, gazing straight up, and her baby, lying stiff and white in her arms, gazed straight up.

'Kreemo,' murmured Mrs Bletchley, like a sleep-walker. With his hat held out perfectly still in his hand, Mr Bowley gazed straight up. All down the Mall people were standing and looking up into the sky. As they looked the whole world became perfectly silent, and a flight of gulls crossed the sky, first one gull leading, then another, and in this extraordinary silence and peace, in this pallor, in this purity, bells struck eleven times, the sound fading up there among the gulls.

The aeroplane turned and raced and swooped exactly where it liked, swiftly, freely, like a skater—

'That's an E,' said Mrs Bletchley—

or a dancer—

'It's toffee,' murmured Mr Bowley—

(and the car went in at the gates and nobody looked at it), and shutting off the smoke, away and away it rushed, and the smoke faded and assembled itself round the broad white shapes of the clouds.

It had gone; it was behind the clouds. There was no sound. The clouds to which the letters E, G, or L had attached themselves moved freely, as if destined to cross from West to East on a mission of the greatest importance which would never be revealed, and yet certainly so it was—a mission of the greatest importance. Then suddenly, as a train comes out of a tunnel, the aeroplane rushed out of the clouds again, the sound boring into the ears of all people in the Mall, in the Green Park, in Piccadilly, in Regent Street, in Regent's Park, and the bar of smoke curved behind and it dropped down, and it soared up and wrote one letter after another—but what word was it writing?

Lucrezia Warren Smith, sitting by her husband's side on a seat in Regent's Park in the Broad Walk, looked up.

'Look, look, Septimus!' she cried. For Dr Holmes had told her to make her husband (who had nothing whatever seriously the matter with him but was a little out of sorts) take an interest in things outside himself.

So, thought Septimus, looking up, they are signalling to me. Not indeed in actual words; that is, he could not read the language yet; but it was plain enough, this beauty, this exquisite beauty, and tears filled his eyes as he looked at the smoke words languishing and melting in the sky and bestowing upon him, in their inexhaustible charity and laughing goodness, one shape after another of unimaginable beauty and signalling their intention to provide him, for nothing, for ever, for looking merely, with beauty, more beauty! Tears ran down his cheeks.

It was toffee; they were advertising toffee, a nursemaid told Rezia. Together they began to spell t . . . o . . . f . . .

'K . . . R . . .' said the nursemaid, and Septimus heard her say 'Kay Arr' close to his ear, deeply, softly, like a mellow organ, but with a roughness in her voice like a grasshopper's, which rasped his spine deliciously and sent running up into his brain waves of sound, which, concussing, broke. A marvellous discovery indeed—that the human voice in certain atmospheric conditions (for one must be scientific, above all scientific) can quicken trees into life! Happily Rezia put her hand down with a tremendous weight on his knee so that he was weighted down, transfixed, or the excitement of the elm trees rising and falling, rising and falling with all their leaves alight and the colour thinning and thickening from blue to the green of a hollow wave, like plumes on horses' heads, feathers on ladies', so proudly they rose and fell, so superbly, would have sent him mad. But he would not go mad. He would shut his eyes; he would see no more.

But they beckoned; leaves were alive; trees were alive. And the leaves being connected by millions of fibres with his own body, there on the seat, fanned it up and down; when the branch stretched he, too, made that statement. The sparrows fluttering, rising, and falling in jagged fountains were part of the pattern; the white and blue, barred with black branches. Sounds made harmonies with premeditation; the spaces between them were as significant as the sounds. A child cried. Rightly far away a horn sounded. All taken together meant the birth of a new religion——

'Septimus!' said Rezia. He started violently. People must notice.

'I am going to walk to the fountain and back,' she said.

For she could stand it no longer. Dr Holmes might say there was nothing the matter. Far rather would she that he were dead! She could not sit beside him when he stared so and did not see her and made everything terrible; sky and tree, children playing, dragging carts, blowing whistles, falling down; all were terrible. And he would not kill himself; and she could tell no one. 'Septimus has been working too hard'—that was all she could say to her own mother. To love makes one solitary, she thought. She could tell nobody, not even Septimus now, and looking back, she saw him sitting in his shabby overcoat alone, on the seat, hunched up, staring. And it was cowardly for a man to say he would kill himself, but Septimus had fought; he was brave; he was not Septimus now. She put on her lace collar. She put on her new hat and he never noticed; and he was happy without her. Nothing could make her happy without him! Nothing! He was selfish. So men are. For he was not ill. Dr Holmes said there was nothing the matter with him. She spread her hand before her. Look! Her wedding ring slipped—she had grown so thin. It was she who suffered—but she had nobody to tell.

Far was Italy and the white houses and the room where her sisters sat making hats, and the streets crowded every evening with people walking, laughing out loud, not half alive like people here, huddled up in Bath chairs, looking at a few ugly flowers stuck in pots!

'For you should see the Milan gardens,' she said aloud. But to whom?

There was nobody. Her words faded. So a rocket fades. Its sparks, having grazed their way into the night, surrender to it, dark descends, pours over the outlines of houses and towers; bleak hillsides soften and fall in. But though they are gone, the night is full of them; robbed of colour, blank of windows, they exist more ponderously, give out what the frank daylight fails to transmit—the trouble and suspense of things conglomerated there in the darkness; huddled together in the darkness; reft of the relief which dawn brings when, washing the walls white and grey, spotting each window-pane, lifting the mist from the fields, showing the red-brown cows peacefully grazing, all is once more decked out to the eye; exists again. I am alone; I am alone! she cried, by the fountain in Regent's Park (staring at the Indian and his cross), as perhaps at midnight, when all boundaries are lost, the country reverts to its ancient shape, as the Romans saw it, lying cloudy, when they landed, and the hills had no names and rivers wound they knew not where—such was her darkness; when suddenly, as if a shelf were shot forth and she stood on it, she said how she was his wife, married years ago in Milan, his wife, and would never, never tell that he was mad! Turning, the shelf fell; down, down she dropped. For he was gone, she thought—gone, as he threatened, to kill himself—to throw himself under a cart! But no; there he was; still sitting alone on the seat, in his shabby overcoat, his legs crossed, staring, talking aloud.

Men must not cut down trees. There is a God. (He noted such revelations on the backs of envelopes.) Change the world. No one kills from hatred. Make it known (he wrote it down). He waited. He listened. A sparrow perched on the railing opposite chirped Septimus, Septimus, four or five times over and went on, drawing its notes out, to sing freshly and piercingly in Greek words how there is no crime and, joined by another sparrow, they sang in voices prolonged and piercing in Greek words, from trees in the meadow of life beyond a river where the dead walk, how there is no death.

There was his hand; there the dead. White things were assembling behind the railings opposite. But he dared not look. Evans was behind the railings!

'What are you saying?' said Rezia suddenly, sitting down by him.

Interrupted again! She was always interrupting.

Away from people—they must get away from people, he said (jumping up), right away over there, where there were chairs beneath a tree and the long slope of the park dipped like a length of green stuff with a ceiling cloth of blue and pink smoke high above, and there was a rampart of far, irregular houses, hazed in smoke, the traffic hummed in a circle, and on the right, dun-coloured animals stretched long necks over the Zoo palings, barking, howling. There they sat down under a tree.

'Look,' she implored him, pointing at a little troop of boys carrying cricket stumps, and one shuffled, spun round on his heel and shuffled, as if he were acting a clown at the music hall.

'Look,' she implored him, for Dr Holmes had told her to make him notice real things, go to a music hall, play cricket—that was the very game, Dr Holmes said, a nice out-of-door game, the very game for her husband.

'Look,' she repeated.

Look, the unseen bade him, the voice which now communicated with him who was the greatest of mankind, Septimus, lately taken from life to death, the Lord who had come to renew society, who lay like a coverlet, a snow blanket smitten only by the sun, for ever unwasted, suffering for ever, the scapegoat, the eternal sufferer, but he did not want it, he moaned, putting from him with a wave of his hand that eternal suffering, that eternal loneliness.

'Look,' she repeated, for he must not talk aloud to himself out of doors.

'Oh, look,' she implored him. But what was there to look at? A few sheep. That was all.

The way to Regent's Park Tube station—could they tell her the way to Regent's Park Tube station—Maisie Johnson wanted to know. She was only up from Edinburgh two days ago.

'Not this way—over there!' Rezia exclaimed, waving her aside, lest she should see Septimus.

Both seemed queer, Maisie Johnson thought. Everything seemed very queer. In London for the first time, come to take up a post at her uncle's in Leadenhall Street, and now walking through Regent's Park in the morning, this couple on the chairs gave her quite a turn: the young woman seeming foreign, the man looking queer, so that should she be very old she would still remember and make it jangle again among her memories how she had walked through Regent's Park on a fine summer's morning fifty years ago. For she was only nineteen and had got her way at last, to come to London; and now how queer it was, this couple she had asked the way of, and the girl started and jerked her hand, and the man—he seemed awfully odd; quarrelling, perhaps; parting for ever, perhaps; something was up, she knew; and now all these people (for she returned to the Broad Walk), the stone basins, the prim flowers, the old men and women, invalids most of them in Bath chairs—all seemed, after Edinburgh, so queer. And Maisie Johnson, as she joined that gently trudging, vaguely gazing, breeze-kissed company—squirrels perching and preening, sparrow fountains fluttering for crumbs, dogs busy with the railings, busy with each other, while the soft warm air washed over them and lent to the fixed unsurprised gaze with which they received life, something whimsical and mollified—Maisie Johnson positively felt she must cry Oh! (for that young man on the seat had given her quite a turn. Something was up, she knew).

Horror! horror! she wanted to cry. (She had left her people; they had warned her what would happen.)

Why hadn't she stayed at home? she cried, twisting the knob of the iron railing.

That girl, thought Mrs Dempster (who saved crusts for the squirrels and often ate her lunch in Regent's Park), don't know a thing yet; and really it seemed to her better to be a little stout, a little slack, a little moderate in one's expectations. Percy drank. Well, better to have a son, thought Mrs Dempster. She had had a hard time of it, and couldn't help smiling at a girl like that. You'll get married, for you're pretty enough, thought Mrs Dempster. Get married, she thought, and then you'll know. Oh, the cooks, and so on. Every man has his ways. But whether I'd have chosen quite like that if I could have known, thought Mrs Dempster, and could not help wishing to whisper a word to Maisie Johnson; to feel on the creased pouch of her worn old face the kiss of pity. For it's been a hard life, thought Mrs Dempster. What hadn't she given to it? Roses; figure; her feet too. (She drew the knobbed lumps beneath her skirt.)

Roses, she thought sardonically. All trash, m'dear. For really, what with eating, drinking, and mating, the bad days and good, life had been no mere matter of roses, and what was more, let me tell you, Carrie Dempster had no wish to change her lot with any woman's in Kentish Town! But, she implored, pity. Pity, for the loss of roses. Pity she asked of Maisie Johnson, standing by the hyacinth beds.

Ah, but that aeroplane! Hadn't Mrs Dempster always longed to see foreign parts? She had a nephew, a missionary. It soared and shot. She always went on the sea at Margate, not out o' sight of land, but she had no patience with women who were afraid of water. It swept and fell. Her stomach was in her mouth. Up again. There's a fine young feller aboard of it, Mrs Dempster wagered, and away and away it went, fast and fading, away and away the aeroplane shot: soaring over Greenwich and all the masts; over the little island of grey churches, St Paul's and the rest, till, on either side of London, fields spread out and dark brown woods where adventurous thrushes, hopping boldly, glancing quickly, snatched the snail and tapped him on a stone, once, twice, thrice.

Away and away the aeroplane shot, till it was nothing but a bright spark; an aspiration; a concentration; a symbol (so it seemed to Mr Bentley, vigorously rolling his strip of turf at Greenwich) of man's soul; of his determination, thought Mr Bentley, sweeping round the cedar tree, to get outside his body, beyond his house, by means of thought, Einstein, speculation, mathematics, the Mendelian theory—away the aeroplane shot.

Then, while a seedy-looking nondescript man carrying a leather bag stood on the steps of St Paul's Cathedral, and hesitated, for within was what balm, how great a welcome, how many tombs with banners waving over them, tokens of victories not over armies, but over, he thought, that plaguy spirit of truth seeking which leaves me at present without a situation, and more than that, the cathedral offers company, he thought, invites you to membership of a society; great men belong to it; martyrs have died for it; why not enter in, he thought, put this leather bag stuffed with pamphlets before an altar, a cross, the symbol of something which has soared beyond seeking and questing and knocking of words together and has become all spirit, disembodied, ghostly—why not enter in? he thought, and while he hesitated out flew the aeroplane over Ludgate Circus.

It was strange; it was still. Not a sound was to be heard above the traffic. Unguided it seemed; sped of its own free will. And now, curving up and up, straight up, like something mounting in ecstasy, in pure delight, out from behind poured white smoke looping, writing a T, and O, an F.

'What are they looking at?' said Clarissa Dalloway to the maid who opened her door.

The hall of the house was cool as a vault. Mrs Dalloway raised her hand to her eyes, and, as the maid shut the door to, and she heard the swish of Lucy's skirts, she felt like a nun who has left the world and feels fold round her the familiar veils and the response to old devotions. The cook whistled in the kitchen. She heard the click of the typewriter. It was her life, and, bending her head over the hall table, she bowed beneath the influence, felt blessed and purified, saying to herself, as she took the pad with the telephone message on it, how moments like this are buds on the tree of life, flowers of darkness they are, she thought (as if some lovely rose had blossomed for her eyes only); not for a moment did she believe in God; but all the more, she thought, taking up the pad, must one repay in daily life to servants, yes, to dogs and canaries, above all to Richard her husband, who was the foundation of it—of the gay sounds, of the green lights, of the cook even whistling, for Mrs Walker was Irish and whistled all day long—one must pay back from this secret deposit of exquisite moments, she thought, lifting the pad, while Lucy stood by her, trying to explain how

'Mr Dalloway, ma'am——'

Clarissa read on the telephone pad, 'Lady Bruton wishes to know if Mr Dalloway will lunch with her today.'

'Mr Dalloway, ma'am, told me to tell you he would be lunching out.'

'Dear!' said Clarissa, and Lucy shared as she meant her to her disappointment (but not the pang); felt the concord between them; took the hint; thought how the gentry love; gilded her own future with calm; and taking Mrs Dalloway's parasol, handled it like a sacred weapon which a goddess, having acquitted herself honourably in the field of battle, sheds, and placed it in the umbrella stand.

'Fear no more,' said Clarissa. Fear no more the heat o' the sun; for the shock of Lady Bruton asking Richard to lunch without her made the moment in which she had stood shiver, as a plant on the river-bed feels the shock of a passing oar and shivers: so she rocked: so she shivered.

Millicent Bruton, whose lunch parties were said to be extraordinarily amusing, had not asked her. No vulgar jealousy could separate her from Richard. But she feared time itself, and read on Lady Bruton's face, as if it had been a dial cut in impassive stone, the dwindling of life; how year by year her share was sliced; how little the margin that remained was capable any longer of stretching, of absorbing, as in the youthful years, the colours, salts, tones of existence, so that she filled the room she entered, and felt often, as she stood hesitating one moment on the threshold of her drawing-room, an exquisite suspense, such as might stay a diver before plunging while the sea darkens and brightens beneath him, and the waves which threaten to break, but only gently split their surface, roll and conceal and encrust as they just turn over the weeds with pearl.

She put the pad on the hall table. She began to go slowly upstairs, with her hand on the banisters, as if she had left a party, where now this friend now that had flashed back her face, her voice; had shut the door and gone out and stood alone, a single figure against the appalling night, or rather, to be accurate, against the stare of this matter-of-fact June morning; soft with the glow of rose petals for some, she knew, and felt it, as she paused by the open staircase window which let in blinds flapping, dogs barking, let in, she thought, feeling herself suddenly shrivelled, aged, breastless, the grinding, blowing, flowering of the day, out of doors, out of the window, out of her body and brain which now failed, since Lady Bruton, whose lunch parties were said to be extraordinarily amusing, had not asked her.

Like a nun withdrawing, or a child exploring a tower, she went, upstairs, paused at the window, came to the bathroom. There was the green linoleum and a tap dripping. There was an emptiness about the heart of life; an attic room. Women must put off their rich apparel. At midday they must disrobe. She pierced the pincushion and laid her feathered yellow hat on the bed. The sheets were clean, tight stretched in a broad white band from side to side. Narrower and narrower would her bed be. The candle was half burnt down and she had read deep in Baron Marbot's *Memoirs*. She had read late at night of the retreat from

Moscow. For the House sat so long that Richard insisted, after her
illness, that she must sleep undisturbed. And really she preferred to read
of the retreat from Moscow. He knew it. So the room was an attic; the
bed narrow; and lying there reading, for she slept badly, she could not
dispel a virginity preserved through childbirth which clung to her like a
sheet. Lovely in girlhood, suddenly there came a moment—for example
on the river beneath the woods at Clieveden—when, through some
contraction of this cold spirit, she had failed him. And then at Constantinople, and again and again. She could see what she lacked. It was not
beauty; it was not mind. It was something central which permeated;
something warm which broke up surfaces and rippled the cold contact
of man and woman, or of women together. For *that* she could dimly
perceive. She resented it, had a scruple picked up Heaven knows where,
or, as she felt, sent by Nature (who is invariably wise); yet she could not
resist sometimes yielding to the charm of a woman, not a girl, of a
woman confessing, as to her they often did, some scrape, some folly.
And whether it was pity, or their beauty, or that she was older, or some
accident—like a faint scent, or a violin next door (so strange is the
power of sounds at certain moments), she did undoubtedly then feel
what men felt. Only for a moment; but it was enough. It was a sudden
revelation, a tinge like a blush which one tried to check and then, as it
spread, one yielded to its expansion, and rushed to the farthest verge
and there quivered and felt the world come closer, swollen with some
astonishing significance, some pressure of rapture, which split its thin
skin and gushed and poured with an extraordinary alleviation over the
cracks and sores. Then, for that moment, she had seen an illumination;
a match burning in a crocus; an inner meaning almost expressed. But
the close withdrew; the hard softened. It was over—the moment.
Against such moments (with women too) there contrasted (as she laid
her hat down) the bed and Baron Marbot and the candle half-burnt.
Lying awake, the floor creaked; the lit house was suddenly darkened,
and if she raised her head she could just hear the click of the handle
released as gently as possible by Richard, who slipped upstairs in his
socks and then, as often as not, dropped his hot-water bottle and swore!
How she laughed!

But this question of love (she thought, putting her coat away), this
falling in love with women. Take Sally Seton; her relation in the old
days with Sally Seton. Had not that, after all, been love?

She sat on the floor—that was her first impression of Sally—she sat
on the floor with her arms round her knees, smoking a cigarette. Where
could it have been? The Mannings'? The Kinloch-Jones's? At some
party (where she could not be certain), for she had a distinct recollection
of saying to the man she was with, 'Who is *that*?' And he had told her,

and said that Sally's parents did not get on (how that shocked her—that one's parents should quarrel!). But all that evening she could not take her eyes off Sally. It was an extraordinary beauty of the kind she most admired, dark, large-eyed, with that quality which, since she hadn't got it herself, she always envied—a sort of abandonment, as if she could say anything, do anything; a quality much commoner in foreigners than in Englishwomen. Sally always said she had French blood in her veins, an ancestor had been with Marie Antoinette, had his head cut off, left a ruby ring. Perhaps that summer she came to stay at Bourton, walking in quite unexpectedly without a penny in her pocket, one night after dinner, and upsetting poor Aunt Helena to such an extent that she never forgave her. There had been some awful quarrel at home. She literally hadn't a penny that night when she came to them—had pawned a brooch to come down. She had rushed off in a passion. They sat up till all hours of the night talking. Sally it was who made her feel, for the first time, how sheltered the life at Bourton was. She knew nothing about sex—nothing about social problems. She had once seen an old man who had dropped dead in a field—she had seen cows just after their calves were born. But Aunt Helena never liked discussion of anything (when Sally gave her William Morris, it had to be wrapped in brown paper). There they sat, hour after hour, talking in her bedroom at the top of the house, talking about life, how they were to reform the world. They meant to found a society to abolish private property, and actually had a letter written, though not sent out. The ideas were Sally's, of course—but very soon she was just as excited—read Plato in bed before breakfast; read Morris; read Shelley by the hour.

Sally's power was amazing, her gift, her personality. There was her way with flowers, for instance. At Bourton they always had stiff little vases all the way down the table. Sally went out, picked hollyhocks, dahlias—all sorts of flowers that had never been seen together—cut their heads off, and made them swim on the top of water in bowls. The effect was extraordinary—coming into dinner in the sunset. (Of course Aunt Helena thought it wicked to treat flowers like that.) Then she forgot her sponge, and ran along the passage naked. That grim old housemaid, Ellen Atkins, went about grumbling—'Suppose any of the gentlemen had seen?' Indeed she did shock people. She was untidy, Papa said.

The strange thing, on looking back, was the purity, the integrity, of her feeling for Sally. It was not like one's feeling for a man. It was completely disinterested, and besides, it had a quality which could only exist between women, between women just grown up. It was protective, on her side; sprang from a sense of being in league together, a presentiment of something that was bound to part them (they spoke of marriage always as a catastrophe), which led to, this chivalry, this protective feeling which was much more on her side than Sally's. For in those days she was completely reckless; did the most idiotic things out of bravado; bicycled round the parapet on the terrace: smoked cigars. Absurd, she was—very absurd. But the charm was overpowering, to her at least, so that she could remember standing in her bedroom at the top of the house holding the hot-water can in her hands and saying aloud, 'She is beneath this roof . . . She is beneath this roof!'

No, the words meant absolutely nothing to her now. She could not even get an echo of her old emotion. But she could remember going cold with excitement and doing her hair in a kind of ecstasy (now the old feeling began to come back to her, as she took out her hairpins, laid them on the dressing-table, began to do her hair), with the rooks flaunting up and down in the pink evening light, and dressing, and going downstairs, and feeling as she crossed the hall 'if it were now to die 'twere now to be most happy'. That was her feeling—Othello's feeling, and she felt it, she was convinced, as strongly as Shakespeare meant Othello to feel it, all because she was coming down to dinner in a white frock to meet Sally Seton!

She was wearing pink gauze—was that possible? She *seemed*, anyhow, all light, glowing, like some bird or air ball that has flown in, attached itself for a moment to a bramble. But nothing is so strange when one is in love (and what was this except being in love?) as the complete indifference of other people. Aunt Helena just wandered off after dinner; Papa read the paper. Peter Walsh might have been there, and old Miss Cummings; Joseph Breitkopf certainly was, for he came every summer, poor old man, for weeks and weeks, and pretended to read German with her, but really played the piano and sang Brahms without any voice.

All this was only a background for Sally. She stood by the fireplace talking, in that beautiful voice which made everything she said sound like a caress, to Papa, who had begun to be attracted rather against his will (he never got over lending her one of his books and finding it soaked on the terrace), when suddenly she said, 'What a shame to sit indoors!' and they all went out on to the terrace and walked up and down. Peter Walsh and Joseph Breitkopf went on about Wagner. She and Sally fell a little behind. Then came the most exquisite moment of her whole life passing a stone urn with flowers in it. Sally stopped; picked a flower; kissed her on the lips. The whole world might have turned upside down! The others disappeared; there she was alone with Sally. And she felt that she had been given a present, wrapped up, and told just to keep it, not to look at it—a diamond, something infinitely precious, wrapped up, which, as they walked (up and down, up and down), she uncovered,

or the radiance burnt through, the revelation, the religious feeling!—
when old Joseph and Peter faced them:

'Star-gazing?' said Peter.

It was like running one's face against a granite wall in the darkness!
It was shocking; it was horrible!

Not for herself. She felt only how Sally was being mauled already,
maltreated; she felt his hostility; his jealousy; his determination to break
into their companionship. All this she saw as one sees a landscape in a
flash of lightning—and Sally (never had she admired her so much!)
gallantly taking her way unvanquished. She laughed. She made old
Joseph tell her the names of the stars, which he liked doing very
seriously. She stood there: she listened. She heard the names of the stars.

'Oh this horror!' she said to herself, as if she had known all along that
something would interrupt, would embitter her moment of happiness.

Yet how much she owed Peter Walsh later. Always when she thought
of him she thought of their quarrels for some reason—because she
wanted his good opinion so much, perhaps. She owed him words:
'sentimental', 'civilized'; they started up every day of her life as if he
guarded her. A book was sentimental; an attitude to life sentimental.
'Sentimental', perhaps she was to be thinking of the past. What would
he think, she wondered, when he came back?

That she had grown older? Would he say that, or would she see him
thinking when he came back, that she had grown older? It was true.
Since her illness she had turned almost white.

Laying her brooch on the table, she had a sudden spasm, as if, while
she mused, the icy claws had had the chance to fix in her. She was not
old yet. She had just broken into her fifty-second year. Months and
months of it were still untouched. June, July, August! Each still
remained almost whole, and, as if to catch the falling drop, Clarissa
(crossing to the dressing-table) plunged into the very heart of the
moment, transfixed it, there—the moment of this June morning on
which was the pressure of all the other mornings, seeing the glass, the
dressing-table, and all the bottles afresh, collecting the whole of her at
one point (as she looked into the glass), seeing the delicate pink face of
the woman who was that very night to give a party; of Clarissa Dalloway;
of herself.

How many million times she had seen her face, and always with the
same imperceptible contraction! She pursed her lips when she looked in
the glass. It was to give her face point. That was her self—pointed;
dart-like; definite. That was her self when some effort, some call on her
to be her self, drew the parts together, she alone knew how different,
how incompatible and composed so for the world only into one centre,
one diamond, one woman who sat in her drawing-room and made a

meeting-point, a radiancy no doubt in some dull lives, a refuge for the lonely to come to, perhaps; she had helped young people, who were grateful to her; had tried to be the same always, never showing a sign of all the other sides of her—faults, jealousies, vanities, suspicions, like this of Lady Bruton not asking her to lunch; which, she thought (combing her hair finally), is utterly base! Now, where was her dress?

Her evening dresses hung in the cupboard. Clarissa, plunging her hand into the softness, gently detached the green dress and carried it to the window. She had torn it. Some one had trod on the skirt. She had felt it give at the Embassy party at the top among the folds. By artificial light the green shone, but lost its colour now in the sun. She would mend it. Her maids had too much to do. She would wear it tonight. She would take her silks, her scissors, her—what was it?—her thimble, of course, down into the drawing-room, for she must also write, and see that things generally were more or less in order.

Strange, she thought, pausing on the landing, and assembling that diamond shape, that single person, strange how a mistress knows the very moment, the very temper of her house! Faint sounds rose in spirals up the well of the stairs; the swish of a mop; tapping; knocking; a loudness when the front door opened; a voice repeating a message in the basement; the chink of silver on a tray; clean silver for the party. All was for the party.

(And Lucy, coming into the drawing-room with her tray held out, put the giant candlesticks on the mantelpiece, the silver casket in the middle, turned the crystal dolphin towards the clock. They would come; they would stand; they would talk in the mincing tones which she could imitate, ladies and gentlemen. Of all, her mistress was loveliest— mistress of silver, of linen, of china, for the sun, the silver, doors off their hinges, Rumpelmayer's men, gave her a sense, as she laid the paper-knife on the inlaid table, of something achieved. Behold! Behold! she said, speaking to her old friends in the baker's shop, where she had first seen service at Caterham, prying into the glass. She was Lady Angela, attending Princess Mary, when in came Mrs Dalloway.)

'Oh, Lucy,' she said, 'the silver does look nice!'

'And how,' she said, turning the crystal dolphin to stand straight, 'how did you enjoy the play last night?' 'Oh, they had to go before the end!' she said. 'They had to be back at ten!' she said. 'So they don't know what happened,' she said. 'That does seem hard luck,' she said (for her servants stayed later, if they asked her). 'That does seem rather a shame,' she said, taking the old bald-looking cushion in the middle of the sofa and putting it in Lucy's arms, and giving her a little push, and crying:

'Take it away! Give it to Mrs Walker with my compliments! Take it away!' she cried.

And Lucy stopped at the drawing-room door, holding the cushion, and said, very shyly, turning a little pink, couldn't she help to mend that dress?

But, said Mrs Dalloway, she had enough on her hands already, quite enough of her own to do without that.

'But, thank you, Lucy, oh, thank you,' said Mrs Dalloway, and thank you, thank you, she went on saying (sitting down on the sofa with her dress over her knees, her scissors, her silks), thank you, thank you, she went on saying in gratitude to her servants generally for helping her to be like this, to be what she wanted, gentle, generous-hearted. Her servants liked her. And then this dress of hers—where was the tear? and now her needle to be threaded. This was a favourite dress, one of Sally Parker's, the last almost she ever made, alas, for Sally had now retired, lived at Ealing, and if ever I have a moment, thought Clarissa (but never would she have a moment any more), I shall go and see her at Ealing. For she was a character, thought Clarissa, a real artist. She thought of little out-of-the-way things; yet her dresses were never queer. You could wear them at Hatfield; at Buckingham Palace. She had worn them at Hatfield; at Buckingham Palace.

Quiet descended on her, calm, content, as her needle, drawing the silk smoothly to its gentle pause, collected the green folds together and attached them, very lightly, to the belt. So on a summer's day waves collect, overbalance, and fall; collect and fall; and the whole world seems to be saying 'that is all' more and more ponderously, until even the heart in the body which lies in the sun on the beach says too, that is all. Fear no more, says the heart. Fear no more, says the heart, committing its burden to some sea, which sighs collectively for all sorrows, and renews, begins, collects, lets fall. And the body alone listens to the passing bee; the wave breaking, the dog barking, far away barking and barking.

'Heavens, the front-door bell!' exclaimed Clarissa, staying her needle. Roused, she listened.

'Mrs Dalloway will see me,' said the elderly man in the hall. 'Oh yes, she will see *me*,' he repeated, putting Lucy aside very benevolently, and running upstairs ever so quickly. 'Yes, yes, yes,' he muttered as he ran upstairs. 'She will see me. After five years in India, Clarissa will see me.'

'Who can—what can—' asked Mrs Dalloway (thinking it was outrageous to be interrupted at eleven o'clock on the morning of the day she was giving a party), hearing a step on the stairs. She heard a hand upon the door. She made to hide her dress, like a virgin protecting chastity, respecting privacy. Now the brass knob slipped. Now the door opened, and in came—for a single second she could not remember what he was called! so surprised she was to see him, so glad, so shy, so utterly taken aback to have Peter Walsh come to her unexpectedly in the morning! (She had not read his letter.)

'And how are you?' said Peter Walsh, positively trembling; taking both her hands; kissing both her hands. She's grown older, he thought, sitting down. I shan't tell her anything about it, he thought, for she's grown older. She's looking at me, he thought, a sudden embarrassment coming over him, though he had kissed her hands. Putting his hand into his pocket, he took out a large pocket-knife and half opened the blade.

Exactly the same, thought Clarissa; the same queer look; the same check suit; a little out of the straight his face is, a little thinner, dryer, perhaps, but he looks awfully well, and just the same.

'How heavenly it is to see you again!' she exclaimed. He had his knife out. That's so like him, she thought.

He had only reached town last night, he said; would have to go down into the country at once; and how was everything, how was everybody—Richard? Elizabeth?

'And what's all this?' he said, tilting his pen-knife towards her green dress.

He's very well dressed, thought Clarissa; yet he always criticizes *me*.

Here she is mending her dress; mending her dress as usual, he thought; here she's been sitting all the time I've been in India; mending her dress; playing about; going to parties; running to the House and back and all that, he thought, growing more and more irritated, more and more agitated, for there's nothing in the world so bad for some women as marriage, he thought; and politics; and having a Conservative husband, like the admirable Richard. So it is, so it is, he thought, shutting his knife with a snap.

'Richard's very well. Richard's at a Committee,' said Clarissa.

And she opened her scissors, and said, did he mind her just finishing what she was doing to her dress, for they had a party that night?

'Which I shan't ask you to,' she said. 'My dear Peter!' she said.

But it was delicious to hear her say that—my dear Peter! Indeed, it was all so delicious—the silver, the chairs; all so delicious!

Why wouldn't she ask him to her party? he asked.

Now of course, thought Clarissa, he's enchanting! perfectly enchanting! Now I remember how impossible it was ever to make up my mind—and why did I make up my mind—not to marry him, she wondered, that awful summer?

'But it's so extraordinary that you should have come this morning!' she cried, putting her hands, one on top of another, down on her dress.

'Do you remember', she said, 'how the blinds used to flap at Bourton?'

'They did,' he said; and he remembered breakfasting alone, very awkwardly, with her father; who had died; and he had not written to Clarissa. But he had never got on well with old Parry, that querulous, weak-kneed old man, Clarissa's father, Justin Parry.

'I often wish I'd got on better with your father,' he said.

'But he never liked anyone who—our friends,' said Clarissa; and could have bitten her tongue for thus reminding Peter that he had wanted to marry her.

Of course I did, thought Peter; it almost broke my heart too, he thought; and was overcome with his own grief, which rose like a moon looked at from a terrace, ghastly beautiful with light from the sunken day. I was more unhappy than I've ever been since, he thought. And as if in truth he were sitting there on the terrace he edged a little towards Clarissa; put his hand out; raised it; let it fall. There above them it hung, that moon. She too seemed to be sitting with him on the terrace, in the moonlight.

'Herbert has it now,' she said. 'I never go there now,' she said.

Then, just as happens on a terrace in the moonlight, when one person begins to feel ashamed that he is already bored, and yet as the other sits silent, very quiet, sadly looking at the moon, does not like to speak, moves his foot, clears his throat, notices some iron scroll on a table leg, stirs a leaf, but says nothing—so Peter Walsh did now. For why go back like this to the past? he thought. Why make him think of it again? Why make him suffer, when she had tortured him so infernally? Why?

'Do you remember the lake?' she said, in an abrupt voice, under the pressure of an emotion which caught her heart, made the muscles of her throat stiff, and contracted her lips in a spasm as she said 'lake'. For she was a child throwing bread to the ducks, between her parents, and at the same time a grown woman coming to her parents who stood by the lake, holding her life in her arms which, as she neared them, grew larger and larger in her arms, until it became a whole life, a complete life, which she put down by them and said, 'This is what I have made of it! This!' And what had she made of it? What, indeed? sitting there sewing this morning with Peter.

She looked at Peter Walsh; her look, passing through all that time and that emotion, reached him doubtfully; settled on him tearfully; and rose and fluttered away, as a bird touches a branch and rises and flutters away. Quite simply she wiped her eyes.

'Yes,' said Peter. 'Yes, yes, yes,' he said, as if she drew up to the surface something which positively hurt him as it rose. Stop! Stop! he wanted to cry. For he was not old; his life was not over; not by any means. He was only just past fifty. Shall I tell her, he thought, or not?

He would like to make a clean breast of it all. But she is too cold, he thought; sewing, with her scissors; Daisy would look ordinary beside Clarissa. And she would think me a failure, which I am in their sense, he thought; in the Dalloways' sense. Oh yes, he had no doubt about that; he was a failure, compared with all this—the inlaid table, the mounted paper-knife, the dolphin and the candlesticks, the chair-covers and the old valuable English tinted prints—he was a failure! I detest the smugness of the whole affair, he thought; Richard's doing, not Clarissa's; save that she married him. (Here Lucy came into the room, carrying silver, more silver, but charming, slender, graceful she looked, he thought, as she stooped to put it down.) And this has been going on all the time! he thought; week after week; Clarissa's life; while I—he thought; and at once everything seemed to radiate from him; journeys; rides; quarrels; adventures; bridge parties; love affairs; work; work, work! and he took out his knife quite openly—his old horn-handled knife which Clarissa could swear he had had these thirty years—and clenched his fist upon it.

What an extraordinary habit that was, Clarissa thought; always playing with a knife. Always making one feel, too, frivolous; empty-minded; a mere silly chatterbox, as he used. But I too, she thought, and, taking up her needle, summoned, like a Queen whose guards have fallen asleep and left her unprotected (she had been quite taken aback by this visit—it had upset her) so that anyone can stroll in and have a look at her where she lies with the brambles curving over her, summoned to her help the things she did; the things she liked; her husband; Elizabeth; herself, in short, which Peter hardly knew now, all to come about her and beat off the enemy.

'Well, and what's happened to you?' she said. So before a battle begins, the horses paw the ground; toss their heads; the light shines on their flanks; their necks curve. So Peter Walsh and Clarissa, sitting side by side on the blue sofa, challenged each other. His powers chafed and tossed in him. He assembled from different quarters all sorts of things; praise; his career at Oxford; his marriage, which she knew nothing whatever about; how he had loved; and altogether done his job.

'Millions of things!' he exclaimed, and, urged by the assembly of powers which were now charging this way and that and giving him the feeling at once frightening and extremely exhilarating of being rushed through the air on the shoulders of people he could no longer see, he raised his hands to his forehead.

Clarissa sat very upright; drew in her breath.

'I am in love,' he said, not to her however, but to someone raised up in the dark so that you could not touch her but must lay your garland down on the grass in the dark.

'In love,' he repeated, now speaking rather dryly to Clarissa Dalloway; 'in love with a girl in India.' He had deposited his garland. Clarissa could make what she would of it.

'In love!' she said. That he at his age should be sucked under in his little bow-tie by that monster! And there's no flesh on his neck; his hands are red; and he's six months older than I am! her eye flashed back to her; but in her heart she felt, all the same; he is in love. He has that, she felt; he is in love.

But the indomitable egotism which for ever rides down the hosts opposed to it, the river which says on, on, on; even though, it admits, there may be no goal for us whatever, still on, on; this indomitable egotism charged her cheeks with colour; made her look very young; very pink; very bright-eyed as she sat with her dress upon her knee, and her needle held to the end of green silk, trembling a little. He was in love! Not with her. With some younger woman, of course.

'And who is she?' she asked.

Now this statue must be brought from its height and set down between them.

'A married woman, unfortunately,' he said; 'the wife of a Major in the Indian Army.'

And with a curious ironical sweetness he smiled as he placed her in this ridiculous way before Clarissa.

(All the same, he is in love, thought Clarissa.)

'She has', he continued, very reasonably, 'two small children; a boy and a girl; and I have come over to see my lawyers about the divorce.'

There they are! he thought. Do what you like with them, Clarissa! There they are! And second by second it seemed to him that the wife of the Major in the Indian Army (his Daisy) and her two small children became more and more lovely as Clarissa looked at them; as if he had set light to a grey pellet on a plate and there had risen up a lovely tree in the brisk sea-salted air of their intimacy (for in some ways no one understood him, felt with him, as Clarissa did)—their exquisite intimacy.

She flattered him; she fooled him, thought Clarissa; shaping the woman, the wife of the Major in the Indian Army, with three strokes of a knife. What a waste! What a folly! All his life long Peter had been fooled like that; first getting sent down from Oxford; next marrying the girl on the boat going out to India; now the wife of a Major—thank Heaven she had refused to marry him! Still, he was in love; her old friend, her dear Peter, he was in love.

'But what are you going to do?' she asked him. Oh, the lawyers and solicitors, Messrs Hooper and Grateley of Lincoln's Inn, they were going to do it, he said. And he actually pared his nails with his pocket-knife.

For Heaven's sake, leave your knife alone! she cried to herself in irrepressible irritation; it was his silly unconventionality, his weakness; his lack of the ghost of a notion what anyone else was feeling that annoyed her, had always annoyed her; and now at his age, how silly!

I know all that, Peter thought; I know what I'm up against, he thought, running his finger along the blade of his knife, Clarissa and Dalloway and all the rest of them; but I'll show Clarissa—and then to his utter surprise, suddenly thrown by those uncontrollable forces, thrown through the air, he burst into tears; wept; wept without the least shame, sitting on the sofa, the tears running down his cheeks.

And Clarissa had leant forward, taken his hand, drawn him to her, kissed him,—actually had felt his face on hers before she could down the brandishing of silver-flashing plumes like pampas grass in a tropic gale in her breast, which, subsiding, left her holding his hand, patting his knee, and feeling as she sat back extraordinarily at her ease with him and light-hearted, all in a clap it came over her, If I had married him, this gaiety would have been mine all day!

It was all over for her. The sheet was stretched and the bed narrow. She had gone up into the tower alone and left them blackberrying in the sun. The door had shut, and there among the dust of fallen plaster and the litter of birds' nests how distant the view had looked, and the sounds came thin and chill (once on Leith Hill, she remembered), and Richard, Richard! she cried, as a sleeper in the night starts and stretches a hand in the dark for help. Lunching with Lady Bruton, it came back to her. He has left me; I am alone for ever, she thought, folding her hands upon her knee.

Peter Walsh had got up and crossed to the window and stood with his back to her, flicking a bandanna handkerchief from side to side. Masterly and dry and desolate he looked, his thin shoulder-blades lifting his coat slightly; blowing his nose violently. Take me with you, Clarissa thought impulsively, as if he were starting directly upon some great voyage; and then, next moment, it was as if the five acts of a play that had been very exciting and moving were now over and she had lived a lifetime in them and had run away, had lived with Peter, and it was now over.

Now it was time to move, and, as a woman gathers her things together, her cloak, her gloves, her opera-glasses, and gets up to go out of the theatre into the street, she rose from the sofa and went to Peter.

And it was awfully strange, he thought, how she still had the power, as she came tinkling, rustling, still had the power, as she came across the room, to make the moon, which he detested, rise at Bourton on the terrace in the summer sky.

'Tell me,' he said, seizing her by the shoulders. 'Are you happy, Clarissa? Does Richard——'

The door opened.

'Here is my Elizabeth,' said Clarissa, emotionally, histrionically, perhaps.

'How d'y do?' said Elizabeth coming forward.

The sound of Big Ben striking the half-hour struck out between them with extraordinary vigour, as if a young man, strong, indifferent, inconsiderate, were swinging dumb-bells this way and that.

'Hullo, Elizabeth!' cried Peter, stuffing his handkerchief into his pocket, going quickly to her, saying 'Good-bye, Clarissa' without looking at her, leaving the room quickly, and running downstairs and opening the hall door.

'Peter! Peter!' cried Clarissa, following him out on to the landing. 'My party! Remember my party tonight!' she cried, having to raise her voice against the roar of the open air, and, overwhelmed by the traffic and the sound of all the clocks striking, her voice crying 'Remember my party tonight!' sounded frail and thin and very far away as Peter Walsh shut the door.

Remember my party, remember my party, said Peter Walsh as he stepped down the street, speaking to himself rhythmically, in time with the flow of the sound, the direct downright sound of Big Ben striking the half-hour. (The leaden circles dissolved in the air.) Oh these parties? he thought; Clarissa's parties. Why does she give these parties? he thought. Not that he blamed her or this effigy of a man in a tail-coat with a carnation in his button-hole coming towards him. Only one person in the world could be as he was, in love. And there he was, this fortunate man, himself, reflected in the plate-glass window of a motor-car manufacturer in Victoria Street. All India lay behind him; plains, mountains; epidemics of cholera; a district twice as big as Ireland; decisions he had come to alone—he, Peter Walsh; who was now really for the first time in his life in love. Clarissa had grown hard, he thought; and a trifle sentimental into the bargain, he suspected, looking at the great motor cars capable of doing—how many miles on how many gallons? For he had a turn for mechanics; had invented a plough in his district, had ordered wheel-barrows from England, but the coolies wouldn't use them, all of which Clarissa knew nothing whatever about.

The way she said 'Here is my Elizabeth!'—that annoyed him. Why not 'Here's Elizabeth' simply? It was insincere. And Elizabeth didn't like it either. (Still the last tremors of the great booming voice shook the air round him; the half-hour; still early; only half-past eleven still.) For he understood young people; he liked them. There was always something cold in Clarissa, he thought. She had always, even as a girl, a sort of timidity, which in middle age becomes conventionality, and then it's all up, it's all up, he thought, looking rather drearily into the glassy depths, and wondering whether by calling at that hour he had annoyed her; overcome with shame suddenly at having been a fool; wept; been emotional; told her everything, as usual, as usual.

As a cloud crosses the sun, silence falls on London; and falls on the mind. Effort ceases. Time flaps on the mast. There we stop; there we stand. Rigid, the skeleton of habit alone upholds the human frame. Where there is nothing, Peter Walsh said to himself; feeling hollowed out, utterly empty within. Clarissa refused me, he thought. He stood there thinking, Clarissa refused me.

Ah, said St Margaret's, like a hostess who comes into her drawing-room on the very stroke of the hour and finds her guests there already. I am not late. No, it is precisely half-past eleven, she says. Yet, though she is perfectly right, her voice, being the voice of the hostess, is reluctant to inflict its individuality. Some grief for the past holds it back; some concern for the present. It is half-past eleven, she says, and the sound of St Margaret's glides into the recesses of the heart and buries itself in ring after ring of sound, like something alive which wants to confide itself, to disperse itself, to be, with a tremor of delight, at rest—like Clarissa herself, thought Peter Walsh, coming downstairs on the stroke of the hour in white. It is Clarissa herself, he thought, with a deep emotion, and an extraordinarily clear, yet puzzling, recollection of her, as if this bell had come into the room years ago, where they sat at some moment of great intimacy, and had gone from one to the other and had left, like a bee with honey, laden with the moment. But what room? What moment? And why had he been so profoundly happy when the clock was striking? Then, as the sound of St Margaret's languished, he thought, she has been ill, and the sound expressed languor and suffering. It was her heart, he remembered; and the sudden loudness of the final stroke tolled for death that surprised in the midst of life, Clarissa falling where she stood, in her drawing-room. No! No! he cried. She is not dead! I am not old, he cried, and marched up Whitehall, as if there rolled down to him, vigorous, unending, his future.

He was not old, or set, or dried in the least. As for caring what they said of him—the Dalloways, the Whitbreads, and their set, he cared not a straw—not a straw (though it was true he would have, some time or other, to see whether Richard couldn't help him to some job). Striding, staring, he glared at the statue of the Duke of Cambridge. He had been sent down from Oxford—true. He had been a Socialist, in some sense a failure—true. Still the future of civilization lies, he thought, in the hands of young men like that; of young men such as he was, thirty years ago;

with their love of abstract principles; getting books sent out to them all the way from London to a peak in the Himalayas; reading science; reading philosophy. The future lies in the hands of young men like that, he thought.

A patter like the patter of leaves in a wood came from behind, and with it a rustling, regular thudding sound, which as it overtook him drummed his thoughts, strict in step, up Whitehall, without his doing. Boys in uniform, carrying guns, marched with their eyes ahead of them, marched, their arms stiff, and on their faces an expression like the letters of a legend written round the base of a statue praising duty, gratitude, fidelity, love of England.

It is, thought Peter Walsh, beginning to keep step with them, a very fine training. But they did not look robust. They were weedy for the most part, boys of sixteen, who might, tomorrow, stand behind bowls of rice, cakes of soap on counters. Now they wore on them unmixed with sensual pleasure or daily preoccupations the solemnity of the wreath which they had fetched from Finsbury Pavement to the empty tomb. They had taken their vow. The traffic respected it; vans were stopped.

I can't keep up with them, Peter Walsh thought, as they marched up Whitehall, and sure enough, on they marched, past him, past everyone, in their steady way, as if one will worked legs and arms uniformly, and life, with its varieties, its irreticences, had been laid under a pavement of monuments and wreaths and drugged into a stiff yet staring corpse by discipline. One had to respect it; one might laugh; but one had to respect it, he thought. There they go, thought Peter Walsh, pausing at the edge of the pavement; and all the exalted statues, Nelson, Gordon, Havelock, the black, the spectacular images of great soldiers stood looking ahead of them, as if they too had made the same renunciation (Peter Walsh felt he, too, had made it the great renunciation), trampled under the same temptations, and achieved at length a marble stare. But the stare Peter Walsh did not want for himself in the least; though he could respect it in others. He could respect it in boys. They don't know the troubles of the flesh yet, he thought, as the marching boys disappeared in the direction of the Strand—all that I've been through, he thought, crossing the road, and standing under Gordon's statue, Gordon whom as a boy he had worshipped; Gordon standing lonely with one leg raised and his arms crossed,—poor Gordon, he thought.

And just because nobody yet knew he was in London, except Clarissa, and the earth, after the voyage, still seemed an island to him, the strangeness of standing alone, alive, unknown, at half-past eleven in Trafalgar Square overcame him. What is it? Where am I? And why, after all, does one do it? he thought, the divorce seeming all moonshine. And down his mind went flat as a marsh, and three great emotions bowled over him; understanding; a vast philanthropy; and finally, as if the result of the others, an irrepressible, exquisite delight; as if inside his brain, by another hand, strings were pulled, shutters moved, and he, having nothing to do with it, yet stood at the opening of endless avenues down which if he chose he might wander. He had not felt so young for years.

He had escaped! was utterly free—as happens in the downfall of habit when the mind, like an unguarded flame, bows and bends and seems about to blow from its holding. I haven't felt so young for years! thought Peter, escaping (only of course for an hour or so) from being precisely what he was, and feeling like a child who runs out of doors, and sees, as he runs, his old nurse waving at the wrong window. But she's extraordinarily attractive, he thought, as, walking across Trafalgar Square in the direction of the Haymarket, came a young woman who, as she passed Gordon's statue, seemed, Peter Walsh thought (susceptible as he was), to shed veil after veil, until she became the very woman he had always had in mind; young, but stately; merry, but discreet; black, but enchanting.

Straightening himself and stealthily fingering his pocket-knife he started after her to follow this woman, this excitement, which seemed even with its back turned to shed on him a light which connected them, which singled him out, as if the random uproar of the traffic had whispered through hollowed hands his name, not Peter, but his private name which he called himself in his own thoughts. 'You,' she said, only 'you', saying it with her white gloves and her shoulders. Then the thin long cloak which the wind stirred as she walked past Dent's shop in Cockspur Street blew out with an enveloping kindness, a mournful tenderness, as of arms that would open and take the tired——

But she's not married; she's young; quite young, thought Peter, the red carnation he had seen her wear as she came across Trafalgar Square burning again in his eyes and making her lips red. But she waited at the kerbstone. There was a dignity about her. She was not worldly, like Clarissa; not rich, like Clarissa. Was she, he wondered as she moved, respectable? Witty, with a lizard's flickering tongue, he thought (for one must invent, must allow oneself a little diversion), a cool waiting wit, a darting wit; not noisy.

She moved; she crossed; he followed her. To embarrass her was the last thing he wished. Still if she stopped he would say 'Come and have an ice,' he would say, and she would answer, perfectly simply, 'Oh yes.'

But other people got between them in the street, obstructing him, blotting her out. He pursued; she changed. There was colour in her cheeks; mockery in her eyes; he was an adventurer, reckless, he thought, swift, daring, indeed (landed as he was last night from India) a romantic buccaneer, careless of all these damned proprieties, yellow dressing-gowns, pipes, fishing-rods, in the shop windows; and respectability and evening parties and spruce old men wearing white slips beneath their waistcoats. He was a buccaneer. On and on she went, across Piccadilly, and up Regent Street, ahead of him, her cloak, her gloves, her shoulders combining with the fringes and the laces and the feather boas in the windows to make the spirit of finery and whimsy which dwindled out of the shops on to the pavement, as the light of a lamp goes wavering at night over hedges in the darkness.

Laughing and delightful, she had crossed Oxford Street and Great Portland Street and turned down one of the little streets, and now, and now, the great moment was approaching, for now she slackened, opened her bag, and with one look in his direction, but not at him, one look that bade farewell, summed up the whole situation and dismissed it triumphantly, for ever, had fitted her key, opened the door, and gone! Clarissa's voice saying, Remember my party, Remember my party, sang in his ears. The house was one of those flat red houses with hanging flower-baskets of vague impropriety. It was over.

Well, I've had my fun; I've had it, he thought, looking up at the swinging baskets of pale geraniums. And it was smashed to atoms—his fun, for it was half made up, as he knew very well; invented, this escapade with the girl; made up, as one makes up the better part of life, he thought—making oneself up; making her up; creating an exquisite amusement, and something more. But odd it was, and quite true; all this one could never share—it smashed to atoms.

He turned; went up the street, thinking to find somewhere to sit, till it was time for Lincoln's Inn—for Messrs Hooper and Grateley. Where should he go? No matter. Up the street, then, towards Regent's Park. His boots on the pavement struck out 'no matter'; for it was early, still very early.

It was a splendid morning too. Like the pulse of a perfect heart, life struck straight through the streets. There was no fumbling—no hesitation. Sweeping and swerving, accurately, punctually, noiselessly, there, precisely at the right instant, the motor car stopped at the door. The girl, silk-stockinged, feathered, evanescent, but not to him particularly attractive (for he had had his fling), alighted. Admirable butlers, tawny chow dogs, halls laid in black and white lozenges with white blinds blowing, Peter saw through the opened door and approved of. A splendid achievement in its own way, after all, London; the season; civilization. Coming as he did from a respectable Anglo-Indian family which for at least three generations had administered the affairs of a continent (it's strange, he thought, what a sentiment I have about that, disliking India, and empire, and army as he did), there were moments when civilization, even of this sort, seemed dear to him as a personal possession; moments of pride in England; in butlers; chow dogs; girls in their security. Ridiculous enough, still there it is, he thought. And the doctors and men of business and capable women all going about their business, punctual, alert, robust, seemed to him wholly admirable, good fellows, to whom one would entrust one's life, companions in the art of living, who would see one through. What with one thing and another, the show was really very tolerable; and he would sit down in the shade and smoke.

There was Regent's Park. Yes. As a child he had walked in Regent's Park—odd, he thought, how the thought of childhood keeps coming back to me—the result of seeing Clarissa, perhaps; for women live much more in the past than we do, he thought. They attach themselves to places; and their fathers—a woman's always proud of her father. Bourton was a nice place, a very nice place, but I could never get on with the old man, he thought. There was quite a scene one night—an argument about something or other, what, he could not remember. Politics presumably.

Yes, he remembered Regent's Park; the long straight walk; the little house where one bought air-balls to the left; an absurd statue with an inscription somewhere or other. He looked for an empty seat. He did not want to be bothered (feeling a little drowsy as he did) by people asking him the time. An elderly grey nurse, with a baby asleep in its perambulator—that was the best he could do for himself; sit down at the far end of the seat by that nurse.

She's a queer-looking girl, he thought, suddenly remembering Elizabeth as she came into the room and stood by her mother. Grown big; quite grown-up, not exactly pretty; handsome rather; and she can't be more than eighteen. Probably she doesn't get on with Clarissa. 'There's my Elizabeth'—that sort of thing—why not 'Here's Elizabeth' simply?—trying to make out, like most mothers, that things are what they're not. She trusts to her charm too much, he thought. She overdoes it.

The rich benignant cigar smoke eddied coolly down his throat; he puffed it out again in rings which breasted the air bravely for a moment; blue, circular—I shall try and get a word alone with Elizabeth tonight, he thought—then began to wobble into hour-glass shapes and taper away; odd shapes they take, he thought. Suddenly he closed his eyes, raised his hand with an effort, and threw away the heavy end of his cigar. A great brush swept smooth across his mind, sweeping across it moving branches, children's voices, the shuffle of feet, and people passing, and humming traffic, rising and falling traffic. Down, down he sank into the plumes and feathers of sleep, sank, and was muffled over.

*

The grey nurse resumed her knitting as Peter Walsh, on the hot seat beside her, began snoring. In her grey dress, moving her hands indefatigably yet quietly, she seemed like the champion of the rights of sleepers, like one of those spectral presences which rise in twilight in woods made of sky and branches. The solitary traveller, haunter of lanes, disturber of ferns, and devastator of great hemlock plants, looking up suddenly, sees the giant figure at the end of the ride.

By conviction an atheist perhaps, he is taken by surprise with moments of extraordinary exaltation. Nothing exists outside us except a state of mind, he thinks; a desire for solace, for relief, for something outside these miserable pigmies, these feeble, these ugly, these craven men and women. But if he can conceive of her, then in some sort she exists, he thinks, and advancing down the path with his eyes upon sky and branches he rapidly endows them with womanhood; sees with amazement how grave they become; how majestically, as the breeze stirs them, they dispense with a dark flutter of the leaves, charity, comprehension, absolution, and then, flinging themselves suddenly aloft, confound the piety of their aspect with a wild carouse.

Such are the visions which proffer great cornucopias full of fruit to the solitary traveller, or murmur in his ear like sirens lolloping away on the green sea waves, or are dashed in his face like bunches of roses, or rise to the surface like pale faces which fishermen flounder through floods to embrace.

Such are the visions which ceaselessly float up, pace beside, put their faces in front of, the actual thing; often overpowering the solitary traveller and taking away from him the sense of the earth, the wish to return, and giving him for substitute a general peace, as if (so he thinks as he advances down the forest ride) all this fever of living were simplicity itself; and myriads of things merged in one thing; and this figure, made of sky and branches as it is, had risen from the troubled sea (he is elderly, past fifty now) as a shape might be sucked up out of the waves to shower down from her magnificent hands, compassion, comprehension, absolution. So, he thinks, may I never go back to the lamplight; to the sitting-room; never finish my book; never knock out my pipe; never ring for Mrs Turner to clear away; rather let me walk straight on to this great figure, who will, with a toss of her head, mount me on her streamers and let me blow to nothingness with the rest.

Such are the visions. The solitary traveller is soon beyond the wood; and there, coming to the door with shaded eyes, possibly to look for his return, with hands raised, with white apron blowing, is an elderly woman who seems (so powerful is this infirmity) to seek, over the desert, a lost son; to search for a rider destroyed; to be the figure of the mother whose sons have been killed in the battles of the world. So, as the solitary traveller advances down the village street where the women stand knitting and the men dig in the garden, the evening seems ominous; the figures still; as if some august fate, known to them, awaited without fear, were about to sweep them into complete annihilation.

Indoors among ordinary things, the cupboard, the table, the window-sill with its geraniums, suddenly the outline of the landlady, bending to remove the cloth, becomes soft with light, an adorable emblem which only the recollection of cold human contacts forbids us to embrace. She takes the marmalade; she shuts it in the cupboard.

'There is nothing more tonight, sir?'

But to whom does the solitary traveller make reply?

So the elderly nurse knitted over the sleeping baby in Regent's Park. So Peter Walsh snored. He woke with extreme suddenness, saying to himself, 'The death of the soul.'

'Lord, Lord!' he said to himself out loud, stretching and opening his eyes. 'The death of the soul.' The words attached themselves to some scene, to some room, to some past he had been dreaming of. It became clearer; the scene, the room, the past he had been dreaming of.

It was at Bourton that summer, early in the 'nineties, when he was so passionately in love with Clarissa. There were a great many people there, laughing and talking, sitting round a table after tea, and the room was bathed in yellow light and full of cigarette smoke. They were talking about a man who had married his housemaid, one of the neighbouring squires, he had forgotten his name. He had married his housemaid, and she had been brought to Bourton to call—an awful visit it had been. She was absurdly overdressed, 'like a cockatoo,' Clarissa had said, imitating her, and she never stopped talking. On and on she went, on and on. Clarissa imitated her. Then somebody said—Sally Seton it was—did it make any real difference to one's feelings to know that before they'd married she had had a baby? (In those days, in mixed company, it was a bold thing to say.) He could see Clarissa now, turning bright pink; somehow contracting; and saying, 'Oh, I shall never be able to speak to her again!' Whereupon the whole party sitting round the tea-table seemed to wobble. It was very uncomfortable.

He hadn't blamed her for minding the fact, since in those days a girl brought up as she was knew nothing, but it was her manner that annoyed him; timid; hard; arrogant; prudish. 'The death of the soul.' He had said that instinctively, ticketing the moment as he used to do— the death of her soul.

Everyone wobbled; everyone seemed to bow, as she spoke, and then to stand up different. He could see Sally Seton, like a child who has been in mischief, leaning forward, rather flushed, wanting to talk, but afraid, and Clarissa did frighten people. (She was Clarissa's greatest friend, always about the place, an attractive creature, handsome, dark, with the reputation in those days of great daring, and he used to give her cigars, which she smoked in her bedroom, and she had either been engaged to somebody or quarrelled with her family, and old Parry disliked them both equally, which was a great bond.) Then Clarissa, still with an air of being offended with them all, got up, made some excuse, and went off, alone. As she opened the door, in came that great shaggy dog which ran after sheep. She flung herself upon him, went into raptures. It was as if she said to Peter—it was all aimed at him, he knew—'I know you thought me absurd about that woman just now; but see how extraordinarily sympathetic I am; see how I love my Rob!'

They had always this queer power of communicating without words. She knew directly he criticized her. Then she would do something quite obvious to defend herself, like this fuss with the dog—but it never took him in, he always saw through Clarissa. Not that he said anything, of course; just sat looking glum. It was the way their quarrels often began.

She shut the door. At once he became extremely depressed. It all seemed useless—going on being in love; going on quarrelling; going on making it up, and he wandered off alone, among outhouses, stables, looking at the horses. (The place was quite a humble one; the Parrys were never very well off; but there were always grooms and stable-boys about—Clarissa loved riding—and an old coachman—what was his name?—an old nurse, old Moody, old Goody, some such name they called her, whom one was taken to visit in a little room with lots of photographs, lots of bird-cages.)

It was an awful evening! He grew more and more gloomy, not about that only; about everything. And he couldn't see her; couldn't explain to her; couldn't have it out. There were always people about—she'd go on as if nothing had happened. That was the devilish part of her—this coldness, this woodenness, something very profound in her, which he had felt again this morning talking to her; an impenetrability. Yet Heaven knows he loved her. She had some queer power of fiddling on one's nerves, turning one's nerves to fiddle-strings, yes.

He had gone into dinner rather late, from some idiotic idea of making himself felt, and had sat down by old Miss Parry—Aunt Helena—Mr Parry's sister, who was supposed to preside. There she sat in her white Cashmere shawl, with her head against the window—a formidable old lady, but kind to him, for he had found her some rare flower, and she was a great botanist, marching off in thick boots with a black tin collecting box slung between her shoulders. He sat down beside her, and couldn't speak. Everything seemed to race past him; he just sat there, eating. And then half-way through dinner he made himself look across at Clarissa for the first time. She was talking to a young man on her right. He had a sudden revelation. 'She will marry that man,' he said to himself. He didn't even know his name.

For of course it was that afternoon, that very afternoon, that Dalloway had come over; and Clarissa called him 'Wickham'; that was the beginning of it all. Somebody had brought him over; and Clarissa got his name wrong. She introduced him to everybody as Wickham. At last he said 'My name is Dalloway!'—that was his first view of Richard—a fair young man, rather awkward, sitting on a deck-chair, and blurting out 'My name is Dalloway!' Sally got hold of it; always after that she called him 'My name is Dalloway!'

He was a prey to revelations at that time. This one—that she would marry Dalloway—was blinding—overwhelming at the moment. There was a sort of—how could he put it?—a sort of ease in her manner to him; something maternal; something gentle. They were talking about politics. All through dinner he tried to hear what they were saying.

Afterwards he could remember standing by old Miss Parry's chair in the drawing-room. Clarissa came up, with her perfect manners, like a real hostess, and wanted to introduce him to someone—spoke as if they had never met before, which enraged him. Yet even then he admired her for it. He admired her courage; her social instinct; he admired her power of carrying things through. 'The perfect hostess,' he said to her, whereupon she winced all over. But he meant her to feel it. He would have done anything to hurt her, after seeing her with Dalloway. So she left him. And he had a feeling that they were all gathered together in a conspiracy against him—laughing and talking—behind his back. There he stood by Miss Parry's chair as though he had been cut out of wood, talking about wild flowers. Never, never had he suffered so infernally! He must have forgotten even to pretend to listen; at last he woke up; he saw Miss Parry looking rather disturbed, rather indignant, with her prominent eyes fixed. He almost cried out that he couldn't attend because he was in Hell! People began going out of the room. He heard them talking about fetching cloaks; about its being cold on the water, and so on. They were going boating on the lake by moonlight—one of Sally's mad ideas. He could hear her describing the moon. And they all went out. He was left quite alone.

'Don't you want to go with them?' said Aunt Helena—poor old lady!—she had guessed. And he turned round and there was Clarissa again. She had come back to fetch him. He was overcome by her generosity—her goodness.

'Come along,' she said. 'They're waiting.'

He had never felt so happy in the whole of his life! Without a word they made it up. They walked down to the lake. He had twenty minutes of perfect happiness. Her voice, her laugh, her dress (something floating, white, crimson), her spirit, her adventurousness; she made them all disembark and explore the island; she startled a hen; she laughed; she sang. And all the time, he knew perfectly well, Dalloway was falling in love with her; she was falling in love with Dalloway; but it didn't seem to matter. Nothing mattered. They sat on the ground and talked—he and Clarissa. They went in and out of each other's minds without any effort. And then in a second it was over. He said to himself as they were getting into the boat, 'She will marry that man,' dully, without any resentment; but it was an obvious thing. Dalloway would marry Clarissa.

Dalloway rowed them in. He said nothing. But somehow as they watched him start, jumping on to his bicycle to ride twenty miles through the woods, wobbling off down the drive, waving his hand and disappearing, he obviously did feel, instinctively, tremendously, strongly, all that; the night; the romance; Clarissa. He deserved to have her.

For himself, he was absurd. His demands upon Clarissa (he could see it now) were absurd. He asked impossible things. He made terrible scenes. She would have accepted him still, perhaps, if he had been less absurd. Sally thought so. She wrote him all that summer long letters; how they had talked of him; how she had praised him, how Clarissa burst into tears! It was an extraordinary summer—all letters, scenes, telegrams—arriving at Bourton early in the morning, hanging about till the servants were up; appalling *tête-à-têtes* with old Mr Parry at breakfast; Aunt Helena formidable but kind; Sally sweeping him off for talks in the vegetable garden; Clarissa in bed with headaches.

The final scene, the terrible scene which he believed had mattered more than anything in the whole of his life (it might be an exaggeration—but still, so it did seem now), happened at three o'clock in the afternoon of a very hot day. It was a trifle that led up to it—Sally at lunch saying something about Dalloway, and calling him 'My name is Dalloway'; whereupon Clarissa suddenly stiffened, coloured, in a way she had, and rapped out sharply, 'We've had enough of that feeble joke.' That was all; but for him it was as if she had said, 'I'm only amusing myself with you; I've an understanding with Richard Dalloway.' So he took it. He had not slept for nights. 'It's got to be finished one way or the other,' he said to himself. He sent a note to her by Sally asking her to meet him by the fountain at three. 'Something very important has happened,' he scribbled at the end of it.

The fountain was in the middle of a little shrubbery, far from the house, with shrubs and trees all round it. There she came, even before the time, and they stood with the fountain between them, the spout (it was broken) dribbling water incessantly. How sights fix themselves upon the mind! For example, the vivid green moss.

She did not move. 'Tell me the truth, tell me the truth,' he kept on saying. He felt as if his forehead would burst. She seemed contracted, petrified. She did not move. 'Tell me the truth,' he repeated, when suddenly that old man Breitkopf popped his head in carrying *The Times*; stared at them; gaped; and went away. They neither of them moved. 'Tell me the truth,' he repeated. He felt that he was grinding against something physically hard; she was unyielding. She was like iron, like flint, rigid up the backbone. And when she said, 'It's no use. It's no use. This is the end'—after he had spoken for hours, it seemed, with the tears running down his cheeks—it was as if she had hit him in the face. She turned, she left him, she went away.

'Clarissa!' he cried. 'Clarissa!' But she never came back. It was over. He went away that night. He never saw her again.

It was awful, he cried, awful, awful!

Still, the sun was hot. Still, one got over things. Still, life had a way of adding day to day. Still, he thought, yawning and beginning to take notice—Regent's Park had changed very little since he was a boy, except for the squirrels—still, presumably there were compensations—when little Elise Mitchell, who had been picking up pebbles to add to the pebble collection which she and her brother were making on the nursery mantelpiece, plumped her handful down on the nurse's knee and scudded off again full tilt into a lady's legs. Peter Walsh laughed out.

But Lucrezia Warren Smith was saying to herself, It's wicked; why should I suffer? she was asking, as she walked down the broad path. No; I can't stand it any longer, she was saying, having left Septimus, who wasn't Septimus any longer, to say hard, cruel, wicked things, to talk to himself, to talk to a dead man, on the seat over there; when the child ran full tilt into her, fell flat, and burst out crying.

That was comforting rather. She stood her upright, dusted her frock, kissed her.

But for herself she had done nothing wrong; she had loved Septimus; she had been happy; she had had a beautiful home, and there her sisters lived still, making hats. Why should *she* suffer?

The child ran straight back to its nurse, and Rezia saw her scolded, comforted, taken up by the nurse who put down her knitting, and the kind-looking man gave her his watch to blow open to comfort her—but why should *she* be exposed? Why not left in Milan? Why tortured? Why?

Slightly waved by tears, the broad path, the nurse, the man in grey, the perambulator, rose and fell before her eyes. To be rocked by this malignant torturer was her lot. But why? She was like a bird sheltering under the thin hollow of a leaf, who blinks at the sun when the leaf moves; starts at the crack of a dry twig. She was exposed; she was surrounded by the enormous trees, vast clouds of an indifferent world, exposed; tortured; and why should she suffer? Why?

She frowned; she stamped her foot. She must go back again to Septimus since it was almost time for them to be going to Sir William Bradshaw. She must go back and tell him, go back to him sitting there on the green chair under the tree, talking to himself, or to that dead man Evans, whom she had only seen once for a moment in the shop. He had seemed a nice quiet man; a great friend of Septimus's, and he had been killed in the War. But such things happen to everyone. Everyone has friends who were killed in the War. Everyone gives up something when they marry. She had given up her home. She had come to live here, in this awful city. But Septimus let himself think about horrible things, as she could too, if she tried. He had grown stranger and stranger. He said people were talking behind the bedroom walls. Mrs Filmer thought it odd. He saw things too—he had seen an old woman's head in the middle of a fern. Yet he could be happy when he chose. They went to Hampton Court on top of a bus, and they were perfectly happy. All the little red and yellow flowers were out on the grass, like floating lamps he said, and talked and chattered and laughed, making up stories. Suddenly he said, 'Now we will kill ourselves,' when they were standing by the river, and he looked at it with a look which she had seen in his eyes when a train went by, or an omnibus—a look as if something fascinated him; and she felt he was going from her and she caught him by the arm. But going home he was perfectly quiet— perfectly reasonable. He would argue with her about killing themselves; and explain how wicked people were; how he could see them making up lies as they passed in the street. He knew all their thoughts, he said; he knew everything. He knew the meaning of the world, he said.

Then when they got back he could hardly walk. He lay on the sofa and made her hold his hand to prevent him from falling down, down, he cried, into the flames! and saw faces laughing at him, calling him horrible disgusting names, from the walls and hands pointing round the screen. Yet they were quite alone. But he began to talk aloud, answering people, arguing, laughing, crying, getting very excited and making her write things down. Perfect nonsense it was; about death; about Miss Isabel Pole. She could stand it no longer. She would go back.

She was close to him now, could see him staring at the sky, muttering, clasping his hands. Yet Dr Holmes said there was nothing the matter with him. What, then, had happened—why had he gone, then, why, when she sat by him, did he start, frown at her, move away, and point at her hand, take her hand, look at it terrified?

Was it that she had taken off her wedding ring? 'My hand has grown so thin,' she said; 'I have put it in my purse,' she told him.

He dropped her hand. Their marriage was over, he thought, with agony, with relief. The rope was cut; he mounted; he was free, as it was decreed that he, Septimus, the lord of men, should be free; alone (since his wife had thrown away her wedding ring; since she had left him), he, Septimus, was alone, called forth in advance of the mass of men to hear the truth, to learn the meaning, which now at last, after all the toils of civilization—Greeks, Romans, Shakespeare, Darwin, and now himself— was to be given whole to . . . 'To whom?' he asked aloud, 'To the Prime Minister,' the voices which rustled above his head replied. The supreme secret must be told to the Cabinet; first, that trees are alive; next, there is no crime; next, love, universal love, he muttered, gasping, trembling, painfully drawing out these profound truths which needed, so deep were they, so difficult, an immense effort to speak out, but the world was entirely changed by them for ever.

No crime; love; he repeated, fumbling for his card and pencil, when a Skye terrier snuffed his trousers and he started in an agony of fear. It was turning into a man! He could not watch it happen! It was horrible, terrible to see a dog become a man! At once the dog trotted away.

Heaven was divinely merciful, infinitely benignant. It spared him, pardoned his weakness. But what was the scientific explanation (for one must be scientific above all things)? Why could he see through bodies, see into the future, when dogs will become men? It was the heat wave presumably, operating upon a brain made sensitive by eons of evolution. Scientifically speaking, the flesh was melted off the world. His body was macerated until only the nerve fibres were left. It was spread like a veil upon a rock.

He lay back in his chair, exhausted but upheld. He lay resting, waiting, before he again interpreted, with effort, with agony, to mankind. He lay very high, on the back of the world. The earth thrilled beneath him. Red flowers grew through his flesh; their stiff leaves rustled by his head. Music began clanging against the rocks up here. It is a motor horn down in the street, he muttered; but up here it cannoned from rock to rock, divided, met in shocks of sound which rose in smooth columns (that music should be visible was a discovery) and became an anthem, an anthem twined round now by a shepherd boy's piping (That's an old man playing a penny whistle by the public-house, he muttered) which, as the boy stood still, came bubbling from his pipe, and then, as he climbed higher, made its exquisite plaint while the traffic passed beneath. This boy's elegy is played among the traffic, thought Septimus.

Now he withdraws up into the snows, and roses hang about him—the thick red roses which grow on my bedroom wall, he reminded himself. The music stopped. He has his penny, he reasoned it out, and has gone on to the next public-house.

But he himself remained high on his rock, like a drowned sailor on a rock. I leant over the edge of the boat and fell down, he thought. I went under the sea. I have been dead, and yet am now alive, but let me rest still, he begged (he was talking to himself again—it was awful, awful!); and as, before waking, the voices of birds and the sound of wheels chime and chatter in a queer harmony, grow louder and louder, and the sleeper feels himself drawing to the shores of life, so he felt himself drawing towards life, the sun growing hotter, cries sounding louder, something tremendous about to happen.

He had only to open his eyes; but a weight was on them; a fear. He strained; he pushed; he looked; he saw Regent's Park before him. Long streamers of sunlight fawned at his feet. The trees waved, brandished. We welcome, the world seemed to say; we accept; we create. Beauty, the world seemed to say. And as if to prove it (scientifically) wherever he looked, at the houses, at the railings, at the antelopes stretching over the palings, beauty sprang instantly. To watch a leaf quivering in the rush of air was an exquisite joy. Up in the sky swallows swooping, swerving, flinging themselves in and out, round and round, yet always with perfect control as if elastics held them; and the flies rising and falling; and the sun spotting now this leaf, now that, in mockery, dazzling it with soft gold in pure good temper; and now and again some chime (it might be a motor horn) tinkling divinely on the grass stalks—all of this, calm and reasonable as it was, made out of ordinary things as it was, was the truth now; beauty, that was the truth now. Beauty was everywhere.

'It is time,' said Rezia.

The word 'time' split its husk; poured its riches over him; and from his lips fell like shells, like shavings from a plane, without his making them, hard, white, imperishable, words, and flew to attach themselves to their places in an ode to Time; an immortal ode to Time. He sang. Evans answered from behind the tree. The dead were in Thessaly, Evans sang, among the orchids. There they waited till the War was over, and now the dead, now Evans himself—

'For God's sake don't come!' Septimus cried out. For he could not look upon the dead.

But the branches parted. A man in grey was actually walking towards them. It was Evans! But no mud was on him; no wounds; he was not changed. I must tell the whole world, Septimus cried, raising his hand (as the dead man in the grey suit came nearer), raising his hand like some colossal figure who has lamented the fate of man for ages in the

desert alone with his hands pressed to his forehead, furrows of despair
on his cheeks, and now sees light on the desert's edge which broadens
and strikes the iron-black figure (and Septimus half rose from his chair),
and with legions of men prostrate behind him he, the giant mourner,
receives for one moment on his face the whole—

'But I am so unhappy, Septimus,' said Rezia, trying to make him sit
down.

The millions lamented; for ages they had sorrowed. He would turn
round, he would tell them in a few moments, only a few moments more,
of this relief, of this joy, of this astonishing revelation—

'The time, Septimus,' Rezia repeated. 'What is the time?'

He was talking, he was starting, this man must notice him. He was
looking at them.

'I will tell you the time,' said Septimus, very slowly, very drowsily,
smiling mysteriously at the dead man in the grey suit. As he sat smiling,
the quarter struck—the quarter to twelve.

And that is being young, Peter Walsh thought as he passed them. To
be having an awful scene—the poor girl looked absolutely desperate—
in the middle of the morning. But what was it about? he wondered;
what had the young man in the overcoat been saying to her to make her
look like that; what awful fix had they got themselves into, both to look
so desperate as that on a fine summer morning? The amusing thing
about coming back to England, after five years, was the way it made,
anyhow the first days, things stand out as if one had never seen them
before; lovers squabbling under a tree; the domestic family life of the
parks. Never had he seen London look so enchanting—the softness of
the distances; the richness; the greenness, the civilization, after India,
he thought, strolling across the grass.

This susceptibility to impressions had been his undoing, no doubt.
Still at his age he had, like a boy or a girl even, these alternations of
mood; good days, bad days, for no reason whatever, happiness from a
pretty face, downright misery at the sight of a frump. After India of
course one fell in love with every woman one met. There was a freshness
about them; even the poorest dressed better than five years ago surely;
and to his eye the fashions had never been so becoming; the long black
cloaks; the slimness; the elegance; and then the delicious and apparently
universal habit of paint. Every woman, even the most respectable, had
roses blooming under glass; lips cut with a knife; curls of Indian ink;
there was design, art, everywhere; a change of some sort had undoubtedly taken place. What did the young people think about? Peter Walsh
asked himself.

Those five years—1918 to 1923—had been, he suspected, somehow
very important. People looked different. Newspapers seemed different.

Now, for instance, there was a man writing quite openly in one of the respectable weeklies about water-closets. That you couldn't have done ten years ago—written quite openly about water-closets in a respectable weekly. And then this taking out a stick of rouge, or a powder-puff, and making up in public. On board ship coming home there were lots of young men and girls—Betty and Bertie he remembered in particular—carrying on quite openly; the old mother sitting and watching them with her knitting, cool as a cucumber. The girl would stand still and powder her nose in front of everyone. And they weren't engaged; just having a good time; no feelings hurt on either side. As hard as nails she was—Betty Whatshername—but a thorough good sort. She would make a very good wife at thirty—she would marry when it suited her to marry; marry some rich man and live in a large house near Manchester.

Who was it now who had done that? Peter Walsh asked himself, turning into the Broad Walk—married a rich man and lived in a large house near Manchester? Somebody who had written him a long, gushing letter quite lately about 'blue hydrangeas'. It was seeing blue hydrangeas that made her think of him and the old days—Sally Seton, of course! It was Sally Seton—the last person in the world one would have expected to marry a rich man and live in a large house near Manchester, the wild, the daring, the romantic Sally!

But of all that ancient lot, Clarissa's friends—Whitbreads, Kindersleys, Cunninghams, Kinloch Jones's—Sally was probably the best. She tried to get hold of things by the right end anyhow. She saw through Hugh Whitbread anyhow—the admirable Hugh—when Clarissa and the rest were at his feet.

'The Whitbreads?' he could hear her saying. 'Who are the Whitbreads? Coal merchants. Respectable trades-people.'

Hugh she detested for some reason. He thought of nothing but his own appearance, she said. He ought to have been a Duke. He would be certain to marry one of the Royal Princesses. And of course Hugh had the most extraordinary, the most natural, the most sublime respect for the British aristocracy of any human being he had ever come across. Even Clarissa had to own that. Oh, but he was such a dear, so unselfish, gave up shooting to please his old mother—remembered his aunts' birthdays, and so on.

Sally, to do her justice, saw through all that. One of the things he remembered best was an argument one Sunday morning at Bourton about women's rights (that antediluvian topic), when Sally suddenly lost her temper, flared up, and told Hugh that he represented all that was most detestable in British middle-class life. She told him that she considered him responsible for the state of 'those poor girls in Piccadilly'—Hugh, the perfect gentleman, poor Hugh!—never did a man look more horrified! She did it on purpose, she said afterwards (for they used to get together in the vegetable garden and compare notes). 'He's read nothing, thought nothing, felt nothing,' he could hear her saying in that very emphatic voice which carried so much farther than she knew. The stable boys had more life in them than Hugh, she said. He was a perfect specimen of the public-school type, she said. No country but England could have produced him. She was really spiteful, for some reason; had some grudge against him. Something had happened—he forgot what—in the smoking-room. He had insulted her—kissed her? Incredible! Nobody believed a word against Hugh, of course. Who could? Kissing Sally in the smoking-room! If it had been some Honourable Edith or Lady Violet, perhaps; but not that ragamuffin Sally without a penny to her name, and a father or a mother gambling at Monte Carlo. For of all the people he had ever met Hugh was the greatest snob—the most obsequious—no, he didn't cringe exactly. He was too much of a prig for that. A first-rate valet was the obvious comparison—somebody who walked behind carrying suitcases; could be trusted to send telegrams—indispensable to hostesses. And he'd found his job—married his Honourable Evelyn; got some little post at Court, looked after the King's cellars, polished the Imperial shoe-buckles, went about in knee-breeches and lace ruffles. How remorseless life is! A little job at Court!

He had married this lady, the Honourable Evelyn, and they lived hereabouts, so he thought (looking at the pompous houses overlooking the Park), for he had lunched there once in a house which had, like all Hugh's possessions, something that no other house could possibly have—linen cupboards it might have been. You had to go and look at them—you had to spend a great deal of time always admiring whatever it was—linen cupboards, pillow-cases, old oak furniture, pictures, which Hugh had picked up for an old song. But Mrs Hugh sometimes gave the show away. She was one of those obscure mouse-like little women who admire big men. She was almost negligible. Then suddenly she would say something quite unexpected—something sharp. She had the relics of the grand manner, perhaps. The steam coal was a little too strong for her—it made the atmosphere thick. And so there they lived, with their linen cupboards and their old masters and their pillow-cases fringed with real lace, at the rate of five or ten thousand a year presumably, while he, who was two years older than Hugh, cadged for a job.

At fifty-three he had to come and ask them to put him into some secretary's office, to find him some usher's job teaching little boys Latin, at the beck and call of some mandarin in an office, something that brought in five hundred a year; for if he married Daisy, even with his pension, they could never do on less. Whitbread could do it presumably;

or Dalloway. He didn't mind what he asked Dalloway. He was a thorough good sort; a bit limited; a bit thick in the head; yes; but a thorough good sort. Whatever he took up he did in the same matter-of-fact sensible way; without a touch of imagination, without a spark of brilliancy, but with the inexplicable niceness of his type. He ought to have been a country gentleman—he was wasted on politics. He was at his best out of doors, with horses and dogs—how good he was, for instance, when that great shaggy dog of Clarissa's got caught in a trap and had its paw half torn off, and Clarissa turned faint and Dalloway did the whole thing; bandaged, made splints; told Clarissa not to be a fool. That was what she liked him for, perhaps—that was what she needed. 'Now, my dear, don't be a fool. Hold this—fetch that,' all the time talking to the dog as if it were a human being.

But how could she swallow all that stuff about poetry? How could she let him hold forth about Shakespeare? Seriously and solemnly Richard Dalloway got on his hind legs and said that no decent man ought to read Shakespeare's sonnets because it was like listening at keyholes (besides, the relationship was not one that he approved). No decent man ought to let his wife visit a deceased wife's sister. Incredible! The only thing to do was to pelt him with sugared almonds—it was at dinner. But Clarissa sucked it all in; thought it so honest of him; so independent of him; Heaven knows if she didn't think him the most original mind she'd ever met!

That was one of the bonds between Sally and himself. There was a garden where they used to walk, a walled-in place, with rose-bushes and giant cauliflowers—he could remember Sally tearing off a rose, stopping to exclaim at the beauty of the cabbage leaves in the moonlight (it was extraordinary how vividly it all came back to him, things he hadn't thought of for years), while she implored him, half laughing of course, to carry off Clarissa, to save her from the Hughs and the Dalloways and all the other 'perfect gentlemen' who would 'stifle her soul' (she wrote reams of poetry in those days), make a mere hostess of her, encourage her worldliness. But one must do Clarissa justice. She wasn't going to marry Hugh anyhow. She had a perfectly clear notion of what she wanted. Her emotions were all on the surface. Beneath, she was very shrewd—a far better judge of character than Sally, for instance, and with it all, purely feminine; with that extraordinary gift, that woman's gift, of making a world of her own wherever she happened to be. She came into a room; she stood, as he had often seen her, in a doorway with lots of people round her. But it was Clarissa one remembered. Not that she was striking; not beautiful at all; there was nothing picturesque about her; she never said anything specially clever; there she was, however; there she was.

No, no, no! He was not in love with her any more! He only felt, after
seeing her that morning, among her scissors and silks, making ready for
the party, unable to get away from the thought of her; she kept coming
back and back like a sleeper jolting against him in a railway carriage;
which was not being in love, of course; it was thinking of her, criticizing
her, starting again, after thirty years, trying to explain her. The obvious
thing to say of her was that she was worldly; cared too much for rank
and society and getting on in the world—which was true in a sense; she
had admitted it to him. (You could always get her to own up if you took
the trouble; she was honest.) What she would say was that she hated
frumps, fogies, failures, like himself presumably; thought people had no
right to slouch about with their hands in their pockets; must do
something, be something; and these great swells, these Duchesses, these
hoary old Countesses one met in her drawing-room, unspeakably remote
as he felt them to be from anything that mattered a straw, stood for
something real to her. Lady Bexborough, she said once, held herself
upright (so did Clarissa herself; she never lounged in any sense of the
word; she was straight as a dart, a little rigid in fact). She said they had
a kind of courage which the older she grew the more she respected. In
all this there was a great deal of Dalloway, of course; a great deal of the
public-spirited, British Empire, tariff-reform, governing-class spirit,
which had grown on her, as it tends to do. With twice his wits, she had
to see things through his eyes—one of the tragedies of married life. With
a mind of her own, she must always be quoting Richard—as if one
couldn't know to a tittle what Richard thought by reading the *Morning
Post* of a morning! These parties, for example, were all for him, or for
her idea of him (to do Richard justice he would have been happier
farming in Norfolk). She made her drawing-room a sort of meeting-
place; she had a genius for it. Over and over again he had seen her take
some raw youth, twist him, turn him, wake him up; set him going.
Infinite numbers of dull people conglomerated round her, of course. But
odd unexpected people turned up; an artist sometimes; sometimes a
writer; queer fish in that atmosphere. And behind it all was that network
of visiting, leaving cards, being kind to people; running about with
bunches of flowers, little presents; So-and-so was going to France—must
have an air-cushion; a real drain on her strength; all that interminable
traffic that women of her sort keep up; but she did it genuinely, from a
natural instinct.

Oddly enough, she was one of the most thorough-going sceptics he
had ever met, and possibly (this was a theory he used to make up to
account for her, so transparent in some ways, so inscrutable in others),
possibly she said to herself, As we are a doomed race, chained to a

sinking ship (her favourite reading as a girl was Huxley and Tyndall, and they were fond of these nautical metaphors), as the whole thing is a bad joke, let us, at any rate, do our part; mitigate the sufferings of our fellow-prisoners (Huxley again); decorate the dungeon with flowers and air-cushions; be as decent as we possibly can. Those ruffians, the Gods, shan't have it all their own way—her notion being that the Gods, who never lost a chance of hurting, thwarting and spoiling human lives, were seriously put out if, all the same, you behaved like a lady. That phase came directly after Sylvia's death—that horrible affair. To see your own sister killed by a falling tree (all Justin Parry's fault—all his carelessness) before your very eyes, a girl too on the verge of life, the most gifted of them, Clarissa always said, was enough to turn one bitter. Later she wasn't so positive, perhaps; she thought there were no Gods; no one was to blame; and so she evolved this atheist's religion of doing good for the sake of goodness.

And of course she enjoyed life immensely. It was her nature to enjoy (though, goodness only knows, she had her reserves; it was a mere sketch, he often felt, that even he, after all these years, could make of Clarissa). Anyhow there was no bitterness in her; none of that sense of moral virtue which is so repulsive in good women. She enjoyed practically everything. If you walked with her in Hyde Park, now it was a bed of tulips, now a child in a perambulator, now some absurd little drama she made up on the spur of the moment. (Very likely she would have talked to those lovers, if she had thought them unhappy.) She had a sense of comedy that was really exquisite, but she needed people, always people, to bring it out, with the inevitable result that she frittered her time away, lunching, dining, giving these incessant parties of hers, talking nonsense, saying things she didn't mean, blunting the edge of her mind, losing her discrimination. There she would sit at the head of the table taking infinite pains with some old buffer who might be useful to Dalloway—they knew the most appalling bores in Europe—or in came Elizabeth and everything must give way to her. She was at a High School, at the inarticulate stage last time he was over, a round-eyed, pale-faced girl, with nothing of her mother in her, a silent, stolid creature, who took it all as a matter of course, let her mother make a fuss of her, and then said 'May I go now?' like a child of four; going off, Clarissa explained, with that mixture of amusement and pride which Dalloway himself seemed to rouse in her, to play hockey. And now Elizabeth was 'out', presumably; thought him an old fogy, laughed at her mother's friends. Ah well, so be it. The compensation of growing old, Peter Walsh thought, coming out of Regent's Park, and holding his hat in his hand, was simply this; that the passions remain as strong as

ever, but one has gained—at last!—the power which adds the supreme
flavour to existence—the power of taking hold of experience, of turning
it round, slowly, in the light.

A terrible confession it was (he put his hat on again), but now, at the
age of fifty-three, one scarcely needed people any more. Life itself, every
moment of it, every drop of it, here, this instant, now, in the sun, in
Regent's Park, was enough. Too much, indeed. A whole lifetime was too
short to bring out, now that one had acquired the power, the full flavour;
to extract every ounce of pleasure, every shade of meaning; which both
were so much more solid than they used to be, so much less personal. It
was impossible that he should ever suffer again as Clarissa had made
him suffer. For hours at a time (pray God that one might say these
things without being overheard!), for hours and days he never thought
of Daisy.

Could it be that he was in love with her, then, remembering the
misery, the torture, the extraordinary passion of those days? It was a
different thing altogether—a much pleasanter thing—the truth being,
of course, that now *she* was in love with *him*. And that perhaps was the
reason why, when the ship actually sailed, he felt an extraordinary relief,
wanted nothing so much as to be alone; was annoyed to find all her little
attentions—cigars, notes, a rug for the voyage—in his cabin. Everyone
if they were honest would say the same; one doesn't want people after
fifty; one doesn't want to go on telling women they are pretty; that's
what most men of fifty would say, Peter Walsh thought, if they were
honest.

But then these astonishing accesses of emotion—bursting into tears
this morning, what was all that about? What could Clarissa have
thought of him? thought him a fool presumably, not for the first time. It
was jealousy that was at the bottom of it—jealousy which survives every
other passion of mankind, Peter Walsh thought, holding his pocket-knife
at arm's length. She had been meeting Major Orde, Daisy said in her
last letter; said it on purpose, he knew; said it to make him jealous; he
could see her wrinkling her forehead as she wrote, wondering what she
could say to hurt him; and yet it made no difference; he was furious! All
this pother of coming to England and seeing lawyers wasn't to marry
her, but to prevent her from marrying anybody else. That was what
tortured him, that was what came over him when he saw Clarissa so
calm, so cold, so intent on her dress or whatever it was; realizing what
she might have spared him, what she had reduced him to—a whimpering, snivelling old ass. But women, he thought, shutting his pocket-
knife, don't know what passion is. They don't know the meaning of it to
men. Clarissa was as cold as an icicle. There she would sit on the sofa

by his side, let him take her hand, give him one kiss on the cheek——
Here he was at the crossing.

A sound interrupted him; a frail quivering sound, a voice bubbling up
without direction, vigour, beginning or end, running weakly and shrilly
and with an absence of all human meaning into

> ee um fah um so
> foo swee too eem oo——

the voice of no age or sex, the voice of an ancient spring spouting from
the earth; which issued, just opposite Regent's Park Tube Station, from
a tall quivering shape, like a funnel, like a rusty pump, like a wind-
beaten tree for ever barren of leaves which lets the wind run up and
down its branches singing

> ee um fah um so
> foo swee too eem oo,

and rocks and creaks and moans in the eternal breeze.

Through all ages—when the pavement was grass, when it was swamp,
through the age of tusk and mammoth, through the age of silent
sunrise—the battered woman—for she wore a skirt—with her right
hand exposed, her left clutching at her side, stood singing of love—love
which has lasted a million years, she sang, love which prevails, and
millions of years ago her lover, who had been dead these centuries, had
walked, she crooned, with her in May; but in the course of ages, long as
summer days, and flaming, she remembered, with nothing but red
asters, he had gone; death's enormous sickle had swept those tremendous
hills, and when at last she laid her hoary and immensely aged head on
the earth, now become a mere cinder of ice, she implored the Gods to
lay by her side a bunch of purple heather, there on her high burial place
which the last rays of the last sun caressed; for then the pageant of the
universe would be over.

As the ancient song bubbled up opposite Regent's Park Tube Station,
still the earth seemed green and flowery; still, though it issued from so
rude a mouth, a mere hole in the earth, muddy too, matted with root
fibres and tangled grasses, still the old bubbling burbling song, soaking
through the knotted roots of infinite ages, and skeletons and treasure,
streamed away in rivulets over the pavement and all along the Maryle-
bone Road, and down towards Euston, fertilizing, leaving a damp stain.

Still remembering how once in some primeval May she had walked
with her lover, this rusty pump, this battered old woman with one hand
exposed for coppers, the other clutching her side, would still be there in
ten million years, remembering how once she had walked in May, where

the sea flows now, with whom it did not matter—he was a man, oh yes, a man who had loved her. But the passage of ages had blurred the clarity of that ancient May day; the bright-petalled flowers were hoar and silver frosted; and she no longer saw, when she implored him (as she did now quite clearly) 'look in my eyes with thy sweet eyes intently', she no longer saw brown eyes, black whiskers or sunburnt face, but only a looming shape, a shadow shape, to which, with the bird-like freshness of the very aged, she still twittered 'give me your hand and let me press it gently' (Peter Walsh couldn't help giving the poor creature a coin as he stepped into his taxi), 'and if someone should see, what matter they?' she demanded; and her fist clutched at her side, and she smiled, pocketing her shilling, and all peering inquisitive eyes seemed blotted out, and the passing generations—the pavement was crowded with bustling middle-class people—vanished, like leaves, to be trodden under, to be soaked and steeped and made mould of by that eternal spring—

> ee um fah um so
> foo swee too eem oo.

'Poor old woman,' said Rezia Warren Smith.

Oh, poor old wretch! she said, waiting to cross.

Suppose it was a wet night? Suppose one's father, or somebody who had known one in better days had happened to pass, and saw one standing there in the gutter? And where did she sleep at night?

Cheerfully, almost gaily, the invincible thread of sound wound up into the air like the smoke from a cottage chimney, winding up clean beech trees and issuing in a tuft of blue smoke among the topmost leaves. 'And if someone should see, what matter they?'

Since she was so unhappy, for weeks and weeks now, Rezia had given meanings to things that happened, almost felt sometimes that she must stop people in the street, if they looked good, kind people, just to say to them 'I am unhappy'; and this old woman singing in the street 'if someone should see, what matter they?' made her suddenly quite sure that everything was going to be right. They were going to Sir William Bradshaw; she thought his name sounded nice; he would cure Septimus at once. And then there was a brewer's cart; and the grey horses had upright bristles of straw in their tails; there were newspaper placards. It was a silly, silly dream, being unhappy.

So they crossed, Mr and Mrs Septimus Warren Smith, and was there, after all, anything to draw attention to them, anything to make a passer-by suspect here is a young man who carries in him the greatest message in the world, and is, moreover, the happiest man in the world, and the most miserable? Perhaps they walked more slowly than other people, and there was something hesitating, trailing, in the man's walk, but what more natural for a clerk, who has not been in the West End on a weekday at this hour for years, than to keep looking at the sky, looking at this, that and the other, as if Portland Place were a room he had come into when the family are away, the chandeliers being hung in holland bags, and the caretaker, as she lets in long shafts of dusty light upon deserted, queer-looking armchairs, lifting one corner of the long blinds, explains to the visitors what a wonderful place it is; how wonderful, but at the same time, he thinks, how strange.

To look at, he might have been a clerk, but of the better sort; for he wore brown boots; his hands were educated; so, too, his profile—his angular, big-nosed, intelligent, sensitive profile; but not his lips altogether, for they were loose; and his eyes (as eyes tend to be), eyes merely; hazel, large; so that he was, on the whole, a border case, neither one thing nor the other; might end with a house at Purley and a motor car, or continue renting apartments in back streets all his life; one of those half-educated, self-educated men whose education is all learnt from books borrowed from public libraries, read in the evening after the day's work, on the advice of well-known authors consulted by letter.

As for the other experiences, the solitary ones, which people go through alone, in their bedrooms, in their offices, walking the fields and the streets of London, he had them; had left home, a mere boy, because of his mother; she lied; because he came down to tea for the fiftieth time with his hands unwashed; because he could see no future for a poet in Stroud; and so, making a confidant of his little sister, had gone to London leaving an absurd note behind him, such as great men have written, and the world has read later when the story of their struggles has become famous.

London has swallowed up many millions of young men called Smith; thought nothing of fantastic Christian names like Septimus with which their parents have thought to distinguish them. Lodging off the Euston Road, there were experiences, again experiences, such as change a face in two years from a pink innocent oval to a face lean, contracted, hostile. But of all this what could the most observant of friends have said except what a gardener says when he opens the conservatory door in the morning and finds a new blossom on his plant: It has flowered; flowered from vanity, ambition, idealism, passion, loneliness, courage, laziness, the usual seeds, which all muddled up (in a room off the Euston Road), made him shy, and stammering, made him anxious to improve himself, made him fall in love with Miss Isabel Pole, lecturing in the Waterloo Road upon Shakespeare.

Was he not like Keats? she asked; and reflected how she might give him a taste of *Antony and Cleopatra* and the rest; lent him books; wrote him scraps of letters; and lit in him such a fire as burns only once in a lifetime, without heat, flickering a red-gold flame infinitely ethereal and insubstantial over Miss Pole; *Antony and Cleopatra*; and the Waterloo Road. He thought her beautiful, believed her impeccably wise; dreamed of her, wrote poems to her, which, ignoring the subject, she corrected in red ink; he saw her, one summer evening, walking in a green dress in a square. 'It has flowered,' the gardener might have said, had he opened the door; had he come in, that is to say, any night about this time, and found him writing; found him tearing up his writing; found him finishing a masterpiece at three o'clock in the morning and running out to pace the streets, and visiting churches, and fasting one day, drinking another, devouring Shakespeare, Darwin, *The History of Civilisation*, and Bernard Shaw.

Something was up, Mr Brewer knew; Mr Brewer, managing clerk at Sibleys and Arrowsmiths, auctioneers, valuers, land and estate agents; something was up, he thought, and, being paternal with his young men, and thinking very highly of Smith's abilities, and prophesying that he would, in ten or fifteen years, succeed to the leather armchair in the inner room under the skylight with the deed-boxes round him, 'if he keeps his health,' said Mr Brewer, and that was the danger—he looked weakly; advised football, invited him to supper and was seeing his way to consider recommending a rise of salary, when something happened which threw out many of Mr Brewer's calculations, took away his ablest young fellows, and eventually, so prying and insidious were the fingers of the European War, smashed a plaster cast of Ceres, ploughed a hole in the geranium beds, and utterly ruined the cook's nerves at Mr Brewer's establishment at Muswell Hill.

Septimus was one of the first to volunteer. He went to France to save an England which consisted almost entirely of Shakespeare's plays and Miss Isabel Pole in a green dress walking in a square. There in the trenches the change which Mr Brewer desired when he advised football was produced instantly; he developed manliness; he was promoted; he drew the attention, indeed the affection of his officer, Evans by name. It was a case of two dogs playing on a hearth-rug; one worrying a paper screw, snarling, snapping, giving a pinch, now and then, at the old dog's ear; the other lying somnolent, blinking at the fire, raising a paw, turning and growling good-temperedly. They had to be together, share with each other, fight with each other, quarrel with each other. But when Evans (Rezia, who had only seen him once, called him 'a quiet man', a sturdy red-haired man, undemonstrative in the company of women), when Evans was killed, just before the Armistice, in Italy, Septimus, far from showing any emotion or recognizing that here was the end of a friendship, congratulated himself upon feeling very little and very reasonably. The War had taught him. It was sublime. He had gone through the whole show, friendship, European War, death, had won promotion, was still under thirty and was bound to survive. He was right there. The last shells missed him. He watched them explode with indifference. When peace came he was in Milan, billeted in the house of an innkeeper with a courtyard, flowers in tubs, little tables in the open, daughters making hats, and to Lucrezia, the younger daughter, he became engaged one evening when the panic was on him—that he could not feel.

For now that it was all over, truce signed, and the dead buried, he had, especially in the evening, these sudden thunder-claps of fear. He could not feel. As he opened the door of the room where the Italian girls sat making hats, he could see them; could hear them; they were rubbing wires among coloured beads in saucers; they were turning buckram shapes this way and that; the table was all strewn with feathers, spangles, silks, ribbons; scissors were rapping on the table; but something failed him; he could not feel. Still, scissors rapping, girls laughing, hats being made protected him; he was assured of safety; he had a refuge. But he could not sit there all night. There were moments of waking in the early morning. The bed was falling; he was falling. Oh for the scissors and the lamplight and the buckram shapes! He asked Lucrezia to marry him, the younger of the two, the gay, the frivolous, with those little artist's fingers that she would hold up and say 'It is all in them.' Silk, feathers, what not, were alive to them.

'It is the hat that matters most,' she would say, when they walked out together. Every hat that passed she would examine; and the cloak and the dress and the way the woman held herself. Ill-dressing, over-dressing she stigmatized, not savagely, rather with impatient movements of the hands, like those of a painter who puts from him some obvious well-meant glaring imposture; and then, generously, but always critically, she would welcome a shop-girl who had turned her little bit of stuff gallantly, or praise, wholly, with enthusiastic and professional understanding, a French lady descending from her carriage, in chinchilla, robes, pearls.

'Beautiful!' she would murmur, nudging Septimus, that he might see. But beauty was behind a pane of glass. Even taste (Rezia liked ices, chocolates, sweet things) had no relish to him. He put down his cup on the little marble table. He looked at people outside; happy they seemed, collecting in the middle of the street, shouting, laughing, squabbling over nothing. But he could not taste, he could not feel. In the tea-shop among the tables and the chattering waiters the appalling fear came over him—he could not feel. He could reason; he could read, Dante for example, quite easily ('Septimus, do put down your book,' said Rezia, gently shutting the *Inferno*), he could add up his bill; his brain was perfect; it must be the fault of the world then—that he could not feel.

'The English are so silent,' Rezia said. She liked it, she said. She respected these Englishmen, and wanted to see London, and the English horses, and the tailor-made suits, and could remember hearing how wonderful the shops were, from an aunt who had married and lived in Soho.

It might be possible, Septimus thought, looking at England from the train window, as they left Newhaven; it might be possible that the world itself is without meaning.

At the office they advanced him to a post of considerable responsibility. They were proud of him; he had won crosses. 'You have done your duty; it is up to us——' began Mr Brewer; and could not finish, so pleasurable was his emotion. They took admirable lodgings off the Tottenham Court Road.

Here he opened Shakespeare once more. That boy's business of the intoxication of language—*Antony and Cleopatra*—had shrivelled utterly. How Shakespeare loathed humanity—the putting on of clothes, the getting of children, the sordidity of the mouth and the belly! This was now revealed to Septimus; the message hidden in the beauty of words. The secret signal which one generation passes, under disguise, to the next is loathing, hatred, despair. Dante the same. Aeschylus (translated) the same. There Rezia sat at the table trimming hats. She trimmed hats for Mrs Filmer's friends; she trimmed hats by the hour. She looked pale, mysterious, like a lily, drowned, under water, he thought.

'The English are so serious,' she would say, putting her arms round Septimus, her cheek against his.

Love between man and woman was repulsive to Shakespeare. The business of copulation was filth to him before the end. But, Rezia said, she must have children. They had been married five years.

They went to the Tower together; to the Victoria and Albert Museum; stood in the crowd to see the King open Parliament. And there were the shops—hat shops, dress shops, shops with leather bags in the window, where she would stand staring. But she must have a boy.

She must have a son like Septimus, she said. But nobody could be like Septimus; so gentle; so serious; so clever. Could she not read Shakespeare too? Was Shakespeare a difficult author? she asked.

One cannot bring children into a world like this. One cannot perpetrate suffering, or increase the breed of these lustful animals, who have no lasting emotions, but only whims and vanities, eddying them now this way, now that.

He watched her snip, shape, as one watches a bird hop, flit in the grass, without daring to move a finger. For the truth is (let her ignore it) that human beings have neither kindness, nor faith, nor charity beyond what serves to increase the pleasure of the moment. They hunt in packs. Their packs scour the desert and vanish screaming into the wilderness. They desert the fallen. They are plastered over with grimaces. There was Brewer at the office, with his waxed moustache, coral tie-pin, white slip, and pleasurable emotions—all coldness and clamminess within,—his geraniums ruined in the War—his cook's nerves destroyed; or Amelia Whatshername, handing round cups of tea punctually at five—a leering, sneering, obscene little harpy; and the Toms and Berties in their starched shirt fronts oozing thick drops of vice. They never saw him drawing pictures of them naked at their antics in his notebook. In the street, vans roared past him; brutality blared out on placards, men were trapped in mines; women burnt alive; and once a maimed file of lunatics being exercised or displayed for the diversion of the populace (who laughed aloud) ambled and nodded and grinned past him, in the Tottenham Court Road, each half apologetically, yet triumphantly, inflicting his hopeless woe. And would *he* go mad?

At tea Rezia told him that Mrs Filmer's daughter was expecting a baby. *She* could not grow old and have no children! She was very lonely, she was very unhappy! She cried for the first time since they were married. Far away he heard her sobbing; he heard it accurately, he noticed it distinctly; he compared it to a piston thumping. But he felt nothing.

His wife was crying, and he felt nothing; only each time she sobbed in this profound, this silent, this hopeless way, he descended another step into the pit.

At last, with a melodramatic gesture which he assumed mechanically and with complete consciousness of its insincerity, he dropped his head on his hands. Now he had surrendered; now other people must help him. People must be sent for. He gave in.

Nothing could rouse him. Rezia put him to bed. She sent for a doctor—Mrs Filmer's Dr Holmes. Dr Holmes examined him. There was nothing whatever the matter, said Dr Holmes. Oh, what a relief! What a kind man, what a good man! thought Rezia. When he felt like that he went to the Music Hall, said Dr Holmes. He took a day off with his wife and played golf. Why not try two tabloids of bromide dissolved in a glass of water at bedtime? These old Bloomsbury houses, said Dr Holmes, tapping the wall, are often full of very fine panelling, which the landlords have the folly to paper over. Only the other day, visiting a patient, Sir Somebody Something, in Bedford Square—

So there was no excuse; nothing whatever the matter, except the sin for which human nature had condemned him to death; that he did not feel. He had not cared when Evans was killed; that was worst; but all the other crimes raised their heads and shook their fingers and jeered and sneered over the rail of the bed in the early hours of the morning at the prostrate body which lay realizing its degradation; how he had married his wife without loving her; had lied to her; seduced her; outraged Miss Isabel Pole, and was so pocked and marked with vice that women shuddered when they saw him in the street. The verdict of human nature on such a wretch was death.

Dr Holmes came again. Large, fresh-coloured, handsome, flicking his boots, looking in the glass, he brushed it all aside—headaches, sleeplessness, fears, dreams—nerve symptoms and nothing more, he said. If Dr Holmes found himself even half a pound below eleven stone six, he asked his wife for another plate of porridge at breakfast. (Rezia would learn to cook porridge.) But, he continued, health is largely a matter in our own control. Throw yourself into outside interests; take up some hobby. He opened Shakespeare—*Antony and Cleopatra*; pushed Shakespeare aside. Some hobby, said Dr Holmes, for did he not owe his own excellent health (and he worked as hard as any man in London) to the fact that he could always switch off from his patients on to old furniture? And what a very pretty comb, if he might say so, Mrs Warren Smith was wearing!

When the damned fool came again, Septimus refused to see him. Did he indeed? said Dr Holmes, smiling agreeably. Really he had to give that charming little lady, Mrs Smith, a friendly push before he could get past her into her husband's bedroom.

'So you're in a funk,' he said agreeably, sitting down by his patient's side. He had actually talked of killing himself to his wife, quite a girl, a foreigner, wasn't she? Didn't that give her a very odd idea of English husbands? Didn't one owe perhaps a duty to one's wife? Wouldn't it be better to do something instead of lying in bed? For he had had forty years' experience behind him; and Septimus could take Dr Holmes's word for it—there was nothing whatever the matter with him. And next time Dr Holmes came he hoped to find Smith out of bed and not making that charming little lady his wife anxious about him.

Human nature, in short, was on him—the repulsive brute, with the blood-red nostrils. Holmes was on him. Dr Holmes came quite regularly every day. Once you stumble, Septimus wrote on the back of a postcard, human nature is on you. Holmes is on you. Their only chance was to escape, without letting Holmes know; to Italy—anywhere, anywhere, away from Dr Holmes.

But Rezia could not understand him. Dr Holmes was such a kind man. He was so interested in Septimus. He only wanted to help them, he said. He had four little children and he had asked her to tea, she told Septimus.

So he was deserted. The whole world was clamouring: Kill yourself, kill yourself, for our sakes. But why should he kill himself for their sakes? Food was pleasant; the sun hot; and this killing oneself, how does one set about it, with a table knife, uglily, with floods of blood,—by sucking a gas-pipe? He was too weak; he could scarcely raise his hand. Besides, now that he was quite alone, condemned, deserted, as those who are about to die are alone, there was a luxury in it, an isolation full of sublimity; a freedom which the attached can never know. Holmes had won of course; the brute with the red nostrils had won. But even Holmes himself could not touch this last relic straying on the edge of the world, this outcast, who gazed back at the inhabited regions, who lay, like a drowned sailor, on the shore of the world.

It was at that moment (Rezia had gone shopping) that the great revelation took place. A voice spoke from behind the screen. Evans was speaking. The dead were with him.

'Evans, Evans!' he cried.

Mr Smith was talking aloud to himself, Agnes the servant girl cried to Mrs Filmer in the kitchen. 'Evans, Evans!' he had said as she brought in the tray. She jumped, she did. She scuttled downstairs.

And Rezia came in, with her flowers, and walked across the room, and put the roses in a vase, upon which the sun struck directly, and went laughing, leaping round the room.

She had had to buy the roses, Rezia said, from a poor man in the street. But they were almost dead already, she said, arranging the roses.

So there was a man outside; Evans presumably; and the roses, which Rezia said were half dead, had been picked by him in the fields of Greece. Communication is health; communication is happiness. Communication, he muttered.

'What are you saying, Septimus?' Rezia asked, wild with terror, for he was talking to himself.

She sent Agnes running for Dr Holmes. Her husband, she said, was mad. He scarcely knew her.

'You brute! You brute!' cried Septimus, seeing human nature, that is Dr Holmes, enter the room.

'Now what's all this about,' said Dr Holmes in the most amiable way in the world. 'Talking nonsense to frighten your wife?' But he would give him something to make him sleep. And if they were rich people, said Dr Holmes, looking ironically round the room, by all means let them go to Harley Street; if they had no confidence in him, said Dr Holmes, looking not quite so kind.

It was precisely twelve o'clock; twelve by Big Ben; whose stroke was wafted over the northern part of London; blent with that of other clocks, mixed in a thin ethereal way with the clouds and wisps of smoke and died up there among the seagulls—twelve o'clock struck as Clarissa Dalloway laid her green dress on her bed, and the Warren Smiths walked down Harley Street. Twelve was the hour of their appointment. Probably, Rezia thought, that was Sir William Bradshaw's house with the grey motor car in front of it. (The leaden circles dissolved in the air.)

Indeed it was—Sir William Bradshaw's motor car; low, powerful, grey with plain initials interlocked on the panel, as if the pomps of heraldry were incongruous, this man being the ghostly helper, the priest of science; and, as the motor car was grey, so, to match its sober suavity, grey furs, silver grey rugs were heaped in it, to keep her ladyship warm while she waited. For often Sir William would travel sixty miles or more down into the country to visit the rich, the afflicted, who could afford the very large fee which Sir William very properly charged for his advice. Her ladyship waited with the rugs about her knees an hour or more, leaning back, thinking sometimes of the patient, sometimes, excusably, of the wall of gold, mounting minute by minute while she waited; the wall of gold that was mounting between them and all shifts and anxieties (she had borne them bravely; they had had their struggles), until she felt wedged on a calm ocean, where only spice winds blow; respected, admired, envied, with scarcely anything left to wish for, though she regretted her stoutness; large dinner-parties every Thursday night to the profession; an occasional bazaar to be opened; Royalty greeted; too little time, alas, with her husband, whose work grew and grew; a boy doing well at Eton; she would have liked a daughter too; interests she had, however, in plenty; child welfare; the after-care of the epileptic, and photography, so that if there was a church building, or a church decaying, she bribed the sexton, got the key and took photographs, which were scarcely to be distinguished from the work of professionals, while she waited.

Sir William himself was no longer young. He had worked very hard; he had won his position by sheer ability (being the son of a shop-keeper); loved his profession; made a fine figurehead at ceremonies and spoke well—all of which had by the time he was knighted given him a heavy look, a weary look (the stream of patients being so incessant, the responsibilities and privileges of his profession so onerous), which weariness, together with his grey hairs, increased the extraordinary distinction of his presence and gave him the reputation (of the utmost importance in dealing with nerve cases) not merely of lightning skill and almost infallible accuracy in diagnosis, but of sympathy; tact; under-standing of the human soul. He could see the first moment they came into the room (the Warren Smiths they were called); he was certain directly he saw the man; it was a case of extreme gravity. It was a case of complete breakdown—complete physical and nervous breakdown, with every symptom in an advanced stage, he ascertained in two or three minutes (writing answers to questions, murmured discreetly, on a pink card).

How long had Dr Holmes been attending him?

Six weeks.

Prescribed a little bromide? Said there was nothing the matter? Ah yes (those general practitioners! thought Sir William. It took half his time to undo their blunders. Some were irreparable).

'You served with great distinction in the War?'

The patient repeated the word 'war' interrogatively.

He was attaching meanings to words of a symbolical kind. A serious symptom to be noted on the card.

'The War?' the patient asked. The European War—that little shindy of schoolboys with gunpowder? Had he served with distinction? He really forgot. In the War itself he had failed.

'Yes, he served with the greatest distinction,' Rezia assured the doctor; 'he was promoted.'

'And they have the very highest opinion of you at your office?' Sir William murmured, glancing at Mr Brewer's very generously worded letter. 'So that you have nothing to worry you, no financial anxiety, nothing?'

He had committed an appalling crime and been condemned to death by human nature.

'I have—I have', he began, 'committed a crime ——'

'He has done nothing wrong whatever,' Rezia assured the doctor. If Mr Smith would wait, said Sir William, he would speak to Mrs Smith in the next room. Her husband was very seriously ill, Sir William said. Did he threaten to kill himself?

Oh, he did, she cried. But he did not mean it, she said. Of course not. It was merely a question of rest, said Sir William; of rest, rest, rest; a long rest in bed. There was a delightful home down in the country where her husband would be perfectly looked after. Away from her? she asked. Unfortunately, yes; the people we care for most are not good for us when we are ill. But he was not mad, was he? Sir William said he never spoke of 'madness'; he called it not having a sense of proportion. But her husband did not like doctors. He would refuse to go there. Shortly and kindly Sir William explained to her the state of the case. He had threatened to kill himself. There was no alternative. It was a question of law. He would lie in bed in a beautiful house in the country. The nurses were admirable. Sir William would visit him once a week. If Mrs

Warren Smith was quite sure she had no more questions to ask—he never hurried his patients—they would return to her husband. She had nothing more to ask—not of Sir William.

So they returned to the most exalted of mankind; the criminal who faced his judges; the victim exposed on the heights; the fugitive; the drowned sailor; the poet of the immortal ode; the Lord who had gone from life to death; to Septimus Warren Smith, who sat in the armchair under the skylight staring at a photograph of Lady Bradshaw in Court dress, muttering messages about beauty.

'We have had our little talk,' said Sir William.

'He says that you are very, very ill,' Rezia cried.

'We have been arranging that you should go into a home,' said Sir William.

'One of Holmes's homes?' sneered Septimus.

The fellow made a distasteful impression. For there was in Sir William, whose father had been a tradesman, a natural respect for breeding and clothing, which shabbiness nettled; again, more profoundly, there was in Sir William, who had never had time for reading, a grudge, deeply buried, against cultivated people who came into his room and intimated that doctors, whose profession is a constant strain upon all the highest faculties, are not educated men.

'One of *my* homes, Mr Warren Smith,' he said, 'where we will teach you to rest.'

And there was just one thing more.

He was quite certain that when Mr Warren Smith was well he was the last man in the world to frighten his wife. But he had talked of killing himself.

'We all have our moments of depression,' said Sir William.

Once you fall, Septimus repeated to himself, human nature is on you. Holmes and Bradshaw are on you. They scour the desert. They fly screaming into the wilderness. The rack and the thumbscrew are applied. Human nature is remorseless.

'Impulses came upon him sometimes?' Sir William asked, with his pencil on a pink card.

That was his own affair, said Septimus.

'Nobody lives for himself alone,' said Sir William, glancing at the photograph of his wife in Court dress.

'And you have a brilliant career before you,' said Sir William. There was Mr Brewer's letter on the table. 'An exceptionally brilliant career.'

But if he confessed? If he communicated? Would they let him off then, Holmes, Bradshaw?

'I—I——' he stammered.

But what was his crime? He could not remember it.

'Yes?' Sir William encouraged him. (But it was growing late.)

Love, trees, there is no crime—what was his message?

He could not remember it.

'I—I——' Septimus stammered.

'Try to think as little about yourself as possible,' said Sir William kindly. Really, he was not fit to be about.

Was there anything else they wished to ask him? Sir William would make all arrangements (he murmured to Rezia) and he would let her know between five and six that evening.

'Trust everything to me,' he said, and dismissed them.

Never, never had Rezia felt such agony in her life! She had asked for help and been deserted! He had failed them! Sir William Bradshaw was not a nice man.

The upkeep of that motor car alone must cost him quite a lot, said Septimus, when they got out into the street.

She clung to his arm. They had been deserted.

But what more did she want?

To his patients he gave three-quarters of an hour; and if in this exacting science which has to do with what, after all, we know nothing about—the nervous system, the human brain—a doctor loses his sense of proportion, as a doctor he fails. Health we must have; and health is proportion; so that when a man comes into your room and says he is Christ (a common delusion), and has a message, as they mostly have, and threatens, as they often do, to kill himself, you invoke proportion; order rest in bed; rest in solitude; silence and rest; rest without friends, without books, without messages; six months' rest; until a man who went in weighing seven stone six comes out weighing twelve.

Proportion, divine proportion, Sir William's goddess, was acquired by Sir William walking hospitals, catching salmon, begetting one son in Harley Street by Lady Bradshaw, who caught salmon herself and took photographs scarcely to be distinguished from the work of professionals. Worshipping proportion, Sir William not only prospered himself but made England prosper, secluded her lunatics, forbade childbirth, penalized despair, made it impossible for the unfit to propagate their views until they, too, shared his sense of proportion—his, if they were men, Lady Bradshaw's if they were women (she embroidered, knitted, spent four nights out of seven at home with her son), so that not only did his colleagues respect him, his subordinates fear him, but the friends and relations of his patients felt for him the keenest gratitude for insisting that these prophetic Christs and Christesses, who prophesied the end of the world, or the advent of God, should drink milk in bed, as Sir William ordered; Sir William with his thirty years' experience of these kinds of cases, and his infallible instinct, this is madness, this sense; his sense of proportion.

But Proportion has a sister, less smiling, more formidable, a Goddess even now engaged—in the heat and sands of India, the mud and swamp of Africa, the purlieus of London, wherever, in short, the climate or the devil tempts men to fall from the true belief which is her own—is even now engaged in dashing down shrines, smashing idols, and setting up in their place her own stern countenance. Conversion is her name and she feasts on the wills of the weakly, loving to impress, to impose, adoring her own features stamped on the face of the populace. At Hyde Park Corner on a tub she stands preaching; shrouds herself in white and walks penitentially disguised as brotherly love through factories and parliaments; offers help, but desires power; smites out of her way roughly the dissentient, or dissatisfied; bestows her blessing on those who, looking upward, catch submissively from her eyes the light of their own. This lady too (Rezia Warren Smith divined it) had her dwelling in Sir William's heart, though concealed, as she mostly is, under some plausible disguise; some venerable name; love, duty, self-sacrifice. How he would work—how toil to raise funds, propagate reforms, initiate institutions! But conversion, fastidious Goddess, loves blood better than brick, and feasts most subtly on the human will. For example, Lady Bradshaw. Fifteen years ago she had gone under. It was nothing you could put your finger on; there had been no scene, no snap; only the slow sinking, water-logged, of her will into his. Sweet was her smile, swift her submission; dinner in Harley Street, numbering eight or nine courses, feeding ten or fifteen guests of the professional classes, was smooth and urbane. Only as the evening wore on a very slight dullness, or uneasiness perhaps, a nervous twitch, fumble, stumble and confusion indicated, what it was really painful to believe—that the poor lady lied. Once, long ago, she had caught salmon freely: now, quick to minister to the craving which lit her husband's eye so oilily for dominion, for power, she cramped, squeezed, pared, pruned, drew back, peeped through: so that without knowing precisely what made the evening disagreeable, and caused this pressure on the top of the head (which might well be imputed to the professional conversation, or the fatigue of a great doctor whose life, Lady Bradshaw said, 'is not his own but his patient's'), disagreeable it was: so that guests, when the clock struck ten, breathed in the air of Harley Street even with rapture; which relief, however, was denied to his patients.

There in the grey room, with the pictures on the wall, and the valuable furniture, under the ground-glass skylight, they learnt the extent of their transgressions: huddled up in armchairs, they watched him go through, for their benefit, a curious exercise with the arms, which he shot out, brought sharply back to his hip, to prove (if the patient was obstinate) that Sir William was master of his own actions, which the patient was not. There some weakly broke down; sobbed, submitted; others, inspired by Heaven knows what intemperate madness, called Sir William to his face a damnable humbug; questioned, even more impiously, life itself. Why live? they demanded. Sir William replied that life was good. Certainly Lady Bradshaw in ostrich feathers hung over the mantelpiece, and as for his income it was quite twelve thousand a year. But to us, they protested, life has given no such bounty. He acquiesced. They lacked a sense of proportion. And perhaps, after all, there is no God? He shrugged his shoulders. In short, this living or not living is an affair of our own? But there they were mistaken. Sir William had a friend in Surrey where they taught, what Sir William frankly admitted was a difficult art—a sense of proportion. There were, moreover, family affection; honour; courage; and a brilliant career. All of these had in Sir William a resolute champion. If they failed, he had to support him police and the good of society, which, he remarked very quietly, would take care, down in Surrey, that these unsocial impulses, bred more than anything by the lack of good blood, were held in control. And then stole out from her hiding-place and mounted her throne that Goddess whose lust is to override opposition, to stamp indelibly in the sanctuaries of others the image of herself. Naked, defenceless, the exhausted, the friendless received the impress of Sir William's will. He swooped; he devoured. He shut people up. It was this combination of decision and humanity that endeared Sir William so greatly to the relations of his victims.

But Rezia Warren Smith cried, walking down Harley Street, that she did not like that man.

Shredding and slicing, dividing and subdividing, the clocks of Harley Street nibbled at the June day, counselled submission, upheld authority, and pointed out in chorus the supreme advantages of a sense of proportion, until the mound of time was so far diminished that a commercial clock, suspended above a shop in Oxford Street, announced, genially and fraternally, as if it were a pleasure to Messrs Rigby and Lowndes to give the information gratis, that it was half-past one.

Looking up, it appeared that each letter of their names stood for one of the hours; subconsciously one was grateful to Rigby and Lowndes for giving one time ratified by Greenwich; and this gratitude (so Hugh Whitbread ruminated, dallying there in front of the shop window) naturally took the form later of buying off Rigby and Lowndes socks or shoes. So he ruminated. It was his habit. He did not go deeply. He brushed surfaces; the dead languages, the living, life in Constantinople,

Paris, Rome; riding, shooting, tennis, it had been once. The malicious asserted that he now kept guard at Buckingham Palace, dressed in silk stockings and knee-breeches, over what nobody knew. But he did it extremely efficiently. He had been afloat on the cream of English society for fifty-five years. He had known Prime Ministers. His affections were understood to be deep. And if it were true that he had not taken part in any of the great movements of the time or held important office, one or two humble reforms stood to his credit; an improvement in public shelters was one; the protection of owls in Norfolk another; servant girls had reason to be grateful to him; and his name at the end of letters to *The Times*, asking for funds, appealing to the public to protect, to preserve, to clear up litter, to abate smoke, and stamp out immorality in parks, commanded respect.

A magnificent figure he cut too, pausing for a moment (as the sound of the half-hour died away) to look critically, magisterially, at socks and shoes; impeccable, substantial, as if he beheld the world from a certain eminence, and dressed to match; but realized the obligations which size, wealth, health entail, and observed punctiliously, even when not abso-lutely necessary, little courtesies, old-fashioned ceremonies, which gave a quality to his manner, something to imitate, something to remember him by, for he would never lunch, for example, with Lady Bruton, whom he had known these twenty years, without bringing her in his outstretched hand a bunch of carnations, and asking Miss Brush, Lady Bruton's secretary, after her brother in South Africa, which, for some reason, Miss Brush, deficient though she was in every attribute of female charm, so much resented that she said 'Thank you, he's doing very well in South Africa,' when, for half-a-dozen years, he had been doing badly in Portsmouth.

Lady Bruton herself preferred Richard Dalloway, who arrived at the same moment. Indeed they met on the doorstep.

Lady Bruton preferred Richard Dalloway of course. He was made of much finer material. But she wouldn't let them run down her poor dear Hugh. She could never forget his kindness—he had been really remark-ably kind—she forgot precisely upon what occasion. But he had been—remarkably kind. Anyhow, the difference between one man and another does not amount to much. She had never seen the sense of cutting people up, as Clarissa Dalloway did—cutting them up and sticking them together again; not at any rate when one was sixty-two. She took Hugh's carnations with her angular grim smile. There was nobody else coming, she said. She had got them there on false pretences, to help her out of a difficulty—

'But let us eat first,' she said.

And so there began a soundless and exquisite passing to and fro through swing doors of aproned, white-capped maids, handmaidens not of necessity, but adepts in a mystery or grand deception practised by hostesses in Mayfair from one-thirty to two, when, with a wave of the hand, the traffic ceases, and there rises instead this profound illusion in the first place about the food—how it is not paid for; and then that the table spreads itself voluntarily with glass and silver, little mats, saucers of red fruit; films of brown cream mask turbot; in casseroles severed chickens swim; coloured, undomestic, the fire burns; and with the wine and the coffee (not paid for) rise jocund visions before musing eyes; gently speculative eyes; eyes to whom life appears musical, mysterious; eyes now kindled to observe genially the beauty of the red carnations which Lady Bruton (whose movements were always angular) had laid beside her plate, so that Hugh Whitbread, feeling at peace with the entire universe and at the same time completely sure of his standing, said, resting his fork:

'Wouldn't they look charming against your lace?'

Miss Brush resented this familiarity intensely. She thought him an underbred fellow. She made Lady Bruton laugh.

Lady Bruton raised the carnations, holding them rather stiffly with much the same attitude with which the General held the scroll in the picture behind her; she remained fixed, tranced. Which was she now, the General's great-granddaughter? great-great-granddaughter? Richard Dalloway asked himself. Sir Roderick, Sir Miles, Sir Talbot—that was it. It was remarkable how in that family the likeness persisted in the women. She should have been a general of dragoons herself. And Richard would have served under her, cheerfully; he had the greatest respect for her; he cherished these romantic views about well-set-up old women of pedigree, and would have liked, in his good-humoured way, to bring some young hot-heads of his acquaintance to lunch with her; as if a type like hers could be bred of amiable tea-drinking enthusiasts! He knew her country. He knew her people. There was a vine, still bearing, which either Lovelace or Herrick—she never read a word of poetry herself, but so the story ran—had sat under. Better wait to put before them the question that bothered her (about making an appeal to the public; if so, in what terms and so on), better wait until they have had their coffee, Lady Bruton thought; and so laid the carnations down beside her plate.

'How's Clarissa?' she asked abruptly.

Clarissa always said that Lady Bruton did not like her. Indeed, Lady Bruton had the reputation of being more interested in politics than people; of talking like a man; of having had a finger in some notorious intrigue of the eighties, which was now beginning to be mentioned in memoirs. Certainly there was an alcove in her drawing-room, and a table in that alcove, and a photograph upon that table of General Sir Talbot Moore, now deceased, who had written there (one evening in the eighties) in Lady Bruton's presence, with her cognisance, perhaps advice, a telegram ordering the British troops to advance upon an historical occasion. (She kept the pen and told the story.) Thus, when she said in her offhand way 'How's Clarissa?' husbands had difficulty in persuading their wives, and indeed, however devoted, were secretly doubtful themselves, of her interest in women who often got in their husbands' way, prevented them from accepting posts abroad, and had to be taken to the seaside in the middle of the session to recover from influenza. Nevertheless her inquiry, 'How's Clarissa?' was known by women infallibly to be a signal from a well-wisher, from an almost silent companion, whose utterances (half a dozen perhaps in the course of a lifetime) signified recognition of some feminine comradeship which went beneath masculine lunch parties and united Lady Bruton and Mrs Dalloway, who seldom met, and appeared when they did meet indifferent and even hostile, in a singular bond.

'I met Clarissa in the Park this morning,' said Hugh Whitbread, diving into the casserole, anxious to pay himself this little tribute, for he had only to come to London and he met everybody at once; but greedy, one of the greediest men she had ever known, Milly Brush thought, who observed men with unflinching rectitude, and was capable of everlasting devotion, to her own sex in particular, being knobbed, scraped, angular, and entirely without feminine charm.

'D'you know who's in town?' said Lady Bruton, suddenly bethinking her. 'Our old friend, Peter Walsh.'

They all smiled. Peter Walsh! And Mr Dalloway was genuinely glad, Milly Brush thought; and Mr Whitbread thought only of his chicken.

Peter Walsh! All three, Lady Bruton, Hugh Whitbread, and Richard Dalloway, remembered the same thing—how passionately Peter had been in love; been rejected; gone to India; come a cropper; made a mess of things; and Richard Dalloway had a very great liking for the dear old fellow too. Milly Brush saw that; saw a depth in the brown of his eyes; saw him hesitate; consider; which interested her, as Mr Dalloway always interested her, for what was he thinking, she wondered, about Peter Walsh?

That Peter Walsh had been in love with Clarissa; that he would go back directly after lunch and find Clarissa; that he would tell her, in so many words, that he loved her. Yes, he would say that.

Milly Brush once might almost have fallen in love with these silences; and Mr Dalloway was always so dependable; such a gentleman too. Now, being forty, Lady Bruton had only to nod, or turn her head a little abruptly, and Milly Brush took the signal, however deeply she might be sunk in these reflections of a detached spirit, of an uncorrupted soul whom life could not bamboozle, because life had not offered her a trinket of the slightest value; not a curl, smile, lip, cheek, nose; nothing whatever; Lady Bruton had only to nod, and Perkins was instructed to quicken the coffee.

'Yes; Peter Walsh has come back,' said Lady Bruton. It was vaguely flattering to them all. He had come back, battered, unsuccessful, to their secure shores. But to help him, they reflected, was impossible; there was some flaw in his character. Hugh Whitbread said one might of course mention his name to So-and-so. He wrinkled lugubriously, consequentially, at the thought of the letters he would write to the heads of Government offices about 'my old friend, Peter Walsh', and so on. But it wouldn't lead to anything—not to anything permanent, because of his character.

'In trouble with some woman,' said Lady Bruton. They had all guessed that *that* was at the bottom of it.

'However,' said Lady Bruton, anxious to leave the subject, 'we shall hear the whole story from Peter himself.'

(The coffee was very slow in coming.)

'The address?' murmured Hugh Whitbread; and there was at once a ripple in the grey tide of service which washed round Lady Bruton day in, day out, collecting, intercepting, enveloping her in a fine tissue which broke concussions, mitigated interruptions, and spread round the house in Brook Street a fine net where things lodged and were picked out accurately, instantly by grey-haired Perkins, who had been with Lady Bruton these thirty years and now wrote down the address; handed it to Mr Whitbread, who took out his pocket-book, raised his eyebrows, and, slipping it in among documents of the highest importance, said that he would get Evelyn to ask him to lunch.

(They were waiting to bring the coffee until Mr Whitbread had finished.)

Hugh was very slow, Lady Bruton thought. He was getting fat, she noticed. Richard always kept himself in the pink of condition. She was getting impatient; the whole of her being was setting positively, undeniably, domineeringly brushing aside all this unnecessary trifling (Peter Walsh and his affairs) upon that subject which engaged her attention, and not merely her attention, but that fibre which was the ramrod of her soul, that essential part of her without which Millicent Bruton would not have been Millicent Bruton; that project for emigrating young people of both sexes born of respectable parents and setting them up with a fair prospect of doing well in Canada. She exaggerated. She had perhaps lost her sense of proportion. Emigration was not to others the obvious remedy, the sublime conception. It was not to them (not to Hugh, or Richard, or even to devoted Miss Brush) the liberator of the pent egotism, which a strong martial woman, well nourished, well descended, of direct impulses, downright feelings, and little introspective power (broad and simple—why could not everyone be broad and simple? she asked), feels rise within her, once youth is past, and must eject upon some object—it may be Emigration, it may be Emancipation; but whatever it be, this object round which the essence of her soul is daily secreted becomes inevitably prismatic, lustrous, half looking-glass, half precious stone; now carefully hidden in case people should sneer at it; now proudly displayed. Emigration had become, in short, largely Lady Bruton.

But she had to write. And one letter to *The Times*, she used to say to Miss Brush, cost her more than to organize an expedition to South Africa (which she had done in the war). After a morning's battle, beginning, tearing up, beginning again, she used to feel the futility of her own womanhood as she felt it on no other occasion, and would turn gratefully to the thought of Hugh Whitbread who possessed—no one could doubt it—the art of writing letters to *The Times*.

A being so differently constituted from herself, with such a command of language; able to put things as editors liked them put; had passions which one could not call simply greed. Lady Bruton often suspended judgement upon men in deference to the mysterious accord in which they, but no woman, stood to the laws of the universe; knew how to put things; knew what was said; so that if Richard advised her, and Hugh wrote for her, she was sure of being somehow right. So she let Hugh eat his soufflé; asked after poor Evelyn; waited until they were smoking, and then said,

'Milly, would you fetch the papers?'

And Miss Brush went out, came back; laid papers on the table; and Hugh produced his fountain pen; his silver fountain pen, which had done twenty years' service, he said, unscrewing the cap. It was still in perfect order; he had shown it to the makers; there was no reason, they said, why it should ever wear out; which was somehow to Hugh's credit, and to the credit of the sentiments which his pen expressed (so Richard Dalloway felt) as Hugh began carefully writing capital letters with rings round them in the margin, and thus marvellously reduced Lady Bruton's tangles to sense, to grammar such as the editor of *The Times*, Lady Bruton felt, watching the marvellous transformation, must respect. Hugh was slow. Hugh was pertinacious. Richard said one must take risks. Hugh proposed modifications in deference to people's feelings, which, he said rather tartly when Richard laughed, 'had to be considered', and read out 'how, therefore, we are of opinion that the times are ripe . . . the superfluous youth of our ever-increasing population . . .

what we owe to the dead . . .' which Richard thought all stuffing and bunkum, but no harm in it, of course, and Hugh went on drafting sentiments in alphabetical order of the highest nobility, brushing the cigar ash from his waistcoat, and summing up now and then the progress they had made until, finally, he read out the draft of a letter which Lady Bruton felt certain was a masterpiece. Could her own meaning sound like that?

Hugh could not guarantee that the editor would put it in; but he would be meeting somebody at luncheon.

Whereupon Lady Bruton, who seldom did a graceful thing, stuffed all Hugh's carnations into the front of her dress, and flinging her hands out called him 'My Prime Minister!' What she would have done without them both she did not know. They rose. And Richard Dalloway strolled off as usual to have a look at the General's portrait, because he meant, whenever he had a moment of leisure, to write a history of Lady Bruton's family.

And Millicent Bruton was very proud of her family. But they could wait, they could wait, she said, looking at the picture; meaning that her family, of military men, administrators, admirals, had been men of action, who had done their duty; and Richard's first duty was to his country, but it was a fine face, she said; and all the papers were ready for Richard down at Aldmixton whenever the time came; the Labour Government, she meant. 'Ah, the news from India!' she cried.

And then, as they stood in the hall taking yellow gloves from the bowl on the malachite table and Hugh was offering Miss Brush with quite unnecessary courtesy some discarded ticket or other compliment, which she loathed from the depths of her heart and blushed brick red, Richard turned to Lady Bruton, with his hat in his hand, and said,

'We shall see you at our party tonight?' whereupon Lady Bruton resumed the magnificence which letter-writing had shattered. She might come; or she might not come. Clarissa had wonderful energy. Parties terrified Lady Bruton. But then, she was getting old. So she intimated, standing at her doorway; handsome; very erect; while her chow stretched behind her, and Miss Brush disappeared into the background with her hands full of papers.

And Lady Bruton went ponderously, majestically, up to her room, lay, one arm extended, on the sofa. She sighed, she snored, not that she was asleep, only drowsy and heavy, drowsy and heavy, like a field of clover in the sunshine this hot June day, with the bees going round and about and the yellow butterflies. Always she went back to those fields down in Devonshire, where she had jumped the brooks on Patty, her pony, with Mortimer and Tom, her brothers. And there were the dogs; there were the rats; there were her father and mother on the lawn under the trees, with the tea-things out, and the beds of dahlias, the hollyhocks, the pampas grass; and they, little wretches, always up to some mischief! stealing back through the shrubbery, so as not to be seen, all bedraggled from some roguery. What old nurse used to say about her frocks!

Ah, dear, she remembered—it was Wednesday in Brook Street. Those kind good fellows, Richard Dalloway, Hugh Whitbread, had gone this hot day through the streets whose growl came up to her lying on the sofa. Power was hers, position, income. She had lived in the forefront of her time. She had had good friends; known the ablest men of her day. Murmuring London flowed up to her, and her hand, lying on the sofa back, curled upon some imaginary baton such as her grandfathers might have held, holding which she seemed, drowsy and heavy, to be commanding battalions marching to Canada, and those good fellows walking across London, that territory of theirs, that little bit of carpet, Mayfair.

And they went further and further from her, being attached to her by a thin thread (since they had lunched with her) which would stretch and stretch, get thinner and thinner as they walked across London; as if one's friends were attached to one's body, after lunching with them, by a thin thread, which (as she dozed there) became hazy with the sound of bells, striking the hour or ringing to service, as a single spider's thread is blotted with raindrops, and, burdened, sags down. So she slept.

And Richard Dalloway and Hugh Whitbread hesitated at the corner of Conduit Street at the very moment that Millicent Bruton, lying on the sofa, let the thread snap; snored. Contrary winds buffeted at the street corner. They looked in at a shop window; they did not wish to buy or to talk but to part, only with contrary winds buffeting the street corner, with some sort of lapse in the tides of the body, two forces meeting in a swirl, morning and afternoon, they paused. Some newspaper placard went up in the air, gallantly, like a kite at first, then paused, swooped, fluttered; and a lady's veil hung. Yellow awnings trembled. The speed of the morning traffic slackened, and single carts rattled carelessly down half-empty streets. In Norfolk, of which Richard Dalloway was half thinking, a soft warm wind blew back the petals; confused the waters; ruffled the flowering grasses. Haymakers, who had pitched beneath hedges to sleep away the morning toil, parted curtains of green blades; moved trembling globes of cow parsley to see the sky; the blue, the steadfast, the blazing summer sky.

Aware that he was looking at a silver two-handled Jacobean mug, and that Hugh Whitbread admired condescendingly, with airs of connoisseurship, a Spanish necklace which he thought of asking the price of in case Evelyn might like it—still Richard was torpid; could not think or move. Life had thrown up this wreckage; shop windows full of coloured paste, and one stood stark with the lethargy of the old, stiff with the rigidity of the old, looking in. Evelyn Whitbread might like to buy this Spanish necklace—so she might. Yawn he must. Hugh was going into the shop.

'Right you are!' said Richard, following.

Goodness knows he didn't want to go buying necklaces with Hugh. But there are tides in the body. Morning meets afternoon. Borne like a frail shallop on deep, deep floods, Lady Bruton's great-grandfather and his memoir and his campaigns in North America were whelmed and sunk. And Millicent Bruton too. She went under. Richard didn't care a straw what became of Emigration; about that letter, whether the editor put it in or not. The necklace hung stretched between Hugh's admirable fingers. Let him give it to a girl, if he must buy jewels—any girl, any girl in the street. For the worthlessness of this life did strike Richard pretty forcibly—buying necklaces for Evelyn. If he'd had a boy he'd have said, Work, work. But he had his Elizabeth; he adored his Elizabeth.

'I should like to see Mr Dubonnet,' said Hugh in his curt worldly way. It appeared that this Dubonnet had the measurements of Mrs Whitbread's neck, or, more strangely still, knew her views upon Spanish jewellery and the extent of her possessions in that line (which Hugh could not remember). All of which seemed to Richard Dalloway awfully odd. For he never gave Clarissa presents, except a bracelet two or three years ago, which had not been a success. She never wore it. It pained him to remember that she never wore it. And as a single spider's thread after wavering here and there attaches itself to the point of a leaf, so Richard's mind, recovering from its lethargy, set now on his wife, Clarissa, whom Peter Walsh had loved so passionately; and Richard had had a sudden vision of her there at luncheon; of himself and Clarissa; of their life together; and he drew the tray of old jewels towards him, and taking up first this brooch, then that ring, 'How much is that?' he asked, but doubted his own taste. He wanted to open the drawing-room door and come in holding out something; a present for Clarissa. Only what? But Hugh was on his legs again. He was unspeakably pompous. Really, after dealing here for thirty-five years he was not going to be put off by a mere boy who did not know his business. For Dubonnet, it seemed, was out, and Hugh would not buy anything until Mr Dubonnet chose to be in; at which the youth flushed and bowed his correct little bow. It was all perfectly correct. And yet Richard couldn't have said that to save his life! Why these people stood that damned insolence he could not conceive. Hugh was becoming an intolerable ass. Richard Dalloway could not stand more than an hour of his society. And, flicking his bowler hat by way of farewell, Richard turned at the corner of Conduit Street eager, yes, very eager, to travel that spider's thread of attachment between himself and Clarissa; he would go straight to her, in Westminster.

But he wanted to come in holding something. Flowers? Yes, flowers, since he did not trust his taste in gold; any number of flowers, roses, orchids, to celebrate what was, reckoning things as you will, an event; this feeling about her when they spoke of Peter Walsh at luncheon; and they never spoke of it; not for years had they spoken of it; which, he thought, grasping his red and white roses together (a vast bunch in tissue paper), is the greatest mistake in the world. The time comes when it can't be said; one's too shy to say it, he thought, pocketing his sixpence or two of change, setting off with his great bunch held against his body to Westminster, to say straight out in so many words (whatever she might think of him), holding out his flowers, 'I love you.' Why not? Really it was a miracle thinking of the war, and thousands of poor chaps, with all their lives before them, shovelled together, already half forgotten; it was a miracle. Here he was walking across London to say to Clarissa in so many words that he loved her. Which one never does say, he thought. Partly one's lazy; partly one's shy. And Clarissa—it was difficult to think of her; except in starts, as at luncheon, when he saw her quite distinctly; their whole life. He stopped at the crossing; and repeated—being simple by nature, and undebauched, because he had tramped, and shot; being pertinacious and dogged, having championed the down-trodden and followed his instincts in the House of Commons; being preserved in his simplicity yet at the same time grown rather speechless, rather stiff—he repeated that it was a miracle that he should have married Clarissa; a miracle—his life had been a miracle, he thought; hesitating to cross. But it did make his blood boil to see little creatures of five or six crossing Piccadilly alone. The police ought to have stopped the traffic at once. He had no illusions about the London police. Indeed, he was collecting evidence of their malpractices; and those costermongers, not allowed to stand their barrows in the streets; and prostitutes, good Lord, the fault wasn't in them, nor in young men either, but in our detestable social system and so forth; all of which he considered, could be seen considering, grey, dogged, dapper, clean, as he walked across the Park to tell his wife that he loved her.

For he would say it in so many words, when he came into the room. Because it is a thousand pities never to say what one feels, he thought, crossing the Green Park and observing with pleasure how in the shade of the trees whole families, poor families, were sprawling; children kicking up their legs; sucking milk; paper bags thrown about, which could easily be picked up (if people objected) by one of those fat gentlemen in livery; for he was of opinion that every park, and every square, during the summer months should be open to children (the grass of the park flushed and faded, lighting up the poor mothers of Westminster and their crawling babies, as if a yellow lamp were moved beneath). But what could be done for female vagrants like that poor creature, stretched on her elbow (as if she had flung herself on the earth, rid of all ties, to observe curiously, to speculate boldly, to consider the whys and the wherefores, impudent, loose-lipped, humorous), he did not know. Bearing his flowers like a weapon, Richard Dalloway approached her; intent he passed her; still there was time for a spark between them—she laughed at the sight of him, he smiled good-humouredly, considering the problem of the female vagrant; not that they would ever speak. But he would tell Clarissa that he loved her, in so many words. He had, once upon a time, been jealous of Peter Walsh; jealous of him and Clarissa. But she had often said to him that she had been right not to marry Peter Walsh; which, knowing Clarissa, was obviously true; she wanted support. Not that she was weak; but she wanted support.

As for Buckingham Palace (like an old prima donna facing the audience all in white) you can't deny it a certain dignity, he considered, nor despise what does, after all, stand to millions of people (a little crowd was waiting at the gate to see the King drive out) for a symbol, absurd though it is; a child with a box of bricks could have done better, he thought; looking at the memorial to Queen Victoria (whom he could remember in her horn spectacles driving through Kensington), its white mound, its billowing motherliness; but he liked being ruled by the descendant of Horsa; he liked continuity; and the sense of handing on the traditions of the past. It was a great age in which to have lived. Indeed, his own life was a miracle; let him make no mistake about it; here he was, in the prime of life, walking to his house in Westminster to tell Clarissa that he loved her. Happiness is this, he thought.

It is this, he said, as he entered Dean's Yard. Big Ben was beginning to strike, first the warning, musical; then the hour, irrevocable. Lunch parties waste the entire afternoon, he thought, approaching his door.

The sound of Big Ben flooded Clarissa's drawing-room, where she sat, ever so annoyed, at her writing-table; worried; annoyed. It was perfectly true that she had not asked Ellie Henderson to her party; but she had done it on purpose. Now Mrs Marsham wrote: 'She had told Ellie Henderson she would ask Clarissa—Ellie so much wanted to come.'

But why should she invite all the dull women in London to her parties? Why should Mrs Marsham interfere? And there was Elizabeth closeted all this time with Doris Kilman. Anything more nauseating she could not conceive. Prayer at this hour with that woman. And the sound of the bell flooded the room with its melancholy wave; which receded,

and gathered itself together to fall once more, when she heard, distract-
ingly, something fumbling, something scratching at the door. Who at
this hour? Three, good Heavens! Three already! For with overpowering
directness and dignity the clock struck three; and she heard nothing
else; but the door handle slipped round and in came Richard! What a
surprise! In came Richard, holding out flowers. She had failed him, once
at Constantinople; and Lady Bruton, whose lunch parties were said to
be extraordinarily amusing, had not asked her. He was holding out
flowers—roses, red and white roses. (But he could not bring himself to
say he loved her; not in so many words.)

But how lovely, she said, taking his flowers. She understood; she
understood without his speaking; his Clarissa. She put them in vases on
the mantelpiece. How lovely they looked, she said. And was it amusing,
she asked? Had Lady Bruton asked after her? Peter Walsh was back.
Mrs Marsham had written. Must she ask Ellie Henderson? That woman
Kilman was upstairs.

'But let us sit down for five minutes,' said Richard.

It all looked so empty. All the chairs were against the wall. What had
they been doing? Oh, it was for the party; no, he had not forgotten the
party. Peter Walsh was back. Oh yes, she had had him. And he was
going to get a divorce; and he was in love with some woman out there.
And he hadn't changed in the slightest. There she was, mending her
dress . . .

'Thinking of Bourton,' she said.

'Hugh was at lunch,' said Richard. She had met him too! Well, he
was getting absolutely intolerable. Buying Evelyn necklaces; fatter than
ever; an intolerable ass.

'And it came over me "I might have married you",' she said, thinking
of Peter sitting there in his little bow-tie; with that knife, opening it,
shutting it. 'Just as he always was, you know.'

They were talking about him at lunch, said Richard. (But he could
not tell her he loved her. He held her hand. Happiness is this, he
thought.) They had been writing a letter to *The Times* for Millicent
Bruton. That was about all Hugh was fit for.

'And our dear Miss Kilman?' he asked. Clarissa thought the roses
absolutely lovely; first bunched together; now of their own accord
starting apart.

'Kilman arrives just as we've done lunch,' she said. 'Elizabeth turns
pink. They shut themselves up. I suppose they're praying.'

Lord! He didn't like it; but these things pass over if you let them.

'In a mackintosh with an umbrella,' said Clarissa.

He had not said 'I love you'; but he held her hand. Happiness is this,
is this, he thought.

'But why should I ask all the dull women in London to my parties?' said Clarissa. And if Mrs Marsham gave a party, did *she* invite her guests?

'Poor Ellie Henderson,' said Richard—it was a very odd thing how much Clarissa minded about her parties, he thought.

But Richard had no notion of the look of a room. However—what was he going to say?

If she worried about these parties he would not let her give them. Did she wish she had married Peter? But he must go.

He must be off, he said, getting up. But he stood for a moment as if he were about to say something; and she wondered what? Why? There were the roses.

'Some Committee?' she asked, as he opened the door.

'Armenians,' he said; or perhaps it was 'Albanians'.

And there is a dignity in people; a solitude; even between husband and wife a gulf; and that one must respect, thought Clarissa, watching him open the door; for one would not part with it oneself, or take it, against his will, from one's husband, without losing one's independence, one's self-respect—something, after all, priceless.

He returned with a pillow and a quilt.

'An hour's complete rest after luncheon,' he said. And he went.

How like him! He would go on saying 'An hour's complete rest after luncheon' to the end of time, because a doctor had ordered it once. It was like him to take what doctors said literally; part of his adorable divine simplicity, which no one had to the same extent; which made him go and do the thing while she and Peter frittered their time away bickering. He was already half-way to the House of Commons, to his Armenians, his Albanians, having settled her on the sofa, looking at his roses. And people would say, 'Clarissa Dalloway is spoilt.' She cared much more for her roses than for the Armenians. Hunted out of existence, maimed, frozen, the victims of cruelty and injustice (she had heard Richard say so over and over again)—no, she could feel nothing for the Albanians, or was it the Armenians? but she loved her roses (didn't that help the Armenians?)—the only flowers she could bear to see cut. But Richard was already at the House of Commons; at his Committee, having settled all her difficulties. But no; alas, that was not true. He did not see the reasons against asking Ellie Henderson. She would do it, of course, as he wished it. Since he had brought the pillow, she would lie down . . . But—but—why did she suddenly feel, for no reason that she could discover, desperately unhappy? As a person who has dropped some grain of pearl or diamond into the grass and parts the tall blades very carefully, this way and that, and searches here and there vainly, and at last spies it there at the roots, so she went through one thing and another; no, it was not Sally Seton saying that Richard would never be in the Cabinet because he had a second-class brain (it came back to her); no, she did not mind that; nor was it to do with Elizabeth either and Doris Kilman; those were facts. It was a feeling, some unpleasant feeling, earlier in the day perhaps; something that Peter had said, combined with some depression of her own, in her bedroom, taking off her hat; and what Richard had said had added to it, but what had he said? There were his roses. Her parties! That was it! Her parties! Both of them criticized her very unfairly, laughed at her very unjustly, for her parties. That was it! That was it!

Well, how was she going to defend herself? Now that she knew what it was, she felt perfectly happy. They thought, or Peter at any rate thought, that she enjoyed imposing herself; liked to have famous people about her; great names; was simply a snob, in short. Well, Peter might think so. Richard merely thought it foolish of her to like excitement when she knew it was bad for her heart. It was childish, he thought. And both were quite wrong. What she liked was simply life.

'That's what I do it for,' she said, speaking aloud, to life.

Since she was lying on the sofa, cloistered, exempt, the presence of this thing which she felt to be so obvious became physically existent; with robes of sound from the street, sunny, with hot breath, whispering, blowing out the blinds. But suppose Peter said to her, 'Yes, yes, but your parties—what's the sense of your parties?' all she could say was (and nobody could be expected to understand): They're an offering; which sounded horribly vague. But who was Peter to make out that life was all plain sailing?—Peter always in love, always in love with the wrong woman? What's your love? she might say to him. And she knew his answer; how it is the most important thing in the world and no woman possibly understood it. Very well. But could any man understand what she meant either? about life? She could not imagine Peter or Richard taking the trouble to give a party for no reason whatever.

But to go deeper, beneath what people said (and these judgements, how superficial, how fragmentary they are!) in her own mind now, what did it mean to her, this thing called life? Oh, it was very queer. Here was So-and-so in South Kensington; someone up in Bayswater; and somebody else, say, in Mayfair. And she felt quite continuously a sense of their existence; and she felt what a waste; and she felt what a pity; and she felt if only they could be brought together; so she did it. And it was an offering; to combine, to create; but to whom?

An offering for the sake of offering, perhaps. Anyhow, it was her gift. Nothing else had she of the slightest importance; could not think, write, even play the piano. She muddled Armenians and Turks; loved success;

hated discomfort; must be liked; talked oceans of nonsense; and to this day, ask her what the Equator was, and she did not know.

All the same, that one day should follow another; Wednesday, Thursday, Friday, Saturday; that one should wake up in the morning; see the sky; walk in the park; meet Hugh Whitbread; then suddenly in came Peter; then these roses; it was enough. After that, how unbelievable death was!—that it must end; and no one in the whole world would know how she had loved it all; how, every instant . . .

The door opened. Elizabeth knew that her mother was resting. She came in very quietly. She stood perfectly still. Was it that some Mongol had been wrecked on the coast of Norfolk (as Mrs Hilbery said), had mixed with the Dalloway ladies, perhaps a hundred years ago? For the Dalloways, in general, were fair-haired; blue-eyed; Elizabeth, on the contrary, was dark; had Chinese eyes in a pale face; an Oriental mystery; was gentle, considerate, still. As a child, she had had a perfect sense of humour; but now at seventeen, why, Clarissa could not in the least understand, she had become very serious; like a hyacinth sheathed in glossy green, with buds just tinted, a hyacinth which has had no sun.

She stood quite still and looked at her mother; but the door was ajar, and outside the door was Miss Kilman, as Clarissa knew; Miss Kilman in her mackintosh listening to whatever they said.

Yes, Miss Kilman stood on the landing, and wore a mackintosh; but had her reasons. First, it was cheap; second, she was over forty; and did not, after all, dress to please. She was poor, moreover; degradingly poor. Otherwise she would not be taking jobs from people like the Dalloways; from rich people, who liked to be kind. Mr Dalloway, to do him justice, had been kind. But Mrs Dalloway had not. She had been merely condescending. She came from the most worthless of all classes—the rich, with a smattering of culture. They had expensive things everywhere; pictures, carpets, lots of servants. She considered that she had a perfect right to anything that the Dalloways did for her.

She had been cheated. Yes, the word was no exaggeration, for surely a girl has a right to some kind of happiness? And she had never been happy, what with being so clumsy and so poor. And then, just as she might have had a chance at Miss Dolby's school, the war came; and she had never been able to tell lies. Miss Dolby thought she would be happier with people who shared her views about the Germans. She had had to go. It was true that the family was of German origin; spelt the name Kiehlman in the eighteenth century; but her brother had been killed. They turned her out because she would not pretend that the Germans were all villains—when she had German friends, when the only happy days of her life had been spent in Germany! And after all, she could read history. She had had to take whatever she could get. Mr Dalloway had come across her working for the Friends. He had allowed her (and that was really generous of him) to teach his daughter history. Also she did a little Extension lecturing and so on. Then Our Lord had come to her (and here she always bowed her head). She had seen the light two years and three months ago. Now she did not envy women like Clarissa Dalloway; she pitied them.

She pitied and despised them from the bottom of her heart, as she stood on the soft carpet, looking at the old engraving of a little girl with a muff. With all this luxury going on, what hope was there for a better state of things? Instead of lying on a sofa—'My mother is resting,' Elizabeth had said—she should have been in a factory; behind a counter; Mrs Dalloway and all the other fine ladies!

Bitter and burning, Miss Kilman had turned into a church two years three months ago. She had heard the Rev. Edward Whittaker preach; the boys sing; had seen the solemn lights descend, and whether it was the music, or the voices (she herself when alone in the evening found comfort in a violin; but the sound was excruciating; she had no ear), the hot and turbulent feelings which boiled and surged in her had been assuaged as she sat there, and she had wept copiously, and gone to call on Mr Whittaker at his private house in Kensington. It was the hand of God, he said. The Lord had shown her the way. So now, whenever the hot and painful feelings boiled within her, this hatred of Mrs Dalloway, this grudge against the world, she thought of God. She thought of Mr Whittaker. Rage was succeeded by calm. A sweet savour filled her veins, her lips parted, and, standing formidable upon the landing in her mackintosh, she looked with steady and sinister serenity at Mrs Dalloway, who came out with her daughter.

Elizabeth said she had forgotten her gloves. That was because Miss Kilman and her mother hated each other. She could not bear to see them together. She ran upstairs to find her gloves.

But Miss Kilman did not hate Mrs Dalloway. Turning her large gooseberry-coloured eyes upon Clarissa, observing her small pink face, her delicate body, her air of freshness and fashion, Miss Kilman felt, Fool! Simpleton! You who have known neither sorrow nor pleasure; who have trifled your life away! And there rose in her an overmastering desire to overcome her; to unmask her. If she could have felled her it would have eased her. But it was not the body; it was the soul and its mockery that she wished to subdue; make feel her mastery. If only she could make her weep; could ruin her; humiliate her; bring her to her knees crying, You are right! But this was God's will, not Miss Kilman's. It was to be a religious victory. So she glared; so she glowered.

Clarissa was really shocked. This a Christian—this woman! This woman had taken her daughter from her! She in touch with invisible presences! Heavy, ugly, commonplace, without kindness or grace, she know the meaning of life!

'You are taking Elizabeth to the Stores?' Mrs Dalloway said.

Miss Kilman said she was. They stood there. Miss Kilman was not going to make herself agreeable. She had always earned her living. Her knowledge of modern history was thorough in the extreme. She did, out of her meagre income, set aside so much for causes she believed in; whereas this woman did nothing, believed nothing; brought up her daughter—but here was Elizabeth, rather out of breath, the beautiful girl.

So they were going to the Stores. Odd it was, as Miss Kilman stood there (and stand she did, with the power and taciturnity of some prehistoric monster armoured for primeval warfare), how, second by second, the idea of her diminished, how hatred (which was for ideas, not people) crumbled, how she lost her malignity, her size, became second by second merely Miss Kilman, in a mackintosh, whom Heaven knows Clarissa would have liked to help.

At this dwindling of the monster, Clarissa laughed. Saying good-bye, she laughed.

Off they went together, Miss Kilman and Elizabeth, downstairs.

With a sudden impulse, with a violent anguish, for this woman was taking her daughter from her, Clarissa leant over the banisters and cried out, 'Remember the party! Remember our party tonight!'

But Elizabeth had already opened the front door; there was a van passing; she did not answer.

Love and religion! thought Clarissa, going back into the drawing-room, tingling all over. How detestable, how detestable they are! For now that the body of Miss Kilman was not before her, it overwhelmed her—the idea. The cruellest things in the world, she thought, seeing them clumsy, hot, domineering, hypocritical, eavesdropping, jealous, infinitely cruel and unscrupulous, dressed in a mackintosh coat, on the landing; love and religion. Had she ever tried to convert anyone herself? Did she not wish everybody merely to be themselves? And she watched out of the window the old lady opposite climbing upstairs. Let her climb upstairs if she wanted to; let her stop; then let her, as Clarissa had often seen her, gain her bedroom, part her curtains, and disappear again into the background. Somehow one respected that—that old woman looking out of the window, quite unconscious that she was being watched. There was something solemn in it—but love and religion would destroy that, whatever it was, the privacy of the soul. The odious Kilman would destroy it. Yet it was a sight that made her want to cry.

Love destroyed too. Everything that was fine, everything that was true went. Take Peter Walsh now. There was a man, charming, clever, with ideas about everything. If you wanted to know about Pope, say, or Addison, or just to talk nonsense, what people were like, what things meant, Peter knew better than anyone. It was Peter who had helped her; Peter who had lent her books. But look at the women he loved—vulgar, trivial, commonplace. Think of Peter in love—he came to see her after all these years, and what did he talk about? Himself. Horrible passion! she thought. Degrading passion! she thought, thinking of Kilman and her Elizabeth walking to the Army and Navy Stores.

Big Ben struck the half-hour.

How extraordinary it was, strange, yes, touching to see the old lady (they had been neighbours ever so many years) move away from the window, as if she were attached to that sound, that string. Gigantic as it was, it had something to do with her. Down, down, into the midst of ordinary things the finger fell, making the moment solemn. She was forced, so Clarissa imagined, by that sound, to move, to go—but where? Clarissa tried to follow her as she turned and disappeared, and could still just see her white cap moving at the back of the bedroom. She was still there, moving about at the other end of the room. Why creeds and prayers and mackintoshes? when, thought Clarissa, that's the miracle, that's the mystery; that old lady, she meant, whom she could see going from chest of drawers to dressing-table. She could still see her. And the supreme mystery which Kilman might say she had solved, or Peter might say he had solved, but Clarissa didn't believe either of them had the ghost of an idea of solving, was simply this: here was one room; there another. Did religion solve that, or love?

Love—but here the other clock, the clock which always struck two minutes after Big Ben, came shuffling in with its lap full of odds and ends, which it dumped down as if Big Ben were all very well with his majesty laying down the law, so solemn, so just, but she must remember all sorts of little things besides—Mrs Marsham, Ellie Henderson, glasses for ices—all sorts of little things came flooding and lapping and dancing in on the wake of that solemn stroke which lay flat like a bar of gold on the sea. Mrs Marsham, Ellie Henderson, glasses for ices. She must telephone now at once.

Volubly, troublously, the late clock sounded, coming in on the wake of Big Ben, with its lap full of trifles. Beaten up, broken up by the assault of carriages, the brutality of vans, the eager advance of myriads of angular men, of flaunting women, the domes and spires of offices and hospitals, the last relics of this lap full of odds and ends seemed to break, like the spray of an exhausted wave, upon the body of Miss Kilman standing still in the street for a moment to mutter 'It is the flesh.'

It was the flesh that she must control. Clarissa Dalloway had insulted her. That she expected. But she had not triumphed; she had not mastered the flesh. Ugly, clumsy, Clarissa Dalloway had laughed at her for being that; and had revived the fleshly desires, for she minded looking as she did beside Clarissa. Nor could she talk as she did. But why wish to resemble her? Why? She despised Mrs Dalloway from the bottom of her heart. She was not serious. She was not good. Her life was a tissue of vanity and deceit. Yet Doris Kilman had been overcome. She had, as a matter of fact, very nearly burst into tears when Clarissa Dalloway laughed at her. 'It is the flesh, it is the flesh,' she muttered (it being her habit to talk aloud), trying to subdue this turbulent and painful feeling as she walked down Victoria Street. She prayed to God. She could not help being ugly; she could not afford to buy pretty clothes. Clarissa Dalloway had laughed—but she would concentrate her mind upon something else until she had reached the pillar-box. At any rate she had got Elizabeth. But she would think of something else; she would think of Russia; until she reached the pillar-box.

How nice it must be, she said, in the country, struggling, as Mr Whittaker had told her, with that violent grudge against the world which had scorned her, sneered at her, cast her off, beginning with this indignity—the infliction of her unlovable body which people could not bear to see. Do her hair as she might, her forehead remained like an egg, bald, white. No clothes suited her. She might buy anything. And for a woman, of course, that meant never meeting the opposite sex. Never would she come first with anyone. Sometimes lately it had seemed to her that, except for Elizabeth, her food was all that she lived for; her comforts; her dinner, her tea; her hot-water bottle at night. But one must fight; vanquish; have faith in God. Mr Whittaker had said she was there for a purpose. But no one knew the agony! He said, pointing to the crucifix, that God knew. But why should she have to suffer when other women, like Clarissa Dalloway, escaped? Knowledge comes through suffering, said Mr Whittaker.

She had passed the pillar-box, and Elizabeth had turned into the cool brown tobacco department of the Army and Navy Stores while she was still muttering to herself what Mr Whittaker had said about knowledge coming through suffering and the flesh. 'The flesh,' she muttered.

What department did she want? Elizabeth interrupted her.

'Petticoats,' she said abruptly, and stalked straight on to the lift.

Up they went. Elizabeth guided her this way and that; guided her in her abstraction as if she had been a great child, an unwieldy battleship. There were the petticoats, brown, decorous, striped, frivolous, solid, flimsy; and she chose, in her abstraction, portentously, and the girl serving thought her mad.

Elizabeth rather wondered, as they did up the parcel, what Miss

Kilman was thinking. They must have their tea, said Miss Kilman, rousing, collecting herself. They had their tea.

Elizabeth rather wondered whether Miss Kilman could be hungry. It was her way of eating, eating with intensity, then looking, again and again, at a plate of sugared cakes on the table next them; then, when a lady and a child sat down and the child took the cake, could Miss Kilman really mind it? Yes, Miss Kilman did mind it. She had wanted that cake—the pink one. The pleasure of eating was almost the only pure pleasure left her, and then to be baffled even in that!

When people are happy they have a reserve, she had told Elizabeth, upon which to draw, whereas she was like a wheel without a tyre (she was fond of such metaphors), jolted by every pebble—so she would say, staying on after the lesson, standing by the fire-place with her bag of books, her 'satchel', she called it, on a Tuesday morning, after the lesson was over. And she talked too about the war. After all, there were people who did not think the English invariably right. There were books. There were meetings. There were other points of view. Would Elizabeth like to come with her to listen to So-and-so? (a most extraordinary-looking old man). Then Miss Kilman took her to some church in Kensington and they had tea with a clergyman. She had lent her books. Law, medicine, politics, all professions are open to women of your generation, said Miss Kilman. But for herself, her career was absolutely ruined, and was it her fault? Good gracious, said Elizabeth, no.

And her mother would come calling to say that a hamper had come from Bourton and would Miss Kilman like some flowers? To Miss Kilman she was always very, very nice, but Miss Kilman squashed the flowers all in a bunch, and hadn't any small talk, and what interested Miss Kilman bored her mother, and Miss Kilman and she were terrible together; and Miss Kilman swelled and looked very plain, but Miss Kilman was frightfully clever. Elizabeth had never thought about the poor. They lived with everything they wanted,—her mother had break-fast in bed every day; Lucy carried it up; and she liked old women because they were Duchesses, and being descended from some Lord. But Miss Kilman said (one of those Tuesday mornings when the lesson was over), 'My grandfather kept an oil and colour shop in Kensington.' Miss Kilman was quite different from anyone she knew; she made one feel so small.

Miss Kilman took another cup of tea. Elizabeth, with her oriental bearing, her inscrutable mystery, sat perfectly upright; no, she did not want anything more. She looked for her gloves—her white gloves. They were under the table. Ah, but she must not go! Miss Kilman could not let her go! this youth, that was so beautiful! this girl, whom she genuinely loved! Her large hand opened and shut on the table.

But perhaps it was a little flat somehow, Elizabeth felt. And really she would like to go.

But said Miss Kilman, 'I've not quite finished yet.'

Of course, then, Elizabeth would wait. But it was rather stuffy in here.

'Are you going to the party tonight?' Miss Kilman said. Elizabeth supposed she was going; her mother wanted her to go. She must not let parties absorb her, Miss Kilman said, fingering the last two inches of a chocolate éclair.

She did not much like parties, Elizabeth said. Miss Kilman opened her mouth, slightly projected her chin, and swallowed down the last inches of the chocolate éclair, then wiped her fingers, and washed the tea round in her cup.

She was about to split asunder, she felt. The agony was so terrific. If she could grasp her, if she could clasp her, if she could make her hers absolutely and for ever and then die; that was all she wanted. But to sit here, unable to think of anything to say; to see Elizabeth turning against her; to be felt repulsive even by her—it was too much; she could not stand it. The thick fingers curled inwards.

'I never go to parties,' said Miss Kilman, just to keep Elizabeth from going. 'People don't ask me to parties'—and she knew as she said it that it was this egotism that was her undoing; Mr Whittaker had warned her; but she could not help it. She had suffered so horribly. 'Why should they ask me?' she said. 'I'm plain, I'm unhappy.' She knew it was idiotic. But it was all those people passing—people with parcels who despised her—who made her say it. However, she was Doris Kilman. She had her degree. She was a woman who had made her way in the world. Her knowledge of modern history was more than respectable.

'I don't pity myself,' she said. 'I pity'—she meant to say 'your mother', but no, she could not, not to Elizabeth. 'I pity other people much more.'

Like some dumb creature who has been brought up to a gate for an unknown purpose, and stands there longing to gallop away, Elizabeth Dalloway sat silent. Was Miss Kilman going to say anything more?

'Don't quite forget me,' said Doris Kilman; her voice quivered. Right away to the end of the field the dumb creature galloped in terror.

The great hand opened and shut.

Elizabeth turned her head. The waitress came. One had to pay at the desk, Elizabeth said, and went off, drawing out, so Miss Kilman felt, the very entrails in her body, stretching them as she crossed the room, and then, with a final twist, bowing her head very politely, she went.

She had gone. Miss Kilman sat at the marble table among the éclairs, stricken once, twice, thrice by shocks of suffering. She had gone. Mrs

Dalloway had triumphed. Elizabeth had gone. Beauty had gone; youth had gone.

So she sat. She got up, blundered off among the little tables, rocking slightly from side to side, and somebody came after her with her petticoat, and she lost her way, and was hemmed in by trunks specially prepared for taking to India; next got among the accouchement sets and baby linen; through all the commodities of the world, perishable and permanent, hams, drugs, flowers, stationery, variously smelling, now sweet, now sour, she lurched; saw herself thus lurching with her hat askew, very red in the face, full length in a looking-glass; and at last came out into the street.

The tower of Westminster Cathedral rose in front of her, the habitation of God. In the midst of the traffic, there was the habitation of God. Doggedly she set off with her parcel to that other sanctuary, the Abbey, where, raising her hands in a tent before her face, she sat beside those driven into shelter too; the variously assorted worshippers, now divested of social rank, almost of sex, as they raised their hands before their faces; but once they removed them, instantly reverent, middle-class, English men and women, some of them desirous of seeing the waxworks.

But Miss Kilman held her tent before her face. Now she was deserted; now rejoined. New worshippers came in from the street to replace the strollers, and still, as people gazed round and shuffled past the tomb of the Unknown Warrior, still she barred her eyes with her fingers and tried in this double darkness, for the light in the Abbey was bodiless, to aspire above the vanities, the desires, the commodities, to rid herself both of hatred and of love. Her hands twitched. She seemed to struggle. Yet to others God was accessible and the path to Him smooth. Mr Fletcher, retired, of the Treasury, Mrs Gorham, widow of the famous KC, approached Him simply, and having done their praying, leant back, enjoyed the music (the organ pealed sweetly), and saw Miss Kilman at the end of the row, praying, praying, and, being still on the threshold of their underworld, thought of her sympathetically as a soul haunting the same territory; a soul cut out of immaterial substance; not a woman, a soul.

But Mr Fletcher had to go. He had to pass her, and being himself neat as a new pin, could not help being a little distressed by the poor lady's disorder; her hair down; her parcel on the floor. She did not at once let him pass. But, as he stood gazing about him, at the white marbles, grey window panes, and accumulated treasures (for he was extremely proud of the Abbey), her largeness, robustness, and power as she sat there shifting her knees from time to time (it was so rough the approach to her God—so tough her desires) impressed him, as they had impressed Mrs Dalloway (she could not get the thought of her out of her mind that afternoon), the Rev. Edward Whittaker, and Elizabeth too.

And Elizabeth waited in Victoria Street for an omnibus. It was so nice to be out of doors. She thought perhaps she need not go home just yet. It was so nice to be out in the air. So she would get on to an omnibus. And already, even as she stood there, in her very well-cut clothes, it was beginning . . . People were beginning to compare her to poplar trees, early dawn, hyacinths, fawns, running water, and garden lilies; and it made her life a burden to her, for she so much preferred being left alone to do what she liked in the country, but they would compare her to lilies, and she had to go to parties, and London was so dreary compared with being alone in the country with her father and the dogs.

Buses swooped, settled, were off—garish caravans, glistening with red and yellow varnish. But which should she get on to? She had no preferences. Of course, she would not push her way. She inclined to be passive. It was expression she needed, but her eyes were fine, Chinese, oriental, and, as her mother said, with such nice shoulders and holding herself so straight, she was always charming to look at; and lately, in the evening especially, when she was interested, for she never seemed excited, she looked almost beautiful, very stately, very serene. What could she be thinking? Every man fell in love with her, and she was really awfully bored. For it was beginning. Her mother could see that— the compliments were beginning. That she did not care more about it— for instance for her clothes—sometimes worried Clarissa, but perhaps it was as well with all those puppies and guinea pigs about having distemper, and it gave her a charm. And now there was this odd friendship with Miss Kilman. Well, thought Clarissa about three o'clock in the morning, reading Baron Marbot for she could not sleep, it proves she has a heart.

Suddenly Elizabeth stepped forward and most competently boarded the omnibus, in front of everybody. She took a seat on top. The impetuous creature—a pirate—started forward, sprang away; she had to hold the rail to steady herself, for a pirate it was, reckless, unscrupulous, bearing down ruthlessly, circumventing dangerously, boldly snatching a passenger, or ignoring a passenger, squeezing eel-like and arrogant in between, and then rushing insolently all sails spread up Whitehall. And did Elizabeth give one thought to poor Miss Kilman who loved her without jealousy, to whom she had been a fawn in the open, a moon in a glade? She was delighted to be free. The fresh air was so delicious. It had been so stuffy in the Army and Navy Stores. And now it was like riding, to be rushing up Whitehall; and to each movement of the omnibus the beautiful body in the fawn-coloured coat responded freely like a rider, like the figure-head of a ship, for the breeze slightly disarrayed her; the heat gave her cheeks the pallor of white painted wood; and her fine eyes, having no eyes to meet, gazed ahead, blank, bright, with the staring, incredible innocence of sculpture.

It was always talking about her own sufferings that made Miss Kilman so difficult. And was she right? If it was being on committees and giving up hours and hours every day (she hardly ever saw him in London) that helped the poor, her father did that, goodness knows—if that was what Miss Kilman meant about being a Christian; but it was so difficult to say. Oh, she would like to go a little farther. Another penny, was it, to the Strand? Here was another penny, then. She would go up the Strand.

She liked people who were ill. And every profession is open to the women of your generation, said Miss Kilman. So she might be a doctor. She might be a farmer. Animals are often ill. She might own a thousand acres and have people under her. She would go and see them in their cottages. This was Somerset House. One might be a very good farmer—and that, strangely enough, though Miss Kilman had her share in it, was almost entirely due to Somerset House. It looked so splendid, so serious, that great grey building. And she liked the feeling of people working. She liked those churches, like shapes of grey paper, breasting the stream of the Strand. It was quite different here from Westminster, she thought, getting off at Chancery Lane. It was so serious; it was so busy. In short, she would like to have a profession. She would become a doctor, a farmer, possibly go into Parliament if she found it necessary, all because of the Strand.

The feet of those people busy about their activities, hands putting stone to stone, minds eternally occupied not with trivial chatterings (comparing women to poplars—which was rather exciting, of course, but very silly), but with thoughts of ships, of business, of law, of administration, and with it all so stately (she was in the Temple), gay (there was the river), pious (there was the Church), made her quite determined, whatever her mother might say, to become either a farmer or a doctor. But she was, of course, rather lazy.

And it was much better to say nothing about it. It seemed so silly. It was the sort of thing that did sometimes happen, when one was alone—buildings without architects' names, crowds of people coming back from the city having more power than single clergymen in Kensington, than any of the books Miss Kilman had lent her, to stimulate what lay slumbrous, clumsy, and shy on the mind's sandy floor, to break surface, as a child suddenly stretches its arms; it was just that, perhaps, a sigh, a stretch of the arms; an impulse, a revelation, which has its effects for ever, and then down again it went to the sandy floor. She must go home. She must dress for dinner. But what was the time?—where was a clock?

She looked up Fleet Street. She walked just a little way towards St Paul's, shyly, like someone penetrating on tiptoe, exploring a strange house by night with a candle, on edge lest the owner should suddenly fling wide his bedroom door and ask her business, nor did she dare wander off into queer alleys, tempting by-streets, any more than in a strange house open doors which might be bedroom doors, or sitting-room doors, or lead straight to the larder. For no Dalloways came down the Strand daily; she was a pioneer, a stray, venturing, trusting.

In many ways, her mother felt, she was extremely immature, like a child still, attached to dolls, to old slippers; a perfect baby; and that was charming. But then, of course, there was in the Dalloway family the tradition of public service. Abbesses, principals, head mistresses, dignitaries, in the republic of women—without being brilliant, any of them, they were that. She penetrated a little farther in the direction of St Paul's. She liked the geniality, sisterhood, motherhood, brotherhood of this uproar. It seemed to her good. The noise was tremendous; and suddenly there were trumpets (the unemployed) blaring, rattling about in the uproar; military music; as if people were marching; yet had they been dying—had some woman breathed her last, and whoever was watching, opening the window of the room where she had just brought off that act of supreme dignity, looked down on Fleet Street, that uproar, that military music would have come triumphing up to him, consolatory, indifferent.

It was not conscious. There was no recognition in it of one's fortune, or fate, and for that very reason even to those dazed with watching for the last shivers of consciousness on the faces of the dying, consoling.

Forgetfulness in people might wound, their ingratitude corrode, but this voice, pouring endlessly, year in, year out, would take whatever it might be; this vow; this van; this life; this procession; would wrap them all about and carry them on, as in the rough stream of a glacier the ice holds a splinter of bone, a blue petal, some oak trees, and rolls them on.

But it was later than she thought. Her mother would not like her to be wandering off alone like this. She turned back down the Strand.

A puff of wind (in spite of the heat, there was quite a wind) blew a thin black veil over the sun and over the Strand. The faces faded; the omnibuses suddenly lost their glow. For although the clouds were of mountainous white so that one could fancy hacking hard chips off with a hatchet, with broad golden slopes, lawns of celestial pleasure gardens, on their flanks, and had all the appearance of settled habitations assembled for the conference of gods above the world, there was a perpetual movement among them. Signs were interchanged, when, as if to fulfil some scheme arranged already, now a summit dwindled, now a whole block of pyramidal size which had kept its station inalterably advanced into the midst or gravely led the procession to fresh anchorage. Fixed though they seemed at their posts, at rest in perfect unanimity, nothing could be fresher, freer, more sensitive superficially than the snow-white or gold-kindled surface; to change, to go, to dismantle the solemn assemblage was immediately possible; and in spite of the grave fixity, the accumulated robustness and solidity, now they struck light to the earth, now darkness.

Calmly and competently, Elizabeth Dalloway mounted the Westminster omnibus.

Going and coming, beckoning, signalling, so the light and shadow, which now made the wall grey, now the bananas bright yellow, now made the Strand grey, now made the omnibuses bright yellow, seemed to Septimus Warren Smith lying on the sofa in the sitting-room; watching the watery gold glow and fade with the astonishing sensibility of some live creature on the roses, on the wallpaper. Outside the trees dragged their leaves like nets through the depths of the air; the sound of water was in the room, and through the waves came the voices of birds singing. Every power poured its treasures on his head, and his hand lay there on the back of the sofa, as he had seen his hand lie when he was bathing, floating, on the top of the waves, while far away on shore he heard dogs barking and barking far away. Fear no more, says the heart in the body; fear no more.

He was not afraid. At every moment Nature signified by some laughing hint like that gold spot which went round the wall—there, there, there—her determination to show, by brandishing her plumes, shaking her tresses, flinging her mantle this way and that, beautifully, always beautifully, and standing close up to breathe through her hollowed hands Shakespeare's words, her meaning.

Rezia, sitting at the table twisting a hat in her hands, watched him; saw him smiling. He was happy, then. But she could not bear to see him smiling. It was not marriage; it was not being one's husband to look strange like that, always to be starting, laughing, sitting hour after hour silent, or clutching her and telling her to write. The table drawer was full of those writings; about war; about Shakespeare; about great discoveries; how there is no death. Lately he had become excited suddenly for no reason (and both Dr Holmes and Sir William Bradshaw said excitement was the worst thing for him), and waved his hands and cried out that he knew the truth! He knew everything! That man, his friend who was killed, Evans, had come, he said. He was singing behind the screen. She wrote it down just as he spoke it. Some things were very beautiful; others sheer nonsense. And he was always stopping in the middle, changing his mind; wanting to add something; hearing something new; listening with his hand up. But she heard nothing.

And once they found the girl who did the room reading one of these papers in fits of laughter. It was a dreadful pity. For that made Septimus cry out about human cruelty—how they tear each other to pieces. The fallen, he said, they tear to pieces. 'Holmes is on us,' he would say, and he would invent stories about Holmes; Holmes eating porridge; Holmes reading Shakespeare—making himself roar with laughter or rage, for Dr Holmes seemed to stand for something horrible to him. 'Human nature', he called him. Then there were the visions. He was drowned, he used to say, and lying on a cliff with the gulls screaming over him. He would look over the edge of the sofa down into the sea. Or he was hearing music. Really it was only a barrel organ or some man crying in the street. But 'Lovely!' he used to cry, and the tears would run down his cheeks, which was to her the most dreadful thing of all, to see a man like Septimus, who had fought, who was brave, crying. And he would lie listening until suddenly he would cry that he was falling down, down into the flames! Actually she would look for flames, it was so vivid. But there was nothing. They were alone in the room. It was a dream, she would tell him, and so quiet him at last, but sometimes she was frightened too. She sighed as she sat sewing.

Her sigh was tender and enchanting, like the wind outside a wood in the evening. Now she put down her scissors; now she turned to take something from the table. A little stir, a little crinkling, a little tapping built up something on the table there, where she sat sewing. Through his eyelashes he could see her blurred outline; her little black body; her face and hands; her turning movements at the table, as she took up a reel, or looked (she was apt to lose things) for her silk. She was making a hat for Mrs Filmer's married daughter, whose name was—he had forgotten her name.

'What is the name of Mrs Filmer's married daughter?' he asked.

'Mrs Peters,' said Rezia. She was afraid it was too small, she said, holding it before her. Mrs Peters was a big woman; but she did not like her. It was only because Mrs Filmer had been so good to them—'She gave me grapes this morning,' she said—that Rezia wanted to do something to show that they were grateful. She had come into the room the other evening and found Mrs Peters, who thought they were out, playing the gramophone.

'Was it true?' he asked. She was playing the gramophone? Yes; she had told him about it at the time; she had found Mrs Peters playing the gramophone.

He began, very cautiously, to open his eyes, to see whether a

gramophone was really there. But real things—real things were too
exciting. He must be cautious. He would not go mad. First he looked at
the fashion papers on the lower shelf, then gradually at the gramophone
with the green trumpet. Nothing could be more exact. And so, gathering
courage, he looked at the sideboard; the plate of bananas; the engraving
of Queen Victoria and the Prince Consort; at the mantelpiece, with the
jar of roses. None of these things moved. All were still; all were real.

'She is a woman with a spiteful tongue,' said Rezia.

'What does Mr Peters do?' Septimus asked.

'Ah,' said Rezia, trying to remember. She thought Mrs Filmer had
said that he travelled for some company. 'Just now he is in Hull,' she
said.

'Just now!' She said that with her Italian accent. She said that herself.
He shaded his eyes so that he might see only a little of her face at a time,
first the chin, then the nose, then the forehead, in case it were deformed,
or had some terrible mark on it. But no, there she was, perfectly natural,
sewing, with the pursed lips that women have, the set, the melancholy
expression, when sewing. But there was nothing terrible about it, he
assured himself, looking a second time, a third time at her face, her
hands, for what was frightening or disgusting in her as she sat there in
broad daylight, sewing? Mrs Peters had a spiteful tongue. Mr Peters
was in Hull. Why, then, rage and prophesy? Why fly scourged and
outcast? Why be made to tremble and sob by the clouds? Why seek
truths and deliver messages when Rezia sat sticking pins into the front
of her dress, and Mr Peters was in Hull? Miracles, revelations, agonies,
loneliness, falling through the sea, down, down into the flames, all were
burnt out, for he had a sense, as he watched Rezia trimming the straw
hat for Mrs Peters, of a coverlet of flowers.

'It's too small for Mrs Peters,' said Septimus.

For the first time for days he was speaking as he used to do! Of course
it was—absurdly small, she said. But Mrs Peters had chosen it.

He took it out of her hands. He said it was an organ grinder's
monkey's hat.

How it rejoiced her, that! Not for weeks had they laughed like this
together, poking fun privately like married people. What she meant was
that if Mrs Filmer had come in, or Mrs Peters or anybody, they would
not have understood what she and Septimus were laughing at.

'There,' she said, pinning a rose to one side of the hat. Never had she
felt so happy! Never in her life!

But that was still more ridiculous, Septimus said. Now the poor
woman looked like a pig at a fair. (Nobody ever made her laugh as
Septimus did.)

What had she got in her work-box? She had ribbons and beads, tassels, artificial flowers. She tumbled them out on the table. He began putting odd colours together—for though he had no fingers, could not even do up a parcel, he had a wonderful eye, and often he was right, sometimes absurd, of course, but sometimes wonderfully right.

'She shall have a beautiful hat!' he murmured, taking up this and that, Rezia kneeling by his side, looking over his shoulder. Now it was finished—that is to say the design; she must stitch it together. But she must be very, very careful, he said, to keep it just as he had made it.

So she sewed. When she sewed, he thought, she made a sound like a kettle on the hob; bubbling, murmuring, always busy, her strong little pointed fingers pinching and poking; her needle flashing straight. The sun might go in and out, on the tassels, on the wallpaper, but he would wait, he thought, stretching out his feet, looking at his ringed sock at the end of the sofa; he would wait in this warm place, this pocket of still air, which one comes on at the edge of a wood sometimes in the evening, when, because of a fall in the ground, or some arrangement of the trees (one must be scientific above all, scientific), warmth lingers, and the air buffets the cheek like the wing of a bird.

'There it is,' said Rezia, twirling Mrs Peters' hat on the tips of her fingers. 'That'll do for the moment. Later . . .' her sentence bubbled away drip, drip, drip, like a contented tap left running.

It was wonderful. Never had he done anything which made him feel so proud. It was so real, it was so substantial, Mrs Peters' hat.

'Just look at it,' he said.

Yes, it would always make her happy to see that hat. He had become himself then, he had laughed then. They had been alone together. Always she would like that hat.

He told her to try it on.

'But I must look so queer!' she cried, running over to the glass and looking first this side, then that. Then she snatched it off again, for there was a tap at the door. Could it be Sir William Bradshaw? Had he sent already?

No! it was only the small girl with the evening paper.

What always happened, then happened—what happened every night of their lives. The small girl sucked her thumb at the door; Rezia went down on her knees; Rezia cooed and kissed; Rezia got a bag of sweets out of the table drawer. For so it always happened. First one thing, then another. So she built it up, first one thing and then another. Dancing, skipping, round and round the room they went. He took the paper. Surrey was all out, he read. There was a heat wave. Rezia repeated: Surrey was all out. There was a heat wave, making it part of the game she was playing with Mrs Filmer's grandchild, both of them laughing, chattering at the same time, at their game. He was very tired. He was very happy. He would sleep. He shut his eyes. But directly he saw nothing the sounds of the game became fainter and stranger and sounded like the cries of people seeking and not finding, and passing farther and farther away. They had lost him!

He started up in terror. What did he see? The plate of bananas on the sideboard. Nobody was there (Rezia had taken the child to its mother; it was bedtime). That was it: to be alone for ever. That was the doom pronounced in Milan when he came into the room and saw them cutting out buckram shapes with their scissors; to be alone for ever.

He was alone with the sideboard and the bananas. He was alone, exposed on this bleak eminence, stretched out—but not on a hill-top; not on a crag; on Mrs Filmer's sitting-room sofa. As for the visions, the faces, the voices of the dead, where were they? There was a screen in front of him, with black bulrushes and blue swallows. Where he had once seen mountains, where he had seen faces, where he had seen beauty, there was a screen.

'Evans!' he cried. There was no answer. A mouse had squeaked, or a curtain rustled. Those were the voices of the dead. The screen, the coal-scuttle, the sideboard remained to him. Let him, then, face the screen, the coal-scuttle and the sideboard . . . but Rezia burst into the room chattering.

Some letter had come. Everybody's plans were changed. Mrs Filmer would not be able to go to Brighton after all. There was no time to let Mrs Williams know, and really Rezia thought it very, very annoying, when she caught sight of the hat and thought . . . perhaps . . . she— might just make a little . . . Her voice died out in contented melody.

'Ah, damn!' she cried (it was a joke of theirs, her swearing); the needle had broken. Hat, child, Brighton, needle. She built it up; first one thing, then another, she built it up, sewing.

She wanted him to say whether by moving the rose she had improved the hat. She sat on the end of the sofa.

They were perfectly happy now, she said suddenly, putting the hat down. For she could say anything to him now. She could say whatever came into her head. That was almost the first thing she had felt about him, that night in the café when he had come in with his English friends. He had come in, rather shyly, looking round him, and his hat had fallen when he hung it up. That she could remember. She knew he was English, though not one of the large Englishmen her sister admired, for he was always thin; but he had a beautiful fresh colour; and with his big nose, his bright eyes, his way of sitting a little hunched, made her think, she had often told him, of a young hawk, that first evening she saw him, when they were playing dominoes, and he had come in—of a young hawk; but with her he was always very gentle. She had never seen him wild or drunk, only suffering sometimes through this terrible war, but even so, when she came in, he would put it all away. Anything, anything in the whole world, any little bother with her work, anything that struck her to say she would tell him, and he understood at once. Her own family even were not the same. Being older than she was and being so clever—how serious he was, wanting her to read Shakespeare before she could even read a child's story in English!—being so much more experienced, he could help her. And she, too, could help him.

But this hat now. And then (it was getting late) Sir William Bradshaw.

She held her hands to her head, waiting for him to say did he like the hat or not, and as she sat there, waiting, looking down, he could feel her mind, like a bird, falling from branch to branch, and always alighting, quite rightly; he could follow her mind, as she sat there in one of those loose lax poses that came to her naturally, and, if he should say anything, at once she smiled, like a bird alighting with all its claws firm upon the bough.

But he remembered. Bradshaw said, 'The people we are most fond of are not good for us when we are ill.' Bradshaw said he must be taught to rest. Bradshaw said they must be separated.

'Must', 'must', why 'must'? What power had Bradshaw over him? 'What right has Bradshaw to say "must" to me?' he demanded.

'It is because you talked of killing yourself,' said Rezia. (Mercifully, she could now say anything to Septimus.)

So he was in their power! Holmes and Bradshaw were on him! The brute with the red nostrils was snuffling into every secret place! 'Must' it could say! Where were his papers? the things he had written?

She brought him his papers, the things he had written, things she had written for him. She tumbled them out on to the sofa. They looked at them together. Diagrams, designs, little men and women brandishing sticks for arms, with wings—were they?—on their backs; circles traced round shillings and sixpences—the suns and stars; zigzagging precipices with mountaineers ascending roped together, exactly like knives and forks; sea pieces with little faces laughing out of what might perhaps be waves: the map of the world. Burn them! he cried. Now for his writings; how the dead sing behind rhododendron bushes; odes to Time; conversations with Shakespeare; Evans, Evans, Evans—his messages from the dead; do not cut down trees; tell the Prime Minister. Universal love: the meaning of the world. Burn them! he cried.

But Rezia laid her hands on them. Some were very beautiful, she thought. She would tie them up (for she had no envelope) with a piece of silk.

Even if they took him, she said, she would go with him. They could not separate them against their wills, she said.

Shuffling the edges straight, she did up the papers, and tied the parcel almost without looking, sitting close, sitting beside him, he thought, as if all her petals were about her. She was a flowering tree; and through her branches looked out the face of a lawgiver, who had reached a sanctuary where she feared no one; not Holmes; not Bradshaw; a miracle, a triumph, the last and greatest. Staggering he saw her mount the appalling staircase, laden with Holmes and Bradshaw, men who never weighed less than eleven stone six, who sent their wives to court, men who made ten thousand a year and talked of proportion; who differed in their verdicts (for Holmes said one thing, Bradshaw another), yet judges they were; who mixed the vision and the sideboard; saw nothing clear, yet ruled, yet inflicted. Over them she triumphed.

'There!' she said. The papers were tied up. No one should get at them. She would put them away.

And, she said, nothing should separate them. She sat down beside him and called him by the name of that hawk or crow which, being malicious and a great destroyer of crops, was precisely like him. No one could separate them, she said.

Then she got up to go into the bedroom to pack their things, but hearing voices downstairs and thinking that Dr Holmes had perhaps called, ran down to prevent him coming up.

Septimus could hear her talking to Holmes on the staircase.

'My dear lady, I have come as a friend,' Holmes was saying.

'No. I will not allow you to see my husband,' she said.

He could see her, like a little hen, with her wings spread barring his passage. But Holmes persevered.

'My dear lady, allow me . . .' Holmes said, putting her aside (Holmes was a powerfully built man).

Holmes was coming upstairs. Holmes would burst open the door. Holmes would say, 'In a funk, eh?' Holmes would get him. But no; not Holmes; not Bradshaw. Getting up rather unsteadily, hopping indeed from foot to foot, he considered Mrs Filmer's nice clean bread-knife with 'Bread' carved on the handle. Ah, but one mustn't spoil that. The gas fire? But it was too late now. Holmes was coming. Razors he might have got, but Rezia, who always did that sort of thing, had packed them. There remained only the window, the large Bloomsbury lodging-house window; the tiresome, the troublesome, and rather melodramatic business of opening the window and throwing himself out. It was their idea of tragedy, not his or Rezia's (for she was with him). Holmes and Bradshaw liked that sort of thing. (He sat on the sill.) But he would wait till the very last moment. He did not want to die. Life was good. The sun hot. Only human beings? Coming down the staircase opposite an old man stopped and stared at him. Holmes was at the door. 'I'll give it you!' he cried, and flung himself vigorously, violently down on to Mrs Filmer's area railings.

'The coward!' cried Dr Holmes, bursting the door open. Rezia ran to the window, she saw; she understood. Dr Holmes and Mrs Filmer collided with each other. Mrs Filmer flapped her apron and made her hide her eyes in the bedroom. There was a great deal of running up and down stairs. Dr Holmes came in—white as a sheet, shaking all over, with a glass in his hand. She must be brave and drink something, he said (What was it? Something sweet), for her husband was horribly mangled, would not recover consciousness, she must not see him, must be spared as much as possible, would have the inquest to go through, poor young woman. Who could have foretold it? A sudden impulse, no one was in the least to blame (he told Mrs Filmer). And why the devil he did it, Dr Holmes could not conceive.

It seemed to her as she drank the sweet stuff that she was opening long windows, stepping out into some garden. But where? The clock was striking—one, two, three: how sensible the sound was; compared with all this thumping and whispering; like Septimus himself. She was falling asleep. But the clock went on striking, four, five, six, and Mrs Filmer waving her apron (they wouldn't bring the body in here, would they?) seemed part of that garden; or a flag. She had once seen a flag slowly rippling out from a mast when she stayed with her aunt at Venice. Men killed in battle were thus saluted, and Septimus had been through the War. Of her memories, most were happy.

She put on her hat, and ran through cornfields—where could it have been?—on to some hill, somewhere near the sea, for there were ships, gulls, butterflies; they sat on a cliff. In London, too, there they sat, and, half dreaming, came to her through the bedroom door, rain falling, whisperings, stirrings among dry corn, the caress of the sea, as it seemed to her, hollowing them in its arched shell and murmuring to her laid on shore, strewn she felt, like flying flowers over some tomb.

'He is dead,' she said, smiling at the poor old woman who guarded her with her honest light-blue eyes fixed on the door. (They wouldn't bring him in here, would they?) But Mrs Filmer pooh-poohed. Oh no, oh no! They were carrying him away now. Ought she not to be told? Married people ought to be together, Mrs Filmer thought. But they must do as the doctor said.

'Let her sleep,' said Dr Holmes, feeling her pulse. She saw the large outline of his body dark against the window. So that was Dr Holmes.

One of the triumphs of civilization, Peter Walsh thought. It is one of the triumphs of civilization, as the light high bell of the ambulance sounded. Swiftly, cleanly, the ambulance sped to the hospital, having picked up instantly, humanely, some poor devil; some one hit on the head, struck down by disease, knocked over perhaps a minute or so ago at one of these crossings, as might happen to oneself. That was civilization. It struck him coming back from the East—the efficiency, the organization, the communal spirit of London. Every cart or carriage of its own accord drew aside to let the ambulance pass. Perhaps it was morbid; or was it not touching rather, the respect which they showed this ambulance with its victim inside—busy men hurrying home, yet instantly bethinking them as it passed of some wife; or presumably how easily it might have been them there, stretched on a shelf with a doctor and a nurse . . . Ah, but thinking became morbid, sentimental, directly one began conjuring up doctors, dead bodies; a little glow of pleasure, a sort of lust, too, over the visual impression warned one not to go on with that sort of thing any more—fatal to art, fatal to friendship. True. And yet, thought Peter Walsh, as the ambulance turned the corner, though the light high bell could be heard down the next street and still farther as it crossed the Tottenham Court Road, chiming constantly, it is the privilege of loneliness; in privacy one may do as one chooses. One might weep if no one saw. It had been his undoing—this susceptibility—in Anglo-Indian society; not weeping at the right time, or laughing either. I have that in me, he thought, standing by the pillar-box, which could now dissolve in tears. Why, heaven knows. Beauty of some sort probably, and the weight of the day, which, beginning with that visit to Clarissa, had exhausted him with its heat, its intensity, and the drip, drip of one impression after another down into that cellar where they stood, deep, dark, and no one would ever know. Partly for that reason, its secrecy, complete and inviolable, he had found life like an unknown garden, full of turns and corners, surprising, yes; really it took one's breath away, these moments; there coming to him by the pillar-box opposite the British Museum one of them, a moment, in which things came together; this ambulance; and life and death. It was as if he were sucked up to some very high roof by that rush of emotion, and the rest of him, like a white shell-sprinkled beach, left bare. It had been his undoing in Anglo-Indian society—this susceptibility.

Clarissa once, going on top of an omnibus with him somewhere, Clarissa superficially at least, so easily moved, now in despair, now in the best of spirits, all aquiver in those days and such good company, spotting queer little scenes, names, people from the top of a bus, for they used to explore London and bring back bags full of treasures from the Caledonian market—Clarissa had a theory in those days—they had heaps of theories, always theories, as young people have. It was to explain the feeling they had of dissatisfaction; not knowing people; not being known. For how could they know each other? You met every day;

then not for six months, or years. It was unsatisfactory, they agreed, how little one knew people. But she said, sitting on the bus going up Shaftesbury Avenue, she felt herself everywhere; not 'here, here, here'; and she tapped the back of the seat; but everywhere. She waved her hand, going up Shaftesbury Avenue. She was all that. So that to know her, or any one, one must seek out the people who completed them; even the places. Odd affinities she had with people she had never spoken to, some woman in the street, some man behind a counter—even trees, or barns. It ended in a transcendental theory which, with her horror of death, allowed her to believe, or say that she believed (for all her scepticism), that since our apparitions, the part of us which appears, are so momentary compared with the other, the unseen part of us, which spreads wide, the unseen might survive, be recovered somehow attached to this person or that, or even haunting certain places, after death. Perhaps—perhaps.

Looking back over that long friendship of almost thirty years her theory worked to this extent. Brief, broken, often painful as their actual meetings had been, what with his absences and interruptions (this morning, for instance, in came Elizabeth, like a long-legged colt, handsome, dumb, just as he was beginning to talk to Clarissa), the effect of them on his life was immeasurable. There was a mystery about it You were given a sharp, acute, uncomfortable grain—the actual meeting; horribly painful as often as not; yet in absence, in the most unlikely places, it would flower out, open, shed its scent, let you touch, taste, look about you, get the whole feel of it and understanding, after years of lying lost. Thus she had come to him; on board ship; in the Himalayas; suggested by the oddest things (so Sally Seton, generous, enthusiastic goose! thought of *him* when she saw blue hydrangeas). She had influenced him more than any person he had ever known. And always in this way coming before him without his wishing it, cool, lady-like, critical; or ravishing, romantic, recalling some field or English harvest. He saw her most often in the country, not in London. One scene after another at Bourton . . .

He had reached his hotel. He crossed the hall, with its mounds of reddish chairs and sofas, its spike-leaved, withered-looking plants. He got his key off the hook. The young lady handed him some letters. He went upstairs—he saw her most often at Bourton, in the late summer, when he stayed there for a week, or fortnight even, as people did in those days. First on top of some hill there she would stand, hands clapped to her hair, her cloak blowing out, pointing, crying to them— She saw the Severn beneath. Or in a wood, making the kettle boil— very ineffective with her fingers; the smoke curtseying, blowing in their faces; her little pink face showing through; begging water from an old woman in a cottage, who came to the door to watch them go. They walked always; the others drove. She was bored driving, disliked all animals, except that dog. They tramped miles along roads. She would break off to get her bearings, pilot him back across country; and all the time they argued, discussed poetry, discussed people, discussed politics (she was a Radical then); never noticing a thing except when she stopped, cried out at a view or a tree, and made him look with her; and so on again, through stubble fields, she walking ahead, with a flower for her aunt, never tired of walking for all her delicacy; to drop down on Bourton in the dusk. Then, after dinner, old Breitkopf would open the piano and sing without any voice, and they would lie sunk in armchairs, trying not to laugh, but always breaking down and laughing, laughing— laughing at nothing. Breitkopf was supposed not to see. And then in the morning, flirting up and down like a wagtail in front of the house . . .

Oh it was a letter from her! This blue envelope; that was her hand. And he would have to read it. Here was another of those meetings, bound to be painful! To read her letter needed the devil of an effort. 'How heavenly it was to see him. She must tell him that.' That was all.

But it upset him. It annoyed him. He wished she hadn't written it. Coming on top of his thoughts, it was like a nudge in the ribs. Why couldn't she let him be? After all, she had married Dalloway, and lived with him in perfect happiness all these years.

These hotels are not consoling places. Far from it. Any number of people had hung up their hats on those pegs. Even the flies, if you thought of it, had settled on other people's noses. As for the cleanliness which hit him in the face, it wasn't cleanliness, so much as bareness, frigidity; a thing that had to be. Some arid matron made her rounds at dawn sniffing, peering, causing blue-nosed maids to scour, for all the world as if the next visitor were a joint of meat to be served on a perfectly clean platter. For sleep, one bed; for sitting in, one armchair; for cleaning one's teeth and shaving one's chin, one tumbler, one looking-glass. Books, letters, dressing-gown, slipped about on the imper- sonality of the horse-hair like incongruous impertinences. And it was Clarissa's letter that made him see all this. 'Heavenly to see you. She must say so!' He folded the paper; pushed it away; nothing would induce him to read it again!

To get that letter to him by six o'clock she must have sat down and written it directly he left her; stamped it; sent somebody to the post. It was, as people say, very like her. She was upset by his visit. She had felt a great deal; had for a moment, when she kissed his hand, regretted, envied him even, remembered possibly (for he saw her look it) something he had said—how they would change the world if she married him perhaps; whereas, it was this; it was middle age; it was mediocrity; then forced herself with her indomitable vitality to put all that aside, there being in her a thread of life which for toughness, endurance, power to overcome obstacles and carry her triumphantly through he had never known the like of. Yes; but there would come a reaction directly he left the room. She would be frightfully sorry for him; she would think what in the world she could do to give him pleasure (short always of the one thing), and he could see her with the tears running down her cheeks going to her writing-table and dashing off that one line which he was to find greeting him . . . 'Heavenly to see you!' And she meant it.

Peter Walsh had now unlaced his boots.

But it would not have been a success, their marriage. The other thing, after all, came so much more naturally.

It was odd; it was true; lots of people felt it. Peter Walsh, who had done just respectably, filled the usual posts adequately, was liked, but thought a little cranky, gave himself airs—it was odd that *he* should have had, especially now that his hair was grey, a contented look; a look of having reserves. It was this that made him attractive to women, who liked the sense that he was not altogether manly. There was something unusual about him, or something behind him. It might be that he was bookish—never came to see you without taking up the book on the table (he was now reading, with his bootlaces trailing on the floor); or that he was a gentleman, which showed itself in the way he knocked the ashes out of his pipe, and in his manners of course to women. For it was very charming and quite ridiculous how easily some girl without a grain of sense could twist him round her finger. But at her own risk. That is to say, though he might be ever so easy, and indeed with his gaiety and good-breeding fascinating to be with, it was only up to a point. She said something—no, no; he saw through that. He wouldn't stand that—no, no. Then he could shout and rock and hold his sides together over some joke with men. He was the best judge of cooking in India. He was a man. But not the sort of man one had to respect—which was a mercy; not like Major Simmons, for instance; not in the least, Daisy thought, when, in spite of her two small children, she used to compare them.

He pulled off his boots. He emptied his pockets. Out came with his pocket-knife a snapshot of Daisy on the verandah; Daisy all in white, with a fox-terrier on her knee; very charming, very dark; the best he had ever seen of her. It did come, after all, so naturally; so much more naturally than Clarissa. No fuss. No bother. No finicking and fidgeting. All plain sailing. And the dark, adorably pretty girl on the verandah exclaimed (he could hear her). Of course, of course she would give him everything! she cried (she had no sense of discretion), everything he wanted! she cried, running to meet him, whoever might be looking. And she was only twenty-four. And she had two children. Well, well!

Well indeed he had got himself into a mess at his age. And it came over him when he woke in the night pretty forcibly. Suppose they did marry? For him it would be all very well, but what about her? Mrs Burgess, a good sort and no chatterbox, in whom he had confided, thought this absence of his in England, ostensibly to see lawyers, might serve to make Daisy reconsider, think what it meant. It was a question of her position, Mrs Burgess said; the social barrier; giving up her children. She'd be a widow with a past one of these days, draggling about in the suburbs, or more likely, indiscriminate (you know, she said, what such women get like, with too much paint). But Peter Walsh pooh-poohed all that. He didn't mean to die yet. Anyhow, she must settle for herself; judge for herself, he thought, padding about the room in his socks, smoothing out his dress-shirt for he might go to Clarissa's party, or he might go to one of the Halls, or he might settle in and read an absorbing book written by a man he used to know at Oxford. And if he did retire, that's what he'd do—write books. He would go to Oxford and poke about in the Bodleian. Vainly the dark, adorably pretty girl ran to the end of the terrace; vainly waved her hand; vainly cried she didn't care a straw what people said. There he was, the man she thought the world of, the perfect gentleman, the fascinating, the distinguished (and his age made not the least difference to her), padding about a room in an hotel in Bloomsbury, shaving, washing, continuing, as he took up cans, put down razors, to poke about in the Bodleian, and get at the truth about one or two little matters that interested him. And he would have a chat with whoever it might be, and so come to disregard more and more precise hours for lunch, and miss engagements; and when Daisy asked him, as she would, for a kiss, a scene, fail to come up to the scratch (though he was genuinely devoted to her)—in short, it might be happier, as Mrs Burgess said, that she should forget him, or merely remember him as he was in August 1922, like a figure standing at the crossroads at dusk, which grows more and more remote as the dog-cart spins away, carrying her securely fastened to the back seat, though her arms are outstretched; and as she sees the figure dwindle and disappear, still she cries out how she would do anything in the world, anything, anything, anything . . .

He never knew what people thought. It became more and more difficult for him to concentrate. He became absorbed; he became busied with his own concerns; now surly, now gay; dependent on women, absent-minded, moody, less and less able (so he thought as he shaved) to understand why Clarissa couldn't simply find them a lodging and be nice to Daisy; introduce her. And then he could just—just do what? just haunt and hover (he was at the moment actually engaged in sorting out various keys, papers), swoop and taste, be alone, in short, sufficient to himself; and yet nobody of course was more dependent upon others (he buttoned his waistcoat); it had been his undoing. He could not keep out of smoking-rooms, liked colonels, liked golf, liked bridge, and above all women's society, and the fineness of their companionship, and their faithfulness and audacity and greatness in loving which, though it had its drawbacks, seemed to him (and the dark, adorably pretty face was on top of the envelopes) so wholly admirable, so splendid a flower to grow on the crest of human life, and yet he could not come up to the scratch, being always apt to see round things (Clarissa had sapped something in him permanently), and to tire very easily of mute devotion and to want variety in love, though it would make him furious if Daisy loved anybody else, furious! for he was jealous, uncontrollably jealous by temperament. He suffered tortures! But where was his knife; his watch; his seals, his note-case, and Clarissa's letter which he would not read again but liked to think of, and Daisy's photograph? And now for dinner.

They were eating.

Sitting at little tables round vases, dressed or not dressed, with their shawls and bags laid beside them, with their air of false composure, for they were not used to so many courses at dinner; and confidence, for they were able to pay for it, and strain, for they had been running about London all day shopping, sightseeing; and their natural curiosity, for they looked round and up as the nice-looking gentleman in horn-rimmed spectacles came in; and their good nature, for they would have been glad to do any little service, such as lend a time-table or impart useful information; and their desire, pulsing in them, tugging at them subterraneously, somehow to establish connections if it were only a birthplace (Liverpool, for example), in common or friends of the same name; with their furtive glances, odd silences, and sudden withdrawals into family jocularity and isolation; there they sat eating dinner when Mr Walsh came in and took his seat at a little table by the curtain.

It was not that he said anything, for being solitary he could only address himself to the waiter; it was his way of looking at the menu, of pointing his forefinger to a particular wine, of hitching himself up to the table, of addressing himself seriously, not gluttonously, to dinner, that won him their respect; which, having to remain unexpressed for the greater part of the meal, flared up at the table where the Morrises sat when Mr Walsh was heard to say at the end of the meal, 'Bartlett pears'. Why he should have spoken so moderately yet firmly, with the air of a disciplinarian well within his rights which are founded upon justice, neither young Charles Morris, nor old Charles, neither Miss Elaine nor Mrs Morris knew. But when he said, 'Bartlett pears', sitting alone at his table, they felt that he counted on their support in some lawful demand;

was champion of a cause which immediately became their own, so that their eyes met his eyes sympathetically, and when they all reached the smoking-room simultaneously, a little talk between them became inevitable.

It was not very profound—only to the effect that London was crowded; had changed in thirty years; that Mr Morris preferred Liverpool; that Mrs Morris had been to the Westminster flower-show, and that they had all seen the Prince of Wales. Yet, thought Peter Walsh, no family in the world can compare with the Morrises; none whatever; and their relations to each other are perfect, and they don't care a hang for the upper classes, and they like what they like, and Elaine is training for the family business, and the boy has won a scholarship at Leeds, and the old lady (who is about his own age) has three more children at home; and they have two motor cars, but Mr Morris still mends the boots on Sunday: it is superb, it is absolutely superb, thought Peter Walsh, swaying a little backwards and forwards with his liqueur glass in his hand among the hairy red chairs and ash-trays, feeling very well pleased with himself, for the Morrises liked him. Yes, they liked a man who said 'Bartlett pears'. They liked him, he felt.

He would go to Clarissa's party. (The Morrises moved off; but they would meet again.) He would go to Clarissa's party, because he wanted to ask Richard what they were doing in India—the conservative duffers. And what's being acted? And music . . . Oh yes, and mere gossip.

For this is the truth about our soul, he thought, our self, who fish-like inhabits deep seas and plies among obscurities threading her way between the boles of giant weeds, over sun-flickered spaces and on and on into gloom, cold, deep, inscrutable; suddenly she shoots to the surface and sports on the wind-wrinkled waves; that is, has a positive need to brush, scrape, kindle herself, gossiping. What did the Government mean—Richard Dalloway would know—to do about India?

Since it was a very hot night and the paper boys went by with placards proclaiming in huge red letters that there was a heat-wave, wicker chairs were placed on the hotel steps and there, sipping, smoking, detached gentlemen sat. Peter Walsh sat there. One might fancy that day, the London day, was just beginning. Like a woman who had slipped off her print dress and white apron to array herself in blue and pearls, the day changed, put off stuff, took gauze, changed to evening, and with the same sigh of exhilaration that a woman breathes, tumbling petticoats on the floor, it too shed dust, heat, colour; the traffic thinned; motor cars, tinkling, darting, succeeded the lumber of vans; and here and there among the thick foliage of the squares an intense light hung. I resign, the evening seemed to say, as it paled and faded above the battlements and prominences, moulded, pointed, of hotel, flat, and block of shops, I fade, she was beginning, I disappear, but London would have none of it, and rushed her bayonets into the sky, pinioned her, constrained her to partnership in her revelry.

For the great revolution of Mr Willett's summer time had taken place since Peter Walsh's last visit to England. The prolonged evening was new to him. It was inspiriting, rather. For as the young people went by with their despatch-boxes, awfully glad to be free, proud too, dumbly, of stepping this famous pavement, joy of a kind, cheap, tinselly, if you like, but all the same rapture, flushed their faces. They dressed well too; pink stockings; pretty shoes. They would now have two hours at the pictures. It sharpened, it refined them, the yellow-blue evening light; and on the leaves in the square shone lurid, livid—they looked as if dipped in sea water—the foliage of a submerged city. He was astonished by the beauty; it was encouraging too, for where the returned Anglo-Indian sat by rights (he knew crowds of them) in the Oriental Club biliously summing up the ruin of the world, here was he, as young as ever; envying young people their summer time and the rest of it, and more than suspecting from the words of a girl, from a housemaid's laughter—intangible things you couldn't lay your hands on—that shift in the whole pyramidal accumulation which in his youth had seemed immovable. On top of them it had pressed, weighed them down, the women especially, like those flowers Clarissa's Aunt Helena used to press between sheets of grey blotting-paper with Littré's dictionary on top, sitting under the lamp after dinner. She was dead now. He had heard of her, from Clarissa, losing the sight of one eye. It seemed so fitting—one of nature's masterpieces—that old Miss Parry should turn to glass. She would die like some bird in a frost gripping her perch. She belonged to a different age, but being so entire, so complete, would always stand up on the horizon, stone-white, eminent, like a lighthouse marking some past stage on this adventurous, long, long voyage, this interminable—(he felt for a copper to buy a paper and read about Surrey and Yorkshire; he had held out that copper millions of times— Surrey was all out once more)—this interminable life. But cricket was no mere game. Cricket was important. He could never help reading about cricket. He read the scores in the stop press first, then how it was a hot day; then about a murder case. Having done things millions of times enriched them, though it might be said to take the surface off. The past enriched, and experience, and having cared for one or two people, and so having acquired the power which the young lack, of cutting short, doing what one likes, not caring a rap what people say and coming and going without any very great expectations (he left his paper on the table and moved off), which however (and he looked for his hat and coat) was not altogether true of him, not tonight, for here he was starting to go to a party, at his age, with the belief upon him that he was about to have an experience. But what?

Beauty anyhow. Not the crude beauty of the eye. It was not beauty pure and simple—Bedford Place leading into Russell Square. It was straightness and emptiness of course; the symmetry of a corridor; but it was also windows lit up, a piano, a gramophone sounding; a sense of pleasure-making hidden, but now and again emerging when, through the uncurtained window, the window left open, one saw parties sitting over tables, young people slowly circling, conversations between men and women, maids idly looking out (a strange comment theirs, when work was done), stockings drying on top ledges, a parrot, a few plants. Absorbing, mysterious, of infinite richness, this life. And in the large square where the cabs shot and swerved so quick, there were loitering couples, dallying, embracing, shrunk up under the shower of a tree; that was moving; so silent, so absorbed, that one passed, discreetly, timidly, as if in the presence of some sacred ceremony to interrupt which would have been impious. That was interesting. And so on into the flare and glare.

His light overcoat blew open, he stepped with indescribable idiosyncrasy, leant a little forward, tripped, with his hands behind his back and his eyes still a little hawk-like; he tripped through London, towards Westminster, observing.

Was everybody dining out, then? Doors were being opened here by a footman to let issue a high-stepping old dame, in buckled shoes, with three purple ostrich feathers in her hair. Doors were being opened for ladies wrapped like mummies in shawls with bright flowers on them, ladies with bare heads. And in respectable quarters with stucco pillars through small front gardens, lightly swathed, with combs in their hair (having run up to see the children), women came; men waited for them, with their coats blowing open, and the motor started. Everybody was going out. What with these doors being opened, and the descent and the start, it seemed as if the whole of London were embarking in little boats moored to the bank, tossing on the waters, as if the whole place were floating off in carnival. And Whitehall was skated over, silver beaten as it was, skated over by spiders, and there was a sense of midges round the arc lamps; it was so hot that people stood about talking. And here in Westminster was a retired Judge, presumably, sitting four square at his house door dressed all in white. An Anglo-Indian presumably.

And here a shindy of brawling women, drunken women; here only a policeman and looming houses, high houses, domed houses, churches, parliaments, and the hoot of a steamer on the river, a hollow misty cry. But it was her street, this, Clarissa's; cabs were rushing round the corner, like water round the piers of a bridge, drawn together, it seemed to him, because they bore people going to her party, Clarissa's party.

The cold stream of visual impressions failed him now as if the eye were a cup that overflowed and let the rest run down its china walls unrecorded. The brain must wake now. The body must contract now, entering the house, the lighted house, where the door stood open, where the motor cars were standing, and bright women descending: the soul must brave itself to endure. He opened the big blade of his pocket-knife.

Lucy came running full tilt downstairs, having just nipped into the drawing-room to smooth a cover, to straighten a chair, to pause a moment and feel whoever came in must think how clean, how bright, how beautifully cared for, when they saw the beautiful silver, the brass fire-irons, the new chair-covers, and the curtains of yellow chintz: she appraised each; heard a roar of voices; people already coming up from dinner; she must fly!

The Prime Minister was coming, Agnes said: so she had heard them say in the dining-room, she said, coming in with a tray of glasses. Did it matter, did it matter in the least, one Prime Minister more or less? It made no difference at this hour of the night to Mrs Walker among the plates, saucepans, cullenders, frying-pans, chicken in aspic, ice-cream freezers, pared crusts of bread, lemons, soup tureens, and pudding basins which, however hard they washed up in the scullery, seemed to be all on top of her, on the kitchen table, on chairs, while the fire blared and roared, the electric lights glared, and still supper had to be laid. All she felt was, one Prime Minister more or less made not a scrap of difference to Mrs Walker.

The ladies were going upstairs already, said Lucy; the ladies were going up, one by one, Mrs Dalloway walking last and almost always sending back some message to the kitchen, 'My love to Mrs Walker,' that was it one night. Next morning they would go over the dishes—the soup, the salmon; the salmon, Mrs Walker knew, as usual underdone, for she always got nervous about the pudding and left it to Jenny; so it happened, the salmon was always underdone. But some lady with fair hair and silver ornaments had said, Lucy said, about the entrée, was it really made at home? But it was the salmon that bothered Mrs Walker, as she spun the plates round and round, and pushed in dampers and pulled out dampers; and there came a burst of laughter from the dining-room; a voice speaking; then another burst of laughter—the gentlemen enjoying themselves when the ladies had gone. The tokay, said Lucy, running in. Mr Dalloway had sent for the tokay, from the Emperor's cellars, the Imperial Tokay.

It was borne through the kitchen. Over her shoulder Lucy reported how Miss Elizabeth looked quite lovely; she couldn't take her eyes off her; in her pink dress, wearing the necklace Mr Dalloway had given her. Jenny must remember the dog, Miss Elizabeth's fox-terrier, which, since it bit, had to be shut up and might, Elizabeth thought, want something. Jenny must remember the dog. But Jenny was not going upstairs with all those people about. There was a motor at the door already! There was a ring at the bell—and the gentlemen still in the dining-room, drinking tokay!

There, they were going upstairs; that was the first to come, and now they would come faster and faster, so that Mrs Parkinson (hired for parties) would leave the hall door ajar, and the hall would be full of gentlemen waiting (they stood waiting, sleeking down their hair) while the ladies took their cloaks off in the room along the passage; where Mrs Barnet helped them, old Ellen Barnet, who had been with the family for forty years, and came every summer to help the ladies, and remembered mothers when they were girls, and though very unassuming did shake hands; said 'milady' very respectfully, yet had a humorous way with her, looking at the young ladies, and ever so tactfully helping Lady Lovejoy, who had some trouble with her underbodice. And they could not help feeling, Lady Lovejoy and Miss Alice, that some little privilege in the matter of brush and comb was awarded them having known Mrs Barnet—'thirty years, milady,' Mrs Barnet supplied her. Young ladies did not use to rouge, said Lady Lovejoy, when they stayed at Bourton in the old days. And Miss Alice didn't need rouge, said Mrs Barnet, looking at her fondly. There Mrs Barnet would sit, in the cloakroom, patting down the furs, smoothing out the Spanish shawls, tidying the dressing-table, and knowing perfectly well, in spite of the furs and the embroideries, which were nice ladies, which were not. The dear old body, said Lady Lovejoy, mounting the stairs, Clarissa's old nurse.

And then Lady Lovejoy stiffened. 'Lady and Miss Lovejoy,' she said to Mr Wilkins (hired for parties). He had an admirable manner, as he bent and straightened himself, bent and straightened himself and announced with perfect impartiality 'Lady and Miss Lovejoy . . . Sir John and Lady Needham . . . Miss Weld . . . Mr Walsh'. His manner was admirable; his family life must be irreproachable, except that it seemed impossible that a being with greenish lips and shaven cheeks could ever have blundered into the nuisance of children.

'How delightful to see you!' said Clarissa. She said it to everyone. How delightful to see you! She was at her worst—effusive, insincere. It was a great mistake to have come. He should have stayed at home and read his book, thought Peter Walsh; should have gone to a music hall; he should have stayed at home, for he knew no one.

Oh dear, it was going to be a failure; a complete failure, Clarissa felt it in her bones as dear old Lord Lexham stood there apologizing for his wife who had caught cold at the Buckingham Palace garden party. She could see Peter out of the tail of her eye, criticizing her, there, in that corner. Why, after all, did she do these things? Why seek pinnacles and stand drenched in fire? Might it consume her anyhow! Burn her to cinders! Better anything, better brandish one's torch and hurl it to earth than taper and dwindle away like some Ellie Henderson! It was extraordinary how Peter put her into these states just by coming and standing in a corner. He made her see herself; exaggerate. It was idiotic. But why did he come, then, merely to criticize? Why always take, never give? Why not risk one's one little point of view? There he was wandering off, and she must speak to him. But she would not get the chance. Life was that—humiliation, renunciation. What Lord Lexham was saying was that his wife would not wear her furs at the garden party because 'my dear, you ladies are all alike'—Lady Lexham being seventy-five at least! It was delicious, how they petted each other, that old couple. She did like old Lord Lexham. She did think it mattered, her party, and it made her feel quite sick to know that it was all going wrong, all falling flat. Anything, any explosion, any horror was better than people wandering aimlessly, standing in a bunch at a corner like Ellie Henderson, not even caring to hold themselves upright.

Gently the yellow curtain with all the birds of Paradise blew out and it seemed as if there were a flight of wings into the room, right out, then sucked back. (For the windows were open.) Was it draughty, Ellie Henderson wondered? She was subject to chills. But it did not matter that she should come down sneezing tomorrow; it was the girls with their naked shoulders she thought of, being trained to think of others by an old father, an invalid, late vicar of Bourton, but he was dead now; and her chills never went to her chest, never. It was the girls she thought of, the young girls with their bare shoulders, she herself having always been a wisp of a creature, with her thin hair and meagre profile; though now, past fifty, there was beginning to shine through some mild beam, something purified into distinction by years of self-abnegation but obscured again, perpetually, by her distressing gentility, her panic fear, which arose from three hundred pounds income, and her weaponless state (she could not earn a penny) and it made her timid, and more and more disqualified year by year to meet well-dressed people who did this sort of thing every night of the season, merely telling their maids 'I'll wear so and so,' whereas Ellie Henderson ran out nervously and bought cheap pink flowers, half-a-dozen, and then threw a shawl over her old black dress. For her invitation to Clarissa's party had come at the last moment. She was not quite happy about it. She had a sort of feeling that Clarissa had not meant to ask her this year.

Why should she? There was no reason really, except that they had always known each other. Indeed, they were cousins. But naturally they had rather drifted apart, Clarissa being so sought after. It was an event to her, going to a party. It was quite a treat just to see the lovely clothes. Wasn't that Elizabeth, grown up, with her hair done in the fashionable way, in the pink dress? Yet she could not be more than seventeen. She was very, very handsome. But girls when they first came out didn't seem to wear white as they used. (She must remember everything to tell Edith.) Girls wore straight frocks, perfectly tight, with skirts well above the ankles. It was not becoming, she thought.

So, with her weak eyesight, Ellie Henderson craned rather forward, and it wasn't so much she who minded not having anyone to talk to (she hardly knew anybody there), for she felt that they were all such interesting people to watch; politicians presumably; Richard Dalloway's friends; but it was Richard himself who felt that he could not let the poor creature go on standing there all the evening by herself.

'Well, Ellie, and how's the world treating *you?*' he said in his genial way, and Ellie Henderson, getting nervous and flushing and feeling that it was extraordinarily nice of him to come and talk to her, said that many people really felt the heat more than the cold.

'Yes, they do,' said Richard Dalloway. 'Yes.'

But what more did one say?

'Hullo, Richard,' said somebody, taking him by the elbow, and, good Lord, there was old Peter, old Peter Walsh. He was delighted to see him—ever so pleased to see him! He hadn't changed a bit. And off they went together walking right across the room, giving each other little pats, as if they hadn't met for a long time, Ellie Henderson thought, watching them go, certain she knew that man's face. A tall man, middle aged, rather fine eyes, dark, wearing spectacles, with a look of John Burrows. Edith would be sure to know.

The curtain with its flight of birds of Paradise blew out again. And Clarissa saw—she saw Ralph Lyon beat it back, and go on talking. So it wasn't a failure after all! it was going to be all right now—her party. It had begun. It had started. But it was still touch and go. She must stand there for the present. People seemed to come in a rush.

Colonel and Mrs Garrod . . . Mr Hugh Whitbread . . . Mr Bowley . . . Mrs Hilbery . . . Lady Mary Maddox . . . Mr Quin . . . intoned Wilkins. She had six or seven words with each, and they went on, they went into the rooms; into something now, not nothing, since Ralph Lyon had beat back the curtain.

And yet for her own part, it was too much of an effort. She was not enjoying it. It was too much like being—just anybody, standing there; anybody could do it; yet this anybody she did a little admire, couldn't help feeling that she had, anyhow, made this happen, that it marked a stage, this post that she felt herself to have become, for oddly enough she had quite forgotten what she looked like, but felt herself a stake driven in at the top of her stairs. Every time she gave a party she had this feeling of being something not herself, and that everyone was unreal in one way; much more real in another. It was, she thought, partly their clothes, partly being taken out of their ordinary ways, partly the background; it was possible to say things you couldn't say anyhow else, things that needed an effort; possible to go much deeper. But not for her; not yet anyhow.

'How delightful to see you!' she said. Dear old Sir Harry! He would know everyone.

And what was so odd about it was the sense one had as they came up the stairs one after another, Mrs Mount and Celia, Herbert Ainsty, Mrs Dakers—oh, and Lady Bruton!

'How awfully good of you to come!' she said, and she meant it—it was odd how standing there one felt them going on, going on, some quite old, some . . .

What name? Lady Rosseter? But who on earth was Lady Rosseter?

'Clarissa!' That voice! It was Sally Seton! Sally Seton! after all these years! She loomed through a mist. For she hadn't looked like *that*, Sally Seton, when Clarissa grasped the hot-water can. To think of her under this roof, under this roof! Not like that!

All on top of each other, embarrassed, laughing, words tumbled out— passing through London; heard from Clara Haydon; what a chance of seeing you! So I thrust myself in—without an invitation . . .

One might put down the hot-water can quite composedly. The lustre had left her. Yet it was extraordinary to see her again, older, happier, less lovely. They kissed each other, first this cheek, then that, by the drawing-room door, and Clarissa turned, with Sally's hand in hers, and saw her rooms full, heard the roar of voices, saw the candlesticks, the blowing curtains, and the roses which Richard had given her.

'I have five enormous boys,' said Sally.

She had the simplest egotism, the most open desire to be thought first always, and Clarissa loved her for being still like that. 'I can't believe it!' she cried, kindling all over with pleasure at the thought of the past.

But alas, Wilkins; Wilkins wanted her; Wilkins was emitting in a voice of commanding authority, as if the whole company must be admonished and the hostess reclaimed from frivolity, one name:

'The Prime Minister,' said Peter Walsh.

The Prime Minister? Was it really? Ellie Henderson marvelled. What a thing to tell Edith!

One couldn't laugh at him. He looked so ordinary. You might have stood him behind a counter and bought biscuits—poor chap, all rigged up in gold lace. And to be fair, as he went his rounds, first with Clarissa, then with Richard escorting him, he did it very well. He tried to look somebody. It was amusing to watch. Nobody looked at him. They just went on talking, yet it was perfectly plain that they all knew, felt to the marrow of their bones, this majesty passing; this symbol of what they all stood for, English society. Old Lady Bruton, and she looked very fine too, very stalwart in her lace, swam up, and they withdrew into a little room which at once became spied upon, guarded, and a sort of stir and rustle rippled through everyone openly: the Prime Minister!

Lord, lord, the snobbery of the English! thought Peter Walsh, standing in the corner. How they loved dressing up in gold lace and doing homage! There! That must be—by Jove it was—Hugh Whitbread, snuffling around the precincts of the great, grown rather fatter, rather whiter, the admirable Hugh!

He looked always as if he were on duty, thought Peter, a privileged but secretive being, hoarding secrets which he would die to defend, though it was only some little piece of tittle-tattle dropped by a court footman which would be in all the papers tomorrow. Such were his rattles, his baubles, in playing with which he had grown white, come to the verge of old age, enjoying the respect and affection of all who had the privilege of knowing this type of the English public-school man. Inevitably one made up things like that about Hugh; that was his style; the style of those admirable letters which Peter had read thousands of miles across the sea in *The Times*, and had thanked God he was out of that pernicious hubble-bubble if it were only to hear baboons chatter and coolies beat their wives. An olive-skinned youth from one of the Universities stood obsequiously by. Him he would patronize, initiate, teach how to get on. For he liked nothing better than doing kindnesses, making the hearts of old ladies palpitate with the joy of being thought of in their age, their affliction, thinking themselves quite forgotten, yet here was dear Hugh driving up and spending an hour talking of the past, remembering trifles, praising the home-made cake, though Hugh might eat cake with a Duchess any day of his life, and, to look at him, probably did spend a good deal of time in that agreeable occupation. The All-judging, the All-merciful, might excuse. Peter Walsh had no mercy. Villains there must be, and, God knows, the rascals who get hanged for battering the brains of a girl out in a train do less harm on the whole than Hugh Whitbread and his kindness! Look at him now, on tip-toe, dancing forward, bowing and scraping, as the Prime Minister and Lady Bruton emerged, intimating for all the world to see that he was privileged to say something, something private, to Lady Bruton as she passed. She stopped. She wagged her fine old head. She was thanking him presumably for some piece of servility. She had her toadies, minor officials in Government offices who ran about putting through little jobs on her behalf, in return for which she gave them luncheon. But she derived from the eighteenth century. She was all right.

And now Clarissa escorted her Prime Minister down the room, prancing, sparkling, with the stateliness of her grey hair. She wore earrings, and a silver-green mermaid's dress. Lolloping on the waves and braiding her tresses she seemed, having that gift still; to be; to exist; to sum it all up in the moment as she passed; turned, caught her scarf in some other woman's dress, unhitched it, laughed, all with the most perfect ease and air of a creature floating in its element. But age had brushed her; even as a mermaid might behold in her glass the setting sun on some very clear evening over the waves. There was a breath of tenderness; her severity, her prudery, her woodenness were all warmed through now, and she had about her as she said good-bye to the thick gold-laced man who was doing his best, and good luck to him, to look important, an inexpressible dignity; an exquisite cordiality; as if she wished the whole world well, and must now, being on the very verge and rim of things, take her leave. So she made him think. (But he was not in love.)

Indeed, Clarissa felt, the Prime Minister had been good to come. And, walking down the room with him, with Sally there and Peter there and Richard very pleased, with all those people rather inclined, perhaps, to envy, she had felt that intoxication of the moment, that dilatation of the nerves of the heart itself till it seemed to quiver, steeped, upright;— yes, but after all it was what other people felt, that; for, though she loved it and felt it tingle and sting, still these semblances, these triumphs (dear old Peter, for example, thinking her so brilliant), had a hollowness; at arm's length they were, not in the heart; and it might be that she was growing old, but they satisfied her no longer as they used; and suddenly, as she saw the Prime Minister go down the stairs, the gilt rim of the Sir Joshua picture of the little girl with a muff brought back Kilman with a rush; Kilman her enemy. That was satisfying; that was real. Ah, how she hated her—hot, hypocritical, corrupt; with all that power; Elizabeth's seducer; the woman who had crept in to steal and defile (Richard would say, What nonsense!). She hated her: she loved her. It was enemies one wanted, not friends—not Mrs Durrant and Clara, Sir

William and Lady Bradshaw, Miss Truelock and Eleanor Gibson (whom she saw coming upstairs). They must find her if they wanted her. She was for the party!

There was her old friend Sir Harry.

'Dear Sir Harry!' she said, going up to the fine old fellow who had produced more bad pictures than any other two Academicians in the whole of St John's Wood (they were always of cattle, standing in sunset pools absorbing moisture, or signifying, for he had a certain range of gesture, by the raising of one foreleg and the toss of the antlers, 'the Approach of the Stranger'—all his activities, dining out, racing, were founded on cattle standing absorbing moisture in sunset pools).

'What are you laughing at?' she asked him. For Willie Titcomb and Sir Harry and Herbert Ainsty were all laughing. But no. Sir Harry could not tell Clarissa Dalloway (much though he liked her; of her type he thought her perfect, and threatened to paint her) his stories of the music-hall stage. He chaffed her about her party. He missed his brandy. These circles, he said, were above him. But he liked her; respected her, in spite of her damnable, difficult, upper-class refinement, which made it impossible to ask Clarissa Dalloway to sit on his knee. And up came that wandering will-o'-the-wisp, that vagous phosphorescence, old Mrs Hilbery, stretching her hands to the blaze of his laughter (about the Duke and the Lady), which, as she heard it across the room, seemed to reassure her on a point which sometimes bothered her if she woke early in the morning and did not like to call her maid for a cup of tea; how it is certain we must die.

'They won't tell us their stories,' said Clarissa.

'Dear Clarissa!' exclaimed Mrs Hilbery. She looked tonight, she said, so like her mother as she first saw her walking in a garden in a grey hat.

And really Clarissa's eyes filled with tears. Her mother, walking in a garden! But alas, she must go.

For there was Professor Brierly, who lectured on Milton, talking to little Jim Hutton (who was unable even for a party like this to compass both tie and waistcoat or make his hair lie flat), and even at this distance they were quarrelling, she could see. For Professor Brierly was a very queer fish. With all those degrees, honours, lectureships between him and the scribblers, he suspected instantly an atmosphere not favourable to his queer compound; his prodigious learning and timidity; his wintry charm without cordiality; his innocence blent with snobbery; he quivered if made conscious, by a lady's unkempt hair, a youth's boots, of an underworld, very creditable doubtless, of rebels, of ardent young people; of would-be geniuses, and intimated with a little toss of the head, with a sniff—Humph!—the value of moderation; of some slight training in the classics in order to appreciate Milton. Professor Brierly (Clarissa could see) wasn't hitting it off with little Jim Hutton (who wore red socks, his black being at the laundry) about Milton. She interrupted.

She said she loved Bach. So did Hutton. That was the bond between them, and Hutton (a very bad poet) always felt that Mrs Dalloway was far the best of the great ladies who took an interest in art. It was odd how strict she was. About music she was purely impersonal. She was rather a prig. But how charming to look at! She made her house so nice, if it weren't for her Professors. Clarissa had half a mind to snatch him off and set him down at the piano in the back room. For he played divinely.

'But the noise!' she said. 'The noise!'

'The sign of a successful party.' Nodding urbanely, the Professor stepped delicately off.

'He knows everything in the whole world about Milton,' said Clarissa.

'Does he indeed?' said Hutton, who would imitate the Professor throughout Hampstead: the Professor on Milton; the Professor on moderation; the Professor stepping delicately off.

But she must speak to that couple, said Clarissa, Lord Gayton and Nancy Blow.

Not that *they* added perceptibly to the noise of the party. They were not talking (perceptibly) as they stood side by side by the yellow curtains. They would soon be off elsewhere, together; and never had very much to say in any circumstances. They looked; that was all. That was enough. They looked so clean, so sound, she with an apricot bloom of powder and paint, but he scrubbed, rinsed, with the eyes of a bird, so that no ball could pass him or stroke surprise him. He struck, he leapt, accurately, on the spot. Ponies' mouths quivered at the end of his reins. He had his honours, ancestral monuments, banners hanging in the church at home. He had his duties; his tenants; a mother and sisters; had been all day at Lord's, and that was what they were talking about— cricket, cousins, the movies—when Mrs Dalloway came up. Lord Gayton liked her most awfully. So did Miss Blow. She had such charming manners.

'It is angelic—it is delicious of you to have come!' she said. She loved Lord's; she loved youth, and Nancy, dressed at enormous expense by the greatest artists in Paris, stood there looking as if her body had merely put forth, of its own accord, a green frill.

'I had meant to have dancing,' said Clarissa.

For the young people could not talk. And why should they? Shout, embrace, swing, be up at dawn; carry sugar to ponies; kiss and caress the snouts of adorable chows; and then, all tingling and streaming, plunge and swim. But the enormous resources of the English language, the power it bestows, after all, of communicating feelings (at their age, she and Peter would have been arguing all the evening), was not for them. They would solidify young. They would be good beyond measure to the people on the estate, but alone, perhaps, rather dull.

'What a pity!' she said. 'I had hoped to have dancing.'

It was so extraordinarily nice of them to have come! But talk of dancing! The rooms were packed.

There was old Aunt Helena in her shawl. Alas, she must leave them— Lord Gayton and Nancy Blow. There was old Miss Parry, her aunt.

For Miss Helena Parry was not dead: Miss Parry was alive. She was past eighty. She ascended staircases slowly with a stick. She was placed in a chair (Richard had seen to it). People who had known Burma in the 'seventies were always led up to her. Where had Peter got to? They used to be such friends. For at the mention of India, or even Ceylon, her eyes (only one was glass) slowly deepened, became blue, beheld, not human beings—she had no tender memories, no proud illusions about Viceroys, Generals, Mutinies—it was orchids she saw, and mountain passes, and herself carried on the backs of coolies in the 'sixties over solitary peaks; or descending to uproot orchids (startling blossoms, never beheld before) which she painted in water-colour; an indomitable Englishwoman, fretful if disturbed by the war, say, which dropped a bomb at her very door, from her deep meditation over orchids and her own figure journeying in the 'sixties in India—but here was Peter.

'Come and talk to Aunt Helena about Burma,' said Clarissa.

And yet he had not had a word with her all the evening!

'We will talk later,' said Clarissa, leading him up to Aunt Helena, in her white shawl, with her stick.

'Peter Walsh,' said Clarissa.

That meant nothing.

Clarissa had asked her. It was tiring; it was noisy; but Clarissa had asked her. So she had come. It was a pity that they lived in London— Richard and Clarissa. If only for Clarissa's health it would have been better to live in the country. But Clarissa had always been fond of society.

'He has been in Burma,' said Clarissa.

Ah! She could not resist recalling what Charles Darwin had said about her little book on the orchids of Burma.

(Clarissa must speak to Lady Bruton.)

No doubt it was forgotten now, her book on the orchids of Burma, but it went into three editions before 1870, she told Peter. She remembered him now. He had been at Bourton (and he had left her, Peter Walsh remembered, without a word in the drawing-room that night when Clarissa had asked him to come boating).

'Richard so much enjoyed his lunch party,' said Clarissa to Lady Bruton.

'Richard was the greatest possible help,' Lady Bruton replied. 'He helped me to write a letter. And how are you?'

'Oh, perfectly well!' said Clarissa. (Lady Bruton detested illness in the wives of politicians.)

'And there's Peter Walsh!' said Lady Bruton (for she could never think of anything to say to Clarissa; though she liked her. She had lots of fine qualities; but they had nothing in common—she and Clarissa. It might have been better if Richard had married a woman with less charm, who would have helped him more in his work. He had lost his chance of the Cabinet). 'There's Peter Walsh!' she said, shaking hands with that agreeable sinner, that very able fellow who should have made a name for himself but hadn't (always in difficulties with women), and, of course, old Miss Parry. Wonderful old lady!

Lady Bruton stood by Miss Parry's chair, a spectral grenadier, draped in black, inviting Peter Walsh to lunch; cordial; but without small talk, remembering nothing whatever about the flora or fauna of India. She had been there, of course; had stayed with three Viceroys; thought some of the Indian civilians uncommonly fine fellows; but what a tragedy it was—the state of India! The Prime Minister had just been telling her (old Miss Parry, huddled up in her shawl, did not care what the Prime Minister had just been telling her), and Lady Bruton would like to have Peter Walsh's opinion, he being fresh from the centre, and she would get Sir Sampson to meet him, for really it prevented her from sleeping at night, the folly of it, the wickedness she might say, being a soldier's daughter. She was an old woman now, not good for much. But her house, her servants, her good friend Milly Brush—did he remember her?—were all there only asking to be used if—if they could be of help, in short. For she never spoke of England, but this isle of men, this dear, dear land, was in her blood (without reading Shakespeare), and if ever a woman could have worn the helmet and shot the arrow, could have led troops to attack, ruled with indomitable justice barbarian hordes and lain under a shield noseless in a church, or made a green grass mound on some primeval hillside, that woman was Millicent Bruton. Debarred by her sex, and some truancy, too, of the logical faculty (she found it impossible to write a letter to *The Times*), she had the thought of Empire always at hand, and had acquired from her association with that armoured goddess her ramrod bearing, her robustness of demeanour, so that one could not figure her even in death parted from the earth or roaming territories over which, in some spiritual shape, the Union Jack had ceased to fly. To be not English even among the dead—no, no! Impossible!

But was it Lady Bruton? (whom she used to know). Was it Peter Walsh grown grey? Lady Rosseter asked herself (who had been Sally Seton). It was old Miss Parry certainly—the old aunt who used to be so cross when she stayed at Bourton. Never should she forget running along the passage naked, and being sent for by Miss Parry! And Clarissa! oh Clarissa! Sally caught her by the arm.

Clarissa stopped beside them.

'But I can't stay,' she said. 'I shall come later. Wait,' she said, looking at Peter and Sally. They must wait, she meant, until all these people had gone.

'I shall come back,' she said, looking at her old friends, Sally and Peter, who were shaking hands, and Sally, remembering the past no doubt, was laughing.

But her voice was wrung of its old ravishing richness; her eyes not aglow as they used to be, when she smoked cigars, when she ran down the passage to fetch her sponge bag without a stitch of clothing on her, and Ellen Atkins asked, What if the gentlemen had met her? But everybody forgave her. She stole a chicken from the larder because she was hungry in the night; she smoked cigars in her bedroom; she left a priceless book in the punt. But everybody adored her (except perhaps Papa). It was her warmth; her vitality—she would paint, she would write. Old women in the village never to this day forgot to ask after 'your friend in the red cloak who seemed so bright'. She accused Hugh Whitbread, of all people (and there he was, her old friend Hugh, talking to the Portuguese Ambassador), of kissing her in the smoking-room to punish her for saying that women should have votes. Vulgar men did, she said. And Clarissa remembered having to persuade her not to denounce him at family prayers—which she was capable of doing with her daring, her recklessness, her melodramatic love of being the centre of everything and creating scenes, and it was bound, Clarissa used to think, to end in some awful tragedy; her death; her martyrdom; instead of which she had married, quite unexpectedly, a bald man with a large buttonhole who owned, it was said, cotton mills at Manchester. And she had five boys!

She and Peter had settled down together. They were talking; it seemed so familiar—that they should be talking. They would discuss the past. With the two of them (more even than with Richard) she shared her past; the garden; the trees; old Joseph Breitkopf singing Brahms without any voice; the drawing-room wallpaper; the smell of the mats. A part of this Sally must always be; Peter must always be. But she must leave them. There were the Bradshaws, whom she disliked.

She must go up to Lady Bradshaw (in grey and silver, balancing like a sea-lion at the edge of its tank, barking for invitations, Duchesses, the typical successful man's wife), she must go up to Lady Bradshaw and say . . .

But Lady Bradshaw anticipated her.

'We are shockingly late, dear Mrs Dalloway; we hardly dared to come in,' she said.

And Sir William, who looked very distinguished, with his grey hair and blue eyes, said yes: they had not been able to resist the temptation. He was talking to Richard about that Bill probably, which they wanted to get through the Commons. Why did the sight of him, talking to Richard, curl her up? He looked what he was, a great doctor. A man absolutely at the head of his profession, very powerful, rather worn. For think what cases came before him—people in the uttermost depths of misery; people on the verge of insanity; husbands and wives. He had to decide questions of appalling difficulty. Yet—what she felt was, one wouldn't like Sir William to see one unhappy. No; not that man.

'How is your son at Eton?' she asked Lady Bradshaw.

He had just missed his eleven, said Lady Bradshaw, because of the mumps. His father minded even more than he did, she thought, 'being', she said, 'nothing but a great boy himself.'

Clarissa looked at Sir William, talking to Richard. He did not look like a boy—not in the least like a boy.

She had once gone with someone to ask his advice. He had been perfectly right; extremely sensible. But Heavens—what a relief to get out to the street again! There was some poor wretch sobbing, she remembered, in the waiting-room. But she did not know what it was about Sir William; what exactly she disliked. Only Richard agreed with her, 'didn't like his taste, didn't like his smell'. But he was extraordinarily able. They were talking about this Bill. Some case Sir William was mentioning, lowering his voice. It had its bearing upon what he was saying about the deferred effects of shell-shock. There must be some provision in the Bill.

Sinking her voice, drawing Mrs Dalloway into the shelter of a common femininity, a common pride in the illustrious qualities of husbands and their sad tendency to overwork, Lady Bradshaw (poor goose—one didn't dislike her) murmured how, 'just as we were starting, my husband was called up on the telephone, a very sad case. A young man (that is what Sir William is telling Mr Dalloway) had killed himself. He had been in the army.' Oh! thought Clarissa, in the middle of my party, here's death, she thought.

She went on, into the little room where the Prime Minister had gone with Lady Bruton. Perhaps there was somebody there. But there was nobody. The chairs still kept the impress of the Prime Minister and Lady Bruton, she turned deferentially, he sitting four-square, authoritatively. They had been talking about India. There was nobody. The party's splendour fell to the floor, so strange it was to come in alone in her finery.

What business had the Bradshaws to talk of death at her party? A young man had killed himself. And they talked of it at her party—the Bradshaws talked of death. He had killed himself—but how? Always her body went through it, when she was told, first, suddenly, of an accident; her dress flamed, her body burnt. He had thrown himself from a window. Up had flashed the ground; through him, blundering, bruising, went the rusty spikes. There he lay with a thud, thud, thud in his brain, and then a suffocation of blackness. So she saw it. But why had he done it? And the Bradshaws talked of it at her party!

She had once thrown a shilling into the Serpentine, never anything more. But he had flung it away. They went on living (she would have to go back; the rooms were still crowded; people kept on coming). They (all day she had been thinking of Bourton, of Peter, of Sally), they would grow old. A thing there was that mattered; a thing, wreathed about with chatter, defaced, obscured in her own life, let drop every day in corruption, lies, chatter. This he had preserved. Death was defiance. Death was an attempt to communicate, people feeling the impossibility of reaching the centre which, mystically, evaded them; closeness drew apart; rapture faded; one was alone. There was an embrace in death.

But this young man who had killed himself—had he plunged holding his treasure? 'If it were now to die, 'twere now to be most happy,' she had said to herself once, coming down, in white.

Or there were the poets and thinkers. Suppose he had had that passion, and had gone to Sir William Bradshaw, a great doctor, yet to her obscurely evil, without sex or lust, extremely polite to women, but capable of some indescribable outrage—forcing your soul, that was it— if this young man had gone to him, and Sir William had impressed him, like that, with his power, might he not then have said (indeed she felt it now), Life is made intolerable; they make life intolerable, men like that?

Then (she had felt it only this morning) there was the terror; the overwhelming incapacity, one's parents giving it into one's hands, this life, to be lived to the end, to be walked with serenely; there was in the depths of her heart an awful fear. Even now, quite often if Richard had not been there reading *The Times*, so that she could crouch like a bird and gradually revive, send roaring up that immeasurable delight, rubbing stick to stick, one thing with another, she must have perished. She had escaped. But that young man had killed himself.

Somehow it was her disaster—her disgrace. It was her punishment to see sink and disappear here a man, there a woman, in this profound darkness, and she forced to stand here in her evening dress. She had schemed; she had pilfered. She was never wholly admirable. She had wanted success, Lady Bexborough and the rest of it. And once she had walked on the terrace at Bourton.

Odd, incredible; she had never been so happy. Nothing could be slow enough; nothing last too long. No pleasure could equal, she thought, straightening the chairs, pushing in one book on the shelf, this having done with the triumphs of youth, lost herself in the process of living, to find it, with a shock of delight, as the sun rose, as the day sank. Many a time had she gone, at Bourton when they were all talking, to look at the sky; or seen it between people's shoulders at dinner; seen it in London when she could not sleep. She walked to the window.

It held, foolish as the idea was, something of her own in it, this country sky, this sky above Westminster. She parted the curtains; she looked. Oh, but how surprising!—in the room opposite the old lady stared straight at her! She was going to bed. And the sky. It will be a solemn sky, she had thought, it will be a dusky sky, turning away its cheek in beauty. But there it was—ashen pale, raced over quickly by tapering vast clouds. It was new to her. The wind must have risen. She was going to bed, in the room opposite. It was fascinating to watch her, moving about, that old lady, crossing the room, coming to the window. Could she see her? It was fascinating, with people still laughing and shouting in the drawing-room, to watch that old woman, quite quietly, going to bed alone. She pulled the blind now. The clock began striking. The young man had killed himself; but she did not pity him; with the clock striking the hour, one, two, three, she did not pity him, with all this going on. There! the old lady had put out her light! the whole house was dark now with this going on, she repeated, and the words came to her, Fear no more the heat of the sun. She must go back to them. But what an extraordinary night! She felt somehow very like him—the young man who had killed himself. She felt glad that he had done it; thrown it away while they went on living. The clock was striking. The leaden circles dissolved in the air. But she must go back. She must assemble. She must find Sally and Peter. And she came in from the little room.

'But where is Clarissa?' said Peter. He was sitting on the sofa with Sally. (After all these years he really could not call her 'Lady Rosseter'.) 'Where's the woman gone to?' he asked. 'Where's Clarissa?'

Sally supposed, and so did Peter for the matter of that, that there were people of importance, politicians, whom neither of them knew unless by sight in the picture papers, whom Clarissa had to be nice to, had to talk to. She was with them. Yet there was Richard Dalloway not in the Cabinet. He hadn't been a success, Sally supposed? For herself, she scarcely ever read the papers. She sometimes saw his name mentioned. But then—well, she lived a very solitary life, in the wilds, Clarissa would say, among great merchants, great manufacturers, men, after all, who did things. She had done things too!

'I have five sons!' she told him.

Lord, lord, what a change had come over her! the softness of motherhood; its egotism too. Last time they met, Peter remembered, had been among the cauliflowers in the moonlight, the leaves 'like rough bronze' she had said, with her literary turn; and she had picked a rose. She had marched him up and down that awful night, after the scene by the fountain; he was to catch the midnight train. Heavens, he had wept!

That was his old trick, opening a pocket-knife, thought Sally, always opening and shutting a knife when he got excited. They had been very, very intimate, she and Peter Walsh, when he was in love with Clarissa, and there was that dreadful, ridiculous scene over Richard Dalloway at lunch. She had called Richard 'Wickham'. Why not call Richard 'Wickham'? Clarissa had flared up! and indeed they had never seen each other since, she and Clarissa, not more than half-a-dozen times perhaps in the last ten years. And Peter Walsh had gone off to India, and she had heard vaguely that he had made an unhappy marriage, and she didn't know whether he had any children, and she couldn't ask him, for he had changed. He was rather shrivelled-looking, but kinder, she felt, and she had a real affection for him, for he was connected with her youth, and she still had a little Emily Brontë he had given her, and he was to write, surely? In those days he was to write.

'Have you written?' she asked him, spreading her hand, her firm and shapely hand, on her knee in a way he recalled.

'Not a word!' said Peter Walsh, and she laughed.

She was still attractive, still a personage, Sally Seton. But who was this Rosseter? He wore two camellias on his wedding day—that was all Peter knew of him. 'They have myriads of servants, miles of conservatories,' Clarissa wrote; something like that. Sally owned it with a shout of laughter.

'Yes, I have ten thousand a year'—whether before the tax was paid or after, she couldn't remember, for her husband, 'whom you must meet,' she said, 'whom you would like,' she said, did all that for her.

And Sally used to be in rags and tatters. She had pawned her great-grandfather's ring which Marie Antoinette had given him—had he got it right?—to come to Bourton.

Oh yes, Sally remembered; she had it still, a ruby ring which Marie Antoinette had given her great-grandfather. She never had a penny to her name in those days, and going to Bourton always meant some frightful pinch. But going to Bourton had meant so much to her—had kept her sane, she believed, so unhappy had she been at home. But that was all a thing of the past—all over now, she said. And Mr Parry was dead; and Miss Parry was still alive. Never had he had such a shock in his life! said Peter. He had been quite certain she was dead. And the marriage had been, Sally supposed, a success? And that very handsome, very self-possessed young woman was Elizabeth, over there, by the curtains, in pink.

(She was like a poplar, she was like a river, she was like a hyacinth, Willie Titcomb was thinking. Oh how much nicer to be in the country and do what she liked! She could hear the poor dog howling, Elizabeth was certain.) She was not a bit like Clarissa, Peter Walsh said.

'Oh, Clarissa!' said Sally.

What Sally felt was simply this. She had owed Clarissa an enormous amount. They had been friends, not acquaintances, friends, and she still saw Clarissa all in white going about the house with her hands full of flowers—to this day tobacco plants made her think of Bourton. But— did Peter understand?—she lacked something. Lacked what was it? She had charm; she had extraordinary charm. But to be frank (and she felt that Peter was an old friend, a real friend—did absence matter? did distance matter? She had often wanted to write to him, but torn it up, yet felt he understood, for people understand without things being said, as one realizes growing old, and old she was, had been that afternoon to see her sons at Eton, where they had the mumps), to be quite frank, then, how could Clarissa have done it?—married Richard Dalloway? a sportsman, a man who cared only for dogs. Literally, when he came into the room he smelt of the stables. And then all this? She waved her hand.

Hugh Whitbread it was, strolling past in his white waistcoat, dim, fat, blind, past everything he looked, except self-esteem and comfort.

'He's not going to recognize *us*,' said Sally, and really she hadn't the courage—so that was Hugh! the admirable Hugh!

'And what does he do?' she asked Peter.

He blacked the King's boots or counted bottles at Windsor, Peter told her. Peter kept his sharp tongue still! But Sally must be frank, Peter said. That kiss now, Hugh's.

On the lips, she assured him, in the smoking-room one evening. She went straight to Clarissa in a rage. Hugh didn't do such things! Clarissa said, the admirable Hugh! Hugh's socks were without exception the most beautiful she had ever seen—and now his evening dress. Perfect! And had he children?

'Everybody in the room has six sons at Eton,' Peter told her, except himself. He, thank God, had none. No sons, no daughters, no wife. Well, he didn't seem to mind, said Sally. He looked younger, she thought, than any of them.

But it had been a silly thing to do, in many ways, Peter said, to marry like that; 'a perfect goose she was,' he said, but, he said, 'we had a splendid time of it,' but how could that be? Sally wondered; what did he mean? and how odd it was to know him and yet not know a single thing that had happened to him. And did he say it out of pride? Very likely, for after all it must be galling for him (though he was an oddity, a sort of sprite, not at all an ordinary man), it must be lonely at his age to have no home, nowhere to go to. But he must stay with them for weeks and weeks. Of course he would; he would love to stay with them, and that was how it came out. All these years the Dalloways had never been once. Time after time they had asked them. Clarissa (for it was Clarissa of course) would not come. For, said Sally, Clarissa was at heart a snob—one had to admit it, a snob. And it was that that was between them, she was convinced. Clarissa thought she had married beneath her, her husband being—she was proud of it—a miner's son. Every penny they had he had earned. As a little boy (her voice trembled) he had carried great sacks.

(And so she would go on, Peter felt, hour after hour; the miner's son; people thought she had married beneath her; her five sons; and what was the other thing—plants, hydrangeas, syringas, very very rare hibiscus lilies that never grow north of the Suez Canal, but she, with one gardener in a suburb near Manchester, had beds of them, positively beds! Now all that Clarissa had escaped, unmaternal as she was.)

A snob was she? Yes, in many ways. Where was she, all this time? It was getting late.

'Yes,' said Sally, 'when I heard Clarissa was giving a party, I felt I couldn't *not* come—must see her again (and I'm staying in Victoria Street, practically next door). So I just came without an invitation. But,' she whispered, 'tell me, do. Who is this?'

It was Mrs Hilbery, looking for the door. For how late it was getting! And, she murmured, as the night grew later, as people went, one found old friends; quiet nooks and corners; and the loveliest views. Did they know, she asked, that they were surrounded by an enchanted garden? Lights and trees and wonderful gleaming lakes and the sky. Just a few fairy lamps, Clarissa Dalloway had said, in the back garden! But she was a magician! It was a park . . . And she didn't know their names, but friends she knew they were, friends without names, songs without words, always the best. But there were so many doors, such unexpected places, she could not find her way.

'Old Mrs Hilbery,' said Peter; but who was that? that lady standing by the curtain all the evening, without speaking? He knew her face; connected her with Bourton. Surely she used to cut up underclothes at the large table in the window? Davidson, was that her name?

'Oh, that is Ellie Henderson,' said Sally. Clarissa was really very hard on her. She was a cousin, very poor. Clarissa *was* hard on people.

She was rather, said Peter. Yet, said Sally, in her emotional way, with a rush of that enthusiasm which Peter used to love her for, yet dreaded a little now, so effusive she might become—how generous to her friends Clarissa was! and what a rare quality one found it, and how sometimes at night or on Christmas Day, when she counted up her blessings, she put that friendship first. They were young; that was it. Clarissa was pure-hearted; that was it. Peter would think her sentimental. So she was. For she had come to feel that it was the only thing worth saying—what one felt. Cleverness was silly. One must say simply what one felt.

'But I do not know', said Peter Walsh, 'what I feel.'

Poor Peter, thought Sally. Why did not Clarissa come and talk to them? That was what he was longing for. She knew it. All the time he was thinking only of Clarissa, and was fidgeting with his knife.

He had not found life simple, Peter said. His relations with Clarissa had not been simple. It had spoilt his life, he said. (They had been so intimate—he and Sally Seton, it was absurd not to say it.) One could not be in love twice, he said. And what could she say? Still, it is better to have loved (but he would think her sentimental—he used to be so sharp). He must come and stay with them in Manchester. That is all very true, he said. All very true. He would love to come and stay with them, directly he had done what he had to do in London.

And Clarissa had cared for him more than she had ever cared for Richard, Sally was positive of that.

'No, no, no!' said Peter (Sally should not have said that—she went too far). That good fellow—there he was at the end of the room, holding forth, the same as ever, dear old Richard. Who was he talking to? Sally asked, that very distinguished-looking man? Living in the wilds as she did, she had an insatiable curiosity to know who people were. But Peter did not know. He did not like his looks, he said, probably a Cabinet Minister. Of them all, Richard seemed to him the best, he said—the most disinterested.

'But what has he done?' Sally asked. Public work, she supposed. And were they happy together? Sally asked (she herself was extremely happy); for, she admitted, she knew nothing about them, only jumped to conclusions, as one does, for what can one know even of the people one lives with every day? she asked. Are we not all prisoners? She had read a wonderful play about a man who scratched on the wall of his cell, and she had felt that was true of life—one scratched on the wall.

Despairing of human relationships (people were so difficult), she often went into her garden and got from her flowers a peace which men and women never gave her. But no; he did not like cabbages; he preferred human beings, Peter said. Indeed, the young are beautiful, Sally said, watching Elizabeth cross the room. How unlike Clarissa at her age! Could he make anything of her? She would not open her lips. Not much, not yet, Peter admitted. She was like a lily, Sally said, a lily by the side of a pool. But Peter did not agree that we know nothing. We know everything, he said; at least he did.

But these two, Sally whispered, these two coming now (and really she must go, if Clarissa did not come soon), this distinguished-looking man and his rather common-looking wife who had been talking to Richard—what could one know about people like that?

'That they're damnable humbugs,' said Peter, looking at them casually. He made Sally laugh.

But Sir William Bradshaw stopped at the door to look at a picture. He looked in the corner for the engraver's name. His wife looked too. Sir William Bradshaw was so interested in art.

When one was young, said Peter, one was too much excited to know people. Now that one was old, fifty-two to be precise (Sally was fifty-five, in body, she said, but her heart was like a girl's of twenty); now that one was mature then, said Peter, one could watch, one could understand, and one did not lose the power of feeling, he said. No, that is true, said Sally. She felt more deeply, more passionately, every year. It increased, he said, alas, perhaps, but one should be glad of it—it went on increasing in his experience. There was someone in India. He would like to tell Sally about her. He would like Sally to know her. She was married, he said. She had two small children. They must all come to Manchester, said Sally—he must promise before they left.

'There's Elizabeth,' he said, 'she feels not half what we feel, not yet.' 'But,' said Sally, watching Elizabeth go to her father, 'one can see they are devoted to each other.' She could feel it by the way Elizabeth went to her father.

For her father had been looking at her, as he stood talking to the Bradshaws, and he had thought to himself who is that lovely girl? And suddenly he realized that it was his Elizabeth, and he had not recognized her, she looked so lovely in her pink frock! Elizabeth had felt him looking at her as she talked to Willie Titcomb. So she went to him and they stood together, now that the party was almost over, looking at the people going, and the rooms getting emptier and emptier, with things scattered on the floor. Even Ellie Henderson was going, nearly last of all, though no one had spoken to her, but she had wanted to see everything, to tell Edith. And Richard and Elizabeth were rather glad it was over, but

Richard was proud of his daughter. And he had not meant to tell her, but he could not help telling her. He had looked at her, he said, and he had wondered, who is that lovely girl? and it was his daughter! That did make her happy. But her poor dog was howling.

'Richard has improved. You are right,' said Sally. 'I shall go and talk to him. I shall say good-night. What does the brain matter,' said Lady Rosseter, getting up, 'compared with the heart?'

'I will come,' said Peter, but he sat on for a moment. What is this terror? what is this ecstasy? he thought to himself. What is it that fills me with extraordinary excitement?

It is Clarissa, he said.

For there she was.

To the Lighthouse

CONTENTS

I

THE WINDOW

'Yes, of course, if it's fine tomorrow,' said Mrs Ramsay. 'But you'll have to be up with the lark,' she added.

To her son these words conveyed an extraordinary joy, as if it were settled the expedition were bound to take place, and the wonder to which he had looked forward, for years and years it seemed, was, after a night's darkness and a day's sail, within touch. Since he belonged, even at the age of six, to that great clan which cannot keep this feeling separate from that, but must let future prospects, with their joys and sorrows, cloud what is actually at hand, since to such people even in earliest childhood any turn in the wheel of sensation has the power to crystallize and transfix the moment upon which its gloom or radiance rests, James Ramsay, sitting on the floor cutting out pictures from the illustrated catalogue of the Army and Navy Stores, endowed the picture of a refrigerator as his mother spoke with heavenly bliss. It was fringed with joy. The wheelbarrow, the lawn-mower, the sound of poplar trees, leaves whitening before rain, rooks cawing, brooms knocking, dresses rustling—all these were so coloured and distinguished in his mind that he had already his private code, his secret language, though he appeared the image of stark and uncompromising severity, with his high forehead and his fierce blue eyes, impeccably candid and pure, frowning slightly at the sight of human frailty, so that his mother, watching him guide his scissors neatly round the refrigerator, imagined him all red and ermine on the Bench or directing a stern and momentous enterprise in some crisis of public affairs.

'But,' said his father, stopping in front of the drawing-room window, 'it won't be fine.'

Had there been an axe handy, a poker, or any weapon that would have gashed a hole in his father's breast and killed him, there and then, James would have seized it. Such were the extremes of emotion that Mr Ramsay excited in his children's breasts by his mere presence; standing, as now, lean as a knife, narrow as the blade of one, grinning sarcastically, not only with the pleasure of disillusioning his son and casting ridicule upon his wife, who was ten thousand times better in every way than he was (James thought), but also with some secret conceit at his own accuracy of judgement. What he said was true. It was always true. He was incapable of untruth; never tampered with a fact; never altered a disagreeable word to suit the pleasure or convenience of any mortal being, least of all of his own children, who, sprung from his loins, should be aware from childhood that life is difficult; facts uncompromising; and the passage to that fabled land where our brightest hopes are extinguished, our frail barks founder in darkness (here Mr Ramsay would straighten his back and narrow his little blue eyes upon the horizon), one that needs, above all, courage, truth, and the power to endure.

'But it may be fine—I expect it will be fine,' said Mrs Ramsay, making some little twist of the reddish-brown stocking she was knitting, impatiently. If she finished it tonight, if they did go to the Lighthouse after all, it was to be given to the Lighthouse keeper for his little boy, who was threatened with a tuberculous hip; together with a pile of old magazines, and some tobacco, indeed whatever she could find lying about, not really wanted, but only littering the room, to give those poor fellows who must be bored to death sitting all day with nothing to do but polish the lamp and trim the wick and rake about on their scrap of garden, something to amuse them. For how would you like to be shut up for a whole month at a time, and possibly more in stormy weather, upon a rock the size of a tennis lawn? she would ask; and to have no letters or newspapers, and to see nobody; if you were married, not to see your wife, not to know how your children were,—if they were ill, if they had fallen down and broken their legs or arms; to see the same dreary waves breaking week after week, and then a dreadful storm coming, and the windows covered with spray, and birds dashed against the lamp, and the whole place rocking, and not be able to put your nose out of doors for fear of being swept into the sea? How would you like that? she asked, addressing herself particularly to her daughters. So she added, rather differently, one must take them whatever comforts one can.

'It's due west,' said the atheist Tansley, holding his bony fingers spread so that the wind blew through them, for he was sharing Mr Ramsay's evening walk up and down, up and down the terrace. That is to say, the wind blew from the worst possible direction for landing at the Lighthouse. Yes, he did say disagreeable things, Mrs Ramsay admitted; it was odious of him to rub this in, and make James still more disappointed; but at the same time, she would not let them laugh at him. 'The atheist', they called him; 'the little atheist'. Rose mocked him; Prue mocked him; Andrew, Jasper, Roger mocked him; even old Badger without a tooth in his head had bit him, for being (as Nancy put it) the hundred and tenth young man to chase them all the way up to the Hebrides when it was ever so much nicer to be alone.

'Nonsense,' said Mrs Ramsay, with great severity. Apart from the habit of exaggeration which they had from her, and from the implication (which was true) that she asked too many people to stay, and had to lodge some in the town, she could not bear incivility to her guests, to young men in particular, who were poor as church mice, 'exceptionally able', her husband said, his great admirers, and come there for a holiday. Indeed, she had the whole of the other sex under her protection; for reasons she could not explain, for their chivalry and valour, for the fact that they negotiated treaties, ruled India, controlled finance; finally for an attitude towards herself which no woman could fail to feel or to find agreeable, something trustful, childlike, reverential; which an old woman could take from a young man without loss of dignity, and woe betide the girl—pray Heaven it was none of her daughters!—who did not feel the worth of it, and all that it implied, to the marrow of her bones.

She turned with severity upon Nancy. He had not chased them, she said. He had been asked.

They must find a way out of it all. There might be some simpler way, some less laborious way, she sighed. When she looked in the glass and saw her hair grey, her cheek sunk, at fifty, she thought, possibly she might have managed things better—her husband; money; his books. But for her own part she would never for a single second regret her decision, evade difficulties, or slur over duties. She was now formidable to behold, and it was only in silence, looking up from their plates, after she had spoken so severely about Charles Tansley, that her daughters— Prue, Nancy, Rose—could sport with infidel ideas which they had brewed for themselves of a life different from hers; in Paris, perhaps; a wilder life; not always taking care of some man or other; for there was in all their minds a mute questioning of deference and chivalry, of the Bank of England and the Indian Empire, of ringed fingers and lace, though to them all there was something in this of the essence of beauty, which called out the manliness in their girlish hearts, and made them, as they sat at table beneath their mother's eyes, honour her strange severity, her extreme courtesy, like a Queen's raising from the mud a beggar's dirty foot and washing it, when she thus admonished them so very severely about that wretched atheist who had chased them to—or, speaking accurately, been invited to stay with them in—the Isle of Skye.

'There'll be no landing at the Lighthouse tomorrow,' said Charles Tansley, clapping his hands together as he stood at the window with her husband. Surely, he had said enough. She wished they would both leave her and James alone and go on talking. She looked at him. He was such a miserable specimen, the children said, all humps and hollows. He couldn't play cricket; he poked; he shuffled. He was a sarcastic brute, Andrew said. They knew what he liked best—to be for ever walking up and down, up and down, with Mr Ramsay, and saying who had won this, who had won that, who was a 'first-rate man' at Latin verses, who was 'brilliant but I think fundamentally unsound', who was undoubtedly the 'ablest fellow in Balliol', who had buried his light temporarily at Bristol or Bedford, but was bound to be heard of later when his

Prolegomena, of which Mr Tansley had the first pages in proof with him if Mr Ramsay would like to see them, to some branch of mathematics or philosophy saw the light of day. That was what they talked about.

She could not help laughing herself sometimes. She said, the other day, something about 'waves mountains high'. Yes, said Charles Tansley, it was a little rough. 'Aren't you drenched to the skin?' she had said. 'Damp, not wet through,' said Mr Tansley, pinching his sleeve, feeling his socks.

But it was not that they minded, the children said. It was not his face; it was not his manners. It was him—his point of view. When they talked about something interesting, people, music, history, anything, even said it was a fine evening so why not sit out of doors, then what they complained of about Charles Tansley was that until he had turned the whole thing round and made it somehow reflect himself and disparage them, put them all on edge somehow with his acid way of peeling the flesh and blood off everything, he was not satisfied. And he would go to picture galleries, they said, and he would ask one, did one like his tie? God knows, said Rose, one did not.

Disappearing as stealthily as stags from the dinner-table directly the meal was over, the eight sons and daughters of Mr and Mrs Ramsay sought their bedrooms, their fastnesses in a house where there was no other privacy to debate anything, everything; Tansley's tie; the passing of the Reform Bill; sea-birds and butterflies; people; while the sun poured into those attics, which a plank alone separated from each other so that every footstep could be plainly heard and the Swiss girl sobbing for her father who was dying of cancer in a valley of the Grisons, and lit up bats, flannels, straw hats, ink-pots, paint-pots, beetles, and the skulls of small birds, while it drew from the long frilled strips of seaweed pinned to the wall a smell of salt and weeds, which was in the towels too, gritty with sand from bathing.

Strife, divisions, difference of opinion, prejudices twisted into the very fibre of being, oh that they should begin so early, Mrs Ramsay deplored. They were so critical, her children. They talked such nonsense. She went from the dining-room, holding James by the hand, since he would not go with the others. It seemed to her such nonsense—inventing differences, when people, heaven knows, were different enough without that. The real differences, she thought, standing by the drawing-room window, are enough, quite enough. She had in mind at the moment, rich and poor, high and low; the great in birth receiving from her, half grudging, some respect, for had she not in her veins the blood of that very noble, if slightly mythical, Italian house, whose daughters, scattered about English drawing-rooms in the nineteenth century, had lisped so charmingly, had stormed so wildly, and all her wit and her bearing and her temper came from them, and not from the sluggish English, or the cold Scotch; but more profoundly she ruminated the other problem, of rich and poor, and the things she saw with her own eyes, weekly, daily, here or in London, when she visited this widow, or that struggling wife in person with a bag on her arm, and a notebook and pencil with which she wrote down in columns carefully ruled for the purpose wages and spendings, employment and unemployment, in the hope that thus she would cease to be a private woman whose charity was half a sop to her own indignation, half a relief to her own curiosity, and become, what with her untrained mind she greatly admired, an investigator elucidating the social problem.

Insoluble questions they were, it seemed to her, standing there, holding James by the hand. He had followed her into the drawing-room, that young man they laughed at; he was standing by the table, fidgeting with something, awkwardly, feeling himself out of things, as she knew without looking round. They had all gone—the children; Minta Doyle and Paul Rayley; Augustus Carmichael; her husband—they had all gone. So she turned with a sigh and said, 'Would it bore you to come with me, Mr Tansley?'

She had a dull errand in the town; she had a letter or two to write; she would be ten minutes perhaps; she would put on her hat. And, with her basket and her parasol, there she was again, ten minutes later, giving out a sense of being ready, of being equipped for a jaunt, which, however, she must interrupt for a moment, as they passed the tennis lawn, to ask Mr Carmichael, who was basking with his yellow cat's eyes ajar, so that like a cat's they seemed to reflect the branches moving or the clouds passing, but to give no inkling of any inner thoughts or emotion whatsoever, if he wanted anything.

For they were making the great expedition, she said, laughing. They were going to the town. 'Stamps, writing-paper, tobacco?' she suggested, stopping by his side. But no, he wanted nothing. His hands clasped themselves over his capacious paunch, his eyes blinked, as if he would have liked to reply kindly to these blandishments (she was seductive but a little nervous) but could not, sunk as he was in a grey-green somnolence which embraced them all, without need of words, in a vast and benevolent lethargy of well-wishing; all the house; all the world; all the people in it, for he had slipped into his glass at lunch a few drops of something, which accounted, the children thought, for the vivid streak of canary-yellow in moustache and beard that were otherwise milk-white. He wanted nothing, he murmured.

He should have been a great philosopher, said Mrs Ramsay, as they went down the road to the fishing village, but he had made an unfortunate marriage. Holding her black parasol very erect, and moving with an indescribable air of expectation, as if she were going to meet someone round the corner, she told the story; an affair at Oxford with some girl; an early marriage; poverty; going to India; translating a little poetry 'very beautifully, I believe', being willing to teach the boys Persian or Hindustanee, but what really was the use of that?—and then lying, as they saw him, on the lawn.

It flattered him; snubbed as he had been, it soothed him that Mrs Ramsay should tell him this. Charles Tansley revived. Insinuating, too, as she did the greatness of man's intellect, even in its decay, the subjection of all wives—not that she blamed the girl, and the marriage had been happy enough, she believed—to their husband's labours, she made him feel better pleased with himself than he had done yet, and he would have liked, had they taken a cab, for example, to have paid the fare. As for her little bag, might he not carry that? No, no, she said, she always carried *that* herself. She did too. Yes, he felt that in her. He felt many things, something in particular that excited him and disturbed him for reasons which he could not give. He would like her to see him, gowned and hooded, walking in a procession. A fellowship, a professorship,—he felt capable of anything and saw himself—but what was she looking at? At a man pasting a bill. The vast flapping sheet flattened itself out, and each shove of the brush revealed fresh legs, hoops, horses, glistening reds and blues, beautifully smooth, until half the wall was covered with the advertisement of a circus; a hundred horsemen, twenty performing seals, lions, tigers . . . Craning forwards, for she was short-sighted, she read out how it . . . 'will visit this town'. It was terribly dangerous work for a one-armed man, she exclaimed, to stand on top of a ladder like that—his left arm had been cut off in a reaping machine two years ago.

'Let us all go!' she cried, moving on, as if all those riders and horses had filled her with child-like exultation and made her forget her pity.

'Let's go,' he said, repeating her words, clicking them out, however, with a self-consciousness that made her wince. 'Let us go to the Circus.' No. He could not say it right. He could not feel it right. But why not? she wondered. What was wrong with him then? She liked him warmly, at the moment. Had they not been taken, she asked, to circuses when they were children? Never, he answered, as if she asked the very thing he wanted to reply to; had been longing all these days to say, how they did not go to circuses. It was a large family, nine brothers and sisters, and his father was a working man; 'My father is a chemist, Mrs Ramsay. He keeps a shop.' He himself had paid his own way since he was thirteen. Often he went without a greatcoat in winter. He could never 'return hospitality' (those were his parched stiff words) at college. He had to make things last twice the time other people did; he smoked the cheapest tobacco; shag; the same the old men smoked on the quays. He worked hard—seven hours a day; his subject was now the influence of something upon somebody—they were walking on and Mrs Ramsay did not quite catch the meaning, only the words, here and there . . . dissertation . . . fellowship . . . readership . . . lectureship. She could not follow the ugly academic jargon, that rattled itself off so glibly, but said to herself that she saw now why going to the circus had knocked him off his perch, poor little man, and why he came out, instantly, with all that about his father and mother and brothers and sisters, and she would see to it that they didn't laugh at him any more; she would tell Prue about it. What he would have liked, she supposed, would have been to say how he had been to Ibsen with the Ramsays. He was an awful prig—oh yes, an insufferable bore. For, though they had reached the town now and were in the main street, with carts grinding past on the cobbles, still he went on talking, about settlements, and teaching, and working men, and helping our own class, and lectures, till she gathered that he had got back entire self-confidence, had recovered from the circus, and was about (and now again she liked him warmly) to tell her—but here, the houses falling away on both sides, they came out on the quay, and the whole bay spread before them and Mrs Ramsay could not help exclaiming, 'Oh, how beautiful!' For the great plateful of blue water was before her; the hoary Lighthouse, distant, austere, in the midst; and on the right, as far as the eye could see, fading and falling, in soft low pleats, the green sand dunes with the wild flowing grasses on them, which always seemed to be running away into some moon country, uninhabited of men.

That was the view, she said, stopping, growing greyer-eyed, that her husband loved.

She paused a moment. But now, she said, artists had come here. There indeed, only a few paces off, stood one of them, in Panama hat and yellow boots, seriously, softly, absorbedly, for all that he was watched by ten little boys, with an air of profound contentment on his round red face, gazing, and then, when he had gazed, dipping; imbuing the tip of his brush in some soft mound of green or pink. Since Mr Paunceforte had been there, three years before, all the pictures were like that she said, green and grey, with lemon-coloured sailing-boats, and pink women on the beach.

But her grandmother's friends, she said, glancing discreetly as they passed, took the greatest pains; first they mixed their own colours, and then they ground them, and then they put damp cloths on them to keep them moist.

So Mr Tansley supposed she meant him to see that that man's picture was skimpy, was that what one said? The colours weren't solid? Was that what one said? Under the influence of that extraordinary emotion which had been growing all the walk, had begun in the garden when he had wanted to take her bag, had increased in the town when he had wanted to tell her everything about himself, he was coming to see himself and everything he had ever known gone crooked a little. It was awfully strange.

.   There he stood in the parlour of the poky little house where she had taken him, waiting for her, while she went upstairs a moment to see a woman. He heard her quick step above; heard her voice cheerful, then low; looked at the mats, tea-caddies, glass shades; waited quite impatiently; looked forward eagerly to the walk home, determined to carry her bag; then heard her come out; shut a door; say they must keep the windows open and the doors shut, ask at the house for anything they wanted (she must be talking to a child), when, suddenly, in she came, stood for a moment silent (as if she had been pretending up there, and for a moment let herself be now), stood quite motionless for a moment against a picture of Queen Victoria wearing the blue ribbon of the Garter; and all at once he realized that it was this: it was this:—she was the most beautiful person he had ever seen.

With stars in her eyes and veils in her hair, with cyclamen and wild violets—what nonsense was he thinking? She was fifty at least; she had eight children. Stepping through fields of flowers and taking to her breast buds that had broken and lambs that had fallen; with the stars in her eyes and the wind in her hair—He took her bag.

'Good-bye, Elsie,' she said, and they walked up the street, she holding her parasol erect and walking as if she expected to meet someone round the corner, while for the first time in his life Charles Tansley felt an extraordinary pride; a man digging in a drain stopped digging and looked at her; let his arm fall down and looked at her; Charles Tansley felt an extraordinary pride; felt the wind and the cyclamen and the violets for he was walking with a beautiful woman for the first time in his life. He had hold of her bag.

2

'No going to the Lighthouse, James,' he said, as he stood by the window, speaking awkwardly, but trying in deference to Mrs Ramsay to soften his voice into some semblance of geniality at least.

Odious little man, thought Mrs Ramsay, why go on saying that?

3

'Perhaps you will wake up and find the sun shining and the birds singing,' she said compassionately, smoothing the little boy's hair, for her husband, with his caustic saying that it would not be fine, had dashed his spirits she could see. This going to the Lighthouse was a passion of his, she saw, and then, as if her husband had not said enough, with his caustic saying that it would not be fine tomorrow, this odious little man went and rubbed it in all over again.

'Perhaps it will be fine tomorrow,' she said, smoothing his hair.

All she could do now was to admire the refrigerator, and turn the pages of the Stores list in the hope that she might come upon something like a rake, or a mowing-machine, which, with its prongs and its handles, would need the greatest skill and care in cutting out. All these young men parodied her husband, she reflected; he said it would rain; they said it would be a positive tornado.

But here, as she turned the page, suddenly her search for the picture of a rake or a mowing-machine was interrupted. The gruff murmur, irregularly broken by the taking out of pipes and the putting in of pipes which had kept on assuring her, though she could not hear what was said (as she sat in the window), that the men were happily talking; this sound which had lasted now half an hour and had taken its place soothingly in the scale of sounds pressing on top of her, such as the tap of balls upon bats, the sharp, sudden bark now and then, 'How's that? How's that?' of the children playing cricket, had ceased; so that the monotonous fall of the waves on the beach, which for the most part beat a measured and soothing tattoo to her thoughts and seemed consolingly to repeat over and over again as she sat with the children the words of some old cradle song, murmured by nature, 'I am guarding you—I am your support', but at other times suddenly and unexpectedly, especially when her mind raised itself slightly from the task actually in hand, had no such kindly meaning, but like a ghostly roll of drums remorselessly beat the measure of life, made one think of the destruction of the island and its engulfment in the sea, and warned her whose day had slipped past in one quick doing after another that it was all ephemeral as a rainbow—this sound which had been obscured and concealed under the other sounds suddenly thundered hollow in her ears and made her look up with an impulse of terror.

They had ceased to talk; that was the explanation. Falling in one second from the tension which had gripped her to the other extreme which, as if to recoup her for her unnecessary expense of emotion, was cool, amused, and even faintly malicious, she concluded that poor Charles Tansley had been shed. That was of little account to her. If her husband required sacrifices (and indeed he did) she cheerfully offered up to him Charles Tansley, who had snubbed her little boy.

One moment more, with her head raised, she listened, as if she waited for some habitual sound, some regular mechanical sound; and then, hearing something rhythmical, half said, half chanted, beginning in the garden, as her husband beat up and down the terrace, something between a croak and a song, she was soothed once more, assured again that all was well, and looking down at the book on her knee found the picture of a pocket knife with six blades which could only be cut out if James was very careful.

Suddenly a loud cry, as of a sleep-walker, half roused, something about

> Stormed at with shot and shell

sung out with the utmost intensity in her ear, made her turn apprehensively to see if anyone heard him. Only Lily Briscoe, she was glad to find; and that did not matter. But the sight of the girl standing on the edge of the lawn painting reminded her; she was supposed to be keeping her head as much in the same position as possible for Lily's picture. Lily's picture! Mrs Ramsay smiled. With her little Chinese eyes and her puckered-up face she would never marry; one could not take her painting very seriously; but she was an independent little creature, Mrs Ramsay liked her for it, and so remembering her promise, she bent her head.

4

Indeed, he almost knocked her easel over, coming down upon her with his hands waving, shouting out 'Boldly we rode and well', but, mercifully, he turned sharp, and rode off, to die gloriously she supposed upon the heights of Balaclava. Never was anybody at once so ridiculous and so alarming. But so long as he kept like that, waving, shouting, she was safe; he would not stand still and look at her picture. And that was what Lily Briscoe could not have endured. Even while she looked at the mass, at the line, at the colour, at Mrs Ramsay sitting in the window with James, she kept a feeler on her surroundings lest someone should creep up, and suddenly she should find her picture looked at. But now, with all her senses quickened as they were, looking, straining, till the colour of the wall and the jacmanna beyond burnt into her eyes, she was aware of someone coming out of the house, coming towards her; but somehow divined, from the footfall, William Bankes, so that though her brush quivered, she did not, as she would have done had it been Mr Tansley, Paul Rayley, Minta Doyle, or practically anybody else, turn her canvas upon the grass, but let it stand. William Bankes stood beside her.

They had rooms in the village, and so, walking in, walking out, parting late on door-mats, had said little things about the soup, about the children, about one thing and another which made them allies; so that when he stood beside her now in his judicial way (he was old enough to be her father too, a botanist, a widower, smelling of soap, very scrupulous and clean) she just stood there. He just stood there. Her shoes were excellent, he observed. They allowed the toes their natural expansion. Lodging in the same house with her, he had noticed too, how orderly she was, up before breakfast and off to paint, he believed, alone: poor, presumably, and without the complexion or the allurement of Miss Doyle certainly, but with a good sense which made her in his eyes superior to that young lady. Now, for instance, when Ramsay bore down on them, shouting, gesticulating, Miss Briscoe, he felt certain, understood.

Someone had blundered.

Mr Ramsay glared at them. He glared at them without seeming to see them. That did make them both vaguely uncomfortable. Together they had seen a thing they had not been meant to see. They had encroached upon a privacy. So, Lily thought, it was probably an excuse of his for moving, for getting out of earshot, that made Mr Bankes almost immediately say something about its being chilly and suggest taking a stroll. She would come, yes. But it was with difficulty that she took her eyes off her picture.

The jacmanna was bright violet; the wall staring white. She would not have considered it honest to tamper with the bright violet and the staring white, since she saw them like that, fashionable though it was, since Mr Paunceforte's visit, to see everything pale, elegant, semi-transparent. Then beneath the colour there was the shape. She could see it all so clearly, so commandingly, when she looked: it was when she took her brush in hand that the whole thing changed. It was in that moment's flight between the picture and her canvas that the demons set on her who often brought her to the verge of tears and made this passage from conception to work as dreadful as any down a dark passage for a child. Such she often felt herself—struggling against terrific odds to maintain her courage; to say: 'But this is what I see; this is what I see', and so to clasp some miserable remnant of her vision to her breast, which a thousand forces did their best to pluck from her. And it was then too, in that chill and windy way, as she began to paint, that there forced themselves upon her other things, her own inadequacy, her insignificance, keeping house for her father off the Brompton Road, and had much ado to control her impulse to fling herself (thank Heaven she had always resisted so far) at Mrs Ramsay's knee and say to her—but what could one say to her? 'I'm in love with you'? No, that was not true. 'I'm in love with this all', waving her hand at the hedge, at the house, at the children? It was absurd, it was impossible. One could not say what one meant. So now she laid her brushes neatly in the box, side by side, and said to William Bankes:

'It suddenly gets cold. The sun seems to give less heat,' she said, looking about her, for it was bright enough, the grass still a soft deep green, the house starred in its greenery with purple passion flowers, and rooks dropping cool cries from the high blue. But something moved, flashed, turned a silver wing in the air. It was September after all, the middle of September, and past six in the evening. So off they strolled down the garden in the usual direction, past the tennis lawn, past the pampas grass, to that break in the thick hedge, guarded by red-hot pokers like brasiers of clear burning coal, between which the blue waters of the bay looked bluer than ever.

They came there regularly every evening drawn by some need. It was as if the water floated off and set sailing thoughts which had grown stagnant on dry land, and gave to their bodies even some sort of physical relief. First, the pulse of colour flooded the bay with blue, and the heart expanded with it and the body swam, only the next instant to be checked and chilled by the prickly blackness on the ruffled waves. Then, up behind the great black rock, almost every evening spurted irregularly, so that one had to watch for it and it was a delight when it came, a fountain of white water; and then, while one waited for that, one watched, on the pale semicircular beach, wave after wave shedding again and again smoothly a film of mother-of-pearl.

They both smiled, standing there. They both felt a common hilarity, excited by the moving waves; and then by the swift cutting race of a sailing boat, which, having sliced a curve in the bay, stopped; shivered; let its sail drop down; and then, with a natural instinct to complete the picture, after this swift movement, both of them looked at the dunes far away, and instead of merriment felt come over them some sadness—because the thing was completed partly, and partly because distant views seem to outlast by a million years (Lily thought) the gazer and to be communing already with a sky which beholds an earth entirely at rest.

Looking at the far sand-hills, William Bankes thought of Ramsay: thought of a road in Westmorland, thought of Ramsay striding along a road by himself hung round with that solitude which seemed to be his natural air. But this was suddenly interrupted, William Bankes remembered (and this must refer to some actual incident), by a hen, straddling her wings out in protection of a covey of little chicks, upon which Ramsay, stopping, pointed his stick and said 'Pretty—pretty', an odd illumination into his heart, Bankes had thought it, which showed his simplicity, his sympathy with humble things; but it seemed to him as if their friendship had ceased, there, on that stretch of road. After that, Ramsay had married. After that, what with one thing and another, the pulp had gone out of their friendship. Whose fault it was he could not say, only, after a time, repetition had taken the place of newness. It was to repeat that they met. But in this dumb colloquy with the sand dunes he maintained that his affection for Ramsay had in no way diminished; but there, like the body of a young man laid up in peat for a century, with the red fresh on his lips, was his friendship, in its acuteness and reality laid up across the bay among the sand-hills.

He was anxious for the sake of this friendship and perhaps too in order to clear himself in his own mind from the imputation of having dried and shrunk—for Ramsay lived in a welter of children, whereas Bankes was childless and a widower—he was anxious that Lily Briscoe should not disparage Ramsay (a great man in his own way) yet should understand how things stood between them. Begun long years ago, their friendship had petered out on a Westmorland road, where the hen spread her wings before her chicks; after which Ramsay had married, and their paths lying different ways, there had been, certainly for no one's fault, some tendency, when they met, to repeat.

Yes. That was it. He finished. He turned from the view. And, turning to walk back the other way, up the drive, Mr Bankes was alive to things which would not have struck him had not those sand-hills revealed to him the body of his friendship lying with the red on its lips laid up in peat—for instance, Cam, the little girl, Ramsay's youngest daughter. She was picking Sweet Alice on the bank. She was wild and fierce. She would not 'give a flower to the gentleman' as the nursemaid told her. No! no! no! she would not! She clenched her fist. She stamped. And Mr Bankes felt aged and saddened and somehow put into the wrong by her about his friendship. He must have dried and shrunk.

The Ramsays were not rich, and it was a wonder how they managed to contrive it all. Eight children! To feed eight children on philosophy! Here was another of them, Jasper this time, strolling past, to have a shot at a bird, he said, nonchalantly, swinging Lily's hand like a pump-handle as he passed, which caused Mr Bankes to say, bitterly, how *she* was a favourite. There was education now to be considered (true, Mrs Ramsay had something of her own perhaps) let alone the daily wear and tear of shoes and stockings which those 'great fellows', all well grown, angular, ruthless youngsters, must require. As for being sure which was which, or in what order they came, that was beyond him. He called them privately after the Kings and Queens of England; Cam the Wicked, James the Ruthless, Andrew the Just, Prue the Fair—for Prue would have beauty, he thought, how could she help it?—and Andrew brains. While he walked up the drive and Lily Briscoe said yes and no and capped his comments (for she was in love with them all, in love with this world) he weighed Ramsay's case, commiserated him, envied him, as if he had seen him divest himself of all those glories of isolation and austerity which crowned him in youth to cumber himself definitely with fluttering wings and clucking domesticities. They gave him something—William Bankes acknowledged that; it would have been pleasant if Cam had stuck a flower in his coat or clambered over his shoulder, as over her father's, to look at a picture of Vesuvius in eruption; but they had also, his old friends could not but feel, destroyed something. What would a stranger think now? What did this Lily Briscoe think? Could one help noticing that habits grew on him? eccentricities, weaknesses perhaps? It was astonishing that a man of his intellect could stoop so low as he did—but that was too harsh a phrase—could depend so much as he did upon people's praise.

'Oh but', said Lily, 'think of his work!'

Whenever she 'thought of his work' she always saw clearly before her a large kitchen table. It was Andrew's doing. She asked him what his father's books were about. 'Subject and object and the nature of reality', Andrew had said. And when she said Heavens, she had no notion what that meant. 'Think of a kitchen table then', he told her, 'when you're not there'.

So she always saw, when she thought of Mr Ramsay's work, a scrubbed kitchen table. It lodged now in the fork of a pear tree, for they had reached the orchard. And with a painful effort of concentration, she focused her mind, not upon the silver-bossed bark of the tree, or upon its fish-shaped leaves, but upon a phantom kitchen table, one of those scrubbed board tables, grained and knotted, whose virtue seems to have been laid bare by years of muscular integrity, which stuck there, its four legs in air. Naturally, if one's days were passed in this seeing of angular essences, this reducing of lovely evenings, with all their flamingo clouds and blue and silver to a white deal four-legged table (and it was a mark of the finest minds so to do), naturally one could not be judged like an ordinary person.

Mr Bankes liked her for bidding him 'think of his work'. He had thought of it, often and often. Times without number, he had said, 'Ramsay is one of those men who do their best work before they are forty.' He had made a definite contribution to philosophy in one little book when he was only five and twenty; what came after was more or less amplification, repetition. But the number of men who make a definite contribution to anything whatsoever is very small, he said, pausing by the pear tree, well brushed, scrupulously exact, exquisitely judicial. Suddenly, as if the movement of his hand had released it, the load of her accumulated impressions of him tilted up, and down poured in a ponderous avalanche all she felt about him. That was one sensation. Then up rose in a fume the essence of his being. That was another. She felt herself transfixed by the intensity of her perception; it was his severity; his goodness. I respect you (she addressed him silently) in every atom; you are not vain; you are entirely impersonal; you are finer than Mr Ramsay; you are the finest human being that I know; you have neither wife nor child (without any sexual feeling, she longed to cherish that loneliness), you live for science (involuntarily, sections of potatoes rose before her eyes); praise would be an insult to you; generous, pure-hearted, heroic man! But simultaneously, she remembered how he had brought a valet all the way up here; objected to dogs on chairs; would prose for hours (until Mr Ramsay slammed out of the room) about salt in vegetables and the iniquity of English cooks.

How then did it work out, all this? How did one judge people, think of them? How did one add up this and that and conclude that it was liking one felt, or disliking? And to those words, what meaning attached, after all? Standing now, apparently transfixed, by the pear tree, impressions poured in upon her of those two men, and to follow her thought was like following a voice which speaks too quickly to be taken down by one's pencil, and the voice was her own voice saying without prompting undeniable, everlasting, contradictory things, so that even the fissures and humps on the bark of the pear tree were irrevocably fixed there for eternity. You have greatness, she continued, but Mr Ramsay has none of it. He is petty, selfish, vain, egotistical; he is spoilt; he is a tyrant; he wears Mrs Ramsay to death; but he has what you (she addressed Mr Bankes) have not; a fiery unworldliness; he knows nothing about trifles; he loves dogs and his children. He has eight. You have none. Did he not come down in two coats the other night and let Mrs Ramsay trim his hair into a pudding basin? All of this danced up and down, like a company of gnats, each separate, but all marvellously controlled in an invisible elastic net—danced up and down in Lily's mind, in and about the branches of the pear tree, where still hung in effigy the scrubbed kitchen table, symbol of her profound respect for Mr Ramsay's mind, until her thought which had spun quicker and quicker exploded of its own intensity; she felt released; a shot went off close at hand, and there came, flying from its fragments, frightened, effusive, tumultuous, a flock of starlings.

'Jasper!' said Mr Bankes. They turned the way the starlings flew, over the terrace. Following the scatter of swift-flying birds in the sky they stepped through the gap in the high hedge straight into Mr Ramsay, who boomed tragically at them, 'Someone had blundered!'

His eyes, glazed with emotion, defiant with tragic intensity, met theirs for a second, and trembled on the verge of recognition; but then, raising his hand half-way to his face as if to avert, to brush off, in an agony of peevish shame, their normal gaze, as if he begged them to withhold for a moment what he knew to be inevitable, as if he impressed upon them his own child-like resentment of interruption, yet even in the moment of discovery was not to be routed utterly, but was determined to hold fast to something of this delicious emotion, this impure rhapsody of which he was ashamed, but in which he revelled—he turned abruptly, slammed his private door on them; and, Lily Briscoe and Mr Bankes, looking uneasily up into the sky, observed that the flock of starlings which Jasper had routed with his gun had settled on the tops of the elm trees.

5

'And even if it isn't fine tomorrow,' said Mrs Ramsay, raising her eyes to glance at William Bankes and Lily Briscoe as they passed, 'it will be another day. And now,' she said, thinking that Lily's charm was her Chinese eyes, aslant in her white, puckered little face, but it would take a clever man to see it, 'and now stand up, and let me measure your leg,' for they might go to the Lighthouse after all, and she must see if the stocking did not need to be an inch or two longer in the leg.

Smiling, for an admirable idea had flashed upon her this very second—William and Lily should marry—she took the heather mixture stocking, with its criss-cross of steel needles at the mouth of it, and measured it against James's leg.

'My dear, stand still,' she said, for in his jealousy, not liking to serve as measuring-block for the Lighthouse keeper's little boy, James fidgeted purposely; and if he did that, how could she see, was it too long, was it too short? she asked.

She looked up—what demon possessed him, her youngest, her cherished?—and saw the room, saw the chairs, thought them fearfully shabby. Their entrails, as Andrew said the other day, were all over the floor; but then what was the point, she asked herself, of buying good chairs to let them spoil up here all through the winter when the house, with only one old woman to see to it, positively dripped with wet? Never mind: the rent was precisely twopence halfpenny; the children loved it; it did her husband good to be three thousand, or if she must be accurate, three hundred miles from his library and his lectures and his disciples; and there was room for visitors. Mats, camp beds, crazy ghosts of chairs and tables whose London life of service was done—they did well enough here; and a photograph or two, and books. Books, she thought, grew of themselves. She never had time to read them. Alas! even the books that had been given her, and inscribed by the hand of the poet himself: 'For her whose wishes must be obeyed' . . . 'The happier Helen of our days' . . . disgraceful to say, she had never read them. And Croom on the Mind and Bates on the Savage Customs of Polynesia ('My dear, stand still,' she said)—neither of those could one send to the Lighthouse. At a certain moment, she supposed, the house would become so shabby that something must be done. If they could be taught to wipe their feet and not bring the beach in with them—that would be something. Crabs, she had to allow, if Andrew really wished to dissect them, or if Jasper believed that one could make soup from seaweed, one could not prevent it; or Rose's objects—shells, reeds, stones; for they were gifted, her children, but all in quite different ways. And the result of it was, she sighed, taking in the whole room from floor to ceiling, as she held the stocking against James's leg, that things got shabbier and got shabbier summer after summer. The mat was fading; the wallpaper was flapping. You couldn't tell any more that those were roses on it. Still, if every door in a house is left perpetually open, and no lockmaker in the whole of Scotland can mend a bolt, things must spoil. What was the use of flinging a green Cashmere shawl over the edge of a picture frame? In two weeks it would be the colour of pea soup. But it was the doors that annoyed her; every door was left open. She listened. The drawing-room door was open; the hall door was open; it sounded as if the bedroom doors were open; and certainly the window on the landing was open, for that she had opened herself. That windows should be open, and doors shut—simple as it was, could none of them remember it? She would go into the maids' bedrooms at night and find them sealed like ovens, except for Marie's, the Swiss girl, who would rather go without a bath than without fresh air, but then at home, she had said, 'the mountains are so beautiful'. She had said that last night looking out of the window with tears in her eyes. 'The mountains are so beautiful.' Her father was dying there, Mrs Ramsay knew. He was leaving them fatherless. Scolding and demonstrating (how to make a bed, how to open a window, with hands that shut and spread like a Frenchwoman's) all had folded itself quietly about her, when the girl spoke, as, after a flight through the sunshine the wings of a bird fold themselves quietly and the blue of its plumage changes from bright steel to soft purple. She had stood there silent for there was nothing to be said. He had cancer of the throat. At the recollection—how she had stood there, how the girl had said, 'At home the mountains are so beautiful', and there was no hope, no hope whatever, she had a spasm of irritation, and speaking sharply, said to James:

'Stand still. Don't be tiresome,' so that he knew instantly that her severity was real, and straightened his leg and she measured it.

The stocking was too short by half an inch at least, making allowance for the fact that Sorley's little boy would be less well grown than James.

'It's too short,' she said, 'ever so much too short.'

Never did anybody look so sad. Bitter and black, halfway down, in the darkness, in the shaft which ran from the sunlight to the depths, perhaps a tear formed; a tear fell; the waters swayed this way and that, received it, and were at rest. Never did anybody look so sad.

But was it nothing but looks? people said. What was there behind it—her beauty, her splendour? Had he blown his brains out, they asked, had he died the week before they were married—some other, earlier lover, of whom rumours reached one? Or was there nothing? nothing but an incomparable beauty which she lived behind, and could do nothing to disturb? For easily though she might have said at some moment of intimacy when stories of great passion, of love foiled, of ambition thwarted came her way how she too had known or felt or been through it herself, she never spoke. She was silent always. She knew then—she knew without having learnt. Her simplicity fathomed what clever people falsified. Her singleness of mind made her drop plumb like a stone, alight exact as a bird, gave her, naturally, this swoop and fall of the spirit upon truth which delighted, eased, sustained—falsely perhaps.

('Nature has but little clay,' said Mr Bankes once, hearing her voice on the telephone, and much moved by it though she was only telling him a fact about a train, 'like that of which she moulded you'. He saw her at the end of the line, Greek, blue-eyed, straight-nosed. How incongruous it seemed to be telephoning to a woman like that. The Graces assembling seemed to have joined hands in meadows of asphodel to compose that face. Yes, he would catch the 10.30 at Euston.

'But she's no more aware of her beauty than a child,' said Mr Bankes, replacing the receiver and crossing the room to see what progress the workmen were making with an hotel which they were building at the back of his house. And he thought of Mrs Ramsay as he looked at that stir among the unfinished walls. For always, he thought, there was something incongruous to be worked into the harmony of her face. She clapped a deer-stalker's hat on her head; she ran across the lawn in goloshes to snatch a child from mischief. So that if it was her beauty merely that one thought of, one must remember the quivering thing, the living thing (they were carrying bricks up a little plank as he watched them), and work it into the picture; or if one thought of her simply as a woman, one must endow her with some freak of idiosyncrasy; or suppose some latent desire to doff her royalty of form as if her beauty bored her and all that men say of beauty, and she wanted only to be like other people, insignificant. He did not know. He did not know. He must go to his work.)

Knitting her reddish-brown hairy stocking, with her head outlined absurdly by the gilt frame, the green shawl which she had tossed over the edge of the frame, and the authenticated masterpiece by Michael Angelo, Mrs Ramsay smoothed out what had been harsh in her manner a moment before, raised his head, and kissed her little boy on the forehead. 'Let's find another picture to cut out,' she said.

6

But what had happened?

Someone had blundered.

Starting from her musing she gave meaning to words which she had held meaningless in her mind for a long stretch of time. 'Someone had blundered'—Fixing her short-sighted eyes upon her husband, who was now bearing down upon her, she gazed steadily until his closeness revealed to her (the jingle mated itself in her head) that something had happened, someone had blundered. But she could not for the life of her think what.

He shivered; he quivered. All his vanity, all his satisfaction in his own splendour, riding fell as a thunderbolt, fierce as a hawk at the head of his men through the valley of death, had been shattered, destroyed. Stormed at by shot and shell, boldly we rode and well, flashed through the valley of death, volleyed and thundered—straight into Lily Briscoe and William Bankes. He quivered; he shivered.

Not for the world would she have spoken to him, realizing, from the familiar signs, his eyes averted, and some curious gathering together of his person, as if he wrapped himself about and needed privacy into which to regain his equilibrium, that he was outraged and anguished. She stroked James's head; she transferred to him what she felt for her husband, and, as she watched him chalk yellow the white dress shirt of a gentleman in the Army and Navy Stores catalogue, thought what a delight it would be to her should he turn out a great artist; and why should he not? He had a splendid forehead. Then, looking up, as her husband passed her once more, she was relieved to find that the ruin was veiled; domesticity triumphed; custom crooned its soothing rhythm, so that when stopping deliberately, as his turn came round again, at the window he bent quizzically and whimsically to tickle James's bare calf with a sprig of something, she twitted him for having dispatched 'that poor young man', Charles Tansley. Tansley had had to go in and write his dissertation, he said.

'James will have to write *his* dissertation one of these days,' he added ironically, flicking his sprig.

Hating his father, James brushed away the tickling spray with which in a manner peculiar to him, compound of severity and humour, he teased his youngest son's bare leg.

She was trying to get these tiresome stockings finished to send to Sorley's little boy tomorrow, said Mrs Ramsay.

There wasn't the slightest possible chance that they could go to the Lighthouse tomorrow, Mr Ramsay snapped out irascibly.

How did he know? she asked. The wind often changed.

The extraordinary irrationality of her remark, the folly of women's minds enraged him. He had ridden through the valley of death, been shattered and shivered; and now she flew in the face of facts, made his children hope what was utterly out of the question, in effect, told lies. He stamped his foot on the stone step. 'Damn you,' he said. But what had she said? Simply that it might be fine tomorrow. So it might.

Not with the barometer falling and the wind due west.

To pursue truth with such astonishing lack of consideration for other people's feelings, to rend the thin veils of civilization so wantonly, so brutally, was to her so horrible an outrage of human decency that, without replying, dazed and blinded, she bent her head as if to let the pelt of jagged hail, the drench of dirty water, bespatter her unrebuked. There was nothing to be said.

He stood by her in silence. Very humbly, at length, he said that he would step over and ask the Coastguards if she liked.

There was nobody whom she reverenced as she reverenced him.

She was quite ready to take his word for it, she said. Only then they need not cut sandwiches—that was all. They came to her, naturally, since she was a woman, all day long with this and that; one wanting this, another that; the children were growing up; she often felt she was nothing but a sponge sopped full of human emotions. Then he said, Damn you. He said, It must rain. He said, It won't rain; and instantly a Heaven of security opened before her. There was nobody she reverenced more. She was not good enough to tie his shoe strings, she felt.

Already ashamed of that petulance, of that gesticulation of the hands when charging at the head of his troops, Mr Ramsay rather sheepishly prodded his son's bare legs once more, and then, as if he had her leave for it, with a movement which oddly reminded his wife of the great sea lion at the Zoo tumbling backwards after swallowing his fish and walloping off so that the water in the tank washes from side to side, he dived into the evening air which already thinner was taking the substance from leaves and hedges but, as if in return, restoring to roses and pinks a lustre which they had not had by day.

'Someone had blundered,' he said again, striding off, up and down the terrace.

But how extraordinarily his note had changed! It was like the cuckoo; 'in June he gets out of tune'; as if he were trying over, tentatively seeking, some phrase for a new mood, and having only this at hand, used it, cracked though it was. But it sounded ridiculous—'Someone had blundered'—said like that, almost as a question, without any conviction, melodiously. Mrs Ramsay could not help smiling, and soon, sure enough, walking up and down, he hummed it, dropped it, fell silent.

He was safe, he was restored to his privacy. He stopped to light his pipe, looked once at his wife and son in the window, and as one raises one's eyes from a page in an express train and sees a farm, a tree, a cluster of cottages as an illustration, a confirmation of something on the printed page to which one returns, fortified, and satisfied, so without his distinguishing either his son or his wife, the sight of them fortified him and satisfied him and consecrated his effort to arrive at a perfectly clear understanding of the problem which now engaged the energies of his splendid mind.

It was a splendid mind. For if thought is like the keyboard of a piano, divided into so many notes, or like the alphabet is ranged in twenty-six letters all in order, then his splendid mind had no sort of difficulty in running over those letters one by one, firmly and accurately, until it had reached, say, the letter Q. He reached Q. Very few people in the whole of England ever reach Q. Here, stopping for one moment by the stone urn which held the geraniums, he saw, but now far far away, like children picking up shells, divinely innocent and occupied with little trifles at their feet and somehow entirely defenceless against a doom which he perceived, his wife and son, together, in the window. They needed his protection; he gave it them. But after Q? What comes next? After Q there are a number of letters the last of which is scarcely visible to mortal eyes, but glimmers red in the distance. Z is only reached once by one man in a generation. Still, if he could reach R it would be something. Here at least was Q. He dug his heels in at Q. Q he was sure of. Q he could demonstrate. If Q then is Q—R—Here he knocked his pipe out, with two or three resonant taps on the ram's horn which made the handle of the urn, and proceeded. 'Then R . . .' He braced himself. He clenched himself.

Qualities that would have saved a ship's company exposed on a broiling sea with six biscuits and a flask of water—endurance and justice, foresight, devotion, skill, came to his help. R is then—what is R?

A shutter, like the leathern eyelid of a lizard, flickered over the intensity of his gaze and obscured the letter R. In that flash of darkness he heard people saying—he was a failure—that R was beyond him. He would never reach R. On to R, once more. R——

Qualities that in a desolate expedition across the icy solitudes of the Polar region would have made him the leader, the guide, the counsellor, whose temper, neither sanguine nor despondent, surveys with equanimity what is to be and faces it, came to his help again. R——

The lizard's eye flickered once more. The veins on his forehead bulged. The geranium in the urn became startlingly visible and, displayed among its leaves, he could see, without wishing it, that old, that obvious distinction between the two classes of men; on the one hand the steady goers of superhuman strength who, plodding and persevering, repeat the whole alphabet in order, twenty-six letters in all, from start to finish; on the other the gifted, the inspired who, miraculously, lump all the letters together in one flash—the way of genius. He had not genius; he laid no claim to that: but he had, or might have had, the power to repeat every letter of the alphabet from A to Z accurately in order. Meanwhile, he stuck at Q. On, then, on to R.

Feelings that would not have disgraced a leader who, now that the snow has begun to fall and the mountain-top is covered in mist, knows that he must lay himself down and die before morning comes, stole upon him, paling the colour of his eyes, giving him, even in the two minutes of his turn on the terrace, the bleached look of withered old age. Yet he would not die lying down; he would find some crag of rock, and there, his eyes fixed on the storm, trying to the end to pierce the darkness, he would die standing. He would never reach R.

He stood stock still, by the urn, with the geranium flowing over it. How many men in a thousand million, he asked himself, reach Z after all? Surely the leader of a forlorn hope may ask himself that, and answer, without treachery to the expedition behind him, 'One perhaps'. One in a generation. Is he to be blamed then if he is not that one? provided he has toiled honestly, given to the best of his power, till he has no more left to give? And his fame lasts how long? It is permissible even for a dying hero to think before he dies how men will speak of him hereafter. His fame lasts perhaps two thousand years. And what are two thousand years? (asked Mr Ramsay ironically, staring at the hedge). What, indeed, if you look from a mountain-top down the long wastes of the ages? The very stone one kicks with one's boot will outlast Shakespeare. His own little light would shine, not very brightly, for a year or two, and would then be merged in some bigger light, and that in a bigger still. (He looked into the darkness, into the intricacy of the twigs.) Who then could blame the leader of that forlorn party which after all has climbed high enough to see the waste of the years and the perishing of stars, if before death stiffens his limbs beyond the power of movement he does a little consciously raise his numbed fingers to his brow, and square his shoulders, so that when the search party comes they will find him dead at his post, the fine figure of a soldier? Mr Ramsay squared his shoulders and stood very upright by the urn.

Who shall blame him, if, so standing for a moment, he dwells upon fame, upon search parties, upon cairns raised by grateful followers over his bones? Finally, who shall blame the leader of the doomed expedition, if, having adventured to the uttermost, and used his strength wholly to the last ounce and fallen asleep not much caring if he wakes or not, he now perceives by some pricking in his toes that he lives, and does not on the whole object to live, but requires sympathy, and whisky, and someone to tell the story of his suffering to at once? Who shall blame him? Who will not secretly rejoice when the hero puts his armour off, and halts by the window and gazes at his wife and son, who very distant at first, gradually come closer and closer, till lips and book and head are clearly before him, though still lovely and unfamiliar from the intensity of his isolation and the waste of ages and the perishing of the stars, and finally putting his pipe in his pocket and bending his magnificent head before her—who will blame him if he does homage to the beauty of the world?

7

But his son hated him. He hated him for coming up to them, for stopping and looking down on them; he hated him for interrupting them; he hated him for the exaltation and sublimity of his gestures; for the magnificence of his head; for his exactingness and egotism (for there he stood, commanding them to attend to him); but most of all he hated the twang and twitter of his father's emotion which, vibrating round them, disturbed the perfect simplicity and good sense of his relations with his mother. By looking fixedly at the page, he hoped to make him move on; by pointing his finger at a word, he hoped to recall his mother's attention, which, he knew angrily, wavered instantly his father stopped. But no. Nothing would make Mr Ramsay move on. There he stood, demanding sympathy.

Mrs Ramsay, who had been sitting loosely, folding her son in her arm, braced herself, and, half turning, seemed to raise herself with an effort, and at once to pour erect into the air a rain of energy, a column of spray, looking at the same time animated and alive as if all her energies were being fused into force, burning and illuminating (quietly though she sat, taking up her stocking again), and into this delicious fecundity, this fountain and spray of life, the fatal sterility of the male plunged itself, like a beak of brass, barren and bare. He wanted sympathy. He was a failure, he said. Mrs Ramsay flashed her needles. Mr Ramsay repeated, never taking his eyes from her face, that he was a failure. She blew the words back at him. 'Charles Tansley . . .' she said. But he must have more than that. It was sympathy he wanted, to be assured of his genius, first of all, and then to be taken within the circle of life, warmed and soothed, to have his senses restored to him, his barrenness made fertile, and all the rooms of the house made full of life—the drawing-room; behind the drawing-room the kitchen; above the kitchen the bedrooms; and beyond them the nurseries; they must be furnished, they must be filled with life.

Charles Tansley thought him the greatest metaphysician of the time, she said. But he must have more than that. He must have sympathy. He must be assured that he too lived in the heart of life; was needed; not here only, but all over the world. Flashing her needles, confident, upright, she created drawing-room and kitchen, set them all aglow; bade him take his ease there, go in and out, enjoy himself. She laughed, she knitted. Standing between her knees, very stiff, James felt all her strength flaring up to be drunk and quenched by the beak of brass, the arid scimitar of the male, which smote mercilessly, again and again, demanding sympathy.

He was a failure, he repeated. Well, look then, feel then. Flashing her needles, glancing round about her, out of the window, into the room, at James himself, she assured him, beyond a shadow of a doubt, by her laugh, her poise, her competence (as a nurse carrying a light across a dark room assures a fractious child), that it was real; the house was full; the garden blowing. If he put implicit faith in her, nothing should hurt him; however deep he buried himself or climbed high, not for a second should he find himself without her. So boasting of her capacity to surround and protect, there was scarcely a shell of herself left for her to know herself by; all was so lavished and spent; and James, as he stood stiff between her knees, felt her rise in a rosy-flowered fruit tree laid with leaves and dancing boughs into which the beak of brass, the arid scimitar of his father, the egotistical man, plunged and smote, demanding sympathy.

Filled with her words, like a child who drops off satisfied, he said, at last, looking at her with humble gratitude, restored, renewed, that he would take a turn; he would watch the children playing cricket. He went.

Immediately, Mrs Ramsay seemed to fold herself together, one petal closed in another, and the whole fabric fell in exhaustion upon itself, so that she had only strength enough to move her finger, in exquisite abandonment to exhaustion, across the page of Grimm's fairy story, while there throbbed through her, like the pulse in a spring which has expanded to its full width and now gently ceases to beat, the rapture of successful creation.

Every throb of this pulse seemed, as he walked away, to enclose her and her husband, and to give to each that solace which two different notes, one high, one low, struck together, seem to give each other as they combine. Yet, as the resonance died, and she turned to the Fairy Tale again, Mrs Ramsay felt not only exhausted in body (afterwards, not at the time, she always felt this) but also there tinged her physical fatigue some faintly disagreeable sensation with another origin. Not that, as she read aloud the story of the Fisherman's Wife, she knew precisely what it came from; nor did she let herself put into words her dissatisfaction when she realized, at the turn of the page when she stopped and heard dully, ominously, a wave fall, how it came from this: she did not like, even for a second, to feel finer than her husband; and further, could not bear not being entirely sure, when she spoke to him, of the truth of what she said. Universities and people wanting him, lectures and books and their being of the highest importance—all that she did not doubt for a moment; but it was their relation, and his coming to her like that, openly, so that anyone could see, that discomposed her; for then people said he depended on her, when they must know that of the two he was infinitely the more important, and what she gave the world, in comparison with what he gave, negligible. But then again, it was the other thing too—not being able to tell him the truth, being afraid, for instance, about the greenhouse roof and the expense it would be, fifty pounds perhaps, to mend it; and then about his books, to be afraid that he might guess, what she a little suspected, that his last book was not quite his best book (she gathered that from William Bankes); and then to hide small daily things, and the children seeing it, and the burden it laid on them—all this diminished the entire joy, the pure joy, of the two notes sounding together, and let the sound die on her ear now with a dismal flatness.

A shadow was on the page; she looked up. It was Augustus Carmichael shuffling past, precisely now, at the very moment when it was painful to be reminded of the inadequacy of human relationships, that the most perfect was flawed, and could not bear the examination which, loving her husband, with her instinct for truth, she turned upon it; when it was painful to feel herself convicted of unworthiness, and impeded in her proper function by these lies, these exaggerations,—it was at this moment when she was fretted thus ignobly in the wake of her exaltation, that Mr Carmichael shuffled past, in his yellow slippers, and some demon in her made it necessary for her to call out, as he passed,

'Going indoors, Mr Carmichael?'

8

He said nothing. He took opium. The children said he had stained his beard yellow with it. Perhaps. What was obvious to her was that the poor man was unhappy, came to them every year as an escape; and yet every year, she felt the same thing; he did not trust her. She said, 'I am going to the town. Shall I get you stamps, paper, tobacco?' and she felt him wince. He did not trust her. It was his wife's doing. She remembered that iniquity of his wife's towards him, which had made her turn to steel and adamant there, in the horrid little room in St John's Wood, when with her own eyes she had seen that odious woman turn him out of the house. He was unkempt; he dropped things on his coat; he had the tiresomeness of an old man with nothing in the world to do; and she turned him out of the room. She said, in her odious way, 'Now, Mrs Ramsay and I want to have a little talk together,' and Mrs Ramsay could see, as if before her eyes, the innumerable miseries of his life. Had he money enough to buy tobacco? Did he have to ask her for it? half a crown? eighteenpence? Oh, she could not bear to think of the little indignities she made him suffer. And always now (why, she could not guess, except that it came probably from that woman somehow) he shrank from her. He never told her anything. But what more could she have done? There was a sunny room given up to him. The children were good to him. Never did she show a sign of not wanting him. She went out of her way indeed to be friendly. Do you want stamps, do you want tobacco? Here's a book you might like and so on. And after all—after all (here insensibly she drew herself together, physically, the sense of her own beauty becoming, as it did so seldom, present to her)—after all, she had not generally any difficulty in making people like her; for instance, George Manning; Mr Wallace; famous as they were, they would come to her of an evening, quietly, and talk alone over her fire. She bore about with her, she could not help knowing it, the torch of her beauty; she carried it erect into any room that she entered; and after all, veil it as she might, and shrink from the monotony of bearing that it imposed on her, her beauty was apparent. She had been admired. She had been loved. She had entered rooms where mourners sat. Tears had flown in her presence. Men, and women too, letting go the multiplicity of things, had allowed themselves with her the relief of simplicity. It injured her that he should shrink. It hurt her. And yet not cleanly, not rightly. That was what she minded, coming as it did on top of her discontent with her husband; the sense she had now when Mr Carmichael shuffled past, just nodding to her question, with a book beneath his arm, in his yellow slippers, that she was suspected; and that all this desire of hers to give, to help, was vanity. For her own self-satisfaction was it that she wished so instinctively to help, to give, that people might say of her, 'O Mrs Ramsay! dear Mrs Ramsay . . . Mrs Ramsay, of course!' and need her and send for her and admire her? Was it not secretly this that she wanted, and therefore when Mr Carmichael shrank away from her, as he did at this moment, making off to some corner where he did acrostics endlessly, she did not feel merely snubbed back in her instinct, but made aware of the pettiness of some part of her, and of human relations how flawed they are, how despicable, how self-seeking, at their best. Shabby and worn out, and not presumably (her cheeks were hollow, her hair was white) any longer a sight that filled the eyes with joy, she had better devote her mind to the story of the Fisherman and his Wife and so pacify that bundle of sensitiveness (none of her children was as sensitive as he was) her son James.

'The man's heart grew heavy,' she read aloud, 'and he would not go. He said to himself, "It is not right," and yet he went. And when he came to the sea the water was quite purple and dark blue, and grey and thick, and no longer so green and yellow, but it was still quiet. And he stood there and said——'

Mrs Ramsay could have wished that her husband had not chosen that moment to stop. Why had he not gone as he said to watch the children playing cricket? But he did not speak; he looked; he nodded; he approved; he went on. He slipped seeing before him that hedge which had over and over again rounded some pause, signified some conclusion, seeing his wife and child, seeing again the urns with the trailing red geraniums which had so often decorated processes of thought, and bore, written up among their leaves, as if they were scraps of paper on which one scribbles notes in the rush of reading—he slipped, seeing all this, smoothly into speculation suggested by an article in *The Times* about the number of Americans who visit Shakespeare's house every year. If Shakespeare had never existed, he asked, would the world have differed much from what it is today? Does the progress of civilization depend upon great men? Is the lot of the average human being better now than in the time of the Pharaohs? Is the lot of the average human being, however, he asked himself, the criterion by which we judge the measure of civilization? Possibly not. Possibly the greatest good requires the existence of a slave class. The liftman in the Tube is an eternal necessity. The thought was distasteful to him. He tossed his head. To avoid it, he would find some way of snubbing the predominance of the arts. He would argue that the world exists for the average human being; that the arts are merely a decoration imposed on the top of human life; they do not express it. Nor is Shakespeare necessary to it. Not knowing precisely why it was that he wanted to disparage Shakespeare and come to the rescue of the man who stands eternally in the door of the lift, he picked a leaf sharply from the hedge. All this would have to be dished up for the young men at Cardiff next month, he thought; here, on his terrace, he was merely foraging and picnicking (he threw away the leaf that he had picked so peevishly) like a man who reaches from his horse to pick a bunch of roses, or stuffs his pockets with nuts as he ambles at his ease through the lanes and fields of a country known to him from boyhood. It was all familiar; this turning, that stile, that cut across the fields. Hours he would spend thus, with his pipe, of an evening, thinking up and down and in and out of the old familiar lanes and commons, which were all stuck about with the history of that campaign there, the life of this statesman here, with poems and with anecdotes, with figures too, this thinker, that soldier; all very brisk and clear; but at length the lane, the field, the common, the fruitful nut-tree and the flowering hedge led him on to that further turn of the road where he dismounted always, tied his horse to a tree, and proceeded on foot alone. He reached the edge of the lawn and looked out on the bay beneath.

It was his fate, his peculiarity, whether he wished it or not, to come out thus on a spit of land which the sea is slowly eating away, and there to stand, like a desolate seabird, alone. It was his power, his gift, suddenly to shed all superfluities, to shrink and diminish so that he looked barer and felt sparer, even physically, yet lost none of his intensity of mind, and so to stand on his little ledge facing the dark of human ignorance, how we know nothing and the sea eats away the ground we stand on—that was his fate, his gift. But having thrown away, when he dismounted, all gestures and fripperies, all trophies of nuts and roses, and shrunk so that not only fame but even his own name was forgotten by him, he kept even in that desolation a vigilance which spared no phantom and luxuriated in no vision, and it was in this guise that he inspired in William Bankes (intermittently) and in Charles Tansley (obsequiously) and in his wife now, when she looked up and saw him standing at the edge of the lawn, profound reverence, and pity, and gratitude too, as a stake driven into the bed of a channel upon which the gulls perch and the waves beat inspires in merry boatloads a feeling of gratitude for the duty it has taken upon itself of marking the channel out there in the floods alone.

'But the father of eight children has no choice . . .' Muttering half aloud, so he broke off, turned, sighed, raised his eyes, sought the figure of his wife reading stories to the little boy; filled his pipe. He turned from the sight of human ignorance and human fate and the sea eating the ground we stand on, which, had he been able to contemplate it fixedly might have led to something; and found consolation in trifles so slight compared with the august theme just now before him that he was disposed to slur that comfort over, to deprecate it, as if to be caught happy in a world of misery was for an honest man the most despicable of crimes. It was true; he was for the most part happy; he had his wife; he had his children; he had promised in six weeks' time to talk 'some nonsense' to the young men of Cardiff about Locke, Hume, Berkeley, and the causes of the French Revolution. But this and his pleasure in it, in the phrases he made, in the ardour of youth, in his wife's beauty, in the tributes that reached him from Swansea, Cardiff, Exeter, South-ampton, Kidderminster, Oxford, Cambridge—all had to be deprecated and concealed under the phrase 'talking nonsense', because, in effect, he had not done the thing he might have done. It was a disguise; it was the refuge of a man afraid to own his own feelings, who could not say, This is what I like—this is what I am; and rather pitiable and distasteful to William Bankes and Lily Briscoe, who wondered why such concealments should be necessary; why he needed always praise; why so brave a man in thought should be so timid in life; how strangely he was venerable and laughable at one and the same time.

Teaching and preaching is beyond human power, Lily suspected. (She was putting away her things.) If you are exalted you must somehow come a cropper. Mrs Ramsay gave him what he asked too easily. Then the change must be so upsetting, Lily said. He comes in from his books and finds us all playing games and talking nonsense. Imagine what a change from the things he thinks about, she said.

He was bearing down upon them. Now he stopped dead and stood looking in silence at the sea. Now he had turned away again.

9

Yes, Mr Bankes said, watching him go. It was a thousand pities. (Lily had said something about his frightening her—he changed from one mood to another so suddenly.) Yes, said Mr Bankes, it was a thousand pities that Ramsay could not behave a little more like other people. (For he liked Lily Briscoe; he could discuss Ramsay with her quite openly.) It was for that reason, he said, that the young don't read Carlyle. A crusty old grumbler who lost his temper if the porridge was cold, why should he preach to us? was what Mr Bankes understood that young people said nowadays. It was a thousand pities if you thought, as he did, that Carlyle was one of the great teachers of mankind. Lily was ashamed to say that she had not read Carlyle since she was at school. But in her opinion one liked Mr Ramsay all the better for thinking that if his little finger ached the whole world must come to an end. It was not *that* she minded. For who could be deceived by him? He asked you quite openly to flatter him, to admire him, his little dodges deceived nobody. What she disliked was his narrowness, his blindness, she said, looking after him.

'A bit of a hypocrite?' Mr Bankes suggested, looking, too, at Mr Ramsay's back, for was he not thinking of his friendship, and of Cam refusing to give him a flower, and of all those boys and girls, and his own house, full of comfort, but, since his wife's death, quiet rather? Of course, he had his work . . . All the same, he rather wished Lily to agree that Ramsay was, as he said, 'a bit of a hypocrite'.

Lily Briscoe went on putting away her brushes, looking up, looking down. Looking up, there he was—Mr Ramsay—advancing towards them, swinging, careless, oblivious, remote. A bit of a hypocrite? she repeated. Oh no—the most sincere of men, the truest (here he was), the best; but, looking down, she thought, he is absorbed in himself, he is tyrannical, he is unjust; and kept looking down, purposely, for only so could she keep steady, staying with the Ramsays. Directly one looked up and saw them, what she called 'being in love' flooded them. They became part of that unreal but penetrating and exciting universe which is the world seen through the eyes of love. The sky stuck to them; the birds sang through them. And, what was even more exciting, she felt, too, as she saw Mr Ramsay bearing down and retreating, and Mrs Ramsay sitting with James in the window and the cloud moving and the tree bending, how life, from being made up of little separate incidents which one lived one by one, became curled and whole like a wave which bore one up with it and threw one down with it, there, with a dash on the beach.

Mr Bankes expected her to answer. And she was about to say something criticizing Mrs Ramsay, how she was alarming, too, in her way, high-handed, or words to that effect, when Mr Bankes made it entirely unnecessary for her to speak by his rapture. For such it was considering his age, turned sixty, and his cleanliness and his impersonality, and the white scientific coat which seemed to clothe him. For him to gaze as Lily saw him gazing at Mrs Ramsay was a rapture, equivalent, Lily felt, to the loves of dozens of young men (and perhaps Mrs Ramsay had never excited the loves of dozens of young men). It was love, she thought, pretending to move her canvas, distilled and filtered; love that never attempted to clutch its object; but, like the love which mathematicians bear their symbols, or poets their phrases, was meant to be spread

over the world and become part of the human gain. So it was indeed.
The world by all means should have shared it, could Mr Bankes have
said why that woman pleased him so; why the sight of her reading a
fairy tale to her boy had upon him precisely the same effect as the
solution of a scientific problem, so that he rested in contemplation of it,
and felt, as he felt when he had proved something absolute about the
digestive system of plants, that barbarity was tamed, the reign of chaos
subdued.

Such a rapture—for by what other name could one call it?—made
Lily Briscoe forget entirely what she had been about to say. It was
nothing of importance; something about Mrs Ramsay. It paled beside
this 'rapture', this silent stare, for which she felt intense gratitude; for
nothing so solaced her, eased her of the perplexity of life, and miraculously raised its burdens, as this sublime power, this heavenly gift, and
one would no more disturb it, while it lasted, than break up the shaft of
sunlight lying level across the floor.

That people should love like this, that Mr Bankes should feel this for
Mrs Ramsay (she glanced at him musing) was helpful, was exalting.
She wiped one brush after another upon a piece of old rag, menially, on
purpose. She took shelter from the reverence which covered all women;
she felt herself praised. Let him gaze; she would steal a look at her
picture.

She could have wept. It was bad, it was bad, it was infinitely bad!
She could have done it differently of course; the colour could have been
thinned and faded; the shapes etherealized; that was how Paunceforte
would have seen it. But then she did not see it like that. She saw the
colour burning on a framework of steel; the light of a butterfly's wing
lying upon the arches of a cathedral. Of all that only a few random
marks scrawled upon the canvas remained. And it would never be seen;
never be hung even, and there was Mr Tansley whispering in her ear,
'Women can't paint, women can't write . . .'

She now remembered what she had been going to say about Mrs
Ramsay. She did not know how she would have put it; but it would
have been something critical. She had been annoyed the other night by
some high-handedness. Looking along the level of Mr Bankes's glance
at her, she thought that no woman could worship another woman in the
way he worshipped; they could only seek shelter under the shade which
Mr Bankes extended over them both. Looking along his beam she added
to it her different ray, thinking that she was unquestionably the loveliest
of people (bowed over her book); the best perhaps; but also, different
too from the perfect shape which one saw there. But why different, and
how different? she asked herself, scraping her palette of all those mounds
of blue and green which seemed to her like clods with no life in them

now, yet she vowed, she would inspire them, force them to move, flow, do her bidding tomorrow. How did she differ? What was the spirit in her, the essential thing, by which, had you found a glove in the corner of a sofa, you would have known it, from its twisted finger, hers indisputably? She was like a bird for speed, an arrow for directness. She was wilful; she was commanding (of course, Lily reminded herself, I am thinking of her relations with women, and I am much younger, an insignificant person, living off the Brompton Road). She opened bedroom windows. She shut doors. (So she tried to start the tune of Mrs Ramsay in her head.) Arriving late at night, with a light tap on one's bedroom door, wrapped in an old fur coat (for the setting of her beauty was always that—hasty, but apt), she would enact again whatever it might be—Charles Tansley losing his umbrella; Mr Carmichael snuffling and sniffing; Mr Bankes saying, 'the vegetable salts are lost'. All this she would adroitly shape; even maliciously twist; and, moving over to the window, in pretence that she must go,—it was dawn, she could see the sun rising,—half turn back, more intimately, but still always laughing, insist that she must, Minta must, they all must marry, since in the whole world, whatever laurels might be tossed to her (but Mrs Ramsay cared not a fig for her painting), or triumphs won by her (probably Mrs Ramsay had had her share of those), and here she saddened, darkened, and came back to her chair, there could be no disputing this: an unmarried woman (she lightly took her hand for a moment), an unmarried woman has missed the best of life. The house seemed full of children sleeping and Mrs Ramsay listening; of shaded lights and regular breathing.

Oh but, Lily would say, there was her father; her home; even, had she dared to say it, her painting. But all this seemed so little, so virginal, against the other. Yet, as the night wore on, and white lights parted the curtains, and even now and then some bird chirped in the garden, gathering a desperate courage she would urge her own exemption from the universal law; plead for it; she liked to be alone; she liked to be herself; she was not made for that; and so have to meet a serious stare from eyes of unparalleled depth, and confront Mrs Ramsay's simple certainty (and she was childlike now) that her dear Lily, her little Brisk, was a fool. Then, she remembered, she had laid her head on Mrs Ramsay's lap and laughed and laughed and laughed, laughed almost hysterically at the thought of Mrs Ramsay presiding with immutable calm over destinies which she completely failed to understand. There she sat, simple, serious. She had recovered her sense of her now—this was the glove's twisted finger. But into what sanctuary had one penetrated? Lily Briscoe had looked up at last, and there was Mrs Ramsay, unwitting entirely what had caused her laughter, still presiding, but now with every trace of wilfulness abolished, and in its stead, something clear as the space which the clouds at last uncover—the little space of sky which sleeps beside the moon.

Was it wisdom? Was it knowledge? Was it, once more, the deceptiveness of beauty, so that all one's perceptions, half-way to truth, were tangled in a golden mesh? or did she lock up within her some secret which certainly Lily Briscoe believed people must have for the world to go on at all? Every one could not be as helter skelter, hand to mouth as she was. But if they knew, could they tell one what they knew? Sitting on the floor with her arms round Mrs Ramsay's knees, close as she could get, smiling to think that Mrs Ramsay would never know the reason of that pressure, she imagined how in the chambers of the mind and heart of the woman who was, physically, touching her, were stood, like the treasures in the tombs of kings, tablets bearing sacred inscriptions, which if one could spell them out would teach one everything, but they would never be offered openly, never made public. What art was there, known to love or cunning, by which one pressed through into those secret chambers? What device for becoming, like waters poured into one jar, inextricably the same, one with the object one adored? Could the body achieve it, or the mind, subtly mingling in the intricate passages of the brain? or the heart? Could loving, as people called it, make her and Mrs Ramsay one? for it was not knowledge but unity that she desired, not inscriptions on tablets, nothing that could be written in any language known to men, but intimacy itself, which is knowledge, she had thought, leaning her head on Mrs Ramsay's knee.

Nothing happened. Nothing! Nothing! as she leant her head against Mrs Ramsay's knee. And yet, she knew knowledge and wisdom were stored in Mrs Ramsay's heart. How then, she had asked herself, did one know one thing or another thing about people, sealed as they were? Only like a bee, drawn by some sweetness or sharpness in the air intangible to touch or taste, one haunted the dome-shaped hive, ranged the wastes of the air over the countries of the world alone, and then haunted the hives with their murmurs and their stirrings; the hives which were people. Mrs Ramsay rose. Lily rose. Mrs Ramsay went. For days there hung about her, as after a dream some subtle change is felt in the person one has dreamt of, more vividly than anything she said, the sound of murmuring and, as she sat in the wicker armchair in the drawing-room window she wore, to Lily's eyes, an august shape; the shape of a dome.

This ray passed level with Mr Bankes's ray straight to Mrs Ramsay sitting reading there with James at her knee. But now while she still looked, Mr Bankes had done. He had put on his spectacles. He had stepped back. He had raised his hand. He had slightly narrowed his clear blue eyes, when Lily, rousing herself, saw what he was at, and winced like a dog who sees a hand raised to strike it. She would have snatched her picture off the easel, but she said to herself, One must. She braced herself to stand the awful trial of someone looking at her picture. One must, she said, one must. And if it must be seen, Mr Bankes was less alarming than another. But that any other eyes should see the residue of her thirty-three years, the deposit of each day's living, mixed with something more secret than she had ever spoken or shown in the course of all those days was an agony. At the same time it was immensely exciting.

Nothing could be cooler and quieter. Taking out a penknife, Mr Bankes tapped the canvas with the bone handle. What did she wish to indicate by the triangular purple shape, 'just there?' he asked.

It was Mrs Ramsay reading to James, she said. She knew his objection—that no one could tell it for a human shape. But she had made no attempt at likeness, she said. For what reason had she introduced them then? he asked. Why indeed?—except that if there, in that corner, it was bright, here, in this, she felt the need of darkness. Simple, obvious, commonplace, as it was, Mr Bankes was interested. Mother and child then—objects of universal veneration, and in this case the mother was famous for her beauty—might be reduced, he pondered, to a purple shadow without irreverence.

But the picture was not of them, she said. Or, not in his sense. There were other senses, too, in which one might reverence them. By a shadow here and a light there, for instance. Her tribute took that form, if, as she vaguely supposed, a picture must be a tribute. A mother and child might be reduced to a shadow without irreverence. A light here required a shadow there. He considered. He was interested. He took it scientifically in complete good faith. The truth was that all his prejudices were on the other side, he explained. The largest picture in his drawing-room, which painters had praised, and valued at a higher price than he had given for it, was of the cherry trees in blossom on the banks of the Kennet. He had spent his honeymoon on the banks of the Kennet, he said. Lily must come and see that picture, he said. But now—he turned, with his glasses raised to the scientific examination of her canvas. The question being one of the relations of masses, of lights and shadows, which, to be honest, he had never considered before, he would like to have it explained—what then did she wish to make of it? And he indicated the scene before them. She looked. She could not show him what she wished to make of it, could not see it even herself, without a brush in her hand. She took up once more her old painting position with the dim eyes and the absent-minded manner, subduing all her impressions as a woman to something much more general; becoming once more under the power of that vision which she had seen clearly once and must now grope for among hedges and houses and mothers and children—her picture. It was a question, she remembered, how to connect this mass on the right hand with that on the left. She might do it by bringing the line of the branch across so; or break the vacancy in the foreground by an object (James perhaps) so. But the danger was that by doing that the unity of the whole might be broken. She stopped; she did not want to bore him; she took the canvas lightly off the easel.

But it had been seen; it had been taken from her. This man had shared with her something profoundly intimate. And, thanking Mr Ramsay for it and Mrs Ramsay for it and the hour and the place, crediting the world with a power which she had not suspected, that one could walk away down that long gallery not alone any more but arm in arm with somebody—the strangest feeling in the world, and the most exhilarating—she nicked the catch of her paint-box to, more firmly than was necessary, and the nick seemed to surround in a circle for ever the paint-box, the lawn, Mr Bankes, and that wild villain, Cam, dashing past.

10

For Cam grazed the easel by an inch; she would not stop for Mr Bankes and Lily Briscoe; though Mr Bankes, who would have liked a daughter of his own, held out his hand; she would not stop for her father, whom she grazed also by an inch; nor for her mother, who called 'Cam! I want you a moment!' as she dashed past. She was off like a bird, bullet, or arrow, impelled by what desire, shot by whom, at what directed, who could say? What, what? Mrs Ramsay pondered, watching her. It might be a vision—of a shell, of a wheelbarrow, of a fairy kingdom on the far side of the hedge; or it might be the glory of speed; no one knew. But when Mrs Ramsay called 'Cam!' a second time, the projectile dropped in mid-career, and Cam came lagging back, pulling a leaf by the way, to her mother.

What was she dreaming about, Mrs Ramsay wondered, seeing her engrossed, as she stood there, with some thought of her own, so that she had to repeat the message twice—ask Mildred if Andrew, Miss Doyle, and Mr Rayley have come back?—The words seemed to be dropped into a well, where, if the waters were clear, they were also so extraordinarily distorting that, even as they descended, one saw them twisting about to make Heaven knows what pattern on the floor of the child's mind. What message would Cam give the cook? Mrs Ramsay wondered. And indeed it was only by waiting patiently, and hearing that there was an old woman in the kitchen with very red cheeks, drinking soup out of a basin, that Mrs Ramsay at last prompted that parrot-like instinct which had picked up Mildred's words quite accurately and could now produce them, if one waited, in a colourless singsong. Shifting from foot to foot, Cam repeated the words, 'No, they haven't, and I've told Ellen to clear away tea.'

Minta Doyle and Paul Rayley had not come back then. That could only mean, Mrs Ramsay thought, one thing. She must accept him, or she must refuse him. This going off after luncheon for a walk, even though Andrew was with them—what could it mean? except that she had decided, rightly, Mrs Ramsay thought (and she was very, very fond of Minta), to accept that good fellow, who might not be brilliant, but then, thought Mrs Ramsay, realizing that James was tugging at her to make her go on reading aloud the Fisherman and his Wife, she did in her own heart infinitely prefer boobies to clever men who wrote dissertations; Charles Tansley for instance. Anyhow it must have happened, one way or the other, by now.

But she read, 'Next morning the wife awoke first, and it was just daybreak, and from her bed she saw the beautiful country lying before her. Her husband was still stretching himself . . .'

But how could Minta say now that she would not have him? Not if she agreed to spend whole afternoons trapesing about the country alone—for Andrew would be off after his crabs—but possibly Nancy was with them. She tried to recall the sight of them standing at the hall door after lunch. There they stood, looking at the sky, wondering about the weather, and she had said, thinking partly to cover their shyness, partly to encourage them to be off (for her sympathies were with Paul),

'There isn't a cloud anywhere within miles,' at which she could feel little Charles Tansley, who had followed them out, snigger. But she did it on purpose. Whether Nancy was there or not, she could not be certain, looking from one to the other in her mind's eye.

She read on: 'Ah, wife,' said the man, 'why should we be King? I do not want to be King.' 'Well,' said the wife, 'if you won't be King, I will; go to the Flounder, for I will be King.'

'Come in or go out, Cam,' she said, knowing that Cam was attracted only by the word 'Flounder' and that in a moment she would fidget and fight with James as usual. Cam shot off. Mrs Ramsay went on reading, relieved, for she and James shared the same tastes and were comfortable together.

'And when he came to the sea, it was quite dark grey, and the water heaved up from below, and smelt putrid. Then he went and stood by it and said,

"Flounder, flounder, in the sea,
Come, I pray thee, here to me;
For my wife, good Ilsabil,
Wills not as I'd have her will."

"Well, what does she want then?" said the Flounder.' And where were they now? Mrs Ramsay wondered, reading and thinking, quite easily, both at the same time; for the story of the Fisherman and his Wife was like the bass gently accompanying a tune, which now and then ran up unexpectedly into the melody. And when should she be told? If nothing happened, she would have to speak seriously to Minta. For she could not go trapesing about all over the country, even if Nancy were with them (she tried again, unsuccessfully, to visualize their backs going down the path, and to count them). She was responsible to Minta's parents—the Owl and the Poker. Her nicknames for them shot into her mind as she read. The Owl and the Poker—yes, they would be annoyed if they heard—and they were certain to hear—that Minta, staying with the Ramsays, had been seen etcetera, etcetera, etcetera. 'He wore a wig in the House of Commons and she ably assisted him at the head of the stairs,' she repeated, fishing them up out of her mind by a phrase which, coming back from some party, she had made to amuse her husband. Dear, dear, Mrs Ramsay said to herself, how did they produce this incongruous daughter? this tomboy Minta, with a hole in her stocking? How did she exist in that portentous atmosphere where the maid was always removing in a dust-pan the sand that the parrot had scattered, and conversation was almost entirely reduced to the exploits—interesting perhaps, but limited after all—of that bird? Naturally, one had asked her to lunch, tea, dinner, finally to stay with them up at Finlay, which had resulted in some friction with the Owl, her mother, and more calling, and more conversation, and more sand, and really at the end of it, she had told enough lies about parrots to last her a lifetime (so she had said to her husband that night, coming back from the party). However, Minta came ... Yes, she came, Mrs Ramsay thought, suspecting some thorn in the tangle of this thought; and disengaging it found it to be this: a woman had once accused her of 'robbing her of her daughter's affections'; something Mrs Doyle had said made her remember that charge again. Wishing to dominate, wishing to interfere, making people do what she wished—that was the charge against her, and she thought it most unjust. How could she help being 'like that' to look at? No one could accuse her of taking pains to impress. She was often ashamed of her own shabbiness. Nor was she domineering, nor was she tyrannical. It was more true about hospitals and drains and the dairy.

About things like that she did feel passionately, and would, if she had
had the chance, have liked to take people by the scruff of their necks
and make them see. No hospital on the whole island. It was a disgrace.
Milk delivered at your door in London positively brown with dirt. It
should be made illegal. A model dairy and a hospital up here—those
two things she would have liked to do, herself. But how? With all these
children? When they were older, then perhaps she would have time;
when they were all at school.

Oh, but she never wanted James to grow a day older or Cam either.
These two she would have liked to keep for ever just as they were,
demons of wickedness, angels of delight, never to see them grow up into
long-legged monsters. Nothing made up for the loss. When she read just
now to James, 'and there were numbers of soldiers with kettle-drums
and trumpets', and his eyes darkened, she thought, why should they
grow up, and lose all that? He was the most gifted, the most sensitive of
her children. But all, she thought, were full of promise. Prue, a perfect
angel with the others, and sometimes now, at night especially, she took
one's breath away with her beauty. Andrew—even her husband admitted that his gift for mathematics was extraordinary. And Nancy and
Roger, they were both wild creatures now, scampering about over the
country all day long. As for Rose, her mouth was too big, but she had a
wonderful gift with her hands. If they had charades, Rose made the
dresses; made everything; liked best arranging tables, flowers, anything.
She did not like it that Jasper should shoot birds; but it was only a
stage; they all went through stages. Why, she asked, pressing her chin
on James's head, should they grow up so fast? Why should they go to
school? She would have liked always to have had a baby. She was
happiest carrying one in her arms. Then people might say she was
tyrannical, domineering, masterful, if they chose; she did not mind.
And, touching his hair with her lips, she thought, he will never be so
happy again, but stopped herself, remembering how it angered her
husband that she should say that. Still, it was true. They were happier
now than they would ever be again. A tenpenny tea set made Cam
happy for days. She heard them stamping and crowing on the floor
above her head the moment they woke. They came bustling along the
passage. Then the door sprang open and in they came, fresh as roses,
staring, wide awake, as if this coming into the dining-room after
breakfast, which they did every day of their lives was a positive event to
them; and so on, with one thing after another, all day long, until she
went up to say good-night to them, and found them netted in their cots
like birds among cherries and raspberries still making up stories about
some little bit of rubbish—something they had heard, something they
had picked up in the garden. They had all their little treasures . . . And

so she went down and said to her husband, Why must they grow up and lose it all? Never will they be so happy again. And he was angry. Why take such a gloomy view of life? he said. It is not sensible. For it was odd; and she believed it to be true; that with all his gloom and desperation he was happier, more hopeful on the whole, than she was. Less exposed to human worries—perhaps that was it. He had always his work to fall back on. Not that she herself was 'pessimistic', as he accused her of being. Only she thought life—and a little strip of time presented itself to her eyes, her fifty years. There it was before her—life. Life: she thought but she did not finish her thought. She took a look at life, for she had a clear sense of it there, something real, something private, which she shared neither with her children nor with her husband. A sort of transaction went on between them, in which she was on one side, and life was on another, and she was always trying to get the better of it, as it was of her; and sometimes they parleyed (when she sat alone); there were, she remembered, great reconciliation scenes; but for the most part, oddly enough, she must admit that she felt this thing that she called life terrible, hostile, and quick to pounce on you if you gave it a chance. There were the eternal problems: suffering; death; the poor. There was always a woman dying of cancer even here. And yet she had said to all these children, You shall go through with it. To eight people she had said relentlessly that (and the bill for the greenhouse would be fifty pounds). For that reason, knowing what was before them—love and ambition and being wretched alone in dreary places— she had often the feeling, why must they grow up and lose it all? And then she said to herself, brandishing her sword at life, nonsense. They will be perfectly happy. And here she was, she reflected, feeling life rather sinister again, making Minta marry Paul Rayley; because whatever she might feel about her own transaction and she had had experiences which need not happen to everyone (she did not name them to herself); she was driven on, too quickly she knew, almost as if it were an escape for her too, to say that people must marry; people must have children.

Was she wrong in this, she asked herself, reviewing her conduct for the past week or two, and wondering if she had indeed put any pressure upon Minta, who was only twenty-four, to make up her mind. She was uneasy. Had she not laughed about it? Was she not forgetting again how strongly she influenced people? Marriage needed—oh all sorts of qualities (the bill for the greenhouse would be fifty pounds); one—she need not name it—*that* was essential; the thing she had with her husband. Had they that?

'Then he put on his trousers and ran away like a madman,' she read. 'But outside a great storm was raging and blowing so hard that he could scarcely keep his feet; houses and trees toppled over, the mountains trembled, rocks rolled into the sea, the sky was pitch black, and it thundered and lightened, and the sea came in with black waves as high as church towers and mountains, and all with white foam at the top.'

She turned the page; there were only a few lines more, so that she would finish the story, though it was past bedtime. It was getting late. The light in the garden told her that; and the whitening of the flowers and something grey in the leaves conspired together to rouse in her a feeling of anxiety. What it was about she could not think at first. Then she remembered; Paul and Minta and Andrew had not come back. She summoned before her again the little group on the terrace in front of the hall door, standing looking up into the sky. Andrew had his net and basket. That meant he was going to catch crabs and things. That meant he would climb out on to a rock; he would be cut off. Or coming back single file on one of those little paths above the cliff one of them might slip. He would roll and then crash. It was growing quite dark.

But she did not let her voice change in the least as she finished the story, and added, shutting the book, and speaking the last words as if she had made them up herself, looking into James's eyes: 'And there they are living still at this very time.'

'And that's the end,' she said, and she saw in his eyes, as the interest of the story died away in them, something else take its place; something wondering, pale, like the reflection of a light, which at once made him gaze and marvel. Turning, she looked across the bay, and there, sure enough, coming regularly across the waves first two quick strokes and then one long steady stroke, was the light of the Lighthouse. It had been lit.

In a moment he would ask her, 'Are we going to the Lighthouse?' And she would have to say, 'No: not tomorrow; your father says not.' Happily, Mildred came in to fetch them, and the bustle distracted them. But he kept looking back over his shoulder as Mildred carried him out, and she was certain that he was thinking, we are not going to the Lighthouse tomorrow; and she thought, he will remember that all his life.

11

No, she thought, putting together some of the pictures he had cut out— a refrigerator, a mowing-machine, a gentleman in evening dress— children never forget. For this reason, it was so important what one said, and what one did, and it was a relief when they went to bed. For now she need not think about anybody. She could be herself, by herself.

And that was what now she often felt the need of—to think; well not even to think. To be silent; to be alone. All the being and the doing, expansive, glittering, vocal, evaporated; and one shrunk, with a sense of solemnity, to being oneself, a wedge-shaped core of darkness, something invisible to others. Although she continued to knit, and sat upright, it was thus that she felt herself; and this self having shed its attachments was free for the strangest adventures. When life sank down for a moment, the range of experience seemed limitless. And to everybody there was always this sense of unlimited resources, she supposed; one after another, she, Lily, Augustus Carmichael, must feel our apparitions, the things you know us by, are simply childish. Beneath it is all dark, it is all spreading, it is unfathomably deep; but now and again we rise to the surface and that is what you see us by. Her horizon seemed to her limitless. There were all the places she had not seen; the Indian plains; she felt herself pushing aside the thick leather curtain of a church in Rome. This core of darkness could go anywhere, for no one saw it. They could not stop it, she thought, exulting. There was freedom, there was peace, there was, most welcome of all, a summoning together, a resting on a platform of stability. Not as oneself did one find rest ever, in her experience (she accomplished here something dexterous with her needles), but as a wedge of darkness. Losing personality, one lost the fret, the hurry, the stir; and there rose to her lips always some exclamation of triumph over life when things came together in this peace, this rest, this eternity; and pausing there she looked out to meet that stroke of the Lighthouse, the long steady stroke, the last of the three, which was her stroke, for watching them in this mood always at this hour one could not help attaching oneself to one thing especially of the things one saw; and this thing, the long steady stroke, was her stroke. Often she found herself sitting and looking, sitting and looking, with her work in her hands until she became the thing she looked at— that light for example. And it would lift up on it some little phrase or other which had been lying in her mind like that—'Children don't forget, children don't forget'—which she would repeat and begin adding to it, It will end, It will end, she said. It will come, it will come, when suddenly she added, We are in the hands of the Lord.

But instantly she was annoyed with herself for saying that. Who had said it? not she; she had been trapped into saying something she did not mean. She looked up over her knitting and met the third stroke and it seemed to her like her own eyes meeting her own eyes, searching as she alone could search into her mind and her heart, purifying out of existence that lie, any lie. She praised herself in praising the light, without vanity, for she was stern, she was searching, she was beautiful like that light. It was odd, she thought, how if one was alone, one leant to things, inanimate things; trees, streams, flowers; felt they expressed one; felt they became one; felt they knew one, in a sense were one; felt an irrational tenderness thus (she looked at that long steady light) as for oneself. There rose, and she looked and looked with her needles suspended, there curled up off the floor of the mind, rose from the lake of one's being, a mist, a bride to meet her lover.

What brought her to say that: 'We are in the hands of the Lord?' she wondered. The insincerity slipping in among the truths roused her, annoyed her. She returned to her knitting again. How could any Lord have made this world? she asked. With her mind she had always seized the fact that there is no reason, order, justice: but suffering, death, the poor. There was no treachery too base for the world to commit; she knew that. No happiness lasted; she knew that. She knitted with firm composure, slightly pursing her lips and, without being aware of it, so stiffened and composed the lines of her face in a habit of sternness that when her husband passed, though he was chuckling at the thought that Hume, the philosopher, grown enormously fat, had stuck in a bog, he could not help noting, as he passed, the sternness at the heart of her beauty. It saddened him, and her remoteness pained him, and he felt, as he passed, that he could not protect her, and, when he reached the hedge, he was sad. He could do nothing to help her. He must stand by and watch her. Indeed, the infernal truth was, he made things worse for her. He was irritable—he was touchy. He had lost his temper over the Lighthouse. He looked into the hedge, into its intricacy, its darkness.

Always, Mrs Ramsay felt, one helped oneself out of solitude reluctantly by laying hold of some little odd or end, some sound, some sight. She listened, but it was all very still; cricket was over; the children were in their baths; there was only the sound of the sea. She stopped knitting; she held the long reddish-brown stocking dangling in her hands a moment. She saw the light again. With some irony in her interrogation, for when one woke at all, one's relations changed, she looked at the steady light, the pitiless, the remorseless, which was so much her, yet so little her, which had her at its beck and call (she woke in the night and saw it bent across their bed, stroking the floor), but for all that she thought, watching it with fascination, hypnotized, as if it were stroking with its silver fingers some sealed vessel in her brain whose bursting would flood her with delight, she had known happiness, exquisite happiness, intense happiness, and it silvered the rough waves a little more brightly, as daylight faded, and the blue went out of the sea and it rolled in waves of pure lemon which curved and swelled and broke upon the beach and the ecstasy burst in her eyes and waves of pure delight raced over the floor of her mind and she felt, It is enough! It is enough!

He turned and saw her. Ah! She was lovely, lovelier now than ever he thought. But he could not speak to her. He could not interrupt her. He wanted urgently to speak to her now that James was gone and she was alone at last. But he resolved, no; he would not interrupt her. She was aloof from him now in her beauty, in her sadness. He would let her be, and he passed her without a word, though it hurt him that she should look so distant, and he could not reach her, he could do nothing to help her. And again he would have passed her without a word had she not, at that very moment, given him of her own free will what she knew he would never ask, and called to him and taken the green shawl off the picture frame, and gone to him. For he wished, she knew, to protect her.

12

She folded the green shawl about her shoulders. She took his arm. His beauty was so great, she said, beginning to speak of Kennedy the gardener at once; he was so awfully handsome, that she couldn't dismiss him. There was a ladder against the greenhouse, and little lumps of putty stuck about, for they were beginning to mend the greenhouse roof. Yes, but as she strolled along with her husband, she felt that that particular source of worry had been placed. She had it on the tip of her tongue to say, as they strolled, 'It'll cost fifty pounds,' but instead, for her heart failed her about money, she talked about Jasper shooting birds, and he said, at once, soothing her instantly, that it was natural in a boy, and he trusted he would find better ways of amusing himself before long. Her husband was so sensible, so just. And so she said, 'Yes; all children go through stages,' and began considering the dahlias in the big bed, and wondering what about next year's flowers, and had he heard the children's nickname for Charles Tansley, she asked. The atheist, they called him, the little atheist. 'He's not a polished specimen,' said Mr Ramsay. 'Far from it,' said Mrs Ramsay.

She supposed it was all right leaving him to his own devices, Mrs Ramsay said, wondering whether it was any use sending down bulbs; did they plant them? 'Oh, he has his dissertation to write,' said Mr Ramsay. She knew all about *that*, said Mrs Ramsay. He talked of nothing else. It was about the influence of somebody upon something. 'Well, it's all he has to count on,' said Mr Ramsay. 'Pray Heaven he won't fall in love with Prue,' said Mrs Ramsay. He'd disinherit her if she married him, said Mr Ramsay. He did not look at the flowers, which his wife was considering, but at a spot about a foot or so above them. There was no harm in him, he added, and was just about to say that anyhow he was the only young man in England who admired his—— when he choked it back. He would not bother her again about his books.

These flowers seemed creditable, Mr Ramsay said, lowering his gaze and noticing something red, something brown. Yes, but then these she had put in with her own hands, said Mrs Ramsay. The question was, what happened if she sent bulbs down; did Kennedy plant them? It was his incurable laziness; she added, moving on. If she stood over him all day long with a spade in her hand, he did sometimes do a stroke of work. So they strolled along, towards the red-hot pokers. 'You're teaching your daughters to exaggerate,' said Mr Ramsay, reproving her. Her Aunt Camilla was far worse than she was, Mrs Ramsay remarked. 'Nobody ever held up your Aunt Camilla as a model of virtue that I'm aware of,' said Mr Ramsay. 'She was the most beautiful woman I ever saw,' said Mrs Ramsay. 'Somebody else was that,' said Mr Ramsay. Prue was going to be far more beautiful than she was, said Mrs Ramsay. He saw no trace of it, said Mr Ramsay. 'Well, then, look tonight,' said Mrs Ramsay. They paused. He wished Andrew could be induced to work harder. He would lose every chance of a scholarship if he didn't. 'Oh scholarships!' she said. Mr Ramsay thought her foolish for saying that, about a serious thing, like a scholarship. He should be very proud of Andrew if he got a scholarship, he said. She would be just as proud of him if he didn't, she answered. They disagreed always about this, but it did not matter. She liked him to believe in scholarships, and he liked her to be proud of Andrew whatever he did. Suddenly she remembered those little paths on the edge of the cliffs.

Wasn't it late? she asked. They hadn't come home yet. He flicked his watch carelessly open. But it was only just past seven. He held his watch open for a moment, deciding that he would tell her what he had felt on the terrace. To begin with, it was not reasonable to be so nervous. Andrew could look after himself. Then, he wanted to tell her that when he was walking on the terrace just now—here he became uncomfortable, as if he were breaking into that solitude, that aloofness, that remoteness of hers . . . But she pressed him. What had he wanted to tell her, she asked, thinking it was about going to the Lighthouse; and that he was sorry he had said 'Damn you'. But no. He did not like to see her look so sad, he said. Only wool-gathering, she protested, flushing a little. They both felt uncomfortable, as if they did not know whether to go on or go back. She had been reading fairy tales to James, she said. No, they could not share that; they could not say that.

They had reached the gap between the two clumps of red-hot pokers, and there was the Lighthouse again, but she would not let herself look at it. Had she known that he was looking at her, she thought, she would not have let herself sit there, thinking. She disliked anything that reminded her that she had been seen sitting thinking. So she looked over her shoulder, at the town. The lights were rippling and running as if they were drops of silver water held firm in a wind. And all the poverty, all the suffering had turned to that, Mrs Ramsay thought. The lights of the town and of the harbour and of the boats seemed like a phantom net floating there to mark something which had sunk. Well, if he could not share her thoughts, Mr Ramsay said to himself, he would be off, then, on his own. He wanted to go on thinking, telling himself the story how Hume was stuck in a bog; he wanted to laugh. But first it was nonsense to be anxious about Andrew. When he was Andrew's age he used to walk about the country all day long, with nothing but a biscuit in his pocket and nobody bothered about him, or thought that he had fallen over a cliff. He said aloud he thought he would be off for a day's walk if the weather held. He had had about enough of Bankes and of Carmichael. He would like a little solitude. Yes, she said. It annoyed him that she did not protest. She knew that he would never do it. He was too old now to walk all day long with a biscuit in his pocket. She worried about the boys, but not about him. Years ago, before he had married, he thought, looking across the bay, as they stood between the clumps of red-hot pokers, he had walked all day. He had made a meal off bread and cheese in a public house. He had worked ten hours at a stretch; an old woman just popped her head in now and again and saw to the fire. That was the country he liked best, over there; those sand-hills dwindling away into darkness. One could walk all day without meeting a soul. There was not a house scarcely, not a single village for miles on end. One could worry things out alone. There were little sandy beaches where no one had been since the beginning of time. The seals sat up and looked at you. It sometimes seemed to him that in a little house out there, alone—he broke off, sighing. He had no right. The father of eight children—he reminded himself. And he would have been a beast and a cur to wish a single thing altered. Andrew would be a better man than he had been. Prue would be a beauty, her mother said. They would stem the flood a bit. That was a good bit of work on the whole—his eight children. They showed he did not damn the poor little universe entirely, for on an evening like this, he thought, looking at the land dwindling away, the little island seemed pathetically small, half swallowed up in the sea.

'Poor little place,' he murmured with a sigh.

She heard him. He said the most melancholy things, but she noticed that directly he had said them he always seemed more cheerful than usual. All this phrase-making was a game, she thought, for if she had said half what he said, she would have blown her brains out by now.

It annoyed her, this phrase-making, and she said to him, in a matter-of-fact way, that it was a perfectly lovely evening. And what was he groaning about, she asked, half laughing, half complaining, for she

guessed what he was thinking—he would have written better books if
he had not married.

He was not complaining, he said. She knew that he did not complain.
She knew that he had nothing whatever to complain of. And he seized
her hand and raised it to his lips and kissed it with an intensity that
brought the tears to her eyes, and quickly he dropped it.

They turned away from the view and began to walk up the path
where the silver-green spear-like plants grew, arm in arm. His arm was
almost like a young man's arm, Mrs Ramsay thought, thin and hard,
and she thought with delight how strong he still was, though he was
over sixty, and how untamed and optimistic, and how strange it was
that being convinced, as he was, of all sorts of horrors, seemed not to
depress him, but to cheer him. Was it not odd, she reflected? Indeed he
seemed to her sometimes made differently from other people, born blind,
deaf, and dumb, to the ordinary things, but to the extraordinary things,
with an eye like an eagle's. His understanding often astonished her. But
did he notice the flowers? No. Did he notice the view? No. Did he even
notice his own daughter's beauty, or whether there was pudding on his
plate or roast beef? He would sit at table with them like a person in a
dream. And his habit of talking aloud, or saying poetry aloud, was
growing on him, she was afraid; for sometimes it was awkward—

Best and brightest, come away!

poor Miss Giddings, when he shouted that at her, almost jumped out of
her skin. But then, Mrs Ramsay, though instantly taking his side against
all the silly Giddingses in the world, then, she thought, intimating by a
little pressure on his arm that he walked up hill too fast for her, and she
must stop for a moment to see whether those were fresh mole-hills on
the bank, then, she thought, stooping down to look, a great mind like
his must be different in every way from ours. All the great men she had
ever known, she thought, deciding that a rabbit must have got in, were
like that, and it was good for young men (though the atmosphere of
lecture-rooms was stuffy and depressing to her beyond endurance
almost) simply to hear him, simply to look at him. But without shooting
rabbits, how was one to keep them down? she wondered. It might be a
rabbit; it might be a mole. Some creature anyhow was ruining her
Evening Primroses. And looking up, she saw above the thin trees the
first pulse of the full-throbbing star, and wanted to make her husband
look at it; for the sight gave her such keen pleasure. But she stopped
herself. He never looked at things. If he did, all he would say would be,
Poor little world, with one of his sighs.

At that moment, he said, 'Very fine,' to please her, and pretended to
admire the flowers. But she knew quite well that he did not admire

them, or even realize that they were there. It was only to please her . . .
Ah, but was that not Lily Briscoe strolling along with William Bankes?
She focused her short-sighted eyes upon the backs of a retreating couple.
Yes, indeed it was. Did that not mean that they would marry? Yes, it
must! What an admirable idea! They must marry!

I 3

He had been to Amsterdam, Mr Bankes was saying as he strolled across
the lawn with Lily Briscoe. He had seen the Rembrandts. He had been
to Madrid. Unfortunately, it was Good Friday and the Prado was shut.
He had been to Rome. Had Miss Briscoe never been to Rome? Oh, she
should—— It would be a wonderful experience for her—the Sistine
Chapel; Michael Angelo; and Padua, with its Giottos. His wife had been
in bad health for many years, so that their sight-seeing had been on a
modest scale.

She had been to Brussels; she had been to Paris, but only for a flying
visit to see an aunt who was ill. She had been to Dresden; there were
masses of pictures she had not seen; however, Lily Briscoe reflected,
perhaps it was better not to see pictures: they only made one hopelessly
discontented with one's own work. Mr Bankes thought one could carry
that point of view too far. We can't all be Titians and we can't all be
Darwins, he said; at the same time he doubted whether you could have
your Darwin and your Titian if it weren't for humble people like
ourselves. Lily would have liked to pay him a compliment; you're not
humble, Mr Bankes, she would have liked to have said. But he did not
want compliments (most men do, she thought), and she was a little
ashamed of her impulse and said nothing while he remarked that
perhaps what he was saying did not apply to pictures. Anyhow, said
Lily, tossing off her little insincerity, she would always go on painting,
because it interested her. Yes, said Mr Bankes, he was sure she would,
and as they reached the end of the lawn he was asking her whether she
had difficulty in finding subjects in London when they turned and saw
the Ramsays. So that is marriage, Lily thought, a man and a woman
looking at a girl throwing a ball. That is what Mrs Ramsay tried to tell
me the other night, she thought. For she was wearing a green shawl,
and they were standing close together watching Prue and Jasper
throwing catches. And suddenly the meaning which, for no reason at
all, as perhaps they are stepping out of the Tube or ringing a doorbell,
descends on people, making them symbolical, making them representative, came upon them, and made them in the dusk standing, looking,
the symbols of marriage, husband and wife. Then, after an instant, the

symbolical outline which transcended the real figures sank down again and they became, as they met them, Mr and Mrs Ramsay watching the children throwing catches. But still for a moment, though Mrs Ramsay greeted them with her usual smile (oh, she's thinking we're going to get married, Lily thought) and said, 'I have triumphed tonight,' meaning that for once Mr Bankes had agreed to dine with them and not run off to his own lodging where his man cooked vegetables properly; still, for one moment, there was a sense of things having been blown apart, of space, of irresponsibility as the ball soared high, and they followed it and lost it and saw the one star and the draped branches. In the failing light they all looked sharp-edged and ethereal and divided by great distances. Then, darting backwards over the vast space (for it seemed as if solidity had vanished altogether), Prue ran full tilt into them and caught the ball brilliantly high up in her left hand, and her mother said, 'Haven't they come back yet?' whereupon the spell was broken. Mr Ramsay felt free now to laugh out loud at Hume, who had stuck in a bog and an old woman rescued him on condition he said the Lord's Prayer, and chuckling to himself he strolled off to his study. Mrs Ramsay, bringing Prue back into the alliance of family life again, from which she had escaped, throwing catches, asked,

'Did Nancy go with them?'

14

(Certainly, Nancy had gone with them, since Minta Doyle had asked it with her dumb look, holding out her hand, as Nancy made off, after lunch, to her attic, to escape the horror of family life. She supposed she must go then. She did not want to go. She did not want to be drawn into it all. For as they walked along the road to the cliff Minta kept on taking her hand. Then she would let it go. Then she would take it again. What was it she wanted? Nancy asked herself. There was something, of course, that people wanted; for when Minta took her hand and held it, Nancy, reluctantly, saw the whole world spread out beneath her, as if it were Constantinople seen through a mist, and then, however heavy-eyed one might be, one must needs ask, 'Is that Santa Sofia?' 'Is that the Golden Horn?' So Nancy asked, when Minta took her hand, 'What is it that she wants? Is it that?' And what was that? Here and there emerged from the mist (as Nancy looked down upon life spread beneath her) a pinnacle, a dome; prominent things, without names. But when Minta dropped her hand, as she did when they ran down the hillside, all that, the dome, the pinnacle, whatever it was that had protruded through the mist, sank down into it and disappeared.

Minta, Andrew observed, was rather a good walker. She wore more sensible clothes than most women. She wore very short skirts and black knickerbockers. She would jump straight into a stream and flounder across. He liked her rashness, but he saw that it would not do—she would kill herself in some idiotic way one of these days. She seemed to be afraid of nothing—except bulls. At the mere sight of a bull in a field she would throw up her arms and fly screaming, which was the very thing to enrage a bull of course. But she did not mind owning up to it in the least; one must admit that. She knew she was an awful coward about bulls, she said. She thought she must have been tossed in her perambulator when she was a baby. She didn't seem to mind what she said or did. Suddenly now she pitched down on the edge of the cliff and began to sing some song about

Damn your eyes, damn your eyes.

They all had to join in and sing the chorus, and shout out together:

Damn your eyes, damn your eyes,

but it would be fatal to let the tide come in and cover up all the good hunting-grounds before they got on to the beach.

'Fatal,' Paul agreed, springing up, and as they went slithering down, he kept quoting the guide-book about 'these islands being justly celebrated for their park-like prospects and the extent and variety of their marine curiosities'. But it would not do altogether, this shouting and damning your eyes, Andrew felt, picking his way down the cliff, this clapping him on the back, and calling him 'old fellow' and all that; it would not altogether do. It was the worst of taking women on walks. Once on the beach they separated, he going out on to the Pope's Nose, taking his shoes off, and rolling his socks in them and letting that couple look after themselves; Nancy waded out to her own rocks and searched her own pools and let that couple look after themselves. She crouched low down and touched the smooth rubber-like sea anemones, who were stuck like lumps of jelly to the side of the rock. Brooding, she changed the pool into the sea, and made the minnows into sharks and whales, and cast vast clouds over this tiny world by holding her hand against the sun, and so brought darkness and desolation, like God himself, to millions of ignorant and innocent creatures, and then took her hand away suddenly and let the sun stream down. Out on the pale criss-crossed sand, high-stepping, fringed, gauntletted, stalked some fantastic leviathan (she was still enlarging the pool), and slipped into the vast fissures of the mountainside. And then, letting her eyes slide imperceptibly above the pool and rest on that wavering line of sea and sky, on the tree trunks which the smoke of steamers made waver upon the horizon, she became with all that power sweeping savagely in and inevitably withdrawing, hypnotized, and the two senses of that vastness and this tininess (the pool had diminished again) flowering within it made her feel that she was bound hand and foot and unable to move by the intensity of feelings which reduced her own body, her own life, and the lives of all the people in the world, for ever, to nothingness. So listening to the waves, crouched over the pool, she brooded.

And Andrew shouted that the sea was coming in, so she leapt splashing through the shallow waves on to the shore and ran up the beach and was carried by her own impetuosity and her desire for rapid movement right behind a rock and there oh heavens! in each other's arms were Paul and Minta! kissing probably. She was outraged, indignant. She and Andrew put on their shoes and stockings in dead silence without saying a thing about it. Indeed they were rather sharp with each other. She might have called him when she saw the crayfish or whatever it was, Andrew grumbled. However, they both felt, it's not our fault. They had not wanted this horrid nuisance to happen. All the same it irritated Andrew that Nancy should be a woman, and Nancy that Andrew should be a man and they tied their shoes very neatly and drew the bows rather tight.

It was not until they had climbed right up on to the top of the cliff again that Minta cried out that she had lost her grandmother's brooch—her grandmother's brooch, the sole ornament she possessed—a weeping willow, it was (they must remember it) set in pearls. They must have seen it, she said, with the tears running down her cheeks, the brooch which her grandmother had fastened her cap with till the last day of her life. Now she had lost it. She would rather have lost anything than that! She would go back and look for it. They all went back. They poked and peered and looked. They kept their heads very low, and said things shortly and gruffly. Paul Rayley searched like a madman all about the rock where they had been sitting. All this pother about a brooch really didn't do at all, Andrew thought, as Paul told him to make a 'thorough search between this point and that'. The tide was coming in fast. The sea would cover the place where they had sat in a minute. There was not a ghost of a chance of their finding it now. 'We shall be cut off!' Minta shrieked, suddenly terrified. As if there were any danger of that! It was the same as the bulls all over again—she had no control over her emotions, Andrew thought. Women hadn't. The wretched Paul had to pacify her. The men (Andrew and Paul at once became manly, and different from usual) took counsel briefly and decided that they would plant Rayley's stick where they had sat and come back at low tide again. There was nothing more that could be done now. If the brooch was there, it would still be there in the morning, they assured her, but Minta still sobbed, all the way up to the top of the cliff. It was her grandmother's brooch; she would rather have lost anything but that, and yet Nancy felt, though it might be true that she minded losing her brooch, she wasn't crying only for that. She was crying for something else. We might all sit down and cry, she felt. But she did not know what for.

They drew ahead together, Paul and Minta, and he comforted her, and said how famous he was for finding things. Once when he was a little boy he had found a gold watch. He would get up at daybreak and he was positive he would find it. It seemed to him that it would be almost dark, and he would be alone on the beach, and somehow it would be rather dangerous. He began telling her, however, that he would certainly find it, and she said that she would not hear of his getting up at dawn: it was lost: she knew that: she had had a presentiment when she put it on that afternoon. And secretly he resolved that he would not tell her, but he would slip out of the house at dawn when they were all asleep and if he could not find it he would go to Edinburgh and buy her another, just like it but more beautiful. He would prove what he could do. And as they came out on the hill and saw the lights of the town beneath them, the lights coming out suddenly one by one seemed like things that were going to happen to him—his marriage, his children, his house; and again he thought, as they came out on to the high road, which was shaded with high bushes, how they would retreat into solitude together, and walk on and on, he always leading her, and she pressing close to his side (as she did now). As they turned by the crossroads he thought what an appalling experience he had been through, and he must tell someone—Mrs Ramsay of course, for it took his breath away to think what he had been and done. It had been far and away the worst moment of his life when he asked Minta to marry him. He would go straight to Mrs Ramsay, because he felt somehow that she was the person who had made him do it. She had made him think he could do anything. Nobody else took him seriously. But she made him believe that he could do whatever he wanted. He had felt her eyes on him all day today, following him about (though she never said a word) as if she were saying, 'Yes, you can do it. I believe in you. I expect it of you.' She had made him feel all that, and directly they got back (he looked for the lights of the house above the bay) he would go to her and say, 'I've done it, Mrs Ramsay; thanks to you.' And so turning into the lane that led to the house he could see lights moving about in the upper windows. They must be awfully late then. People were getting ready for dinner. The house was all lit up, and the lights after the darkness made his eyes feel full, and he said to himself, childishly, as he walked up the drive, Lights, lights, lights, and repeated in a dazed way, Lights, lights, lights, as they came into the house, staring about him with his face quite stiff. But, good heavens, he said to himself, putting his hand to his tie, I must not make a fool of myself.)

15

'Yes,' said Prue, in her considering way, answering her mother's question, 'I think Nancy did go with them.'

16

Well then, Nancy had gone with them, Mrs Ramsay supposed, wondering, as she put down a brush, took up a comb, and said 'Come in' to a tap at the door (Jasper and Rose came in), whether the fact that Nancy was with them made it less likely or more likely that anything would happen; it made it less likely, somehow, Mrs Ramsay felt, very irrationally, except that after all holocaust on such a scale was not probable. They could not all be drowned. And again she felt alone in the presence of her old antagonist, life.

Jasper and Rose said that Mildred wanted to know whether she should wait dinner.

'Not for the Queen of England,' said Mrs Ramsay emphatically.

'Not for the Empress of Mexico,' she added, laughing at Jasper; for he shared his mother's vice: he, too, exaggerated.

And if Rose liked, she said, while Jasper took the message, she might choose which jewels she was to wear. When there are fifteen people sitting down to dinner, one cannot keep things waiting for ever. She was now beginning to feel annoyed with them for being so late; it was inconsiderate of them, and it annoyed her on top of her anxiety about them, that they should choose this very night to be out late, when, in fact, she wished the dinner to be particularly nice, since William Bankes had at last consented to dine with them; and they were having Mildred's masterpiece—Bœuf en Daube. Everything depended upon things being served up the precise moment they were ready. The beef, the bayleaf, and the wine—all must be done to a turn. To keep it waiting was out of the question. Yet of course tonight, of all nights, out they went, and they came in late, and things had to be sent out, things had to be kept hot; the Bœuf en Daube would be entirely spoilt.

Jasper offered her an opal necklace; Rose a gold necklace. Which looked best against her black dress? Which did indeed? said Mrs Ramsay absent-mindedly, looking at her neck and shoulders (but avoiding her face), in the glass. And then, while the children rummaged among her things, she looked out of the window at a sight which always amused her—the rooks trying to decide which tree to settle on. Every time, they seemed to change their minds and rose up into the air again, because, she thought, the old rook, the father rook, old Joseph was her name for him, was a bird of a very trying and difficult disposition. He was a disreputable old bird, with half his wing feathers missing. He was like some seedy old gentleman in a top hat she had seen playing the horn in front of a public house.

'Look!' she said, laughing. They were actually fighting. Joseph and Mary were fighting. Anyhow they all went up again, and the air was shoved aside by their black wings and cut into exquisite scimitar shapes. The movement of the wings beating out, out, out—she could never describe it accurately enough to please herself—was one of the loveliest of all to her. Look at that, she said to Rose, hoping that Rose would see it more clearly than she could. For one's children so often gave one's own perceptions a little thrust forwards.

But which was it to be? They had all the trays of her jewel-case open. The gold necklace, which was Italian, or the opal necklace, which Uncle James had brought her from India; or should she wear her amethysts?

'Choose, dearests, choose,' she said, hoping that they would make haste.

But she let them take their time to choose: she let Rose, particularly, take up this and then that, and hold her jewels against the black dress, for this little ceremony of choosing jewels, which was gone through every night, was what Rose liked best, she knew. She had some hidden reason of her own for attaching great importance to this choosing what her mother was to wear. What was the reason, Mrs Ramsay wondered, standing still to let her clasp the necklace she had chosen, divining, through her own past, some deep, some buried, some quite speechless feeling that one had for one's mother at Rose's age. Like all feelings felt for oneself, Mrs Ramsay thought, it made one sad. It was so inadequate, what one could give in return; and what Rose felt was quite out of proportion to anything she actually was. And Rose would grow up; and Rose would suffer, she supposed, with these deep feelings, and she said she was ready now, and they would go down, and Jasper, because he was the gentleman, should give her his arm, and Rose, as she was the lady, should carry her handkerchief (she gave her the handkerchief), and what else? oh, yes, it might be cold: a shawl. Choose me a shawl, she said, for that would please Rose, who was bound to suffer so. 'There,' she said, stopping by the window on the landing, 'there they are again.' Joseph had settled on another tree-top. 'Don't you think they mind', she said to Jasper, 'having their wings broken?' Why did he want to shoot poor old Joseph and Mary? He shuffled a little on the stairs, and felt rebuked, but not seriously, for she did not understand the fun of shooting birds; that they did not feel; and being his mother she lived away in another division of the world, but he rather liked her stories about Mary and Joseph. She made him laugh. But how did she know that those were Mary and Joseph? Did she think the same birds came to the same trees every night? he asked. But here, suddenly, like all grown-up people, she ceased to pay him the least attention. She was listening to a clatter in the hall.

'They've come back!' she exclaimed, and at once she felt much more annoyed with them than relieved. Then she wondered, had it happened? She would go down and they would tell her—but no. They could not tell her anything, with all these people about. So she must go down and begin dinner and wait. And, like some queen who, finding her people gathered in the hall, looks down upon them, and descends among them, and acknowledges their tributes silently, and accepts their devotion and their prostration before her (Paul did not move a muscle but looked straight before him as she passed), she went down, and crossed the hall and bowed her head very slightly, as if she accepted what they could not say: their tribute to her beauty.

But she stopped. There was a smell of burning. Could they have let the Bœuf en Daube overboil, she wondered? pray heaven not! when the great clangour of the gong announced solemnly, authoritatively, that all those scattered about, in attics, in bedrooms, on little perches of their own, reading, writing, putting the last smooth to their hair, or fastening dresses, must leave all that, and the little odds and ends on their washing-tables and dressing-tables, and the novels on the bed-tables, and the diaries which were so private, and assemble in the dining-room for dinner.

17

But what have I done with my life? thought Mrs Ramsay, taking her place at the head of the table, and looking at all the plates making white circles on it. 'William, sit by me,' she said. 'Lily,' she said, wearily, 'over there.' They had that—Paul Rayley and Minta Doyle—she, only this—an infinitely long table and plates and knives. At the far end, was her husband, sitting down, all in a heap, frowning. What at? She did not know. She did not mind. She could not understand how she had ever felt any emotion or any affection for him. She had a sense of being past everything, through everything, out of everything, as she helped the soup, as if there was an eddy—there—and one could be in it, or one could be out of it, and she was out of it. It's all come to an end, she thought, while they came in one after another, Charles Tansley—'Sit there, please,' she said—Augustus Carmichael—and sat down. And meanwhile she waited, passively, for someone to answer her, for something to happen. But this is not a thing, she thought, ladling out soup, that one says.

Raising her eyebrows at the discrepancy—that was what she was thinking, this was what she was doing—ladling out soup—she felt, more and more strongly, outside that eddy; or as if a shade had fallen, and, robbed of colour, she saw things truly. The room (she looked round it) was very shabby. There was no beauty anywhere. She forbore to look at Mr Tansley. Nothing seemed to have merged. They all sat separate. And the whole of the effort of merging and flowing and creating rested on her. Again she felt, as a fact without hostility, the sterility of men, for if she did not do it nobody would do it, and so, giving herself the little shake that one gives a watch that has stopped, the old familiar pulse began beating, as the watch begins ticking—one, two, three, one, two, three. And so on and so on, she repeated, listening to it, sheltering and fostering the still feeble pulse as one might guard a weak flame with a newspaper. And so then, she concluded, addressing herself by bending silently in his direction to William Bankes—poor man! who had no wife and no children, and dined alone in lodgings except for tonight; and in pity for him, life being now strong enough to bear her on again, she began all this business, as a sailor not without weariness sees the wind fill his sail and yet hardly wants to be off again and thinks how, had the ship sunk, he would have whirled round and round and found rest on the floor of the sea.

'Did you find your letters? I told them to put them in the hall for you,' she said to William Bankes.

Lily Briscoe watched her drifting into that strange no-man's land where to follow people is impossible and yet their going inflicts such a chill on those who watch them that they always try at least to follow them with their eyes as one follows a fading ship until the sails have sunk beneath the horizon.

How old she looks, how worn she looks, Lily thought, and how remote. Then when she turned to William Bankes, smiling, it was as if the ship had turned and the sun had struck its sails again, and Lily thought with some amusement because she was relieved, Why does she pity him? For that was the impression she gave, when she told him that his letters were in the hall. Poor William Bankes, she seemed to be saying, as if her own weariness had been partly pitying people, and the life in her, her resolve to live again, had been stirred by pity. And it was not true, Lily thought; it was one of those misjudgements of hers that seemed to be instinctive and to arise from some need of her own rather than of other people's. He is not in the least pitiable. He has his work, Lily said to herself. She remembered, all of a sudden as if she had found a treasure, that she too had her work. In a flash she saw her picture, and thought, Yes, I shall put the tree further in the middle; then I shall avoid that awkward space. That's what I shall do. That's what has been puzzling me. She took up the salt cellar and put it down again on a flower in the pattern in the table-cloth, so as to remind herself to move the tree.

'It's odd that one scarcely gets anything worth having by post, yet one always wants one's letters,' said Mr Bankes.

What damned rot they talk, thought Charles Tansley, laying down his spoon precisely in the middle of his plate, which he had swept clean, as if, Lily thought (he sat opposite to her with his back to the window precisely in the middle of view), he were determined to make sure of his meals. Everything about him had that meagre fixity, that bare unloveliness. But nevertheless, the fact remained, it was almost impossible to dislike anyone if one looked at them. She liked his eyes; they were blue, deep set, frightening.

'Do you write many letters, Mr Tansley?' asked Mrs Ramsay, pitying him too, Lily supposed; for that was true of Mrs Ramsay—she pitied men always as if they lacked—something—women never, as if they had something. He wrote to his mother; otherwise he did not suppose he wrote one letter a month, said Mr Tansley, shortly.

For he was not going to talk the sort of rot these people wanted him to talk. He was not going to be condescended to by these silly women. He had been reading in his room, and now he came down and it all seemed to him silly, superficial, flimsy. Why did they dress? He had come down in his ordinary clothes. He had not got any dress clothes. 'One never gets anything worth having by post'—that was the sort of thing they were always saying. They made men say that sort of thing. Yes, it was pretty well true, he thought. They never got anything worth having from one year's end to another. They did nothing but talk, talk, talk, eat, eat, eat. It was the women's fault. Women made civilization impossible with all their 'charm', all their silliness.

'No going to the Lighthouse tomorrow, Mrs Ramsay,' he said asserting himself. He liked her; he admired her; he still thought of the man in the drain-pipe looking up at her; but he felt it necessary to assert himself.

He was really, Lily Briscoe thought, in spite of his eyes, but then look at his nose, look at his hands, the most uncharming human being she had ever met. Then why did she mind what he said? Women can't write, women can't paint—what did that matter coming from him, since clearly it was not true to him but for some reason helpful to him, and that was why he said it? Why did her whole being bow, like corn under a wind, and erect itself again from this abasement only with a great and rather painful effort? She must make it once more. There's the sprig on the table-cloth; there's my painting; I must move the tree to the middle; that matters—nothing else. Could she not hold fast to that, she asked herself, and not lose her temper, and not argue; and if she wanted a little revenge take it by laughing at him?

'Oh, Mr Tansley,' she said, 'do take me to the Lighthouse with you. I should so love it.'

She was telling lies he could see. She was saying what she did not mean to annoy him, for some reason. She was laughing at him. He was in his old flannel trousers. He had no others. He felt very rough and isolated and lonely. He knew that she was trying to tease him for some reason; she didn't want to go to the Lighthouse with him; she despised him: so did Prue Ramsay; so did they all. But he was not going to be made a fool of by women, so he turned deliberately in his chair and looked out of the window and said, all in a jerk, very rudely, it would be too rough for her tomorrow. She would be sick.

It annoyed him that she should have made him speak like that, with Mrs Ramsay listening. If only he could be alone in his room working, he thought, among his books. That was where he felt at his ease. And he had never run a penny into debt; he had never cost his father a penny since he was fifteen; he had helped them at home out of his savings; he was educating his sister. Still, he wished he had known how to answer Miss Briscoe properly; he wished it had not come out all in a jerk like that. 'You'd be sick.' He wished he could think of something to say to Mrs Ramsay, something which would show her that he was not just a dry prig. That was what they all thought him. He turned to her. But Mrs Ramsay was talking about people he had never heard of to William Bankes.

'Yes, take it away,' she said briefly, interrupting what she was saying to Mr Bankes to speak to the maid. 'It must have been fifteen—no, twenty years ago—that I last saw her,' she was saying, turning back to him again as if she could not lose a moment of their talk, for she was absorbed by what they were saying. So he had actually heard from her this evening! And was Carrie still living at Marlow, and was everything still the same? Oh she could remember it as if it were yesterday—going on the river, feeling very cold. But if the Mannings made a plan they stuck to it. Never should she forget Herbert killing a wasp with a teaspoon on the bank! And it was still going on, Mrs Ramsay mused, gliding like a ghost among the chairs and tables of that drawing-room on the banks of the Thames where she had been so very, very cold twenty years ago; but now she went among them like a ghost; and it fascinated her, as if, while she had changed, that particular day, now become very still and beautiful, had remained there, all these years. Had Carrie written to him herself? she asked.

'Yes. She says they're building a new billiard room,' he said. No! No! That was out of the question! Building a billiard room! It seemed to her impossible.

Mr Bankes could not see that there was anything very odd about it. They were very well off now. Should he give her love to Carrie?

'Oh,' said Mrs Ramsay with a little start, 'No,' she added, reflecting that she did not know this Carrie who built a new billiard room. But how strange, she repeated, to Mr Bankes's amusement, that they should be going on there still. For it was extraordinary to think that they had been capable of going on living all these years when she had not thought of them more than once all that time. How eventful her own life had been, during those same years. Yet perhaps Carrie Manning had not thought about her either. The thought was strange and distasteful.

'People soon drift apart,' said Mr Bankes, feeling, however, some satisfaction when he thought that after all he knew both the Mannings and the Ramsays. He had not drifted apart, he thought, laying down his spoon and wiping his clean shaven lips punctiliously. But perhaps he was rather unusual, he thought, in this; he never let himself get into a groove. He had friends in all circles . . . Mrs Ramsay had to break off here to tell the maid something about keeping food hot. That was why he preferred dining alone. All these interruptions annoyed him. Well, thought William Bankes, preserving a demeanour of exquisite courtesy and merely spreading the fingers of his left hand on the table-cloth as a mechanic examines a tool beautifully polished and ready for use in an interval of leisure, such are the sacrifices one's friends ask of one. It would have hurt her if he had refused to come. But it was not worth it for him. Looking at his hand he thought that if he had been alone dinner would have been almost over now; he would have been free to work. Yes, he thought, it is a terrible waste of time. The children were dropping in still. 'I wish one of you would run up to Roger's room,' Mrs Ramsay was saying. How trifling it all is, how boring it all is, he thought, compared with the other thing—work. Here he sat drumming his fingers on the table-cloth when he might have been—he took a flashing bird's-eye view of his work. What a waste of time it all was to be sure! Yet, he thought, she is one of my oldest friends. I am by way of being devoted to her. Yet now, at this moment her presence meant absolutely nothing to him: her beauty meant nothing to him; her sitting with her little boy at the window—nothing, nothing. He wished only to be alone and to take up that book. He felt uncomfortable; he felt treacherous, that he could sit by her side and feel nothing for her. The truth was that he did not enjoy family life. It was in this sort of state that one asked oneself, What does one live for? Why, one asked oneself, does one take all these pains for the human race to go on? Is it so very desirable? Are we attractive as a species? Not so very, he thought, looking at those rather untidy boys. His favourite, Cam, was in bed, he supposed. Foolish questions, vain questions, questions one never asked if one was occupied. Is human life this? Is human life that? One never had time to think about it. But here he was asking himself that sort of question, because Mrs Ramsay was giving orders to servants, and also because it had struck him, thinking how surprised Mrs Ramsay was that Carrie Manning should still exist, that friendships, even the best of them, are frail things. One drifts apart. He reproached himself again. He was sitting beside Mrs Ramsay and he had nothing in the world to say to her.

'I'm so sorry,' said Mrs Ramsay, turning to him at last. He felt rigid and barren, like a pair of boots that has been soaked and gone dry so that you can hardly force your feet into them. Yet he must force his feet into them. He must make himself talk. Unless he were very careful, she would find out this treachery of his; that he did not care a straw for her, and that would not be at all pleasant, he thought. So he bent his head courteously in her direction.

'How you must detest dining in this bear garden,' she said, making use, as she did when she was distracted, of her social manner. So, when there is a strife of tongues at some meeting, the chairman, to obtain unity, suggests that every one shall speak in French. Perhaps it is bad French; French may not contain the words that express the speaker's thoughts; nevertheless speaking French imposes some order, some uniformity. Replying to her in the same language, Mr Bankes said, 'No, not at all,' and Mr Tansley, who had no knowledge of this language, even spoken thus in words of one syllable, at once suspected its insincerity. They did talk nonsense, he thought, the Ramsays; and he pounced on this fresh instance with joy, making a note which, one of these days, he would read aloud, to one or two friends. There, in a society where one could say what one liked he would sarcastically describe 'staying with the Ramsays' and what nonsense they talked. It was worth while doing it once, he would say; but not again. The women bored one so, he would say. Of course Ramsay had dished himself by marrying a beautiful woman and having eight children. It would shape itself something like that, but now, at this moment, sitting stuck there with an empty seat beside him nothing had shaped itself at all. It was all in scraps and fragments. He felt extremely, even physically, uncomfortable. He wanted somebody to give him a chance of asserting himself.

He wanted it so urgently that he fidgeted in his chair, looked at this person, then at that person, tried to break into their talk, opened his mouth and shut it again. They were talking about the fishing industry. Why did no one ask him his opinion? What did they know about the fishing industry?

Lily Briscoe knew all that. Sitting opposite him could she not see, as in an X-ray photograph, the ribs and thigh bones of the young man's desire to impress himself lying dark in the mist of his flesh—that thin mist which convention had laid over his burning desire to break into the conversation? But, she thought, screwing up her Chinese eyes, and remembering how he sneered at women, 'can't paint, can't write', why should I help him to relieve himself?

There is a code of behaviour she knew, whose seventh article (it may be) says that on occasions of this sort it behoves the woman, whatever her own occupation may be, to go to the help of the young man opposite so that he may expose and relieve the thigh bones, the ribs, of his vanity, of his urgent desire to assert himself; as indeed it is their duty, she reflected, in her old maidenly fairness, to help us, suppose the Tube were to burst into flames. Then, she thought, I should certainly expect Mr Tansley to get me out. But how would it be, she thought, if neither of us did either of these things? So she sat there smiling.

'You're not planning to go to the Lighthouse, are you, Lily?' said Mrs Ramsay. 'Remember poor Mr Langley; he had been round the world dozens of times, but he told me he never suffered as he did when my husband took him there. Are you a good sailor, Mr Tansley?' she asked.

Mr Tansley raised a hammer: swung it high in air; but realizing, as it descended, that he could not smite that butterfly with such an instrument as this, said only that he had never been sick in his life. But in that one sentence lay compact, like gunpowder, that his grandfather was a fisherman; his father a chemist; that he had worked his way up entirely himself; that he was proud of it; that he was Charles Tansley—a fact that nobody there seemed to realize; but one of these days every single person would know it. He scowled ahead of him. He could almost pity these mild cultivated people, who would be blown sky high, like bales of wool and barrels of apples, one of these days by the gunpowder that was in him.

'Will you take me, Mr Tansley?' said Lily, quickly, kindly, for, of course, if Mrs Ramsay said to her, as in effect she did, 'I am drowning, my dear, in seas of fire. Unless you apply some balm to the anguish of this hour and say something nice to that young man there, life will run upon the rocks—indeed I hear the grating and the growling at this minute. My nerves are taut as fiddle strings. Another touch and they will snap'—when Mrs Ramsay said all this, as the glance in her eyes said it, of course for the hundred and fiftieth time Lily Briscoe had to renounce the experiment—what happens if one is not nice to that young man there—and be nice.

Judging the turn in her mood correctly—that she was friendly to him now—he was relieved of his egotism, and told her how he had been thrown out of a boat when he was a baby; how his father used to fish him out with a boat-hook; that was how he had learnt to swim. One of his uncles kept the light on some rock or other off the Scottish coast, he said. He had been there with him in a storm. This was said loudly in a pause. They had to listen to him when he said that he had been with his uncle in a lighthouse in a storm. Ah, thought Lily Briscoe, as the conversation took this auspicious turn, and she felt Mrs Ramsay's gratitude (for Mrs Ramsay was free now to talk for a moment herself), ah, she thought, but what haven't I paid to get it for you? She had not been sincere.

She had done the usual trick—been nice. She would never know him. He would never know her. Human relations were all like that, she thought, and the worst (if it had not been for Mr Bankes) were between men and women. Inevitably these were extremely insincere. Then her eye caught the salt cellar, which she had placed there to remind her, and she remembered that next morning she would move the tree further towards the middle, and her spirits rose so high at the thought of painting tomorrow that she laughed out loud at what Mr Tansley was saying. Let him talk all night if he liked it.

'But how long do they leave men on a Lighthouse?' she asked. He told her. He was amazingly well informed. And as he was grateful, and as he liked her, and as he was beginning to enjoy himself, so now, Mrs Ramsay thought, she could return to that dream land, that unreal but fascinating place, the Mannings' drawing-room at Marlow twenty years ago; where one moved about without haste or anxiety, for there was no future to worry about. She knew what had happened to them, what to her. It was like reading a good book again, for she knew the end of that story, since it had happened twenty years ago, and life, which shot down even from this dining-room table in cascades, heaven knows where, was sealed up there, and lay, like a lake, placidly between its banks. He said they had built a billiard room—was it possible? Would William go on talking about the Mannings? She wanted him to. But no—for some reason he was no longer in the mood. She tried. He did not respond. She could not force him. She was disappointed.

'The children are disgraceful,' she said, sighing. He said something about punctuality being one of the minor virtues which we do not acquire until later in life.

'If at all,' said Mrs Ramsay merely to fill up space, thinking what an old maid William was becoming. Conscious of his treachery, conscious of her wish to talk about something more intimate, yet out of mood for it at present, he felt come over him the disagreeableness of life, sitting there, waiting. Perhaps the others were saying something interesting? What were they saying?

That the fishing season was bad; that the men were emigrating. They were talking about wages and unemployment. The young man was abusing the government. William Bankes, thinking what a relief it was to catch on to something of this sort when private life was disagreeable, heard him say something about 'one of the most scandalous acts of the present government'. Lily was listening; Mrs Ramsay was listening; they were all listening. But already bored, Lily felt that something was lacking; Mr Bankes felt that something was lacking. Pulling her shawl round her, Mrs Ramsay felt that something was lacking. All of them bending themselves to listen thought, 'Pray heaven that the inside of my mind may not be exposed,' for each thought, 'The others are feeling this. They are outraged and indignant with the government about the fishermen. Whereas, I feel nothing at all.' But perhaps, thought Mr Bankes, as he looked at Mr Tansley, here is the man. One was always waiting for the man. There was always a chance. At any moment the leader might arise; the man of genius, in politics as in anything else. Probably he will be extremely disagreeable to us old fogies, thought Mr Bankes, doing his best to make allowances, for he knew by some curious physical sensation, as of nerves erect in his spine, that he was jealous, for himself partly, partly more probably for his work, for his point of view, for his science; and therefore he was not entirely open-minded or altogether fair, for Mr Tansley seemed to be saying, You have wasted your lives. You are all of you wrong. Poor old fogies, you're hopelessly behind the times. He seemed to be rather cocksure, this young man; and his manners were bad. But Mr Bankes bade himself observe, he had courage; he had ability; he was extremely well up in the facts. Probably, Mr Bankes thought, as Tansley abused the government, there is a good deal in what he says.

'Tell me now . . .' he said. So they argued about politics, and Lily looked at the leaf on the table-cloth; and Mrs Ramsay, leaving the argument entirely in the hands of the two men, wondered why she was so bored by this talk, and wished, looking at her husband at the other end of the table, that he would say something. One word, she said to herself. For if he said a thing, it would make all the difference. He went to the heart of things. He cared about fishermen and their wages. He could not sleep for thinking of them. It was altogether different when he spoke; one did not feel then, pray heaven you don't see how little I care, because one did care. Then, realizing that it was because she admired him so much that she was waiting for him to speak, she felt as if somebody had been praising her husband to her and their marriage, and she glowed all over without realizing that it was she herself who had praised him. She looked at him thinking to find this shown in his face; he would be looking magnificent . . . But not in the least! He was screwing his face up, he was scowling and frowning, and flushing with anger. What on earth was it about? she wondered. What could be the matter? Only that poor old Augustus had asked for another plate of soup—that was all. It was unthinkable, it was detestable (so he signalled to her across the table) that Augustus should be beginning his soup over again. He loathed people eating when he had finished. She saw his anger fly like a pack of hounds into his eyes, his brow, and she knew that in a moment something violent would explode, and then—but thank goodness! she saw him clutch himself and clap a brake on the wheel, and the whole of his body seemed to emit sparks but not words. He sat there scowling. He had said nothing, he would have her observe. Let her give him the credit for that! But why after all should poor Augustus not ask for another plate of soup? He had merely touched Ellen's arm and said:

'Ellen, please, another plate of soup,' and then Mr Ramsay scowled like that.

And why not? Mrs Ramsay demanded. Surely they could let Augustus have his soup if he wanted it. He hated people wallowing in food, Mr Ramsay frowned at her. He hated everything dragging on for hours like this. But he had controlled himself, Mr Ramsay would have her observe, disgusting though the sight was. But why show it so plainly, Mrs Ramsay demanded (they looked at each other down the long table sending these questions and answers across, each knowing exactly what the other felt). Everybody could see, Mrs Ramsay thought. There was Rose gazing at her father, there was Roger gazing at his father; both would be off in spasms of laughter in another second, she knew, and so she said promptly (indeed it was time):

'Light the candles,' and they jumped up instantly and went and fumbled at the sideboard.

Why could he never conceal his feelings? Mrs Ramsay wondered, and she wondered if Augustus Carmichael had noticed. Perhaps he had; perhaps he had not. She could not help respecting the composure with which he sat there, drinking his soup. If he wanted soup, he asked for soup. Whether people laughed at him or were angry with him he was the same. He did not like her, she knew that; but partly for that very reason she respected him, and looking at him, drinking soup, very large and calm in the failing light, and monumental, and contemplative, she wondered what he did feel then, and why he was always content and dignified; and she thought how devoted he was to Andrew, and would call him into his room, and, Andrew said, 'show him things'. And there he would lie all day long on the lawn brooding presumably over his poetry, till he reminded one of a cat watching birds, and then he clapped his paws together when he had found the word, and her husband said, 'Poor old Augustus—he's a true poet,' which was high praise from her husband.

Now eight candles were stood down the table, and after the first stoop the flames stood upright and drew with them into visibility the long table entire, and in the middle a yellow and purple dish of fruit. What had she done with it, Mrs Ramsay wondered, for Rose's arrangement of the grapes and pears, of the horny pink-lined shell, of the bananas, made her think of a trophy fetched from the bottom of the sea, of Neptune's banquet, of the bunch that hangs with vine leaves over the shoulder of Bacchus (in some picture), among the leopard skins and the torches lolloping red and gold . . . Thus brought up suddenly into the light it seemed possessed of great size and depth, was like a world in which one could take one's staff and climb up hills, she thought, and go down into valleys, and to her pleasure (for it brought them into sympathy momentarily) she saw that Augustus too feasted his eyes on the same plate of fruit, plunged in, broke off a bloom there, a tassel here, and returned, after feasting, to his hive. That was his way of looking, different from hers. But looking together united them.

Now all the candles were lit, and the faces on both sides of the table were brought nearer by the candle light, and composed, as they had not been in the twilight, into a party round a table, for the night was now shut off by panes of glass, which, far from giving any accurate view of the outside world, rippled it so strangely that here, inside the room, seemed to be order and dry land; there, outside, a reflection in which things wavered and vanished, waterily.

Some change at once went through them all, as if this had really happened, and they were all conscious of making a party together in a hollow, on an island; had their common cause against the fluidity out there. Mrs Ramsay who had been uneasy, waiting for Paul and Minta to come in, and unable, she felt, to settle to things, now felt her uneasiness changed to expectation. For now they must come, and Lily Briscoe, trying to analyse the cause of the sudden exhilaration, compared it with that moment on the tennis lawn, when solidity suddenly vanished, and such vast spaces lay between them; and now the same effect was got by the many candles in the sparely furnished room, and the uncurtained windows, and the bright masklike look of faces seen by candlelight. Some weight was taken off them; anything might happen, she felt. They must come now, Mrs Ramsay thought, looking at the door, and at that instant, Minta Doyle, Paul Rayley, and a maid carrying a great dish in her hands came in together. They were awfully late; they were horribly late, Minta said, as they found their way to different ends of the table.

'I lost my brooch—my grandmother's brooch,' said Minta with a sound of lamentation in her voice, and a suffusion in her large brown eyes, looking down, looking up, as she sat by Mr Ramsay, which roused his chivalry so that he bantered her.

How could she be such a goose, he asked, as to scramble about the rocks in jewels?

She was by way of being terrified of him—he was so fearfully clever, and the first night when she had sat by him, and he talked about George Eliot, she had been really frightened, for she had left the third volume of *Middlemarch* in the train and she never knew what happened in the end; but afterwards she got on perfectly, and made herself out even more ignorant than she was, because he liked telling her she was a fool. And so tonight, directly he laughed at her, she was not frightened. Besides, she knew, directly she came into the room, that the miracle had happened; she wore her golden haze. Sometimes she had it; sometimes not. She never knew why it came or why it went, or if she had it until she came into the room and then she knew instantly by the way some man looked at her. Yes, tonight she had it, tremendously; she knew that by the way Mr Ramsay told her not to be a fool. She sat beside him, smiling.

It must have happened then, thought Mrs Ramsay; they are engaged. And for a moment she felt what she had never expected to feel again— jealousy. For he, her husband, felt it too—Minta's glow; he liked these girls, these golden-reddish girls, with something flying, something a little wild and harum-scarum about them, who didn't 'scrape their hair off', weren't, as he said about poor Lily Briscoe, 'skimpy'. There was some quality which she herself had not, some lustre, some richness, which attracted him, amused him, led him to make favourites of girls like Minta. They might cut his hair for him, plait him watch-chains, or interrupt him at his work, hailing him (she heard them), 'Come along, Mr Ramsay; it's our turn to beat them now,' and out he came to play tennis.

But indeed she was not jealous, only, now and then, when she made herself look in her glass a little resentful that she had grown old, perhaps, by her own fault. (The bill for the greenhouse and all the rest of it.) She was grateful to them for laughing at him. ('How many pipes have you smoked today, Mr Ramsay?' and so on), till he seemed a young man; a man very attractive to women, not burdened, not weighed down with the greatness of his labours and the sorrows of the world and his fame or his failure, but again as she had first known him, gaunt but gallant; helping her out of a boat, she remembered; with delightful ways, like that (she looked at him, and he looked astonishingly young, teasing Minta). For herself—'Put it down there,' she said, helping the Swiss girl to place gently before her the huge brown pot in which was the Bœuf en Daube—for her own part she liked her boobies. Paul must sit by her. She had kept a place for him. Really, she sometimes thought she liked the boobies best. They did not bother one with their dissertations. How much they missed, after all, these very clever men! How dried up they did become, to be sure. There was something, she thought as he sat down, very charming about Paul. His manners were delightful to her, and his sharp cut nose and his bright blue eyes. He was so considerate. Would he tell her—now that they were all talking again—what had happened?

'We went back to look for Minta's brooch,' he said, sitting down by her. 'We'—that was enough. She knew from the effort, the rise in his voice to surmount a difficult word that it was the first time he had said 'we'. 'We' did this, 'we' did that. They'll say that all their lives, she thought, and an exquisite scent of olives and oil and juice rose from the great brown dish as Marthe, with a little flourish, took the cover off. The cook had spent three days over that dish. And she must take great care, Mrs Ramsay thought, diving into the soft mass, to choose a specially tender piece for William Bankes. And she peered into the dish, with its shiny walls and its confusion of savoury brown and yellow meats, and its bay leaves and its wine, and thought, This will celebrate the occasion—a curious sense rising in her, at once freakish and tender, of celebrating a festival, as if two emotions were called up in her, one profound—for what could be more serious than the love of man for woman, what more commanding, more impressive, bearing in its bosom the seeds of death; at the same time these lovers, these people entering into illusion glittering eyed, must be danced round with mockery, decorated with garlands.

'It is a triumph,' said Mr Bankes, laying his knife down for a moment. He had eaten attentively. It was rich; it was tender. It was perfectly cooked. How did she manage these things in the depths of the country? he asked her. She was a wonderful woman. All his love, all his reverence had returned; and she knew it.

'It is a French recipe of my grandmother's,' said Mrs Ramsay, speaking with a ring of great pleasure in her voice. Of course it was French. What passes for cookery in England is an abomination (they agreed). It is putting cabbages in water. It is roasting meat till it is like leather. It is cutting off the delicious skins of vegetables. 'In which,' said Mr Bankes, 'all the virtue of the vegetable is contained.' And the waste, said Mrs Ramsay. A whole French family could live on what an English cook throws away. Spurred on by her sense that William's affection had come back to her, and that everything was all right again, and that her suspense was over, and that now she was free both to triumph and to mock, she laughed, she gesticulated, till Lily thought, How childlike, how absurd she was, sitting up there with all her beauty opened again in her, talking about the skins of vegetables. There was something frightening about her. She was irresistible. Always she got her own way in the end, Lily thought. Now she had brought this off—Paul and Minta, one might suppose, were engaged. Mr Bankes was dining here. She put a spell on them all, by wishing, so simply, so directly; and Lily contrasted that abundance with her own poverty of spirit, and supposed that it was partly that belief (for her face was all lit up—without looking young, she looked radiant) in this strange, this terrifying thing, which made Paul Rayley, the centre of it, all of a tremor, yet abstract, absorbed, silent. Mrs Ramsay, Lily felt, as she talked about the skins of vegetables, exalted that, worshipped that; held her hands over it to warm them, to protect it, and yet, having brought it all about, somehow laughed, led her victims, Lily felt, to the altar. It came over her too now—the emotion, the vibration of love. How inconspicuous she felt herself by Paul's side! He, glowing, burning; she, aloof, satirical; he, bound for adventure; she, moored to the shore; he, launched, incautious; she solitary, left out—and, ready to implore a share, if it were disaster, in his disaster, she said shyly:

'When did Minta lose her brooch?'

He smiled the most exquisite smile, veiled by memory, tinged by dreams. He shook his head. 'On the beach,' he said.

'I'm going to find it,' he said, 'I'm getting up early.' This being kept secret from Minta, he lowered his voice, and turned his eyes to where she sat, laughing, beside Mr Ramsay.

Lily wanted to protest violently and outrageously her desire to help him, envisaging how in the dawn on the beach she would be the one to pounce on the brooch half-hidden by some stone, and thus herself be included among the sailors and adventurers. But what did he reply to her offer? She actually said with an emotion that she seldom let appear, 'Let me come with you'; and he laughed. He meant yes or no—either perhaps. But it was not his meaning—it was the odd chuckle he gave, as if he had said, Throw yourself over the cliff if you like, I don't care. He turned on her cheek the heat of love, its horror, its cruelty, its unscrupulosity. It scorched her, and Lily, looking at Minta being charming to Mr Ramsay at the other end of the table, flinched for her exposed to those fangs, and was thankful. For at any rate, she said to herself, catching sight of the salt cellar on the pattern, she need not marry, thank Heaven: she need not undergo that degradation. She was saved from that dilution. She would move the tree rather more to the middle.

Such was the complexity of things. For what happened to her, especially staying with the Ramsays, was to be made to feel violently two opposite things at the same time; that's what you feel, was one; that's what I feel was the other, and then they fought together in her mind, as now. It is so beautiful, so exciting, this love, that I tremble on the verge of it, and offer, quite out of my own habit, to look for a brooch on a beach; also it is the stupidest, the most barbaric of human passions, and turns a nice young man with a profile like a gem (Paul's was exquisite) into a bully with a crowbar (he was swaggering, he was insolent) in the Mile End Road. Yet she said to herself, from the dawn of time odes have been sung to love; wreaths heaped and roses; and if you asked nine people out of ten they would say they wanted nothing but this; while the women, judging from her own experience, would all the time be feeling, This is not what we want; there is nothing more tedious, puerile, and inhumane than love; yet it is also beautiful and necessary. Well then, well then? she asked, somehow expecting the others to go on with the argument, as if in an argument like this one threw one's own little bolt which fell short obviously and left the others to carry it on. So she listened again to what they were saying in case they should throw any light upon the question of love.

'Then,' said Mr Bankes, 'there is that liquid the English call coffee.'

'Oh coffee!' said Mrs Ramsay. But it was much rather a question (she was thoroughly roused, Lily could see, and talked very emphatically) of real butter and clean milk. Speaking with warmth and eloquence she described the iniquity of the English dairy system, and in what state milk was delivered at the door, and was about to prove her charges, for she had gone into the matter, when all round the table, beginning with Andrew in the middle, like a fire leaping from tuft to tuft of furze, her children laughed; her husband laughed; she was laughed at, fire-encircled, and forced to vail her crest, dismount her batteries, and only retaliate by displaying the raillery and ridicule of the table to Mr Bankes as an example of what one suffered if one attacked the prejudices of the British Public.

Purposely, however, for she had it on her mind that Lily, who had helped her with Mr Tansley, was out of things, she exempted her from the rest; said 'Lily anyhow agrees with me,' and so drew her in, a little fluttered, a little startled. (For she was thinking about love.) They were both out of things, Mrs Ramsay had been thinking, both Lily and Charles Tansley. Both suffered from the glow of the other two. He, it was clear, felt himself utterly in the cold; no woman would look at him with Paul Rayley in the room. Poor fellow! Still, he had his dissertation, the influence of somebody upon something: he could take care of himself. With Lily it was different. She faded, under Minta's glow; became more inconspicuous than ever, in her little grey dress with her little puckered face and her little Chinese eyes. Everything about her was so small. Yet, thought Mrs Ramsay, comparing her with Minta, as she claimed her help (for Lily should bear her out she talked no more about her dairies than her husband did about his boots—he would talk by the hour about his boots), of the two Lily at forty will be the better. There was in Lily a thread of something; a flare of something; something of her own which Mrs Ramsay liked very much indeed, but no man would, she feared. Obviously, not, unless it were a much older man, like William Bankes. But then he cared, well, Mrs Ramsay sometimes thought that he cared, since his wife's death, perhaps for her. He was not 'in love' of course; it was one of those unclassified affections of which there are so many. Oh but nonsense, she thought; William must marry Lily. They have so many things in common. Lily is so fond of flowers. They are both cold and aloof and rather self-sufficing. She must arrange for them to take a long walk together.

Foolishly, she had set them opposite each other. That could be remedied tomorrow. If it were fine, they should go for a picnic. Everything seemed possible. Everything seemed right. Just now (but this cannot last, she thought, dissociating herself from the moment while they were all talking about boots) just now she had reached security; she hovered like a hawk suspended; like a flag floated in an element of joy which filled every nerve of her body fully and sweetly, not noisily, solemnly rather, for it arose, she thought, looking at them all eating there, from husband and children and friends; all of which rising in this profound stillness (she was helping William Bankes to one very small piece more and peered into the depths of the earthenware pot) seemed now for no special reason to stay there like a smoke, like a fume rising upwards, holding them safe together. Nothing need be said; nothing could be said. There it was, all round them. It partook, she felt, carefully helping Mr Bankes to a specially tender piece, of eternity; as she had already felt about something different once before that afternoon; there is a coherence in things, a stability; something, she meant, is immune from change, and shines out (she glanced at the window with its ripple of reflected lights) in the face of the flowing, the fleeting, the spectral, like a ruby; so that again tonight she had the feeling she had had once today already, of peace, of rest. Of such moments, she thought, the thing is made that remains for ever after. This would remain.

'Yes,' she assured William Bankes, 'there is plenty for everybody.'

'Andrew,' she said, 'hold your plate lower, or I shall spill it.' (The

Bœuf en Daube was a perfect triumph.) Here, she felt, putting the spoon down, was the still space that lies about the heart of things, where one could move or rest; could wait now (they were all helped) listening; could then, like a hawk which lapses suddenly from its high station, flaunt and sink on laughter easily, resting her whole weight upon what at the other end of the table her husband was saying about the square root of one thousand two hundred and fifty-three, which happened to be the number on his railway ticket.

What did it all mean? To this day she had no notion. A square root? What was that? Her sons knew. She leant on them; on cubes and square roots; that was what they were talking about now; on Voltaire and Madame de Staël; on the character of Napoleon; on the French system of land tenure; on Lord Rosebery; on Creevey's Memoirs: she let it uphold her and sustain her, this admirable fabric of the masculine intelligence, which ran up and down, crossed this way and that, like iron girders spanning the swaying fabric, upholding the world, so that she could trust herself to it utterly, even shut her eyes, or flicker them for a moment, as a child staring up from its pillow winks at the myriad layers of the leaves of a tree. Then she woke up. It was still being fabricated. William Bankes was praising the Waverley novels.

He read one of them every six months, he said. And why should that make Charles Tansley angry? He rushed in (all, thought Mrs Ramsay, because Prue will not be nice to him) and denounced the Waverley novels when he knew nothing about it, nothing about it whatsoever, Mrs Ramsay thought, observing him rather than listening to what he said. She could see how it was from his manner—he wanted to assert himself, and so it would always be with him till he got his Professorship or married his wife, and so need not be always saying, 'I—I—I.' For that was what his criticism of poor Sir Walter, or perhaps it was Jane Austen, amounted to. 'I—I—I.' He was thinking of himself and the impression he was making, as she could tell by the sound of his voice, and his emphasis and his uneasiness. Success would be good for him. At any rate they were off again. Now she need not listen. It could not last she knew, but at the moment her eyes were so clear that they seemed to go round the table unveiling each of these people, and their thoughts and their feelings, without effort like a light stealing under water so that its ripples and the reeds in it and the minnows balancing themselves, and the sudden silent trout are all lit up hanging, trembling. So she saw them; she heard them; but whatever they said had also this quality, as if what they said was like the movement of a trout when, at the same time, one can see the ripple and the gravel, something to the right, something to the left; and the whole is held together; for whereas in active life she would be netting and separating one thing from another; she would be saying she liked the Waverley novels or had not read them; she would be urging herself forward; now she said nothing. For the moment she hung suspended.

'Ah, but how long do you think it'll last?' said somebody. It was as if she had antennae trembling out from her, which, intercepting certain sentences, forced them upon her attention. This was one of them. She scented danger for her husband. A question like that would lead, almost certainly, to something being said which reminded him of his own failure. How long would he be read—he would think at once. William Bankes (who was entirely free from all such vanity) laughed, and said he attached no importance to changes in fashion. Who could tell what was going to last—in literature or indeed in anything else?

'Let us enjoy what we do enjoy,' he said. His integrity seemed to Mrs Ramsay quite admirable. He never seemed for a moment to think, But how does this affect me? But then if you had the other temperament, which must have praise, which must have encouragement, naturally you began (and she knew that Mr Ramsay was beginning) to be uneasy; to want somebody to say, Oh, but your work will last, Mr Ramsay, or something like that. He showed his uneasiness quite clearly now by saying, with some irritation, that, anyhow, Scott (or was it Shakespeare?) would last him his lifetime. He said it irritably. Everybody, she thought, felt a little uncomfortable, without knowing why. Then Minta Doyle, whose instinct was fine, said bluffly, absurdly, that she did not believe that any one really enjoyed reading Shakespeare. Mr Ramsay said grimly (but his mind was turned away again) that very few people liked it as much as they said they did. But, he added, there is considerable merit in some of the plays nevertheless, and Mrs Ramsay saw that it would be all right for the moment anyhow; he would laugh at Minta, and she, Mrs Ramsay saw, realizing his extreme anxiety about himself, would, in her own way, see that he was taken care of, and praise him, somehow or other. But she wished it was not necessary: perhaps it was her fault that it was necessary. Anyhow, she was free now to listen to what Paul Rayley was trying to say about books one had read as a boy. They lasted, he said. He had read some of Tolstoi at school. There was one he always remembered, but he had forgotten the name. Russian names were impossible, said Mrs Ramsay. 'Vronsky,' said Paul. He remembered that because he always thought it such a good name for a villain. 'Vronsky,' said Mrs Ramsay; 'O, *Anna Karenina*,' but that did not take them very far; books were not in their line. No, Charles Tansley would put them both right in a second about books, but it was all so mixed up with, Am I saying the right thing? Am I making a good impression? that, after all, one knew more about him than about Tolstoi, whereas what Paul said was about the thing simply, not himself. Like all stupid people, he had a kind of modesty too, a consideration for what you were feeling, which, once in a way at least, she found attractive. Now he was thinking, not about himself or about Tolstoi, but whether she was cold, whether she felt a draught, whether she would like a pear.

No, she said, she did not want a pear. Indeed she had been keeping guard over the dish of fruit (without realizing it) jealously, hoping that nobody would touch it. Her eyes had been going in and out among the curves and shadows of the fruit, among the rich purples of the lowland grapes, then over the horny ridge of the shell, putting a yellow against a purple, a curved shape against a round shape, without knowing why she did it, or why, every time she did it, she felt more and more serene; until, oh, what a pity that they should do it—a hand reached out, took a pear, and spoilt the whole thing. In sympathy she looked at Rose. She looked at Rose sitting between Jasper and Prue. How odd that one's child should do that!

How odd to see them sitting there, in a row, her children, Jasper, Rose, Prue, Andrew, almost silent, but with some joke of their own going on, she guessed, from the twitching at their lips. It was something quite apart from everything else, something they were hoarding up to laugh over in their own room. It was not about their father, she hoped. No, she thought not. What was it, she wondered, sadly rather, for it seemed to her that they would laugh when she was not there. There was all that hoarded behind those rather set, still, mask-like faces, for they did not join in easily; they were like watchers, surveyors, a little raised or set apart from the grown-up people. But when she looked at Prue tonight, she saw that this was not now quite true of her. She was just beginning, just moving, just descending. The faintest light was on her face, as if the glow of Minta opposite, some excitement, some anticipation of happiness was reflected in her, as if the sun of the love of men and women rose over the rim of the table-cloth, and without knowing what it was she bent towards it and greeted it. She kept looking at Minta, shyly, yet curiously, so that Mrs Ramsay looked from one to the other and said, speaking to Prue in her own mind. You will be as happy as she is one of these days. You will be much happier, she added, because you are my daughter, she meant; her own daughter must be happier than other people's daughters. But dinner was over. It was time to go. They were only playing with things on their plates. She would wait until they had done laughing at some story her husband was telling. He was having a joke with Minta about a bet. Then she would get up.

She liked Charles Tansley, she thought, suddenly; she liked his laugh. She liked him for being so angry with Paul and Minta. She liked his awkwardness. There was a lot in that young man after all. And Lily, she thought, putting her napkin beside her plate, she always has some joke of her own. One need never bother about Lily. She waited. She tucked her napkin under the edge of her plate. Well, were they done now? No. That story had led to another story. Her husband was in great spirits tonight, and wishing, she supposed, to make it all right with old Augustus after that scene about the soup, had drawn him in—they were telling stories about someone they had both known at college. She looked at the window in which the candle flames burnt brighter now that the panes were black, and looking at that outside the voices came to her very strangely, as if they were voices at a service in a cathedral, for she did not listen to the words. The sudden bursts of laughter and then one voice (Minta's) speaking alone, reminded her of men and boys crying out the Latin words of a service in some Roman Catholic cathedral. She waited. Her husband spoke. He was repeating something, and she knew it was poetry from the rhythm and the ring of exaltation and melancholy in his voice:

> Come out and climb the garden path,
>   Luriana Lurilee.
> The China rose is all abloom and buzzing with the yellow bee.

The words (she was looking at the window) sounded as if they were floating like flowers on water out there, cut off from them all, as if no one had said them, but they had come into existence of themselves.

> And all the lives we ever lived and all the lives to be
> Are full of trees and changing leaves.

She did not know what they meant, but, like music, the words seemed to be spoken by her own voice, outside her self, saying quite easily and naturally what had been in her mind the whole evening while she said different things. She knew, without looking round, that everyone at the table was listening to the voice saying:

> I wonder if it seems to you
>   Luriana, Lurilee

with the same sort of relief and pleasure that she had, as if this were, at last, the natural thing to say, this were their own voice speaking.

But the voice stopped. She looked round. She made herself get up. Augustus Carmichael had risen and, holding his table napkin so that it looked like a long white robe he stood chanting:

> To see the Kings go riding by
> Over lawn and daisy lea
> With their palm leaves and cedar sheaves,
>   Luriana, Lurilee,

and as she passed him he turned slightly towards her repeating the last words:

> Luriana, Lurilee,

and bowed to her as if he did her homage. Without knowing why, she felt that he liked her better than he had ever done before; and with a feeling of relief and gratitude she returned his bow and passed through the door which he held open for her.

It was necessary now to carry everything a step further. With her foot on the threshold she waited a moment longer in a scene which was vanishing even as she looked, and then, as she moved and took Minta's arm and left the room, it changed, it shaped itself differently; it had become, she knew, giving one last look at it over her shoulder, already the past.

18

As usual, Lily thought. There was always something that had to be done at that precise moment, something that Mrs Ramsay had decided for reasons of her own to do instantly, it might be with everyone standing about making jokes, as now, not being able to decide whether they were going into the smoking-room, into the drawing-room, up to the attics. Then one saw Mrs Ramsay in the midst of this hubbub standing there with Minta's arm in hers, bethink her 'Yes, it is time for that now,' and so make off at once with an air of secrecy to do something alone. And directly she went a sort of disintegration set in; they wavered about, went different ways, Mr Bankes took Charles Tansley by the arm and went off to finish on the terrace the discussion they had begun at dinner about politics, thus giving a turn to the whole poise of the evening, making the weight fall in a different direction, as if, Lily thought, seeing them go, and hearing a word or two about the policy of the Labour Party, they had gone up on to the bridge of the ship and were taking their bearings; the change from poetry to politics struck her like that; so Mr Bankes and Charles Tansley went off, while the others stood looking at Mrs Ramsay going upstairs in the lamplight alone. Where, Lily wondered, was she going so quickly?

Not that she did in fact run or hurry; she went indeed rather slowly. She felt rather inclined just for a moment to stand still after all that chatter, and pick out one particular thing; the thing that mattered; to detach it; separate it off; clean it of all the emotions and odds and ends of things, and so hold it before her, and bring it to the tribunal where, ranged about in conclave, sat the judges she had set up to decide these things. Is it good, is it bad, is it right or wrong? Where are we going to? and so on. So she righted herself after the shock of the event, and quite unconsciously and incongruously, used the branches of the elm trees outside to help her to stabilize her position. Her world was changing: they were still. The event had given her a sense of movement. All must be in order. She must get that right and that right, she thought, insensibly, approving of the dignity of the trees' stillness, and now again of the superb upward rise (like the beak of a ship up a wave) of the elm branches as the wind raised them. For it was windy (she stood a moment to look out). It was windy, so that the leaves now and then brushed open a star, and the stars themselves seemed to be shaking and darting light and trying to flash out between the edges of the leaves. Yes, that was done then, accomplished; and as with all things done, become solemn. Now one thought of it, cleared of chatter and emotion, it seemed always to have been, only was shown now, and so being shown struck everything into stability. They would, she thought, going on again, however long they lived, come back to this night; this moon; this wind; this house: and to her too. It flattered her, where she was most susceptible of flattery, to think how, wound about in their hearts, however long they lived she would be woven; and this, and this, and this, she thought, going upstairs, laughing, but affectionately, at the sofa on the landing (her mother's) at the rocking-chair (her father's); at the map of the Hebrides. All that would be revived again in the lives of Paul and Minta; 'the Rayleys'—she tried the new name over; and she felt, with her hand on the nursery door, that community of feeling with other people which emotion gives as if the walls of partition had become so thin that practically (the feeling was one of relief and happiness) it was all one stream, and chairs, tables, maps, were hers, were theirs, it did not matter whose, and Paul and Minta would carry it on when she was dead.

She turned the handle, firmly, lest it should squeak, and went in, pursing her lips slightly, as if to remind herself that she must not speak aloud. But directly she came in she saw, with annoyance, that the precaution was not needed. The children were not asleep. It was most annoying. Mildred should be more careful. There was James wide awake and Cam sitting bolt upright, and Mildred out of bed in her bare feet, and it was almost eleven and they were all talking. What was the matter? It was that horrid skull again. She had told Mildred to move it, but Mildred, of course, had forgotten, and now there was Cam wide awake and James wide awake quarrelling when they ought to have been asleep hours ago. What had possessed Edward to send them this horrid skull? She had been so foolish as to let them nail it up there. It was nailed fast, Mildred said, and Cam couldn't go to sleep with it in the room, and James screamed if she touched it.

Then Cam must go to sleep (it had great horns said Cam—) must go to sleep and dream of lovely palaces, said Mrs Ramsay, sitting down on the bed by her side. She could see the horns, Cam said, all over the room. It was true. Wherever they put the light (and James could not sleep without a light) there was always a shadow somewhere.

'But think, Cam, it's only an old pig,' said Mrs Ramsay, 'a nice black pig like the pigs at the farm.' But Cam thought it was a horrid thing, branching at her all over the room.

'Well then,' said Mrs Ramsay, 'we will cover it up,' and they all watched her go to the chest of drawers, and open the little drawers quickly one after another, and not seeing anything that would do, she quickly took her own shawl off and wound it round the skull, round and round and round, and then she came back to Cam and laid her head almost flat on the pillow beside Cam's and said how lovely it looked now; how the fairies would love it; it was like a bird's nest; it was like a beautiful mountain such as she had seen abroad, with valleys and flowers and bells ringing and birds singing and little goats and antelopes . . . She could see the words echoing as she spoke them rhythmically in Cam's mind, and Cam was repeating after her how it was like a mountain, a bird's nest, a garden, and there were little antelopes, and her eyes were opening and shutting, and Mrs Ramsay went on saying still more monotonously, and more rhythmically and more nonsensically, how she must shut her eyes and go to sleep and dream of mountains and valleys and stars falling and parrots and antelopes and gardens, and everything lovely, she said, raising her head very slowly and speaking more and more mechanically, until she sat upright and saw that Cam was asleep.

Now, she whispered, crossing over to his bed, James must go to sleep too, for see, she said, the boar's skull was still there; they had not touched it; they had done just what he wanted; it was there quite unhurt. He made sure that the skull was still there under the shawl. But he wanted to ask her something more. Would they go to the Lighthouse tomorrow?

No, not tomorrow, she said, but soon, she promised him; the next fine day. He was very good. He lay down. She covered him up. But he would never forget, she knew, and she felt angry with Charles Tansley, with her husband, and with herself, for she had raised his hopes. Then feeling for her shawl and remembering that she had wrapped it round the boar's skull, she got up, and pulled the window down another inch or two, and heard the wind, and got a breath of the perfectly indifferent chill night air and murmured good-night to Mildred and left the room and let the tongue of the door slowly lengthen in the lock and went out.

She hoped he would not bang his books on the floor above their heads, she thought, still thinking how annoying Charles Tansley was. For neither of them slept well; they were excitable children, and since he said things like that about the Lighthouse, it seemed to her likely that he would knock a pile of books over just as they were going to sleep, clumsily sweeping them off the table with his elbow. For she supposed that he had gone upstairs to work. Yet he looked so desolate; yet she would feel relieved when he went; yet she would see that he was better treated tomorrow; yet he was admirable with her husband; yet his manners certainly wanted improving; yet she liked his laugh—thinking this, as she came downstairs, she noticed that she could now see the moon itself through the staircase window—the yellow harvest moon—and turned, and they saw her, standing above them on the stairs.

'That's my mother,' thought Prue. Yes; Minta should look at her; Paul Rayley should look at her. That is the thing itself, she felt, as if there were only one person like that in the world; her mother. And, from having been quite grown up, a moment before, talking with the others, she became a child again, and what they had been doing was a game, and would her mother sanction their game, or condemn it, she wondered. And thinking what a chance it was for Minta and Paul and Lily to see her, and feeling what an extraordinary stroke of fortune it was for her to have her, and how she would never grow up and never leave home, she said, like a child, 'We thought of going down to the beach to watch the waves.'

Instantly, for no reason at all, Mrs Ramsay became like a girl of twenty, full of gaiety. A mood of revelry suddenly took possession of her. Of course they must go; of course they must go, she cried, laughing; and running down the last three or four steps quickly, she began turning from one to the other and laughing and drawing Minta's wrap round her and saying she only wished she could come too, and would they be very late, and had any of them got a watch?

'Yes, Paul has,' said Minta. Paul slipped a beautiful gold watch out of a little wash-leather case to show her. And as he held it in the palm of his hand before her, he felt, 'She knows all about it. I need not say anything.' He was saying to her as he showed her the watch, 'I've done it, Mrs Ramsay. I owe it all to you.' And seeing the gold watch lying in his hand, Mrs Ramsay felt, How extraordinarily lucky Minta is! She is marrying a man who has a gold watch in a wash-leather bag!

'How I wish I could come with you!' she cried. But she was withheld by something so strong that she never even thought of asking herself what it was. Of course it was impossible for her to go with them. But she would have liked to go, had it not been for the other thing, and tickled by the absurdity of her thought (how lucky to marry a man with a wash-leather bag for his watch) she went with a smile on her lips into the other room, where her husband sat reading.

19

Of course, she said to herself, coming into the room, she had to come here to get something she wanted. First she wanted to sit down in a particular chair under a particular lamp. But she wanted something more, though she did not know, could not think what it was that she wanted. She looked at her husband (taking up her stocking and beginning to knit), and saw that he did not want to be interrupted— that was clear. He was reading something that moved him very much. He was half smiling and then she knew he was controlling his emotion. He was tossing the pages over. He was acting it—perhaps he was thinking himself the person in the book. She wondered what book it was. Oh, it was one of old Sir Walter's, she saw, adjusting the shade of her lamp so that the light fell on her knitting. For Charles Tansley had been saying (she looked up as if she expected to hear the crash of books on the floor above) had been saying that people don't read Scott any more. Then her husband thought, 'That's what they'll say of me;' so he went and got one of those books. And if he came to the conclusion 'That's true' what Charles Tansley said, he would accept it about Scott. (She could see that he was weighing, considering, putting this with that as he read.) But not about himself. He was always uneasy about himself. That troubled her. He would always be worrying about his own books— will they be read, are they good, why aren't they better, what do people think of me? Not liking to think of him so, and wondering if they had guessed at dinner why he suddenly became irritable when they talked about fame and books lasting, wondering if the children were laughing at that, she twitched the stocking out, and all the fine gravings came drawn with steel instruments about her lips and forehead, and she grew still like a tree which has been tossing and quivering and now, when the breeze falls, settles, leaf by leaf, into quiet.

It didn't matter, any of it, she thought. A great man, a great book, fame—who could tell? She knew nothing about it. But it was his way with him, his truthfulness—for instance at dinner she had been thinking quite instinctively, If only he would speak! She had complete trust in him. And dismissing all this, as one passes in diving now a weed, now a straw, now a bubble, she felt again, sinking deeper, as she had felt in the hall when the others were talking, There is something I want—

something I have come to get, and she fell deeper and deeper without knowing quite what it was, with her eyes closed. And she waited a little, knitting, wondering, and slowly those words they had said at dinner, 'the China rose is all abloom and buzzing with the honey bee', began washing from side to side of her mind rhythmically, and as they washed, words, like little shaded lights, one red, one blue, one yellow, lit up in the dark of her mind, and seemed leaving their perches up there to fly across and across, or to cry out and to be echoed; so she turned and felt on the table beside her for a book.

> And all the lives we ever lived
> And all the lives to be,
> Are full of trees and changing leaves,

she murmured, sticking her needles into the stocking. And she opened the book and began reading here and there at random, and as she did so she felt that she was climbing backwards, upwards, shoving her way up under petals that curved over her, so that she only knew this is white, or this is red. She did not know at first what the words meant at all.

> Steer, hither steer your winged pines, all beaten Mariners

she read and turned the page, swinging herself, zigzagging this way and that, from one line to another as from one branch to another, from one red and white flower to another, until a little sound roused her—her husband slapping his thighs. Their eyes met for a second; but they did not want to speak to each other. They had nothing to say, but something seemed, nevertheless, to go from him to her. It was the life, it was the power of it, it was the tremendous humour, she knew, that made him slap his thighs. Don't interrupt me, he seemed to be saying, don't say anything; just sit there. And he went on reading. His lips twitched. It filled him. It fortified him. He clean forgot all the little rubs and digs of the evening, and how it bored him unutterably to sit still while people ate and drank interminably, and his being so irritable with his wife and so touchy and minding when they passed his books over as if they didn't exist at all. But now, he felt, it didn't matter a damn who reached Z (if thought ran like an alphabet from A to Z). Somebody would reach it— if not he, then another. This man's strength and sanity, his feeling for straightforward simple things, these fishermen, the poor old crazed creature in Mucklebackit's cottage made him feel so vigorous, so relieved of something that he felt roused and triumphant and could not choke back his tears. Raising the book a little to hide his face he let them fall and shook his head from side to side and forgot himself completely (but not one or two reflections about morality and French novels and English novels and Scott's hands being tied but his view perhaps being as true as the other view) forgot his own bothers and failures completely in poor Steenie's drowning and Mucklebackit's sorrow (that was Scott at his best) and the astonishing delight and feeling of vigour that it gave him.

Well, let them improve upon that, he thought as he finished the chapter. He felt that he had been arguing with somebody, and had got the better of him. They could not improve upon that, whatever they might say; and his own position became more secure. The lovers were fiddlesticks, he thought, collecting it all in his mind again. That's fiddlesticks, that's first-rate, he thought, putting one thing beside another. But he must read it again. He could not remember the whole shape of the thing. He had to keep his judgement in suspense. So he returned to the other thought—if young men did not care for this, naturally they did not care for him either. One ought not to complain, thought Mr Ramsay, trying to stifle his desire to complain to his wife that young men did not admire him. But he was determined; he would not bother her again. Here he looked at her reading. She looked very peaceful, reading. He liked to think that everyone had taken themselves off and that he and she were alone. The whole of life did not consist in going to bed with a woman, he thought, returning to Scott and Balzac, to the English novel and the French novel.

Mrs Ramsay raised her head and like a person in a light sleep seemed to say that if he wanted her to wake she would, she really would, but otherwise, might she go on sleeping, just a little longer, just a little longer? She was climbing up those branches, this way and that, laying hands on one flower and then another.

> Nor praise the deep vermilion in the rose,

she read, and so reading she was ascending, she felt, on to the top, on to the summit. How satisfying! How restful! All the odds and ends of the day stuck to this magnet; her mind felt swept, felt clean. And then there it was, suddenly entire shaped in her hands, beautiful and reasonable, clear and complete, the essence sucked out of life and held rounded here—the sonnet.

But she was becoming conscious of her husband looking at her. He was smiling at her, quizzically, as if he were ridiculing her gently for being asleep in broad daylight, but at the same time he was thinking, Go on reading. You don't look sad now, he thought. And he wondered what she was reading, and exaggerated her ignorance, her simplicity, for he liked to think that she was not clever, not book-learned at all. He wondered if she understood what she was reading. Probably not, he thought. She was astonishingly beautiful. Her beauty seemed to him, if that were possible, to increase.

> Yet seem'd it winter still, and, you away,
> As with your shadow I with these did play,

she finished.

'Well?' she said, echoing his smile dreamily, looking up from her book.

> As with your shadow I with these did play,

she murmured putting the book on the table.

What had happened she wondered, as she took up her knitting, since she had last seen him alone? She remembered dressing, and seeing the moon; Andrew holding his plate too high at dinner; being depressed by something William had said; the birds in the trees; the sofa on the landing; the children being awake; Charles Tansley waking them with his books falling—oh no, that she had invented; and Paul having a wash-leather case for his watch. Which should she tell him about?

'They're engaged,' she said, beginning to knit, 'Paul and Minta.'

'So I guessed,' he said. There was nothing very much to be said about it. Her mind was still going up and down, up and down with the poetry; he was still feeling very vigorous, very forthright, after reading about Steenie's funeral. So they sat silent. Then she became aware that she wanted him to say something.

Anything, anything, she thought, going on with her knitting. Anything will do.

'How nice it would be to marry a man with a wash-leather bag for his watch,' she said, for that was the sort of joke they had together.

He snorted. He felt about this engagement as he always felt about any engagement; the girl is much too good for that young man. Slowly it came into her head, why is it then that one wants people to marry? What was the value, the meaning of things? (Every word they said now would be true.) Do say something, she thought, wishing only to hear his voice. For the shadow, the thing folding them in was beginning, she felt, to close round her again. Say anything, she begged, looking at him, as if for help.

He was silent, swinging the compass on his watch-chain to and fro, and thinking of Scott's novels and Balzac's novels. But through the crepuscular walls of their intimacy, for they were drawing together, involuntarily, coming side by side, quite close, she could feel his mind like a raised hand shadowing her mind; and he was beginning now that her thoughts took a turn he disliked—towards this 'pessimism' as he called it—to fidget, though he said nothing, raising his hand to his forehead, twisting a lock of hair, letting it fall again.

'You won't finish that stocking tonight,' he said, pointing to her stocking. That was what she wanted—the asperity in his voice reproving her. If he says it's wrong to be pessimistic probably it is wrong, she thought; the marriage will turn out all right.

'No,' she said, flattening the stocking out upon her knee, 'I shan't finish it.'

And what then? For she felt that he was still looking at her, but that his look had changed. He wanted something—wanted the thing she always found it so difficult to give him; wanted her to tell him that she loved him. And that, no, she could not do. He found talking so much easier than she did. He could say things—she never could. So naturally it was always he that said the things, and then for some reason he would mind this suddenly, and would reproach her. A heartless woman he called her; she never told him that she loved him. But it was not so—it was not so. It was only that she never could say what she felt. Was there no crumb on his coat? Nothing she could do for him? Getting up she stood at the window with the reddish-brown stocking in her hands, partly to turn away from him, partly because she did not mind looking now, with him watching, at the Lighthouse. For she knew that he had turned his head as she turned; he was watching her. She knew that he was thinking, You are more beautiful than ever. And she felt herself very beautiful. Will you not tell me just for once that you love me? He was thinking that, for he was roused, what with Minta and his book, and its being the end of the day and their having quarrelled about going to the Lighthouse. But she could not do it; she could not say it. Then, knowing that he was watching her, instead of saying anything she turned, holding her stocking, and looked at him. And as she looked at him she began to smile, for though she had not said a word, he knew, of course he knew, that she loved him. He could not deny it. And smiling she looked out of the window and said (thinking to herself, Nothing on earth can equal this happiness)—

'Yes, you were right. It's going to be wet tomorrow.' She had not said it, but he knew it. And she looked at him smiling. For she had triumphed again.

II

TIME PASSES

1

'Well, we must wait for the future to show,' said Mr Bankes, coming in from the terrace.

'It's almost too dark to see,' said Andrew, coming up from the beach.

'One can hardly tell which is the sea and which is the land,' said Prue.

'Do we leave that light burning?' said Lily as they took their coats off indoors.

'No,' said Prue, 'not if everyone's in.'

'Andrew,' she called back, 'just put out the light in the hall.'

One by one the lamps were all extinguished, except that Mr Carmichael, who liked to lie awake a little reading Virgil, kept his candle burning rather longer than the rest.

2

So with the lamps all put out, the moon sunk, and a thin rain drumming on the roof a downpouring of immense darkness began. Nothing, it seemed, could survive the flood, the profusion of darkness which, creeping in at keyholes and crevices, stole round window blinds, came into bedrooms, swallowed up here a jug and basin, there a bowl of red and yellow dahlias, there the sharp edges and firm bulk of a chest of drawers. Not only was furniture confounded; there was scarcely anything left of body or mind by which one could say 'This is he' or 'This is she'. Sometimes a hand was raised as if to clutch something or ward off something, or somebody groaned, or somebody laughed aloud as if sharing a joke with nothingness.

Nothing stirred in the drawing-room or in the dining-room or on the staircase. Only through the rusty hinges and swollen sea-moistened woodwork certain airs, detached from the body of the wind (the house was ramshackle after all) crept round corners and ventured indoors. Almost one might imagine them, as they entered the drawing-room, questioning and wondering, toying with the flap of hanging wallpaper, asking, would it hang much longer, when would it fall? Then smoothly brushing the walls, they passed on musingly as if asking the red and yellow roses on the wallpaper whether they would fade, and questioning (gently, for there was time at their disposal) the torn letters in the wastepaper basket, the flowers, the books, all of which were now open to them and asking, Were they allies? Were they enemies? How long would they endure?

So some random light directing them from an uncovered star, or wandering ship, or the Lighthouse even, with its pale footfall upon stair and mat, the little airs mounted the staircase and nosed round bedroom doors. But here surely, they must cease. Whatever else may perish and disappear what lies here is steadfast. Here one might say to those sliding lights, those fumbling airs, that breathe and bend over the bed itself, here you can neither touch nor destroy. Upon which, wearily, ghostlily, as if they had feather-light fingers and the light persistency of feathers, they would look, once, on the shut eyes and the loosely clasping fingers, and fold their garments wearily and disappear. And so, nosing, rubbing, they went to the window on the staircase, to the servants' bedrooms, to the boxes in the attics; descending, blanched the apples on the dining-room table, fumbled the petals of roses, tried the picture on the easel, brushed the mat and blew a little sand along the floor. At length, desisting, all ceased together, gathered together, all sighed together; all together gave off an aimless gust of lamentation to which some door in the kitchen replied; swung wide; admitted nothing; and slammed to.

[Here Mr Carmichael, who was reading Virgil, blew out his candle. It was past midnight.]

3

But what after all is one night? A short space, especially when the darkness dims so soon, and so soon a bird sings, a cock crows, or a faint green quickens, like a turning leaf, in the hollow of the wave. Night, however, succeeds to night. The winter holds a pack of them in store and deals them equally, evenly, with indefatigable fingers. They lengthen; they darken. Some of them hold aloft clear planets, plates of brightness. The autumn trees, ravaged as they are, take on the flash of tattered flags kindling in the gloom of cool cathedral caves where gold letters on marble pages describe death in battle and how bones bleach and burn far away in Indian sands. The autumn trees gleam in the yellow moonlight, in the light of the harvest moons, the light which mellows the energy of labour, and smooths the stubble, and brings the wave lapping blue to the shore.

It seemed now as if, touched by human penitence and all its toil, divine goodness had parted the curtain and displayed behind it, single, distinct, the hare erect; the wave falling; the boat rocking, which, did we deserve them, should be ours always. But alas, divine goodness, twitching the cord, draws the curtain; it does not please him; he covers his treasures in a drench of hail, and so breaks them, so confuses them that it seems impossible that their calm should ever return or that we should ever compose from their fragments a perfect whole or read in the littered pieces the clear words of truth. For our penitence deserves a glimpse only; our toil respite only.

The nights now are full of wind and destruction; the trees plunge and bend and their leaves fly helter skelter until the lawn is plastered with them and they lie packed in gutters and choke rain pipes and scatter damp paths. Also the sea tosses itself and breaks itself, and should any sleeper fancying that he might find on the beach an answer to his doubts, a sharer of his solitude, throw off his bedclothes and go down by himself to walk on the sand, no image with semblance of serving and divine promptitude comes readily to hand bringing the night to order and making the world reflect the compass of the soul. The hand dwindles in his hand; the voice bellows in his ear. Almost it would appear that it is useless in such confusion to ask the night those questions as to what, and why, and wherefore, which tempt the sleeper from his bed to seek an answer.

[Mr Ramsay stumbling along a passage stretched his arms out one dark morning, but, Mrs Ramsay having died rather suddenly the night before, he stretched his arms out. They remained empty.]

4

So with the house empty and the doors locked and the mattresses rolled round, those stray airs, advance guards of great armies, blustered in, brushed bare boards, nibbled and fanned, met nothing in bedroom or drawing-room that wholly resisted them but only hangings that flapped, wood that creaked, the bare legs of tables, saucepans and china already furred, tarnished, cracked. What people had shed and left—a pair of shoes, a shooting cap, some faded skirts and coats in wardrobes—those alone kept the human shape and in the emptiness indicated how once they were filled and animated; how once hands were busy with hooks and buttons; how once the looking-glass had held a face; had held a world hollowed out in which a figure turned, a hand flashed, the door opened, in came children rushing and tumbling; and went out again. Now, day after day, light turned, like a flower reflected in water, its clear image on the wall opposite. Only the shadows of the trees, flourishing in the wind, made obeisance on the wall, and for a moment darkened the pool in which light reflected itself; or birds, flying, made a soft spot flutter slowly across the bedroom floor.

So loveliness reigned and stillness, and together made the shape of loveliness itself, a form from which life had parted; solitary like a pool at evening, far distant, seen from a train window, vanishing so quickly that the pool, pale in the evening, is scarcely robbed of its solitude, though once seen. Loveliness and stillness clasped hands in the bedroom, and among the shrouded jugs and sheeted chairs even the prying of the wind, and the soft nose of the clammy sea airs, rubbing, snuffling, iterating, and reiterating their questions—'Will you fade? Will you perish?'—scarcely disturbed the peace, the indifference, the air of pure integrity, as if the question they asked scarcely needed that they should answer: we remain.

Nothing it seemed could break that image, corrupt that innocence, or disturb the swaying mantle of silence which, week after week, in the empty room, wove into itself the falling cries of birds, ships hooting, the drone and hum of the fields, a dog's bark, a man's shout, and folded them round the house in silence. Once only a board sprang on the landing; once in the middle of the night with a roar, with a rupture, as after centuries of quiescence, a rock rends itself from the mountain and hurtles crashing into the valley, one fold of the shawl loosened and swung to and fro. Then again peace descended; and the shadow wavered; light bent to its own image in adoration on the bedroom wall; when Mrs McNab, tearing the veil of silence with hands that had stood in the wash-tub, grinding it with boots that had crunched the shingle, came as directed to open all windows, and dust the bedrooms.

5

As she lurched (for she rolled like a ship at sea) and leered (for her eyes fell on nothing directly, but with a sidelong glance that deprecated the scorn and anger of the world—she was witless, she knew it), as she clutched the banisters and hauled herself upstairs and rolled from room to room, she sang. Rubbing the glass of the long looking-glass and leering sideways at her swinging figure a sound issued from her lips— something that had been gay twenty years before on the stage perhaps, had been hummed and danced to, but now, coming from the toothless, bonneted, caretaking woman, was robbed of meaning, was like the voice of witlessness, humour, persistency itself, trodden down but springing up again, so that as she lurched, dusting, wiping, she seemed to say how it was one long sorrow and trouble, how it was getting up and going to bed again, and bringing things out and putting them away again. It was not easy or snug this world she had known for close on seventy years. Bowed down she was with weariness. How long, she asked, creaking and groaning on her knees under the bed, dusting the boards, how long

shall it endure? but hobbled to her feet again, pulled herself up, and
again with her sidelong leer which slipped and turned aside even from
her own face, and her own sorrows, stood and gaped in the glass,
aimlessly smiling, and began again the old amble and hobble, taking up
mats, putting down china, looking sideways in the glass, as if, after all,
she had her consolations, as if indeed there twined about her dirge some
incorrigible hope. Visions of joy there must have been at the wash-tub,
say with her children (yet two had been base-born and one had deserted
her), at the public-house, drinking; turning over scraps in her drawers.
Some cleavage of the dark there must have been, some channel in the
depths of obscurity through which light enough issued to twist her face
grinning in the glass and make her, turning to her job again, mumble
out the old music hall song. Meanwhile the mystic, the visionary, walked
the beach, stirred a puddle, looked at a stone, and asked themselves
'What am I?' 'What is this?' and suddenly an answer was vouchsafed
them (what it was they could not say): so that they were warm in the
frost and had comfort in the desert. But Mrs McNab continued to drink
and gossip as before.

6

The spring without a leaf to toss, bare and bright like a virgin fierce in
her chastity, scornful in her purity, was laid out on fields wide-eyed and
watchful and entirely careless of what was done or thought by the
beholders.

[Prue Ramsay, leaning on her father's arm, was given in marriage
that May. What, people said, could have been more fitting? And, they
added, how beautiful she looked!]

As summer neared, as the evenings lengthened, there came to the
wakeful, the hopeful, walking the beach, stirring the pool, imaginations
of the strangest kind—of flesh turned to atoms which drove before the
wind, of stars flashing in their hearts, of cliff, sea, cloud, and sky brought
purposely together to assemble outwardly the scattered parts of the
vision within. In those mirrors, the minds of men, in those pools of
uneasy water, in which clouds for ever turn and shadows form, dreams
persisted, and it was impossible to resist the strange intimation which
every gull, flower, tree, man and woman, and the white earth itself
seemed to declare (but if questioned at once to withdraw) that good
triumphs, happiness prevails, order rules; or to resist the extraordinary
stimulus to range hither and thither in search of some absolute good,
some crystal of intensity, remote from the known pleasures and familiar
virtues, something alien to the processes of domestic life, single, hard,

bright, like a diamond in the sand, which would render the possessor secure. Moreover, softened and acquiescent, the spring with her bees humming and gnats dancing threw her cloak about her, veiled her eyes, averted her head, and among passing shadows and flights of small rain seemed to have taken upon her a knowledge of the sorrows of mankind.

[Prue Ramsay died that summer in some illness connected with childbirth, which was indeed a tragedy, people said. They said nobody deserved happiness more.]

And now in the heat of summer the wind sent its spies about the house again. Flies wove a web in the sunny rooms; weeds that had grown close to the glass in the night tapped methodically at the window pane. When darkness fell, the stroke of the Lighthouse, which had laid itself with such authority upon the carpet in the darkness, tracing its pattern, came now in the softer light of spring mixed with moonlight gliding gently as if it laid its caress and lingered stealthily and looked and came lovingly again. But in the very lull of this loving caress, as the long stroke leant upon the bed, the rock was rent asunder; another fold of the shawl loosened; there it hung, and swayed. Through the short summer nights and the long summer days, when the empty rooms seemed to murmur with the echoes of the fields and the hum of flies, the long streamer waved gently, swayed aimlessly; while the sun so striped and barred the rooms and filled them with yellow haze that Mrs McNab, when she broke in and lurched about, dusting, sweeping, looked like a tropical fish oaring its way through sun-lanced waters.

But slumber and sleep though it might there came later in the summer ominous sounds like the measured blows of hammers dulled on felt, which, with their repeated shocks still further loosened the shawl and cracked the tea-cups. Now and again some glass tinkled in the cupboard as if a giant voice had shrieked so loud in its agony that tumblers stood inside a cupboard vibrated too. Then again silence fell; and then, night after night, and sometimes in plain mid-day when the roses were bright and light turned on the wall its shape clearly there seemed to drop into this silence this indifference, this integrity, the thud of something falling.

[A shell exploded. Twenty or thirty young men were blown up in France, among them Andrew Ramsay, whose death, mercifully, was instantaneous.]

At that season those who had gone down to pace the beach and ask of the sea and sky what message they reported or what vision they affirmed had to consider among the usual tokens of divine bounty—the sunset on the sea, the pallor of dawn, the moon rising, fishing-boats against the moon, and children pelting each other with handfuls of grass, something out of harmony with this jocundity, this serenity. There was the silent apparition of an ashen-coloured ship for instance, come, gone; there was a purplish stain upon the bland surface of the sea as if something had boiled and bled, invisibly, beneath. This intrusion into a scene calculated to stir the most sublime reflections and lead to the most comfortable conclusions stayed their pacing. It was difficult blandly to overlook them, to abolish their significance in the landscape; to continue, as one walked by the sea, to marvel how beauty outside mirrored beauty within.

Did Nature supplement what man advanced? Did she complete what he began? With equal complacence she saw his misery, condoned his meanness, and acquiesced in his torture. That dream, then, of sharing, completing, finding in solitude on the beach an answer, was but a reflection in a mirror, and the mirror itself was but the surface glassiness which forms in quiescence when the nobler powers sleep beneath? Impatient, despairing yet loth to go (for beauty offers her lures, her consolations), to pace the beach was impossible; contemplation was unendurable; the mirror was broken.

[Mr Carmichael brought out a volume of poems that spring, which had an unexpected success. The war, people said, had revived their interest in poetry.]

7

Night after night, summer and winter, the torment of storms, the arrow-like stillness of fine weather, held their court without interference. Listening (had there been anyone to listen) from the upper rooms of the empty house only gigantic chaos streaked with lightning could have been heard tumbling and tossing, as the winds and waves disported themselves like the amorphous bulks of leviathans whose brows are pierced by no light of reason, and mounted one on top of another, and lunged and plunged in the darkness or the daylight (for night and day, month and year ran shapelessly together) in idiot games, until it seemed as if the universe were battling and tumbling, in brute confusion and wanton lust aimlessly by itself.

In spring the garden urns, casually filled with wind-blown plants, were gay as ever. Violets came and daffodils. But the stillness and the brightness of the day were as strange as the chaos and tumult of night, with the trees standing there, and the flowers standing there, looking before them, looking up, yet beholding nothing, eyeless, and thus terrible.

8

Thinking no harm, for the family would not come, never again, some said, and the house would be sold at Michaelmas perhaps, Mrs McNab stooped and picked a bunch of flowers to take home with her. She laid them on the table while she dusted. She was fond of flowers. It was a pity to let them waste. Suppose the house were sold (she stood arms akimbo in front of the looking-glass) it would want seeing to—it would. There it had stood all these years without a soul in it. The books and things were mouldy, for, what with the war and help being hard to get, the house had not been cleaned as she could have wished. It was beyond one person's strength to get it straight now. She was too old. Her legs pained her. All those books needed to be laid out on the grass in the sun; there was plaster fallen in the hall; the rain-pipe had blocked over the study window and let the water in; the carpet was ruined quite. But people should come themselves; they should have sent somebody down to see. For there were clothes in the cupboards; they had left clothes in all the bedrooms. What was she to do with them? They had the moth in them—Mrs Ramsay's things. Poor lady! She would never want *them* again. She was dead, they said, years ago, in London. There was the old grey cloak she wore gardening (Mrs McNab fingered it). She could see her, as she came up the drive with the washing, stooping over her flowers (the garden was a pitiful sight now, all run to riot, and rabbits scuttling at you out of the beds)—she could see her with one of the children by her in that grey cloak. There were boots and shoes; and a brush and comb left on the dressing-table, for all the world as if she expected to come back tomorrow. (She had died very sudden at the end, they said.) And once they had been coming, but had put off coming, what with the war, and travel being so difficult these days; they had never come all these years; just sent her money; but never wrote, never came, and expected to find things as they had left them, ah dear! Why the dressing-table drawers were full of things (she pulled them open), handkerchiefs, bits of ribbon. Yes, she could see Mrs Ramsay as she came up the drive with the washing.

'Good-evening, Mrs McNab,' she would say.

She had a pleasant way with her. The girls all liked her. But dear, many things had changed since then (she shut the drawer); many families had lost their dearest. So she was dead; and Mr Andrew killed; and Miss Prue dead too, they said, with her first baby; but everyone had lost someone these years. Prices had gone up shamefully, and didn't come down again neither. She could well remember her in her grey cloak.

'Good-evening, Mrs McNab,' she said, and told cook to keep a plate of milk soup for her—quite thought she wanted it, carrying that heavy basket all the way up from town. She could see her now, stooping over her flowers; (and faint and flickering, like a yellow beam or the circle at the end of a telescope, a lady in a grey cloak, stooping over her flowers, went wandering over the bedroom wall, up the dressing-table, across the washstand, as Mrs McNab hobbled and ambled, dusting, straightening).

And cook's name now? Mildred? Marian?—some name like that. Ah, she had forgotten—she did forget things. Fiery, like all red-haired women. Many a laugh they had had. She was always welcome in the kitchen. She made them laugh, she did. Things were better then than now.

She sighed; there was too much work for one woman. She wagged her head this side and that. This had been the nursery. Why, it was all damp in here; the plaster was falling. Whatever did they want to hang a beast's skull there? gone mouldy too. And rats in all the attics. The rain came in. But they never sent; never came. Some of the locks had gone, so the doors banged. She didn't like to be up here at dusk alone neither. It was too much for one woman, too much, too much. She creaked, she moaned. She banged the door. She turned the key in the lock, and left the house shut up, locked, alone.

9

The house was left; the house was deserted. It was left like a shell on a sand-hill to fill with dry salt grains now that life had left it. The long night seemed to have set in; the trifling airs, nibbling, the clammy breaths, fumbling, seemed to have triumphed. The saucepan had rusted and the mat decayed. Toads had nosed their way in. Idly, aimlessly, the swaying shawl swung to and fro. A thistle thrust itself between the tiles in the larder. The swallows nested in the drawing-room; the floor was strewn with straw; the plaster fell in shovelfuls; rafters were laid bare; rats carried off this and that to gnaw behind the wainscots. Tortoiseshell butterflies burst from the chrysalis and pattered their life out on the window-pane. Poppies sowed themselves among the dahlias; the lawn waved with long grass; giant artichokes towered among roses; a fringed carnation flowered among the cabbages; while the gentle tapping of a weed at the window had become, on winters' nights, a drumming from sturdy trees and thorned briars which made the whole room green in summer.

What power could now prevent the fertility, the insensibility of nature? Mrs McNab's dream of a lady, of a child, of a plate of milk soup? It had wavered over the walls like a spot of sunlight and vanished. She had locked the door; she had gone. It was beyond the strength of one woman, she said. They never sent. They never wrote. There were things up there rotting in the drawers—it was a shame to leave them so, she said. The place was gone to rack and ruin. Only the Lighthouse beam entered the rooms for a moment, sent its sudden stare over bed and wall in the darkness of winter, looked with equanimity at the thistle and the swallow, the rat and the straw. Nothing now withstood them; nothing said no to them. Let the wind blow; let the poppy seed itself and the carnation mate with the cabbage. Let the swallow build in the drawing-room, and the thistle thrust aside the tiles, and the butterfly sun itself on the faded chintz of the armchairs. Let the broken glass and the china lie out on the lawn and be tangled over with grass and wild berries.

For now had come that moment, that hesitation when dawn trembles and night pauses, when if a feather alight in the scale it will be weighed down. One feather, and the house, sinking, falling, would have turned and pitched downwards to the depths of darkness. In the ruined room, picnickers would have lit their kettles; lovers sought shelter there, lying on the bare boards; and the shepherd stored his dinner on the bricks; and the tramp slept with his coat round him to ward off the cold. Then the roof would have fallen; briars and hemlocks would have blotted out path, step, and window; would have grown, unequally but lustily over the mound, until some trespasser, losing his way, could have told only by a red-hot poker among the nettles, or a scrap of china in the hemlock, that here once someone had lived; there had been a house.

If the feather had fallen, if it had tipped the scale downwards, the whole house would have plunged to the depths to lie upon the sands of oblivion. But there was a force working; something not highly conscious; something that leered, something that lurched; something not inspired to go about its work with dignified ritual or solemn chanting. Mrs McNab groaned; Mrs Bast creaked. They were old; they were stiff; their legs ached. They came with their brooms and pails at last; they got to work. All of a sudden, would Mrs McNab see that the house was ready, one of the young ladies wrote: would she get this done; would she get that done; all in a hurry. They might be coming for the summer; had left everything to the last; expected to find things as they had left them. Slowly and painfully, with broom and pail, mopping, scouring, Mrs McNab, Mrs Bast stayed the corruption and the rot; rescued from the pool of Time that was fast closing over them now a basin, now a cupboard; fetched up from oblivion all the Waverley novels and a tea-set one morning; in the afternoon restored to sun and air a brass fender and a set of steel fire-irons. George, Mrs Bast's son, caught the rats, and cut the grass. They had the builders. Attended with the creaking of hinges and the screeching of bolts, the slamming and banging of damp-swollen woodwork, some rusty laborious birth seemed to be taking place, as the women, stooping, rising, groaning, singing, slapped and slammed, upstairs now now down the cellars. Oh, they said, the work!

They drank their tea in the bedroom sometimes, or in the study; breaking off work at mid-day with the smudge on their faces, and their old hands clasped and cramped with the broom handles. Flopped on chairs they contemplated now the magnificent conquest over taps and bath; now the more arduous, more partial triumph over long rows of books, black as ravens once, now white-stained, breeding pale mush-rooms and secreting furtive spiders. Once more, as she felt the tea warm in her, the telescope fitted itself to Mrs McNab's eyes, and in a ring of light she saw the old gentleman, lean as a rake, wagging his head, as she came up with the washing, talking to himself, she supposed, on the lawn. He never noticed her. Some said he was dead; some said she was dead. Which was it? Mrs Bast didn't know for certain either. The young gentleman was dead. That she was sure. She had read his name in the papers.

There was the cook now, Mildred, Marian, some such name as that—a red-headed woman, quick-tempered like all her sort, but kind, too, if you knew the way with her. Many a laugh they had had together. She saved a plate of soup for Maggie; a bite of ham, sometimes; whatever was over. They lived well in those days. They had everything they wanted (glibly, jovially, with the tea hot in her, she unwound her ball of memories, sitting in the wicker armchair by the nursery fender). There was always plenty doing, people in the house, twenty staying sometimes, and washing up till long past midnight.

Mrs Bast (she had never known them; had lived in Glasgow at that time) wondered, putting her cup down, whatever they hung that beast's skull there for? Shot in foreign parts no doubt.

It might well be, said Mrs McNab, wantoning on with her memories; they had friends in eastern countries; gentlemen staying there, ladies in evening dress; she had seen them once through the dining-room door all sitting at dinner. Twenty she dared say in all their jewellery, and she asked to stay help wash up, might be till after midnight.

Ah, said Mrs Bast, they'd find it changed. She leant out of the window. She watched her son George scything the grass. They might well ask, what had been done to it? seeing how old Kennedy was supposed to have charge of it, and then his leg got so bad after he fell from the cart; and perhaps then no one for a year, or the better part of one; and then Davie Macdonald, and seeds might be sent, but who should say if they were ever planted? They'd find it changed.

She watched her son scything. He was a great one for work—one of those quiet ones. Well they must be getting along with the cupboards, she supposed. They hauled themselves up.

At last, after days of labour within, of cutting and digging without, dusters were flicked from the windows, the windows were shut to, keys were turned all over the house; the front door was banged; it was finished.

And now as if the cleaning and the scrubbing and the scything and the mowing had drowned it there rose that half-heard melody, that intermittent music which the ear half catches but lets fall; a bark, a bleat; irregular, intermittent, yet somehow related; the hum of an insect, the tremor of cut grass, dissevered yet somehow belonging; the jar of a dor beetle, the squeak of a wheel, loud, low, but mysteriously related; which the ear strains to bring together and is always on the verge of harmonizing but they are never quite heard, never fully harmonized, and at last, in the evening, one after another the sounds die out, and the harmony falters, and silence falls. With the sunset sharpness was lost, and like mist rising, quiet rose, quiet spread, the wind settled; loosely the world shook itself down to sleep, darkly here without a light to it, save what came green suffused through leaves, or pale on the white flowers by the window.

[Lily Briscoe had her bag carried up to the house late one evening in September. Mr Carmichael came by the same train.]

10

Then indeed peace had come. Messages of peace breathed from the sea to the shore. Never to break its sleep any more, to lull it rather more deeply to rest and whatever the dreamers dreamt holily, dreamt wisely, to confirm—what else was it murmuring—as Lily Briscoe laid her head on the pillow in the clean still room and heard the sea. Through the open window the voice of the beauty of the world came murmuring, too softly to hear exactly what it said—but what mattered if the meaning were plain?—entreating the sleepers (the house was full again; Mrs Beckwith was staying there, also Mr Carmichael), if they would not actually come down to the beach itself at least to lift the blind and look out. They would see then night flowing down in purple; his head crowned; his sceptre jewelled; and how in his eyes a child might look.

And if they still faltered (Lily was tired out with travelling and slept almost at once; but Mr Carmichael read a book by candlelight), if they still said no, that it was vapour this splendour of his, and the dew had more power than he, and they preferred sleeping; gently then without complaint, or argument, the voice would sing its song. Gently the waves would break (Lily heard them in her sleep); tenderly the light fell (it seemed to come through her eyelids). And it all looked, Mr Carmichael thought, shutting his book, falling asleep, much as it used to look years ago.

Indeed the voice might resume, as the curtains of dark wrapped themselves over the house, over Mrs Beckwith, Mr Carmichael, and Lily Briscoe so that they lay with several folds of blackness on their eyes, why not accept this, be content with this, acquiesce and resign? The sigh of all the seas breaking in measure round the isles soothed them; the night wrapped them; nothing broke their sleep, until, the birds beginning and the dawn weaving their thin voices into its whiteness, a cart grinding, a dog somewhere barking, the sun lifted the curtains, broke the veil on their eyes, and Lily Briscoe stirring in her sleep clutched at her blankets as a faller clutches at the turf on the edge of a cliff. Her eyes opened wide. Here she was again, she thought, sitting bolt upright in bed. Awake.

III

THE LIGHTHOUSE

What does it mean then, what can it all mean? Lily Briscoe asked herself, wondering whether, since she had been left alone, it behoved her to go to the kitchen to fetch another cup of coffee or wait here. What does it mean?—a catchword that was, caught up from some book, fitting her thought loosely, for she could not, this first morning with the Ramsays, contract her feelings, could only make a phrase resound to cover the blankness of her mind until these vapours had shrunk. For really, what did she feel, come back after all these years and Mrs Ramsay dead? Nothing, nothing—nothing that she could express at all.

She had come late last night when it was all mysterious, dark. Now she was awake, at her old place at the breakfast table, but alone. It was very early too, not yet eight. There was this expedition—they were going to the Lighthouse, Mr Ramsay, Cam, and James. They should have gone already—they had to catch the tide or something. And Cam was not ready and James was not ready and Nancy had forgotten to order the sandwiches and Mr Ramsay had lost his temper and banged out of the room.

'What's the use of going now?' he had stormed.

Nancy had vanished. There he was, marching up and down the terrace in a rage. One seemed to hear doors slamming and voices calling all over the house. Now Nancy burst in, and asked, looking round the room, in a queer half dazed, half desperate way, 'What does one send to the Lighthouse?' as if she were forcing herself to do what she despaired of ever being able to do.

What does one send to the Lighthouse indeed! At any other time Lily could have suggested reasonably tea, tobacco, newspapers. But this morning everything seemed so extraordinarily queer that a question like Nancy's—What does one send to the Lighthouse?—opened doors in one's mind that went banging and swinging to and fro and made one keep asking, in a stupefied gape, What does one send? What does one do? Why is one sitting here after all?

Sitting alone (for Nancy went out again) among the clean cups at the long table she felt cut off from other people, able only to go on watching, asking, wondering. The house, the place, the morning, all seemed strangers to her. She had no attachment here, she felt, no relations with it, anything might happen, and whatever did happen, a step outside, a voice calling ('It's not in the cupboard; it's on the landing,' someone cried), was a question, as if the link that usually bound things together had been cut, and they floated up here, down there, off, anyhow. How aimless it was, how chaotic, how unreal it was, she thought, looking at her empty coffee cup. Mrs Ramsay dead; Andrew killed; Prue dead too—repeat it as she might, it roused no feeling in her. And we all get together in a house like this on a morning like this, she said, looking out of the window—it was a beautiful still day.

Suddenly Mr Ramsay raised his head as he passed and looked straight at her, with his distraught wild gaze which was yet so penetrating, as if he saw you, for one second, for the first time, for ever; and she pretended to drink out of her empty coffee cup so as to escape him—to escape his demand on her, to put aside a moment longer that imperious need. And he shook his head at her, and strode on ('Alone' she heard him say, 'Perished' she heard him say) and like everything else this strange morning the words became symbols, wrote themselves all over the grey-green walls. If only she could put them together, she felt, write them out in some sentence, then she would have got at the truth of things. Old Mr Carmichael came padding softly in, fetched his coffee, took his cup and made off to sit in the sun. The extraordinary unreality was frightening; but it was also exciting. Going to the Lighthouse. But what does one send to the Lighthouse? Perished. Alone. The grey-green light on the wall opposite. The empty places. Such were some of the parts, but how bring them together? she asked. As if any interruption would break the frail shape she was building on the table she turned her back to the window lest Mr Ramsay should see her. She must escape somehow, be alone somewhere. Suddenly she remembered. When she had sat there last ten years ago there had been a little sprig or leaf pattern on the table-cloth, which she had looked at in a moment of revelation. There had been a problem about a foreground of a picture. Move the tree to the middle, she had said. She had never finished that picture. It had been knocking about in her mind all these years. She would paint that picture now. Where were her paints, she wondered? Her paints, yes. She had left them in the hall last night. She would start at once. She got up quickly, before Mr Ramsay turned.

She fetched herself a chair. She pitched her easel with her precise old maidish movements on the edge of the lawn, not too close to Mr Carmichael, but close enough for his protection. Yes, it must have been precisely here that she had stood ten years ago. There was the wall; the hedge; the tree. The question was of some relation between those masses. She had borne it in her mind all these years. It seemed as if the solution had come to her: she knew now what she wanted to do.

But with Mr Ramsay bearing down on her, she could do nothing. Every time he approached—he was walking up and down the terrace—ruin approached, chaos approached. She could not paint. She stooped, she turned; she took up this rag; she squeezed that tube. But all she did was to ward him off a moment. He made it impossible for her to do anything. For if she gave him the least chance, if he saw her disengaged a moment, looking his way a moment, he would be on her, saying, as he had said last night, 'You find us much changed.' Last night he had got up and stopped before her, and said that. Dumb and staring though they had all sat, the six children whom they used to call after the Kings and Queens of England—the Red, the Fair, the Wicked, the Ruthless,—she felt how they raged under it. Kind old Mrs Beckwith said something sensible. But it was a house full of unrelated passions—she had felt that all the evening. And on top of this chaos Mr Ramsay got up, pressed her hand, and said: 'You will find us much changed' and none of them had moved or had spoken; but had sat there as if they were forced to let him say it. Only James (certainly the Sullen) scowled at the lamp; and Cam screwed her handkerchief round her finger. Then he reminded them that they were going to the Lighthouse tomorrow. They must be ready, in the hall, on the stroke of half-past seven. Then, with his hand on the door, he stopped; he turned upon them. Did they not want to go? he demanded. Had they dared say No (he had some reason for wanting it) he would have flung himself tragically backwards into the bitter waters of despair. Such a gift he had for gesture. He looked like a king in exile. Doggedly James said yes. Cam stumbled more wretchedly. Yes, oh yes, they'd both be ready, they said. And it struck her, this was tragedy—not palls, dust, and the shroud; but children coerced, their spirits subdued. James was sixteen, Cam seventeen, perhaps. She had looked round for someone who was not there, for Mrs Ramsay, presumably. But there was only kind Mrs Beckwith turning over her sketches under the lamp. Then, being tired, her mind still rising and falling with the sea, the taste and smell that places have after long absence possessing her, the candles wavering in her eyes, she had lost herself and gone under. It was a wonderful night, starlit; the waves sounded as they went upstairs; the moon surprised them, enormous, pale, as they passed the staircase window. She had slept at once.

She set her clean canvas firmly upon the easel, as a barrier, frail, but she hoped sufficiently substantial to ward off Mr Ramsay and his exactingness. She did her best to look, when his back was turned, at her picture; that line there, that mass there. But it was out of the question. Let him be fifty feet away, let him not even speak to you, let him not even see you, he permeated, he prevailed, he imposed himself. He changed everything. She could not see the colour; she could not see the lines; even with his back turned to her, she could only think, But he'll be down on me in a moment, demanding—something she felt she could not give him. She rejected one brush; she chose another. When would those children come? When would they all be off? she fidgeted. That man, she thought, her anger rising in her, never gave; that man took. She, on the other hand, would be forced to give. Mrs Ramsay had given. Giving, giving, giving, she had died—and had left all this. Really, she was angry with Mrs Ramsay. With the brush slightly trembling in her fingers she looked at the hedge, the step, the wall. It was all Mrs Ramsay's doing. She was dead. Here was Lily, at forty-four, wasting her time, unable to do a thing, standing there, playing at painting, playing at the one thing one did not play at, and it was all Mrs Ramsay's fault. She was dead. The step where she used to sit was empty. She was dead.

But why repeat this over and over again? Why be always trying to bring up some feeling she had not got? There was a kind of blasphemy in it. It was all dry: all withered: all spent. They ought not to have asked her; she ought not to have come. One can't waste one's time at forty-four, she thought. She hated playing at painting. A brush, the one dependable thing in a world of strife, ruin, chaos—that one should not play with, knowingly even: she detested it. But he made her. You shan't touch your canvas, he seemed to say, bearing down on her, till you've given me what I want of you. Here he was, close upon her again, greedy, distraught. Well, thought Lily in despair, letting her right hand fall at her side, it would be simpler then to have it over. Surely she could imitate from recollection the glow, the rhapsody, the self-surrender she had seen on so many women's faces (on Mrs Ramsay's, for instance) when on some occasion like this they blazed up—she could remember the look on Mrs Ramsay's face—into a rapture of sympathy, of delight in the reward they had, which, though the reason of it escaped her, evidently conferred on them the most supreme bliss of which human nature was capable. Here he was, stopped by her side. She would give him what she could.

2

She seemed to have shrivelled slightly, he thought. She looked a little skimpy, wispy; but not unattractive. He liked her. There had been some talk of her marrying William Bankes once, but nothing had come of it. His wife had been fond of her. He had been a little out of temper too at breakfast. And then, and then—this was one of those moments when an enormous need urged him, without being conscious what it was, to approach any woman, to force them, he did not care how, his need was so great, to give him what he wanted: sympathy.

Was anybody looking after her? he said. Had she everything she wanted?

'Oh, thanks, everything,' said Lily Briscoe nervously. No; she could not do it. She ought to have floated off instantly upon some wave of sympathetic expansion: the pressure on her was tremendous. But she remained stuck. There was an awful pause. They both looked at the sea. Why, thought Mr Ramsay, should she look at the sea when I am here? She hoped it would be calm enough for them to land at the Lighthouse, she said. The Lighthouse! The Lighthouse! What's that got to do with it? he thought impatiently. Instantly, with the force of some primeval gust (for really he could not restrain himself any longer), there issued from him such a groan that any other woman in the whole world would have done something, said something—all except myself, thought Lily, girding at herself bitterly, who am not a woman, but a peevish, ill-tempered, dried-up old maid presumably.

Mr Ramsay sighed to the full. He waited. Was she not going to say anything? Did she not see what he wanted from her? Then he said he had a particular reason for wanting to go to the Lighthouse. His wife used to send the men things. There was a poor boy with a tuberculous hip, the lightkeeper's son. He sighed profoundly. He sighed significantly. All Lily wished was that this enormous flood of grief, this insatiable hunger for sympathy, this demand that she should surrender herself up to him entirely, and even so he had sorrows enough to keep her supplied for ever, should leave her, should be diverted (she kept looking at the house, hoping for an interruption) before it swept her down in its flow.

'Such expeditions', said Mr Ramsay, scraping the ground with his toe, 'are very painful.' Still Lily said nothing. (She is a stock, she is a stone, he said to himself.) 'They are very exhausting,' he said, looking, with a sickly look that nauseated her (he was acting, she felt, this great man was dramatizing himself), at his beautiful hands. It was horrible, it was indecent. Would they never come, she asked, for she could not sustain this enormous weight of sorrow, support these heavy draperies of grief (he had assumed a pose of extreme decrepitude; he even tottered a little as he stood there) a moment longer.

Still she could say nothing; the whole horizon seemed swept bare of objects to talk about; could only feel, amazedly, as Mr Ramsay stood there, how his gaze seemed to fall dolefully over the sunny grass and discolour it, and cast over the rubicund, drowsy, entirely contented figure of Mr Carmichael, reading a French novel on a deck-chair, a veil of crape, as if such an existence, flaunting its prosperity in a world of woe, were enough to provoke the most dismal thoughts of all. Look at him, he seemed to be saying, look at me; and indeed, all the time he was feeling, Think of me, think of me. Ah, could that bulk only be wafted alongside of them, Lily wished; had she only pitched her easel a yard or two closer to him; a man, any man, would staunch this effusion, would stop these lamentations. A woman, she had provoked this horror; a woman, she should have known how to deal with it. It was immensely to her discredit, sexually, to stand there dumb. One said—what did one say?—Oh, Mr Ramsay! Dear Mr Ramsay! That was what that kind old lady who sketched, Mrs Beckwith, would have said instantly, and rightly. But no. They stood there, isolated from the rest of the world. His immense self-pity, his demand for sympathy poured and spread itself in pools at her feet, and all she did, miserable sinner that she was, was to draw her skirts a little closer round her ankles, lest she should get wet. In complete silence she stood there, grasping her paint brush.

Heaven could never be sufficiently praised! She heard sounds in the house. James and Cam must be coming. But Mr Ramsay, as if he knew that his time ran short, exerted upon her solitary figure the immense pressure of his concentrated woe; his age; his frailty; his desolation; when suddenly, tossing his head impatiently, in his annoyance—for, after all, what woman could resist him?—he noticed that his boot-laces were untied. Remarkable boots they were too, Lily thought, looking down at them: sculptured; colossal; like everything that Mr Ramsay wore, from his frayed tie to his half-buttoned waistcoat, his own indisputably. She could see them walking to his room of their own accord, expressive in his absence of pathos, surliness, ill-temper, charm.

'What beautiful boots!' she exclaimed. She was ashamed of herself. To praise his boots when he asked her to solace his soul; when he had shown her his bleeding hands, his lacerated heart, and asked her to pity them, then to say, cheerfully, 'Ah, but what beautiful boots you wear!' deserved, she knew, and she looked up expecting to get it, in one of his sudden roars of ill-temper, complete annihilation.

Instead, Mr Ramsay smiled. His pall, his draperies, his infirmities fell from him. Ah yes, he said, holding his foot up for her to look at, they were first-rate boots. There was only one man in England who could make boots like that. Boots are among the chief curses of mankind, he said. 'Bootmakers make it their business', he exclaimed, 'to cripple and torture the human foot.' They are also the most obstinate and perverse of mankind. It had taken him the best part of his youth to get boots made as they should be made. He would have her observe (he lifted his right foot and then his left) that she had never seen boots made quite that shape before. They were made of the finest leather in the world, also. Most leather was mere brown paper and cardboard. He looked complacently at his foot, still held in the air. They had reached, she felt, a sunny island where peace dwelt, sanity reigned and the sun for ever shone, the blessed island of good boots. Her heart warmed to him. 'Now let me see if you can tie a knot,' he said. He poohpoohed her feeble system. He showed her his own invention. Once you tied it, it never came undone. Three times he knotted her shoe; three times he unknotted it.

Why, at this completely inappropriate moment, when he was stooping over her shoe, should she be so tormented with sympathy for him that, as she stooped too, the blood rushed to her face, and, thinking of her callousness (she had called him a play-actor) she felt her eyes swell and tingle with tears? Thus occupied he seemed to her a figure of infinite pathos. He tied knots. He bought boots. There was no helping Mr Ramsay on the journey he was going. But now just as she wished to say something, could have said something, perhaps, here they were—Cam and James. They appeared on the terrace. They came, lagging, side by side, a serious, melancholy couple.

But why was it like *that* that they came? She could not help feeling annoyed with them; they might have come more cheerfully; they might have given him what, now that they were off, she would not have the chance of giving him. For she felt a sudden emptiness; a frustration. Her feeling had come too late; there it was ready; but he no longer needed it. He had become a very distinguished, elderly man, who had no need of her whatsoever. She felt snubbed. He slung a knapsack round his shoulders. He shared out the parcels—there were a number of them, ill tied, in brown paper. He sent Cam for a cloak. He had all the appearance of a leader making ready for an expedition. Then, wheeling about, he led the way with his firm military tread, in those wonderful boots, carrying brown paper parcels, down the path, his children following him. They looked, she thought, as if fate had devoted them to some stern enterprise, and they went to it, still young enough to be drawn acquiescent in their father's wake, obediently, but with a pallor in their eyes which made her feel that they suffered something beyond their years in silence. So they passed the edge of the lawn, and it seemed to Lily that she watched a procession go, drawn on by some stress of common feeling which made it, faltering and flagging as it was, a little company bound together and strangely impressive to her. Politely, but very distantly, Mr Ramsay raised his hand and saluted her as they passed.

But what a face, she thought, immediately finding the sympathy which she had not been asked to give troubling her for expression. What had made it like that? Thinking, night after night, she supposed—about the reality of kitchen tables, she added, remembering the symbol which in her vagueness as to what Mr Ramsay did think about Andrew had given her. (He had been killed by the splinter of a shell instantly, she bethought her.) The kitchen table was something visionary, austere; something bare, hard, not ornamental. There was no colour to it; it was all edges and angles; it was uncompromisingly plain. But Mr Ramsay kept always his eyes fixed upon it, never allowed himself to be distracted or deluded, until his face became worn too and ascetic and partook of this unornamented beauty which so deeply impressed her. Then, she recalled (standing where he had left her, holding her brush), worries had fretted it—not so nobly. He must have had his doubts about that table, she supposed; whether the table was a real table; whether it was worth the time he gave to it; whether he was able after all to find it. He had had doubts, she felt, or he would have asked less of people. That was what they talked about late at night sometimes, she suspected; and then next day Mrs Ramsay looked tired, and Lily flew into a rage with him over some absurd little thing. But now he had nobody to talk to about that table, or his boots, or his knots; and he was like a lion seeking whom he could devour, and his face had that touch of desperation, of exaggeration in it which alarmed her, and made her pull her skirts about her. And then, she recalled, there was that sudden revivification, that sudden flare (when she praised his boots), that sudden recovery of vitality and interest in ordinary human things, which too passed and changed (for he was always changing, and hid nothing) into that other final phase which was new to her and had, she owned, made herself ashamed of her own irritability, when it seemed as if he had shed worries and ambitions, and the hope of sympathy and the desire for praise, had entered some other region, was drawn on, as if by curiosity, in dumb colloquy, whether with himself or another, at the head of that little procession out of one's range. An extraordinary face! The gate banged.

3

So they're gone, she thought, sighing with relief and disappointment. Her sympathy seemed to fly back in her face, like a bramble sprung. She felt curiously divided, as if one part of her were drawn out there—it was a still day, hazy; the Lighthouse looked this morning at an immense distance; the other had fixed itself doggedly, solidly, here on the lawn. She saw her canvas as if it had floated up and placed itself white and uncompromising directly before her. It seemed to rebuke her with its cold stare for all this hurry and agitation; this folly and waste of emotion; it drastically recalled her and spread through her mind first a peace, as her disorderly sensations (he had gone and she had been so sorry for him and she had said nothing) trooped off the field; and then, emptiness. She looked blankly at the canvas, with its uncompromising white stare; from the canvas to the garden. There was something (she stood screwing up her little Chinese eyes in her small puckered face) something she remembered in the relations of those lines cutting across, slicing down, and in the mass of the hedge with its green cave of blues and browns, which had stayed in her mind; which had tied a knot in her mind so that at odds and ends of time, involuntarily, as she walked along the Brompton Road, as she brushed her hair, she found herself painting that picture, passing her eye over it, and untying the knot in imagination. But there was all the difference in the world between this planning airily away from the canvas, and actually taking her brush and making the first mark.

She had taken the wrong brush in her agitation at Mr Ramsay's presence, and her easel, rammed into the earth so nervously, was at the wrong angle. And now that she had put that right, and in so doing had subdued the impertinences and irrelevances that plucked her attention and made her remember how she was such and such a person, had such and such relations to people, she took her hand and raised her brush. For a moment it stayed trembling in a painful but exciting ecstasy in the air. Where to begin?—that was the question; at what point to make the first mark? One line placed on the canvas committed her to innumerable risks, to frequent and irrevocable decisions. All that in idea seemed simple became in practice immediately complex; as the waves shape themselves symmetrically from the cliff top, but to the swimmer among them are divided by steep gulfs, and foaming crests. Still the risk must be run; the mark made.

With a curious physical sensation, as if she were urged forward and at the same time must hold herself back, she made her first quick decisive stroke. The brush descended. It flickered brown over the white canvas; it left a running mark. A second time she did it—a third time. And so pausing and so flickering, she attained a dancing rhythmical movement, as if the pauses were one part of the rhythm and the strokes another, and all were related; and so, lightly and swiftly pausing, striking, she scored her canvas with brown running nervous lines which had no sooner settled there than they enclosed (she felt it looming out at her) a space. Down in the hollow of one wave she saw the next wave towering higher and higher above her. For what could be more formidable than that space? Here she was again, she thought, stepping back to look at it, drawn out of gossip, out of living, out of community with people into the presence of this formidable ancient enemy of hers—this other thing, this truth, this reality, which suddenly laid hands on her, emerged stark at the back of appearances and commanded her attention. She was half unwilling, half reluctant. Why always be drawn out and haled away? Why not left in peace, to talk to Mr Carmichael on the lawn? It was an exacting form of intercourse anyhow. Other worshipful objects were content with worship; men, women, God, all let one kneel prostrate; but this form, were it only the shape of a white lamp-shade looming on a wicker table, roused one to perpetual combat, challenged one to a fight in which one was bound to be worsted. Always (it was in her nature, or in her sex, she did not know which) before she exchanged the fluidity of life for the concentration of painting she had a few moments of nakedness when she seemed like an unborn soul, a soul reft of body, hesitating on some windy pinnacle and exposed without protection to all the blasts of doubt. Why then did she do it? She looked at the canvas, lightly scored with running lines. It would be hung in the servants' bedrooms. It would be rolled up and stuffed under a sofa. What was the good of doing it then, and she heard some voice saying she couldn't paint, saying she couldn't create, as if she were caught up in one of those habitual currents which after a certain time forms experience in the mind, so that one repeats words without being aware any longer who originally spoke them.

Can't paint, can't write, she murmured monotonously, anxiously considering what her plan of attack should be. For the mass loomed before her; it protruded; she felt it pressing on her eyeballs. Then, as if some juice necessary for the lubrication of her faculties were spontaneously squirted, she began precariously dipping among the blues and umbers, moving her brush hither and thither, but it was now heavier and went slower, as if it had fallen in with some rhythm which was dictated to her (she kept looking at the hedge, at the canvas) by what she saw, so that while her hand quivered with life, this rhythm was strong enough to bear her along with it on its current. Certainly she was losing consciousness of outer things. And as she lost consciousness of outer things, and her name and her personality and her appearance, and whether Mr Carmichael was there or not, her mind kept throwing up from its depths, scenes, and names, and sayings, and memories and ideas, like a fountain spurting over that glaring, hideously difficult white space, while she modelled it with greens and blues.

Charles Tansley used to say that, she remembered, women can't paint, can't write. Coming up behind her he had stood close beside her, a thing she hated, as she painted here on this very spot. 'Shag tobacco,' he said, 'fivepence an ounce,' parading his poverty, his principles. (But the war had drawn the sting of her femininity. Poor devils one thought, poor devils of both sexes, getting into such messes.) He was always carrying a book about under his arm—a purple book. He 'worked'. He sat, she remembered, working in a blaze of sun. At dinner he would sit right in the middle of the view. And then, she reflected, there was that scene on the beach. One must remember that. It was a windy morning. They had all gone to the beach. Mrs Ramsay sat and wrote letters by a rock. She wrote and wrote. 'Oh,' she said, looking up at last at something floating in the sea, 'is it a lobster pot? Is it an upturned boat?' She was so short-sighted that she could not see, and then Charles Tansley became as nice as he could possibly be. He began playing ducks and drakes. They chose little flat black stones and sent them skipping over the waves. Every now and then Mrs Ramsay looked up over her spectacles and laughed at them. What they said she could not remember, but only she and Charles throwing stones and getting on very well all of a sudden and Mrs Ramsay watching them. She was highly conscious of that. Mrs Ramsay, she thought, stepping back and screwing up her eyes. (It must have altered the design a good deal when she was sitting on the step with James. There must have been a shadow.) Mrs Ramsay. When she thought of herself and Charles throwing ducks and drakes and of the whole scene on the beach, it seemed to depend somehow upon Mrs Ramsay sitting under the rock, with a pad on her knee, writing letters. (She wrote innumerable letters, and sometimes the wind took them and she and Charles just saved a page from the sea.) But what a power was in the human soul! she thought. That woman sitting there, writing under the rock resolved everything into simplicity; made these angers, irritations fall off like old rags; she brought together this and that and then this, and so made out of that miserable silliness and spite (she and Charles squabbling, sparring, had been silly and spiteful) something—this scene on the beach for example, this moment of friendship and liking—which survived, after all these years, complete, so that she dipped into it to re-fashion her memory of him, and it stayed in the mind almost like a work of art.

'Like a work of art,' she repeated, looking from her canvas to the drawing-room steps and back again. She must rest for a moment. And, resting, looking from one to the other vaguely, the old question which traversed the sky of the soul perpetually, the vast, the general question which was apt to particularize itself at such moments as these, when she released faculties that had been on the strain, stood over her, paused over her, darkened over her. What is the meaning of life? That was all— a simple question; one that tended to close in on one with years. The great revelation had never come. The great revelation perhaps never did come. Instead there were little daily miracles, illuminations, matches struck unexpectedly in the dark; here was one. This, that, and the other; herself and Charles Tansley and the breaking wave; Mrs Ramsay bringing them together; Mrs Ramsay saying 'Life stand still here'; Mrs Ramsay making of the moment something permanent (as in another sphere Lily herself tried to make of the moment something permanent)— this was of the nature of a revelation. In the midst of chaos there was shape; this external passing and flowing (she looked at the clouds going and the leaves shaking) was stuck into stability. Life stand still here,

Mrs Ramsay said. 'Mrs Ramsay! Mrs Ramsay!' she repeated. She owed this revelation to her.

All was silence. Nobody seemed yet to be stirring in the house. She looked at it there sleeping in the early sunlight with its windows green and blue with the reflected leaves. The faint thought she was thinking of Mrs Ramsay seemed in consonance with this quiet house; this smoke; this fine early morning air. Faint and unreal, it was amazingly pure and exciting. She hoped nobody would open the window or come out of the house, but that she might be left alone to go on thinking, to go on painting. She turned to her canvas. But impelled by some curiosity, driven by the discomfort of the sympathy which she held undischarged, she walked a pace or so to the end of the lawn to see whether, down there on the beach, she could see that little company setting sail. Down there among the little boats which floated, some with their sails furled, some slowly, for it was very calm, moving away, there was one rather apart from the others. The sail was even now being hoisted. She decided that there in that very distant and entirely silent little boat Mr Ramsay was sitting with Cam and James. Now they had got the sail up; now after a little flagging and hesitation the sails filled and, shrouded in profound silence, she watched the boat take its way with deliberation past the other boats out to sea.

4

The sails flapped over their heads. The water chuckled and slapped the sides of the boat, which drowsed motionless in the sun. Now and then the sails rippled with a little breeze in them, but the ripple ran over them and ceased. The boat made no motion at all. Mr Ramsay sat in the middle of the boat. He would be impatient in a moment, James thought, and Cam thought, looking at their father, who sat in the middle of the boat between them (James steered; Cam sat alone in the bow) with his legs tightly curled. He hated hanging about. Sure enough, after fidgeting a second or two, he said something sharp to Macalister's boy, who got out his oars and began to row. But their father, they knew, would never be content until they were flying along. He would keep looking for a breeze, fidgeting, saying things under his breath, which Macalister and Macalister's boy would overhear, and they would both be made horribly uncomfortable. He had made them come. He had forced them to come. In their anger they hoped that the breeze would never rise, that he might be thwarted in every possible way, since he had forced them to come against their wills.

All the way down to the beach they had lagged behind together, though he bade them 'Walk up, walk up', without speaking. Their heads were bent down, their heads were pressed down by some remorseless gale. Speak to him they could not. They must come; they must follow. They must walk behind him carrying brown paper parcels. But they vowed, in silence, as they walked, to stand by each other and carry out the great compact—to resist tyranny to the death. So there they would sit, one at one end of the boat, one at the other, in silence. They would say nothing, only look at him now and then where he sat with his legs twisted, frowning and fidgeting, and pishing and pshawing and muttering things to himself, and waiting impatiently for a breeze. And they hoped it would be calm. They hoped he would be thwarted. They hoped the whole expedition would fail, and they would have to put back, with their parcels, to the beach.

But now, when Macalister's boy had rowed a little way out, the sails slowly swung round, the boat quickened itself, flattened itself, and shot off. Instantly, as if some great strain had been relieved, Mr Ramsay uncurled his legs, took out his tobacco pouch, handed it with a little grunt to Macalister, and felt, they knew, for all they suffered, perfectly content. Now they would sail on for hours like this, and Mr Ramsay would ask old Macalister a question—about the great storm last winter probably—and old Macalister would answer it, and they would puff their pipes together, and Macalister would take a tarry rope in his fingers, tying or untying some knot, and the boy would fish, and never say a word to anyone. James would be forced to keep his eye all the time on the sail. For if he forgot, then the sail puckered, and shivered, and the boat slackened, and Mr Ramsay would say sharply, 'Look out! Look out!' and old Macalister would turn slowly on his seat. So they heard Mr Ramsay asking some question about the great storm at Christmas. 'She comes driving round the point,' old Macalister said, describing the great storm last Christmas, when ten ships had been driven into the bay for shelter, and he had seen 'one there, one there, one there' (he pointed slowly round the bay. Mr Ramsay followed him, turning his head.) He had seen three men clinging to the mast. Then she was gone. 'And at last we shoved her off,' he went on (but in their anger and their silence they only caught a word here and there, sitting at opposite ends of the boat, united by their compact to fight tyranny to the death). At last they had shoved her off, they had launched the lifeboat, and they had got her out past the point—Macalister told the story; and though they only caught a word here and there, they were conscious all the time of their father—how he leant forward, how he brought his voice into tune with Macalister's voice; how, puffing at his pipe, and looking there and there where Macalister pointed, he relished the thought of the storm and the dark night and the fishermen striving there. He liked that men should labour and sweat on the windy beach at night, pitting muscle and brain against the waves and the wind; he liked men to work like that, and women to keep house, and sit beside sleeping children indoors, while men were drowned, out there in a storm. So James could tell, so Cam could tell (they looked at him, they looked at each other), from his toss and his vigilance and the ring in his voice, and the little tinge of Scottish accent which came into his voice, making him seem like a peasant himself, as he questioned Macalister about the eleven ships that had been driven into the bay in a storm. Three had sunk.

He looked proudly where Macalister pointed; and Cam thought, feeling proud of him without knowing quite why, had he been there he would have launched the lifeboat, he would have reached the wreck, Cam thought. He was so brave, he was so adventurous, Cam thought. But she remembered. There was the compact; to resist tyranny to the death. Their grievance weighed them down. They had been forced; they had been bidden. He had borne them down once more with his gloom and his authority, making them do his bidding, on this fine morning, come, because he wished it, carrying these parcels to the Lighthouse; take part in those rites he went through for his own pleasure in memory of dead people, which they hated, so that they lagged after him, and all the pleasure of the day was spoilt.

Yes, the breeze was freshening. The boat was leaning, the water was sliced sharply and fell away in green cascades, in bubbles, in cataracts. Cam looked down into the foam, into the sea with all its treasure in it, and its speed hypnotized her, and the tie between her and James sagged a little. It slackened a little. She began to think, How fast it goes. Where are we going? and the movement hypnotized her, while James, with his eye fixed on the sail and on the horizon, steered grimly. But he began to think as he steered that he might escape; he might be quit of it all. They might land somewhere; and be free then. Both of them, looking at each other for a moment, had a sense of escape and exaltation, what with the speed and the change. But the breeze bred in Mr Ramsay too the same excitement, and, as old Macalister turned to fling his line overboard, he cried aloud, 'We perished,' and then again, 'each alone'. And then with his usual spasm of repentance or shyness, pulled himself up, and waved his hand towards the shore.

'See the little house,' he said pointing, wishing Cam to look. She raised herself reluctantly and looked. But which was it? She could no longer make out, there on the hillside, which was their house. All looked distant and peaceful and strange. The shore seemed refined, far away, unreal. Already the little distance they had sailed had put them far from it and given it the changed look, the composed look, of something receding in which one has no longer any part. Which was their house? She could not see it.

'But I beneath a rougher sea,' Mr Ramsay murmured. He had found the house and so seeing it, he had also seen himself there; he had seen himself walking on the terrace, alone. He was walking up and down between the urns; and he seemed to himself very old, and bowed. Sitting in the boat he bowed, he crouched himself, acting instantly his part— the part of a desolate man, widowed, bereft; and so called up before him in hosts people sympathizing with him; staged for himself as he sat in the boat, a little drama; which required of him decrepitude and exhaustion and sorrow (he raised his hands and looked at the thinness of them, to confirm his dream) and then there was given him in abundance women's sympathy, and he imagined how they would soothe him and sympathize with him, and so getting in his dream some reflection of the exquisite pleasure women's sympathy was to him, he sighed and said gently and mournfully,

> But I beneath a rougher sea
> Was whelmed in deeper gulfs than he,

so that the mournful words were heard quite clearly by them all. Cam half started on her seat. It shocked her—it outraged her. The movement roused her father; and he shuddered, and broke off, exclaiming: 'Look! Look!' so urgently that James also turned his head to look over his shoulder at the island. They all looked. They looked at the island.

But Cam could see nothing. She was thinking how all those paths and the lawn, thick and knotted with the lives they had lived there, were gone: were rubbed out; were past; were unreal, and now this was real; the boat and the sail with its patch; Macalister with his earrings; the noise of the waves—all this was real. Thinking this, she was murmuring to herself 'We perished, each alone,' for her father's words broke and broke again in her mind, when her father, seeing her gazing so vaguely, began to tease her. Didn't she know the points of the compass? he asked. Didn't she know the North from the South? Did she really think they lived right out there? And he pointed again, and showed her where their house was, there, by those trees. He wished she would try to be more accurate, he said: 'Tell me—which is East, which is West?' he said, half laughing at her, half scolding her, for he could not understand the state of mind of anyone, not absolutely imbecile, who did not know the points of the compass. Yet she did not know. And seeing her gazing, with her vague, now rather frightened, eyes fixed where no house was Mr Ramsay forgot his dream; how he walked up and down between the urns on the terrace; how the arms were stretched out to him. He thought, women are always like that; the vagueness of their minds is hopeless; it was a thing he had never been able to understand; but so it was. It had been so with her—his wife. They could not keep anything clearly fixed in their minds. But he had been wrong to be angry with her; moreover, did he not rather like this vagueness in women? It was part of their extraordinary charm. I will make her smile at me, he thought. She looks frightened. She was so silent. He clutched his fingers, and determined that his voice and his face and all the quick expressive gestures which had been at his command making people pity him and praise him all these years should subdue themselves. He would make her smile at him. He would find some simple easy thing to say to her. But what? For, wrapped up in his work as he was, he forgot the sort of thing one said. There was a puppy. They had a puppy. Who was looking after the puppy today? he asked. Yes, thought James pitilessly, seeing his sister's head against the sail, now she will give way. I shall be left to fight the tyrant alone. The compact would be left to him to carry out. Cam would never resist tyranny to the death, he thought grimly, watching her face, sad, sulky, yielding. And as sometimes happens when a cloud falls on a green hillside and gravity descends and there among all the surrounding hills is gloom and sorrow, and it seems as if the hills themselves must ponder the fate of the clouded, the darkened, either in pity, or maliciously rejoicing in her dismay: so Cam now felt herself overcast, as she sat there among calm, resolute people and wondered how to answer her father about the puppy; how to resist his entreaty—forgive me, care for me; while James the lawgiver, with the tablets of eternal wisdom laid open on his knee (his hand on the tiller had become symbolical to her), said, Resist him. Fight him. He said so rightly; justly. For they must fight tyranny to the death, she thought. Of all human qualities she reverenced justice most. Her brother was most god-like, her father most suppliant. And to which did she yield, she thought, sitting between them, gazing at the shore whose points were all unknown to her, and thinking how the lawn and the terrace and the house were smoothed away now and peace dwelt there.

'Jasper,' she said sullenly. He'd look after the puppy.

And what was she going to call him? her father persisted. He had had a dog when he was a little boy, called Frisk. She'll give way, James thought, as he watched a look come upon her face, a look he remembered. They look down, he thought, at their knitting or something. Then suddenly they look up. There was a flash of blue, he remembered, and then somebody sitting with him laughed, surrendered, and he was very angry. It must have been his mother, he thought, sitting on a low chair, with his father standing over her. He began to search among the infinite series of impressions which time had laid down, leaf upon leaf, fold upon fold softly, incessantly upon his brain; among scents, sounds; voices, harsh, hollow, sweet; and lights passing, and brooms tapping; and the wash and hush of the sea, how a man had marched up and down and stopped dead, upright, over them. Meanwhile, he noticed, Cam dabbled her fingers in the water, and stared at the shore and said nothing. No, she won't give way, he thought; she's different, he thought. Well, if Cam would not answer him, he would not bother her, Mr Ramsay decided, feeling in his pocket for a book. But she would answer him; she wished, passionately, to move some obstacle that lay upon her tongue and to say, Oh yes, Frisk. I'll call him Frisk. She wanted even to say, Was that the dog that found its way over the moor alone? But try as she might, she could think of nothing to say like that, fierce and loyal to the compact, yet passing on to her father, unsuspected by James, a private token of the love she felt for him. For she thought, dabbling her hand (and now Macalister's boy had caught a mackerel, and it lay kicking on the floor, with blood on its gills) for she thought, looking at James who kept his eyes dispassionately on the sail, or glanced now and then for a second at the horizon, you're not exposed to it, to this pressure and division of feeling, this extraordinary temptation. Her father was feeling in his pockets; in another second, he would have found his book. For no one attracted her more; his hands were beautiful to her and his feet, and his voice, and his words, and his haste, and his temper, and his oddity, and his passion, and his saying straight out before everyone, we perish, each alone, and his remoteness. (He had opened his book.) But what remained intolerable, she thought, sitting upright, and watching Macalister's boy tug the hook out of the gills of another fish, was that crass blindness and tyranny of his which had poisoned her childhood and raised bitter storms, so that even now she woke in the night trembling with rage and remembered some command of his; some insolence: 'Do this,' 'Do that,' his dominance: his 'Submit to me.'

So she said nothing, but looked doggedly and sadly at the shore, wrapped in its mantle of peace; as if the people there had fallen asleep, she thought; were free like smoke, were free to come and go like ghosts. They have no suffering there, she thought.

5

Yes, that is their boat, Lily Briscoe decided, standing on the edge of the lawn. It was the boat with greyish-brown sails, which she saw now flatten itself upon the water and shoot off across the bay. There he sits, she thought, and the children are quite silent still. And she could not reach him either. The sympathy she had not given him weighed her down. It made it difficult for her to paint.

She had always found him difficult. She had never been able to praise him to his face, she remembered. And that reduced their relationship to something neutral, without that element of sex in it which made his manner to Minta so gallant, almost gay. He would pick a flower for her, lend her his books. But could he believe that Minta read them? She dragged them about the garden, sticking in leaves to mark the place.

'D'you remember, Mr Carmichael?' she was inclined to ask, looking at the old man. But he had pulled his hat half over his forehead; he was asleep, or he was dreaming, or he was lying there catching words, she supposed.

'D'you remember?' she felt inclined to ask him as she passed him, thinking again of Mrs Ramsay on the beach; the cask bobbing up and down; and the pages flying. Why, after all these years had that survived, ringed round, lit up, visible to the last detail, with all before it blank and all after it blank, for miles and miles?

'Is it a boat? Is it a cork?' she would say, Lily repeated, turning back, reluctantly again, to her canvas. Heaven be praised for it, the problem of space remained, she thought, taking up her brush again. It glared at her. The whole mass of the picture was poised upon that weight. Beautiful and bright it should be on the surface, feathery and evanescent, one colour melting into another like the colours on a butterfly's wing; but beneath the fabric must be clamped together with bolts of iron. It was to be a thing you could ruffle with your breath; and a thing you could not dislodge with a team of horses. And she began to lay on a red, a grey, and she began to model her way into the hollow there. At the same time, she seemed to be sitting beside Mrs Ramsay on the beach.

'Is is a boat? Is it a cask?' Mrs Ramsay said. And she began hunting round for her spectacles. And she sat, having found them, silent, looking out to sea. And Lily, painting steadily, felt as if a door had opened, and one went in and stood gazing silently about in a high cathedral-like place, very dark, very solemn. Shouts came from a world far away. Steamers vanished in stalks of smoke on the horizon. Charles threw stones and sent them skipping.

Mrs Ramsay sat silent. She was glad, Lily thought, to rest in silence, uncommunicative; to rest in the extreme obscurity of human relationships. Who knows what we are, what we feel? Who knows even at the moment of intimacy. This is knowledge? Aren't things spoilt then, Mrs Ramsay may have asked (it seemed to have happened so often, this silence by her side) by saying them? Aren't we more expressive thus? The moment at least seemed extraordinarily fertile. She rammed a little hole in the sand and covered it up, by way of burying in it the perfection of the moment. It was like a drop of silver in which one dipped and illumined the darkness of the past.

Lily stepped back to get her canvas—so—into perspective. It was an odd road to be walking, this of painting. Out and out one went, further and further, until at last one seemed to be on a narrow plank, perfectly alone, over the sea. And as she dipped into the blue paint, she dipped too into the past there. Now Mrs Ramsay got up, she remembered. It was time to go back to the house—time for luncheon. And they all walked up from the beach together, she walking behind with William Bankes, and there was Minta in front of them with a hole in her stocking. How that little round hole of pink heel seemed to flaunt itself before them! How William Bankes deplored it, without, so far as she could remember, saying anything about it! It meant to him the annihilation of womanhood, and dirt and disorder, and servants leaving and beds not made at mid-day—all the things he most abhorred. He had a way of shuddering and spreading his fingers out as if to cover an unsightly object, which he did now—holding his hand in front of him. And Minta walked on ahead, and presumably Paul met her and she went off with Paul in the garden.

The Rayleys, thought Lily Briscoe, squeezing her tube of green paint. She collected her impressions of the Rayleys. Their lives appeared to her in a series of scenes; one, on the staircase at dawn. Paul had come in and gone to bed early; Minta was late. There was Minta, wreathed, tinted, garish on the stairs about three o'clock in the morning. Paul came out in his pyjamas carrying a poker in case of burglars. Minta was eating a sandwich, standing half-way up by a window, in the cadaverous early morning light, and the carpet had a hole in it. But what did they say? Lily asked herself, as if by looking she could hear them. Something violent. Minta went on eating her sandwich, annoyingly, while he spoke. He spoke indignant, jealous words, abusing her, in a mutter so as not to wake the children, the two little boys. He was withered, drawn; she flamboyant, careless. For things had worked loose after the first year or so; the marriage had turned out rather badly.

And this, Lily thought, taking the green paint on her brush, this making up scenes about them, is what we call 'knowing' people, 'thinking' of them, 'being fond' of them! Not a word of it was true; she had made it up; but it was what she knew them by all the same. She went on tunnelling her way into her picture, into the past.

Another time, Paul said he 'played chess in coffee-houses'. She had built up a whole structure of imagination on that saying too. She remembered how, as he said it, she thought how he rang up the servant, and she said 'Mrs Rayley's out, sir', and he decided that he would not come home either. She saw him sitting in the corner of some lugubrious place where the smoke attached itself to the red plush seats, and the waitresses got to know you, playing chess with a little man who was in the tea trade and lived at Surbiton, but that was all Paul knew about him. And then Minta was out when he came home and then there was that scene on the stairs, when he got the poker in case of burglars (no doubt to frighten her too) and spoke so bitterly, saying she had ruined his life. At any rate when she went down to see them at a cottage near Rickmansworth, things were horribly strained. Paul took her down the garden to look at the Belgian hares which he bred, and Minta followed them, singing, and put her bare arm on his shoulder, lest he should tell her anything.

Minta was bored by hares, Lily thought. But Minta never gave herself away. She never said things like that about playing chess in coffee-houses. She was far too conscious, far too wary. But to go on with their story—they had got through the dangerous stage by now. She had been staying with them last summer some time and the car broke down and Minta had to hand him his tools. He sat on the road mending the car, and it was the way she gave him the tools—business-like, straight-forward, friendly—that proved it was all right now. They were 'in love' no longer; no, he had taken up with another woman, a serious woman, with her hair in a plait and a case in her hand (Minta had described her gratefully, almost admiringly), who went to meetings and shared Paul's views (they had got more and more pronounced) about the taxation of land values and a capital levy. Far from breaking up the marriage, that alliance had righted it. They were excellent friends, obviously, as he sat on the road and she handed him his tools.

So that was the story of the Rayleys, Lily smiled. She imagined herself telling it to Mrs Ramsay, who would be full of curiosity to know what had become of the Rayleys. She would feel a little triumphant, telling Mrs Ramsay that the marriage had not been a success.

But the dead, thought Lily, encountering some obstacle in her design which made her pause and ponder, stepping back a foot or so, Oh the dead! she murmured, one pitied them, one brushed them aside, one had even a little contempt for them. They are at our mercy. Mrs Ramsay has faded and gone, she thought. We can over-ride her wishes, improve away her limited, old-fashioned ideas. She recedes further and further from us. Mockingly she seemed to see her there at the end of the corridor of years saying, of all incongruous things, 'Marry, marry!' (sitting very upright early in the morning with the birds beginning to cheep in the garden outside). And one would have to say to her, It has all gone against your wishes. They're happy like that; I'm happy like this. Life has changed completely. At that all her being, even her beauty, became for a moment, dusty and out of date. For a moment Lily, standing there, with the sun hot on her back, summing up the Rayleys, triumphed over Mrs Ramsay, who would never know how Paul went to coffee-houses and had a mistress; how he sat on the ground and Minta handed him his tools; how she stood here painting, had never married, not even William Bankes.

Mrs Ramsay had planned it. Perhaps, had she lived, she would have compelled it. Already that summer he was 'the kindest of men'. He was 'the first scientist of his age, my husband says'. He was also 'poor William—it makes me so unhappy, when I go to see him, to find nothing nice in his house—no one to arrange the flowers'. So they were sent for walks together, and she was told, with that faint touch of irony that made Mrs Ramsay slip through one's fingers, that she had a scientific mind; she liked flowers; she was so exact. What was this mania of hers for marriage? Lily wondered, stepping to and fro from her easel.

(Suddenly, as suddenly as a star slides in the sky, a reddish light seemed to burn in her mind, covering Paul Rayley, issuing from him. It rose like a fire sent up in token of some celebration by savages on a distant beach. She heard the roar and the crackle. The whole sea for miles round ran red and gold. Some winy smell mixed with it and intoxicated her, for she felt again her own headlong desire to throw herself off the cliff and be drowned looking for a pearl brooch on a beach. And the roar and the crackle repelled her with fear and disgust, as if while she saw its splendour and power she saw too how it fed on the treasure of the house, greedily, disgustingly, and she loathed it. But for a sight, for a glory it surpassed everything in her experience, and burnt year after year like a signal fire on a desert island at the edge of the sea, and one had only to say 'in love' and instantly, as happened now, up rose Paul's fire again. And it sank and she said to herself, laughing, 'The Rayleys'; how Paul went to coffee-houses and played chess.)

She had only escaped by the skin of her teeth though, she thought. She had been looking at the table-cloth, and it had flashed upon her that she would move the tree to the middle, and need never marry anybody, and she had felt an enormous exultation. She had felt now she could stand up to Mrs Ramsay—a tribute to the astonishing power that Mrs Ramsay had over one. Do this, she said, and one did it. Even her shadow at the window with James was full of authority. She remembered how William Bankes had been shocked by her neglect of the significance of mother and son. Did she not admire their beauty? he said. But William, she remembered, had listened to her with his wise child's eyes when she explained how it was not irreverence: how a light there needed a shadow there and so on. She did not intend to disparage a subject which, they agreed, Raphael had treated divinely. She was not cynical. Quite the contrary. Thanks to his scientific mind he understood—a proof of disinterested intelligence which had pleased her and comforted her enormously. One could talk of painting then seriously to a man. Indeed, his friendship had been one of the pleasures of her life. She loved William Bankes.

They went to Hampton Court and he always left her, like the perfect gentleman he was, plenty of time to wash her hands, while he strolled by the river. That was typical of their relationship. Many things were left unsaid. Then they strolled through the courtyards, and admired, summer after summer, the proportions and the flowers, and he would tell her things, about perspective, about architecture, as they walked, and he would stop to look at a tree, or the view over the lake, and admire a child (it was his great grief—he had no daughter) in the vague aloof way that was natural to a man who spent so much time in laboratories that the world when he came out seemed to dazzle him, so that he walked slowly, lifted his hand to screen his eyes and paused, with his head thrown back, merely to breathe the air. Then he would tell her how his housekeeper was on her holiday; he must buy a new carpet for the staircase. Perhaps she would go with him to buy a new carpet for the staircase. And once something led him to talk about the Ramsays and he had said how when he first saw her she had been wearing a grey hat; she was not more than nineteen or twenty. She was astonishingly beautiful. There he stood looking down the avenue at Hampton Court, as if he could see her there among the fountains.

She looked now at the drawing-room step. She saw, through William's eyes, the shape of a woman, peaceful and silent, with downcast eyes. She sat musing, pondering (she was in grey that day, Lily thought). Her eyes were bent. She would never lift them. Yes, thought Lily, looking intently, I must have seen her look like that, but not in grey; nor so still, nor so young, nor so peaceful. The figure came readily enough. She was astonishingly beautiful, William said. But beauty was not everything. Beauty had this penalty—it came too readily, came too completely. It stilled life—froze it. One forgot the little agitations; the flush, the pallor, some queer distortion, some light or shadow, which made the face unrecognizable for a moment and yet added a quality one saw for ever after. It was simpler to smooth that all out under the cover of beauty. But what was the look she had, Lily wondered, when she clapped her deer-stalker's hat on her head, or ran across the grass, or scolded Kennedy, the gardener? Who could tell her? Who could help her?

Against her will she had come to the surface, and found herself half out of the picture, looking, a little dazedly, as if at unreal things, at Mr Carmichael. He lay on his chair with his hands clasped above his paunch not reading, or sleeping, but basking like a creature gorged with existence. His book had fallen on to the grass.

She wanted to go straight up to him and say, 'Mr Carmichael!' Then he would look up benevolently as always, from his smoky vague green eyes. But one only woke people if one knew what one wanted to say to them. And she wanted to say not one thing, but everything. Little words that broke up the thought and dismembered it said nothing. 'About life, about death; about Mrs Ramsay'—no, she thought, one could say nothing to nobody. The urgency of the moment always missed its mark. Words fluttered sideways and struck the object inches too low. Then one gave it up; then the idea sunk back again; then one became like most middle-aged people, cautious, furtive, with wrinkles between the eyes and a look of perpetual apprehension. For how could one express in words these emotions of the body? express that emptiness there? (She was looking at the drawing-room steps; they looked extraordinarily empty.) It was one's body feeling, not one's mind. The physical sensations that went with the bare look of the steps had become suddenly extremely unpleasant. To want and not to have, sent all up her body a hardness, a hollowness, a strain. And then to want and not to have—to want and want—how that wrung the heart, and wrung it again and again! Oh Mrs Ramsay! she called out silently, to that essence which sat by the boat, that abstract one made of her, that woman in grey, as if to abuse her for having gone, and then having gone, come back again. It had seemed so safe, thinking of her. Ghost, air, nothingness, a thing you could play with easily and safely at any time of day or night, she had been that, and then suddenly she put her hand out and wrung the heart thus. Suddenly, the empty drawing-room steps, the frill of the chair inside, the puppy tumbling on the terrace, the whole wave and whisper of the garden became like curves and arabesques flourishing round a centre of complete emptiness.

'What does it mean? How do you explain it all?' she wanted to say, turning to Mr Carmichael again. For the whole world seemed to have dissolved in this early morning hour into a pool of thought, a deep basin of reality, and one could almost fancy that had Mr Carmichael spoken, a little tear would have rent the surface of the pool. And then? Something would emerge. A hand would be shoved up, a blade would be flashed. It was nonsense of course.

A curious notion came to her that he did after all hear the things she could not say. He was an inscrutable old man, with the yellow stain on his beard, and his poetry, and his puzzles, sailing serenely through a world which satisfied all his wants, so that she thought he had only to put down his hand where he lay on the lawn to fish up anything he wanted. She looked at her picture. That would have been his answer, presumably—how 'you' and 'I' and 'she' pass and vanish; nothing stays; all changes; but not words, not paint. Yet it would be hung in the attics, she thought; it would be rolled up and flung under a sofa; yet even so, even of a picture like that, it was true. One might say, even of this scrawl, not of that actual picture, perhaps, but of what it attempted, that it 'remained for ever', she was going to say, or, for the word spoken sounded even to herself, too boastful, to hint, wordlessly; when, looking at the picture, she was surprised to find that she could not see it. Her eyes were full of a hot liquid (she did not think of tears at first) which, without disturbing the firmness of her lips, made the air thick, rolled down her cheeks. She had perfect control of herself—Oh yes!—in every other way. Was she crying then for Mrs Ramsay, without being aware of any unhappiness? She addressed old Mr Carmichael again. What was it then? What did it mean? Could things thrust their hands up and grip one; could the blade cut; the fist grasp? Was there no safety? No learning by heart of the ways of the world? No guide, no shelter, but all was miracle, and leaping from the pinnacle of a tower into the air? Could it be, even for elderly people, that this was life?—startling, unexpected, unknown? For one moment she felt that if they both got up, here, now on the lawn, and demanded an explanation, why was it so short, why was it so inexplicable, said it with violence, as two fully equipped human beings from whom nothing should be hid might speak, then, beauty would roll itself up; the space would fill; those empty flourishes would form into shape; if they shouted loud enough Mrs Ramsay would return. 'Mrs Ramsay!' she said aloud, 'Mrs Ramsay!' The tears ran down her face.

6

[Macalister's boy took one of the fish and cut a square out of its side to bait his hook with. The mutilated body (it was alive still) was thrown back into the sea.]

7

'Mrs Ramsay!' Lily cried, 'Mrs Ramsay!' But nothing happened. The pain increased. That anguish could reduce one to such a pitch of imbecility, she thought! Anyhow the old man had not heard her. He remained benignant, calm—if one chose to think it, sublime. Heaven be praised, no one had heard her cry that ignominious cry, stop pain, stop! She had not obviously taken leave of her senses. No one had seen her step off her strip of board into the waters of annihilation. She remained a skimpy old maid, holding a paint-brush on the lawn.

And now slowly the pain of the want, and the bitter anger (to be called back, just as she thought she would never feel sorrow for Mrs Ramsay again. Had she missed her among the coffee cups at breakfast? not in the least) lessened; and of their anguish left, as antidote, a relief that was balm in itself, and also, but more mysteriously, a sense of someone there, of Mrs Ramsay, relieved for a moment of the weight that the world had put on her, staying lightly by her side and then (for this was Mrs Ramsay in all her beauty) raising to her forehead a wreath of white flowers with which she went. Lily squeezed her tubes again. She attacked that problem of the hedge. It was strange how clearly she saw her, stepping with her usual quickness across the fields among whose folds, purplish and soft, among whose flowers, hyacinths or lilies, she vanished. It was some trick of the painter's eye. For days after she had heard of her death she had seen her thus, putting her wreath to her forehead and going unquestionably with her companion, a shadow, across the fields. The sight, the phrase, had its power to console. Wherever she happened to be, painting, here, in the country or in London, the vision would come to her, and her eyes, half closing, sought something to base her vision on. She looked down the railway carriage, the omnibus; took a line from shoulder or cheek; looked at the windows opposite; at Piccadilly, lamp-strung in the evening. All had been part of the fields of death. But always something it might be a face, a voice, a paper boy crying *Standard, News*—thrust through, snubbed her, waked her, required and got in the end an effort of attention, so that the vision must be perpetually remade. Now again, moved as she was by some instinctive need of distance and blue, she looked at the bay beneath her, making hillocks of the blue bars of the waves, and stony fields of the purpler spaces. Again she was roused as usual by something incongruous. There was a brown spot in the middle of the bay. It was a boat. Yes, she realized that after a second. But whose boat? Mr Ramsay's boat, she replied. Mr Ramsay; the man who had marched past her, with his hand raised, aloof, at the head of a procession, in his beautiful boots, asking her for sympathy, which she had refused. The boat was now half-way across the bay.

So fine was the morning except for a streak of wind here and there that the sea and sky looked all one fabric, as if sails were stuck high up in the sky, or the clouds had dropped down into the sea. A steamer far out at sea had drawn in the air a great scroll of smoke which stayed there curving and circling decoratively, as if the air were a fine gauze which held things and kept them softly in its mesh, only gently swaying them this way and that. And as happens sometimes when the weather is very fine, the cliffs looked as if they were conscious of the ships, and the ships looked as if they were conscious of the cliffs, as if they signalled to each other some secret message of their own. For sometimes quite close to the shore, the Lighthouse looked this morning in the haze an enormous distance away.

'Where are they now?' Lily thought, looking out to sea. Where was he, that very old man who had gone past her silently, holding a brown paper parcel under his arm? The boat was in the middle of the bay.

8

They don't feel a thing there, Cam thought, looking at the shore, which, rising and falling, became steadily more distant and more peaceful. Her hand cut a trail in the sea, as her mind made the green swirls and streaks into patterns and, numbed and shrouded, wandered in imagination in that underworld of waters where the pearls stuck in clusters to white sprays, where in the green light a change came over one's entire mind and one's body shone half transparent enveloped in a green cloak.

Then the eddy slackened round her hand. The rush of the water ceased; the world became full of little creaking and squeaking sounds. One heard the waves breaking and flapping against the side of the boat as if they were anchored in harbour. Everything became very close to one. For the sail, upon which James had his eyes fixed until i⁺ had become to him like a person whom he knew, sagged entirely; there they came to a stop, flapping about waiting for a breeze, in the hot sun, miles from shore, miles from the Lighthouse. Everything in the whole world seemed to stand still. The Lighthouse became immovable, and the line of the distant shore became fixed. The sun grew hotter and everybody seemed to come very close together and to feel each other's presence, which they had almost forgotten. Macalister's fishing-line went plumb down into the sea. But Mr Ramsay went on reading with his legs curled under him.

He was reading a little shiny book with covers mottled like a plover's egg. Now and again, as they hung about in that horrid calm, he turned a page. And James felt that each page was turned with a peculiar gesture aimed at him: now assertively, now commandingly; now with the intention of making people pity him; and all the time, as his father read and turned one after another of those little pages, James kept dreading the moment when he would look up and speak sharply to him about something or other. Why were they lagging about here? he would demand, or something quite unreasonable like that. And if he does, James thought, then I shall take a knife and strike him to the heart.

He had always kept this old symbol of taking a knife and striking his father to the heart. Only now, as he grew older, and sat staring at his father in an impotent rage, it was not him, that old man reading, whom he wanted to kill, but it was the thing that descended on him—without his knowing it perhaps: that fierce sudden black-winged harpy, with its talons and its beak all cold and hard, that struck and struck at you (he could feel the beak on his bare legs, where it had struck when he was a child) and then made off, and there he was again, an old man, very sad, reading his book. That he would kill, that he would strike to the heart. Whatever he did—(and he might do anything, he felt, looking at the Lighthouse and the distant shore) whether he was in a business, in a bank, a barrister, a man at the head of some enterprise, that he would fight, that he would track down and stamp out—tyranny, despotism, he called it—making people do what they did not want to do, cutting off their right to speak. How could any of them say, But I won't, when he said, Come to the Lighthouse. Do this. Fetch me that. The black wings spread, and the hard beak tore. And then next moment, there he sat reading his book; and he might look up—one never knew—quite reasonably. He might talk to the Macalisters. He might be pressing a sovereign into some frozen old woman's hand in the street, James thought; he might be shouting out at some fisherman's sports; he might be waving his arms in the air with excitement. Or he might sit at the head of the table dead silent from one end of dinner to the other. Yes, thought James, while the boat slapped and dawdled there in the hot sun; there was a waste of snow and rock very lonely and austere; and there he had come to feel, quite often lately, when his father said something which surprised the others, were two pairs of footprints only; his own and his father's. They alone knew each other. What then was this terror, this hatred? Turning back among the many leaves which the past had folded in him, peering into the heart of that forest where light and shade so chequer each other that all shape is distorted, and one blunders, now with the sun in one's eyes, now with a dark shadow, he sought an image to cool and detach and round off his feeling in a concrete shape. Suppose then that as a child sitting helpless in a perambulator, or on someone's knee, he had seen a waggon crush ignorantly and innocently, someone's foot? Suppose he had seen the foot first, in the grass, smooth, and whole; then the wheel; and the same foot, purple, crushed. But the wheel was innocent. So now, when his father came striding down the passage knocking them up early in the morning to go to the Lighthouse down it came over his foot, over Cam's foot, over anybody's foot. One sat and watched it.

But whose foot was he thinking of, and in what garden did all this happen? For one had settings for these scenes; trees that grew there;

flowers; a certain light; a few figures. Everything tended to set itself in a garden where there was none of this gloom and none of this throwing of hands about; people spoke in an ordinary tone of voice. They went in and out all day long. There was an old woman gossiping in the kitchen; and the blinds were sucked in and out by the breeze; all was blowing, all was growing; and over all those plates and bowls and tall brandishing red and yellow flowers a very thin yellow veil would be drawn, like a vine leaf, at night. Things became stiller and darker at night. But the leaf-like veil was so fine that lights lifted it, voices crinkled it; he could see through it a figure stooping, hear, coming close, going away, some dress rustling, some chain tinkling.

It was in this world that the wheel went over the person's foot. Something, he remembered, stayed and darkened over him; would not move; something flourished up in the air, something arid and sharp descended even there, like a blade, a scimitar, smiting through the leaves and flowers even of that happy world and making them shrivel and fall.

'It will rain,' he remembered his father saying. 'You won't be able to go to the Lighthouse.'

The Lighthouse was then a silvery, misty-looking tower with a yellow eye that opened suddenly and softly in the evening. Now—

James looked at the Lighthouse. He could see the white-washed rocks; the tower, stark and straight; he could see that it was barred with black and white; he could see windows in it; he could even see washing spread on the rocks to dry. So that was the Lighthouse, was it?

No, the other was also the Lighthouse. For nothing was simply one thing. The other was the Lighthouse too. It was sometimes hardly to be seen across the bay. In the evening one looked up and saw the eye opening and shutting and the light seemed to reach them in that airy sunny garden where they sat.

But he pulled himself up. Whenever he said 'they' or 'a person', and then began hearing the rustle of someone coming, the tinkle of someone going, he became extremely sensitive to the presence of whoever might be in the room. It was his father now. The strain became acute. For in one moment if there was no breeze, his father would slap the covers of his book together, and say: 'What's happening now? What are we dawdling about here for, eh?' as, once before he had brought his blade down among them on the terrace and she had gone stiff all over, and if there had been an axe handy, a knife, or anything with a sharp point he would have seized it and struck his father through the heart. His mother had gone stiff all over, and then, her arm slackening, so that he felt she listened to him no longer, she had risen somehow and gone away and left him there, impotent, ridiculous, sitting on the floor grasping a pair of scissors.

Not a breath of wind blew. The water chuckled and gurgled in the bottom of the boat where three or four mackerel beat their tails up and down in a pool of water not deep enough to cover them. At any moment Mr Ramsay (James scarcely dared look at him) might rouse himself, shut his book, and say something sharp; but for the moment he was reading, so that James stealthily, as if he were stealing downstairs on bare feet, afraid of waking a watch-dog by a creaking board, went on thinking what was she like, where did she go that day? He began following her from room to room and at last they came to a room where in a blue light, as if the reflection came from many china dishes, she talked to somebody; he listened to her talking. She talked to a servant, saying simply whatever came into her head. 'We shall need a big dish tonight. Where is it—the blue dish?' She alone spoke the truth; to her alone could he speak it. That was the source of her everlasting attraction for him, perhaps; she was a person to whom one could say what came into one's head. But all the time he thought of her, he was conscious of his father following his thought, shadowing it, making it shiver and falter.

At last he ceased to think; there he sat with his hand on the tiller in the sun, staring at the Lighthouse, powerless to move, powerless to flick off these grains of misery which settled on his mind one after another. A rope seemed to bind him there, and his father had knotted it and he could only escape by taking a knife and plunging it . . . But at that moment the sail swung slowly round, filled slowly out, the boat seemed to shake herself, and then to move off half conscious in her sleep, and then she woke and shot through the waves. The relief was extraordinary. They all seemed to fall away from each other again and to be at their ease and the fishing-lines slanted taut across the side of the boat. But his father did not rouse himself. He only raised his right hand mysteriously high in the air, and let it fall upon his knee again as if he were conducting some secret symphony.

9

[The sea without a stain on it, thought Lily Briscoe, still standing and looking out over the bay. The sea is stretched like silk across the bay. Distance had an extraordinary power; they had been swallowed up in it, she felt, they were gone for ever, they had become part of the nature of things. It was so calm; it was so quiet. The steamer itself had vanished, but the great scroll of smoke still hung in the air and drooped like a flag mournfully in valediction.]

10

It was like that then, the island, thought Cam, once more drawing her fingers through the waves. She had never seen it from out at sea before. It lay like that on the sea, did it, with a dent in the middle and two sharp crags, and the sea swept in there, and spread away for miles and miles on either side of the island. It was very small; shaped something like a leaf stood on end. So we took a little boat, she thought, beginning to tell herself a story of adventure about escaping from a sinking ship. But with the sea streaming through her fingers, a spray of seaweed vanishing behind them, she did not want to tell herself seriously a story; it was the sense of adventure and escape that she wanted, for she was thinking, as the boat sailed on, how her father's anger about the points of the compass, James's obstinacy about the compact, and her own anguish, all had slipped, all had passed, all had streamed away. What then came next? Where were they going? From her hand, ice cold, held deep in the sea, there spurted up a fountain of joy at the change, at the escape, at the adventure (that she should be alive, that she should be there). And the drops falling from this sudden and unthinking fountain of joy fell here and there on the dark, the slumbrous shapes in her mind; shapes of a world not realized but turning in their darkness, catching here and there, a spark of light; Greece, Rome, Constantinople. Small as it was, and shaped something like a leaf stood on end with the gold sprinkled waters flowing in and about it, it had, she supposed, a place in the universe—even that little island? The old gentlemen in the study she thought could have told her. Sometimes she strayed in from the garden purposely to catch them at it. There they were (it might be Mr Carmichael or Mr Bankes, very old, very stiff) sitting opposite each other in their low armchairs. They were crackling in front of them the pages of *The Times*, when she came in from the garden, all in a muddle, about something someone had said about Christ; a mammoth had been dug up in a London street; what was the great Napoleon like? Then they took all this with their clean hands (they wore grey-coloured clothes; they smelt of heather) and they brushed the scraps together, turning the paper, crossing their knees, and said something now and then very brief. In a kind of trance she would take a book from the shelf and stand there, watching her father write, so equally, so neatly from one side of the page to another, with a little cough now and then, or something said briefly to the other old gentleman opposite. And she thought, standing there with her book open, here one could let whatever one thought expand like a leaf in water; and if it did well here, among the old gentlemen smoking and *The Times* crackling, then it was right. And watching her father as he wrote in his study, she thought (now sitting in the boat) he was most lovable, he was most wise; he was not vain nor a tyrant. Indeed, if he saw she was there, reading a book, he would ask her, as gently as any one could, Was there nothing he could give her?

Lest this should be wrong, she looked at him reading the little book with the shiny cover mottled like a plover's egg. No; it was right. Look at him now, she wanted to say aloud to James. (But James had his eye on the sail.) He is a sarcastic brute, James would say. He brings the talk round to himself and his books, James would say. He is intolerably egotistical. Worst of all, he is a tyrant. But look! she said, looking at him. Look at him now. She looked at him reading the little book with his legs curled; the little book whose yellowish pages she knew, without knowing what was written on them. It was small; it was closely printed; on the fly-leaf, she knew, he had written that he had spent fifteen francs on dinner; the wine had been so much; he had given so much to the waiter; all was added up neatly at the bottom of the page. But what might be written in the book which had rounded its edges off in his pocket, she did not know. What he thought they none of them knew. But he was absorbed in it, so that when he looked up, as he did now for an instant, it was not to see anything; it was to pin down some thought more exactly. That done, his mind flew back again and he plunged into his reading. He read, she thought, as if he were guiding something, or wheedling a large flock of sheep, or pushing his way up and up a single narrow path; and sometimes he went fast and straight, and broke his way through the thicket, and sometimes it seemed a branch struck at him, a bramble blinded him, but he was not going to let himself be beaten by that; on he went, tossing over page after page. And she went on telling herself a story about escaping from a sinking ship, for she was safe, while he sat there; safe, as she felt herself when she crept in from the garden, and took a book down, and the old gentleman, lowering the paper suddenly, said something very brief over the top of it about the character of Napoleon.

She gazed back over the sea, at the island. But the leaf was losing its sharpness. It was very small; it was very distant. The sea was more important now than the shore. Waves were all round them, tossing and sinking, with a log wallowing down one wave; a gull riding on another. About here, she thought, dabbling her fingers in the water, a ship had sunk, and she murmured, dreamily, half asleep, how we perished, each alone.

So much depends then, thought Lily Briscoe, looking at the sea which had scarcely a stain on it, which was so soft that the sails and the clouds seemed set in its blue, so much depends, she thought, upon distance: whether people are near us or far from us; for her feeling for Mr Ramsay changed as he sailed further and further across the bay. It seemed to be elongated, stretched out; he seemed to become more and more remote. He and his children seemed to be swallowed up in that blue, that distance; but here, on the lawn, close at hand, Mr Carmichael suddenly grunted. She laughed. He clawed his book up from the grass. He settled into his chair again puffing and blowing like some sea monster. That was different altogether, because he was so near. And now again all was quiet. They must be out of bed by this time, she supposed, looking at the house, but nothing appeared there. But then, she remembered, they had always made off directly a meal was over, on business of their own. It was all in keeping with this silence, this emptiness, and the unreality of the early morning hour. It was a way things had sometimes, she thought, lingering for a moment and looking at the long glittering windows and the plume of blue smoke: they became unreal. So coming back from a journey, or after an illness, before habits had spun themselves across the surface, one felt that same unreality, which was so startling; felt something emerge. Life was most vivid then. One could be at one's ease. Mercifully one need not say, very briskly, crossing the lawn to greet old Mrs Beckwith, who would be coming out to find a corner to sit in, 'Oh good-morning, Mrs Beckwith! What a lovely day! Are you going to be so bold as to sit in the sun? Jasper's hidden the chairs. Do let me find you one!' and all the rest of the usual chatter. One need not speak at all. One glided, one shook one's sails (there was a good deal of movement in the bay, boats were starting off) between things, beyond things. Empty it was not, but full to the brim. She seemed to be standing up to the lips in some substance, to move and float and sink in it, yes, for these waters were unfathomably deep. Into them had spilled so many lives. The Ramsays'; the children's; and all sorts of waifs and strays of things besides. A washerwoman with her basket; a rook; a red-hot poker; the purples and grey-greens of flowers; some common feeling which held the whole together.

It was some such feeling of completeness perhaps which, ten years ago, standing almost where she stood now, had made her say that she must be in love with the place. Love had a thousand shapes. There might be lovers whose gift it was to choose out the elements of things and place them together and so, giving them a wholeness not theirs in life, make of some scene, or meeting of people (all now gone and separate), one of those globed compacted things over which thought lingers, and love plays.

Her eyes rested on the brown speck of Mr Ramsay's sailing boat. They would be at the Lighthouse by lunch-time she supposed. But the wind had freshened, and, as the sky changed slightly and the sea changed slightly and the boats altered their positions, the view, which a moment before had seemed miraculously fixed, was now unsatisfactory. The wind had blown the trail of smoke about; there was something displeasing about the placing of the ships.

The disproportion there seemed to upset some harmony in her own mind. She felt an obscure distress. It was confirmed when she turned to her picture. She had been wasting her morning. For whatever reason she could not achieve that razor edge of balance between two opposite forces; Mr Ramsay and the picture; which was necessary. There was something perhaps wrong with the design? Was it, she wondered, that the line of the wall wanted breaking, was it that the mass of the trees was too heavy? She smiled ironically; for had she not thought, when she began, that she had solved her problem?

What was the problem then? She must try to get hold of something that evaded her. It evaded her when she thought of Mrs Ramsay; it evaded her now when she thought of her picture. Phrases came. Visions came. Beautiful phrases. But what she wished to get hold of was that very jar on the nerves, the thing itself before it has been made anything. Get that and start afresh; get that and start afresh; she said desperately, pitching herself firmly again before her easel. It was a miserable machine, an inefficient machine, she thought, the human apparatus for painting or for feeling; it always broke down at the critical moment; heroically, one must force it on. She stared, frowning. There was the hedge, sure enough. But one got nothing by soliciting urgently. One got only a glare in the eye from looking at the line of the wall, or from thinking—she wore a grey hat. She was astonishingly beautiful. Let it come, she thought, if it will come. For there are moments when one can neither think nor feel. And if one can neither think nor feel, she thought, where is one?

Here on the grass, on the ground, she thought, sitting down, and examining with her brush a little colony of plantains. For the lawn was very rough. Here sitting on the world, she thought, for she could not shake herself free from the sense that everything this morning was happening for the first time, perhaps for the last time, as a traveller, even though he is half asleep, knows, looking out of the train window, that he must look now, for he will never see that town, or that mule-cart, or that woman at work in the fields, again. The lawn was the world; they were up here together, on this exalted station, she thought, looking at old Mr Carmichael, who seemed (though they had not said a word all this time) to share her thoughts. And she would never see him again perhaps. He was growing old. Also, she remembered, smiling at the slipper that dangled from his foot, he was growing famous. People said that his poetry was 'so beautiful'. They went and published things he had written forty years ago. There was a famous man now called Carmichael, she smiled, thinking how many shapes one person might wear, how he was that in the newspapers, but here the same as he had always been. He looked the same—greyer, rather. Yes, he looked the same, but somebody had said, she recalled, that when he had heard of Andrew Ramsay's death (he was killed in a second by a shell; he should have been a great mathematician) Mr Carmichael had 'lost all interest in life'. What did it mean—that? she wondered. Had he marched through Trafalgar Square grasping a big stick? Had he turned pages over and over, without reading them, sitting in his room in St John's Wood alone? She did not know what he had done, when he heard that Andrew was killed, but she felt it in him all the same. They only mumbled at each other on staircases; they looked up at the sky and said it will be fine or it won't be fine. But this was one way of knowing people, she thought: to know the outline, not the detail, to sit in one's garden and look at the slopes of a hill running purple down into the distant heather. She knew him in that way. She knew that he had changed somehow. She had never read a line of his poetry. She thought that she knew how it went though, slowly and sonorously. It was seasoned and mellow. It was about the desert and the camel. It was about the palm tree and the sunset. It was extremely impersonal; it said something about death; it said very little about love. There was an aloofness about him. He wanted very little of other people. Had he not always lurched rather awkwardly past the drawing-room window with some newspaper under his arm, trying to avoid Mrs Ramsay whom for some reason he did not much like? On that account, of course, she would always try to make him stop. He would bow to her. He would halt unwillingly and bow profoundly. Annoyed that he did not want anything of her, Mrs Ramsay would ask him (Lily could hear her) wouldn't he like a coat, a rug, a newspaper? No, he wanted nothing. (Here he bowed.) There was some quality in her which he did not much like. It was perhaps her masterfulness, her positiveness, something matter-of-fact in her. She was so direct.

(A noise drew her attention to the drawing-room window—the squeak of a hinge. The light breeze was toying with the window.)

There must have been people who disliked her very much, Lily thought (Yes; she realized that the drawing-room step was empty, but it had no effect on her whatever. She did not want Mrs Ramsay now.)— People who thought her too sure, too drastic. Also her beauty offended people probably. How monotonous, they would say, and the same always! They preferred another type—the dark, the vivacious. Then she was weak with her husband. She let him make those scenes. Then she was reserved. Nobody knew exactly what had happened to her. And (to go back to Mr Carmichael and his dislike) one could not imagine Mrs Ramsay standing painting, lying reading, a whole morning on the lawn. It was unthinkable. Without saying a word, the only token of her errand a basket on her arm, she went off to the town, to the poor, to sit in some stuffy little bedroom. Often and often Lily had seen her go silently in the midst of some game, some discussion, with her basket on her arm, very upright. She had noted her return. She had thought, half laughing (she was so methodical with the tea cups) half moved (her beauty took one's breath away), eyes that are closing in pain have looked on you. You have been with them there.

And then Mrs Ramsay would be annoyed because somebody was late, or the butter not fresh, or the teapot chipped. And all the time she was saying that the butter was not fresh one would be thinking of Greek temples, and how beauty had been with them there. She never talked of it—she went, punctually, directly. It was her instinct to go, an instinct like the swallows for the south, the artichokes for the sun, turning her infallibly to the human race, making her nest in its heart. And this, like all instincts, was a little distressing to people who did not share it; to Mr Carmichael perhaps, to herself certainly. Some notion was in both of them about the ineffectiveness of action, the supremacy of thought. Her going was a reproach to them, gave a different twist to the world, so that they were led to protest, seeing their own prepossessions disappear, and clutch at them vanishing. Charles Tansley did that too: it was part of the reason why one disliked him. He upset the proportions of one's world. And what had happened to him, she wondered, idly stirring the plantains with her brush. He had got his fellowship. He had married; he lived at Golder's Green.

She had gone one day into a Hall and heard him speaking during the war. He was denouncing something: he was condemning somebody. He was preaching brotherly love. And all she felt was how could he love his kind who did not know one picture from another, who had stood behind her smoking shag ('fivepence an ounce, Miss Briscoe') and making it his business to tell her women can't write, women can't paint, not so much that he believed it, as that for some odd reason he wished it? There he was, lean and red and raucous, preaching love from a platform (there were ants crawling about among the plantains which she disturbed with her brush—red, energetic ants, rather like Charles Tansley). She had looked at him ironically from her seat in the half-empty hall, pumping love into that chilly space, and suddenly, there was the old cask or whatever it was bobbing up and down among the waves and Mrs Ramsay looking for her spectacle case among the pebbles. 'Oh dear! What a nuisance! Lost again. Don't bother, Mr Tansley. I lose thousands every summer,' at which he pressed his chin back against his collar, as if afraid to sanction such exaggeration, but could stand it in her whom he liked, and smiled very charmingly. He must have confided in her on one of those long expeditions when people got separated and walked back alone. He was educating his little sister, Mrs Ramsay had told her. It was immensely to his credit. Her own idea of him was grotesque, Lily knew well, stirring the plantains with her brush. Half one's notions of other people were, after all, grotesque. They served private purposes of one's own. He did for her instead of a whipping-boy. She found herself flagellating his lean flanks when she was out of temper. If she wanted to be serious about him she had to help herself to Mrs Ramsay's sayings, to look at him through her eyes.

She raised a little mountain for the ants to climb over. She reduced them to a frenzy of indecision by this interference in their cosmogony. Some ran this way, others that.

One wanted fifty pairs of eyes to see with, she reflected. Fifty pairs of eyes were not enough to get round that one woman with, she thought. Among them, must be one that was stone blind to her beauty. One wanted most some secret sense, fine as air, with which to steal through keyholes and surround her where she sat knitting, talking, sitting silent in the window alone; which took to itself and treasured up like the air which held the smoke of the steamer, her thoughts, her imaginations, her desires. What did the hedge mean to her, what did the garden mean to her, what did it mean to her when a wave broke? (Lily looked up, as she had seen Mrs Ramsay look up; she too heard a wave falling on the beach.) And then what stirred and trembled in her mind when the children cried, 'How's that? How's that?' cricketing? She would stop knitting for a second. She would look intent. Then she would lapse again, and suddenly Mr Ramsay stopped dead in his pacing in front of her, and some curious shock passed through her and seemed to rock her in profound agitation on its breast when stopping there he stood over her, and looked down at her. Lily could see him.

He stretched out his hand and raised her from her chair. It seemed somehow as if he had done it before; as if he had once bent in the same way and raised her from a boat which, lying a few inches off some island, had required that the ladies should thus be helped on shore by the gentlemen. An old-fashioned scene that was, which required, very nearly, crinolines and peg-top trousers. Letting herself be helped by him, Mrs Ramsay had thought (Lily supposed) the time has come now; Yes, she would say it now. Yes, she would marry him. And she stepped slowly, quietly on shore. Probably she said one word only, letting her hand rest still in his. I will marry you, she might have said, with her hand in his; but no more. Time after time the same thrill had passed between them—obviously it had, Lily thought, smoothing a way for her ants. She was not inventing; she was only trying to smooth out something she had been given years ago folded up; something she had seen. For in the rough and tumble of daily life, with all those children about, all those visitors, one had constantly a sense of repetition—of one thing falling where another had fallen, and so setting up an echo which chimed in the air and made it full of vibrations.

But it would be a mistake, she thought, thinking how they walked off together, she in her green shawl, he with his tie flying, arm in arm, past the greenhouse, to simplify their relationship. It was no monotony of bliss—she with her impulses and quicknesses; he with his shudders and glooms. Oh no. The bedroom door would slam violently early in the morning. He would start from the table in a temper. He would whizz his plate through the window. Then all through the house there would be a sense of doors slamming and blinds fluttering as if a gusty wind were blowing and people scudded about trying in a hasty way to fasten hatches and make things shipshape. She had met Paul Rayley like that one day on the stairs. They had laughed and laughed, like a couple of children, all because Mr Ramsay, finding an earwig in his milk at breakfast had sent the whole thing flying through the air on to the terrace outside. 'An earwig,' Prue murmured, awestruck, 'in his milk.' Other people might find centipedes. But he had built round him such a fence of sanctity, and occupied the space with such a demeanour of majesty that an earwig in his milk was a monster.

But it tired Mrs Ramsay, it cowed her a little—the plates whizzing and the doors slamming. And there would fall between them sometimes long rigid silences, when, in a state of mind which annoyed Lily in her, half plaintive, half resentful, she seemed unable to surmount the tempest calmly, or to laugh as they laughed, but in her weariness perhaps concealed something. She brooded and sat silent. After a time he would hang stealthily about the places where she was—roaming under the window where she sat writing letters or talking, for she would take care to be busy when he passed, and evade him, and pretend not to see him. Then he would turn smooth as silk, affable, urbane, and try to win her so. Still she would hold off, and now she would assert for a brief season some of those prides and airs the due of her beauty which she was generally utterly without; would turn her head; would look so, over her shoulder, always with some Minta, Paul, or William Bankes at her side. At length, standing outside the group the very figure of a famished wolfhound (Lily got up off the grass and stood looking at the steps, at the window, where she had seen him), he would say her name, once only, for all the world like a wolf barking in the snow, but still she held back; and he would say it once more, and this time something in the tone would rouse her, and she would go to him, leaving them all of a sudden, and they would walk off together among the pear trees, the cabbages, and the raspberry beds. They would have it out together. But with what attitudes and with what words? Such a dignity was theirs in this relationship that, turning away, she and Paul and Minta would hide their curiosity and their discomfort, and begin picking flowers, throwing balls, chattering, until it was time for dinner, and there they were, he at one end of the table, she at the other, as usual.

'Why don't some of you take up botany? . . . With all those legs and arms why doesn't one of you . . . ?' So they would talk as usual, laughing, among the children. All would be as usual, save only for some quiver, as of a blade in the air, which came and went between them as if the usual sight of the children sitting round their soup plates had freshened itself in their eyes after that hour among the pears and the cabbages. Especially, Lily thought, Mrs Ramsay would glance at Prue. She sat in the middle between brothers and sisters, always so occupied, it seemed, seeing that nothing went wrong that she scarcely spoke herself. How Prue must have blamed herself for that earwig in the milk! How white she had gone when Mr Ramsay threw his plate through the window! How she drooped under those long silences between them! Anyhow, her mother now would seem to be making it up to her; assuring her that everything was well; promising her that one of these days that same happiness would be hers. She had enjoyed it for less than a year, however.

She had let the flowers fall from her basket, Lily thought, screwing up her eyes and standing back as if to look at her picture, which she was not touching, however, with all her faculties in a trance, frozen over superficially but moving underneath with extreme speed.

She let her flowers fall from her basket, scattered and tumbled them on to the grass and, reluctantly and hesitatingly, but without question or complaint—had she not the faculty of obedience to perfection?— went too. Down fields, across valleys, white, flower-strewn—that was how she would have painted it. The hills were austere. It was rocky; it was steep. The waves sounded hoarse on the stones beneath. They went, the three of them together, Mrs Ramsay walking rather fast in front, as if she expected to meet someone round the corner.

Suddenly the window at which she was looking was whitened by some light stuff behind it. At last then somebody had come into the drawing-room; somebody was sitting in the chair. For Heaven's sake, she prayed, let them sit still there and not come floundering out to talk to her. Mercifully, whoever it was stayed still inside; had settled by some stroke of luck so as to throw an odd-shaped triangular shadow over the step. It altered the composition of the picture a little. It was interesting. It might be useful. Her mood was coming back to her. One must keep on looking without for a second relaxing the intensity of emotion, the determination not to be put off, not to be bamboozled. One must hold the scene—so—in a vice and let nothing come in and spoil it. One wanted, she thought, dipping her brush deliberately, to be on a level with ordinary experience, to feel simply that's a chair, that's a table, and yet at the same time, It's a miracle, it's an ecstasy. The problem might be solved after all. Ah, but what had happened? Some wave of white went over the window pane. The air must have stirred some flounce in the room. Her heart leapt at her and seized her and tortured her.

'Mrs Ramsay! Mrs Ramsay!' she cried, feeling the old horror come back—to want and want and not to have. Could she inflict that still? And then, quietly, as if she refrained, that too became part of ordinary experience, was on a level with the chair, with the table. Mrs Ramsay—it was part of her perfect goodness to Lily—sat there quite simply, in the chair, flicked her needles to and fro, knitted her reddish-brown stocking, cast her shadow on the step. There she sat.

And as if she had something she must share, yet could hardly leave her easel, so full her mind was of what she was thinking, of what she was seeing. Lily went past Mr Carmichael holding her brush to the edge of the lawn. Where was that boat now? Mr Ramsay? She wanted him.

12

Mr Ramsay had almost done reading. One hand hovered over the page as if to be in readiness to turn it the very instant he had finished it. He sat there bareheaded with the wind blowing his hair about, extraordinarily exposed to everything. He looked very old. He looked, James thought, getting his head now against the Lighthouse, now against the waste of waters running away into the open, like some old stone lying on the sand; he looked as if he had become physically what was always at the back of both of their minds—that loneliness which was for both of them the truth about things.

He was reading very quickly, as if he were eager to get to the end. Indeed they were very close to the Lighthouse now. There it loomed up, stark and straight, glaring white and black, and one could see the waves breaking in white splinters like smashed glass upon the rocks. One could see lines and creases in the rocks. One could see the windows clearly; a dab of white on one of them, and a little tuft of green on the rock. A man had come out and looked at them through a glass and gone in again. So it was like that, James thought, the Lighthouse one had seen across the bay all these years; it was a stark tower on a bare rock. It satisfied him. It confirmed some obscure feeling of his about his own character. The old ladies, he thought, thinking of the garden at home, went dragging their chairs about on the lawn. Old Mrs Beckwith, for example, was always saying how nice it was and how sweet it was and how they ought to be so proud and they ought to be so happy, but as a matter of fact James thought, looking at the Lighthouse stood there on its rock, it's like that. He looked at his father reading fiercely with his legs curled tight. They shared that knowledge. 'We are driving before a gale—we must sink,' he began saying to himself, half aloud exactly as his father said it.

Nobody seemed to have spoken for an age. Cam was tired of looking at the sea. Little bits of black cork had floated past; the fish were dead in the bottom of the boat. Still her father read, and James looked at him and she looked at him, and they vowed that they would fight tyranny to the death, and he went on reading quite unconscious of what they thought. It was thus that he escaped, she thought. Yes, with his great forehead and his great nose, holding his little mottled book firmly in front of him, he escaped. You might try to lay hands on him, but then like a bird, he spread his wings, he floated off to settle out of your reach somewhere far away on some desolate stump. She gazed at the immense expanse of the sea. The island had grown so small that it scarcely looked like a leaf any longer. It looked like the top of a rock which some big wave would cover. Yet in its frailty were all those paths, those terraces, those bedrooms—all those innumerable things. But as, just before sleep, things simplify themselves so that only one of all the myriad details has power to assert itself, so, she felt, looking drowsily at the island, all those paths and terraces and bedrooms were fading and disappearing, and nothing was left but a pale blue censer swinging rhythmically this way and that across her mind. It was a hanging garden; it was a valley, full of birds, and flowers, and antelopes . . . She was falling asleep.

'Come now,' said Mr Ramsay, suddenly shutting his book.

Come where? To what extraordinary adventure? She woke with a start. To land somewhere, to climb somewhere? Where was he leading them? For after his immense silence the words startled them. But it was absurd. He was hungry, he said. It was time for lunch. Besides, look, he said. There's the Lighthouse. 'We're almost there.'

'He's doing very well,' said Macalister, praising James. 'He's keeping her very steady.'

But his father never praised him, James thought grimly.

Mr Ramsay opened the parcel and shared out the sandwiches among them. Now he was happy, eating bread and cheese with these fishermen. He would have liked to live in a cottage and lounge about in the harbour spitting with the other old men, James thought, watching him slice his cheese into thin yellow sheets with his penknife.

This is right, this is it, Cam kept feeling, as she peeled her hard-boiled egg. Now she felt as she did in the study when the old men were reading *The Times*. Now I can go on thinking whatever I like, and I shan't fall over a precipice or be drowned, for there he is, keeping his eye on me, she thought.

At the same time they were sailing so fast along by the rocks that it was very exciting—it seemed as if they were doing two things at once; they were eating their lunch here in the sun and they were also making for safety in a great storm after a shipwreck. Would the water last? Would the provisions last? she asked herself, telling herself a story but knowing at the same time what was the truth.

They would soon be out of it, Mr Ramsay was saying to old Macalister, but their children would see some strange things. Macalister said he was seventy-five last March; Mr Ramsay was seventy-one. Macalister said he had never seen a doctor; he had never lost a tooth. And that's the way I'd like my children to live—Cam was sure that her father was thinking that, for he stopped her throwing a sandwich into the sea and told her, as if he were thinking of the fishermen and how they live, that if she did not want it she should put it back in the parcel. She should not waste it. He said it so wisely, as if he knew so well the things that happened in the world, that she put it back at once, and then he gave her, from his own parcel, a gingerbread nut, as if he were a great Spanish gentleman, she thought, handing a flower to a lady at a window (so courteous his manner was). But he was shabby, and simple, eating bread and cheese; and yet he was leading them on a great expedition where, for all she knew, they would be drowned.

'That was where she sunk,' said Macalister's boy suddenly.

'Three men were drowned where we are now,' said the old man. He had seen them clinging to the mast himself. And Mr Ramsay taking a look at the spot was about, James and Cam were afraid, to burst out:

But I beneath a rougher sea,

and if he did, they could not bear it; they would shriek aloud; they could not endure another explosion of the passion that boiled in him; but to their surprise all he said was 'Ah' as if he thought to himself, But why make a fuss about that? Naturally men are drowned in a storm, but it is a perfectly straightforward affair, and the depths of the sea (he sprinkled the crumbs from his sandwich paper over them) are only water after all. Then having lighted his pipe he took out his watch. He looked at it attentively; he made, perhaps, some mathematical calculation. At last he said, triumphantly:

'Well done!' James had steered them like a born sailor.

There! Cam thought, addressing herself silently to James. You've got it at last. For she knew that this was what James had been wanting, and she knew that now he had got it he was so pleased that he would not look at her or at his father or at anyone. There he sat with his hand on the tiller sitting bolt upright, looking rather sulky and frowning slightly. He was so pleased that he was not going to let anybody take away a grain of his pleasure. His father had praised him. They must think that he was perfectly indifferent. But you've got it now, Cam thought.

They had tacked, and they were sailing swiftly, buoyantly on long rocking waves which handed them on from one to another with an extraordinary lilt and exhilaration beside the reef. On the left a row of rocks showed brown through the water which thinned and became greener and on one, a higher rock, a wave incessantly broke and spurted a little column of drops which fell down in a shower. One could hear the slap of the water and the patter of falling drops and a kind of hushing and hissing sound from the waves rolling and gambolling and slapping the rocks as if they were wild creatures who were perfectly free and tossed and tumbled and sported like this for ever.

Now they could see two men on the Lighthouse, watching them and making ready to meet them.

Mr Ramsay buttoned his coat, and turned up his trousers. He took the large, badly packed, brown paper parcel which Nancy had got ready and sat with it on his knee. Thus in complete readiness to land he sat looking back at the island. With his long-sighted eyes perhaps he could see the dwindled leaf-like shape standing on end on a plate of gold quite clearly. What could he see? Cam wondered. It was all a blur to her. What was he thinking now? she wondered. What was it he sought, so fixedly, so intently, so silently? They watched him, both of them, sitting bareheaded with his parcel on his knee staring and staring at the frail blue shape which seemed like the vapour of something that had burnt itself away. What do you want? they both wanted to ask. They both wanted to say, Ask us anything and we will give it you. But he did not ask them anything. He sat and looked at the island and he might be thinking, We perished, each alone, or he might be thinking, I have reached it. I have found it, but he said nothing.

Then he put on his hat.

'Bring those parcels,' he said, nodding his head at the things Nancy had done up for them to take to the Lighthouse. 'The parcels for the Lighthouse men,' he said. He rose and stood in the bow of the boat, very straight and tall, for all the world, James thought, as if he were saying, 'There is no God,' and Cam thought, as if he were leaping into space, and they both rose to follow him as he sprang, lightly like a young man, holding his parcel, on to the rock.

I 3

'He must have reached it,' said Lily Briscoe aloud, feeling suddenly completely tired out. For the Lighthouse had become almost invisible, had melted away into a blue haze, and the effort of looking at it and the effort of thinking of him landing there, which both seemed to be one and the same effort, had stretched her body and mind to the utmost. Ah, but she was relieved. Whatever she had wanted to give him, when he left her that morning, she had given him at last.

'He has landed,' she said aloud. 'It is finished.' Then, surging up, puffing slightly, old Mr Carmichael stood beside her, looking like an old pagan God, shaggy, with weeds in his hair and the trident (it was only a French novel) in his hand. He stood by her on the edge of the lawn, swaying a little in his bulk, and said, shading his eyes with his hand: 'They will have landed,' and she felt that she had been right. They had not needed to speak. They had been thinking the same things and he had answered her without her asking him anything. He stood there spreading his hands over all the weakness and suffering of mankind; she thought he was surveying, tolerantly, compassionately, their final destiny. Now he has crowned the occasion, she thought, when his hand slowly fell, as if she had seen him let fall from his great height a wreath of violets and asphodels which, fluttering slowly, lay at length upon the earth.

Quickly, as if she were recalled by something over there, she turned to her canvas. There it was—her picture. Yes, with all its green and blues, its lines running up and across, its attempt at something. It would be hung in the attics, she thought; it would be destroyed. But what did that matter? she asked herself, taking up her brush again. She looked at the steps; they were empty; she looked at her canvas; it was blurred. With a sudden intensity, as if she saw it clear for a second, she drew a line there, in the centre. It was done; it was finished. Yes, she thought, laying down her brush in extreme fatigue, I have had my vision.

The Waves

The sun had not yet risen. The sea was indistinguishable from the sky, except that the sea was slightly creased as if a cloth had wrinkles in it. Gradually as the sky whitened a dark line lay on the horizon dividing the sea from the sky and the grey cloth became barred with thick strokes moving, one after another, beneath the surface, following each other, pursuing each other, perpetually.

As they neared the shore each bar rose, heaped itself, broke and swept a thin veil of white water across the sand. The wave paused, and then drew out again, sighing like a sleeper whose breath comes and goes unconsciously. Gradually the dark bar on the horizon became clear as if the sediment in an old wine-bottle had sunk and left the glass green. Behind it, too, the sky cleared as if the white sediment there had sunk, or as if the arm of a woman couched beneath the horizon had raised a lamp and flat bars of white, green and yellow spread across the sky like the blades of a fan. Then she raised her lamp higher and the air seemed to become fibrous and to tear away from the green surface flickering and flaming in red and yellow fibres like the smoky fire that roars from a bonfire. Gradually the fibres of the burning bonfire were fused into one haze, one incandescence which lifted the weight of the woollen grey sky on top of it and turned it to a million atoms of soft blue. The surface of the sea slowly became transparent and lay rippling and sparkling until the dark stripes were almost rubbed out. Slowly the arm that held the lamp raised it higher and then higher until a broad flame became visible; an arc of fire burnt on the rim of the horizon, and all round it the sea blazed gold.

The light struck upon the trees in the garden, making one leaf transparent and then another. One bird chirped high up; there was a pause; another chirped lower down. The sun sharpened the walls of the house, and rested like the tip of a fan upon a white blind and made a blue finger-print of shadow under the leaf by the bedroom window. The blind stirred slightly, but all within was dim and unsubstantial. The birds sang their blank melody outside.

'I see a ring,' said Bernard, 'hanging above me. It quivers and hangs in a loop of light.'

'I see a slab of pale yellow,' said Susan, 'spreading away until it meets a purple stripe.'

'I hear a sound,' said Rhoda, 'cheep, chirp; cheep chirp; going up and down.'

'I see a globe,' said Neville, 'hanging down in a drop against the enormous flanks of some hill.'

'I see a crimson tassel,' said Jinny, 'twisted with gold threads.'

'I hear something stamping,' said Louis. 'A great beast's foot is chained. It stamps, and stamps, and stamps.'

'Look at the spider's web on the corner of the balcony,' said Bernard. 'It has beads of water on it, drops of white light.'

'The leaves are gathered round the window like pointed ears,' said Susan.

'A shadow falls on the path,' said Louis, 'like an elbow bent.'

'Islands of light are swimming on the grass,' said Rhoda. 'They have fallen through the trees.'

'The birds' eyes are bright in the tunnels between the leaves,' said Neville.

'The stalks are covered with harsh, short hairs,' said Jinny, 'and drops of water have stuck to them.'

'A caterpillar is curled in a green ring,' said Susan, 'notched with blunt feet.'

'The grey-shelled snail draws across the path and flattens the blades behind him,' said Rhoda.

'And burning lights from the window-panes flash in and out on the grasses,' said Louis.

'Stones are cold to my feet,' said Neville. 'I feel each one, round or pointed, separately.'

'The back of my hand burns,' said Jinny, 'but the palm is clammy and damp with dew.'

'Now the cock crows like a spurt of hard, red water in the white tide,' said Bernard.

'Birds are singing up and down and in and out all round us,' said Susan.

'The beast stamps; the elephant with its foot chained; the great brute on the beach stamps,' said Louis.

'Look at the house,' said Jinny, 'with all its windows white with blinds.'

'Cold water begins to run from the scullery tap,' said Rhoda, 'over the mackerel in the bowl.'

'The walls are cracked with gold cracks,' said Bernard, 'and there are blue, finger-shaped shadows of leaves beneath the windows.'

'Now Mrs Constable pulls up her thick black stockings,' said Susan.

'When the smoke rises, sleep curls off the roof like a mist,' said Louis.

'The birds sang in chorus first,' said Rhoda. 'Now the scullery door is unbarred. Off they fly. Off they fly like a fling of seed. But one sings by the bedroom window alone.'

'Bubbles form on the floor of the saucepan,' said Jinny. 'Then they rise, quicker and quicker, in a silver chain to the top.'

'Now Billy scrapes the fish-scales with a jagged knife on to a wooden board,' said Neville.

'The dining-room window is dark blue now,' said Bernard, 'and the air ripples above the chimneys.'

'A swallow is perched on the lightning-conductor,' said Susan. 'And Biddy has smacked down the bucket on the kitchen flags.'

'That is the first stroke of the church bell,' said Louis. 'Then the others follow; one, two; one, two; one, two.'

'Look at the table-cloth, flying white along the table,' said Rhoda. 'Now there are rounds of white china, and silver streaks beside each plate.'

'Suddenly a bee booms in my ear,' said Neville. 'It is here; it is past.'

'I burn, I shiver,' said Jinny, 'out of this sun, into this shadow.'

'Now they have all gone,' said Louis. 'I am alone. They have gone into the house for breakfast, and I am left standing by the wall among the flowers. It is very early, before lessons. Flower after flower is specked on the depths of green. The petals are harlequins. Stalks rise from the black hollows beneath. The flowers swim like fish made of light upon the dark, green waters. I hold a stalk in my hand. I am the stalk. My roots go down to the depths of the world, through earth dry with brick, and damp earth, through veins of lead and silver. I am all fibre. All tremors shake me, and the weight of the earth is pressed to my ribs. Up here my eyes are green leaves, unseeing. I am a boy in grey flannels with a belt fastened by a brass snake up here. Down there my eyes are the lidless eyes of a stone figure in a desert by the Nile. I see women passing with red pitchers to the river; I see camels swaying and men in turbans. I hear tramplings, tremblings, stirrings round me.

'Up here Bernard, Neville, Jinny and Susan (but not Rhoda) skim the flower-beds with their nets. They skim the butterflies from the nodding tops of the flowers. They brush the surface of the world. Their nets are full of fluttering wings. "Louis! Louis! Louis!" they shout. But they cannot see me. I am on the other side of the hedge. There are only little eye-holes among the leaves. Oh Lord, let them pass. Lord, let them lay their butterflies on a pocket-handkerchief on the gravel. Let them count out their tortoise-shells, their red admirals and cabbage whites. But let me be unseen. I am green as a yew tree in the shade of the hedge. My hair is made of leaves. I am rooted to the middle of the earth. My body is a stalk. I press the stalk. A drop oozes from the hole at the mouth and slowly, thickly, grows larger and larger. Now something pink passes the eye-hole. Now an eye-beam is slid through the chink. Its beam strikes me. I am a boy in a grey flannel suit. She has found me. I am struck on the nape of the neck. She has kissed me. All is shattered.'

'I was running,' said Jinny, 'after breakfast. I saw leaves moving in a hole in the hedge. I thought "That is a bird on its nest." I parted them and looked; but there was no bird on a nest. The leaves went on moving. I was frightened. I ran past Susan, past Rhoda, and Neville and Bernard in the tool-house talking. I cried as I ran, faster and faster. What moved the leaves? What moves my heart, my legs? And I dashed in here, seeing you green as a bush, like a branch, very still, Louis, with your eyes fixed. "Is he dead?" I thought, and kissed you, with my heart jumping under my pink frock like the leaves, which go on moving, though there is nothing to move them. Now I smell geraniums; I smell earth mould. I dance. I ripple. I am thrown over you like a net of light. I lie quivering flung over you.'

'Through the chink in the hedge,' said Susan, 'I saw her kiss him. I raised my head from my flower-pot and looked through a chink in the hedge. I saw her kiss him. I saw them, Jinny and Louis, kissing. Now I will wrap my agony inside my pocket-handkerchief. It shall be screwed tight into a ball. I will go to the beech wood alone, before lessons. I will not sit at a table, doing sums. I will not sit next Jinny and next Louis. I will take my anguish and lay it upon the roots under the beech trees. I will examine it and take it between my fingers. They will not find me. I shall eat nuts and peer for eggs through the brambles and my hair will be matted and I shall sleep under hedges and drink water from ditches and die there.'

'Susan has passed us,' said Bernard. 'She has passed the tool-house door with her handkerchief screwed into a ball. She was not crying, but her eyes, which are so beautiful, were narrow as cats' eyes before they spring. I shall follow her, Neville. I shall go gently behind her, to be at hand, with my curiosity, to comfort her when she bursts out in a rage and thinks, "I am alone".

'Now she walks across the field with a swing, nonchalantly, to deceive us. Then she comes to the dip; she thinks she is unseen; she begins to run with her fists clenched in front of her. Her nails meet in the ball of her pocket-handkerchief. She is making for the beech woods out of the light. She spreads her arms as she comes to them and takes to the shade like a swimmer. But she is blind after the light and trips and flings herself down on the roots under the trees, where the light seems to pant in and out, in and out. The branches heave up and down. There is agitation and trouble here. There is gloom. The light is fitful. There is anguish here. The roots make a skeleton on the ground, with dead leaves heaped in the angles. Susan has spread her anguish out. Her pocket-handkerchief is laid on the roots of the beech trees and she sobs, sitting crumpled where she has fallen.'

'I saw her kiss him,' said Susan. 'I looked between the leaves and saw her. She danced in flecked with diamonds light as dust. And I am squat, Bernard, I am short. I have eyes that look close to the ground and see insects in the grass. The yellow warmth in my side turned to stone when I saw Jinny kiss Louis. I shall eat grass and die in a ditch in the brown water where dead leaves have rotted.'

'I saw you go,' said Bernard. 'As you passed the door of the tool-house I heard you cry "I am unhappy". I put down my knife. I was making boats out of firewood with Neville. And my hair is untidy, because when Mrs Constable told me to brush it there was a fly in a web, and I asked, "Shall I free the fly? Shall I let the fly be eaten?" So I am late always. My hair is unbrushed and these chips of wood stick in it. When I heard you cry I followed you, and saw you put down your handkerchief, screwed up, with its rage, with its hate, knotted in it. But soon that will cease. Our bodies are close now. You hear me breathe. You see the beetle too carrying off a leaf on its back. It runs this way, then that way, so that even your desire while you watch the beetle, to possess one single thing (it is Louis now) must waver, like the light in and out of the beech leaves; and then words, moving darkly, in the depths of your mind will break up this knot of hardness, screwed in your pocket-handkerchief.'

'I love,' said Susan, 'and I hate. I desire one thing only. My eyes are hard. Jinny's eyes break into a thousand lights. Rhoda's are like those pale flowers to which moths come in the evening. Yours grow full and brim and never break. But I am already set on my pursuit. I see insects in the grass. Though my mother still knits white socks for me and hems pinafores and I am a child, I love and I hate.'

'But when we sit together, close,' said Bernard, 'we melt into each other with phrases. We are edged with mist. We make an unsubstantial territory.'

'I see the beetle,' said Susan. 'It is black, I see; it is green, I see; I am tied down with single words. But you wander off; you slip away; you rise up higher, with words and words in phrases.'

'Now,' said Bernard, 'let us explore. There is the white house lying among the trees. It lies down there ever so far beneath us. We shall sink like swimmers just touching the ground with the tips of their toes. We shall sink through the green air of the leaves, Susan. We sink as we run. The waves close over us, the beech leaves meet above our heads. There is the stable clock with its gilt hands shining. Those are the flats and heights of the roofs of the great house. There is the stable-boy clattering in the yard in rubber boots. That is Elvedon.

'Now we have fallen through the tree-tops to the earth. The air no longer rolls its long, unhappy, purple waves over us. We touch earth; we tread ground. That is the close-clipped hedge of the ladies' garden. There they walk at noon, with scissors, clipping roses. Now we are in the ringed wood with the wall round it. This is Elvedon. I have seen signposts at the cross-roads with one arm pointing "To Elvedon". No one has been there. The ferns smell very strong, and there are red funguses growing beneath them. Now we wake the sleeping daws who have never seen a human form; now we tread on rotten oak apples, red with age and slippery. There is a ring of wall round this wood; nobody comes here. Listen! That is the flop of a giant toad in the undergrowth; that is the patter of some primeval fir-cone falling to rot among the ferns.

'Put your foot on this brick. Look over the wall. That is Elvedon. The lady sits between the two long windows, writing. The gardeners sweep the lawn with giant brooms. We are the first to come here. We are the discoverers of an unknown land. Do not stir; if the gardeners saw us they would shoot us. We should be nailed like stoats to the stable door. Look! Do not move. Grasp the ferns tight on the top of the wall.'

'I see the lady writing. I see the gardeners sweeping,' said Susan. 'If we died here, nobody would bury us.'

'Run!' said Bernard. 'Run! The gardener with the black beard has seen us! We shall be shot! We shall be shot like jays and pinned to the wall! We are in a hostile country. We must escape to the beech wood. We must hide under the trees. I turned a twig as we came. There is a secret path. Bend as low as you can. Follow without looking back. They will think we are foxes. Run!

'Now we are safe. Now we can stand upright again. Now we can stretch our arms in this high canopy, in this vast wood. I hear nothing. That is only the murmur of the waves in the air. That is a wood-pigeon breaking cover in the tops of the beech trees. The pigeon beats the air; the pigeon beats the air with wooden wings.'

'Now you trail away,' said Susan, 'making phrases. Now you mount like an air-ball's string, higher and higher through the layers of the leaves, out of reach. Now you lag. Now you tug at my skirts, looking back, making phrases. You have escaped me. Here is the garden. Here is the hedge. Here is Rhoda on the path rocking petals to and fro in her brown basin.'

'All my ships are white,' said Rhoda. 'I do not want red petals of hollyhocks or geranium. I want white petals that float when I tip the basin up. I have a fleet now swimming from shore to shore. I will drop a twig in as a raft for a drowning sailor. I will drop a stone in and see bubbles rise from the depths of the sea. Neville has gone and Susan has gone; Jinny is in the kitchen garden picking currants with Louis perhaps. I have a short time alone, while Miss Hudson spreads our copy-books on the schoolroom table. I have a short space of freedom. I have picked all the fallen petals and made them swim. I have put raindrops in some. I will plant a lighthouse here, a head of Sweet Alice. And I will now rock the brown basin from side to side so that my ships may ride the waves. Some will founder. Some will dash themselves against the cliffs. One sails alone. That is my ship. It sails into icy caverns where the sea-bear barks and stalactites swing green chains. The waves rise; their crests curl; look at the lights on the mastheads. They have scattered, they have foundered, all except my ship, which mounts the wave and sweeps before the gale and reaches the islands where the parrots chatter and the creepers . . .'

'Where is Bernard?' said Neville. 'He has my knife. We were in the tool-shed making boats, and Susan came past the door. And Bernard dropped his boat and went after her taking my knife, the sharp one that cuts the keel. He is like a dangling wire, a broken bell-pull, always twangling. He is like the seaweed hung outside the window, damp now, now dry. He leaves me in the lurch; he follows Susan; and if Susan cries he will take my knife and tell her stories. The big blade is an emperor; the broken blade a Negro. I hate dangling things; I hate dampish things. I hate wandering and mixing things together. Now the bell rings and we shall be late. Now we must drop our toys. Now we must go in together. The copy-books are laid out side by side on the green baize table.'

'I will not conjugate the verb,' said Louis, 'until Bernard has said it. My father is a banker in Brisbane and I speak with an Australian accent. I will wait and copy Bernard. He is English. They are all English. Susan's father is a clergyman. Rhoda has no father. Bernard and Neville are the sons of gentlemen. Jinny lives with her grandmother in London. Now they suck their pens. Now they twist their copy-books, and, looking sideways at Miss Hudson, count the purple buttons on her bodice. Bernard has a chip in his hair. Susan has a red look in her eyes.

Both are flushed. But I am pale; I am neat, and my knickerbockers are drawn together by a belt with a brass snake. I know the lesson by heart. I know more than they will ever know. I know my cases and my genders; I could know everything in the world if I wished. But I do not wish to come to the top and say my lesson. My roots are threaded, like fibres in a flower-pot, round and round about the world. I do not wish to come to the top and live in the light of this great clock, yellow-faced, which ticks and ticks. Jinny and Susan, Bernard and Neville bind themselves into a thong with which to lash me. They laugh at my neatness, at my Australian accent. I will now try to imitate Bernard softly lisping Latin.'

'Those are white words,' said Susan, 'like stones one picks up by the seashore.'

'They flick their tails right and left as I speak them,' said Bernard. 'They wag their tails; they flick their tails; they move through the air in flocks, now this way, now that way, moving all together, now dividing, now coming together.'

'Those are yellow words, those are fiery words,' said Jinny. 'I should like a fiery dress, a yellow dress, a fulvous dress to wear in the evening.'

'Each tense,' said Neville, 'means differently. There is an order in this world; there are distinctions, there are differences in this world, upon whose verge I step. For this is only a beginning.'

'Now Miss Hudson,' said Rhoda, 'has shut the book. Now the terror is beginning. Now taking her lump of chalk she draws figures, six, seven, eight, and then a cross and then a line on the blackboard. What is the answer? The others look; they look with understanding. Louis writes; Susan writes; Neville writes; Jinny writes; even Bernard has now begun to write. But I cannot write. I see only figures. The others are handing in their answers, one by one. Now it is my turn. But I have no answer. The others are allowed to go. They slam the door. Miss Hudson goes. I am left alone to find an answer. The figures mean nothing now. Meaning has gone. The clock ticks. The two hands are convoys marching through a desert. The black bars on the clock face are green oases. The long hand has marched ahead to find water. The other, painfully stumbles among hot stones in the desert. It will die in the desert. The kitchen door slams. Wild dogs bark far away. Look, the loop of the figure is beginning to fill with time; it holds the world in it. I begin to draw a figure and the world is looped in it, and I myself am outside the loop; which I now join—so—and seal up, and make entire. The world is entire, and I am outside of it, crying, "Oh save me, from being blown for ever outside the loop of time!"'

'There Rhoda sits staring at the blackboard,' said Louis, 'in the schoolroom, while we ramble off, picking here a bit of thyme, pinching here a leaf of southernwood while Bernard tells a story. Her shoulder-blades meet across her back like the wings of a small butterfly. And as she stares at the chalk figures, her mind lodges in those white circles, it steps through those white loops into emptiness, alone. They have no meaning for her. She has no answer for them. She has no body as the others have. And I, who speak with an Australian accent, whose father is a banker in Brisbane, do not fear her as I fear the others.'

'Let us now crawl,' said Bernard, 'under the canopy of the currant leaves, and tell stories. Let us inhabit the underworld. Let us take possession of our secret territory, which is lit by pendant currants like candelabra, shining red on one side, black on the other. Here, Jinny, if we curl up close, we can sit under the canopy of the currant leaves and watch the censers swing. This is our universe. The others pass down the carriage-drive. The skirts of Miss Hudson and Miss Curry sweep by like candle extinguishers. Those are Susan's white socks. Those are Louis' neat sand-shoes firmly printing the gravel. Here come warm gusts of decomposing leaves, of rotting vegetation. We are in a swamp now; in a malarial jungle. There is an elephant white with maggots, killed by an arrow shot dead in its eye. The bright eyes of hopping birds—eagles, vultures—are apparent. They take us for fallen trees. They pick at a worm—that is a hooded cobra—and leave it with a festering brown scar to be mauled by lions. This is our world, lit with crescents and stars of light; and great petals half transparent block the openings like purple windows. Everything is strange. Things are huge and very small. The stalks of flowers are thick as oak trees. Leaves are high as the domes of vast cathedrals. We are giants, lying here, who can make forests quiver.'

'This is here,' said Jinny, 'this is now. But soon we shall go. Soon Miss Curry will blow her whistle. We shall walk. We shall part. You will go to school. You will have masters wearing crosses with white ties. I shall have a mistress in a school on the East Coast who sits under a portrait of Queen Alexandra. That is where I am going, and Susan and Rhoda. This is only here; this is only now. Now we lie under the currant bushes and every time the breeze stirs we are mottled all over. My hand is like a snake's skin. My knees are pink floating islands. Your face is like an apple tree netted under.'

'The heat is going,' said Bernard, 'from the Jungle. The leaves flap black wings over us. Miss Curry has blown her whistle on the terrace. We must creep out from the awning of the currant leaves and stand upright. There are twigs in your hair, Jinny. There is a green caterpillar on your neck. We must form, two by two. Miss Curry is taking us for a brisk walk, while Miss Hudson sits at her desk settling her accounts.'

'It is dull,' said Jinny, 'walking along the high road with no windows to look at, with no bleared eyes of blue glass let into the pavement.'

'We must form into pairs,' said Susan, 'and walk in order, not shuffling our feet, not lagging, with Louis going first to lead us, because Louis is alert and not a wool-gatherer.'

'Since I am supposed,' said Neville, 'to be too delicate to go with them, since I get so easily tired and then am sick, I will use this hour of solitude, this reprieve from conversation, to coast round the purlieus of the house and recover, if I can, by standing on the same stair half-way up the landing, what I felt when I heard about the dead man through the swing-door last night when cook was shoving in and out the dampers. He was found with his throat cut. The apple-tree leaves became fixed in the sky; the moon glared; I was unable to lift my foot up the stair. He was found in the gutter. His blood gurgled down the gutter. His jowl was white as a dead codfish. I shall call this stricture, this rigidity, "death among the apple trees" for ever. There were the floating, pale-grey clouds; and the immitigable tree; the implacable tree with its greaved silver bark. The ripple of my life was unavailing. I was unable to pass by. There was an obstacle. "I cannot surmount this unintelligible obstacle", I said. And the others passed on. But we are doomed, all of us, by the apple trees, by the immitigable tree which we cannot pass.

'Now the stricture and rigidity are over; and I will continue to make my survey of the purlieus of the house in the late afternoon, in the sunset, when the sun makes oleaginous spots on the linoleum, and a crack of light kneels on the wall, making the chair legs look broken.'

'I saw Florrie in the kitchen garden,' said Susan, 'as we came back from our walk, with the washing blown out round her, the pyjamas, the drawers, the night-gowns blown tight. And Ernest kissed her. He was in his green baize apron, cleaning silver; and his mouth was sucked like a purse in wrinkles and he seized her with the pyjamas blown out hard between them. He was blind as a bull, and she swooned in anguish, only little veins streaking her white cheeks red. Now though they pass plates of bread and butter and cups of milk at tea-time I see a crack in the earth and hot steam hisses up; and the urn roars as Ernest roared, and I am blown out hard like the pyjamas, even while my teeth meet in the soft bread and butter, and I lap the sweet milk. I am not afraid of heat, nor of the frozen winter. Rhoda dreams, sucking a crust soaked in milk; Louis regards the wall opposite with snail-green eyes; Bernard moulds his bread into pellets and calls them "people". Neville with his clean and decisive ways has finished. He has rolled his napkin and slipped it through the silver ring. Jinny spins her fingers on the table-cloth, as if they were dancing in the sunshine, pirouetting. But I am not afraid of the heat or of the frozen winter.'

'Now,' said Louis, 'we all rise; we all stand up. Miss Curry spreads wide the black book on the harmonium. It is difficult not to weep as we sing, as we pray that God may keep us safe while we sleep, calling ourselves little children. When we are sad and trembling with apprehension it is sweet to sing together, leaning slightly, I towards Susan, Susan towards Bernard, clasping hands, afraid of much, I of my accent, Rhoda of figures; yet resolute to conquer.'

'We troop upstairs like ponies,' said Bernard, 'stamping, clattering one behind another to take our turns in the bathroom. We buffet, we tussle, we spring up and down on the hard, white beds. My turn has come. I come now.

'Mrs Constable, girt in a bath-towel, takes her lemon-coloured sponge and soaks it in water; it turns chocolate-brown; it drips; and, holding it high above me, shivering beneath her, she squeezes it. Water pours down the runnel of my spine. Bright arrows of sensation shoot on either side. I am covered with warm flesh. My dry crannies are wetted; my cold body is warmed; it is sluiced and gleaming. Water descends and sheets me like an eel. Now hot towels envelop me, and their roughness, as I rub my back, makes my blood purr. Rich and heavy sensations form on the roof of my mind; down showers the day—the woods; and Elvedon; Susan and the pigeon. Pouring down the walls of my mind, running together, the day falls copious, resplendent. Now I tie my pyjamas loosely round me, and lie under this thin sheet afloat in the shallow light which is like a film of water drawn over my eyes by a wave. I hear through it far off, far away, faint and far, the chorus beginning; wheels; dogs; men shouting; church bells; the chorus beginning.'

'As I fold up my frock and my chemise,' said Rhoda, 'so I put off my hopeless desire to be Susan, to be Jinny. But I will stretch my toes so that they touch the rail at the end of the bed; I will assure myself, touching the rail, of something hard. Now I cannot sink; cannot altogether fall through the thin sheet now. Now I spread my body on this frail mattress and hang suspended. I am above the earth now. I am no longer upright, to be knocked against and damaged. All is soft, and bending. Walls and cupboards whiten and bend their yellow squares on top of which a pale glass gleams. Out of me now my mind can pour. I can think of my Armadas sailing on the high waves. I am relieved of hard contacts and collisions. I sail on alone under white cliffs. Oh, but I sink, I fall! That is the corner of the cupboard; that is the nursery looking-glass. But they stretch, they elongate. I sink down on the black plumes of sleep; its thick wings are pressed to my eyes. Travelling through darkness I see the stretched flower-beds, and Mrs Constable runs from behind the corner of the pampas-grass to say my aunt has come to fetch me in a carriage. I mount; I escape; I rise on spring-heeled boots over the tree-tops. But I am now fallen into the carriage at the hall door, where she sits nodding yellow plumes with eyes hard like glazed marbles. Oh, to awake from dreaming! Look, there is the chest of drawers. Let me pull myself out of these waters. But they heap themselves on me; they sweep me between their great shoulders; I am turned; I am tumbled; I am stretched, among these long lights, these long waves, these endless paths, with people pursuing, pursuing.'

The sun rose higher. Blue waves, green waves swept a quick fan over the beach, circling the spike of sea-holly and leaving shallow pools of light here and there on the sand. A faint black rim was left behind them. The rocks which had been misty and soft hardened and were marked with red clefts.

Sharp stripes of shadow lay on the grass, and the dew dancing on the tips of the flowers and leaves made the garden like a mosaic of single sparks not yet formed into one whole. The birds, whose breasts were specked canary and rose, now sang a strain or two together, wildly, like skaters rollicking arm-in-arm, and were suddenly silent, breaking asunder.

The sun laid broader blades upon the house. The light touched something green in the window corner and made it a lump of emerald, a cave of pure green like stoneless fruit. It sharpened the edges of chairs and tables and stitched white table-cloths with fine gold wires. As the light increased a bud here and there split asunder and shook out flowers, green veined and quivering, as if the effort of opening had set them rocking, and pealing a faint carillon as they beat their frail clappers against their white walls. Everything became softly amorphous, as if the china of the plate flowed and the steel of the knife were liquid. Meanwhile the concussion of the waves breaking fell with muffled thuds, like logs falling, on the shore.

'Now,' said Bernard, 'the time has come. The day has come. The cab is at the door. My huge box bends George's bandy-legs even wider. The horrible ceremony is over, the tips, and the good-byes in the hall. Now there is this gulping ceremony with my mother, this hand-shaking ceremony with my father; now I must go on waving, I must go on waving, till we turn the corner. Now that ceremony is over. Heaven be praised, all ceremonies are over. I am alone; I am going to school for the first time.

'Everybody seems to be doing things for this moment only; and never again. Never again. The urgency of it all is fearful. Everybody knows I am going to school, going to school for the first time. "That boy is going to school for the first time", says the housemaid, cleaning the steps. I must not cry. I must behold them indifferently. Now the awful portals of the station gape; "the moon-faced clock regards me". I must make phrases and phrases and so interpose something hard between myself and the stare of housemaids, the stare of clocks, staring faces, indifferent faces, or I shall cry. There is Louis, there is Neville, in long coats, carrying handbags, by the booking-office. They are composed. But they look different.'

'Here is Bernard,' said Louis. 'He is composed; he is easy. He swings his bag as he walks. I will follow Bernard, because he is not afraid. We are drawn through the booking-office on to the platform as a stream draws twigs and straws round the piers of a bridge. There is the very powerful, bottle-green engine without a neck, all back and thighs, breathing steam. The guard blows his whistle; the flag is dipped; without an effort, of its own momentum, like an avalanche started by a gentle push, we start forward. Bernard spreads a rug and plays knuckle-bones. Neville reads. London crumbles. London heaves and surges. There is a bristling of chimneys and towers. There a white church; there a mast among the spires. There a canal. Now there are open spaces with asphalt paths upon which it is strange that people should now be walking. There is a hill striped with red houses. A man crosses a bridge with a dog at his heels. Now the red boy begins firing at a pheasant. The blue boy shoves him aside. "My uncle is the best shot in England. My cousin is Master of Foxhounds." Boasting begins. And I cannot boast, for my father is a banker in Brisbane, and I speak with an Australian accent.'

'After all this hubbub,' said Neville, 'all this scuffling and hubbub, we have arrived. This is indeed a moment—this is indeed a solemn moment. I come, like a lord to his halls appointed. That is our founder; our illustrious founder, standing in the courtyard with one foot raised. I salute our founder. A noble Roman air hangs over these austere quadrangles. Already the lights are lit in the form rooms. Those are laboratories perhaps; and that a library, where I shall explore the exactitude of the Latin language, and step firmly upon the well-laid sentences, and pronounce the explicit, the sonorous hexameters of Virgil, of Lucretius; and chant with a passion that is never obscure or formless the loves of Catullus, reading from a big book, a quarto with margins. I shall lie, too, in the fields among the tickling grasses. I shall lie with my friends under the towering elm trees.

'Behold, the Headmaster. Alas, that he should excite my ridicule. He is too sleek, he is altogether too shiny and black, like some statue in a public garden. And on the left side of his waistcoat, his taut, his drum-like waistcoat, hangs a crucifix.'

'Old Crane,' said Bernard, 'now rises to address us. Old Crane, the Headmaster, has a nose like a mountain at sunset, and a blue cleft in his chin, like a wooded ravine, which some tripper has fired; like a wooded ravine seen from the train window. He sways slightly, mouthing out his tremendous and sonorous words. I love tremendous and sonorous words. But his words are too hearty to be true. Yet he is by this time convinced of their truth. And when he leaves the room, lurching rather heavily from side to side, and hurls his way through the swing-doors, all the masters, lurching rather heavily from side to side, hurl themselves also through the swing-doors. This is our first night at school, apart from our sisters.'

'This is my first night at school,' said Susan, 'away from my father, away from my home. My eyes swell; my eyes prick with tears. I hate the smell of pine and linoleum. I hate the wind-bitten shrubs and the sanitary tiles. I hate the cheerful jokes and the glazed look of everyone. I left my squirrel and my doves for the boy to look after. The kitchen door slams, and shot patters among the leaves when Percy fires at the rooks. All here is false; all is meretricious. Rhoda and Jinny sit far off in brown serge, and look at Miss Lambert who sits under a picture of Queen Alexandra reading from a book before her. There is also a blue scroll of needlework embroidered by some old girl. If I do not purse my lips, if I do not screw my handkerchief, I shall cry.'

'The purple light,' said Rhoda, 'in Miss Lambert's ring passes to and

fro across the black stain on the white page of the Prayer Book. It is a
vinous, it is an amorous light. Now that our boxes are unpacked in the
dormitories, we sit herded together under maps of the entire world.
There are desks with wells for the ink. We shall write our exercises in
ink here. But here I am nobody. I have no face. This great company, all
dressed in brown serge, has robbed me of my identity. We are all
callous, unfriended. I will seek out a face, a composed, a monumental
face, and will endow it with omniscience, and wear it under my dress
like a talisman and then (I promise this) I will find some dingle in a
wood where I can display my assortment of curious treasures. I promise
myself this. So I will not cry.'

'That dark woman,' said Jinny, 'with high cheek-bones, has a shiny
dress, like a shell, veined, for wearing in the evening. That is nice for
summer, but for winter I should like a thin dress shot with red threads
that would gleam in the firelight. Then when the lamps were lit, I
should put on my red dress and it would be thin as a veil, and would
wind about my body, and billow out as I came into the room,
pirouetting. It would make a flower shape as I sank down, in the middle
of the room, on a gilt chair. But Miss Lambert wears an opaque dress,
that falls in a cascade from her snow-white ruffle as she sits under a
picture of Queen Alexandra pressing one white finger firmly on the
page. And we pray.'

'Now we march, two by two,' said Louis, 'orderly, processional, into
chapel. I like the dimness that falls as we enter the sacred building. I
like the orderly progress. We file in; we seat ourselves. We put off our
distinctions as we enter. I like it now, when, lurching slightly, but only
from his momentum, Dr Crane mounts the pulpit and reads the lesson
from a Bible spread on the back of the brass eagle. I rejoice; my heart
expands in his bulk, in his authority. He lays the whirling dust clouds
in my tremulous, my ignominiously agitated mind—how we danced
round the Christmas tree and handing parcels they forgot me, and the
fat woman said, "This little boy has no present", and gave me a shiny
Union Jack from the top of the tree, and I cried with fury—to be
remembered with pity. Now all is laid by his authority, his crucifix, and
I feel come over me the sense of the earth under me, and my roots going
down and down till they wrap themselves round some hardness at the
centre. I recover my continuity, as he reads. I become a figure in the
procession, a spoke in the huge wheel that turning, at last erects me,
here and now. I have been in the dark; I have been hidden; but when
the wheel turns (as he reads) I rise into this dim light where I just
perceive, but scarcely, kneeling boys, pillars and memorial brasses.
There is no crudity here, no sudden kisses.'

'The brute menaces my liberty,' said Neville, 'when he prays.

Unwarmed by imagination, his words fall cold on my head like paving-stones, while the gilt cross heaves on his waistcoat. The words of authority are corrupted by those who speak them. I gibe and mock at this sad religion, at these tremulous, grief-stricken figures advancing, cadaverous and wounded, down a white road shadowed by fig trees where boys sprawl in the dust—naked boys; and goatskins distended with wine hang at the tavern door. I was in Rome travelling with my father at Easter; and the trembling figure of Christ's mother was borne niddle-noddling along the streets; there went by also the stricken figure of Christ in a glass case.

'Now I will lean sideways as if to scratch my thigh. So I shall see Percival. There he sits, upright among the smaller fry. He breathes through his straight nose rather heavily. His blue and oddly inexpressive eyes are fixed with pagan indifference upon the pillar opposite. He would make an admirable churchwarden. He should have a birch and beat little boys for misdemeanours. He is allied with the Latin phrases on the memorial brasses. He sees nothing; he hears nothing. He is remote from us all in a pagan universe. But look—he flicks his hand to the back of his neck. For such gestures one falls hopelessly in love for a lifetime. Dalton, Jones, Edgar and Bateman flick their hands to the back of their necks likewise. But they do not succeed.'

'At last,' said Bernard, 'the growl ceases. The sermon ends. He has minced the dance of the white butterflies at the door to powder. His rough and hairy voice is like an unshaven chin. Now he lurches back to his seat like a drunken sailor. It is an action that all the other masters will try to imitate; but, being flimsy, being floppy, wearing grey trousers, they will only succeed in making themselves ridiculous. I do not despise them. Their antics seem pitiable in my eyes. I note the fact for future reference with many others in my notebook. When I am grown up I shall carry a notebook—a fat book with many pages, methodically lettered. I shall enter my phrases. Under B shall come "Butterfly powder". If, in my novel, I describe the sun on the window-sill, I shall look under B and find butterfly powder. That will be useful. The tree "shades the window with green fingers". That will be useful. But alas! I am so soon distracted—by a hair like twisted candy, by Celia's Prayer Book, ivory covered. Louis can contemplate nature, unwinking, by the hour. Soon I fail, unless talked to. "The lake of my mind, unbroken by oars, heaves placidly and soon sinks into an oily somnolence." That will be useful.'

'Now we move out of this cool temple, into the yellow playing-fields,' said Louis. 'And, as it is a half-holiday (the Duke's birthday) we will settle among the long grasses, while they play cricket. Could I be "they" I would choose it; I would buckle on my pads and stride across the playing-field at the head of the batsmen. Look now, how everybody follows Percival. He is heavy. He walks clumsily down the field, through the long grass, to where the great elm trees stand. His magnificence is that of some mediaeval commander. A wake of light seems to lie on the grass behind him. Look at us trooping after him, his faithful servants, to be shot like sheep, for he will certainly attempt some forlorn enterprise and die in battle. My heart turns rough; it abrades my side like a file with two edges: one, that I adore his magnificence; the other I despise his slovenly accents—I who am so much his superior—and am jealous.'

'And now,' said Neville, 'let Bernard begin. Let him burble on, telling us stories, while we lie recumbent. Let him describe what we have all seen so that it becomes a sequence. Bernard says there is always a story. I am a story. Louis is a story. There is the story of the boot-boy, the story of the man with one eye, the story of the woman who sells winkles. Let him burble on with his story while I lie back and regard the stiff-legged figures of the padded batsmen through the trembling grasses. It seems as if the whole world were flowing and curving—on the earth the trees, in the sky the clouds. I look up, through the trees, into the sky. The match seems to be played up there. Faintly among the soft, white clouds I hear the cry "Run", I hear the cry "How's that?" The clouds lose tufts of whiteness as the breeze dishevels them. If that blue could stay for ever; if that hole could remain for ever; if this moment could stay for ever——

'But Bernard goes on talking. Up they bubble—images. "Like a camel", . . . "a vulture". The camel is a vulture; the vulture a camel; for Bernard is a dangling wire, loose, but seductive. Yes, for when he talks, when he makes his foolish comparisons, a lightness comes over one. One floats, too, as if one were that bubble; one is freed; I have escaped, one feels. Even the chubby little boys (Dalton, Larpent and Baker) feel the same abandonment. They like this better than the cricket. They catch the phrases as they bubble. They let the feathery grasses tickle their noses. And then we all feel Percival lying heavy among us. His curious guffaw seems to sanction our laughter. But now he has rolled himself over in the long grass. He is, I think, chewing a stalk between his teeth. He feels bored; I too feel bored. Bernard at once perceives that we are bored. I detect a certain effort, an extravagance in his phrase, as if he said "Look!" but Percival says "No". For he is always the first to detect insincerity; and is brutal in the extreme. The sentence tails off feebly. Yes, the appalling moment has come when Bernard's power fails him and there is no longer any sequence and he sags and twiddles a bit of string and falls silent, gaping as if about to burst into tears. Among the tortures and devastations of life is this then—our friends are not able to finish their stories.'

'Now let me try,' said Louis, 'before we rise, before we go to tea, to fix the moment in one effort of supreme endeavour. This shall endure. We are parting; some to tea; some to the nets; I to show my essay to Mr Barker. This will endure. From discord, from hatred (I despise dabblers in imagery—I resent the power of Percival intensely) my shattered mind is pieced together by some sudden perception. I take the trees, the clouds, to be witnesses of my complete integration. I, Louis, I, who shall walk the earth these seventy years, am born entire, out of hatred, out of discord. Here on this ring of grass we have sat together, bound by the tremendous power of some inner compulsion. The trees wave, the clouds pass. The time approaches when these soliloquies shall be shared. We shall not always give out a sound like a beaten gong as one sensation strikes and then another. Children, our lives have been gongs striking; clamour and boasting; cries of despair; blows on the nape of the neck in gardens.

'Now grass and trees, the travelling air blowing empty spaces in the blue which they then recover, shaking the leaves which then replace themselves, and our ring here, sitting, with our arms binding our knees, hint at some other order, and better, which makes a reason everlastingly. This I see for a second, and shall try tonight to fix in words, to forge in a ring of steel, though Percival destroys it, as he blunders off, crushing the grasses, with the small fry trotting subservient after him. Yet it is Percival I need; for it is Percival who inspires poetry.'

'For how many months,' said Susan, 'for how many years, have I run up these stairs, in the dismal days of winter, in the chilly days of spring? Now it is midsummer. We go upstairs to change into white frocks to play tennis—Jinny and I with Rhoda following after. I count each step as I mount, counting each step something done with. So each night I tear off the old day from the calendar, and screw it tight into a ball. I do this vindictively, while Betty and Clara are on their knees. I do not pray. I revenge myself upon the day. I wreak my spite upon its image. You are dead now, I say, school day, hated day. They have made all the days of June—this is the twenty-fifth—shiny and orderly, with gongs, with lessons, with orders to wash, to change, to work, to eat. We listen to missionaries from China. We drive off in brakes along the asphalt pavement, to attend concerts in halls. We are shown galleries and pictures.

'At home the hay waves over the meadows. My father leans upon the stile, smoking. In the house one door bangs and then another, as the summer air puffs along the empty passages. Some old picture perhaps swings on the wall. A petal drops from the rose in the jar. The farm wagons strew the hedges with tufts of hay. All this I see, I always see, as I pass the looking-glass on the landing, with Jinny in front and Rhoda lagging behind. Jinny dances. Jinny always dances in the hall on the ugly, the encaustic tiles; she turns cartwheels in the playground; she picks some flower forbiddenly, and sticks it behind her ear so that Miss Perry's dark eyes smoulder with admiration, for Jinny, not me. Miss Perry loves Jinny; and I could have loved her, but now love no one, except my father, my doves and the squirrel whom I left in the cage at home for the boy to look after.'

'I hate the small looking-glass on the stairs,' said Jinny. 'It shows our heads only; it cuts off our heads. And my lips are too wide, and my eyes are too close together; I show my gums too much when I laugh. Susan's head, with its fell look, with its grass-green eyes which poets will love, Bernard said, because they fall upon close white stitching, put mine out; even Rhoda's face, mooning, vacant, is completed, like those white petals she used to swim in her bowl. So I skip up the stairs past them, to the next landing, where the long glass hangs and I see myself entire. I see my body and head in one now; for even in this serge frock they are one, my body and my head. Look, when I move my head I ripple all down my narrow body; even my thin legs ripple like a stalk in the wind. I flicker between the set face of Susan and Rhoda's vagueness; I leap like one of those flames that run between the cracks of the earth; I move, I dance; I never cease to move and to dance. I move like the leaf that moved in the hedge as a child and frightened me. I dance over these streaked, these impersonal, distempered walls with their yellow skirting as firelight dances over teapots. I catch fire even from women's cold eyes. When I read, a purple rim runs round the black edge of the textbook. Yet I cannot follow any word through its changes. I cannot follow any thought from present to past. I do not stand lost, like Susan, with tears in my eyes remembering home; or lie, like Rhoda, crumpled among the ferns, staining my pink cotton green, while I dream of plants that flower under the sea, and rocks through which the fish swim slowly. I do not dream.

'Now let us be quick. Now let me be the first to pull off these coarse clothes. Here are my clean white stockings. Here are my new shoes. I bind my hair with a white ribbon, so that when I leap across the court the ribbon will stream out in a flash, yet curl round my neck, perfectly in its place. Not a hair shall be untidy.'

'That is my face,' said Rhoda, 'in the looking-glass behind Susan's shoulder—that face is my face. But I will duck behind her to hide it, for I am not here. I have no face. Other people have faces; Susan and Jinny have faces; they are here. Their world is the real world. The things they lift are heavy. They say Yes, they say No; whereas I shift and change and am seen through in a second. If they meet a housemaid she looks at them without laughing. But she laughs at me. They know what to say if spoken to. They laugh really; they get angry really; while I have to look first and do what other people do when they have done it.

'See now with what extraordinary certainty Jinny pulls on her stockings, simply to play tennis. That I admire. But I like Susan's way better, for she is more resolute, and less ambitious of distinction than Jinny. Both despise me for copying what they do; but Susan sometimes teaches me, for instance, how to tie a bow, while Jinny has her own knowledge but keeps it to herself. They have friends to sit by. They have things to say privately in corners. But I attach myself only to names and faces; and hoard them like amulets against disaster. I choose out across the hall some unknown face and can hardly drink my tea when she whose name I do not know sits opposite. I choke. I am rocked from side to side by the violence of my emotion. I imagine these nameless, these immaculate people, watching me from behind bushes. I leap high to excite their admiration. At night, in bed, I excite their complete wonder. I often die pierced with arrows to win their tears. If they should say, or I should see from a label on their boxes, that they were in Scarborough last holidays, the whole town runs gold, the whole pavement is illuminated. Therefore I hate looking-glasses which show me my real face. Alone, I often fall down into nothingness. I must push my foot stealthily lest I should fall off the edge of the world into nothingness. I have to bang my head against some hard door to call myself back to the body.'

'We are late,' said Susan. 'We must wait our turn to play. We will pitch here in the long grass and pretend to watch Jinny and Clara, Betty and Mavis. But we will not watch them. I hate watching other people play games. I will make images of all the things I hate most and bury them in the ground. This shiny pebble is Madame Carlo, and I will bury her deep because of her fawning and ingratiating manners, because of the sixpence she gave me for keeping my knuckles flat when I played my scales. I buried her sixpence. I would bury the whole school: the gymnasium; the classroom; the dining-room that always smells of meat; and the chapel. I would bury the red-brown tiles and the oily portraits of old men—benefactors, founders of schools. There are some trees I like; the cherry tree with lumps of clear gum on the bark; and one view from the attic towards some far hills. Save for these, I would bury it all as I bury these ugly stones that are always scattered about this briny coast, with its piers and its trippers. At home, the waves are mile long. On winter nights we hear them booming. Last Christmas a man was drowned sitting alone in his cart.'

'When Miss Lambert passes,' said Rhoda, 'talking to the clergyman, the others laugh and imitate her hunch behind her back; yet everything changes and becomes luminous. Jinny leaps higher too when Miss Lambert passes. Suppose she saw that daisy, it would change. Wherever she goes, things are changed under her eyes; and yet when she has gone is not the thing the same again? Miss Lambert is taking the clergyman through the wicket-gate to her private garden; and when she comes to the pond, she sees a frog on a leaf, and that will change. All is solemn, all is pale where she stands, like a statue in a grove. She lets her tasselled silken cloak slip down, and only her purple ring still glows, her vinous, her amethystine ring. There is this mystery about people when they leave us. When they leave us I can companion them to the pond and make them stately. When Miss Lambert passes, she makes the daisy change; and everything runs like streaks of fire when she carves the beef. Month by month things are losing their hardness; even my body now lets the light through; my spine is soft like wax near the flame of the candle. I dream; I dream.'

'I have won the game,' said Jinny. 'Now it is your turn. I must throw myself on the ground and pant. I am out of breath with running, with triumph. Everything in my body seems thinned out with running and triumph. My blood must be bright red, whipped up, slapping against my ribs. My soles tingle, as if wire rings opened and shut in my feet. I see every blade of grass very clear. But the pulse drums so in my forehead, behind my eyes, that everything dances—the net, the grass; your faces leap like butterflies; the trees seem to jump up and down. There is nothing staid, nothing settled, in this universe. All is rippling, all is dancing; all is quickness and triumph. Only, when I have lain alone on the hard ground, watching you play your game, I begin to feel the wish to be singled out; to be summoned, to be called away by one person who comes to find me, who is attracted towards me, who cannot keep himself from me, but comes to where I sit on my gilt chair, with my frock billowing round me like a flower. And withdrawing into an alcove, sitting alone on a balcony we talk together.

'Now the tide sinks. Now the trees come to earth; the brisk waves that slap my ribs rock more gently, and my heart rides at anchor, like a sailing-boat whose sails slide slowly down on to the white deck. The game is over. We must go to tea now.'

'The boasting boys,' said Louis, 'have gone now in a vast team to play cricket. They have driven off in their great brake, singing in chorus. All their heads turn simultaneously at the corner by the laurel bushes. Now they are boasting. Larpent's brother played football for Oxford; Smith's father made a century at Lords. Archie and Hugh; Parker and Dalton; Larpent and Smith; then again Archie and Hugh; Parker and Dalton; Larpent and Smith—the names repeat themselves; the names are the same always. They are the volunteers; they are the cricketers; they are the officers of the Natural History Society. They are always forming into fours and marching in troops with badges on their caps; they salute simultaneously passing the figure of their general. How majestic is their order, how beautiful is their obedience! If I could follow, if I could be with them, I would sacrifice all I know. But they also leave butterflies trembling with their wings pinched off; they throw dirty pocket-handkerchiefs clotted with blood screwed up into corners. They make little boys sob in dark passages. They have big red ears that stand out under their caps. Yet that is what we wish to be, Neville and I. I watch them go with envy. Peeping from behind a curtain, I note the simultaneity of their movements with delight. If my legs were reinforced by theirs, how they would run! If I had been with them and won matches and rowed in great races, and galloped all day, how I should thunder out songs at midnight! In what a torrent the words would rush from my throat!'

'Percival has gone now,' said Neville. 'He is thinking of nothing but the match. He never waved his hand as the brake turned the corner by the laurel bush. He despises me for being too weak to play (yet he is always kind to my weakness). He despises me for not caring if they win or lose except that he cares. He takes my devotion; he accepts my tremulous, no doubt abject offering, mixed with contempt as it is for his mind. For he cannot read. Yet when I read Shakespeare or Catullus, lying in the long grass, he understands more than Louis. Not the words—but what are words? Do I not know already how to rhyme, how to imitate Pope, Dryden, even Shakespeare? But I cannot stand all day in the sun with my eyes on the ball; I cannot feel the flight of the ball through my body and think only of the ball. I shall be a clinger to the outsides of words all my life. Yet I could not live with him and suffer his stupidity. He will coarsen and snore. He will marry and there will be scenes of tenderness at breakfast. But now he is young. Not a thread, not a sheet of paper lies between him and the sun, between him and the rain, between him and the moon as he lies naked, tumbled, hot, on his bed. Now as they drive along the high road in their brake his face is mottled red and yellow. He will throw off his coat and stand with his legs apart, with his hands ready, watching the wicket. And he will pray, "Lord let us win"; he will think of one thing only, that they should win.

'How could I go with them in a brake to play cricket? Only Bernard could go with them, but Bernard is too late to go with them. He is always too late. He is prevented by his incorrigible moodiness from going with them. He stops, when he washes his hands, to say, "There is a fly in that web. Shall I rescue that fly; shall I let the spider eat it?" He is shaded with innumerable perplexities, or he would go with them to play cricket, and would lie in the grass, watching the sky, and would start when the ball was hit. But they would forgive him; for he would tell them a story.'

'They have bowled off,' said Bernard, 'and I am too late to go with them. The horrid little boys, who are also so beautiful, whom you and Louis, Neville, envy so deeply, have bowled off with their heads all turned the same way. But I am unaware of these profound distinctions. My fingers slip over the keyboard without knowing which is black and which white. Archie makes easily a hundred; I by a fluke make sometimes fifteen. But what is the difference between us? Wait though, Neville; let me talk. The bubbles are rising like the silver bubbles from the floor of a saucepan; image on top of image. I cannot sit down to my book, like Louis, with ferocious tenacity. I must open the little trap-door and let out these linked phrases in which I run together whatever happens, so that instead of incoherence there is perceived a wandering thread, lightly joining one thing to another. I will tell you the story of the doctor.

'When Dr Crane lurches through the swing-doors after prayers he is convinced, it seems, of his immense superiority; and indeed, Neville, we cannot deny that his departure leaves us not only with a sense of relief, but also with a sense of something removed, like a tooth. Now let us follow him as he heaves through the swing-door to his own apartments. Let us imagine him in his private room over the stables undressing. He unfastens his sock suspenders (let us be trivial, let us be intimate). Then with a characteristic gesture (it is difficult to avoid these ready-made phrases, and they are, in his case, somehow appropriate) he takes the silver, he takes the coppers from his trouser pockets and places them there, and there, on his dressing-table. With both arms stretched on the arms of his chair he reflects (this is his private moment; it is here we must try to catch him): shall he cross the pink bridge into his bedroom or shall he not cross it? The two rooms are united by a bridge of rosy light from the lamp at the bedside where Mrs Crane lies with her hair on the pillow reading a French memoir. As she reads, she sweeps her hand with an abandoned and despairing gesture over her forehead, and sighs, "Is this all?" comparing herself with some French duchess. Now, says the doctor, in two years I shall retire. I shall clip yew hedges in a west country garden. An admiral I might have been; or a judge; not a schoolmaster. What forces, he asks, staring at the gas-fire with his shoulders hunched up more hugely than we know them (he is in his shirt-sleeves remember), have brought me to this? What vast forces? he thinks, getting into the stride of his majestic phrases as he looks over his shoulder at the window. It is a stormy night; the branches of the chestnut trees are ploughing up and down. Stars flash between them. What vast forces of good and evil have brought me here? he asks, and sees with sorrow that his chair has worn a little hole in the pile of the purple carpet. So there he sits, swinging his braces. But stories that follow people into their private rooms are difficult. I cannot go on with this story. I twiddle a piece of string; I turn over four or five coins in my trouser pocket.'

'Bernard's stories amuse me,' said Neville, 'at the start. But when they tail off absurdly and he gapes, twiddling a bit of string, I feel my own solitude. He sees everyone with blurred edges. Hence I cannot talk to him of Percival. I cannot expose my absurd and violent passion to his sympathetic understanding. It too would make a "story". I need someone whose mind falls like a chopper on a block; to whom the pitch of absurdity is sublime, and a shoe-string adorable. To whom can I expose the urgency of my own passion? Louis is too cold, too universal. There is nobody—here among these grey arches, and moaning pigeons, and cheerful games and tradition and emulation, all so skilfully organized to prevent feeling alone. Yet I am struck still as I walk by sudden premonitions of what is to come. Yesterday, passing the open door leading into the private garden, I saw Fenwick with his mallet raised. The steam from the tea-urn rose in the middle of the lawn. There were banks of blue flowers. Then suddenly descended upon me the obscure, the mystic sense of adoration, of completeness that triumphed over chaos. Nobody saw my poised and intent figure as I stood at the open door. Nobody guessed the need I had to offer my being to one god; and perish, and disappear. His mallet descended; the vision broke.

'Should I seek out some tree? Should I desert these form rooms and libraries, and the broad yellow page in which I read Catullus, for woods and fields? Should I walk under beech trees, or saunter along the river bank, where the trees meet united like lovers in the water? But nature is too vegetable, too vapid. She has only sublimities and vastitudes and water and leaves. I begin to wish for firelight, privacy, and the limbs of one person.'

'I begin to wish,' said Louis, 'for night to come. As I stand here with my hand on the grained oak panel of Mr Wickham's door I think myself the friend of Richelieu, or the Duke of St Simon holding out a snuff-box to the King himself. It is my privilege. My witticisms "run like wildfire through the court". Duchesses tear emeralds from their earrings out of admiration—but these rockets rise best in darkness, in my cubicle at night. I am now a boy only with a colonial accent holding my knuckles against Mr Wickham's grained oak door. The day has been full of ignominies and triumphs concealed from fear of laughter. I am the best scholar in the school. But when darkness comes I put off this unenviable body—my large nose, my thin lips, my colonial accent— and inhabit space. I am then Virgil's companion, and Plato's. I am then the last scion of one of the great houses of France. But I am also one who will force himself to desert these windy and moonlit territories, these midnight wanderings, and confront grained oak doors. I will achieve in my life—Heaven grant that it be not long—some gigantic amalgamation between the two discrepancies so hideously apparent to me. Out of my suffering I will do it. I will knock. I will enter.'

'I have torn off the whole of May and June,' said Susan, 'and twenty days of July. I have torn them off and screwed them up so that they no longer exist, save as a weight in my side. They have been crippled days, like moths with shrivelled wings unable to fly. There are only eight days left. In eight days' time I shall get out of the train and stand on the platform at six twenty-five. Then my freedom will unfurl, and all these restrictions that wrinkle and shrivel—hours and order and discipline, and being here and there exactly at the right moment—will crack asunder. Out the day will spring, as I open the carriage-door and see my father in his old hat and gaiters. I shall tremble. I shall burst into tears. Then next morning I shall get up at dawn. I shall let myself out by the kitchen door. I shall walk on the moor. The great horses of the phantom riders will thunder behind me and stop suddenly. I shall see the swallow skim the grass. I shall throw myself on a bank by the river and watch the fish slip in and out among the reeds. The palms of my hands will be printed with pine-needles. I shall there unfold and take out whatever it is I have made here; something hard. For something has grown in me here, through the winters and summers, on staircases, in bedrooms. I do not want, as Jinny wants, to be admired. I do not want people, when I come in, to look up with admiration. I want to give, to be given, and solitude in which to unfold my possessions.

'Then I shall come back through the trembling lanes under the arches of the nut leaves. I shall pass an old woman wheeling a perambulator full of sticks; and the shepherd. But we shall not speak. I shall come back through the kitchen garden, and see the curved leaves of the cabbages pebbled with dew, and the house in the garden, blind with curtained windows. I shall go upstairs to my room, and turn over my own things, locked carefully in the wardrobe: my shells; my eggs; my curious grasses. I shall feed my doves and my squirrel. I shall go to the kennel and comb my spaniel. So gradually I shall turn over the hard thing that has grown here in my side. But here bells ring; feet shuffle perpetually.'

'I hate darkness and sleep and night,' said Jinny, 'and lie longing for the day to come. I long that the week should be all one day without divisions. When I wake early—and the birds wake me—I lie and watch the brass handles on the cupboard grow clear; then the basin; then the towel-horse. As each thing in the bedroom grows clear, my heart beats quicker. I feel my body harden, and become pink, yellow, brown. My hands pass over my legs and body. I feel its slopes, its thinness. I love to hear the gong roar through the house and the stir begin—here a thud, there a patter. Doors slam; water rushes. Here is another day, here is another day, I cry, as my feet touch the floor. It may be a bruised day, an imperfect day. I am often scolded. I am often in disgrace for idleness, for laughing; but even as Miss Matthews grumbles at my feather-headed carelessness, I catch sight of something moving—a speck of sun perhaps on a picture, or the donkey drawing the mowing-machine across the lawn; or a sail that passes between the laurel leaves, so that I am never cast down. I cannot be prevented from pirouetting behind Miss Matthews into prayers.

'Now, too, the time is coming when we shall leave school and wear long skirts. I shall wear necklaces and a white dress without sleeves at night. There will be parties in brilliant rooms; and one man will single me out and will tell me what he has told no other person. He will like me better than Susan or Rhoda. He will find in me some quality, some peculiar thing. But I shall not let myself be attached to one person only. I do not want to be fixed, to be pinioned. I tremble, I quiver, like the leaf in the hedge, as I sit dangling my feet, on the edge of the bed, with a new day to break open. I have fifty years, I have sixty years to spend. I have not yet broken into my hoard. This is the beginning.'

'There are hours and hours,' said Rhoda, 'before I can put out the light and lie suspended on my bed above the world, before I can let the day drop down, before I can let my tree grow, quivering in green pavilions above my head. Here I cannot let it grow. Somebody knocks through it. They ask questions, they interrupt, they throw it down.

'Now I will go to the bathroom and take off my shoes and wash; but as I wash, as I bend my head down over the basin, I will let the Russian Empress's veil flow about my shoulders. The diamonds of the Imperial crown blaze on my forehead. I hear the roar of the hostile mob as I step out on to the balcony. Now I dry my hands, vigorously, so that Miss, whose name I forget, cannot suspect that I am waving my fist at an infuriated mob. "I am your Empress, people." My attitude is one of defiance. I am fearless. I conquer.

'But this is a thin dream. This is a papery tree. Miss Lambert blows it down. Even the sight of her vanishing down the corridor blows it to atoms. It is not solid; it gives me no satisfaction—this Empress dream. It leaves me, now that it has fallen, here in the passage rather shivering. Things seem paler. I will go now into the library and take out some book, and read and look; and read again and look. Here is a poem about a hedge. I will wander down it and pick flowers, green cowbind and the moonlight-coloured May, wild roses and ivy serpentine. I will clasp them in my hands and lay them on the desk's shiny surface. I will sit by the river's trembling edge and look at the water-lilies, broad and bright, which lit the oak that overhung the hedge with moonlight beams of their own watery light. I will pick flowers; I will bind flowers in one garland and clasp them and present them—Oh! to whom? There is some check in the flow of my being; a deep stream presses on some obstacle; it jerks; it tugs; some knot in the centre resists. Oh, this is pain, this is anguish! I faint, I fail. Now my body thaws; I am unsealed, I am incandescent. Now the stream pours in a deep tide fertilizing, opening the shut, forcing the tight-folded, flooding free. To whom shall I give all that now flows through me, from my warm, my porous body? I will gather my flowers and present them—Oh! to whom?

'Sailors loiter on the parade, and amorous couples; the omnibuses rattle along the sea front to the town. I will give; I will enrich; I will return to the world this beauty. I will bind my flowers in one garland and advancing with my hand outstretched will present them—Oh! to whom?'

'Now we have received,' said Louis, 'for this is the last day of the last term—Neville's and Bernard's and my last day—whatever our masters have had to give us. The introduction has been made; the world presented. They stay, we depart. The great Doctor, whom of all men I most revere, swaying a little from side to side among the tables, the bound volumes, has dealt out Horace, Tennyson, the complete works of Keats and Matthew Arnold, suitably inscribed. I respect the hand which gave them. He speaks with complete conviction. To him his words are true, though not to us. Speaking in the gruff voice of deep emotion, fiercely, tenderly, he has told us that we are about to go. He has bid us "quit ourselves like men". (On his lips quotations from the Bible, from *The Times*, seem equally magnificent.) Some will do this; others that. Some will not meet again. Neville, Bernard and I shall not meet here again. Life will divide us. But we have formed certain ties. Our boyish, our irresponsible years are over. But we have forged certain links. Above all, we have inherited traditions. These stone flags have been worn for six hundred years. On these walls are inscribed the names of men of war, of statesmen, of some unhappy poets (mine shall be among them). Blessings be on all traditions, on all safeguards and circumscriptions! I am most grateful to you men in black gowns, and you, dead, for your leading, for your guardianship; yet after all, the problem remains. The differences are not yet solved. Flowers toss their heads outside the window. I see wild birds, and impulses wilder than the wildest birds strike from my wild heart. My eyes are wild; my lips tight pressed. The bird flies; the flower dances; but I hear always the sullen thud of the waves; and the chained beast stamps on the beach. It stamps and stamps.'

'This is the final ceremony,' said Bernard. 'This is the last of all our ceremonies. We are overcome by strange feelings. The guard holding his flag is about to blow his whistle; the train breathing steam in another moment is about to start. One wants to say something, to feel something, absolutely appropriate to the occasion. One's mind is primed; one's lips are pursed. And then a bee drifts in and hums round the flowers in the bouquet which Lady Hampton, the wife of the General, keeps smelling to show her appreciation of the compliment. If the bee were to sting her nose? We are all deeply moved; yet irreverent; yet penitent; yet anxious to get it over; yet reluctant to part. The bee distracts us; its casual flight seems to deride our intensity. Humming vaguely, skimming widely, it is settled now on the carnation. Many of us will not meet again. We shall not enjoy certain pleasures again, when we are free to go to bed, or to sit up, when I need no longer smuggle in bits of candle-ends and immoral literature. The bee now hums round the head of the great Doctor. Larpent, John, Archie, Percival, Baker and Smith—I have liked them enormously. I have known one mad boy only. I have hated one mean boy only. I enjoy in retrospect my terribly awkward breakfasts at the Headmaster's table with toast and marmalade. He alone does not notice the bee. If it were to settle on his nose he would flick it off with one magnificent gesture. Now he has made his joke; now his voice has almost broken but not quite. Now we are dismissed—Louis, Neville and I for ever. We take our highly polished books, scholastically inscribed in a little crabbed hand. We rise, we disperse; the pressure is removed. The bee has become an insignificant, a disregarded insect, flown through the open window into obscurity. Tomorrow we go.'

'We are about to part,' said Neville. 'Here are the boxes; here are the cabs. There is Percival in his billycock hat. He will forget me. He will leave my letters lying about among guns and dogs unanswered. I shall send him poems and he will perhaps reply with a picture post card. But it is for that that I love him. I shall propose meeting—under a clock, by some Cross; and shall wait, and he will not come. It is for that that I love him. Oblivious, almost entirely ignorant, he will pass from my life. And I shall pass, incredible as it seems, into other lives; this is only an escapade perhaps, a prelude only. I feel already, though I cannot endure the Doctor's pompous mummery and faked emotions, that things we have only dimly perceived draw near. I shall be free to enter the garden where Fenwick raises his mallet. Those who have despised me shall acknowledge my sovereignty. But by some inscrutable law of my being sovereignty and the possession of power will not be enough; I shall always push through curtains to privacy, and want some whispered words alone. Therefore I go, dubious, but elate; apprehensive of intolerable pain; yet I think bound in my adventuring to conquer after huge suffering, bound, surely, to discover my desire in the end. There, for the last time, I see the statue of our pious founder with the doves about his head. They will wheel for ever about his head, whitening it, while the organ moans in the chapel. So I take my seat; and, when I have found my place in the corner of our reserved compartment, I will shade my eyes with a book to hide one tear; I will shade my eyes to observe; to peep at one face. It is the first day of the summer holidays.'

'It is the first day of the summer holidays,' said Susan. 'But the day is still rolled up. I will not examine it until I step out on to the platform in the evening. I will not let myself even smell it until I smell the cold green air off the fields. But already these are not school fields; these are not school hedges; the men in these fields are doing real things; they fill carts with real hay; and those are real cows, not school cows. But the carbolic smell of corridors and the chalky smell of schoolrooms is still in my nostrils. The glazed, shiny look of matchboard is still in my eyes. I must wait for fields and hedges, and woods and fields, and steep railway cuttings, sprinkled with gorse bushes, and trucks in sidings, and tunnels and suburban gardens with women hanging out washing, and then fields again and children swinging on gates, to cover it over, to bury it deep, this school that I have hated.

'I will not send my children to school nor spend a night all my life in London. Here in this vast station everything echoes and booms hollowly. The light is like the yellow light under an awning. Jinny lives here. Jinny takes her dog for walks on these pavements. People here shoot through the streets silently. They look at nothing but shop-windows. Their heads bob up and down all at about the same height. The streets are laced together with telegraph wires. The houses are all glass, all festoons and glitter; now all front doors and lace curtains, all pillars and white steps. But now I pass on, out of London again; the fields begin again; and the houses, and women hanging washing, and trees and fields. London is now veiled, now vanished, now crumbled, now fallen. The carbolic and the pitch-pine begin to lose their savour. I smell corn and turnips. I undo a paper packet tied with a piece of white cotton. The egg-shells slide into the cleft between my knees. Now we stop at station after station, rolling out milk cans. Now women kiss each other and help with baskets. Now I will let myself lean out of the window. The air rushes down my nose and throat—the cold air, the salt air with the smell of turnip fields in it. And there is my father, with his back turned, talking to a farmer. I tremble. I cry. There is my father in gaiters. There is my father.'

'I sit snug in my own corner going north,' said Jinny, 'in this roaring express which is yet so smooth that it flattens hedges, lengthens hills. We flash past signal-boxes; we make the earth rock slightly from side to side. The distance closes for ever in a point; and we for ever open the distance wide again. The telegraph poles bob up incessantly; one is felled, another rises. Now we roar and swing into a tunnel. The gentleman pulls up the window. I see reflections on the shining glass which lines the tunnel. I see him lower his paper. He smiles at my reflection in the tunnel. My body instantly of its own accord puts forth a frill under his gaze. My body lives a life of its own. Now the black window glass is green again. We are out of the tunnel. He reads his paper. But we have exchanged the approval of our bodies. There is then a great society of bodies, and mine is introduced; mine has come into the room where the gilt chairs are. Look—all the windows of the villas and their white-tented curtains dance; and the men sitting in the hedges in the cornfields with knotted blue handkerchiefs are aware too, as I am aware, of heat and rapture. One waves as we pass him. There are bowers and arbours in these villa gardens and young men in shirt-sleeves on ladders trimming roses. A man on a horse canters over the field. His horse plunges as we pass. And the rider turns to look at us. We roar again through blackness. And I lie back; I give myself up to rapture; I think that at the end of the tunnel I enter a lamp-lit room with chairs, into one of which I sink, much admired, my dress billowing round me. But behold, looking up, I meet the eyes of a sour woman, who suspects me of rapture. My body shuts in her face, impertinently, like a parasol. I open my body, I shut my body at my will. Life is beginning. I now break into my hoard of life.'

'It is the first day of the summer holidays,' said Rhoda. 'And now, as the train passes by these red rocks, by this blue sea, the term, done with, forms itself into one shape behind me. I see its colour. June was white. I see the fields white with daisies, and white with dresses; and tennis courts marked with white. Then there was wind and violent thunder.

There was a star riding through clouds one night, and I said to the star, "Consume me". That was at midsummer, after the garden party and my humiliation at the garden party. Wind and storm coloured July. Also, in the middle, cadaverous, awful, lay the grey puddle in the courtyard, when, holding an envelope in my hand, I carried a message. I came to the puddle. I could not cross it. Identity failed me. We are nothing, I said, and fell. I was blown like a feather, I was wafted down tunnels. Then very gingerly, I pushed my foot across. I laid my hand against a brick wall. I returned very painfully, drawing myself back into my body over the grey, cadaverous space of the puddle. This is life then to which I am committed.

'So I detach the summer term. With intermittent shocks, sudden as the springs of a tiger, life emerges heaving its dark crest from the sea. It is to this we are attached; it is to this we are bound, as bodies to wild horses. And yet we have invented devices for filling up the crevices and disguising these fissures. Here is the ticket collector. Here are two men; three women; there is a cat in a basket; myself with my elbow on the window-sill—this is here and now. We draw on, we make off, through whispering fields of golden corn. Women in the fields are surprised to be left behind there, hoeing. The train now stamps heavily, breathes stertorously, as it climbs up and up. At last we are on the top of the moor. Only a few wild sheep live here; a few shaggy ponies; yet we are provided with every comfort; with tables to hold our newspapers, with rings to hold our tumblers. We come carrying these appliances with us over the top of the moor. Now we are on the summit. Silence will close behind us. If I look back over that bald head, I can see silence already closing and the shadows of clouds chasing each other over the empty moor; silence closes over our transient passage. This I say is the present moment; this is the first day of the summer holidays. This is part of the emerging monster to whom we are attached.'

'Now we are off,' said Louis. 'Now I hang suspended without attachments. We are nowhere. We are passing through England in a train. England slips by the window, always changing from hill to wood, from rivers and willows to towns again. And I have no firm ground to which I go. Bernard and Neville, Percival, Archie, Larpent and Baker go to Oxford or Cambridge, to Edinburgh, Rome, Paris, Berlin, or to some American University. I go vaguely, to make money vaguely. Therefore a poignant shadow, a keen accent, falls on these golden bristles, on these poppy-red fields, this flowing corn that never overflows its boundaries; but runs rippling to the edge. This is the first day of a new life, another

spoke of the rising wheel. But my body passes vagrant as a bird's
shadow. I should be transient as the shadow on the meadow, soon
fading, soon darkening and dying there where it meets the wood, were it
not that I coerce my brain to form in my forehead; I force myself to
state, if only in one line of unwritten poetry, this moment; to mark this
inch in the long, long history that began in Egypt, in the time of the
Pharaohs, when women carried red pitchers to the Nile. I seem already
to have lived many thousand years. But if I now shut my eyes, if I fail
to realize the meeting-place of past and present, that I sit in a third-
class railway carriage full of boys going home for the holidays, human
history is defrauded of a moment's vision. Its eye, that would see
through me, shuts—if I sleep now, through slovenliness, or cowardice,
burying myself in the past, in the dark; or acquiesce, as Bernard
acquiesces, telling stories; or boast, as Percival, Archie, John, Walter,
Lathom, Larpent, Roper, Smith boast—the names are the same always,
the names of the boasting boys. They are all boasting, all talking, except
Neville, who slips a look occasionally over the edge of a French novel,
and so will always slip into cushioned firelit rooms, with many books
and one friend, while I tilt on an office chair behind a counter. Then I
shall grow bitter and mock at them. I shall envy them their continuance
down the safe traditional ways under the shade of old yew trees while I
consort with cockneys and clerks, and tap the pavements of the city.

'But now disembodied, passing over fields without lodgement—(there
is a river; a man fishes; there is a spire, there is the village street with its
bow-windowed inn)—all is dreamlike and dim to me. These hard
thoughts, this envy, this bitterness, make no lodgement in me. I am the
ghost of Louis, an ephemeral passer-by, in whose mind dreams have
power, and garden sounds when in the early morning petals float on
fathomless depths and the birds sing. I dash and sprinkle myself with
the bright waters of childhood. Its thin veil quivers. But the chained
beast stamps and stamps on the shore.'

'Louis and Neville,' said Bernard, 'both sit silent. Both are absorbed.
Both feel the presence of other people as a separating wall. But if I find
myself in company with other people, words at once make smoke rings—
see how phrases at once begin to wreathe off my lips. It seems that a
match is set to a fire; something burns. An elderly and apparently
prosperous man, a traveller, now gets in. And I at once wish to approach
him; I instinctively dislike the sense of his presence, cold, unassimilated,
among us. I do not believe in separation. We are not single. Also I wish
to add to my collection of valuable observations upon the true nature of
human life. My book will certainly run to many volumes, embracing
every known variety of man and woman. I fill my mind with whatever
happens to be the contents of a room or a railway carriage as one fills a

fountain-pen in an inkpot. I have a steady unquenchable thirst. Now I feel by imperceptible signs, which I cannot yet interpret but will later, that his defiance is about to thaw. His solitude shows signs of cracking. He has passed a remark about a country house. A smoke ring issues from my lips (about crops) and circles him, bringing him into contact. The human voice has a disarming quality—(we are not single, we are one). As we exchange these few but amiable remarks about country houses, I furbish him up and make him concrete. He is indulgent as a husband but not faithful; a small builder who employs a few men. In local society he is important; is already a councillor, and perhaps in time will be mayor. He wears a large ornament, like a double tooth torn up by the roots, made of coral, hanging at his watch-chain. Walter J. Trumble is the sort of name that would fit him. He has been in America, on a business trip with his wife, and a double room in a smallish hotel cost him a whole month's wages. His front tooth is stopped with gold.

'The fact is that I have little aptitude for reflection. I require the concrete in everything. It is so only that I lay hands upon the world. A good phrase, however, seems to me to have an independent existence. Yet I think it is likely that the best are made in solitude. They require some final refrigeration which I cannot give them, dabbling always in warm soluble words. My method, nevertheless, has certain advantages over theirs. Neville is repelled by the grossness of Trumble. Louis, glancing, tripping with the high step of a disdainful crane, picks up words as if in sugar-tongs. It is true that his eyes—wild, laughing, yet desperate—express something that we have not gauged. There is about both Neville and Louis a precision, an exactitude, that I admire and shall never possess. Now I begin to be aware that action is demanded. We approach a junction; at a junction I have to change. I have to board a train for Edinburgh. I cannot precisely lay fingers on this fact—it lodges loosely among my thoughts like a button, like a small coin. Here is the jolly old boy who collects tickets. I had one—I had one certainly. But it does not matter. Either I shall find it, or I shall not find it. I examine my note-case. I look in all my pockets. These are the things that for ever interrupt the process upon which I am eternally engaged of finding some perfect phrase that fits this very moment exactly.'

'Bernard has gone,' said Neville, 'without a ticket. He has escaped us, making a phrase, waving his hand. He talked as easily to the horse-breeder or to the plumber as to us. The plumber accepted him with devotion. "If he had a son like that," he was thinking, "he would manage to send him to Oxford." But what did Bernard feel for the plumber? Did he not only wish to continue the sequence of the story which he never stops telling himself? He began it when he rolled his bread into pellets as a child. One pellet was a man, one was a woman.

We are all pellets. We are all phrases in Bernard's story, things he writes down in his notebook under A or under B. He tells our story with extraordinary understanding, except of what we most feel. For he does not need us. He is never at our mercy. There he is, waving his arms on the platform. The train has gone without him. He has missed his connection. He has lost his ticket. But that does not matter. He will talk to the barmaid about the nature of human destiny. We are off; he has forgotten us already; we pass out of his view; we go on, filled with lingering sensations, half bitter, half sweet, for he is somehow to be pitied, breasting the world with half-finished phrases, having lost his ticket: he is also to be loved.

'Now I pretend again to read. I raise my book, till it almost covers my eyes. But I cannot read in the presence of horse-dealers and plumbers. I have no power of ingratiating myself. I do not admire that man; he does not admire me. Let me at least be honest. Let me denounce this piffling, trifling, self-satisfied world; these horse-hair seats; these coloured photographs of piers and parades. I could shriek aloud at the smug self-satisfaction, at the mediocrity of this world, which breeds horse-dealers with coral ornaments hanging from their watch-chains. There is that in me which will consume them entirely. My laughter shall make them twist in their seats; shall drive them howling before me. No; they are immortal. They triumph. They will make it impossible for me always to read Catullus in a third-class railway carriage. They will drive me in October to take refuge in one of the universities, where I shall become a don; and go with schoolmasters to Greece; and lecture on the ruins of the Parthenon. It would be better to breed horses and live in one of those red villas than to run in and out of the skulls of Sophocles and Euripides like a maggot, with a high-minded wife, one of those University women. That, however, will be my fate. I shall suffer. I am already at eighteen capable of such contempt that horse-breeders hate me. That is my triumph; I do not compromise. I am not timid; I have no accent. I do not finick about fearing what people think of "my father a banker at Brisbane" like Louis.

'Now we draw near the centre of the civilized world. There are the familiar gasometers. There are the public gardens intersected by asphalt paths. There are the lovers lying shamelessly mouth to mouth on the burnt grass. Percival is now almost in Scotland; his train draws through the red moors; he sees the long line of the Border hills and the Roman wall. He reads a detective novel, yet understands everything.

'The train slows and lengthens, as we approach London, the centre, and my heart draws out too, in fear, in exultation. I am about to meet— what? What extraordinary adventure waits me, among these mail vans, these porters, these swarms of people calling taxis? I feel insignificant, lost, but exultant. With a soft shock we stop. I will let the others get out before me. I will sit still one moment before I emerge into that chaos, that tumult. I will not anticipate what is to come. The huge uproar is in my ears. It sounds and resounds, under this glass roof like the surge of a sea. We are cast down on the platform with our handbags. We are whirled asunder. My sense of self almost perishes; my contempt. I become drawn in, tossed down, thrown sky-high. I step out on to the platform, grasping tightly all that I possess—one bag.'

The sun rose. Bars of yellow and green fell on the shore, gilding the ribs of the eaten-out boat and making the sea-holly and its mailed leaves gleam blue as steel. Light almost pierced the thin swift waves as they raced fan-shaped over the beach. The girl who had shaken her head and made all the jewels, the topaz, the aquamarine, the water-coloured jewels with sparks of fire in them, dance, now bared her brows and with wide-opened eyes drove a straight pathway over the waves. Their quivering mackerel sparkling was darkened; they massed themselves; their green hollows deepened and darkened and might be traversed by shoals of wandering fish. As they splashed and drew back they left a black rim of twigs and cork on the shore and straws and sticks of wood, as if some light shallop had foundered and burst its sides and the sailor had swum to land and bounded up the cliff and left his frail cargo to be washed ashore.

In the garden the birds that had sung erratically and spasmodically in the dawn on that tree, on that bush, now sang together in chorus, shrill and sharp; now together, as if conscious of companionship, now alone as if to the pale blue sky. They swerved, all in one flight, when the black cat moved among the bushes, when the cook threw cinders on the ash heap and startled them. Fear was in their song, and apprehension of pain, and joy to be snatched quickly now at this instant. Also they sang emulously in the clear morning air, swerving high over the elm tree, singing together as they chased each other, escaping, pursuing, pecking each other as they turned high in the air. And then tiring of pursuit and flight, lovelily they came descending, delicately declining, dropped down and sat silent on the tree, on the wall, with their bright eyes glancing, and their heads turned this way, that way; aware, awake; intensely conscious of one thing, one object in particular.

Perhaps it was a snail shell, rising in the grass like a grey cathedral, a swelling building burnt with dark rings and shadowed green by the grass. Or perhaps they saw the splendour of the flowers making a light of flowing purple over the beds, through which dark tunnels of purple shade were driven between the stalks. Or they fixed their gaze on the small bright apple leaves, dancing yet withheld, stiffly sparkling among the pink-tipped blossoms. Or they saw the rain drop on the hedge, pendent but not falling, with a whole house bent in it, and towering elms; or, gazing straight at the sun, their eyes became gold beads.

Now glancing this side, that side, they looked deeper, beneath the flowers, down the dark avenues into the unlit world where the leaf rots and the flower has fallen. Then one of them, beautifully darting, accurately alighting, spiked the soft, monstrous body of the defenceless worm, pecked again and yet again, and left it to fester. Down there among the roots where the flowers decayed, gusts of dead smells were wafted; drops formed on the bloated sides of swollen things. The skin of rotten fruit broke, and matter oozed too thick to run. Yellow excretions were exuded by slugs, and now and again an amorphous body with a head at either end swayed slowly from side to side. The gold-eyed birds darting in between the leaves observed that purulence, that wetness, quizzically. Now and then they plunged the tips of their beaks savagely into the sticky mixture.

Now, too, the rising sun came in at the window, touching the red-edged curtain, and began to bring out circles and lines. Now in the growing light its whiteness settled in the plate; the blade condensed its gleam. Chairs and cupboards loomed behind so that though each was separate they seemed inextricably involved. The looking-glass whitened its pool upon the wall. The real flower on the window-sill was attended by a phantom flower. Yet the phantom was part of the flower, for when a bud broke free the paler flower in the glass opened a bud too.

The wind rose. The waves drummed on the shore, like turbaned warriors, like turbaned men with poisoned assegais who, whirling their arms on high, advance upon the feeding flocks, the white sheep.

'The complexity of things becomes more close,' said Bernard, 'here at college, where the stir and pressure of life are so extreme, where the excitement of mere living becomes daily more urgent. Every hour something new is unburied in the great bran-pie. What am I? I ask. This? No, I am that. Especially now, when I have left a room, and people talking, and the stone flags ring out with my solitary footsteps, and I behold the moon rising, sublimely, indifferently, over the ancient chapel—then it becomes clear that I am not one and simple, but complex and many. Bernard, in public, bubbles; in private, is secretive. That is what they do not understand, for they are now undoubtedly discussing me, saying I escape them, am evasive. They do not understand that I have to effect different transitions; have to cover the entrances and exits of several different men who alternately act their parts as Bernard. I am abnormally aware of circumstances. I can never read a book in a railway carriage without asking, Is he a builder? Is she unhappy? I was aware today acutely that poor Simes, with his pimple, was feeling, how bitterly, that his chance of making a good impression upon Billy Jackson was remote. Feeling this painfully, I invited him to dinner with ardour. This he will attribute to an admiration which is not mine. That is true. But "joined to the sensibility of a woman" (I am here quoting my own biographer) "Bernard possessed the logical sobriety of a man". Now people who make a single impression, and that, in the main, a good one (for there seems to be a virtue in simplicity), are those who keep their equilibrium in mid-stream. (I instantly see fish with their noses one way, the stream rushing past another.) Canon, Lycett, Peters, Hawkins, Larpent, Neville—all fish in mid-stream. But *you* understand, *you*, my self, who always comes at a call (that would be a harrowing experience to call and for no one to come; that would make the midnight hollow, and explains the expression of old men in clubs— they have given up calling for a self who does not come), you understand that I am only superficially represented by what I was saying tonight. Underneath, and, at the moment when I am most disparate, I am also integrated. I sympathize effusively; I also sit, like a toad in a hole, receiving with perfect coldness whatever comes. Very few of you who are now discussing me have the double capacity to feel, to reason. Lycett, you see, believes in running after hares; Hawkins has spent a most industrious afternoon in the library. Peters has his young lady at the circulating library. You are all engaged, involved, drawn in, and absolutely energized to the top of your bent—all save Neville, whose mind is far too complex to be roused by any single activity. I also am too complex. In my case something remains floating, unattached.

'Now, as a proof of my susceptibility to atmosphere, here, as I come into my room, and turn on the light, and see the sheet of paper, the table, my gown lying negligently over the back of the chair, I feel that I am that dashing yet reflective man, that bold and deleterious figure, who, lightly throwing off his cloak, seizes his pen and at once flings off the following letter to the girl with whom he is passionately in love.

'Yes, all is propitious. I am now in the mood. I can write the letter straight off which I have begun ever so many times. I have just come in; I have flung down my hat and my stick; I am writing the first thing that comes into my head without troubling to put the paper straight. It is going to be a brilliant sketch which, she must think, was written without a pause, without an erasure. Look how unformed the letters are—there is a careless blot. All must be sacrificed to speed and carelessness. I will write a quick, running, small hand, exaggerating the down stroke of the "y" and crossing the "t" thus—with a dash. The date shall be only Tuesday, the 17th, and then a question mark. But also I must give her the impression that though he—for this is not myself—is writing in such an off-hand, such a slap-dash way, there is some subtle suggestion of intimacy and respect. I must allude to talks we have had together— bring back some remembered scene. But I must seem to her (this is very important) to be passing from thing to thing with the greatest ease in the world. I shall pass from the service for the man who was drowned (I have a phrase for that) to Mrs Moffat and her sayings (I have a note of them), and so to some reflections apparently casual but full of profundity (profound criticism is often written casually) about some book I have been reading, some out-of-the-way book. I want her to say as she brushes her hair or puts out the candle, "Where did I read that? Oh, in Bernard's letter." It is the speed, the hot, molten effect, the laval flow of sentence into sentence that I need. Who am I thinking of? Byron of course. I am, in some ways, like Byron. Perhaps a sip of Byron will help to put me in the vein. Let me read a page. No; this is dull; this is scrappy. This is rather too formal. Now I am getting the hang of it. Now I am getting his beat into my brain (the rhythm is the main thing in writing). Now, without pausing I will begin, on the very lilt of the stroke——.

'Yet it falls flat. It peters out. I cannot get up steam enough to carry me over the transition. My true self breaks off from my assumed. And if I begin to re-write it, she will feel "Bernard is posing as a literary man;

Bernard is thinking of his biographer" (which is true). No, I will write the letter tomorrow directly after breakfast.

'Now let me fill my mind with imaginary pictures. Let me suppose that I am asked to stay at Restover, King's Laughton, Station Langley three miles. I arrive in the dusk. In the courtyard of this shabby but distinguished house there are two or three dogs, slinking, long-legged. There are faded rugs in the hall; a military gentleman smokes a pipe as he paces the terrace. The note is of distinguished poverty and military connections. A hunter's hoof on the writing-table—a favourite horse. "Do you ride?" "Yes, sir, I love riding." "My daughter expects us in the drawing-room." My heart pounds against my ribs. She is standing at a low table; she has been hunting; she munches sandwiches like a tomboy. I make a fairly good impression on the Colonel. I am not too clever, he thinks; I am not too raw. Also I play billiards. Then the nice maid who has been with the family thirty years comes in. The pattern on the plates is of Oriental long-tailed birds. Her mother's portrait in muslin hangs over the fireplace. I can sketch the surroundings up to a point with extraordinary ease. But can I make it work? Can I hear her voice—the precise tone with which, when we are alone, she says "Bernard"? And then what next?

'The truth is that I need the stimulus of other people. Alone, over my dead fire, I tend to see the thin places in my own stories. The real novelist, the perfectly simple human being, could go on, indefinitely, imagining. He would not integrate, as I do. He would not have this devastating sense of grey ashes in a burnt-out grate. Some blind flaps in my eyes. Everything becomes impervious. I cease to invent.

'Let me recollect. It has been on the whole a good day. The drop that forms on the roof of the soul in the evening is round, many-coloured. There was the morning, fine; there was the afternoon, walking. I like views of spires across grey fields. I like glimpses between people's shoulders. Things kept popping into my head. I was imaginative, subtle. After dinner, I was dramatic. I put into concrete form many things that we had dimly observed about our common friends. I made my transitions easily. But now let me ask myself the final question, as I sit over this grey fire, with its naked promontories of black coal, which of these people am I? It depends so much upon the room. When I say to myself, "Bernard", who comes? A faithful, sardonic man, disillusioned, but not embittered. A man of no particular age or calling. Myself, merely. It is he who now takes the poker and rattles the cinders so that they fall in showers through the grate. "Lord", he says to himself, watching them fall, "what a pother!" and then he adds, lugubriously, but with some sense of consolation, "Mrs Moffat will come and sweep it all up——" I fancy I shall often repeat to myself that phrase, as I rattle and bang through life, hitting first this side of the carriage, then the other, "Oh, yes, Mrs Moffat will come and sweep it all up". And so to bed.'

'In a world which contains the present moment,' said Neville, 'why discriminate? Nothing should be named lest by so doing we change it. Let it exist, this bank, this beauty, and I, for one instant, steeped in pleasure. The sun is hot. I see the river. I see trees specked and burnt in the autumn sunlight. Boats float past, through the red, through the green. Far away a bell tolls, but not for death. There are bells that ring for life. A leaf falls, from joy. Oh, I am in love with life! Look how the willow shoots its fine sprays into the air! Look how through them a boat passes, filled with indolent, with unconscious, with powerful young men. They are listening to the gramophone; they are eating fruit out of paper bags. They are tossing the skins of bananas, which then sink eel-like, into the river. All they do is beautiful. There are cruets behind them and ornaments; their rooms are full of oars and oleographs but they have turned all to beauty. That boat passes under the bridge. Another comes. Then another. That is Percival, lounging on the cushions, monolithic, in giant repose. No, it is only one of his satellites, imitating his monolithic, his giant repose. He alone is unconscious of their tricks, and when he catches them at it he buffets them good-humouredly with a blow of his paw. They, too, have passed under the bridge through "the fountains of the pendant trees", through its fine strokes of yellow and plum colour. The breeze stirs; the curtain quivers; I see behind the leaves the grave, yet eternally joyous buildings, which seem porous, not gravid; light, though set so immemorially on the ancient turf. Now begins to rise in me the familiar rhythm; words that have lain dormant now lift, now toss their crests, and fall and rise, and fall and rise again. I am a poet, yes. Surely I am a great poet. Boats and youth passing and distant trees, "the falling fountains of the pendant trees". I see it all. I feel it all. I am inspired. My eyes fill with tears. Yet even as I feel this, I lash my frenzy higher and higher. It foams. It becomes artificial, insincere. Words and words and words, how they gallop—how they lash their long manes and tails, but for some fault in me I cannot give myself to their backs; I cannot fly with them, scattering women and string bags. There is some flaw in me—some fatal hesitancy, which, if I pass it over, turns to foam and falsity. Yet it is incredible that I should not be a great poet. What did I write last night if it was not good poetry? Am I too fast, too facile? I do not know. I do not know myself sometimes, or how to measure and name and count out the grains that make me what I am.

'Something now leaves me; something goes from me to meet that figure who is coming, and assures me that I know him before I see who it is. How curiously one is changed by the addition, even at a distance, of a friend. How useful an office one's friends perform when they recall us. Yet how painful to be recalled, to be mitigated, to have one's self adulterated, mixed up, become part of another. As he approaches I become not myself but Neville mixed with somebody—with whom?— with Bernard? Yes, it is Bernard, and it is to Bernard that I shall put the question, Who am I?'

'How strange,' said Bernard, 'the willow looks seen together. I was Byron, and the tree was Byron's tree, lachrymose, down-showering, lamenting. Now that we look at the tree together, it has a combined look, each branch distinct, and I will tell you what I feel, under the compulsion of your clarity.

'I feel your disapproval, I feel your force. I become, with you, an untidy, an impulsive human being whose bandanna handkerchief is for ever stained with the grease of crumpets. Yes, I hold Gray's *Elegy* in one hand; with the other I scoop out the bottom crumpet, that has absorbed all the butter and sticks to the bottom of the plate. This offends you; I feel your distress acutely. Inspired by it and anxious to regain your good opinion, I proceed to tell you how I have just pulled Percival out of bed; I describe his slippers, his table, his guttered candle; his surly and complaining accents as I pull the blankets off his feet; he burrowing like some vast cocoon meanwhile. I describe all this in such a way that, centred as you are upon some private sorrow (for a hooded shape presides over our encounter), you give way, you laugh and delight in me. My charm and flow of language, unexpected and spontaneous as it is, delights me too. I am astonished, as I draw the veil off things with words, how much, how infinitely more than I can say, I have observed. More and more bubbles into my mind as I talk, images and images. This, I say to myself, is what I need; why, I ask, can I not finish the letter that I am writing? For my room is always scattered with unfinished letters. I begin to suspect, when I am with you, that I am among the most gifted of men. I am filled with the delight of youth, with potency, with the sense of what is to come. Blundering, but fervid, I see myself buzzing round flowers, humming down scarlet cups, making blue funnels resound with my prodigious booming. How richly I shall enjoy my youth (you make me feel). And London. And freedom. But stop. You are not listening. You are making some protest, as you slide, with an inexpressibly familiar gesture, your hand along your knee. By such signs we diagnose our friends' diseases. "Do not, in your affluence and plenty," you seem to say, "pass me by." "Stop," you say. "Ask me what I suffer."

'Let me then create you. (You have done as much for me.) You lie on this hot bank, in this lovely, this fading, this still bright October day, watching boat after boat float through the combed-out twigs of the willow tree. And you wish to be a poet; and you wish to be a lover. But the splendid clarity of your intelligence, and the remorseless honesty of your intellect (these Latin words I owe you; these qualities of yours make me shift a little uneasily and see the faded patches, the thin strands in my own equipment) bring you to a halt. You indulge in no mystifications. You do not fog yourself with rosy clouds, or yellow.

'Am I right? Have I read the little gesture of your left hand correctly? If so, give me your poems; hand over the sheets you wrote last night in such a fervour of inspiration that you now feel a little sheepish. For you distrust inspiration, yours or mine. Let us go back together, over the bridge, under the elm trees, to my room, where, with walls round us and red serge curtains drawn, we can shut out these distracting voices, scents and savours of lime trees, and other lives; these pert shop-girls, disdainfully tripping, these shuffling, heavy-laden old women; these furtive glimpses of some vague and vanishing figure—it might be Jinny, it might be Susan, or was that Rhoda disappearing down the avenue? Again, from some slight twitch I guess your feeling; I have escaped you; I have gone buzzing like a swarm of bees, endlessly vagrant, with none of your power of fixing remorselessly upon a single object. But I will return.'

'When there are buildings like these,' said Neville, 'I cannot endure that there should be shop-girls. Their titter, their gossip, offends me; breaks into my stillness, and nudges me, in moments of purest exultation, to remember our degradation.

'But now we have regained our territory after that brief brush with the bicycles and the lime scent and the vanishing figures in the distracted street. Here we are masters of tranquillity and order; inheritors of proud tradition. The lights are beginning to make yellow slits across the square. Mists from the river are filling these ancient spaces. They cling, gently, to the hoary stone. The leaves now are thick in country lanes, sheep cough in the damp fields; but here in your room we are dry. We talk privately. The fire leaps and sinks, making some knob bright.

'You have been reading Byron. You have been marking the passages that seem to approve of your own character. I find marks against all those sentences which seem to express a sardonic yet passionate nature; a moth-like impetuosity dashing itself against hard glass. You thought, as you drew your pencil there, "I too throw off my cloak like that. I too snap my fingers in the face of destiny." Yet Byron never made tea as you do, who fill the pot so that when you put the lid on the tea spills over. There is a brown pool on the table—it is running among your books and papers. Now you mop it up, clumsily, with your pocket-handkerchief. You then stuff your handkerchief back into your pocket—that is not Byron; that is you; that is so essentially you that if I think of you in twenty years' time, when we are both famous, gouty and intolerable, it will be by that scene: and if you are dead, I shall weep. Once you were Tolstoy's young man; now you are Byron's young man; perhaps you will be Meredith's young man; then you will visit Paris in the Easter vacation and come back wearing a black tie, some detestable Frenchman whom nobody has ever heard of. Then I shall drop you.

'I am one person—myself. I do not impersonate Catullus, whom I adore. I am the most slavish of students, with here a dictionary, there a notebook in which I enter curious uses of the past participle. But one cannot go on for ever cutting these ancient inscriptions clearer with a knife. Shall I always draw the red serge curtain close and see my book, laid like a block of marble, pale under the lamp? That would be a glorious life, to addict oneself to perfection; to follow the curve of the sentence wherever it might lead, into deserts, under drifts of sand, regardless of lures, of seductions; to be poor always and unkempt; to be ridiculous in Piccadilly.

'But I am too nervous to end my sentence properly. I speak quickly, as I pace up and down, to conceal my agitation. I hate your greasy handkerchiefs—you will stain your copy of *Don Juan*. You are not listening to me. You are making phrases about Byron. And while you gesticulate, with your cloak, your cane, I am trying to expose a secret told to nobody yet, I am asking you (as I stand with my back to you) to take my life in your hands and tell me whether I am doomed always to cause repulsion in those I love?

'I stand with my back to you fidgeting. No, my hands are now perfectly still. Precisely, opening a space in the bookcase, I insert *Don Juan*; there. I would rather be loved, I would rather be famous than follow perfection through the sand. But am I doomed to cause disgust? Am I a poet? Take it. The desire which is loaded behind my lips, cold as lead, fell as a bullet, the thing I aim at shop-girls, women, the pretence, the vulgarity of life (because I love it) shoots at you as I throw—catch it—my poem.'

'He has shot like an arrow from the room,' said Bernard. 'He has left me his poem. O friendship, I too will press flowers between the pages of Shakespeare's sonnets! O friendship, how piercing are your darts—there, there, again there. He looked at me, turning to face me; he gave me his poem. All mists curl off the roof of my being. That confidence I shall keep to my dying day. Like a long wave, like a roll of heavy waters, he went over me, his devastating presence—dragging me open, laying bare the pebbles on the shore of my soul. It was humiliating; I was turned to small stones. All semblances were rolled up. "You are not Byron; you are your self." To be contracted by another person into a single being—how strange.

'How strange to feel the line that is spun from us lengthening its fine filament across the misty spaces of the intervening world. He is gone; I stand here, holding his poem. Between us is this line. But now, how comfortable, how reassuring to feel that alien presence removed, that scrutiny darkened and hooded over! How grateful to draw the blinds, and admit no other presence; to feel returning from the dark corners in which they took refuge, those shabby inmates, those familiars, whom, with his superior force, he drove into hiding. The mocking, the observant spirits who, even in the crisis and stab of the moment, watched on my behalf now come flocking home again. With their addition, I am Bernard; I am Byron; I am this, that and the other. They darken the air and enrich me, as of old, with their antics, their comments, and cloud the fine simplicity of my moment of emotion. For I am more selves than Neville thinks. We are not simple as our friends would have us to meet their needs. Yet love is simple.

'Now they have returned, my inmates, my familiars. Now the stab, the rent in my defences that Neville made with his astonishing fine rapier, is repaired. I am almost whole now; and see how jubilant I am, bringing into play all that Neville ignores in me. I feel, as I look from the window, parting the curtains, "That would give him no pleasure; but it rejoices me". (We use our friends to measure our own stature.) My scope embraces what Neville never reaches. They are shouting hunting-songs over the way. They are celebrating some run with the beagles. The little boys in caps who always turned at the same moment when the brake went round the corner are clapping each other on the shoulder and boasting. But Neville, delicately avoiding interference, stealthily, like a conspirator, hastens back to his room. I see him sunk in his low chair gazing at the fire which has assumed for the moment an architectural solidity. If life, he thinks, could wear that permanence, if life could have that order—for above all he desires order, and detests my Byronic untidiness; and so draws his curtain; and bolts his door. His eyes (for he is in love; the sinister figure of love presided at our encounter) fill with longing; fill with tears. He snatches the poker and with one blow destroys that momentary appearance of solidity in the burning coals. All changes. And youth and love. The boat has floated through the arch of the willows and is now under the bridge. Percival, Tony, Archie, or another, will go to India. We shall not meet again. Then he stretches his hand for his copy-book—a neat volume bound in mottled paper—and writes feverishly long lines of poetry, in the manner of whomever he admires most at the moment.

'But I want to linger; to lean from the window; to listen. There again comes that rollicking chorus. They are now smashing china—that also is the convention. The chorus, like a torrent jumping rocks, brutally assaulting old trees, pours with splendid abandonment headlong over precipices. On they roll; on they gallop; after hounds, after footballs; they pump up and down attached to oars like sacks of flour. All divisions are merged—they act like one man. The gusty October wind blows the uproar in bursts of sound and silence across the court. Now again they are smashing the china—that is the convention. An old, unsteady woman carrying a bag trots home under the fire-red windows. She is half afraid that they will fall on her and tumble her into the gutter. Yet she pauses as if to warm her knobbed, her rheumaticky hands at the bonfire which flares away with streams of sparks and bits of blown paper. The old woman pauses against the lit window. A contrast. That I see and Neville does not see; that I feel and Neville does not feel. Hence he will reach perfection and I shall fail and shall leave nothing behind me but imperfect phrases littered with sand.

'I think of Louis now. What malevolent yet searching light would Louis throw upon this dwindling autumn evening, upon this china-smashing and trolling of hunting-songs, upon Neville, Byron and our life here? His thin lips are somewhat pursed; his cheeks are pale; he pores in an office over some obscure commercial document. "My father, a banker at Brisbane"—being ashamed of him he always talks of him—failed. So he sits in an office, Louis, the best scholar in the school. But I seeking contrasts often feel his eye on us, his laughing eye, his wild eye, adding us up like insignificant items in some grand total which he is for ever pursuing in his office. And one day, taking a fine pen and dipping it in red ink, the addition will be complete; our total will be known; but it will not be enough.

'Bang! They have thrown a chair now against the wall. We are damned then. My case is dubious too. Am I not indulging in unwarranted emotions? Yes, as I lean out of the window and drop my cigarette so that it twirls lightly to the ground, I feel Louis watching even my cigarette. And Louis says, "That means something. But what?" '

'People go on passing,' said Louis. 'They pass the window of this eating-shop incessantly. Motor-cars, vans, motor-omnibuses; and again motor-omnibuses, vans, motor-cars—they pass the window. In the background I perceive shops and houses; also the grey spires of a city church. In the foreground are glass shelves set with plates of buns and ham sandwiches. All is somewhat obscured by steam from a tea-urn. A meaty, vapourish smell of beef and mutton, sausages and mash, hangs down like a damp net in the middle of the eating-house. I prop my book against a bottle of Worcester sauce and try to look like the rest.

'Yet I cannot. (They go on passing, they go on passing in disorderly procession.) I cannot read my book, or order my beef, with conviction. I repeat, "I am an average Englishman; I am an average clerk", yet I look at the little men at the next table to be sure that I do what they do. Supple-faced, with rippling skins, that are always twitching with the multiplicity of their sensations, prehensile like monkeys, greased to this particular moment, they are discussing with all the right gestures the sale of a piano. It blocks up the hall; so he would take a tenner. People go on passing; they go on passing against the spires of the church and the plates of ham sandwiches. The streamers of my consciousness waver out and are perpetually torn and distressed by their disorder. I cannot therefore concentrate on my dinner. "I would take a tenner. The case is handsome; but it blocks up the hall." They dive and plunge like guillemots whose feathers are slippery with oil. All excesses beyond that norm are vanity. That is the mean; that is the average. Meanwhile the hats bob up and down; the door perpetually shuts and opens. I am conscious of flux, of disorder; of annihilation and despair. If this is all, this is worthless. Yet I feel, too, the rhythm of the eating-house. It is like a waltz tune, eddying in and out, round and round. The waitresses, balancing trays, swing in and out, round and round, dealing plates of greens, of apricot and custard, dealing them at the right time, to the right customers. The average men, including her rhythm in their rhythm ("I would take a tenner; for it blocks up the hall") take their greens, take their apricots and custard. Where then is the break in this continuity? What the fissure through which one sees disaster? The circle is unbroken; the harmony complete. Here is the central rhythm; here the common mainspring. I watch it expand, contract; and then expand again. Yet I am not included. If I speak, imitating their accent, they prick their ears, waiting for me to speak again, in order that they may place me—if I come from Canada or Australia, I, who desire above all things to be taken to the arms with love, am alien, external. I, who would wish to feel close over me the protective waves of the ordinary, catch with the tail of my eye some far horizon; am aware of hats bobbing up and down in perpetual disorder. To me is addressed the plaint of the wandering and distracted spirit (a woman with bad teeth falters at the counter), "Bring us back to the fold, we who pass so disjectedly, bobbing up and down, past windows with plates of ham sandwiches in the foreground." Yes; I will reduce you to order.

'I will read in the book that is propped against the bottle of Worcester sauce. It contains some forged rings, some perfect statements, a few words, but poetry. You, all of you, ignore it. What the dead poet said, you have forgotten. And I cannot translate it to you so that its binding power ropes you in, and makes it clear to you that you are aimless; and the rhythm is cheap and worthless; and so remove that degradation which, if you are unaware of your aimlessness, pervades you, making you senile, even while you are young. To translate that poem so that it is easily read is to be my endeavour. I, the companion of Plato, of Virgil, will knock at the grained oak door. I oppose to what is passing this ramrod of beaten steel. I will not submit to this aimless passing of billycock hats and Homburg hats and all the plumed and variegated head-dresses of women. (Susan, whom I respect, would wear a plain straw hat on a summer's day.) And the grinding and the steam that runs in unequal drops down the window-pane; and the stopping and the starting with a jerk of motor-omnibuses; and the hesitations at counters; and the words that trail drearily without human meaning; I will reduce you to order.

'My roots go down through veins of lead and silver, through damp, marshy places that exhale odours, to a knot made of oak roots bound together in the centre. Sealed and blind, with earth stopping my ears, I have yet heard rumours of wars; and the nightingale; have felt the hurrying of many troops of men flocking hither and thither in quest of civilization like flocks of birds migrating seeking the summer; I have seen women carrying red pitchers to the banks of the Nile. I woke in a garden, with a blow on the nape of my neck, a hot kiss, Jinny's; remembering all this as one remembers confused cries and toppling pillars and shafts of red and black in some nocturnal conflagration. I am for ever sleeping and waking. Now I sleep; now I wake. I see the gleaming tea-urn; the glass cases full of pale-yellow sandwiches; the men in round coats perched on stools at the counter; and also behind them, eternity. It is a stigma burnt on my quivering flesh by a cowled man with a red-hot iron. I see this eating-shop against the packed and fluttering birds' wings, many feathered, folded, of the past. Hence my pursed lips, my sickly pallor; my distasteful and uninviting aspect as I turn my face with hatred and bitterness upon Bernard and Neville, who saunter under yew trees; who inherit armchairs; and draw their curtains close, so that lamplight falls on their books.

'Susan, I respect; because she sits stitching. She sews under a quiet lamp in a house where the corn sighs close to the window and gives me safety. For I am the weakest, the youngest of them all. I am a child looking at his feet and the little runnels that the stream has made in the gravel. That is a snail, I say; that is a leaf. I delight in the snails; I delight in the leaf. I am always the youngest, the most innocent, the most trustful. You are all protected. I am naked. When the waitress with the plaited wreaths of hair swings past, she deals you your apricots and custard unhesitatingly, like a sister. You are her brothers. But when I get up, brushing the crumbs from my waistcoat, I slip too large a tip, a shilling, under the edge of my plate, so that she may not find it till I am gone, and her scorn, as she picks it up with laughter, may not strike on me till I am past the swing-doors.'

'Now the wind lifts the blind,' said Susan, 'jars, bowls, matting and the shabby armchair with the hole in it are now become distinct. The usual faded ribbons sprinkle the wallpaper. The bird chorus is over, only one bird now sings close to the bedroom window. I will pull on my stockings and go quietly past the bedroom doors, and down through the kitchen, out through the garden past the greenhouse into the field. It is still early morning. The mist is on the marshes. The day is stark and stiff as a linen shroud. But it will soften; it will warm. At this hour, this still early hour, I think I am the field, I am the barn, I am the trees; mine are the flocks of birds, and this young hare who leaps, at the last moment when I step almost on him. Mine is the heron that stretches its vast wings lazily; and the cow that creaks as it pushes one foot before another munching; and the wild, swooping swallow; and the faint red in the sky, and the green when the red fades; the silence and the bell; the call of the man fetching cart-horses from the fields—all are mine.

'I cannot be divided, or kept apart. I was sent to school; I was sent to Switzerland to finish my education. I hate linoleum; I hate fir trees and mountains. Let me now fling myself on this flat ground under a pale sky where the clouds pace slowly. The cart grows gradually larger as it comes along the road. The sheep gather in the middle of the field. The birds gather in the middle of the road—they need not fly yet. The wood smoke rises. The starkness of the dawn is going out of it. Now the day stirs. Colour returns. The day waves yellow with all its crops. The earth hangs heavy beneath me.

'But who am I, who lean on this gate and watch my setter nose in a circle? I think sometimes (I am not twenty yet) I am not a woman, but the light that falls on this gate, on this ground. I am the seasons, I think sometimes, January, May, November; the mud, the mist, the dawn. I cannot be tossed about, or float gently, or mix with other people. Yet now, leaning here till the gate prints my arm, I feel the weight that has formed itself in my side. Something has formed, at school, in Switzerland, some hard thing. Not sighs and laughter, not circling and ingenious phrases; not Rhoda's strange communications when she looks past us, over our shoulders; nor Jinny's pirouetting, all of a piece, limbs and body. What I give is fell. I cannot float gently, mixing with other people. I like best the stare of shepherds met in the road; the stare of gipsy women beside a cart in a ditch suckling their children as I shall suckle my children. For soon in the hot midday when the bees hum round the hollyhocks my lover will come. He will stand under the cedar tree. To his one word I shall answer my one word. What has formed in me I shall give him. I shall have children; I shall have maids in aprons; men with pitchforks; a kitchen where they bring the ailing lambs to warm in baskets, where the hams hang and the onions glisten. I shall be like my mother, silent in a blue apron locking up the cupboards.

'Now I am hungry. I will call my setter. I think of crusts and bread and butter and white plates in a sunny room. I will go back across the fields. I will walk along this grass path with strong, even strides, now swerving to avoid the puddle, now leaping lightly to a clump. Beads of wet form on my rough skirt; my shoes become supple and dark. The stiffness has gone from the day; it is shaded with grey, green and umber. The birds no longer settle on the high road.

'I return, like a cat or fox returning, whose fur is grey with rime, whose pads are hardened by the coarse earth. I push through the cabbages, making their leaves squeak and their drops spill. I sit waiting for my father's footsteps as he shuffles down the passage pinching some herb between his fingers. I pour out cup after cup while the unopened flowers hold themselves erect on the table among the pots of jam, the loaves and the butter. We are silent.

'I go then to the cupboard, and take the damp bags of rich sultanas; I lift the heavy flour on to the clean scrubbed kitchen table. I knead; I stretch; I pull, plunging my hands in the warm inwards of the dough. I let the cold water stream fanwise through my fingers. The fire roars; the flies buzz in a circle. All my currants and rices, the silver bags and the blue bags, are locked again in the cupboard. The meat is stood in the oven; the bread rises in a soft dome under the clean towel. I walk in the afternoon down to the river. All the world is breeding. The flies are going from grass to grass. The flowers are thick with pollen. The swans ride the stream in order. The clouds, warm now, sun-spotted, sweep over the hills, leaving gold in the water, and gold on the necks of the swans. Pushing one foot before the other, the cows munch their way across the field. I feel through the grass for the white-domed mushroom; and break its stalk and pick the purple orchid that grows beside it and lay the orchid by the mushroom with the earth at its root, and so home to make the kettle boil for my father among the just reddened roses on the tea-table.

'But evening comes and the lamps are lit. And when evening comes and the lamps are lit they make a yellow fire in the ivy. I sit with my sewing by the table. I think of Jinny; of Rhoda; and hear the rattle of wheels on the pavement as the farm horses plod home; I hear traffic roaring in the evening wind. I look at the quivering leaves in the dark garden and think "They dance in London. Jinny kisses Louis."'

'How strange,' said Jinny, 'that people should sleep, that people should put out the lights and go upstairs. They have taken off their dresses, they have put on white night-gowns. There are no lights in any of these houses. There is a line of chimney-pots against the sky; and a street lamp or two burning, as lamps burn when nobody needs them. The only people in the streets are poor people hurrying. There is no one coming or going in this street; the day is over. A few policemen stand at the corners. Yet night is beginning. I feel myself shining in the dark. Silk is on my knee. My silk legs rub smoothly together. The stones of a necklace lie cold on my throat. My feet feel the pinch of shoes. I sit bolt upright so that my hair may not touch the back of the seat. I am arrayed, I am prepared. This is the momentary pause; the dark moment. The fiddlers have lifted their bows.

'Now the car slides to a stop. A strip of pavement is lighted. The door is opening and shutting. People are arriving; they do not speak; they hasten in. There is the swishing sound of cloaks falling in the hall. This is the prelude, this is the beginning. I glance, I peep, I powder. All is exact, prepared. My hair is swept in one curve. My lips are precisely red. I am ready now to join men and women on the stairs, my peers. I pass them, exposed to their gaze, as they are to mine. Like lightning we look but do not soften or show signs of recognition. Our bodies communicate. This is my calling. This is my world. All is decided and ready; the servants, standing here, and again here, take my name, my fresh, my unknown name, and toss it before me. I enter.

'Here are gilt chairs in the empty, the expectant rooms, and flowers, stiller, statelier, than flowers that grow, spread green, spread white, against the walls. And on one small table is one bound book. This is what I have dreamt; this is what I have foretold. I am native here. I tread naturally on thick carpets. I slide easily on smooth-polished floors, I now begin to unfurl, in this scent, in this radiance, as a fern when its curled leaves unfurl. I stop. I take stock of this world. I look among the groups of unknown people. Among the lustrous green, pink, pearl-grey women stand upright the bodies of men. They are black and white; they are grooved beneath their clothes with deep rills. I feel again the reflection in the window of the tunnel; it moves. The black-and-white figures of unknown men look at me as I lean forward; as I turn aside to look at a picture, they turn too. Their hands go fluttering to their ties. They touch their waistcoats, their pocket-handkerchiefs. They are very young. They are anxious to make a good impression. I feel a thousand capacities spring up in me. I am arch, gay, languid, melancholy by turns. I am rooted, but I flow. All gold, flowing that way, I say to this one, "Come". Rippling black, I say to that one, "No". One breaks off from his station under the glass cabinet. He approaches. He makes towards me. This is the most exciting moment I have ever known. I flutter. I ripple. I stream like a plant in the river, flowing this way, flowing that way, but rooted, so that he may come to me. "Come," I say, "come." Pale, with dark hair, the one who is coming is melancholy, romantic. And I am arch and fluent and capricious; for he is melancholy, he is romantic. He is here; he stands at my side.

'Now with a little jerk, like a limpet broken from a rock, I am broken off: I fall with him; I am carried off. We yield to this slow flood. We go in and out of this hesitating music. Rocks break the current of the dance; it jars, it shivers. In and out, we are swept now into this large figure; it holds us together; we cannot step outside its sinuous, its hesitating, its abrupt, its perfectly encircling walls. Our bodies, his hard, mine flowing, are pressed together within its body; it holds us together; and then lengthening out, in smooth, in sinuous folds, rolls us between it, on and on. Suddenly the music breaks. My blood runs on but my body stands still. The room reels past my eyes. It stops.

'Come, then, let us wander whirling to the gilt chairs. The body is stronger than I thought. I am dizzier than I supposed. I do not care for anything in the world. I do not care for anybody save this man whose name I do not know. Are we not acceptable, moon? Are we not lovely sitting together here, I in my satin; he in black and white? My peers may look at me now. I look straight back at you, men and women. I am one of you. This is my world. Now I take this thin-stemmed glass and sip. Wine has a drastic, an astringent taste. I cannot help wincing as I drink. Scent and flowers, radiance and heat, are distilled here to a fiery, to a yellow liquid. Just behind my shoulder-blades some dry thing, wide-eyed, gently closes, gradually lulls itself to sleep. This is rapture; this is relief. The bar at the back of my throat lowers itself. Words crowd and cluster and push forth one on top of another. It does not matter which. They jostle and mount on each other's shoulders. The single and the solitary mate, tumble and become many. It does not matter what I say. Crowding, like a fluttering bird, one sentence crosses the empty space between us. It settles on his lips. I fill my glass again. I drink. The veil drops between us. I am admitted to the warmth and privacy of another soul. We are together, high up, on some Alpine pass. He stands melancholy on the crest of the road. I stoop. I pick a blue flower and fix it, standing on tiptoe to reach him, in his coat. There! That is my moment of ecstasy. Now it is over.

'Now slackness and indifference invade us. Other people brush past. We have lost consciousness of our bodies uniting under the table. I also like fair-haired men with blue eyes. The door opens. The door goes on opening. Now I think, next time it opens the whole of my life will be changed. Who comes? But it is only a servant, bringing glasses. That is an old man—I should be a child with him. That is a great lady—with her I should dissemble. There are girls of my own age, for whom I feel the drawn swords of an honourable antagonism. For these are my peers. I am a native of this world. Here is my risk, here is my adventure. The door opens. O come, I say to this one, rippling gold from head to heels. "Come", and he comes towards me.'

'I shall edge behind them,' said Rhoda, 'as if I saw someone I know. But I know no one. I shall twitch the curtain and look at the moon. Draughts of oblivion shall quench my agitation. The door opens; the tiger leaps. The door opens; terror rushes in; terror upon terror, pursuing me. Let me visit furtively the treasures I have laid apart. Pools lie on the other side of the world reflecting marble columns. The swallow dips her wing in dark pools. But here the door opens and people come; they come towards me. Throwing faint smiles to mask their cruelty, their indifference, they seize me. The swallow dips her wings; the moon rides through the blue seas alone. I must take his hand; I must answer. But what answer shall I give? I am thrust back to stand burning in this clumsy, this ill-fitting body, to receive the shafts of his indifference and his scorn, I who long for marble columns and pools on the other side of the world where the swallow dips her wings.

'Night has wheeled a little further over the chimney-pots. I see out of the window over his shoulder some unembarrassed cat, not drowned in light, not trapped in silk, free to pause, to stretch, and to move again. I hate all details of the individual life. But I am fixed here to listen. An immense pressure is on me. I cannot move without dislodging the weight of centuries. A million arrows pierce me. Scorn and ridicule pierce me. I, who could beat my breast against the storm and let the hail choke me joyfully, am pinned down here; am exposed. The tiger leaps. Tongues with their whips are upon me. Mobile, incessant, they flicker over me. I must prevaricate and fence them off with lies. What amulet is there against this disaster? What face can I summon to lay cool upon this heat? I think of names on boxes; of mothers from whose wide knees skirts descend; of glades where the many-backed steep hills come down. Hide me, I cry, protect me, for I am the youngest, the most naked of you all. Jinny rides like a gull on the wave, dealing her looks adroitly here and there, saying this, saying that, with truth. But I lie; I prevaricate.

'Alone, I rock my basins; I am mistress of my fleet of ships. But here, twisting the tassels of this brocaded curtain in my hostess's window, I am broken into separate pieces; I am no longer one. What then is the knowledge that Jinny has as she dances; the assurance that Susan has as, stooping quietly beneath the lamplight, she draws the white cotton through the eye of her needle? They say, Yes; they say, No; they bring their fists down with a bang on the table. But I doubt; I tremble; I see the wild thorn tree shake its shadow in the desert.

'Now I will walk, as if I had an end in view, across the room, to the balcony under the awning. I see the sky, softly feathered with its sudden effulgence of moon. I also see the railings of the square, and two people without faces, leaning like statues against the sky. There is, then, a world immune from change. When I have passed through this drawing-room flickering with tongues that cut me like knives, making me stammer, making me lie, I find faces rid of features, robed in beauty. The lovers crouch under the plane tree. The policeman stands sentinel at the corner. A man passes. There is, then, a world immune from change. But I am not composed enough, standing on tiptoe on the verge of fire, still scorched by the hot breath, afraid of the door opening and the leap of the tiger, to make even one sentence. What I say is perpetually contradicted. Each time the door opens I am interrupted. I am not yet twenty-one. I am to be broken. I am to be derided all my life. I am to be cast up and down among these men and women, with their twitching faces, with their lying tongues, like a cork on a rough sea. Like a ribbon of weed I am flung far every time the door opens. I am the foam that sweeps and fills the uttermost rims of the rocks with whiteness; I am also a girl, here in this room.'

The sun, risen, no longer couched on a green mattress darting a fitful glance through watery jewels, bared its face and looked straight over the waves. They fell with a regular thud. They fell with the concussion of horses' hooves on the turf. Their spray rose like the tossing of lances and assegais over the riders' heads. They swept the beach with steel blue and diamond-tipped water. They drew in and out with the energy, the muscularity, of an engine which sweeps its force out and in again. The sun fell on cornfields and woods. Rivers became blue and many-plaited, lawns that sloped down to the water's edge became green as birds' feathers softly ruffling their plumes. The hills, curved and controlled, seemed bound back by thongs, as a limb is laced by muscles; and the woods which bristled proudly on their flanks were like the curt, clipped mane on the neck of a horse.

In the garden where the trees stood thick over flower-beds, ponds, and greenhouses the birds sang in the hot sunshine, each alone. One sang under the bedroom window; another on the topmost twig of the lilac bush; another on the edge of the wall. Each sang stridently, with passion, with vehemence, as if to let the song burst out of it, no matter if it shattered the song of another bird with harsh discord. Their round eyes bulged with brightness; their claws gripped the twig or rail. They sang, exposed without shelter, to the air and the sun, beautiful in their new plumage, shell-veined or brightly mailed, here barred with soft blues, here splashed with gold, or striped with one bright feather. They sang as if the song were urged out of them by the pressure of the morning. They sang as if the edge of being were sharpened and must cut, must split the softness of the blue-green light, the dampness of the wet earth; the fumes and steams of the greasy kitchen vapour; the hot breath of mutton and beef; the richness of pastry and fruit; the damp shreds and peelings thrown from the kitchen bucket, from which a slow steam oozed on the rubbish heap. On all the sodden, the damp-spotted, the curled with wetness, they descended, dry-beaked, ruthless, abrupt. They swooped suddenly from the lilac bough or the fence. They spied a snail and tapped the shell against a stone. They tapped furiously, methodically, until the shell broke and something slimy oozed from the crack. They swept and soared sharply in flights high into the air, twittering short, sharp notes, and perched in the upper branches of some tree, and looked down upon leaves and spires beneath, and the country white with blossom, flowing with grass, and the sea which beat like a drum that raises a regiment of plumed and turbaned soldiers. Now and again their songs ran together in swift scales like the interlacings of a mountain stream whose waters, meeting, foam and then mix, and hasten quicker and quicker down the same channel, brushing the same broad leaves. But there is a rock; they sever.

The sun fell in sharp wedges inside the room. Whatever the light touched became dowered with a fanatical existence. A plate was like a white lake. A knife looked like a dagger of ice. Suddenly tumblers revealed themselves upheld by streaks of light. Tables and chairs rose to the surface as if they had been sunk under water and rose, filmed with red, orange, purple like the bloom on the skin of ripe fruit. The veins on the glaze of the china, the grain of the wood, the fibres of the matting became more and more finely engraved. Everything was without shadow. A jar was so green that the eye seemed sucked up through a funnel by its intensity and stuck to it like a limpet. Then shapes took on mass and edge. Here was the boss of a chair; here the bulk of a cupboard. And as the light increased, flocks of shadow were driven before it and conglomerated and hung in many-pleated folds in the background.

'How fair, how strange,' said Bernard, 'glittering, many-pointed and many-domed London lies before me under mist. Guarded by gasometers, by factory chimneys, she lies sleeping as we approach. She folds the ant-heap to her breast. All cries, all clamour, are softly enveloped in silence. Not Rome herself looks more majestic. But we are aimed at her. Already her maternal somnolence is uneasy. Ridges fledged with houses rise from the mist. Factories, cathedrals, glass domes, institutions and theatres erect themselves. The early train from the north is hurled at her like a missile. We draw a curtain as we pass. Blank expectant faces stare at us as we rattle and flash through stations. Men clutch their news-papers a little tighter, as our wind sweeps them, envisaging death. But we roar on. We are about to explode in the flanks of the city like a shell in the side of some ponderous, maternal, majestic animal. She hums and murmurs; she awaits us.

'Meanwhile as I stand looking from the train window, I feel strangely, persuasively, that because of my great happiness (being engaged to be married) I am become part of this speed, this missile hurled at the city. I am numbed to tolerance and acquiescence. My dear sir, I could say, why do you fidget, taking down your suitcase and pressing into it the cap that you have worn all night? Nothing we can do will avail. Over us all broods a splendid unanimity. We are enlarged and solemnized and brushed into uniformity as with the grey wing of some enormous goose (it is a fine but colourless morning) because we have only one desire— to arrive at the station. I do not want the train to stop with a thud. I do not want the connection which has bound us together sitting opposite each other all night long to be broken. I do not want to feel that hate and rivalry have resumed their sway; and different desires. Our com-munity in the rushing train, sitting together with only one wish, to arrive at Euston, was very welcome. But behold! It is over. We have attained our desire. We have drawn up at the platform. Hurry and confusion and the wish to be first through the gate into the lift assert themselves. But I do not wish to be first through the gate, to assume the burden of individual life. I, who have been since Monday, when she accepted me, charged in every nerve with a sense of identity, who could not see a tooth-brush in a glass without saying, "*My* tooth-brush", now wish to unclasp my hands and let fall my possessions, and merely stand here in the street, taking no part, watching the omnibuses, without desire; without envy; with what would be boundless curiosity about human destiny if there were any longer an edge to my mind. But it has none. I have arrived; am accepted. I ask nothing.

'Having dropped off satisfied like a child from the breast, I am at liberty now to sink down, deep, into what passes, this omnipresent, general life. (How much, let me note, depends upon trousers; the intelligent head is entirely handicapped by shabby trousers.) One observes curious hesitations at the door of the lift. This way, that way, the other? Then individuality asserts itself. They are off. They are all impelled by some necessity. Some miserable affair of keeping an appointment, of buying a hat, severs these beautiful human beings once so united. For myself, I have no aim. I have no ambition. I will let myself be carried on by the general impulse. The surface of my mind slips along like a pale-grey stream reflecting what passes. I cannot remember my past, my nose, or the colour of my eyes, or what my general opinion of myself is. Only in moments of emergency, at a crossing, at a kerb, the wish to preserve my body springs out and seizes me and stops me, here, before this omnibus. We insist, it seems, on living. Then again, indifference descends. The roar of the traffic, the passage of undifferentiated faces, this way and that way, drugs me into dreams; rubs the features from faces. People might walk through me. And, what is this moment of time, this particular day in which I have found myself caught? The growl of traffic might be any uproar—forest trees or the roar of wild beasts. Time has whizzed back an inch or two on its reel; our short progress has been cancelled. I think also that our bodies are in truth naked. We are only lightly covered with buttoned cloth; and beneath these pavements are shells, bones and silence.

'It is, however, true that my dreaming, my tentative advance like one carried beneath the surface of a stream, is interrupted, torn, pricked and plucked at by sensations, spontaneous and irrelevant, of curiosity, greed, desire, irresponsible as in sleep. (I covet that bag—etc.) No, but I wish to go under; to visit the profound depths; once in a while to exercise my prerogative not always to act, but to explore; to hear vague, ancestral sounds of boughs creaking, of mammoths; to indulge impossible desires to embrace the whole world with the arms of understanding—impossible to those who act. Am I not, as I walk, trembling with strange oscillations and vibrations of sympathy, which, unmoored as I am from a private being, bid me embrace these engrossed flocks; these starers and trippers; these errand-boys and furtive and fugitive girls who, ignoring their doom, look in at shop-windows? But I am aware of our ephemeral passage.

'It is, however, true that I cannot deny a sense that life for me is now mysteriously prolonged. Is it that I may have children, may cast a fling of seed wider, beyond this generation, this doom-encircled population, shuffling each other in endless competition along the street? My daughters shall come here, in other summers; my sons shall turn new fields. Hence we are not raindrops, soon dried by the wind; we make gardens blow and forests roar; we come up differently, for ever and ever. This, then, serves to explain my confidence, my central stability, otherwise so monstrously absurd as I breast the stream of this crowded thoroughfare, making always a passage for myself between people's bodies, taking advantage of safe moments to cross. It is not vanity; for I am emptied of ambition; I do not remember my special gifts, or idiosyncrasy, or the marks I bear on my person; eyes, nose or mouth. I am not, at this moment, myself.

'Yet behold, it returns. One cannot extinguish that persistent smell. It steals in through some crack in the structure—one's identity. I am not part of the street—no, I observe the street. One splits off, therefore. For instance, up that back street a girl stands waiting; for whom? A romantic story. On the wall of that shop is fixed a small crane, and for what reason, I ask, was that crane fixed there? and invent a purple lady swelling, circumambient, hauled from a barouche landau by a perspiring husband sometime in the sixties. A grotesque story. That is, I am a natural coiner of words, a blower of bubbles through one thing and another. And, striking off these observations spontaneously, I elaborate myself; differentiate myself and, listening to the voice that says as I stroll past, "Look! Take note of that!" I conceive myself called upon to provide, some winter's night, a meaning for all my observations—a line that runs from one to another, a summing up that completes. But soliloquies in back streets soon pall. I need an audience. That is my downfall. That always ruffles the edge of the final statement and prevents it from forming. I cannot seat myself in some sordid eating-house and order the same glass day after day and imbue myself entirely in one fluid—this life. I make my phrase and run off with it to some furnished room where it will be lit by dozens of candles. I need eyes on me to draw out these frills and furbelows. To be myself (I note) I need the illumination of other people's eyes, and therefore cannot be entirely sure what is my self. The authentics, like Louis, like Rhoda, exist most completely in solitude. They resent illumination, reduplication. They toss their pictures once painted face downward on the field. On Louis's words the ice is packed thick. His words issue pressed, condensed, enduring.

'I wish, then, after this somnolence to sparkle, many-faceted under the light of my friends' faces. I have been traversing the sunless territory of non-identity. A strange land. I have heard in my moment of appeasement, in my moment of obliterating satisfaction, the sigh, as it goes in, comes out, of the tide that draws beyond this circle of bright light, this drumming of insensate fury. I have had one moment of enormous peace. This perhaps is happiness. Now I am drawn back by pricking sensations; by curiosity, greed (I am hungry) and the irresistible desire to be myself. I think of people to whom I could say things: Louis, Neville, Susan, Jinny and Rhoda. With them I am many-sided. They retrieve me from darkness. We shall meet tonight, thank Heaven. Thank Heaven, I need not be alone. We shall dine together. We shall say good-bye to Percival, who goes to India. The hour is still distant, but I feel already those harbingers, those outriders, figures of one's friends in absence. I see Louis, stone-carved, sculpturesque; Neville, scissor-cutting, exact; Susan with eyes like lumps of crystal; Jinny dancing like a flame, febrile, hot, over dry earth; and Rhoda the nymph of the fountain always wet. These are fantastic pictures—these are figments, these visions of friends in absence, grotesque, dropsical, vanishing at the first touch of the toe of a real boot. Yet they drum me alive. They brush off these vapours. I begin to be impatient of solitude—to feel its draperies hang sweltering, unwholesome about me. Oh, to toss them off and be active! Anybody will do. I am not fastidious. The crossing-sweeper will do; the postman; the waiter in this French restaurant; better still the genial proprietor, whose geniality seems reserved for oneself. He mixes the salad with his own hands for some privileged guest. Which is the privileged guest, I ask, and why? And what is he saying to the lady in ear rings; is she a friend or a customer? I feel at once, as I sit down at a table, the delicious jostle of confusion, of uncertainty, of possibility, of speculation. Images breed instantly. I am embarrassed by my own fertility. I could describe every chair, table, luncher here copiously, freely. My mind hums hither and thither with its veil of words for everything. To speak, about wine even to the waiter, is to bring about an explosion. Up goes the rocket. Its golden grain falls, fertilizing, upon the rich soil of my imagination. The entirely unexpected nature of this explosion—that is the joy of intercourse. I, mixed with an unknown Italian waiter—what am I? There is no stability in this world. Who is to say what meaning there is in anything? Who is to foretell the flight of a word? It is a balloon that sails over tree-tops. To speak of knowledge is futile. All is experiment and adventure. We are for ever mixing ourselves with unknown quantities. What is to come? I know not. But as I put down my glass I remember: I am engaged to be married. I am to dine with my friends tonight. I am Bernard, myself.'

'It is now five minutes to eight,' said Neville. 'I have come early. I have taken my place at the table ten minutes before the time in order to taste every moment of anticipation; to see the door open and to say, "Is it Percival? No; it is not Percival." There is a morbid pleasure in saying:

"No, it is not Percival". I have seen the door open and shut twenty times already; each time the suspense sharpens. This is the place to which he is coming. This is the table at which he will sit. Here, incredible as it seems, will be his actual body. This table, these chairs, this metal vase with its three red flowers are about to undergo an extraordinary transformation. Already the room, with its swing-doors, its tables heaped with fruit, with cold joints, wears the wavering, unreal appearance of a place where one waits expecting something to happen. Things quiver as if not yet in being. The blankness of the white table-cloth glares. The hostility, the indifference of other people dining here is oppressive. We look at each other; see that we do not know each other, stare, and go off. Such looks are lashes. I feel the whole cruelty and indifference of the world in them. If he should not come I could not bear it. I should go. Yet somebody must be seeing him now. He must be in some cab; he must be passing some shop. And every moment he seems to pump into this room this prickly light, this intensity of being, so that things have lost their normal uses—this knife-blade is only a flash of light, not a thing to cut with. The normal is abolished.

'The door opens, but he does not come. That is Louis hesitating there. That is his strange mixture of assurance and timidity. He looks at himself in the looking-glass as he comes in; he touches his hair; he is dissatisfied with his appearance. He says, "I am a Duke—the last of an ancient race". He is acrid, suspicious, domineering, difficult (I am comparing him with Percival). At the same time he is formidable, for there is laughter in his eyes. He has seen me. Here he is.'

'There is Susan,' said Louis. 'She does not see us. She has not dressed, because she despises the futility of London. She stands for a moment at the swing-door, looking about her like a creature dazed by the light of a lamp. Now she moves. She has the stealthy yet assured movements (even among tables and chairs) of a wild beast. She seems to find her way by instinct in and out among these little tables, touching no one, disregarding waiters, yet comes straight to our table in the corner. When she sees us (Neville, and myself) her face assumes a certainty which is alarming, as if she had what she wanted. To be loved by Susan would be to be impaled by a bird's sharp beak, to be nailed to a barnyard door. Yet there are moments when I could wish to be speared by a beak, to be nailed to a barnyard door, positively, once and for all.

'Rhoda comes now, from nowhere, having slipped in while we were not looking. She must have made a tortuous course, taking cover now behind a waiter, now behind some ornamental pillar, so as to put off as long as possible the shock of recognition, so as to be secure for one more moment to rock her petals in her basin. We wake her. We torture her. She dreads us, she despises us, yet comes cringing to our sides because for all our cruelty there is always some name, some face, which sheds a radiance, which lights up her pavements and makes it possible for her to replenish her dreams.'

'The door opens, the door goes on opening,' said Neville, 'yet he does not come.'

'There is Jinny,' said Susan. 'She stands in the door. Everything seems stayed. The waiter stops. The diners at the table by the door look. She seems to centre everything; round her tables, lines of doors, windows, ceilings, ray themselves, like rays round the star in the middle of a smashed window-pane. She brings things to a point, to order. Now she sees us, and moves, and all the rays ripple and flow and waver over us, bringing in new tides of sensation. We change. Louis puts his hand to his tie. Neville, who sits waiting with agonized intensity, nervously straightens the forks in front of him. Rhoda sees her with surprise, as if on some far horizon a fire blazed. And I, though I pile my mind with damp grass, with wet fields, with the sound of rain on the roof and the gusts of wind that batter at the house in winter and so protect my soul against her, feel her derision steal round me, feel her laughter curl its tongues of fire round me and light up unsparingly my shabby dress, my square-tipped finger-nails, which I at once hide under the table-cloth.'

'He has not come,' said Neville. 'The door opens and he does not come. That is Bernard. As he pulls off his coat he shows, of course, the blue shirt under his arm-pits. And then, unlike the rest of us, he comes in without pushing open a door, without knowing that he comes into a room full of strangers. He does not look in the glass. His hair is untidy, but he does not know it. He has no perception that we differ, or that this table is his goal. He hesitates on his way here. Who is that? he asks himself, for he half knows a woman in an opera cloak. He half knows everybody; he knows nobody (I compare him with Percival). But now, perceiving us, he waves a benevolent salute; he bears down with such benignity, with such love of mankind (crossed with humour at the futility of "loving mankind"), that, if it were not for Percival, who turns all this to vapour, one would feel, as the others already feel: Now is our festival; now we are together. But without Percival there is no solidity. We are silhouettes, hollow phantoms moving mistily without a background.'

'The swing-door goes on opening,' said Rhoda. 'Strangers keep on coming, people we shall never see again, people who brush us disagreeably with their familiarity, their indifference, and the sense of a world continuing without us. We cannot sink down, we cannot forget our faces. Even I who have no face, who make no difference when I come in (Susan and Jinny change bodies and faces), flutter unattached, without anchorage anywhere, unconsolidated, incapable of composing any blankness or continuity or wall against which these bodies move. It is because of Neville and his misery. The sharp breath of his misery scatters my being. Nothing can settle; nothing can subside. Every time the door opens he looks fixedly at the table—he dare not raise his eyes—then looks for one second and says, "He has not come". But here he is.'

'Now,' said Neville, 'my tree flowers. My heart rises. All oppression is relieved. All impediment is removed. The reign of chaos is over. He has imposed order. Knives cut again.'

'Here is Percival,' said Jinny. 'He has not dressed.'

'Here is Percival,' said Bernard, 'smoothing his hair, not from vanity (he does not look in the glass), but to propitiate the god of decency. He is conventional; he is a hero. The little boys trooped after him across the playing-fields. They blew their noses as he blew his nose, but unsuccessfully, for he is Percival. Now, when he is about to leave us, to go to India, all these trifles come together. He is a hero. Oh yes, that is not to be denied, and when he takes his seat by Susan, whom he loves, the occasion is crowned. We who yelped like jackals biting at each other's heels now assume the sober and confident air of soldiers in the presence of their captain. We who have been separated by our youth (the oldest is not yet twenty-five), who have sung like eager birds each his own song and tapped with the remorseless and savage egotism of the young our own snail-shell till it cracked (I am engaged), or perched solitary outside some bedroom window and sang of love, of fame and other single experiences so dear to the callow bird with a yellow tuft on its beak, now come nearer; and shuffling closer on our perch in this restaurant where everybody's interests are at variance, and the incessant passage of traffic chafes us with distractions, and the door opening perpetually its glass cage solicits us with myriad temptations and offers insults and wounds to our confidence—sitting together here we love each other and believe in our own endurance.'

'Now let us issue from the darkness of solitude,' said Louis.

'Now let us say, brutally and directly, what is in our minds,' said Neville. 'Our isolation, our preparation, is over. The furtive days of secrecy and hiding, the revelations on staircases, moments of terror and ecstasy.'

'Old Mrs Constable lifted her sponge and warmth poured over us,' said Bernard. 'We became clothed in this changing, this feeling garment of flesh.'

'The boot-boy made love to the scullery-maid in the kitchen garden,' said Susan, 'among the blown-out washing.'

'The breath of the wind was like a tiger panting,' said Rhoda.

'The man lay livid with his throat cut in the gutter,' said Neville.

'And going upstairs I could not raise my foot against the immitigable apple tree with its silver leaves held stiff.'

'The leaf danced in the hedge without anyone to blow it,' said Jinny.

'In the sun-baked corner,' said Louis, 'the petals swam on depths of green.'

'At Elvedon the gardeners swept and swept with their great brooms, and the woman sat at a table writing,' said Bernard.

'From these close-furled balls of string we draw now every filament,' said Louis, 'remembering, when we meet.'

'And then,' said Bernard, 'the cab came to the door, and, pressing our new bowler hats tightly over our eyes to hide our unmanly tears, we drove through streets in which even the housemaids looked at us, and our names painted in white letters on our boxes proclaimed to all the world that we were going to school with the regulation number of socks and drawers, on which our mothers for some nights previously had stitched our initials, in our boxes. A second severance from the body of our mother.'

'And Miss Lambert, Miss Cutting and Miss Bard,' said Jinny, 'monumental ladies, white-ruffed, stone-coloured, enigmatic, with amethyst rings moving like virginal tapers, dim glow-worms over the pages of French, geography and arithmetic, presided; and there were maps, green-baize boards, and rows of shoes on a shelf.'

'Bells rang punctually,' said Susan, 'maids scuffled and giggled. There was a drawing in of chairs and a drawing out of chairs on the linoleum. But from one attic there was a blue view, a distant view of a field unstained by the corruption of this regimented, unreal existence.'

'Down from our heads veils fell,' said Rhoda. 'We clasped the flowers with their green leaves rustling in garlands.'

'We changed, we became unrecognizable,' said Louis. 'Exposed to all these different lights, what we had in us (for we are all so different) came intermittently, in violent patches, spaced by blank voids, to the surface as if some acid had dropped unequally on the plate. I was this, Neville that, Rhoda different again, and Bernard too.'

'Then canoes slipped through palely tinted yellow branches,' said Neville, 'and Bernard, advancing in his casual way against breadths of green, against houses of very ancient foundation, tumbled in a heap on the ground beside me. In an access of emotion—winds are not more raving, nor lightning more sudden—I took my poem, I flung my poem, I slammed the door behind me.'

'I, however,' said Louis, 'losing sight of you, sat in my office and tore the date from the calendar, and announced to the world of ship-brokers, corn-chandlers and actuaries that Friday the tenth, or Tuesday the eighteenth, had dawned on the city of London.'

'Then,' said Jinny, 'Rhoda and I, exposed in bright dresses, with a few precious stones nestling on a cold ring round our throats, bowed, shook hands and took a sandwich from a plate with a smile.'

'The tiger leapt, and the swallow dipped her wings in dark pools on the other side of the world,' said Rhoda.

'But here and now we are together,' said Bernard. 'We have come together, at a particular time, to this particular spot. We are drawn into this communion by some deep, some common emotion. Shall we call it, conveniently, "love"? Shall we say "love of Percival" because Percival is going to India?

'No, that is too small, too particular a name. We cannot attach the width and spread of our feelings to so small a mark. We have come together (from the North, from the South, from Susan's farm, from Louis's house of business) to make one thing, not enduring—for what endures?—but seen by many eyes simultaneously. There is a red carnation in that vase. A single flower as we sat here waiting, but now a seven-sided flower, many-petalled, red, puce, purple-shaded, stiff with silver-tinted leaves—a whole flower to which every eye brings its own contribution.'

'After the capricious fires, the abysmal dullness of youth,' said Neville, 'the light falls upon real objects now. Here are knives and forks. The world is displayed, and we too, so that we can talk.'

'We differ, it may be too profoundly,' said Louis, 'for explanation. But let us attempt it. I smoothed my hair when I came in, hoping to look like the rest of you. But I cannot, for I am not single and entire as you are. I have lived a thousand lives already. Every day I unbury—I dig up. I find relics of myself in the sand that women made thousands of years ago, when I heard songs by the Nile and the chained beast stamping. What you see beside you, this man, this Louis, is only the cinders and refuse of something once splendid. I was an Arab prince; behold my free gestures. I was a great poet in the time of Elizabeth. I was a Duke at the court of Louis the Fourteenth. I am very vain, very confident; I have an immeasurable desire that women should sigh in sympathy. I have eaten no lunch today in order that Susan may think me cadaverous and that Jinny may extend to me the exquisite balm of her sympathy. But while I admire Susan and Percival, I hate the others, because it is for them that I do these antics, smoothing my hair, concealing my accent. I am the little ape who chatters over a nut, and you are the dowdy women with shiny bags of stale buns; I am also the caged tiger, and you are the keepers with red-hot bars. That is, I am fiercer and stronger than you are, yet the apparition that appears above ground after ages of non-entity will be spent in terror lest you should laugh at me, in veerings with the wind against the soot storms, in efforts to make a steel ring of clear poetry that shall connect the gulls and the women with bad teeth, the church spire and the bobbing billycock hats as I see them when I take my luncheon and prop my poet—is it Lucretius?—against a cruet and the gravy-splashed bill of fare.'

'But you will never hate me,' said Jinny. 'You will never see me, even across a room full of gilt chairs and ambassadors, without coming to me across the room to seek my sympathy. When I came in just now everything stood still in a pattern. Waiters stopped, diners raised their forks and held them. I had the air of being prepared for what would happen. When I sat down you put your hands to your ties, you hid them under the table. But I hide nothing. I am prepared. Every time the door opens I cry "More!" But my imagination is the bodies. I can imagine nothing beyond the circle cast by my body. My body goes before me, like a lantern down a dark lane, bringing one thing after another out of darkness into a ring of light. I dazzle you; I make you believe that this is all.'

'But when you stand in the door,' said Neville, 'you inflict stillness, demanding admiration, and that is a great impediment to the freedom of intercourse. You stand in the door making us notice you. But none of you saw me approach. I came early; I came quickly and directly, *here*, to sit by the person whom I love. My life has a rapidity that yours lack. I am like a hound on the scent. I hunt from dawn to dusk. Nothing, not the pursuit of perfection through the sand, nor fame, nor money, has meaning for me. I shall have riches; I shall have fame. But I shall never have what I want, for I lack bodily grace and the courage that comes with it. The swiftness of my mind is too strong for my body. I fail before I reach the end and fall in a heap, damp, perhaps disgusting. I excite pity in the crises of life, not love. Therefore I suffer horribly. But I do not suffer, as Louis does, to make myself a spectacle. I have too fine a sense of fact to allow myself these juggleries, these pretences. I see everything—except one thing—with complete clarity. That is my saving. That is what gives my suffering an unceasing excitement. That is what makes me dictate, even when I am silent. And since I am, in one respect, deluded, since the person is always changing, though not the desire, and I do not know in the morning by whom I shall sit at night, I am never stagnant; I rise from my worst disasters, I turn, I change. Pebbles bounce off the mail of my muscular, my extended body. In this pursuit I shall grow old.'

'If I could believe,' said Rhoda, 'that I should grow old in pursuit and change, I should be rid of my fear: nothing persists. One moment does not lead to another. The door opens and the tiger leaps. You did not see me come. I circled round the chairs to avoid the horror of the spring. I am afraid of you all. I am afraid of the shock of sensation that leaps upon me, because I cannot deal with it as you do—I cannot make one moment merge in the next. To me they are all violent, all separate; and if I fall under the shock of the leap of the moment you will be on me, tearing me to pieces. I have no end in view. I do not know how to run minute to minute and hour to hour, solving them by some natural force until they make the whole and indivisible mass that you call life. Because you have an end in view—one person, is it, to sit beside, an idea is it, your beauty is it? I do not know—your days and hours pass like the boughs of forest trees and the smooth green of forest rides to a hound running on the scent. But there is no single scent, no single body for me to follow. And I have no face. I am like the foam that races over the beach or the moonlight that falls arrowlike here on a tin can, here on a spike of the mailed sea-holly, or a bone or a half-eaten boat. I am whirled down caverns, and flap like paper against endless corridors, and must press my hand against the wall to draw myself back.

'But since I wish above all things to have lodgement, I pretend, as I go upstairs lagging behind Jinny and Susan, to have an end in view. I pull on my stockings as I see them pull on theirs. I wait for you to speak and then speak like you. I am drawn here across London to a particular spot, to a particular place, not to see you or you or you, but to light my fire at the general blaze of you who live wholly, indivisibly and without caring.'

'When I came into the room tonight,' said Susan, 'I stopped, I peered about like an animal with its eyes near to the ground. The smell of carpets and furniture and scent disgusts me. I like to walk through the wet fields alone, or to stop at a gate and watch my setter nose in a circle, and to ask: Where is the hare? I like to be with people who twist herbs, and spit into the fire, and shuffle down long passages in slippers like my father. The only sayings I understand are cries of love, hate, rage and pain. This talking is undressing an old woman whose dress had seemed to be part of her, but now, as we talk, she turns pinkish underneath, and has wrinkled thighs and sagging breasts. When you are silent you are again beautiful. I shall never have anything but natural happiness. It will almost content me. I shall go to bed tired. I shall lie like a field bearing crops in rotation; in the summer heat will dance over me; in the winter I shall be cracked with the cold. But heat and cold will follow each other naturally without my willing or unwilling. My children will carry me on; their teething, their crying, their going to school and coming back will be like the waves of the sea under me. No day will be without its movement. I shall be lifted higher than any of you on the backs of the seasons. I shall possess more than Jinny, more than Rhoda, by the time I die. But on the other hand, where you are various and dimple a million times to the ideas and laughter of others, I shall be sullen, storm-tinted and all one purple. I shall be debased and hide-bound by the bestial and beautiful passion of maternity. I shall push the fortunes of my children unscrupulously. I shall hate those who see their faults. I shall lie basely to help them. I shall let them wall me away from you, from you and from you. Also, I am torn with jealousy. I hate Jinny because she shows me that my hands are red, my nails bitten. I love with such ferocity that it kills me when the object of my love shows by a phrase that he can escape. He escapes, and I am left clutching at a string that slips in and out among the leaves on the tree-tops. I do not understand phrases.'

'Had I been born,' said Bernard, 'not knowing that one word follows another I might have been, who knows, perhaps anything. As it is, finding sequences everywhere, I cannot bear the pressure of solitude. When I cannot see words curling like rings of smoke round me I am in darkness—I am nothing. When I am alone I fall into lethargy, and say to myself dismally as I poke the cinders through the bars of the grate, Mrs Moffat will come. She will come and sweep it all up. When Louis is alone he sees with astonishing intensity, and will write some words that may outlast us all. Rhoda loves to be alone. She fears us because we shatter the sense of being which is so extreme in solitude—see how she grasps her fork—her weapon against us. But I only come into existence when the plumber, or the horse-dealer, or whoever it may be, says something which sets me alight. Then how lovely the smoke of my phrase is, rising and falling, flaunting and falling, upon red lobsters and yellow fruit, wreathing them into one beauty. But observe how meretri-cious the phrase is—made up of what evasions and old lies. Thus my character is in part made of the stimulus which other people provide, and is not mine, as yours are. There is some fatal streak, some wandering and irregular vein of silver, weakening it. Hence the fact that used to enrage Neville at school, that I left him. I went with the boasting boys with little caps and badges, driving off in big brakes—there are some here tonight, dining together, correctly dressed, before they go off in perfect concord to the music hall; I loved them. For they bring me into existence as certainly as you do. Hence, too, when I am leaving you and the train is going, you feel that it is not the train that is going, but I, Bernard, who does not care, who does not feel, who has no ticket, and has lost perhaps his purse. Susan, staring at the string that slips in and out among the leaves of the beech trees, cries: "He is gone! He has escaped me!" For there is nothing to lay hold of. I am made and remade continually. Different people draw different words from me.

'Thus there is not one person but fifty people whom I want to sit beside tonight. But I am the only one of you who is at home here without taking liberties. I am not gross; I am not a snob. If I lie open to the pressure of society I often succeed with the dexterity of my tongue in putting something difficult into the currency. See my little toys, twisted out of nothing in a second, how they entertain. I am no hoarder—I shall leave only a cupboard of old clothes when I die—and I am almost indifferent to the minor vanities of life which cause Louis so much torture. But I have sacrificed much. Veined as I am with iron, with silver and streaks of common mud, I cannot contract into the firm fist which those clench who do not depend upon stimulus. I am incapable of the denials, the heroisms of Louis and Rhoda. I shall never succeed, even in talk, in making a perfect phrase. But I shall have contributed more to the passing moment than any of you; I shall go into more rooms, more different rooms, than any of you. But because there is something that comes from outside and not from within I shall be forgotten; when my voice is silent you will not remember me, save as the echo of a voice that once wreathed the fruit into phrases.'

'Look,' said Rhoda; 'listen. Look how the light becomes richer, second by second, and bloom and ripeness lie everywhere; and our eyes, as they range round this room with all its tables, seem to push through curtains of colour, red, orange, umber and queer ambiguous tints, which yield like veils and close behind them, and one thing melts into another.'

'Yes,' said Jinny, 'our senses have widened. Membranes, webs of nerve that lay white and limp, have filled and spread themselves and float round us like filaments, making the air tangible and catching in them far-away sounds unheard before.'

'The roar of London,' said Louis, 'is round us. Motor-cars, vans, omnibuses pass and repass continuously. All are merged in one turning wheel of single sound. All separate sounds—wheels, bells, the cries of drunkards, of merry-makers—are churned into one sound, steel blue, circular. Then a siren hoots. At that shores slip away, chimneys flatten themselves, the ship makes for the open sea.'

'Percival is going,' said Neville. 'We sit here, surrounded, lit up, many-coloured; all things—hands, curtains, knives and forks, other people dining—run into each other. We are walled in here. But India lies outside.'

'I see India,' said Bernard. 'I see the low, long shore; I see the tortuous lanes of stamped mud that lead in and out among ramshackle pagodas; I see the gilt and crenellated buildings which have an air of fragility and decay as if they were temporarily run up buildings in some Oriental exhibition. I see a pair of bullocks who drag a low cart along the sun-baked road. The cart sways incompetently from side to side. Now one wheel sticks in the rut, and at once innumerable natives in loin-cloths swarm round it, chattering excitedly. But they do nothing.

Time seems endless, ambition vain. Over all broods a sense of the uselessness of human exertion. There are strange sour smells. An old man in a ditch continues to chew betel and to contemplate his navel. But now, behold, Percival advances; Percival rides a flea-bitten mare, and wears a sun helmet. By applying the standards of the West, by using the violent language that is natural to him, the bullock-cart is righted in less than five minutes. The Oriental problem is solved. He rides on; the multitude cluster round him, regarding him as if he were— what indeed he is—a God.'

'Unknown, with or without a secret, it does not matter,' said Rhoda, 'he is like a stone fallen into a pond round which minnows swarm. Like minnows, we who had been shooting this way, that way, all shot round him when he came. Like minnows, conscious of the presence of a great stone, we undulate and eddy contentedly. Comfort steals over us. Gold runs in our blood. One, two; one, two; the heart beats in serenity, in confidence, in some trance of well-being, in some rapture of benignity; and look—the outermost parts of the earth—pale shadows on the utmost horizon, India for instance, rise into our purview. The world that had been shrivelled, rounds itself; remote provinces are fetched up out of darkness; we see muddy roads, twisted jungle, swarms of men, and the vulture that feeds on some bloated carcass as within our scope, part of our proud and splendid province, since Percival, riding alone on a flea-bitten mare, advances down a solitary path, has his camp pitched among desolate trees, and sits alone, looking at the enormous mountains.'

'It is Percival,' said Louis, 'sitting silent as he sat among the tickling grasses when the breeze parted the clouds and they formed again, who makes us aware that these attempts to say, "I am this, I am that", which we make, coming together, like separated parts of one body and soul, are false. Something has been left out from fear. Something has been altered, from vanity. We have tried to accentuate differences. From the desire to be separate we have laid stress upon our faults, and what is particular to us. But there is a chain whirling round, round, in a steel-blue circle beneath.'

'It is hate, it is love,' said Susan. 'That is the furious coal-black stream that makes us dizzy if we look down into it. We stand on a ledge here, but if we look down we turn giddy.'

'It is love,' said Jinny, 'it is hate, such as Susan feels for me because I kissed Louis once in the garden; because equipped as I am, I make her think when I come in, "My hands are red", and hide them. But our hatred is almost indistinguishable from our love.'

'Yet these roaring waters,' said Neville, 'upon which we build our

crazy platforms are more stable than the wild, the weak and inconsequent cries that we utter when, trying to speak, we rise; when we reason
and jerk out these false sayings, "I am this; I am that!" Speech is false.

'But I eat. I gradually lose all knowledge of particulars as I eat. I am
becoming weighed down with food. These delicious mouthfuls of roast
duck, fitly piled with vegetables, following each other in exquisite
rotation of warmth, weight, sweet and bitter, past my palate, down my
gullet, into my stomach, have stabilized my body. I feel quiet, gravity,
control. All is solid now. Instinctively my palate now requires and
anticipates sweetness and lightness, something sugared and evanescent;
and cool wine, fitting glove-like over those finer nerves that seem to
tremble from the roof of my mouth and make it spread (as I drink) into
a domed cavern, green with vine leaves, musk-scented, purple with
grapes. Now I can look steadily into the mill-race that foams beneath.
By what particular name are we to call it? Let Rhoda speak, whose face
I see reflected mistily in the looking-glass opposite; Rhoda whom I
interrupted when she rocked her petals in a brown basin, asking for the
pocket-knife that Bernard had stolen. Love is not a whirlpool to her. She
is not giddy when she looks down. She looks far away over our heads,
beyond India.'

'Yes, between your shoulders, over your heads, to a landscape,' said
Rhoda, 'to a hollow where the many-backed steep hills come down like
birds' wings folded. There, on the short, firm turf, are bushes, dark
leaved, and against their darkness I see a shape, white, but not of stone,
moving, perhaps alive. But it is not you, it is not you, it is not you; not
Percival, Susan, Jinny, Neville or Louis. When the white arm rests upon
the knee it is a triangle; now it is upright—a column; now a fountain,
falling. It makes no sign, it does not beckon, it does not see us. Behind
it roars the sea. It is beyond our reach. Yet there I venture. There I go
to replenish my emptiness, to stretch my nights and fill them fuller and
fuller with dreams. And for a second even now, even here, I reach my
object and say, "Wander no more. All else is trial and make-believe.
Here is the end." But these pilgrimages, these moments of departure,
start always in your presence, from this table, these lights, from Percival
and Susan, here and now. Always I see the grove over your heads,
between your shoulders, or from a window when I have crossed the
room at a party and stand looking down into the street.'

'But his slippers?' said Neville. 'And his voice downstairs in the hall?
And catching sight of him when he does not see one? One waits and he
does not come. It gets later and later. He has forgotten. He is with
someone else. He is faithless, his love meant nothing. Oh, then the
agony—then the intolerable despair! And then the door opens. He is
here.'

'Rippling gold, I say to him, "Come",' said Jinny. 'And he comes; he crosses the room to where I sit, with my dress like a veil billowing round me on the gilt chair. Our hands touch, our bodies burst into fire. The chair, the cup, the table—nothing remains unlit. All quivers, all kindles, all burns clear.'

('Look, Rhoda,' said Louis, 'they have become nocturnal, rapt. Their eyes are like moths' wings moving so quickly that they do not seem to move at all.'

'Horns and trumpets,' said Rhoda, 'ring out. Leaves unfold; the stags blare in the thicket. There is a dancing and a drumming, like the dancing and the drumming of naked men with assagais.'

'Like the dance of savages,' said Louis, 'round the camp-fire. They are savage; they are ruthless. They dance in a circle, flapping bladders. The flames leap over their painted faces, over the leopard skins and the bleeding limbs which they have torn from the living body.'

'The flames of the festival rise high,' said Rhoda. 'The great procession passes, flinging green boughs and flowering branches. Their horns spill blue smoke; their skins are dappled red and yellow in the torchlight. They throw violets. They deck the beloved with garlands and with laurel leaves, there on the ring of turf where the steep-backed hills come down. The procession passes. And while it passes, Louis, we are aware of downfalling, we forebode decay. The shadow slants. We who are conspirators, withdrawn together to lean over some cold urn, note how the purple flame flows downwards.'

'Death is woven in with the violets,' said Louis. 'Death and again death.')

'How proudly we sit here,' said Jinny, 'we who are not yet twenty-five! Outside the trees flower; outside the women linger; outside the cabs swerve and sweep. Emerged from the tentative ways, the obscurities and dazzle of youth, we look straight in front of us, ready for what may come (the door opens, the door keeps on opening). All is real; all is firm without shadow or illusion. Beauty rides our brows. There is mine, there is Susan's. Our flesh is firm and cool. Our differences are clear-cut as the shadows of rocks in full sunlight. Beside us lie crisp rolls, yellow-glazed and hard; the table-cloth is white; and our hands lie half curled, ready to contract. Days and days are to come; winter days, summer days; we have scarcely broken into our hoard. Now the fruit is swollen beneath the leaf. The room is golden, and I say to him, "Come".'

'He has red ears,' said Louis, 'and the smell of meat hangs down in a damp net while the city clerks take snacks at the lunch bar.'

'With infinite time before us,' said Neville, 'we ask what shall we do? Shall we loiter down Bond Street, looking here and there, and buying perhaps a fountain-pen because it is green, or asking how much is the ring with the blue stone? Or shall we sit indoors and watch the coals turn crimson? Shall we stretch our hands for books and read here a passage and there a passage? Shall we shout with laughter for no reason? Shall we push through flowering meadows and make daisy chains? Shall we find out when the next train starts for the Hebrides and engage a reserved compartment? All is to come.'

'For you,' said Bernard, 'but yesterday I walked bang into a pillar-box. Yesterday I became engaged.'

'How strange,' said Susan, 'the little heaps of sugar look by the side of our plates. Also the mottled peelings of pears, and the plush rims to the looking-glasses. I had not seen them before. Everything is now set; everything is fixed. Bernard is engaged. Something irrevocable has happened. A circle has been cast on the waters; a chain is imposed. We shall never flow freely again.'

'For one moment only,' said Louis. 'Before the chain breaks, before disorder returns, see us fixed, see us displayed, see us held in a vice.

'But now the circle breaks. Now the current flows. Now we rush faster than before. Now passions that lay in wait down there in the dark weeds which grow at the bottom rise and pound us with their waves. Pain and jealousy, envy and desire, and something deeper than they are, stronger than love and more subterranean. The voice of action speaks. Listen, Rhoda (for we are conspirators, with our hands on the cold urn), to the casual, quick, exciting voice of action, of hounds running on the scent. They speak now without troubling to finish their sentences. They talk a little language such as lovers use. An imperious brute possesses them. The nerves thrill in their thighs. Their hearts pound and churn in their sides. Susan screws her pocket-handkerchief. Jinny's eyes dance with fire.'

'They are immune,' said Rhoda, 'from picking fingers and searching eyes. How easily they turn and glance; what poses they take of energy and pride! What life shines in Jinny's eyes; how fell, how entire Susan's glance is, searching for insects at the roots! Their hair shines lustrous. Their eyes burn like the eyes of animals brushing through leaves on the scent of the prey. The circle is destroyed. We are thrown asunder.'

'But soon, too soon,' said Bernard, 'this egotistic exultation fails. Too soon the moment of ravenous identity is over, and the appetite for happiness, and happiness, and still more happiness is glutted. The stone is sunk; the moment is over. Round me there spreads a wide margin of indifference. Now open in my eyes a thousand eyes of curiosity. Anyone now is at liberty to murder Bernard, who is engaged to be married, so long as they leave untouched this margin of unknown territory, this forest of the unknown world. Why, I ask (whispering discreetly), do women dine alone together there? Who are they? And what has brought them on this particular evening to this particular spot? The youth in the corner, judging from the nervous way in which he puts his hand from time to time to the back of his head, is from the country. He is suppliant, and so anxious to respond suitably to the kindness of his father's friend, his host, that he can scarcely enjoy now what he will enjoy very much at about half-past eleven tomorrow morning. I have also seen that lady powder her nose three times in the midst of an absorbing conversation—about love perhaps, about the unhappiness of their dearest friend perhaps. "Ah, but the state of my nose!" she thinks, and out comes her powder-puff, obliterating in its passage all the most fervent feelings of the human heart. There remains, however, the insoluble problem of the solitary man with the eyeglass; of the elderly lady drinking champagne alone. Who and what are these unknown people? I ask. I could make a dozen stories of what he said, of what she said—I can see a dozen pictures. But what are stories? Toys I twist, bubbles I blow, one ring passing through another. And sometimes I begin to doubt if there are stories. What is my story? What is Rhoda's? What is Neville's? There are facts, as, for example: "The handsome young man in the grey suit, whose reserve contrasted so strangely with the loquacity of the others, now brushed the crumbs from his waistcoat and, with a characteristic gesture at once commanding and benign, made a sign to the waiter, who came instantly and returned a moment later with the bill discreetly folded upon a plate". That is the truth; that is the fact, but beyond it all is darkness and conjecture.'

'Now once more,' said Louis, 'as we are about to part, having paid our bill, the circle in our blood, broken so often, so sharply, for we are so different, closes in a ring. Something is made. Yes, as we rise and fidget, a little nervously, we pray, holding in our hands this common feeling, "Do not move, do not let the swing-door cut to pieces the thing that we have made, that globes itself here, among these lights, these peelings, this litter of breadcrumbs and people passing. Do not move, do not go. Hold it for ever."'

'Let us hold it for one moment,' said Jinny; 'love, hatred, by whatever name we call it, this globe whose walls are made of Percival, of youth and beauty, and something so deep sunk within us that we shall perhaps never make this moment out of one man again.'

'Forests and far countries on the other side of the world,' said Rhoda, 'are in it; seas and jungles; the howlings of jackals and moonlight falling upon some high peak where the eagle soars.'

'Happiness is in it,' said Neville, 'and the quiet of ordinary things. A table, a chair, a book with a paper-knife stuck between the pages. And the petal falling from the rose, and the light flickering as we sit silent, or, perhaps, bethinking us of some trifle, suddenly speak.'

'Week-days are in it,' said Susan, 'Monday, Tuesday, Wednesday; the horses going up to the fields, and the horses returning; the rooks rising and falling, and catching the elm-trees in their net, whether it is April, whether it is November.'

'What is to come is in it,' said Bernard. 'That is the last drop and the brightest that we let fall like some supernal quicksilver into the swelling and splendid moment created by us from Percival. What is to come? I ask, brushing the crumbs from my waistcoat, what is outside? We have proved, sitting eating, sitting talking, that we can add to the treasury of moments. We are not slaves bound to suffer incessantly unrecorded petty blows on our bent backs. We are not sheep either, following a master. We are creators. We too have made something that will join the innumerable congregations of past time. We too, as we put on our hats and push open the door, stride not into chaos, but into a world that our own force can subjugate and make part of the illumined and everlasting road.

'Look, Percival, while they fetch the taxi, at the prospect which you are so soon to lose. The street is hard and burnished with the churning of innumerable wheels. The yellow canopy of our tremendous energy hangs like a burning cloth above our heads. Theatres, music halls and lamps in private houses make that light.'

'Peaked clouds,' said Rhoda, 'voyage over a sky dark like polished whalebone.'

'Now the agony begins; now the horror has seized me with its fangs,' said Neville. 'Now the cab comes; now Percival goes. What can we do to keep him? How bridge the distance between us? How fan the fire so that it blazes for ever? How signal to all time to come that we, who stand in the street, in the lamplight, loved Percival? Now Percival is gone.'

The sun had risen to its full height. It was no longer half seen and guessed at, from hints and gleams, as if a girl couched on her green-sea mattress tired her brows with water-globed jewels that sent lances of opal-tinted light falling and flashing in the uncertain air like the flanks of a dolphin leaping, or the flash of a falling blade. Now the sun burnt uncompromising, undeniable. It struck upon the hard sand, and the rocks became furnaces of red heat; it searched each pool and caught the minnow hiding in the cranny, and showed the rusty cartwheel, the white bone, or the boot without laces stuck, black as iron, in the sand. It gave to everything its exact measure of colour; to the sandhills their innumerable glitter, to the wild grasses their glancing green; or it fell upon the arid waste of the desert, here wind-scourged into furrows, here swept into desolate cairns, here sprinkled with stunted dark-green jungle trees. It lit up the smooth gilt mosque, the frail pink-and-white card houses of the southern village, and the long-breasted, white-haired women who knelt in the river bed beating wrinkled cloths upon stones. Steamers thudding slowly over the sea were caught in the level stare of the sun, and it beat through the yellow awnings upon passengers who dozed or paced the deck, shading their eyes to look for the land, while day after day, compressed in its oily throbbing sides, the ship bore them on monotonously over the waters.

The sun beat on the crowded pinnacles of southern hills and glared into deep, stony river beds where the water was shrunk beneath the high slung bridge so that washerwomen kneeling on hot stones could scarcely wet their linen; and lean mules went picking their way among the chattering grey stones with panniers slung across their narrow shoulders. At midday the heat of the sun made the hills grey as if shaved and singed in an explosion, while, further north, in cloudier and rainier countries hills smoothed into slabs as with the back of a spade had a light in them as if a warder, deep within, went from chamber to chamber carrying a green lamp. Through atoms of grey-blue air the sun struck at English fields and lit up marshes and pools, a white gull on a stake, the slow sail of shadows over blunt-headed woods and young corn and flowing hayfields. It beat on the orchard wall, and every pit and grain of the brick was silver pointed, purple, fiery as if soft to touch, as if touched it must melt into hot-baked grains of dust. The currants hung against the wall in ripples and cascades of polished red; plums swelled out their leaves, and all the blades of the grass were run together in one fluent green blaze. The trees' shadow was sunk to a dark pool at the root. Light descending in floods dissolved the separate foliation into one green mound.

The birds sang passionate songs addressed to one ear only and then stopped. Bubbling and chuckling they carried little bits of straw and twig to the dark knots in the higher branches of the trees. Gilt and purpled they perched in the garden where cones of laburnum and purple shook down gold and lilac, for now at midday the garden was all blossom and profusion and even the tunnels under the plants were green and purple and tawny as the sun beat through the red petal, or the broad yellow petal, or was barred by some thickly furred green stalk.

The sun struck straight upon the house, making the white walls glare between the dark windows. Their panes, woven thickly with green branches, held circles of impenetrable darkness. Sharp-edged wedges of light lay upon the window-sill and showed inside the room plates with blue rings, cups with curved handles, the bulge of a great bowl, the criss-cross pattern in the rug, and the formidable corners and lines of cabinets and bookcases. Behind their conglomeration hung a zone of shadow in which might be a further shape to be disencumbered of shadow or still denser depths of darkness.

The waves broke and spread their waters swiftly over the shore. One after another they massed themselves and fell; the spray tossed itself back with the energy of their fall. The waves were steeped deep-blue save for a pattern of diamond-pointed light on their backs which rippled as the backs of great horses ripple with muscles as they move. The waves fell; withdrew and fell again, like the thud of a great beast stamping.

'He is dead,' said Neville. 'He fell. His horse tripped. He was thrown. The sails of the world have swung round and caught me on the head. All is over. The lights of the world have gone out. There stands the tree which I cannot pass.

'Oh, to crumple this telegram in my fingers—to let the light of the world flood back—to say this has not happened! But why turn one's head hither and thither? This is the truth. This is the fact. His horse stumbled; he was thrown. The flashing trees and white rails went up in a shower. There was a surge; a drumming in his ears. Then the blow; the world crashed; he breathed heavily. He died where he fell.

'Barns and summer days in the country, rooms where we sat—all now lie in the unreal world which is gone. My past is cut from me. They came running. They carried him to some pavilion, men in riding-boots, men in sun helmets; among unknown men he died. Loneliness and silence often surrounded him. He often left me. And then, returning, "See where he comes!" I said.

'Women shuffle past the window as if there were no gulf cut in the street; no tree with stiff leaves which we cannot pass. We deserve then to be tripped by molehills. We are infinitely abject, shuffling past with our eyes shut. But why should I submit? Why try to lift my foot and mount the stair? This is where I stand; here, holding the telegram. The past, summer days and rooms where we sat, stream away like burnt paper with red eyes in it. Why meet and resume? Why talk and eat and make up other combinations with other people? From this moment I am solitary. No one will know me now. I have three letters, "I am about to play quoits with a colonel, so no more", thus he ends our friendship, shouldering his way through the crowd with a wave of his hand. This farce is worth no more formal celebration. Yet if someone had but said: "Wait"; had pulled the strap three holes tighter—he would have done justice for fifty years, and sat in Court and ridden alone at the head of troops and denounced some monstrous tyranny, and come back to us.

'Now I say there is a grinning, there is a subterfuge. There is something sneering behind our backs. That boy almost lost his footing as he leapt on the bus. Percival fell; was killed; is buried; and I watch people passing; holding tight to the rails of omnibuses; determined to save their lives.

'I will not lift my foot to climb the stair. I will stand for one moment beneath the immitigable tree, alone with the man whose throat is cut, while downstairs the cook shoves in and out the dampers. I will not climb the stair. We are doomed, all of us. Women shuffle past with shopping-bags. People keep on passing. Yet you shall not destroy me. For this moment, this one moment, we are together. I press you to me. Come, pain, feed on me. Bury your fangs in my flesh. Tear me asunder. I sob, I sob.'

'Such is the incomprehensible combination,' said Bernard, 'such is the complexity of things, that as I descend the staircase I do not know which is sorrow, which joy. My son is born; Percival is dead. I am upheld by pillars, shored up on either side by stark emotions; but which is sorrow, which is joy? I ask, and do not know, only that I need silence, and to be alone and to go out, and to save one hour to consider what has happened to my world, what death has done to my world.

'This then is the world that Percival sees no longer. Let me look. The butcher delivers meat next door; two old men stumble along the pavement; sparrows alight. The machine then works; I note the rhythm, the throb, but as a thing in which I have no part, since he sees it no longer. (He lies pale and bandaged in some room.) Now then is my chance to find out what is of great importance, and I must be careful, and tell no lies. About him my feeling was: he sat there in the centre. Now I go to that spot no longer. The place is empty.

'Oh yes, I can assure you, men in felt hats and women carrying baskets—you have lost something that would have been very valuable to you. You have lost a leader whom you would have followed; and one of you has lost happiness and children. He is dead who would have given you that. He lies on a camp-bed, bandaged, in some hot Indian hospital while coolies squatted on the floor agitate those fans—I forget how they call them. But this is important; "You are well out of it", I said, while the doves descended over the roofs and my son was born, as if it were a fact. I remember, as a boy, his curious air of detachment. And I go on to say (my eyes fill with tears and then are dry), "But this is better than one had dared to hope". I say, addressing what is abstract, facing me eyeless at the end of the avenue, in the sky, "Is this the utmost you can do?" Then we have triumphed. You have done your utmost, I say, addressing that blank and brutal face (for he was twenty-five and should have lived to be eighty) without avail. I am not going to lie down and weep away a life of care. (An entry to be made in my pocket-book; contempt for those who inflict meaningless death.) Further, this is important; that I should be able to place him in trifling and ridiculous situations, so that he may not feel himself absurd, perched on a great horse. I must be able to say, "Percival, a ridiculous name". At the same time let me tell you, men and women, hurrying to the tube station, you would have had to respect him. You would have had to form up and follow behind him. How strange to oar one's way through crowds seeing life through hollow eyes, burning eyes.

'Yet already signals begin, beckonings, attempts to lure me back. Curiosity is knocked out for only a short time. One cannot live outside the machine for more perhaps than half an hour. Bodies, I note, already begin to look ordinary; but what is behind them differs—the perspective. Behind that newspaper placard is the hospital; the long room with black men pulling ropes; and then they bury him. Yet since it says a famous actress has been divorced, I ask instantly, Which? Yet I cannot take out my penny; I cannot buy a paper; I cannot suffer interruption yet.

'I ask, if I shall never see you again and fix my eyes on that solidity, what form will our communication take? You have gone across the court, further and further, drawing finer and finer the thread between us. But you exist somewhere. Something of you remains. A judge. That is, if I discover a new vein in myself I shall submit it to you privately. I shall ask, What is your verdict? You shall remain the arbiter. But for how long? Things will become too difficult to explain: there will be new things; already my son. I am now at the zenith of an experience. It will decline. Already I no longer cry with conviction, "What luck!" Exaltation, the flight of doves descending, is over. Chaos, detail return. I am no longer amazed by names written over shop-windows. I do not feel Why hurry? Why catch trains? The sequence returns; one thing leads to another—the usual order.

'Yes, but I still resent the usual order. I will not let myself be made yet to accept the sequence of things. I will walk; I will not change the rhythm of my mind by stopping, by looking; I will walk. I will go up these steps into the gallery and submit myself to the influence of minds like mine outside the sequence. There is little time left to answer the question; my powers flag; I become torpid. Here are pictures. Here are cold madonnas among their pillars. Let them lay to rest the incessant activity of the mind's eye, the bandaged head, the men with ropes, so that I may find something unvisual beneath. Here are gardens; and Venus among her flowers; here are saints and blue madonnas. Mercifully these pictures make no reference; they do not nudge; they do not point. Thus they expand my consciousness of him and bring him back to me differently. I remember his beauty. "Look, where he comes", I said.

'Lines and colours almost persuade me that I too can be heroic, I, who make phrases so easily, am so soon seduced, love what comes next, and cannot clench my fist, but vacillate weakly making phrases according to my circumstances. Now, through my own infirmity I recover what he was to me: my opposite. Being naturally truthful, he did not see the point of these exaggerations, and was borne on by a natural sense of the

fitting, was indeed a great master of the art of living so that he seems to
have lived long, and to have spread calm round him, indifference one
might almost say, certainly to his own advancement, save that he had
also great compassion. A child playing—a summer evening—doors will
open and shut, will keep opening and shutting, through which I see
sights that make me weep. For they cannot be imparted. Hence our
loneliness; hence our desolation. I turn to that spot in my mind and find
it empty. My own infirmities oppress me. There is no longer him to
oppose them.

'Behold, then, the blue madonna streaked with tears. This is my
funeral service. We have no ceremonies, only private dirges and no
conclusions, only violent sensations, each separate. Nothing that has
been said meets our case. We sit in the Italian room at the National
Gallery picking up fragments. I doubt that Titian ever felt this rat
gnaw. Painters live lives of methodical absorption, adding stroke to
stroke. They are not like poets—scapegoats; they are not chained to the
rock. Hence the silence, the sublimity. Yet that crimson must have burnt
in Titian's gizzard. No doubt he rose with the great arms holding the
cornucopia, and fell, in that descent. But the silence weighs on me—the
perpetual solicitation of the eye. The pressure is intermittent and
muffled. I distinguish too little and too vaguely. The bell is pressed and
I do not ring or give out irrelevant clamours all jangled. I am titillated
inordinately by some splendour; the ruffled crimson against the green
lining; the march of pillars; the orange light behind the black, pricked
ears of the olive trees. Arrows of sensation strike from my spine, but
without order.

'Yet something is added to my interpretation. Something lies deeply
buried. For one moment I thought to grasp it. But bury it, bury it; let it
breed, hidden in the depths of my mind some day to fructify. After a
long lifetime, loosely, in a moment of revelation, I may lay hands on it,
but now the idea breaks in my hand. Ideas break a thousand times for
once that they globe themselves entire. They break; they fall over me.
"Line and colours they survive, therefore . . ."

'I am yawning. I am glutted with sensations. I am exhausted with the
strain and the long, long time—twenty-five minutes, half an hour—that
I have held myself alone outside the machine. I grow numb; I grow stiff.
How shall I break up this numbness which discredits my sympathetic
heart? There are others suffering—multitudes of people suffering.
Neville suffers. He loved Percival. But I can no longer endure extremi-
ties; I want someone with whom to laugh, with whom to yawn, with
whom to remember how he scratched his head; someone he was at ease
with and liked (not Susan, whom he loved, but Jinny rather). In her
room also I could do penance. I could ask, Did he tell you how I refused

him when he asked me to go to Hampton Court that day? Those are the thoughts that will wake me leaping in anguish in the middle of the night—the crimes for which one would do penance in all the markets of the world bareheaded; that one did not go to Hampton Court that day.

'But now I want life round me, and books and little ornaments, and the usual sounds of tradesmen calling on which to pillow my head after this exhaustion, and shut my eyes after this revelation. I will go straight, then, down the stairs, and hail the first taxi and drive to Jinny.'

'There is the puddle,' said Rhoda, 'and I cannot cross it. I hear the rush of the great grindstone within an inch of my head. Its wind roars in my face. All palpable forms of life have failed me. Unless I can stretch and touch something hard, I shall be blown down the eternal corridors for ever. What, then, can I touch? What brick, what stone? and so draw myself across the enormous gulf into my body safely?

'Now the shadow has fallen and the purple light slants downwards. The figure that was robed in beauty is now clothed in ruin. The figure that stood in the grove where the steep-backed hills come down falls in ruin, as I told them when they said they loved his voice on the stair, and his old shoes and moments of being together.

'Now I will walk down Oxford Street envisaging a world rent by lightning; I will look at oaks cracked asunder and red where the flowering branch has fallen. I will go to Oxford Street and buy stockings for a party. I will do the usual things under the lightning flash. On the bare ground I will pick violets and bind them together and offer them to Percival, something given him by me. Look now at what Percival has given me. Look at the street now that Percival is dead. The houses are lightly founded to be puffed over by a breath of air. Reckless and random the cars race and roar and hunt us to death like bloodhounds. I am alone in a hostile world. The human face is hideous. This is to my liking. I want publicity and violence and to be dashed like a stone on the rocks. I like factory chimneys and cranes and lorries. I like the passing of face and face and face, deformed, indifferent. I am sick of prettiness; I am sick of privacy. I ride rough waters and shall sink with no one to save me.

'Percival, by his death, has made me this present, has revealed this terror, has left me to undergo this humiliation—faces and faces, served out like soup-plates by scullions; coarse, greedy, casual; looking in at shop-windows with pendent parcels; ogling, brushing, destroying everything, leaving even our love impure, touched now by their dirty fingers.

'Here is the shop where they sell stockings. And I could believe that beauty is once more set flowing. Its whisper comes down these aisles, through these laces, breathing among baskets of coloured ribbons. There are then warm hollows grooved in the heart of the uproar; alcoves of silence where we can shelter under the wing of beauty from truth which I desire. Pain is suspended as a girl silently slides open a drawer. And then, she speaks; her voice wakes me. I shoot to the bottom among the weeds and see envy, jealousy, hatred and spite scuttle like crabs over the sand as she speaks. These are our companions. I will pay my bill and take my parcel.

'This is Oxford Street. Here are hate, jealousy, hurry, and indifference frothed into the wild semblance of life. These are our companions. Consider the friends with whom we sit and eat. I think of Louis, reading the sporting column of an evening newspaper, afraid of ridicule; a snob. He says, looking at the people passing, he will shepherd us if we will follow. If we submit he will reduce us to order. Thus he will smooth out the death of Percival to his satisfaction, looking fixedly over the cruet, past the houses at the sky. Bernard, meanwhile, flops red-eyed into some armchair. He will have out his notebook; under D, he will enter "Phrases to be used on the deaths of friends". Jinny, pirouetting across the room, will perch on the arm of his chair and ask, "Did he love me?" "More than he loved Susan?" Susan, engaged to her farmer in the country, will stand for a second with the telegram before her, holding a plate; and then, with a kick of her heel, slam to the oven door. Neville, after staring at the window through his tears, will see through his tears, and ask, "Who passes the window?"—"What lovely boy?" This is my tribute to Percival; withered violets, blackened violets.

'Where shall I go then? To some museum, where they keep rings under glass cases, where there are cabinets, and the dresses that queens have worn? Or shall I go to Hampton Court and look at the red walls and courtyards and the seemliness of herded yew trees making black pyramids symmetrically on the grass among flowers? There shall I recover beauty, and impose order upon my raked, my dishevelled soul? But what can one make in loneliness? Alone I should stand on the empty grass and say, Rooks fly; somebody passes with a bag; there is a gardener with a wheelbarrow. I should stand in a queue and smell sweat, and scent as horrible as sweat; and be hung with other people like a joint of meat among other joints of meat.

'Here is a hall where one pays money and goes in, where one hears music among somnolent people who have come here after lunch on a hot afternoon. We have eaten beef and pudding enough to live for a week without tasting food. Therefore we cluster like maggots on the back of something that will carry us on. Decorous, portly—we have white hair waved under our hats; slim shoes; little bags; clean-shaven cheeks; here and there a military moustache; not a speck of dust has been allowed to settle anywhere on our broadcloth. Swaying and opening programmes, with a few words of greeting to friends, we settle down, like walruses stranded on rocks, like heavy bodies incapable of waddling to the sea, hoping for a wave to lift us, but we are too heavy, and too much dry shingle lies between us and the sea. We lie gorged with food, torpid in the heat. Then, swollen but contained in slippery satin, the sea-green woman comes to our rescue. She sucks in her lips, assumes an air of intensity, inflates herself and hurls herself precisely at the right moment as if she saw an apple and her voice was the arrow into the note, "Ah!"

'An axe has split a tree to the core; the core is warm; sound quivers within the bark. "Ah!" cried a woman to her lover, leaning from her window in Venice. "Ah, ah!" she cried, and again she cries "Ah!" She has provided us with a cry. But only a cry. And what is a cry? Then the beetle-shaped men come with their violins; wait; count; nod; down come their bows. And there is ripple and laughter like the dance of olive trees and their myriad-tongued grey leaves when a seafarer, biting a twig between his lips where the many-backed steep hills come down, leaps on shore.

'"Like" and "like" and "like"—but what is the thing that lies beneath the semblance of the thing? Now that lightning has gashed the tree and the flowering branch has fallen and Percival, by his death, has made me this gift, let me see the thing. There is a square; there is an oblong. The players take the square and place it upon the oblong. They place it very accurately; they make a perfect dwelling-place. Very little is left outside. The structure is now visible; what is inchoate is here stated; we are not so various or so mean; we have made oblongs and stood them upon squares. This is our triumph; this is our consolation.

'The sweetness of this content overflowing runs down the walls of my mind, and liberates understanding. Wander no more, I say; this is the end. The oblong has been set upon the square; the spiral is on top. We have been hauled over the shingle, down to the sea. The players come again. But they are mopping their faces. They are no longer so spruce or so debonair. I will go. I will set aside this afternoon. I will make a pilgrimage. I will go to Greenwich. I will fling myself fearlessly into trams, into omnibuses. As we lurch down Regent Street, and I am flung upon this woman, upon this man, I am not injured, I am not outraged by the collision. A square stands upon an oblong. Here are mean streets where chaffering goes on in street markets, and every sort of iron rod, bolt and screw is laid out, and people swarm off the pavement, pinching raw meat with thick fingers. The structure is visible. We have made a dwelling-place.

'These, then, are the flowers that grow among the rough grasses of the field which the cows trample, wind-bitten, almost deformed, without fruit or blossom. These are what I bring, torn up by the roots from the

pavement of Oxford Street, my penny bunch, my penny bunch of violets.
Now from the window of the tram I see masts among chimneys; there is
the river; there are ships that sail to India. I will walk by the river. I
will pace this embankment, where an old man reads a newspaper in a
glass shelter. I will pace this terrace and watch the ships bowling down
the tide. A woman walks on deck, with a dog barking round her. Her
skirts are blown; her hair is blown; they are going out to sea; they are
leaving us; they are vanishing this summer evening. Now I will
relinquish; now I will let loose. Now I will at last free the checked, the
jerked-back desire to be spent, to be consumed. We will gallop together
over desert hills where the swallow dips her wings in dark pools and the
pillars stand entire. Into the wave that dashes upon the shore, into the
wave that flings its white foam to the uttermost corners of the earth, I
throw my violets, my offering to Percival.'

The sun no longer stood in the middle of the sky. Its light slanted, falling obliquely. Here it caught on the edge of a cloud and burnt it into a slice of light, a blazing island on which no foot could rest. Then another cloud was caught in the light and another and another, so that the waves beneath were arrow-struck with fiery feathered darts that shot erratically across the quivering blue.

The topmost leaves of the tree were crisped in the sun. They rustled stiffly in the random breeze. The birds sat still save that they flicked their heads sharply from side to side. Now they paused in their song as if glutted with sound, as if the fullness of midday had gorged them. The dragon-fly poised motionless over a reed, then shot its blue stitch further through the air. The far hum in the distance seemed made of the broken tremor of fine wings dancing up and down on the horizon. The river water held the reeds now fixed as if glass had hardened round them; and then the glass wavered and the reeds swept low. Pondering, sunken headed, the cattle stood in the fields and cumbrously moved one foot and then another. In the bucket near the house the tap stopped dripping, as if the bucket were full, and then the tap dripped one, two, three separate drops in succession.

The windows showed erratically spots of burning fire, the elbow of one branch, and then some tranquil space of pure clarity. The blind hung red at the window's edge and within the room daggers of light fell upon chairs and tables making cracks across their lacquer and polish. The green pot bulged enormously, with its white window elongated in its side. Light driving darkness before it spilt itself profusely upon the corners and bosses; and yet heaped up darkness in mounds of unmoulded shape.

The waves massed themselves, curved their backs and crashed. Up spurted stones and shingle. They swept round the rocks, and the spray, leaping high, spattered the walls of a cave that had been dry before, and left pools inland, where some fish stranded lashed its tail as the wave drew back.

'I have signed my name,' said Louis, 'already twenty times. I, and again I, and again I. Clear, firm, unequivocal, there it stands, my name. Clear-cut and unequivocal am I too. Yet a vast inheritance of experience is packed in me. I have lived thousands of years. I am like a worm that has eaten its way through the wood of a very old oak beam. But now I am compact; now I am gathered together this fine morning.

'The sun shines from a clear sky. But twelve o'clock brings neither rain nor sunshine. It is the hour when Miss Johnson brings me my letters in a wire tray. Upon these white sheets I indent my name. The whisper of leaves, water running down gutters, green depths flecked with dahlias or zinnias; I, now a duke, now Plato, companion of Socrates; the tramp of dark men and yellow men migrating east, west, north and south; the eternal procession, women going with attaché cases down the Strand as they went once with pitchers to the Nile; all the furled and close-packed leaves of my many-folded life are now summed in my name; incised cleanly and barely on the sheet. Now a full-grown man; now upright standing in sun or rain. I must drop heavy as a hatchet and cut the oak with my sheer weight, for if I deviate, glancing this way, or that way, I shall fall like snow and be wasted.

'I am half in love with the typewriter and the telephone. With letters and cables and brief but courteous commands on the telephone to Paris, Berlin, New York, I have fused my many lives into one; I have helped by my assiduity and decision to score those lines on the map there by which the different parts of the world are laced together. I love punctually at ten to come into my room; I love the purple glow of the dark mahogany; I love the table and its sharp edge; and the smooth-running drawers. I love the telephone with its lip stretched to my whisper, and the date on the wall; and the engagement book. Mr Prentice at four; Mr Eyres sharp at four-thirty.

'I like to be asked to come to Mr Burchard's private room and report on our commitments to China. I hope to inherit an armchair and a Turkey carpet. My shoulder is to the wheel; I roll the dark before me, spreading commerce where there was chaos in the far parts of the world. If I press on, from chaos making order, I shall find myself where Chatham stood, and Pitt, Burke and Sir Robert Peel. Thus I expunge certain stains, and erase old defilements; the woman who gave me a flag from the top of the Christmas tree; my accent; beatings and other tortures; the boasting boys; my father, a banker at Brisbane.

'I have read my poet in an eating-house, and, stirring my coffee, listened to the clerks making bets at the little tables, watched the women hesitating at the counter. I said that nothing should be irrelevant, like a piece of brown paper dropped casually on the floor. I said their journeys should have an end in view; they should earn their two pound ten a week at the command of an august master; some hand, some robe, should fold us about in the evening. When I have healed these fractures and comprehended these monstrosities so that they need neither excuse nor apology, which both waste our strength, I shall give back to the street and the eating-shop what they lost when they fell on these hard times and broke on these stony beaches. I shall assemble a few words and forge round us a hammered ring of beaten steel.

'But now I have not a moment to spare. There is no respite here, no shadow made of quivering leaves, or alcove to which one can retreat from the sun, to sit, with a lover, in the cool of the evening. The weight of the world is on our shoulders; its vision is through our eyes; if we blink or look aside, or turn back to finger what Plato said or remember Napoleon and his conquests, we inflict on the world the injury of some obliquity. This is life; Mr Prentice at four; Mr Eyres at four-thirty. I like to hear the soft rush of the lift and the thud with which it stops on my landing and the heavy male tread of responsible feet down the corridors. So by dint of our united exertions we send ships to the remotest parts of the globe; replete with lavatories and gymnasiums. The weight of the world is on our shoulders. This is life. If I press on, I shall inherit a chair and a rug; a place in Surrey with glass houses, and some rare conifer, melon or flowering tree which other merchants will envy.

'Yet I still keep my attic room. There I open the usual little book; there I watch the rain glisten on the tiles till they shine like a policeman's waterproof; there I see the broken windows in poor people's houses; the lean cats; some slattern squinting in a cracked looking-glass as she arranges her face for the street corner; there Rhoda sometimes comes. For we are lovers.

'Percival has died (he died in Egypt; he died in Greece; all deaths are one death). Susan has children; Neville mounts rapidly to the conspicuous heights. Life passes. The clouds change perpetually over our houses. I do this, do that, and again do this and then that. Meeting and parting, we assemble different forms, make different patterns. But if I do not nail these impressions to the board and out of the many men in me make one; exist here and now and not in streaks and patches, like scattered snow wreaths on far mountains; and ask Miss Johnson as I pass through the office about the movies and take my cup of tea and accept also my favourite biscuit, then I shall fall like snow and be wasted.

'Yet when six o'clock comes and I touch my hat to the commissionaire, being always too effusive in ceremony since I desire so much to be accepted; and struggle, leaning against the wind, buttoned up, with my jaws blue and my eyes running water, I wish that a little typist would cuddle on my knees; I think that my favourite dish is liver and bacon; and so am apt to wander to the river, to the narrow streets where there are frequent public-houses, and the shadows of ships passing at the end of the street, and women fighting. But I say to myself, recovering my sanity, Mr Prentice at four; Mr Eyres at four-thirty. The hatchet must fall on the block; the oak must be cleft to the centre. The weight of the world is on my shoulders. Here is the pen and the paper; on the letters in the wire basket I sign my name, I, I, and again I.'

'Summer comes, and winter,' said Susan. 'The seasons pass. The pear fills itself and drops from the tree. The dead leaf rests on its edge. But steam has obscured the window. I sit by the fire watching the kettle boil. I see the pear tree through the streaked steam on the window-pane.

'Sleep, sleep, I croon, whether it is summer or winter, May or November. Sleep I sing—I, who am unmelodious and hear no music save rustic music when a dog barks, a bell tinkles, or wheels crunch upon the gravel. I sing my song by the fire like an old shell murmuring on the beach. Sleep, sleep, I say, warning off with my voice all who rattle milk-cans, fire at rooks, shoot rabbits, or in any way bring the shock of destruction near this wicker cradle, laden with soft limbs, curled under a pink coverlet.

'I have lost my indifference, my blank eyes, my pear-shaped eyes that saw to the root. I am no longer January, May or any other season, but am all spun to a fine thread round the cradle, wrapping in a cocoon made of my own blood the delicate limbs of my baby. Sleep, I say, and feel within me uprush some wilder, darker violence, so that I would fell down with one blow any intruder, any snatcher, who should break into this room and wake the sleeper.

'I pad about the house all day long in apron and slippers, like my mother who died of cancer. Whether it is summer, whether it is winter, I no longer know by the moor grass, and the heath flower; only by the steam on the window-pane, or the frost on the window-pane. When the lark peels high his ring of sound and it falls through the air like an apple paring, I stoop; I feed my baby. I, who used to walk through beech woods noting the jay's feather turning blue as it falls, past the shepherd and the tramp, who stared at the woman squatted beside a tilted cart in a ditch, go from room to room with a duster. Sleep, I say, desiring sleep to fall like a blanket of down and cover these weak limbs; demanding that life shall sheathe its claws and gird its lightning and pass by, making of my own body a hollow, a warm shelter for my child to sleep in. Sleep, I say, sleep. Or I go to the window, I look at the rook's high nest; and the pear tree. "His eyes will see when mine are shut", I think. "I shall go mixed with them beyond my body and shall see India. He will come home, bringing trophies to be laid at my feet. He will increase my possessions."

'But I never rise at dawn and see the purple drops in the cabbage leaves; the red drops in the roses. I do not watch the setter nose in a circle, or lie at night watching the leaves hide the stars and the stars move and the leaves hang still. The butcher calls; the milk has to be stood under a shade lest it should sour.

'Sleep, I say, sleep, as the kettle boils and its breath comes thicker and thicker issuing in one jet from the spout. So life fills my veins. So life pours through my limbs. So I am driven forward, till I could cry, as I move from dawn to dusk opening and shutting, "No more. I am glutted with natural happiness." Yet more will come, more children; more cradles, more baskets in the kitchen and hams ripening; and onions glistening; and more beds of lettuce and potatoes. I am blown like a leaf by the gale; now brushing the wet grass, now whirled up. I am glutted with natural happiness; and wish sometimes that the fullness would pass from me and the weight of the sleeping house rise, when we sit reading, and I stay the thread at the eye of my needle. The lamp kindles a fire in the dark pane. A fire burns in the heart of the ivy. I see a lit-up street in the evergreens. I hear traffic in the brush of the wind down the lane, and broken voices, and laughter, and Jinny who cries as the door opens, "Come, Come!"

'But no sound breaks the silence of our house, where the fields sigh close to the door. The wind washes through the elm trees; a moth hits the lamp; a cow lows; a crack of sound starts in the rafter, and I push my thread through the needle and murmur, "Sleep".'

'Now is the moment,' said Jinny. 'Now we have met, and have come together. Now let us talk, let us tell stories. Who is he? Who is she? I am infinitely curious and do not know what is to come. If you, whom I meet for the first time, were to say to me, "The coach starts at four from Piccadilly", I would not stay to fling a few necessaries in a bandbox, but would come at once.

'Let us sit here under the cut flowers, on the sofa by the picture. Let us decorate our Christmas tree with facts and again with facts. People are so soon gone; let us catch them. That man there, by the cabinet; he lives, you say, surrounded by china pots. Break one and you shatter a thousand pounds. And he loved a girl in Rome and she left him. Hence the pots, old junk found in lodging-houses or dug from the desert sands. And since beauty must be broken daily to remain beautiful, and he is static, his life stagnates in a china sea. It is strange though; for once, as a young man, he sat on damp ground and drank rum with soldiers.

'One must be quick and add facts deftly, like toys to a tree, fixing them with a twist of the fingers. He stoops, how he stoops, even over an azalea. He stoops over the old woman even, because she wears diamonds in her ears, and, bundling about her estate in a pony carriage, directs who is to be helped, what tree felled, and who turned out tomorrow. (I have lived my life, I must tell you, all these years, and I am now past thirty, perilously, like a mountain goat, leaping from crag to crag; I do not settle long anywhere; I do not attach myself to one person in particular; but you will find that if I raise my arm, some figure at once breaks off and will come.) And that man is a judge; and that man is a millionaire, and that man, with the eyeglass, shot his governess through the heart with an arrow when he was ten years old. Afterwards he rode through deserts with despatches, took part in revolutions and now collects materials for a history of his mother's family, long settled in Norfolk. That little man with a blue chin has a right hand that is withered. But why? We do not know. That woman, you whisper discreetly, with the pearl pagodas hanging from her ears, was the pure flame who lit the life of one of our statesmen; now since his death she sees ghosts, tells fortunes, and has adopted a coffee-coloured youth whom she calls the Messiah. That man with the drooping moustache, like a cavalry officer, lived a life of the utmost debauchery (it is all in some memoir) until one day he met a stranger in a train who converted him between Edinburgh and Carlisle by reading the Bible.

'Thus, in a few seconds, deftly, adroitly, we decipher the hieroglyphs written on other people's faces. Here, in this room, are the abraded and battered shells cast on the shore. The door goes on opening. The room fills and fills with knowledge, anguish, many kinds of ambition, much indifference, some despair. Between us, you say, we could build cathedrals, dictate policies, condemn men to death, and administer the affairs of several public offices. The common fund of experience is very deep. We have between us scores of children of both sexes, whom we are educating, going to see at school with the measles, and bringing up to inherit our houses. In one way or another we make this day, this Friday, some by going to the Law Courts; others to the city; others to the nursery; others by marching and forming fours. A million hands stitch, raise hods with bricks. The activity is endless. And tomorrow it begins again; tomorrow we make Saturday. Some take train for France; others ship for India. Some will never come into this room again. One may die tonight. Another will beget a child. From us every sort of building, policy, venture, picture, poem, child, factory, will spring. Life comes; life goes; we make life. So you say.

'But we who live in the body see with the body's imagination things in outline. I see rocks in bright sunshine. I cannot take these facts into some cave and, shading my eyes, grade their yellows, blues, umbers into one substance. I cannot remain seated for long. I must jump up and go. The coach may start from Piccadilly. I drop all these facts—diamonds, withered hands, china pots and the rest of it—as a monkey drops nuts from its naked paws. I cannot tell you if life is this or that. I am going to push out into the heterogeneous crowd. I am going to be buffeted; to be flung up, and flung down, among men, like a ship on the sea.

'For now my body, my companion, which is always sending its signals, the rough black "No", the golden "Come", in rapid running arrows of sensation, beckons. Someone moves. Did I raise my arm? Did I look? Did my yellow scarf with the strawberry spots float and signal? He has broken from the wall. He follows. I am pursued through the forest. All is rapt, all is nocturnal, and the parrots go screaming through the branches. All my senses stand erect. Now I feel the roughness of the fibre of the curtain through which I push; now I feel the cold iron railing and its blistered paint beneath my palm. Now the cool tide of darkness breaks its waters over me. We are out of doors. Night opens; night traversed by wandering moths; night hiding lovers roaming to adventure. I smell roses; I smell violets; I see red and blue just hidden. Now gravel is under my shoes; now grass. Up reel the tall backs of houses guilty with lights. All London is uneasy with flashing lights. Now let us sing our love song—Come, come, come. Now my gold signal is like a dragon-fly flying taut. Jug, jug, jug, I sing like the nightingale whose melody is crowded in the too narrow passage of her throat. Now I hear crash and rending of boughs and the crack of antlers as if the beasts of the forest were all hunting, all rearing high and plunging down among the thorns. One has pierced me. One is driven deep within me.

'And velvet flowers and leaves whose coolness has been stood in water wash me round, and sheathe me, embalming me.'

'Why, look,' said Neville, 'at the clock ticking on the mantelpiece? Time passes, yes. And we grow old. But to sit with you, alone with you, here in London, in this firelit room, you there, I here, is all. The world ransacked to its uttermost ends, and all its heights stripped and gathered of their flowers, holds no more. Look at the firelight running up and down the gold thread in the curtain. The fruit it circles droops heavy. It falls on the toe of your boot, it gives your face a red rim—I think it is the firelight and not your face; I think those are books against the wall, and that a curtain, and that perhaps an armchair. But when you come everything changes. The cups and saucers changed when you came in this morning. There can be no doubt, I thought, pushing aside the newspaper, that our mean lives, unsightly as they are, put on splendour and have meaning only under the eyes of love.

'I rose. I had done my breakfast. There was the whole day before us, and as it was fine, tender, non-committal, we walked through the Park to the Embankment, along the Strand to St Paul's, then to the shop where I bought an umbrella, always talking, and now and then stopping to look. But can this last? I said to myself, by a lion in Trafalgar Square, by the lion seen once and for ever;—so I revisit my past life, scene by scene; there is an elm tree, and there lies Percival. For ever and ever, I swore. Then darted in the usual doubt. I clutched your hand. You left me. The descent into the Tube was like death. We were cut up, we were dissevered by all those faces and the hollow wind that seemed to roar down there over desert boulders. I sat staring in my own room. By five I knew that you were faithless. I snatched the telephone and the buzz, buzz, buzz of its stupid voice in your empty room battered my heart down, when the door opened and there you stood. That was the most perfect of our meetings. But these meetings, these partings, finally destroy us.

'Now this room seems to me central, something scooped out of the eternal night. Outside lines twist and intersect, but round us, wrapping us about. Here we are centred. Here we can be silent, or speak without raising our voices. Did you notice that and then that? we say. He said that, meaning. . . . She hesitated, and I believe suspected. Anyhow, I heard voices, a sob on the stair late at night. It is the end of their relationship. Thus we spin round us infinitely fine filaments and construct a system. Plato and Shakespeare are included, also quite obscure people, people of no importance whatsoever. I hate men who wear crucifixes on the left side of their waistcoats. I hate ceremonies and lamentations and the sad figure of Christ trembling beside another trembling and sad figure. Also the pomp and the indifference and the emphasis, always on the wrong place, of people holding forth under chandeliers in full evening dress, wearing stars and decorations. Some spray in a hedge, though, or a sunset over a flat winter field, or again the way some old woman sits, arms akimbo, in an omnibus with a basket—those we point at for the other to look at. It is so vast an alleviation to be able to point for another to look at. And then not to talk. To follow the dark paths of the mind and enter the past, to visit books, to brush aside their branches and break off some fruit. And you take it and marvel, as I take the careless movements of your body and marvel at its ease, its power—how you fling open windows and are dexterous with your hands. For alas! my mind is a little impeded, it soon tires; I fall damp, perhaps disgusting, at the goal.

'Alas! I could not ride about India in a sun helmet and return to a bungalow. I cannot tumble, as you do, like half-naked boys on the deck of a ship, squirting each other with hose-pipes. I want this fire, I want this chair. I want someone to sit beside after the day's pursuit and all its anguish, after its listenings, and its waitings, and its suspicions. After quarrelling and reconciliation I need privacy—to be alone with you, to set this hubbub in order. For I am as neat as a cat in my habits. We must oppose the waste and deformity of the world, its crowds eddying round and round disgorged and trampling. One must slip paper-knives, even, exactly through the pages of novels, and tie up packets of letters neatly with green silk, and brush up the cinders with a hearth broom. Everything must be done to rebuke the horror of deformity. Let us read writers of Roman severity and virtue; let us seek perfection through the sand. Yes, but I love to slip the virtue and severity of the noble Romans under the grey light of your eyes, and dancing grasses and summer breezes and the laughter and shouts of boys at play—of naked cabin-boys squirting each other with hose-pipes on the decks of ships. Hence I am not a disinterested seeker, like Louis, after perfection through the sand. Colours always stain the page; clouds pass over it. And the poem, I think, is only your voice speaking. Alcibiades, Ajax, Hector and Percival are also you. They loved riding, they risked their lives wantonly, they were not great readers either. But you are not Ajax or Percival. They did not wrinkle their noses and scratch their foreheads with your precise gesture. You are you. That is what consoles me for the lack of many things—I am ugly, I am weak—and the depravity of the world, and the flight of youth and Percival's death, and bitterness and rancour and envies innumerable.

'But if one day you do not come after breakfast, if one day I see you in some looking-glass perhaps looking after another, if the telephone buzzes and buzzes in your empty room, I shall then, after unspeakable anguish, I shall then—for there is no end to the folly of the human heart—seek another, find another, you. Meanwhile, let us abolish the ticking of time's clock with one blow. Come closer.'

The sun had now sunk lower in the sky. The islands of cloud had gained in density and drew themselves across the sun so that the rocks went suddenly black, and the trembling sea-holly lost its blue and turned silver, and shadows were blown like grey cloths over the sea. The waves no longer visited the further pools or reached the dotted black line which lay irregularly upon the beach. The sand was pearl white, smoothed and shining.

Birds swooped and circled high up in the air. Some raced in the furrows of the wind and turned and sliced through them as if they were one body cut into a thousand shreds. Birds fell like a net descending on the tree-tops. Here one bird taking its way alone made wing for the marsh and sat solitary on a white stake, opening its wings and shutting them.

Some petals had fallen in the garden. They lay shell-shaped on the earth. The dead leaf no longer stood upon its edge, but had been blown, now running, now pausing, against some stalk. Through all the flowers the same wave of light passed in a sudden flaunt and flash as if a fin cut the green glass of a lake. Now and again some level and masterly blast blew the multitudinous leaves up and down and then, as the wind flagged, each blade regained its identity. The flowers, burning their bright discs in the sun, flung aside the sunlight as the wind tossed them, and then some heads too heavy to rise again drooped slightly.

The afternoon sun warmed the fields, poured blue into the shadows and reddened the corn. A deep varnish was laid like a lacquer over the fields. A cart, a horse, a flock of rooks—whatever moved in it was rolled round in gold. If a cow moved a leg it stirred ripples of red gold, and its horns seemed lined with light. Sprays of flaxen-haired corn lay on the hedges, brushed from the shaggy carts that came up from the meadows short legged and primeval looking. The round-headed clouds never dwindled as they bowled along, but kept every atom of their rotundity. Now, as they passed, they caught a whole village in the fling of their net and, passing, let it fly free again. Far away on the horizon, among the million grains of blue-grey dust, burnt one pane, or stood the single line of one steeple or one tree.

The red curtains and the white blinds blew in and out, flapping against the edge of the window, and the light which entered by flaps and breadths unequally had in it some brown tinge, and some abandonment as it blew through the blowing curtains in gusts. Here it browned a cabinet, there reddened a chair, here it made the window waver in the side of the green jar.

All for a moment wavered and bent in uncertainty and ambiguity, as if a great moth sailing through the room had shadowed the immense solidity of chairs and tables with floating wings.

'And time,' said Bernard, 'lets fall its drop. The drop that has formed on the roof of the soul falls. On the roof of my mind time, forming, lets fall its drop. Last week, as I stood shaving, the drop fell. I, standing with my razor in my hand, became suddenly aware of the merely habitual nature of my action (this is the drop forming) and congratulated my hands, ironically, for keeping at it. Shave, shave, shave, I said. Go on shaving. The drop fell. All through the day's work, at intervals, my mind went to an empty place, saying, "What is lost? What is over?" And "Over and done with," I muttered, "over and done with", solacing myself with words. People noticed the vacuity of my face and the aimlessness of my conversation. The last words of my sentence tailed away. And as I buttoned on my coat to go home I said more dramatically, "I have lost my youth".

'It is curious how, at every crisis, some phrase which does not fit insists upon coming to the rescue—the penalty of living in an old civilization with a notebook. This drop falling has nothing to do with losing my youth. This drop falling is time tapering to a point. Time, which is a sunny pasture covered with a dancing light, time, which is widespread as a field at midday, becomes pendent. Time tapers to a point. As a drop falls from a glass heavy with some sediment, time falls. These are the true cycles, these are the true events. Then as if all the luminosity of the atmosphere were withdrawn I see to the bare bottom. I see what habit covers. I lie sluggish in bed for days. I dine out and gape like a codfish. I do not trouble to finish my sentences, and my actions, usually so uncertain, acquire a mechanical precision. On this occasion, passing an office, I went in and bought, with all the composure of a mechanical figure, a ticket for Rome.

'Now I sit on a stone seat in these gardens surveying the eternal city, and the little man who was shaving in London five days ago looks already like a heap of old clothes. London has also crumbled. London consists of fallen factories and a few gasometers. At the same time I am not involved in this pageantry. I see the violet-sashed priests and the picturesque nursemaids; I notice externals only. I sit here like a convalescent, like a very simple man who knows only words of one syllable. "The sun is hot". I say. "The wind is cold." I feel myself carried round like an insect on top of the earth and could swear that, sitting here, I feel its hardness, its turning movement. I have no desire to go the opposite way from the earth. Could I prolong this sense another six inches I have a foreboding that I should touch some queer territory. But I have a very limited proboscis. I never wish to prolong these states of detachment; I dislike them; I also despise them. I do not wish to be a man who sits for fifty years on the same spot thinking of his navel. I wish to be harnessed to a cart, a vegetable-cart that rattles over the cobbles.

'The truth is that I am not one of those who find their satisfaction in one person, or in infinity. The private room bores me, also the sky. My being only glitters when all its facets are exposed to many people. Let them fail and I am full of holes, dwindling like burnt paper. Oh, Mrs Moffat, Mrs Moffat, I say, come and sweep it all up. Things have dropped from me. I have outlived certain desires; I have lost friends, some by death—Percival—others through sheer inability to cross the street. I am not so gifted as at one time seemed likely. Certain things lie beyond my scope. I shall never understand the harder problems of philosophy. Rome is the limit of my travelling. As I drop asleep at night it strikes me sometimes with a pang that I shall never see savages in Tahiti spearing fish by the light of a blazing cresset, or a lion spring in the jungle, or a naked man eating raw flesh. Nor shall I learn Russian or read the Vedas. I shall never again walk bang into the pillar-box. (But still a few stars fall through my night, beautifully, from the violence of that concussion.) But as I think, truth has come nearer. For many years I crooned complacently, "My children . . . my wife . . . my house . . . my dog". As I let myself in with the latch-key I would go through that familiar ritual and wrap myself in those warm coverings. Now that lovely veil has fallen. I do not want possessions now. (Note: an Italian washerwoman stands on the same rung of physical refinement as the daughter of an English duke.)

'But let me consider. The drop falls; another stage has been reached. Stage upon stage. And why should there be an end of stages? and where do they lead? To what conclusion? For they come wearing robes of solemnity. In these dilemmas the devout consult those violet-sashed and sensual-looking gentry who are trooping past me. But for ourselves, we resent teachers. Let a man get up and say, "Behold, this is the truth", and instantly I perceive a sandy cat filching a piece of fish in the background. Look, you have forgotten the cat, I say. So Neville, at school, in the dim chapel, raged at the sight of the doctor's crucifix. I, who am always distracted, whether by a cat or by a bee buzzing round the bouquet that Lady Hampden keeps so diligently pressed to her nose, at once make up a story and so obliterate the angles of the crucifix. I have made up thousands of stories; I have filled innumerable notebooks with phrases to be used when I have found the true story, the one story to which all these phrases refer. But I have never yet found that story. And I begin to ask, Are there stories?

'Look now from this terrace at the swarming population beneath. Look at the general activity and clamour. That man is in difficulties with his mule. Half a dozen good-natured loafers offer their services. Others pass by without looking. They have as many interests as there are threads in a skein. Look at the sweep of the sky, bowled over by round white clouds. Imagine the leagues of level land and the aqueducts and the broken Roman pavement and the tombstones in the Campagna, and beyond the Campagna, the sea, then again more land, then the sea. I could break off any detail in all that prospect—say the mule-cart—and describe it with the greatest ease. But why describe a man in trouble with his mule? Again, I could invent stories about that girl coming up the steps. "She met him under the dark archway. . . . 'It is over,' he said, turning from the cage where the china parrot hangs." Or simply, "That was all". But why impose my arbitrary design? Why stress this and shape that and twist up little figures like the toys men sell in trays in the street? Why select this, out of all that—one detail?

'Here am I shedding one of my life-skins, and all they will say is, "Bernard is spending ten days in Rome". Here am I marching up and down this terrace alone, unoriented. But observe how dots and dashes are beginning, as I walk, to run themselves into continuous lines, how things are losing the bald, the separate identity that they had as I walked up those steps. The great red pot is now a reddish streak in a wave of yellowish green. The world is beginning to move past me like the banks of a hedge when the train starts, like the waves of the sea when a steamer moves. I am moving too, am becoming involved in the general sequence when one thing follows another and it seems inevitable that the tree should come, then the telegraph-pole, then the break in the hedge. And as I move, surrounded, included and taking part, the usual phrases begin to bubble up, and I wish to free these bubbles from the trap-door in my head, and direct my steps therefore towards that man, the back of whose head is half familiar to me. We were together at school. We shall undoubtedly meet. We shall certainly lunch together. We shall talk. But wait, one moment wait.

'These moments of escape are not to be despised. They come too seldom. Tahiti becomes possible. Leaning over this parapet I see far out a waste of water. A fin turns. This bare visual impression is unattached to any line of reason, it springs up as one might see the fin of a porpoise on the horizon. Visual impressions often communicate thus briefly statements that we shall in time to come uncover and coax into words. I note under F., therefore, "Fin in a waste of waters". I, who am perpetually making notes in the margin of my mind for some final statement, make this mark, waiting for some winter's evening.

'Now I shall go and lunch somewhere, I shall hold my glass up, I shall look through the wine, I shall observe with more than my usual detachment, and when a pretty woman enters the restaurant and comes down the room between the tables I shall say to myself, "Look where she comes against a waste of waters". A meaningless observation, but to me, solemn, slate-coloured, with a fatal sound of ruining worlds and waters falling to destruction.

'So, Bernard (I recall you, you the usual partner in my enterprises), let us begin this new chapter, and observe the formation of this new, this unknown, strange, altogether unidentified and terrifying experience—the new drop—which is about to shape itself. Larpent is that man's name.'

'In this hot afternoon,' said Susan, 'here in this garden, here in this field where I walk with my son, I have reached the summit of my desires. The hinge of the gate is rusty; he heaves it open. The violent passions of childhood, my tears in the garden when Jinny kissed Louis, my rage in the schoolroom, which smelt of pine, my loneliness in foreign places, when the mules came clattering in on their pointed hoofs and the Italian women chattered at the fountain, shawled, with carnations twisted in their hair, are rewarded by security, possession, familiarity. I have had peaceful, productive years. I possess all I see. I have grown trees from the seed. I have made ponds in which goldfish hide under the broad-leaved lilies. I have netted over strawberry beds and lettuce beds, and stitched the pears and the plums into white bags to keep them safe from the wasps. I have seen my sons and daughters, once netted over like fruit in their cots, break the meshes and walk with me, taller than I am, casting shadows on the grass.

'I am fenced in, planted here like one of my own trees. I say, "My son", I say, "My daughter", and even the ironmonger looking up from his counter strewn with nails, paint and wire-fencing respects the shabby car at the door with its butterfly nets, pads and bee-hives. We hang mistletoe over the clock at Christmas, weigh our blackberries and mushrooms, count out jam-pots, and stand year by year to be measured against the shutter in the drawing-room window. I also make wreaths of white flowers, twisting silver-leaved plants among them for the dead, attaching my card with sorrow for the dead shepherd, with sympathy for the wife of the dead carter; and sit by the beds of dying women, who murmur their last terrors, who clutch my hand; frequenting rooms intolerable except to one born as I was and early acquainted with the farmyard and the dung-heap and the hens straying in and out, and the mother with two rooms and growing children. I have seen the windows run with heat, I have smelt the sink.

'I ask now, standing with my scissors among my flowers, Where can the shadow enter? What shock can loosen my laboriously gathered, relentlessly pressed down life? Yet sometimes I am sick of natural happiness, and fruit growing, and children scattering the house with oars, guns, skulls, books won for prizes and other trophies. I am sick of the body, I am sick of my own craft, industry and cunning, of the unscrupulous ways of the mother who protects, who collects under her jealous eyes at one long table her own children, always her own.

'It is when spring comes, cold, showery, with sudden yellow flowers— then as I look at the meat under the blue shade and press the heavy silver bags of tea, of sultanas, I remember how the sun rose, and the swallows skimmed the grass, and phrases that Bernard made when we were children, and the leaves shook over us, many-folded, very light, breaking the blue of the sky, scattering wandering lights upon the skeleton roots of the beech trees where I sat, sobbing. The pigeon rose. I jumped up and ran after the words that trailed like the dangling string from an air ball, up and up, from branch to branch escaping. Then like a cracked bowl the fixity of my morning broke, and putting down the bag of flour I thought, Life stands round me like a glass round the imprisoned reed.

'I hold scissors and snip off the hollyhocks, who went to Elvedon and trod on rotten oak-apples, and saw the lady writing and the gardeners with their great brooms. We ran back panting lest we should be shot and nailed like stoats to the wall. Now I measure, I preserve. At night I sit in the armchair and stretch my arm for my sewing; and hear my husband snore; and look up when the light from a passing car dazzles the windows and feel the waves of my life tossed, broken, round me who am rooted; and hear cries, and see others' lives eddying like straws round the piers of a bridge while I push my needle in and out and draw my thread through the calico.

'I think sometimes of Percival who loved me. He rode and fell in India. I think sometimes of Rhoda. Uneasy cries wake me at dead of night. But for the most part I walk content with my sons. I cut the dead petals from hollyhocks. Rather squat, grey before my time, but with clear eyes, pear-shaped eyes, I pace my fields.'

'Here I stand,' said Jinny, 'in the Tube station where everything that is desirable meets—Piccadilly South Side, Piccadilly North Side, Regent Street and the Haymarket. I stand for a moment under the pavement in the heart of London. Innumerable wheels rush and feet press just over my head. The great avenues of civilization meet here and strike this way and that. I am in the heart of life. But look—there is my body in that looking-glass. How solitary, how shrunk, how aged! I am no longer young. I am no longer part of the procession. Millions descend those stairs in a terrible descent. Great wheels churn inexorably urging them downwards. Millions have died. Percival died. I still move. I still live. But who will come if I signal?

'Little animal that I am, sucking my flanks in and out with fear, I stand here, palpitating, trembling. But I will not be afraid. I will bring the whip down on my flanks. I am not a whimpering little animal making for the shadow. It was only for a moment, catching sight of myself before I had time to prepare myself as I always prepare myself for the sight of myself, that I quailed. It is true; I am not young—I shall soon raise my arm in vain and my scarf will fall to my side without having signalled. I shall not hear the sudden sigh in the night and feel through the dark someone coming. There will be no reflections in window-panes in dark tunnels. I shall look into faces, and I shall see them seek some other face. I admit, for one moment the soundless flight of upright bodies down the moving stairs like the pinioned and terrible descent of some army of the dead downwards and the churning of the great engines remorselessly forwarding us, all of us, onwards, made me cower and run for shelter.

'But now I swear, making deliberately in front of the glass those slight preparations that equip me, I will not be afraid. Think of the superb omnibuses, red and yellow, stopping and starting, punctually in order. Think of the powerful and beautiful cars that now slow to a foot's pace and now shoot forward; think of men, think of women, equipped, prepared, driving onward. This is the triumphant procession; this is the army of victory with banners and brass eagles and heads crowned with laurel-leaves won in battle. They are better than savages in loin-cloths, and women whose hair is dank, whose long breasts sag, with children tugging at their long breasts. These broad thoroughfares—Piccadilly South, Piccadilly North, Regent Street and the Haymarket—are sanded paths of victory driven through the jungle. I too, with my little patent-leather shoes, my handkerchief that is but a film of gauze, my reddened lips and my finely pencilled eyebrows, march to victory with the band.

'Look how they show off clothes here even under ground in a perpetual radiance. They will not let the earth even lie wormy and sodden. There are gauzes and silks illumined in glass cases and underclothes trimmed with a million close stitches of fine embroidery. Crimson, green, violet, they are dyed all colours. Think how they organize, roll out, smooth, dip in dyes, and drive tunnels blasting the rock. Lifts rise and fall; trains stop, trains start as regularly as the waves of the sea. This is what has my adhesion. I am a native of this world, I follow its banners. How could I run for shelter when they are so magnificently adventurous, daring, curious, too, and strong enough in the midst of effort to pause and scrawl with a free hand a joke upon the wall? Therefore I will powder my face and redden my lips. I will make the angle of my eyebrows sharper than usual. I will rise to the surface, standing erect with the others in Piccadilly Circus. I will sign with a sharp gesture to a cab whose driver will signify by some indescribable alacrity his understanding of my signals. For I still excite eagerness. I still feel the bowing of men in the street like the silent stoop of the corn when the light wind blows, ruffling it red.

'I will drive to my own house. I will fill the vases with lavish, with luxurious, with extravagant flowers nodding in great bunches. I will place one chair there, another here. I will put ready cigarettes, glasses and some gaily covered new unread book in case Bernard comes, or Neville or Louis. But perhaps it will not be Bernard, Neville or Louis, but somebody new, somebody unknown, somebody I passed on a staircase and, just turning as we passed, I murmured, "Come". He will come this afternoon; somebody I do not know, somebody new. Let the silent army of the dead descend. I march forward.'

'I no longer need a room now,' said Neville, 'or walls and firelight. I am no longer young. I pass Jinny's house without envy, and smile at the young man who arranges his tie a little nervously on the doorstep. Let the dapper young man ring the bell; let him find her. I shall find her if I want her; if not, I pass on. The old corrosion has lost its bite—envy, intrigue and bitterness have been washed out. We have lost our glory too. When we were young we sat anywhere, on bare benches in draughty halls with the doors always banging. We tumbled about half naked like boys on the deck of a ship squirting each other with hose-pipes. Now I could swear that I like people pouring profusely out of the Tube when the day's work is done, unanimous, indiscriminate, uncounted. I have picked my own fruit. I look dispassionately.

'After all, we are not responsible. We are not judges. We are not called upon to torture our fellows with thumbscrews and irons; we are not called upon to mount pulpits and lecture them on pale Sunday afternoons. It is better to look at a rose, or to read Shakespeare as I read him here in Shaftesbury Avenue. Here's the fool, here's the villain, here in a car comes Cleopatra, burning on her barge. Here are figures of the damned too, noseless men by the police-court wall, standing with their feet in fire, howling. This is poetry if we do not write it. They act their parts infallibly, and almost before they open their lips I know what they are going to say, and wait the divine moment when they speak the word that must have been written. If it were only for the sake of the play, I could walk Shaftesbury Avenue for ever.

'Then coming from the street, entering some room, there are people talking, or hardly troubling to talk. He says, she says, somebody else says things have been said so often that one word is now enough to lift a whole weight. Argument, laughter, old grievances—they fall through the air, thickening it. I take a book and read half a page of anything. They have not mended the spout of the teapot yet. The child dances, dressed in her mother's clothes.

'But then Rhoda, or it may be Louis, some fasting and anguished spirit, passes through and out again. They want a plot, do they? They want a reason? It is not enough for them, this ordinary scene. It is not enough to wait for the thing to be said as if it were written; to see the sentence lay its dab of clay precisely on the right place, making character; to perceive, suddenly, some group in outline against the sky. Yet if they want violence, I have seen death and murder and suicide all in one room. One comes in, one goes out. There are sobs on the staircase. I have heard threads broken and knots tied and the quiet stitching of white cambric going on and on on the knees of a woman. Why ask, like Louis, for a reason, or fly like Rhoda to some far grove and part the leaves of the laurels and look for statues? They say that one must beat one's wings against the storm in the belief that beyond this welter the sun shines; the sun falls sheer into pools that are fledged with willows. (Here it is November; the poor hold out matchboxes in wind-bitten fingers.) They say truth is to be found there entire, and virtue, that shuffles along here, down blind alleys, is to be had there perfect. Rhoda flies with her neck outstretched and blind fanatic eyes, past us. Louis, now so opulent, goes to his attic window among the blistered roofs and gazes where she has vanished, but must sit down in his office among the typewriters and the telephone and work it all out for our instruction, for our regeneration, and the reform of an unborn world.

'But now in this room, which I enter without knocking, things are said as if they had been written. I go to the bookcase. If I choose, I read half a page of anything. I need not speak. But I listen. I am marvellously on the alert. Certainly, one cannot read this poem without effort. The page is often corrupt and mud-stained, and torn and stuck together with faded leaves, with scraps of verbena or geranium. To read this poem one must have myriad eyes, like one of those lamps that turn on slabs of racing water at midnight in the Atlantic, when perhaps only a spray of seaweed pricks the surface, or suddenly the waves gape and up shoulders a monster. One must put aside antipathies and jealousies and not interrupt. One must have patience and infinite care and let the light sound, whether of spiders' delicate feet on a leaf or the chuckle of water in some irrelevant drain-pipe, unfold too. Nothing is to be rejected in fear or horror. The poet who has written this page (what I read with

people talking) has withdrawn. There are no commas or semi-colons.
The lines do not run in convenient lengths. Much is sheer nonsense.
One must be sceptical, but throw caution to the winds and when the
door opens accept absolutely. Also sometimes weep; also cut away
ruthlessly with a slice of the blade soot, bark, hard accretions of all sorts.
And so (while they talk) let down one's net deeper and deeper and
gently draw in and bring to the surface what he said and she said and
make poetry.

'Now I have listened to them talking. They have gone now. I am
alone. I could be content to watch the fire burn for ever, like a dome,
like a furnace; now some spike of wood takes the look of a scaffold, or
pit, or happy valley; now it is a serpent curled crimson with white scales.
The fruit on the curtain swells beneath the parrot's beak. Cheep, cheep,
creaks the fire, like the cheep of insects in the middle of a forest. Cheep,
cheep, it clicks while out there the branches thrash the air, and now,
like a volley of shot, a tree falls. These are the sounds of a London night.
Then I hear the one sound I wait for. Up and up it comes, approaches,
hesitates, stops at my door. I cry, "Come in. Sit by me. Sit on the edge
of the chair." Swept away by the old hallucination, I cry, "Come closer,
closer".'

'I come back from the office,' said Louis. 'I hang my coat here, place
my stick there—I like to fancy that Richelieu walked with such a cane.
Thus I divest myself of my authority. I have been sitting at the right
hand of a director at a varnished table. The maps of our successful
undertakings confront us on the wall. We have laced the world together
with our ships. The globe is strung with our lines. I am immensely
respectable. All the young ladies in the office acknowledge my entrance.
I can dine where I like now, and without vanity may suppose that I
shall soon acquire a house in Surrey, two cars, a conservatory and some
rare species of melon. But I still return, I still come back to my attic,
hang up my hat and resume in solitude that curious attempt which I
have made since I brought down my fist on my master's grained oak
door. I open a little book. I read one poem. One poem is enough.

O western wind . . .

O western wind, you are at enmity with my mahogany table and spats,
and also, alas, with the vulgarity of my mistress, the little actress, who
has never been able to speak English correctly—

O western wind, when wilt thou blow . . .

'Rhoda, with her intense abstraction, with her unseeing eyes the
colour of snail's flesh, does not destroy you, western wind, whether she
comes at midnight when the stars blaze or at the most prosaic hour of

midday. She stands at the window and looks at the chimney-pots and
the broken windows in the houses of poor people—

O western wind, when wilt thou blow . . .

'My task, my burden, has always been greater than other people's. A
pyramid has been set on my shoulders. I have tried to do a colossal
labour. I have driven a violent, an unruly, a vicious team. With my
Australian accent I have sat in eating-shops and tried to make the clerks
accept me, yet never forgotten my solemn and severe convictions and
the discrepancies and incoherences that must be resolved. As a boy I
dreamt of the Nile, was reluctant to awake, yet brought down my fist on
the grained oak door. It would have been happier to have been born
without a destiny, like Susan, like Percival, whom I most admire.

O western wind, when wilt thou blow,
That the small rain down can rain?

'Life has been a terrible affair for me. I am like some vast sucker,
some glutinous, some adhesive, some insatiable mouth. I have tried to
draw from the living flesh the stone lodged at the centre. I have known
little natural happiness, though I chose my mistress in order that, with
her cockney accent, she might make me feel at my ease. But she only
tumbled the floor with dirty under-linen, and the charwoman and the
shop-boys called after me a dozen times a day, mocking my prim and
supercilious gait.

O western wind, when wilt thou blow,
That the small rain down can rain?

'What has my destiny been, the sharp-pointed pyramid that has
pressed on my ribs all these years? That I remember the Nile and the
women carrying pitchers on their heads; that I feel myself woven in and
out of the long summers and winters that have made the corn flow and
have frozen the streams. I am not a single and passing being. My life is
not a moment's bright spark like that on the surface of a diamond. I go
beneath ground tortuously, as if a warder carried a lamp from cell to
cell. My destiny has been that I remember and must weave together,
must plait into one cable the many threads, the thin, the thick, the
broken, the enduring of our long history, of our tumultuous and varied
day. There is always more to be understood; a discord to be listened for;
a falsity to be reprimanded. Broken and soot-stained are these roofs with
their chimney cowls, their loose slates, their slinking cats and attic
windows. I pick my way over broken glass, among blistered tiles, and
see only vile and famished faces.

'Let us suppose that I make reason of it all—one poem on a page, and then die. I can assure you it will not be unwillingly. Percival died. Rhoda left me. But I shall live to be gaunt and sere, to tap my way, much respected, with my gold-headed cane along the pavements of the city. Perhaps I shall never die, shall never attain even that continuity and permanence—

> O western wind, when wilt thou blow,
>   That the small rain down can rain?

'Percival was flowering with green leaves and was laid in the earth with all his branches still sighing in the summer wind. Rhoda, with whom I shared silence when the others spoke, she who hung back and turned aside when the herd assembled and galloped with orderly, sleek backs over the rich pastures, has gone now like the desert heat. When the sun blisters the roofs of the city I think of her; when the dry leaves patter to the ground; when the old men come with pointed sticks and pierce little bits of paper as we pierced her—

> O western wind, when wilt thou blow,
>   That the small rain down can rain?
> Christ, that my love were in my arms,
>   And I in my bed again!

I return now to my book; I return now to my attempt.'

'Oh, life, how I have dreaded you,' said Rhoda, 'oh, human beings, how I have hated you! How you have nudged, how you have interrupted, how hideous you have looked in Oxford Street, how squalid sitting opposite each other staring in the Tube! Now as I climb this mountain, from the top of which I shall see Africa, my mind is printed with brown-paper parcels and your faces. I have been stained by you and corrupted. You smelt so unpleasant too, lining up outside doors to buy tickets. All were dressed in indeterminate shades of grey and brown, never even a blue feather pinned to a hat. None had the courage to be one thing rather than another. What dissolution of the soul you demanded in order to get through one day, what lies, bowings, scrapings, fluency and servility! How you chained me to one spot, one hour, one chair, and sat yourselves down opposite! How you snatched from me the white spaces that lie between hour and hour and rolled them into dirty pellets and tossed them into the waste-paper basket with your greasy paws. Yet those were my life.

'But I yielded. Sneers and yawns were covered with my hand. I did not go out into the street and break a bottle in the gutter as a sign of rage. Trembling with ardour, I pretended that I was not surprised. What you did, I did. If Susan and Jinny pulled up their stockings like that, I pulled mine up like that also. So terrible was life that I held up shade after shade. Look at life through this, look at life through that; let there be rose leaves, let there be vine leaves—I covered the whole street, Oxford Street, Piccadilly Circus, with the blaze and ripple of my mind, with vine leaves and rose leaves. There were boxes too, standing in the passage when the school broke up. I stole secretly to read the labels and dream of names and faces. Harrogate, perhaps, Edinburgh, perhaps, was ruffled with golden glory where some girl whose name I forget stood on the pavement. But it was the name only. I left Louis; I feared embraces. With fleeces, with vestments, I have tried to cover the blue-black blade. I implored day to break into night. I have longed to see the cupboard dwindle, to feel the bed soften, to float suspended, to perceive lengthened trees, lengthened faces, a green bank on a moor and two figures in distress saying good-bye. I flung words in fans like those the sower throws over the ploughed fields when the earth is bare. I desired always to stretch the night and fill it fuller and fuller with dreams.

'Then in some Hall I parted the boughs of music and saw the house we have made; the square stood upon the oblong. "The house which contains all", I said, lurching against people's shoulders in an omnibus after Percival died; yet I went to Greenwich. Walking on the embankment, I prayed that I might thunder for ever on the verge of the world where there is no vegetation, but here and there a marble pillar. I threw my bunch into the spreading wave. I said, "Consume me, carry me to the furthest limit". The wave has broken; the bunch is withered. I seldom think of Percival now.

'Now I climb this Spanish hill; and I will suppose that this mule-back is my bed and that I lie dying. There is only a thin sheet between me now and the infinite depths. The lumps in the mattress soften beneath me. We stumble up—we stumble on. My path has been up and up, towards some solitary tree with a pool beside it on the very top. I have sliced the waters of beauty in the evening when the hills close themselves like birds' wings folded. I have picked sometimes a red carnation, and wisps of hay. I have sunk alone on the turf and fingered some old bone and thought: When the wind stoops to brush this height, may there be nothing found but a pinch of dust.

'The mule stumbles up and on. The ridge of the hill rises like mist, but from the top I shall see Africa. Now the bed gives under me. The sheets spotted with yellow holes let me fall through. The good woman with a face like a white horse at the end of the bed makes a valedictory movement and turns to go. Who then comes with me? Flowers only, the cowbind and the moonlight-coloured May. Gathering them loosely in a sheaf I made of them a garland and gave them—Oh, to whom? We launch out now over the precipice. Beneath us lie the lights of the herring fleet. The cliffs vanish. Rippling small, rippling grey, innumerable waves spread beneath us. I touch nothing. I see nothing. We may sink and settle on the waves. The sea will drum in my ears. The white petals will be darkened with sea water. They will float for a moment and then sink. Rolling me over the waves will shoulder me under. Everything falls in a tremendous shower, dissolving me.

'Yet that tree has bristling branches; that is the hard line of a cottage roof. Those bladder shapes painted red and yellow are faces. Putting my foot to the ground I step gingerly and press my hand against the hard door of a Spanish inn.'

The sun was sinking. The hard stone of the day was cracked and light poured through its splinters. Red and gold shot through the waves, in rapid running arrows, feathered with darkness. Erratically rays of light flashed and wandered, like signals from sunken islands, or darts shot through laurel groves by shameless, laughing boys. But the waves, as they neared the shore, were robbed of light, and fell in one long concussion, like a wall falling, a wall of grey stone, unpierced by any chink of light.

A breeze rose; a shiver ran through the leaves; and thus stirred they lost their brown density and became grey or white as the tree shifted its mass, winked and lost its domed uniformity. The hawk poised on the topmost branch flicked its eyelids and rose and sailed and soared far away, the wild plover cried in the marshes, evading, circling, and crying further off in loneliness. The smoke of trains and chimneys was stretched and torn and became part of the fleecy canopy that hung over the sea and the fields.

Now the corn was cut. Now only a brisk stubble was left of all its flowing and waving. Slowly a great owl launched itself from the elm tree and swung and rose, as if on a line that dipped, to the height of the cedar. On the hills the slow shadows now broadened, now shrank, as they passed over. The pool on the top of the moor lay blank. No furry face looked there, or hoof splashed, or hot muzzle seethed in the water. A bird, perched on an ash-coloured twig, sipped a beak full of cold water. There was no sound of cropping, and no sound of wheels, but only the sudden roar of the wind letting its sails fill and brushing the tops of the grasses. One bone lay rain-pocked and sun-bleached till it shone like a twig that the sea has polished. The tree, that had burnt foxy red in spring and in midsummer bent pliant leaves to the south wind, was now black as iron, and as bare.

The land was so distant that no shining roof or glittering window could be any longer seen. The tremendous weight of the shadowed earth had engulfed such frail fetters, such snail-shell encumbrances. Now there was only the liquid shadow of the cloud, the buffeting of the rain, a single darting spear of sunshine, or the sudden bruise of the rainstorm. Solitary trees marked distant hills like obelisks.

The evening sun, whose heat had gone out of it and whose burning spot of intensity had been diffused, made chairs and tables mellower and inlaid them with lozenges of brown and yellow. Lined with shadows their weight seemed more ponderous, as if colour, tilted, had run to one side. Here lay knife, fork and glass, but lengthened, swollen, and made portentous. Rimmed in a gold circle the looking-glass held the scene immobile as if everlasting in its eye.

Meanwhile the shadows lengthened on the beach; the blackness deepened. The iron black boot became a pool of deep blue. The rocks lost their hardness. The water that stood round the old boat was dark as if mussels had been steeped in it. The foam had turned livid and left here and there a white gleam of pearl on the misty sand.

'Hampton Court,' said Bernard. 'Hampton Court. This is our meeting-place. Behold the red chimneys, the square battlements of Hampton Court. The tone of my voice as I say "Hampton Court" proves that I am middle-aged. Ten years, fifteen years ago, I should have said "Hampton Court?" with interrogation—what will it be like? Will there be lakes, mazes? Or with anticipation, What is going to happen to me here? Whom shall I meet? Now, Hampton Court—Hampton Court—the words beat a gong in the space which I have so laboriously cleared with half a dozen telephone messages and post cards, give off ring after ring of sound, booming, sonorous: and pictures rise—summer after-noons, boats, old ladies holding their skirts up, one urn in winter, some daffodils in March—these all float to the top of the waters that now lie deep on every scene.

'There at the door by the Inn, our meeting-place, they are already standing—Susan, Louis, Rhoda, Jinny and Neville. They have come together already. In a moment, when I have joined them, another arrangement will form, another pattern. What now runs to waste, forming scenes profusely, will be checked, stated. I am reluctant to suffer that compulsion. Already at fifty yards distance I feel the order of my being changed. The tug of the magnet of their society tells upon me. I come nearer. They do not see me. Now Rhoda sees me, but she pretends, with her horror of the shock of meeting, that I am a stranger. Now Neville turns. Suddenly, raising my hand, saluting Neville, I cry, "I too have pressed flowers between the pages of Shakespeare's sonnets", and am churned up. My little boat bobs unsteadily upon the chopped and tossing waves. There is no panacea (let me note) against the shock of meeting.

'It is uncomfortable too, joining ragged edges, raw edges; only gradually, as we shuffle and trample into the Inn, taking coats and hats off, does meeting become agreeable. Now we assemble in the long, bare dining-room that overlooks some park, some green space still fantastic-ally lit by the setting sun so that there is a gold bar between the trees, and sit ourselves down.'

'Now sitting side by side,' said Neville, 'at this narrow table, now before the first emotion is worn smooth, what do we feel? Honestly now, openly and directly as befits old friends meeting with difficulty, what do we feel on meeting? Sorrow. The door will not open; he will not come.

And we are laden. Being now all of us middle-aged, loads are on us. Let us put down our loads. What have you made of life, we ask, and I? You, Bernard; you, Susan; you, Jinny; and Rhoda and Louis? The lists have been posted on the doors. Before we break these rolls, and help ourselves to fish and salad, I feel in my private pocket and find my credentials—what I carry to prove my superiority. I have passed. I have papers in my private pocket that prove it. But your eyes, Susan, full of turnips and cornfields, disturb me. These papers in my private pocket—the clamour that proves that I have passed—make a faint sound like that of a man clapping in an empty field to scare away rooks. Now it has died down altogether, under Susan's stare (the clapping, the reverberation that I have made), and I hear only the wind sweeping over the ploughed land and some bird singing—perhaps some intoxicated lark. Has the waiter heard of me, or those furtive everlasting couples, now loitering, now holding back and looking at the trees which are not yet dark enough to shelter their prostrate bodies? No; the sound of clapping has failed.

'What then remains, when I cannot pull out my papers and make you believe by reading aloud my credentials that I have passed? What remains is what Susan brings to light under the acid of her green eyes, her crystal, pear-shaped eyes. There is always somebody, when we come together, and the edges of meeting are still sharp, who refuses to be submerged; whose identity therefore one wishes to make crouch beneath one's own. For me now, it is Susan. I talk to impress Susan. Listen to me, Susan.

'When someone comes in at breakfast, even the embroidered fruit on my curtain swells so that parrots can peck it; one can break it off between one's thumb and finger. The thin, skimmed milk of early morning turns opal, blue, rose. At that hour your husband—the man who slapped his gaiters, pointing with his whip at the barren cow—grumbles. You say nothing. You see nothing. Custom blinds your eyes. At that hour your relationship is mute, null, dun-coloured. Mine at that hour is warm and various. There are no repetitions for me. Each day is dangerous. Smooth on the surface, we are all bone beneath like snakes coiling. Suppose we read *The Times*; suppose we argue. It is an experience. Suppose it is winter. The snow falling loads down the roof and seals us together in a red cave. The pipes have burst. We stand a yellow tin bath in the middle of the room. We rush helter-skelter for basins. Look there—it has burst again over the bookcase. We shout with laughter at the sight of ruin. Let solidity be destroyed. Let us have no possessions. Or is it summer? We may wander to a lake and watch Chinese geese waddling flat-footed to the water's edge or see a bone-like city church with young green trembling before it. (I choose at random; I choose the obvious.) Each sight is an arabesque scrawled suddenly to illustrate some hazard and marvel of intimacy. The snow, the burst pipe, the tin bath, the Chinese goose—these are signs swung high aloft upon which, looking back, I read the character of each love; how each was different.

'You meanwhile—for I want to diminish your hostility, your green eyes fixed on mine, and your shabby dress, your rough hands, and all the other emblems of your maternal splendour—have stuck like a limpet to the same rock. Yet it is true, I do not want to hurt you; only to refresh and furbish up my own belief in myself that failed at your entry. Change is no longer possible. We are committed. Before, when we met in a restaurant in London with Percival, all simmered and shook; we could have been anything. We have chosen now, or sometimes it seems the choice was made for us—a pair of tongs pinched us between the shoulders. I chose. I took the print of life not outwardly, but inwardly upon the raw, the white, the unprotected fibre. I am clouded and bruised with the print of minds and faces and things so subtle that they have smell, colour, texture, substance, but no name. I am merely "Neville" to you, who see the narrow limits of my life and the line it cannot pass. But to myself I am immeasurable; a net whose fibres pass imperceptibly beneath the world. My net is almost indistinguishable from that which it surrounds. It lifts whales—huge leviathans and white jellies, what is amorphous and wandering; I detect, I perceive. Beneath my eyes opens—a book; I see to the bottom; the heart—I see to the depths. I know what loves are trembling into fire; how jealousy shoots its green flashes hither and thither; how intricately love crosses love; love makes knots; love brutally tears them apart. I have been knotted; I have been torn apart.

'But there was another glory once, when we watched for the door to open, and Percival came; when we flung ourselves unattached on the edge of a hard bench in a public room.'

'There was the beech wood,' said Susan, 'Elvedon, and the gilt hands of the clock sparkling among the trees. The pigeons broke the leaves. The changing travelling lights wandered over me. They escaped me. Yet look, Neville, whom I discredit in order to be myself, at my hand on the table. Look at the gradations of healthy colour here on the knuckles, here on the palm. My body has been used daily, rightly, like a tool by a good workman, all over. The blade is clean, sharp, worn in the centre. (We battle together like beasts fighting in a field, like stags making their horns clash.) Seen through your pale and yielding flesh, even apples and bunches of fruit must have a filmed look as if they stood under glass. Lying deep in a chair with one person, one person only, but one person who changes, you see one inch of flesh only; its nerves, fibres, the sullen or quick flow of blood on it; but nothing entire. You do not see a house in a garden; a horse in a field; a town laid out, as you bend like an old woman straining her eyes over her darning. But I have seen life in blocks, substantial, huge; its battlements and towers, factories and gasometers; a dwelling-place made from time immemorial after an hereditary pattern. These things remain square, prominent, undissolved in my mind. I am not sinuous or suave; I sit among you abrading your softness with my hardness, quenching the silver-grey flickering moth-wing quiver of words with the green spurt of my clear eyes.

'Now we have clashed our antlers. This is the necessary prelude; the salute of old friends.'

'The gold has faded between the trees,' said Rhoda, 'and a slice of green lies behind them, elongated like the blade of a knife seen in dreams, or some tapering island on which nobody sets foot. Now the cars begin to wink and flicker, coming down the avenue. Lovers can draw into the darkness now; the boles of the trees are swollen, are obscene with lovers.'

'It was different once,' said Bernard. 'Once we could break the current as we chose. How many telephone calls, how many post cards, are now needed to cut this hole through which we come together, united, at Hampton Court? How swift life runs from January to December! We are all swept on by the torrent of things grown so familiar that they cast no shade; we make no comparisons; think scarcely ever of I or of you; and in this unconsciousness attain the utmost freedom from friction and part the weeds that grow over the mouths of sunken channels. We have to leap like fish, high in the air, in order to catch the train from Waterloo. And however high we leap we fall back again into the stream. I shall never now take ship for the South Sea Islands. A journey to Rome is the limit of my travelling. I have sons and daughters. I am wedged into my place in the puzzle.

'But it is only my body—this elderly man here whom you call Bernard—that is fixed irrevocably—so I desire to believe. I think more disinterestedly than I could when I was young and must dig furiously like a child rummaging in a bran-pie to discover my self. "Look, what is this? And this? Is this going to be a fine present? Is that all?" and so on. Now I know what the parcels hold; and do not care much. I throw my mind out in the air as a man throws seeds in great fan-flights, falling through the purple sunset, falling on the pressed and shining ploughland which is bare.

'A phrase. An imperfect phrase. And what are phrases? They have left me very little to lay on the table, beside Susan's hand; to take from my pocket, with Neville's credentials. I am not an authority on law, or medicine, or finance. I am wrapped round with phrases, like damp straw; I glow, phosphorescent. And each of you feels when I speak, "I am lit up. I am glowing." The little boys used to feel "That's a good one, that's a good one", as the phrases bubbled up from my lips under the elm trees in the playing-fields. They too bubbled up; they also escaped with my phrases. But I pine in solitude. Solitude is my undoing.

'I pass from house to house like the friars in the Middle Ages who cozened the wives and girls with beads and ballads. I am a traveller, a pedlar, paying for my lodging with a ballad; I am an indiscriminate, an easily pleased guest; often putting up in the best room in a four-poster; then lying in a barn on a haystack. I don't mind the fleas and find no fault with silk either. I am very tolerant. I am not a moralist. I have too great a sense of the shortness of life and its temptations to rule red lines. Yet I am not so indiscriminate as you think, judging me—as you judge me—from my fluency. I have a little dagger of contempt and severity hidden up my sleeve. But I am apt to be deflected. I make stories. I twist up toys out of anything. A girl sits at a cottage door; she is waiting; for whom? Seduced, or not seduced? The Headmaster sees the hole in the carpet. He sighs. His wife, drawing her fingers through the waves of her still abundant hair, reflects—et cetera. Waves of hands, hesitations at street corners, someone dropping a cigarette into the gutter—all are stories. But which is the true story? That I do not know. Hence I keep my phrases hung like clothes in a cupboard, waiting for someone to wear them. Thus waiting, thus speculating, making this note and then another, I do not cling to life. I shall be brushed like a bee from a sunflower. My philosophy, always accumulating, welling up moment by moment, runs like quicksilver a dozen ways at once. But Louis, wild-eyed but severe, in his attic, in his office, has formed unalterable conclusions upon the true nature of what is to be known.'

'It breaks,' said Louis, 'the thread I try to spin; your laughter breaks it, your indifference, also your beauty. Jinny broke the thread when she kissed me in the garden years ago. The boasting boys mocked me at school for my Australian accent and broke it. "This is the meaning," I say; and then start with a pang—vanity. "Listen", I say, "to the nightingale, who sings among the trampling feet; the conquests and migrations. Believe——" and then am twitched asunder. Over broken tiles and splinters of glass I pick my way. Different lights fall, making the ordinary leopard-spotted and strange. This moment of reconciliation, when we meet together united, this evening moment, with its wine and shaking leaves, and youth coming up from the river in white flannels, carrying cushions, is to me black with the shadows of dungeons and the tortures and infamies practised by man upon man. So imperfect are my senses that they never blot out with one purple the serious charge that my reason adds and adds against us, even as we sit here. What is the solution, I ask myself, and the bridge? How can I reduce these dazzling, these dancing apparitions to one line capable of linking all in one? So I ponder; and you meanwhile observe maliciously my pursed lips, my sallow cheeks and my invariable frown.

'But I beg you also to notice my cane and my waistcoat. I have inherited a desk of solid mahogany in a room hung with maps. Our steamers have won an enviable reputation for their cabins replete with luxury. We supply swimming-baths and gymnasiums. I wear a white waistcoat now and consult a little book before I make an engagement.

'This is the arch and ironical manner in which I hope to distract you from my shivering, my tender, and infinitely young and unprotected soul. For I am always the youngest; the most naïvely surprised; the one who runs in advance in apprehension and sympathy with discomfort or ridicule—should there be a smut on a nose, or a button undone. I suffer for all humiliations. Yet I am also ruthless, marmoreal. I do not see how you can say that it is fortunate to have lived. Your little excitements, your childish transports, when a kettle boils, when the soft air lifts Jinny's spotted scarf and it floats web-like, are to me like silk streamers thrown in the eyes of the charging bull. I condemn you. Yet my heart yearns towards you. I would go with you through the fires of death. Yet am happiest alone. I luxuriate in gold and purple vestments. Yet I prefer a view over chimney-pots; cats scraping their mangy sides upon blistered chimney-stacks; broken windows; and the hoarse clangour of bells from the steeple of some brick chapel.'

'I see what is before me,' said Jinny. 'This scarf, these wine-coloured spots. This glass. This mustard pot. This flower. I like what one touches, what one tastes. I like rain when it has turned to snow and become palpable. And being rash, and much more courageous than you are, I do not temper my beauty with meanness lest it should scorch me. I gulp it down entire. It is made of flesh; it is made of stuff. My imagination is the body's. Its visions are not fine-spun and white with purity like Louis's. I do not like your lean cats and your blistered chimney-pots. The scrannel beauties of your roof-tops repel me. Men and women, in uniforms, wigs and gowns, bowler hats and tennis shirts beautifully open at the neck, the infinite variety of women's dresses (I note all clothes always) delight me. I eddy with them, in and out, in and out, into rooms, into halls, here, there, everywhere, wherever they go. This man lifts the hoof of a horse. This man shoves in and out the drawers of his private collection. I am never alone. I am attended by a regiment of my fellows. My mother must have followed the drum, my father the sea. I am like a little dog that trots down the road after the regimental band, but stops to snuff a tree-trunk, to sniff some brown stain, and suddenly careers across the street after some mongrel cur and then holds one paw up while it sniffs an entrancing whiff of meat from the butcher's shop.

My traffics have led me into strange places. Men, how many, have broken from the wall and come to me. I have only to hold my hand up. Straight as a dart they have come to the place of assignation—perhaps a chair on a balcony, perhaps a shop at a street corner. The torments, the divisions of your lives have been solved for me night after night, sometimes only by the touch of a finger under the table-cloth as we sat dining—so fluid has my body become, forming even at the touch of a finger into one full drop, which fills itself, which quivers, which flashes, which falls in ecstasy.

'I have sat before a looking-glass as you sit writing, adding up figures at desks. So, before the looking-glass in the temple of my bedroom, I have judged my nose and my chin; my lips that open too wide and show too much gum. I have looked. I have noted. I have chosen what yellow or white, what shine or dullness, what loop or straightness suits. I am volatile for one, rigid for another, angular as an icicle in silver, or voluptuous as a candle flame in gold. I have run violently like a whip flung out to the extreme end of my tether. His shirt front, there in the corner, has been white; then purple; smoke and flame have wrapped us about; after a furious conflagration—yet we scarcely raised our voices, sitting on the hearth-rug, as we murmured all the secrets of our hearts as into shells so that nobody might hear in the sleeping-house, but I heard the cook stir once, and once we thought the ticking of the clock was a footfall—we have sunk to ashes, leaving no relics, no unburnt bones, no wisps of hair to be kept in lockets such as your intimacies leave behind them. Now I turn grey; now I turn gaunt; but I look at my face at midday sitting in front of the looking-glass in broad daylight, and note precisely my nose, my chin, my lips that open too wide and show too much gum. But I am not afraid.'

'There were lamp-posts,' said Rhoda, 'and trees that had not yet shed their leaves on the way from the station. The leaves might have hidden me still. But I did not hide behind them. I walked straight up to you instead of circling round to avoid the shock of sensation as I used. But it is only that I have taught my body to do a certain trick. Inwardly I am not taught; I fear, I hate, I love, I envy and despise you, but I never join you happily. Coming up from the station, refusing to accept the shadow of the trees and the pillar-boxes, I perceived, from your coats and umbrellas, even at a distance, how you stand embedded in a substance made of repeated moments run together; are committed, have an attitude, with children, authority, fame, love, society; where I have nothing. I have no face.

'Here in this dining-room you see the antlers and the tumblers; the salt-cellars; the yellow stains on the table-cloth. "Waiter!" says Bernard. "Bread!" says Susan. And the waiter comes; he brings bread. But I see the side of a cup like a mountain and only parts of antlers, and the brightness on the side of that jug like a crack in darkness with wonder and terror. Your voices sound like trees creaking in a forest. So with your faces and their prominences and hollows. How beautiful, standing at a distance immobile at midnight against the railings of some square! Behind you is a white crescent of foam, and fishermen on the verge of the world are drawing in nets and casting them. A wind ruffles the topmost leaves of primeval trees. (Yet here we sit at Hampton Court.) Parrots shrieking break the intense stillness of the jungle. (Here the trams start.) The swallow dips her wings in midnight pools. (Here we talk.) That is the circumference that I try to grasp as we sit together. Thus I must undergo the penance of Hampton Court at seven thirty precisely.

'But since these rolls of bread and wine bottles are needed by me, and your faces with their hollows and prominences are beautiful, and the table-cloth and its yellow stain, far from being allowed to spread in wider and wider circles of understanding that may at last (so I dream, falling off the edge of the earth at night when my bed floats suspended) embrace the entire world, I must go through the antics of the individual. I must start when you pluck at me with your children, your poems, your chilblains or whatever it is that you do and suffer. But I am not deluded. After all these callings hither and thither, these pluckings and searchings, I shall fall alone through this thin sheet into gulfs of fire. And you will not help me. More cruel than the old torturers, you will let me fall, and will tear me to pieces when I am fallen. Yet there are moments when the walls of the mind grow thin; when nothing is unabsorbed, and I could fancy that we might blow so vast a bubble that the sun might set and rise in it and we might take the blue of midday and the black of midnight and be cast off and escape from here and now.'

'Drop upon drop,' said Bernard, 'silence falls. It forms on the roof of the mind and falls into pools beneath. For ever alone, alone, alone— hear silence fall and sweep its rings to the farthest edges. Gorged and replete, solid with middle-aged content, I, whom loneliness destroys, let silence fall, drop by drop.

'But now silence falling pits my face, wastes my nose like a snowman stood out in a yard in the rain. As silence falls I am dissolved utterly and become featureless and scarcely to be distinguished from another. It does not matter. What matters? We have dined well. The fish, the veal cutlets, the wine have blunted the sharp tooth of egotism. Anxiety is at rest. The vainest of us, Louis perhaps, does not care what people think. Neville's tortures are at rest. Let others prosper—that is what he thinks. Susan hears the breathing of all her children safe asleep. Sleep, sleep, she murmurs. Rhoda has rocked her ships to shore. Whether they have foundered, whether they have anchored, she cares no longer. We are ready to consider any suggestion that the world may offer quite impartially. I reflect now that the earth is only a pebble flicked off accidentally from the face of the sun and that there is no life anywhere in the abysses of space.'

'In this silence,' said Susan, 'it seems as if no leaf would ever fall, or bird fly.'

'As if the miracle had happened,' said Jinny, 'and life were stayed here and now.'

'And,' said Rhoda, 'we had no more to live.'

'But listen,' said Louis, 'to the world moving through abysses of infinite space. It roars; the lighted strip of history is past and our Kings and Queens; we are gone; our civilization; the Nile; and all life. Our separate drops are dissolved; we are extinct, lost in the abysses of time, in the darkness.'

'Silence falls; silence falls,' said Bernard. 'But now listen; tick, tick; hoot, hoot; the world has hailed us back to it. I heard for one moment the howling winds of darkness as we passed beyond life. Then tick, tick (the clock); then hoot, hoot (the cars). We are landed; we are on shore; we are sitting, six of us, at a table. It is the memory of my nose that recalls me. I rise; "Fight," I cry, "fight!" remembering the shape of my own nose, and strike with this spoon upon this table pugnaciously.'

'Oppose ourselves to this illimitable chaos,' said Neville, 'this formless imbecility. Making love to a nursemaid behind a tree, that soldier is more admirable than all the stars. Yet sometimes one trembling star comes in the clear sky and makes me think the world beautiful and we maggots deforming even the trees with our lust.'

('Yet, Louis,' said Rhoda, 'how short a time silence lasts. Already they are beginning to smooth their napkins by the side of their plates. "Who comes?" says Jinny; and Neville sighs, remembering that Percival comes no more. Jinny has taken out her looking-glass. Surveying her face like an artist, she draws a powder-puff down her nose, and after one moment of deliberation has given precisely that red to the lips that the lips need. Susan, who feels scorn and fear at the sight of these preparations, fastens the top button of her coat, and unfastens it. What is she making ready for? For something, but something different.'

'They are saying to themselves,' said Louis, '"It is time. I am still vigorous", they are saying, "My face shall be cut against the black of infinite space". They do not finish their sentences. "It is time", they keep saying. "The gardens will be shut." And going with them, Rhoda, swept into their current, we shall perhaps drop a little behind.'

'Like conspirators who have something to whisper,' said Rhoda.)

'It is true, and I know for a fact,' said Bernard, 'as we walk down this avenue, that a King, riding, fell over a molehill here. But how strange it seems to set against the whirling abysses of infinite space a little figure with a golden teapot on his head. Soon one recovers belief in figures: but not at once in what they put on their heads. Our English past—one inch of light. Then people put teapots on their heads and say, "I am a King!" No, I try to recover, as we walk, the sense of time, but with that streaming darkness in my eyes I have lost my grip. This Palace seems light as a cloud set for a moment on the sky. It is a trick of the mind—to put Kings on their thrones, one following another, with crowns on their heads. And we ourselves, walking six abreast, what do we oppose, with this random flicker of light in us that we call brain and feeling, how can we do battle against this flood; what has permanence? Our lives too stream away, down the unlighted avenues, past the strip of time, unidentified. Once Neville threw a poem at my head. Feeling a sudden conviction of immortality, I said, "I too know what Shakespeare knew". But that has gone.'

'Unreasonably, ridiculously,' said Neville, 'as we walk, time comes back. A dog does it, prancing. The machine works. Age makes hoary that gateway. Three hundred years now seem more than a moment vanished against that dog. King William mounts his horse wearing a wig, and the court ladies sweep the turf with their embroidered panniers. I am beginning to be convinced, as we walk, that the fate of Europe is of immense importance, and, ridiculous as it still seems, that all depends upon the battle of Blenheim. Yes; I declare, as we pass through this gateway, it is the present moment; I am become a subject of King George.'

'While we advance down this avenue,' said Louis, 'I leaning slightly upon Jinny, Bernard arm-in-arm with Neville, and Susan with her hand in mine, it is difficult not to weep, calling ourselves little children, praying that God may keep us safe while we sleep. It is sweet to sing together, clasping hands, afraid of the dark, while Miss Curry plays the harmonium.'

'The iron gates have rolled back,' said Jinny. 'Time's fangs have ceased their devouring. We have triumphed over the abysses of space, with rouge, with powder, with flimsy pocket-handkerchiefs.'

'I grasp, I hold fast,' said Susan. 'I hold firmly to this hand, anyone's, with love, with hatred; it does not matter which.'

'The still mood, the disembodied mood is on us,' said Rhoda, 'and we enjoy this momentary alleviation (it is not often that one has no anxiety) when the walls of the mind become transparent. Wren's palace, like the quartet played to the dry and stranded people in the stalls, makes an oblong. A square is stood upon the oblong and we say, "This is our dwelling-place. The structure is now visible. Very little is left outside."'

'The flower,' said Bernard, 'the red carnation that stood in the vase on the table of the restaurant when we dined together with Percival, is become a six-sided flower; made of six lives.'

'A mysterious illumination,' said Louis, 'visible against those yew trees.'

'Built up with much pain, many strokes,' said Jinny.

'Marriage, death, travel, friendship,' said Bernard; 'town and country; children and all that; a many-sided substance cut out of this dark; a many-faceted flower. Let us stop for a moment; let us behold what we have made. Let it blaze against the yew trees. One life. There. It is over. Gone out.'

'Now they vanish,' said Louis. 'Susan with Bernard. Neville with Jinny. You and I, Rhoda, stop for a moment by this stone urn. What song shall we hear now that these couples have sought the groves, and Jinny, pointing with her gloved hand, pretends to notice the water-lilies, and Susan, who has always loved Bernard, says to him, "My ruined life, my wasted life". And Neville, taking Jinny's little hand, with the cherry-coloured finger-nails, by the lake, by the moonlit water, cries, "Love, love", and she answers, imitating the bird, "Love, love?" What song do we hear?'

'They vanish, towards the lake,' said Rhoda. 'They slink away over the grass furtively, yet with assurance as if they asked of our pity their ancient privilege—not to be disturbed. The tide in the soul, tipped, flows that way; they cannot help deserting us. The dark has closed over their bodies. What song do we hear—the owl's, the nightingale's, the wren's? The steamer hoots; the light on the electric rails flashes; the trees gravely bow and bend. The flare hangs over London. Here is an old woman, quietly returning, and a man, a late fisherman, comes down the terrace with his rod. Not a sound, not a movement must escape us.'

'A bird flies homeward,' said Louis. 'Evening opens her eyes and gives one quick glance among the bushes before she sleeps. How shall we put it together, the confused and composite message that they send back to us, and not they only, but many dead, boys and girls, grown men and women, who have wandered here, under one king or another?'

'A weight has dropped into the night,' said Rhoda, 'dragging it down. Every tree is big with a shadow that is not the shadow of the tree behind it. We hear a drumming on the roofs of a fasting city when the Turks are hungry and uncertain tempered. We hear them crying with sharp, stag-like barks, "Open, open". Listen to the trams squealing and to the flashes from the electric rails. We hear the beech trees and the birch trees raise their branches as if the bride had let her silken nightdress fall and come to the doorway saying, "Open, open".'

'All seems alive,' said Louis. 'I cannot hear death anywhere tonight.

Stupidity, on that man's face, age, on that woman's, would be strong enough, one would think, to resist the incantation, and bring in death. But where is death tonight? All the crudity, odds and ends, this and that, have been crushed like glass splinters into the blue, the red-fringed tide, which, drawing into the shore, fertile with innumerable fish, breaks at our feet.'

'If we could mount together, if we could perceive from a sufficient height,' said Rhoda, 'if we could remain untouched without any support—but you, disturbed by faint clapping sounds of praise and laughter, and I, resenting compromise and right and wrong on human lips, trust only in solitude and the violence of death and thus are divided.'

'For ever,' said Louis, 'divided. We have sacrificed the embrace among the ferns, and love, love, love by the lake, standing, like conspirators who have drawn apart to share some secret, by the urn. But now look, as we stand here, a ripple breaks on the horizon. The net is raised higher and higher. It comes to the top of the water. The water is broken by silver, by quivering little fish. Now leaping, now lashing, they are laid on shore. Life tumbles its catch upon the grass. There are figures coming towards us. Are they men or are they women? They still wear the ambiguous draperies of the flowing tide in which they have been immersed.'

'Now,' said Rhoda, 'as they pass that tree, they regain their natural size. They are only men, only women. Wonder and awe change as they put off the draperies of the flowing tide. Pity returns, as they emerge into the moonlight, like the relics of an army, our representatives, going every night (here or in Greece) to battle, and coming back every night with their wounds, their ravaged faces. Now light falls on them again. They have faces. They become Susan and Bernard, Jinny and Neville, people we know. Now what a shrinkage takes place! Now what a shrivelling, what an humiliation! The old shivers run through me, hatred and terror, as I feel myself grappled to one spot by these hooks they cast on us; these greetings, recognitions, pluckings of the finger and searchings of the eyes. Yet they have only to speak, and their first words, with the remembered tone and the perpetual deviation from what one expects, and their hands moving and making a thousand past days rise again in the darkness, shake my purpose.'

'Something flickers and dances,' said Louis. 'Illusion returns as they approach down the avenue. Rippling and questioning begin. What do I think of you—what do you think of me? Who are you? Who am I?— that quivers again its uneasy air over us, and the pulse quickens and the eye brightens and all the insanity of personal existence without which life would fall flat and die, begins again. They are on us. The southern sun flickers over this urn; we push off in to the tide of the violent and cruel sea. Lord help us to act our parts as we greet them returning—Susan and Bernard, Neville and Jinny.'

'We have destroyed something by our presence,' said Bernard, 'a world perhaps.'

'Yet we scarcely breathe,' said Neville, 'spent as we are. We are in that passive and exhausted frame of mind when we only wish to rejoin the body of our mother from whom we have been severed. All else is distasteful, forced and fatiguing. Jinny's yellow scarf is moth-coloured in this light; Susan's eyes are quenched. We are scarcely to be distinguished from the river. One cigarette end is the only point of emphasis among us. And sadness tinges our content, that we should have left you, torn the fabric; yielded to the desire to press out, alone, some bitterer, some blacker juice, which was sweet too. But now we are worn out.'

'After our fire,' said Jinny, 'there is nothing left to put in lockets.'

'Still I gape,' said Susan, 'like a young bird, unsatisfied, for something that has escaped me.'

'Let us stay for a moment,' said Bernard, 'before we go. Let us pace the terrace by the river almost alone. It is nearly bed-time. People have gone home. Now how comforting it is to watch the lights coming out in the bedrooms of small shopkeepers on the other side of the river. There is one—there is another. What do you think their takings have been today? Only just enough to pay for the rent, for light and food and the children's clothing. But just enough. What a sense of the tolerableness of life the lights in the bedrooms of small shopkeepers give us! Saturday comes, and there is just enough to pay perhaps for seats at the Pictures. Perhaps before they put out the light they go into the little garden and look at the giant rabbit couched in its wooden hut. That is the rabbit they will have for Sunday dinner. Then they put out the light. Then they sleep. And for thousands of people sleep is nothing but warmth and silence and one moment's sport with some fantastic dream. "I have posted my letter," the greengrocer thinks, "to the Sunday newspaper. Suppose I win five hundred pounds in the football competition? And we shall kill the rabbit. Life is pleasant. Life is good. I have posted the letter. We shall kill the rabbit." And he sleeps.

'That goes on. Listen. There is a sound like the knocking of railway trucks in a siding. That is the happy concatenation of one event following another in our lives. Knock, knock, knock. Must, must, must. Must go, must sleep, must wake, must get up—sober, merciful word which we pretend to revile, which we press tight to our hearts, without which we should be undone. How we worship that sound like the knocking together of trucks in a siding!

'Now far off down the river I hear the chorus; the song of the boasting boys, who are coming back in large charabancs from a day's outing on the decks of crowded steamers. Still they are singing as they used to sing, across the court, on winters' nights, or with the windows open in summer, getting drunk, breaking the furniture, wearing little striped caps, all turning their heads the same way as the brake rounded the corner; and I wished to be with them.

'What with the chorus, and the spinning water and the just perceptible murmur of the breeze we are slipping away. Little bits of ourselves are crumbling. There! Something very important fell then. I cannot keep myself together. I shall sleep. But we must go; must catch our train; must walk back to the station—must, must, must. We are only bodies jogging along side by side. I exist only in the soles of my feet and in the tired muscles of my thighs. We have been walking for hours it seems. But where? I cannot remember. I am like a log slipping smoothly over some waterfall. I am not a judge. I am not called upon to give my opinion. Houses and trees are all the same in this grey light. Is that a post? Is that a woman walking? Here is the station, and if the train were to cut me in two, I should come together on the further side, being one, being indivisible. But what is odd is that I still clasp the return half of my ticket to Waterloo firmly between the fingers of my right hand, even now, even sleeping '

Now the sun had sunk. Sky and sea were indistinguishable. The waves breaking spread their white fans far out over the shore, sent white shadows into the recesses of sonorous caves and then rolled back sighing over the shingle.

The tree shook its branches and a scattering of leaves fell to the ground. There they settled with perfect composure on the precise spot where they would await dissolution. Black and grey were shot into the garden from the broken vessel that had once held red light. Dark shadows blackened the tunnels between the stalks. The thrush was silent and the worm sucked itself back into its narrow hole. Now and again a whitened and hollow straw was blown from an old nest and fell into the dark grasses among the rotten apples. The light had faded from the tool-house wall and the adder's skin hung from the nail empty. All the colours in the room had overflown their banks. The precise brush stroke was swollen and lop-sided; cupboards and chairs melted their brown masses into one huge obscurity. The height from floor to ceiling was hung with vast curtains of shaking darkness. The looking-glass was pale as the mouth of a cave shadowed by hanging creepers.

The substance had gone from the solidity of the hills. Travelling lights drove a plumy wedge among unseen and sunken roads, but no lights opened among the folded wings of the hills, and there was no sound save the cry of a bird seeking some lonelier tree. At the cliff's edge there was an equal murmur of air that had been brushed through forests, of water that had been cooled in a thousand glassy hollows of mid-ocean.

As if there were waves of darkness in the air, darkness moved on, covering houses, hills, trees, as waves of water wash round the sides of some sunken ship. Darkness washed down streets, eddying round single figures, engulfing them; blotting out couples clasped under the showery darkness of elm trees in full summer foliage. Darkness rolled its waves along grassy rides and over the wrinkled skin of the turf, enveloping the solitary thorn tree and the empty snail shells at its foot. Mounting higher, darkness blew along the bare upland slopes, and met the fretted and abraded pinnacles of the mountain where the snow lodges for ever on the hard rock even when the valleys are full of running streams and yellow vine leaves, and girls, sitting on verandahs, look up at the snow, shading their faces with their fans. Them, too, darkness covered.

'Now to sum up,' said Bernard. 'Now to explain to you the meaning of my life. Since we do not know each other (though I met you once, I think, on board a ship going to Africa), we can talk freely. The illusion is upon me that something adheres for a moment, has roundness, weight, depth, is completed. This, for the moment, seems to be my life. If it were possible, I would hand it to you entire. I would break it off as one breaks off a bunch of grapes. I would say, "Take it. This is my life."

'But unfortunately, what I see (this globe, full of figures) you do not see. You see me, sitting at a table opposite you, a rather heavy, elderly man, grey at the temples. You see me take my napkin and unfold it. You see me pour myself out a glass of wine. And you see behind me the door opening, and people passing. But in order to make you understand, to give you my life, I must tell you a story—and there are so many, and so many—stories of childhood, stories of school, love, marriage, death, and so on; and none of them are true. Yet like children we tell each other stories, and to decorate them we make up these ridiculous, flamboyant, beautiful phrases. How tired I am of stories, how tired I am of phrases that come down beautifully with all their feet on the ground! Also, how I distrust neat designs of life that are drawn upon half-sheets of note-paper. I begin to long for some little language such as lovers use, broken words, inarticulate words, like the shuffling of feet on the pavement. I begin to seek some design more in accordance with those moments of humiliation and triumph that come now and then undeniably. Lying in a ditch on a stormy day, when it has been raining, then enormous clouds come marching over the sky, tattered clouds, wisps of cloud. What delights me then is the confusion, the height, the indifference and the fury. Great clouds always changing, and movement; something sulphurous and sinister, bowled up, helter-skelter; towering, trailing, broken off, lost, and I forgotten, minute, in a ditch. Of story, of design, I do not see a trace then.

'But meanwhile, while we eat, let us turn over these scenes as children turn over the pages of a picture-book and the nurse says, pointing: "That's a cow. That's a boat." Let us turn over the pages, and I will add, for your amusement, a comment in the margin.

'In the beginning, there was the nursery, with windows opening on to a garden, and beyond that the sea. I saw something brighten—no doubt the brass handle of a cupboard. Then Mrs Constable raised the sponge above her head, squeezed it, and out shot, right, left, all down the spine, arrows of sensation. And so, as long as we draw breath, for the rest of time, if we knock against a chair, a table, or a woman, we are pierced with arrows of sensation—if we walk in a garden, if we drink this wine. Sometimes indeed, when I pass a cottage with a light in the window where a child has been born, I could implore them not to squeeze the sponge over that new body. Then, there was the garden and the canopy of the currant leaves which seemed to enclose everything; flowers, burning like sparks upon the depths of green; a rat wreathing with maggots under a rhubarb leaf; the fly going buzz, buzz, buzz upon the nursery ceiling, and plates upon plates of innocent bread and butter. All these things happen in one second and last for ever. Faces loom. Dashing round the corner. "Hullo", one says, "there's Jinny. That's Neville. That's Louis in grey flannel with a snake belt. That's Rhoda." She had a basin in which she sailed petals of white flowers. It was Susan who cried, that day when I was in the tool-house with Neville; and I felt my indifference melt. Neville did not melt. "Therefore," I said, "I am myself, not Neville", a wonderful discovery. Susan cried and I followed her. Her wet pocket-handkerchief, and the sight of her little back heaving up and down like a pump-handle, sobbing for what was denied her, screwed my nerves up. "That is not to be borne", I said, as I sat beside her on the roots that were hard as skeletons. I then first became aware of the presence of those enemies who change, but are always there; the forces we fight against. To let oneself be carried on passively is unthinkable. "That's your course, world," one says, "mine is this." So, "Let's explore", I cried, and jumped up, and ran downhill with Susan and saw the stable-boy clattering about the yard in great boots. Down below, through the depths of the leaves, the gardeners swept the lawns with great brooms. The lady sat writing. Transfixed, stopped dead, I thought, "I cannot interfere with a single stroke of those brooms. They sweep and they sweep. Nor with the fixity of that woman writing." It is strange that one cannot stop gardeners sweeping nor dislodge a woman. There they have remained all my life. It is as if one had woken in Stonehenge surrounded by a circle of great stones, these enemies, these presences. Then a wood-pigeon flew out of the trees. And being in love for the first time, I made a phrase—a poem about a wood-pigeon— a single phrase, for a hole had been knocked in my mind, one of those sudden transparencies through which one sees everything. Then more bread and butter and more flies droning round the nursery ceiling on which quivered islands of light, ruffled, opalescent, while the pointed fingers of the lustre dripped blue pools on the corner of the mantelpiece. Day after day as we sat at tea we observed these sights.

'But we were all different. The wax—the virginal wax that coats the spine melted in different patches for each of us. The growl of the boot-boy making love to the tweeny among the gooseberry bushes; the clothes blown out hard on the line; the dead man in the gutter; the apple tree, stark in the moonlight; the rat swarming with maggots; the lustre dripping blue—our white wax was streaked and stained by each of these differently. Louis was disgusted by the nature of human flesh; Rhoda by our cruelty; Susan could not share; Neville wanted order; Jinny love; and so on. We suffered terribly as we became separate bodies.

'Yet I was preserved from these excesses and have survived many of my friends, am a little stout, grey, rubbed on the thorax as it were, because it is the panorama of life, seen not from the roof, but from the third-storey window, that delights me, not what one woman says to one man, even if that man is myself. How could I be bullied at school therefore? How could they make things hot for me? There was the Doctor lurching into chapel, as if he trod a battleship in a gale of wind, shouting out his commands through a megaphone, since people in authority always become melodramatic—I did not hate him like Neville, or revere him like Louis. I took notes as we sat together in chapel. There were pillars, shadows, memorial brasses, boys scuffling and swopping stamps behind Prayer Books; the sound of a rusty pump; the Doctor booming, about immortality and quitting ourselves like men; and Percival scratching his thigh. I made notes for stories; drew portraits in the margin of my pocket-book and thus became still more separate. Here are one or two of the figures I saw.

'Percival sat staring straight ahead of him that day in chapel. He also had a way of flicking his hand to the back of his neck. His movements were always remarkable. We all flicked our hands to the backs of our heads—unsuccessfully. He had the kind of beauty which defends itself from any caress. As he was not in the least precocious, he read whatever was written up for our edification without any comment, and thought with that magnificent equanimity (Latin words come naturally) that was to preserve him from so many meannesses and humiliations, that Lucy's flaxen pigtails and pink cheeks were the height of female beauty. Thus preserved, his taste later was of extreme fineness. But there should be music, some wild carol. Through the window should come a hunting-song from some rapid unapprehended life—a sound that shouts among the hills and dies away. What is startling, what is unexpected, what we cannot account for, what turns symmetry to nonsense—that comes suddenly to my mind, thinking of him. The little apparatus of observation is unhinged. Pillars go down; the Doctor floats off; some sudden exaltation possesses me. He was thrown, riding in a race, and when I came along Shaftesbury Avenue tonight, those insignificant and scarcely formulated faces that bubble up out of the doors of the Tube, and many obscure Indians, and people dying of famine and disease, and women who have been cheated, and whipped dogs and crying children—all these seemed to me bereft. He would have done justice. He would have protected. About the age of forty he would have shocked the authorities. No lullaby has ever occurred to me capable of singing him to rest.

'But let me dip again and bring up in my spoon another of these minute objects which we call optimistically, "characters of our friends"—Louis. He sat staring at the preacher. His being seemed conglobulated in his brow, his lips were pressed; his eyes were fixed, but suddenly they flashed with laughter. Also he suffered from chilblains, the penalty of an imperfect circulation. Unhappy, unfriended, in exile he would sometimes, in moments of confidence, describe how the surf swept over the beaches of his home. The remorseless eye of youth fixed itself upon his swollen joints. Yes, but we were also quick to perceive how cutting, how apt, how severe he was, how naturally, when we lay under the elm trees pretending to watch cricket, we waited his approval, seldom given. His ascendancy was resented, as Percival's was adored. Prim, suspicious, lifting his feet like a crane, there was yet a legend that he had smashed a door with his naked fist. But his peak was too bare, too stony for that kind of mist to cling to it. He was without those simple attachments by which one is connected with another. He remained aloof; enigmatic; a scholar capable of that inspired accuracy which has something formidable about it. My phrases (how to describe the moon) did not meet with his approval. On the other hand, he envied me to the point of desperation for being at my ease with servants. Not that the sense of his own deserts failed him. That was commensurate with his respect for discipline. Hence his success, finally. His life, though, was not happy. But look—his eye turns white as he lies in the palm of my hand. Suddenly the sense of what people are leaves one. I return him to the pool where he will acquire lustre.

'Neville next—lying on his back staring up at the summer sky. He floated among us like a piece of thistledown, indolently haunting the sunny corner of the playing-field, not listening, yet not remote. It was through him that I have nosed round without ever precisely touching the Latin classics and have also derived some of those persistent habits of thought which make us irredeemably lop-sided—for instance about crucifixes, that they are the mark of the devil. Our half-loves and half-hates and ambiguities on these points were to him indefensible treacheries. The swaying and sonorous Doctor, whom I made to sit swinging his braces over a gas-fire, was to him nothing but an instrument of the inquisition. So he turned with a passion that made up for his indolence upon Catullus, Horace, Lucretius, lying lazily dormant, yes, but regardant, noticing, with rapture, cricketers, while with a mind like the tongue of an ant-eater, rapid, dexterous, glutinous, he searched out every curl and twist of those Roman sentences, and sought out one person, always one person to sit beside.

'And the long skirts of the masters' wives would come swishing by, mountainous, menacing; and our hands would fly to our caps. And immense dullness would descend unbroken, monotonous. Nothing, nothing, nothing broke with its fin that leaden waste of waters. Nothing would happen to lift that weight of intolerable boredom. The terms went on. We grew; we changed; for, of course, we are animals. We are not always aware by any means; we breathe, eat, sleep automatically. We exist not only separately but in undifferentiated blobs of matter. With one scoop a whole brakeful of boys is swept up and goes cricketing, footballing. An army marches across Europe. We assemble in parks and halls and sedulously oppose any renegade (Neville, Louis, Rhoda) who sets up a separate existence. And I am so made that, while I hear one or two distinct melodies, such as Louis sings, or Neville, I am also drawn irresistibly to the sound of the chorus chanting its old, chanting its almost wordless, almost senseless song that comes across courts at night; which we hear now booming round us as cars and omnibuses take people to theatres. (Listen; the cars rush past this restaurant; now and then, down the river, a siren hoots, as a steamer makes for the sea.) If a bagman offers me snuff in a train I accept. I like the copious, shapeless, warm, not so very clever, but extremely easy and rather coarse aspect of things; the talk of men in clubs and public-houses, of miners half naked in drawers—the forthright, perfectly unassuming, and without end in view except dinner, love, money and getting along tolerably; that which is without great hopes, ideals or anything of that kind; what is unassuming except to make a tolerably good job of it. I like all that. So I joined them, when Neville sulked or Louis, as I quite agree sublimely, turned on his heel.

'Thus, not equally by any means or with order, but in great streaks my waxen waistcoat melted, here one drop, there another. Now through this transparency became visible those wondrous pastures, at first so moon-white, radiant, where no foot has been; meadows of the rose, the crocus, of the rock and the snake too; of the spotted and swart; the embarrassing, the binding and tripping up. One leaps out of bed, throws up the window; with what a whirr the birds rise! You know that sudden rush of wings, that exclamation, carol, and confusion; the riot and babble of voices; and all the drops are sparkling, trembling, as if the garden were a splintered mosaic, vanishing, twinkling; not yet formed into one whole; and a bird sings close to the window. I heard those songs. I followed those phantoms. I saw Joans, Dorothys, Miriams, I forget their names, passing down avenues, stopping on the crest of bridges to look down into the river. And from among them rise one or two distinct figures, birds who sang with the rapt egotism of youth by the window; broke their snails on stones, dipped their beaks in sticky, viscous matter; hard, avid, remorseless; Jinny, Susan, Rhoda. They had been educated on the east coast or on the south coast. They had grown long pigtails and acquired the look of startled foals, which is the mark of adolescence.

'Jinny was the first to come sidling up to the gate to eat sugar. She nipped it off the palms of one's hands very cleverly, but her ears were laid back as if she might bite. Rhoda was wild—Rhoda one never could catch. She was both frightened and clumsy. It was Susan who first became wholly woman, purely feminine. It was she who dropped on my face those scalding tears which are terrible, beautiful; both, neither. She was born to be the adored of poets, since poets require safety; someone who sits sewing, who says, "I hate, I love", who is neither comfortable nor prosperous, but has some quality in accordance with the high but unemphatic beauty of pure style which those who create poetry so particularly admire. Her father trailed from room to room and down flagged corridors in his flapping dressing-gown and worn slippers. On still nights a wall of water fell with a roar a mile off. The ancient dog could scarcely heave himself up on to his chair. And some witless servant could be heard laughing at the top of the house as she whirred the wheel of the sewing-machine round and round.

'That I observed even in the midst of my anguish when, twisting her pocket-handkerchief, Susan cried, "I love; I hate". "A worthless servant", I observed, "laughs upstairs in the attic", and that little piece of dramatization shows how incompletely we are merged in our own experiences. On the outskirts of every agony sits some observant fellow who points; who whispers as he whispered to me that summer morning in the house where the corn comes up to the window, "The willow grows on the turf by the river. The gardeners sweep with great brooms and the lady sits writing." Thus he directed me to that which is beyond and outside our own predicament; to that which is symbolic, and thus perhaps permanent, if there is any permanence in our sleeping, eating, breathing, so animal, so spiritual and tumultuous lives.

'The willow tree grew by the river. I sat on the smooth turf with Neville, with Larpent, with Baker, Romsey, Hughes, Percival and Jinny. Through its fine plumes specked with little pricked ears of green in spring, of orange in autumn, I saw boats; buildings; I saw hurrying, decrepit women. I buried match after match in the turf decidedly to mark this or that stage in the process of understanding (it might be philosophy; science; it might be myself) while the fringe of my intelligence floating unattached caught those distant sensations which after a time the mind draws in and works upon; the chime of bells; general murmurs; vanishing figures; one girl on a bicycle who, as she rode, seemed to lift the corner of a curtain concealing the populous undifferentiated chaos of life which surged behind the outlines of my friends and the willow tree.

'The tree alone resisted our eternal flux. For I changed and changed; was Hamlet, was Shelley, was the hero, whose name I now forget, of a novel by Dostoevsky; was for a whole term, incredibly, Napoleon; but was Byron chiefly. For many weeks at a time it was my part to stride into rooms and fling gloves and coat on the back of chairs, scowling slightly. I was always going to the bookcase for another sip of the divine specific. Therefore, I let fly my tremendous battery of phrases upon somebody quite inappropriate—a girl now married, now buried; every book, every window-seat was littered with the sheets of my unfinished letters to the woman who made me Byron. For it is difficult to finish a letter in somebody else's style. I arrived all in a lather at her house; exchanged tokens but did not marry her, being no doubt unripe for that intensity.

'Here again there should be music. Not that wild hunting-song, Percival's music; but a painful, guttural, visceral, also soaring, lark-like, pealing song to replace these flagging, foolish transcripts—how much too deliberate! how much too reasonable!—which attempt to describe the flying moment of first love. A purple slide is slipped over the day. Look at a room before she comes and after. Look at the innocents outside pursuing their way. They neither see nor hear; yet on they go. Moving oneself in this radiant yet gummy atmosphere, how conscious one is of every movement—something adheres, something sticks to one's hands, taking up a newspaper even. Then there is the being eviscerated—drawn out, spun like a spider's web and twisted in agony round a thorn. Then a thunder-clap of complete indifference; the light blown out; then the return of measureless irresponsible joy; certain fields seem to glow green for ever, and innocent landscapes appear as if in the light of the first dawn—one patch of green, for example, up at Hampstead; and all faces are lit up, all conspire in a hush of tender joy; and then the mystic sense of completion and then that rasping, dog-fish skin-like roughness—those black arrows of shivering sensation, when she misses the post, when she does not come. Out rush a bristle of horned suspicions, horror, horror, horror—but what is the use of painfully elaborating these consecutive sentences when what one needs is nothing consecutive but a bark, a groan? And years later to see a middle-aged woman in a restaurant taking off her cloak.

'But to return. Let us again pretend that life is a solid substance, shaped like a globe, which we turn about in our fingers. Let us pretend that we can make out a plain and logical story, so that when one matter is despatched—love for instance—we go on, in an orderly manner, to the next. I was saying there was a willow tree. Its shower of falling branches, its creased and crooked bark had the effect of what remains outside our illusions yet cannot stay them, is changed by them for the moment, yet shows through stable, still, and with a sternness that our lives lack. Hence the comment it makes; the standard it supplies, and the reason why, as we flow and change, it seems to measure. Neville, for example, sat with me on the turf. But can anything be as clear as all that, I would say, following his gaze, through the branches, to a punt on the river, and a young man eating bananas from a paper bag? The scene was cut out with such intensity and so permeated with the quality of his vision that for a moment I could see it too; the punt, the bananas, the young man, through the branches of the willow tree. Then it faded.

'Rhoda came wandering vaguely. She would take advantage of any scholar in a blowing gown, or donkey rolling the turf with slippered feet to hide behind. What fear wavered and hid itself and blew to a flame in the depths of her grey, her startled, her dreaming eyes? Cruel and vindictive as we are, we are not bad to that extent. We have our fundamental goodness surely or to talk as I talk freely to someone I hardly know would be impossible—we should cease. The willow as she saw it grew on the verge of a grey desert where no bird sang. The leaves shrivelled as she looked at them, tossed in agony as she passed them. The trams and omnibuses roared hoarse in the street, ran over rocks and sped foaming away. Perhaps one pillar, sunlit, stood in her desert by a pool where wild beasts come down stealthily to drink.

'Then Jinny came. She flashed her fire over the tree. She was like a crinkled poppy, febrile, thirsty with the desire to drink dry dust. Darting, angular, not in the least impulsive, she came prepared. So little flames zigzag over the cracks in the dry earth. She made the willows dance, but not with illusion; for she saw nothing that was not there. It was a tree; there was the river; it was afternoon; here we were; I in my serge suit; she in green. There was no past, no future; merely the moment in its ring of light, and our bodies; and the inevitable climax, the ecstasy.

'Louis, when he let himself down on the grass, cautiously spreading (I do not exaggerate) a mackintosh square, made one acknowledge his presence. It was formidable. I had the intelligence to salute his integrity; his research with bony fingers wrapped in rags because of chilblains for some diamond of indissoluble veracity. I buried boxes of burnt matches in holes in the turf at his feet. His grim and caustic tongue reproved my indolence. He fascinated me with his sordid imagination. His heroes wore bowler-hats and talked about selling pianos for tenners. Through his landscape the tram squealed; the factory poured its acrid fumes. He haunted mean streets and towns where women lay drunk, naked, on counterpanes on Christmas day. His words falling from a shot-tower hit the water and up it spurted. He found one word, one only for the moon. Then he got up and went; we all got up; we all went. But I, pausing, looked at the tree, and as I looked in autumn at the fiery and yellow branches, some sediment formed; I formed; a drop fell; I fell—that is, from some completed experience I had emerged.

'I rose and walked away—I, I, I; not Byron, Shelley, Dostoevsky, but I, Bernard. I even repeated my own name once or twice. I went, swinging my stick, into a shop, and bought—not that I love music—a picture of Beethoven in a silver frame. Not that I love music, but because the whole of life, its masters, its adventurers, then appeared in long ranks of magnificent human beings behind me; and I was the inheritor; I, the continuer; I, the person miraculously appointed to carry it on. So, swinging my stick, with my eyes filmed, not with pride, but with humility rather, I walked down the street. The first whirr of wings had gone up, the carol, the exclamation; and now one enters; one goes into the house, the dry, uncompromising, inhabited house, the place with all its traditions, its objects, its accumulations of rubbish, and treasures displayed upon tables. I visited the family tailor, who remembered my uncle. People turned up in great quantities, not cut out, like the first faces (Neville, Louis, Jinny, Susan, Rhoda), but confused, featureless, or changed their features so fast that they seemed to have none. And blushing yet scornful, in the oddest condition of raw rapture and scepticism, I took the blow; the mixed sensations; the complex and disturbing and utterly unprepared for impacts of life all over, in all places, at the same time. How upsetting! How humiliating never to be sure what to say next, and those painful silences, glaring as dry deserts, with every pebble apparent; and then to say what one ought not to have said, and then to be conscious of a ramrod of incorruptible sincerity which one would willingly exchange for a shower of smooth pence, but could not, there at that party, where Jinny sat quite at her ease, rayed out on a gilt chair.

'Then says some lady with an impressive gesture, "Come with me". She leads one into a private alcove and admits one to the honour of her intimacy. Surnames change to Christian names; Christian names to nicknames. What is to be done about India, Ireland or Morocco? Old gentlemen answer the question standing decorated under chandeliers. One finds oneself surprisingly supplied with information. Outside the undifferentiated forces roar; inside we are very private, very explicit, have a sense indeed, that it is here, in this little room, that we make whatever day of the week it may be. Friday or Saturday. A shell forms upon the soft soul, nacreous, shiny, upon which sensations tap their beaks in vain. On me it formed earlier than on most. Soon I could carve my pear when other people had done dessert. I could bring my sentence to a close in a hush of complete silence. It is at that season too that perfection has a lure. One can learn Spanish, one thinks, by tying a string to the right toe and waking early. One fills up the little compartments of one's engagement book with dinner at eight; luncheon at one-thirty. One has shirts, socks, ties laid out on one's bed.

'But it is a mistake, this extreme precision, this orderly and military progress; a convenience, a lie. There is always deep below it, even when we arrive punctually at the appointed time with our white waistcoats and polite formalities, a rushing stream of broken dreams, nursery rhymes, street cries, half-finished sentences and sights—elm trees, willow trees, gardeners sweeping, women writing—that rise and sink even as we hand a lady down to dinner. While one straightens the fork so precisely on the table-cloth, a thousand faces mop and mow. There is nothing one can fish up in a spoon; nothing one can call an event. Yet it is alive too and deep, this stream. Immersed in it I would stop between one mouthful and the next, and look intently at a vase, perhaps with one red flower, while a reason struck me, a sudden revelation. Or I would say, walking along the Strand, "That's the phrase I want", as some beautiful, fabulous phantom bird, fish or cloud with fiery edges swam up to enclose once and for all some notion haunting me, after which on I trotted taking stock with renewed delight of ties and things in shop-windows.

'The crystal, the globe of life as one calls it, far from being hard and cold to the touch, has walls of thinnest air. If I press them all will burst. Whatever sentence I extract whole and entire from this cauldron is only a string of six little fish that let themselves be caught while a million others leap and sizzle, making the cauldron bubble like boiling silver, and slip through my fingers. Faces recur, faces and faces—they press their beauty to the walls of my bubble—Neville, Susan, Louis, Jinny, Rhoda and a thousand others. How impossible to order them rightly; to detach one separately, or to give the effect of the whole—again like music. What a symphony with its concord and its discord, and its tunes on top and its complicated bass beneath, then grew up! Each played his own tune, fiddle, flute, trumpet, drum or whatever the instrument might be. With Neville, "Let's discuss Hamlet". With Louis, science. With Jinny, love. Then suddenly, in a moment of exasperation, off to Cumberland with a quiet man for a whole week in an inn, with the rain running down the window-panes and nothing but mutton and mutton and again mutton for dinner. Yet that week remains a solid stone in the welter of unrecorded sensation. It was then we played dominoes; then we quarrelled about tough mutton. Then we walked on the fell. And a little girl, peeping round the door, gave me that letter, written on blue paper, in which I learnt that the girl who had made me Byron was to marry a squire. A man in gaiters, a man with a whip, a man who made speeches about fat oxen at dinner—I exclaimed derisively and looked at the racing clouds, and felt my own failure; my desire to be free; to escape; to be bound; to make an end; to continue; to be Louis; to be myself; and walked out in my mackintosh alone, and felt grumpy under the eternal hills and not in the least sublime; and came home and blamed the meat and packed and so back again to the welter; to the torture.

'Nevertheless, life is pleasant, life is tolerable. Tuesday follows Monday; then comes Wednesday. The mind grows rings; the identity becomes robust; pain is absorbed in growth. Opening and shutting, shutting and opening, with increasing hum and sturdiness, the haste and fever of youth are drawn into service until the whole being seems to expand in and out like the mainspring of a clock. How fast the stream flows from January to December! We are swept on by the torrent of things grown so familiar that they cast no shadow. We float, we float. . . .

'However, since one must leap (to tell you this story), I leap, here, at this point, and alight now upon some perfectly commonplace object— say the poker and tongs, as I saw them sometime later, after that lady who had made me Byron had married, under the light of one whom I will call the third Miss Jones. She is the girl who wears a certain dress expecting one at dinner, who picks a certain rose, who makes one feel "Steady, steady, this is a matter of some importance", as one shaves. Then one asks, "How does she behave to children?" One observes that she is a little clumsy with her umbrella; but minded when the mole was caught in the trap; and finally, would not make the loaf at breakfast (I was thinking of the interminable breakfasts of married life as I shaved) altogether prosaic—it would not surprise one sitting opposite this girl to see a dragon-fly perched on the loaf at breakfast. Also she inspired me with a desire to rise in the world; also she made me look with curiosity at the hitherto repulsive faces of new-born babies. And the little fierce beat—tick-tack, tick-tack—of the pulse of one's mind took on a more majestic rhythm. I roamed down Oxford Street. We are the continuers, we are the inheritors, I said, thinking of my sons and daughters; and if the feeling is so grandiose as to be absurd and one conceals it by jumping on to a bus or buying the evening paper, it is still a curious element in the ardour with which one laces up one's boots, with which one now addresses old friends committed to different careers. Louis, the attic-dweller; Rhoda, the nymph of the fountain always wet; both contradicted what was then so positive to me; both gave the other side of what seemed to me so evident (that we marry, that we domesticate);

for which I loved them, pitied them, and also deeply envied them their different lot.

'Once I had a biographer, dead long since, but if he still followed my footsteps with his old flattering intensity he would here say, "About this time Bernard married and bought a house. . . . His friends observed in him a growing tendency to domesticity. . . . The birth of children made it highly desirable that he should augment his income." That is the biographic style, and it does to tack together torn bits of stuff, stuff with raw edges. After all, one cannot find fault with the biographic style if one begins letters "Dear Sir", ends them "yours faithfully"; one cannot despise these phrases laid like Roman roads across the tumult of our lives, since they compel us to walk in step like civilized people with the slow and measured tread of policemen though one may be humming any nonsense under one's breath at the same time—"Hark, hark, the dogs do bark", "Come away, come away, death", "Let me not to the marriage of true minds", and so on. "He attained some success in his profession. . . . He inherited a small sum of money from an uncle"— that is how the biographer continues, and if one wears trousers and hitches them up with braces, one has to say that, though it is tempting now and then to go blackberrying; tempting to play ducks and drakes with all these phrases. But one has to say that.

'I became, I mean, a certain kind of man, scoring my path across life as one treads a path across the fields. My boots became worn a little on the left side. When I came in, certain rearrangements took place. "Here's Bernard!" How differently different people say that! There are many rooms—many Bernards. There was the charming, but weak; the strong, but supercilious; the brilliant, but remorseless; the very good fellow, but, I make no doubt, the awful bore; the sympathetic, but cold; the shabby, but—go into the next room—the foppish, worldly, and too well dressed. What I was to myself was different; was none of these. I am inclined to pin myself down most firmly there before the loaf at breakfast with my wife, who being now entirely my wife and not at all the girl who wore when she hoped to meet me a certain rose, gave me that feeling of existing in the midst of unconsciousness such as the tree-frog must have couched on the right shade of green leaf. "Pass" . . . I would say. "Milk" . . . she might answer, or "Mary's coming" . . .— simple words for those who have inherited the spoils of all the ages but not as said then, day after day, in the full tide of life, when one feels complete, entire, at breakfast. Muscles, nerves, intestines, blood-vessels, all that makes the coil and spring of our being, the unconscious hum of the engine, as well as the dart and flicker of the tongue, functioned superbly. Opening, shutting; shutting, opening; eating, drinking; some-times speaking—the whole mechanism seemed to expand, to contract, like the mainspring of a clock. Toast and butter, coffee and bacon, *The Times* and letters—suddenly the telephone rang with urgency and I rose deliberately and went to the telephone. I took up the black mouth. I marked the ease with which my mind adjusted itself to assimilate the message—it might be (one has these fancies) to assume command of the British Empire; I observed my composure; I remarked with what magnificent vitality the atoms of my attention dispersed, swarmed round the interruption, assimilated the message, adapted themselves to a new state of affairs and had created, by the time I put back the receiver, a richer, stronger, a more complicated world in which I was called upon to act my part and had no doubt whatever that I could do it. Clapping my hat on my head, I strode into a world inhabited by vast numbers of men who had also clapped their hats on their heads, and as we jostled and encountered in trains and tubes we exchanged the knowing wink of competitors and comrades braced with a thousand snares and dodges to achieve the same end—to earn our livings.

'Life is pleasant. Life is good. The mere process of life is satisfactory. Take the ordinary man in good health. He likes eating and sleeping. He likes the snuff of fresh air and walking at a brisk pace down the Strand. Or in the country there's a cock crowing on a gate; there's a foal galloping round a field. Something always has to be done next. Tuesday follows Monday; Wednesday Tuesday. Each spreads the same ripple of well-being, repeats the same curve of rhythm; covers fresh sand with a chill or ebbs a little slackly without. So the being grows rings; identity becomes robust. What was fiery and furtive like a fling of grain cast into the air and blown hither and thither by wild gusts of life from every quarter is now methodical and orderly and flung with a purpose—so it seems.

'Lord, how pleasant! Lord, how good! How tolerable is the life of little shopkeepers, I would say, as the train drew through the suburbs and one saw lights in bedroom windows. Active, energetic as a swarm of ants, I said, as I stood at the window and watched workers, bag in hand, stream into town. What hardness, what energy and violence of limb, I thought, seeing men in white drawers scouring after a football on a patch of snow in January. Now being grumpy about some small matter—it might be the meat—it seemed luxurious to disturb with a little ripple the enormous stability, whose quiver, for our child was about to be born, increased its joy, of our married life. I snapped at dinner. I spoke unreasonably as if, being a millionaire, I could throw away five shillings; or, being a perfect steeple-jack, stumbled over a footstool on purpose. Going up to bed we settled our quarrel on the stairs, and standing by the window looking at a sky clear like the inside of a blue stone, "Heaven be praised," I said, "we need not whip this prose into poetry. The little language is enough." For the space of the prospect and its clarity seemed to offer no impediment whatsoever, but to allow our lives to spread out and out beyond all bristling of roofs and chimneys to the flawless verge.

'Into this crashed death—Percival's. "Which is happiness?" I said (our child had been born), "which pain?" referring to the two sides of my body, as I came downstairs, making a purely physical statement. Also I made note of the state of the house; the curtain blowing; the cook singing; the wardrobe showing through the half-opened door. I said, "Give him (myself) another moment's respite" as I went downstairs. "Now in this drawing-room he is going to suffer. There is no escape." But for pain words are lacking. There should be cries, cracks, fissures, whiteness passing over chintz covers, interference with the sense of time, of space; the sense also of extreme fixity in passing objects; and sounds very remote and then very close; flesh being gashed and blood spurting, a joint suddenly twisted—beneath all of which appears something very important, yet remote, to be just held in solitude. So I went out. I saw the first morning he would never see—the sparrows were like toys dangled from a string by a child. To see things without attachment, from the outside, and to realize their beauty in itself—how strange! And then the sense that a burden has been removed; pretence and make-believe and unreality are gone, and lightness has come with a kind of transparency, making oneself invisible and things seen through as one walks—how strange. "And now what other discovery will there be?" I said, and in order to hold it tight ignored newspaper placards and went and looked at pictures. Madonnas and pillars, arches and orange trees, still as on the first day of creation, but acquainted with grief, there they hung, and I gazed at them. "Here," I said, "we are together without interruption." This freedom, this immunity, seemed then a conquest, and stirred in me such exaltation that I sometimes go there, even now, to bring back exaltation and Percival. But it did not last. What torments one is the horrible activity of the mind's eye—how he fell, how he looked, where they carried him; men in loin-cloths, pulling ropes; the bandages and the mud. Then comes the terrible pounce of memory, not to be foretold, not to be warded off—that I did not go with him to Hampton Court. That claw scratched; that fang tore; I did not go. In spite of his impatiently protesting that it did not matter; why interrupt, why spoil our moment of uninterrupted community?—Still, I repeated sullenly, I did not go, and so, driven out of the sanctuary by these officious devils, went to Jinny because she had a room; a room with little tables, with little ornaments scattered on little tables. There I confessed, with tears—I had not gone to Hampton Court. And she, remembering other things, to me trifles but torturing to her, showed me how life withers when there are things we cannot share. Soon, too, a maid came in with a note, and as she turned to answer it and I felt my own curiosity to know what she was writing and to whom, I saw the first leaf fall on his grave. I saw us push beyond this moment, and leave it behind us for ever. And then sitting side by side on the sofa we remembered inevitably what had been said by others; "the lily of the day is fairer far in May"; we compared Percival to a lily—Percival whom I wanted to lose his hair, to shock the authorities, to grow old with me; he was already covered with lilies.

'So the sincerity of the moment passed; so it became symbolical; and that I could not stand. Let us commit any blasphemy of laughter and criticism rather than exude this lily-sweet glue; and cover him with phrases, I cried. Therefore I broke off, and Jinny, who was without future, or speculation, but respected the moment with complete integrity, gave her body a flick with the whip, powdered her face (for which I loved her), and waved to me as she stood on the doorstep, pressing her hand to her hair so that the wind might not disorder it, a gesture for which I honoured her, as if it confirmed our determination—not to let lilies grow.

'I observed with disillusioned clarity the despicable non-entity of the street; its porches; its window curtains; the drab clothes, the cupidity and complacency of shopping women; and old men taking the air in comforters; the caution of people crossing; the universal determination to go on living, when really, fools and gulls that you are, I said, any slate may fly from a roof, any car may swerve, for there is neither rhyme nor reason when a drunk man staggers about with a club in his hand— that is all. I was like one admitted behind the scenes: like one shown how the effects are produced. I returned, however, to my own snug home and was warned by the parlourmaid to creep upstairs in my stockings. The child was asleep. I went to my room.

'Was there no sword, nothing with which to batter down these walls, this protection, this begetting of children and living behind curtains, and becoming daily more involved and committed, with books and pictures? Better burn one's life out like Louis, desiring perfection; or like Rhoda leave us, flying past us to the desert; or choose one out of millions and one only like Neville; better be like Susan and love and hate the heat of the sun or the frost-bitten grass; or be like Jinny, honest, an animal. All had their rapture; their common feeling with death; something that stood them in stead. Thus I visited each of my friends in turn, trying, with fumbling fingers, to prise open their locked caskets. I went from one to the other holding my sorrow—no, not my sorrow but the incomprehensible nature of this our life—for their inspection. Some people go to priests; others to poetry; I to my friends, I to my own heart,

I to seek among phrases and fragments something unbroken—I to whom there is not beauty enough in moon or tree; to whom the touch of one person with another is all, yet who cannot grasp even that, who am so imperfect, so weak, so unspeakably lonely. There I sat.

'Should this be the end of the story? a kind of sigh? a last ripple of the wave? A trickle of water to some gutter where, burbling, it dies away? Let me touch the table—so—and thus recover my sense of the moment. A sideboard covered with cruets; a basket full of rolls; a plate of bananas—these are comfortable sights. But if there are no stories, what end can there be, or what beginning? Life is not susceptible perhaps to the treatment we give it when we try to tell it. Sitting up late at night it seems strange not to have more control. Pigeon-holes are not then very useful. It is strange how force ebbs away and away into some dry creek. Sitting alone, it seems we are spent; our waters can only just surround feebly that spike of sea-holly; we cannot reach that further pebble so as to wet it. It is over, we are ended. But wait—I sat all night waiting—an impulse again runs through us; we rise, we toss back a mane of white spray; we pound on the shore; we are not to be confined. That is, I shaved and washed; did not wake my wife, and had breakfast; put on my hat, and went out to earn my living. After Monday, Tuesday comes.

'Yet some doubt remained, some note of interrogation. I was surprised, opening a door, to find people thus occupied; I hesitated, taking a cup of tea, whether one said milk or sugar. And the light of the stars falling, as it falls now, on my hand after travelling for millions upon millions of years—I could get a cold shock from that for a moment—not more, my imagination is too feeble. But some doubt remained. A shadow flitted through my mind like moths' wings among chairs and tables in a room in the evening. When, for example, I went to Lincolnshire that summer to see Susan and she advanced towards me across the garden with the lazy movement of a half-filled sail, with the swaying movement of a woman with child, I thought, "It goes on; but why?" We sat in the garden; the farm carts came up dripping with hay; there was the usual country gabble of rooks and doves; fruit was netted and covered over; the gardener dug. Bees boomed down the purple tunnels of flowers; bees embedded themselves on the golden shields of sunflowers. Little twigs were blown across the grass. How rhythmical, and half conscious and like something wrapped in mist it was; but to me hateful, like a net folding one's limbs in its meshes, cramping. She who had refused Percival lent herself to this, to this covering over.

'Sitting down on a bank to wait for my train, I thought then how we surrender, how we submit to the stupidity of nature. Woods covered in thick green leafage lay in front of me. And by some flick of a scent or a sound on a nerve, the old image—the gardeners sweeping, the lady writing—returned. I saw the figures beneath the beech trees at Elvedon. The gardeners swept; the lady at the table sat writing. But I now made the contribution of maturity to childhood's intuitions—satiety and doom; the sense of what is unescapable in our lot; death; the knowledge of limitations; how life is more obdurate than one had thought it. Then, when I was a child, the presence of an enemy had asserted itself; the need for opposition had stung me. I had jumped up and cried, "Let's explore". The horror of the situation was ended.

'Now what situation was there to end? Dullness and doom. And what to explore? The leaves and the wood concealed nothing. If a bird rose I should no longer make a poem—I should repeat what I had seen before. Thus if I had a stick with which to point to indentations in the curve of being, this is the lowest; here it coils useless on the mud where no tide comes—here, where I sit with my back to a hedge, and my hat over my eyes, while the sheep advance remorselessly in that wooden way of theirs, step by step on stiff, pointed legs. But if you hold a blunt blade to a grindstone long enough, something spurts—a jagged edge of fire; so held to lack of reason, aimlessness, the usual, all massed together, out spurted in one flame hatred, contempt. I took my mind, my being, the old dejected, almost inanimate object, and lashed it about among these odds and ends, sticks and straws, detestable little bits of wreckage, flotsam and jetsam, floating on the oily surface. I jumped up. I said, "Fight! Fight!" I repeated. It is the effort and the struggle, it is the perpetual warfare, it is the shattering and piecing together—this is the daily battle, defeat or victory, the absorbing pursuit. The trees, scattered, put on order; the thick green of the leaves thinned itself to a dancing light. I netted them under with a sudden phrase. I retrieved them from formlessness with words.

'The train came in. Lengthening down the platform, the train came to a stop. I caught my train. And so back to London in the evening. How satisfactory, the atmosphere of common sense and tobacco; old women clambering into the third-class carriage with their baskets; the sucking at pipes; the good-nights and see you tomorrows of friends parting at wayside stations, and then the lights of London—not the flaring ecstasy of youth, not that tattered violet banner, but still the lights of London all the same; hard, electric lights, high up in offices; street lamps laced along dry pavements; flares roaring above street markets. I like all this when I have despatched the enemy for a moment.

'Also I like to find the pageant of existence roaring, in a theatre for instance. The clay-coloured, earthy nondescript animal of the field here erects himself and with infinite ingenuity and effort puts up a fight against the green woods and green fields and sheep advancing with measured tread, munching. And, of course, windows in the long grey streets were lit up; strips of carpet cut the pavement; there were swept and garnished rooms, fire, food, wine, talk. Men with withered hands, women with pearl pagodas hanging from their ears, came in and went out. I saw old men's faces carved into wrinkles and sneers by the work of the world; beauty cherished so that it seemed newly sprung even in age; and youth so apt for pleasure that pleasure, one thought, must exist; it seemed that grass-lands must roll for it; and the sea be chopped up into little waves; and the woods rustle with bright-coloured birds for youth, for youth expectant. There one met Jinny and Hal, Tom and Betty; there we had our jokes and shared our secrets; and never parted in the doorway without arranging to meet again in some other room as the occasion, as the time of the year, suggested. Life is pleasant; life is good. After Monday comes Tuesday, and Wednesday follows.

'Yes, but after a time with a difference. It may be that something in the look of the room one night, in the arrangement of the chairs, suggests it. It seems comfortable to sink down on a sofa in a corner, to look, to listen. Then it happens that two figures standing with their backs to the window appear against the branches of a spreading willow. With a shock of emotion one feels, "There are figures without features robed in beauty". In the pause that follows while the ripples spread, the girl to whom one should be talking says to herself, "He is old". But she is wrong. It is not age; it is that a drop has fallen; another drop. Time has given the arrangement another shake. Out we creep from the arch of the currant leaves, out into a wider world. The true order of things—this is our perpetual illusion—is now apparent. Thus in a moment, in a drawing-room, our life adjusts itself to the majestic march of day across the sky.

'It was for this reason that instead of pulling on my patent-leather shoes and finding a tolerable tie, I sought Neville. I sought my oldest friend, who had known me when I was Byron; when I was Meredith's young man, and also that hero in a book by Dostoevsky whose name I have forgotten. I found him alone, reading. A perfectly neat table; a curtain pulled methodically straight; a paper-knife dividing a French volume—nobody, I thought, ever changes the attitude in which we saw them first, or the clothes. Here he has sat in this chair, in these clothes, ever since we first met. Here was freedom; here was intimacy; the firelight broke off some round apple on the curtain. There we talked; sat talking; sauntered down that avenue, the avenue which runs under the trees, under the thick-leaved murmuring trees, the trees that are hung with fruit, which we have trodden so often together, so that now the turf is bare round some of those trees, round certain plays and poems, certain favourites of ours—the turf is trodden bare by our incessant unmethodical pacing. If I have to wait, I read; if I wake in the night, I feel along the shelf for a book. Swelling, perpetually augmented, there is a vast accumulation of unrecorded matter in my head. Now and then I break off a lump, Shakespeare it may be, it may be some old woman called Peck; and say to myself, smoking a cigarette in bed, "That's Shakespeare. That's Peck"—with a certainty of recognition and a shock of knowledge which is endlessly delightful, though not to be imparted. So we shared our Pecks, our Shakespeares; compared each other's versions; allowed each other's insight to set our own Peck or Shakespeare in a better light; and then sank into one of those silences which are now and again broken by a few words, as if a fin rose in the wastes of silence; and then the fin, the thought, sinks back into the depths, spreading round it a little ripple of satisfaction, content.

'Yes, but suddenly one hears a clock tick. We who had been immersed in this world became aware of another. It is painful. It was Neville who changed our time. He, who had been thinking with the unlimited time of the mind, which stretches in a flash from Shakespeare to ourselves, poked the fire and began to live by that other clock which marks the approach of a particular person. The wide and dignified sweep of his mind contracted. He became on the alert. I could feel him listening to sounds in the street. I noted how he touched a cushion. From the myriads of mankind and all time past he had chosen one person, one moment in particular. A sound was heard in the hall. What he was saying wavered in the air like an uneasy flame. I watched him disentangle one footstep from other footsteps; wait for some particular mark of identification and glance with the swiftness of a snake at the handle of the door. (Hence the astonishing acuteness of his perceptions; he has been trained always by one person.) So concentrated a passion shot out others like foreign matter from a still, sparkling fluid. I became aware of my own vague and cloudy nature full of sediment, full of doubt, full of phrases and notes to be made in pocket-books. The folds of the curtain became still, statuesque; the paperweight on the table hardened; the threads on the curtain sparkled; everything became definite, external, a scene in which I had no part. I rose, therefore; I left him.

'Heavens! how they caught me as I left the room, the fangs of that old pain! the desire for someone not there. For whom? I did not know at first; then remembered Percival. I had not thought of him for months. Now to laugh with him, to laugh with him at Neville—that was what I wanted, to walk off arm-in-arm together laughing. But he was not there. The place was empty.

'It is strange how the dead leap out on us at street corners, or in dreams.

'This fitful gust blowing so sharp and cold upon me sent me that night across London to visit other friends, Rhoda and Louis, desiring company, certainty, contact. I wondered, as I mounted the stairs, what was their relationship? What did they say alone? I figured her awkward with the tea-kettle. She gazed over the slate roofs—the nymph of the fountain always wet, obsessed with visions, dreaming. She parted the curtain to look at the night. "Away!" she said. "The moor is dark beneath the moon." I rang; I waited. Louis perhaps poured out milk in a saucer for the cat; Louis, whose bony hands shut like the sides of a dock closing themselves with a slow anguish of effort upon an enormous tumult of waters, who knew what has been said by the Egyptian, the Indian, by men with high cheek-bones and solitaries in hair shirts. I knocked: I waited; there was no answer. I tramped down the stone stairs again. Our friends—how distant, how mute, how seldom visited and little known. And I, too, am dim to my friends and unknown; a phantom, sometimes seen, often not. Life is a dream surely. Our flame, the will-o'-the-wisp that dances in a few eyes, is soon to be blown out and all will fade. I recalled my friends. I thought of Susan. She had bought fields. Cucumbers and tomatoes ripened in her hothouses. The vine that had been killed by last year's frost was putting out a leaf or two. She walked heavily with her sons across her meadows. She went about the land attended by men in gaiters, pointing with her stick at a roof, at hedges, at walls fallen into disrepair. The pigeons followed her, waddling, for the grain that she let fall from her capable, earthy fingers. "But I no longer rise at dawn", she said. Then Jinny—entertaining, no doubt, some new young man. They reached the crisis of the usual conversation. The room would be darkened; chairs arranged. For she still sought the moment. Without illusions, hard and clear as crystal, she rode at the day with her breast bared. She let its spikes pierce her. When the lock whitened on her forehead she twisted it fearlessly among the rest. So when they come to bury her nothing will be out of order. Bits of ribbons will be found curled up. But still the door opens. Who is coming in? she asks, and rises to meet him, prepared, as on those first spring nights when the tree under the big London houses where respectable citizens were going soberly to bed scarcely sheltered her love; and the squeak of trams mixed with her cry of delight and the rippling of leaves had to shade her languor, her delicious lassitude as she sank down cooled by all the sweetness of nature satisfied. Our friends, how seldom visited, how little known—it is true; and yet, when I meet an unknown person, and try to break off, here at this table, what I call "my life", it is not one life that I look back upon; I am not one person; I am many people; I do not altogether know who I am—Jinny, Susan, Neville, Rhoda, or Louis; or how to distinguish my life from theirs.

'So I thought that night in early autumn when we came together and dined once more at Hampton Court. Our discomfort was at first considerable, for each by that time was committed to a statement, and the other person coming along the road to the meeting-place dressed like this or that, with a stick or without, seemed to contradict it. I saw Jinny look at Susan's earthy fingers and then hide her own; I, considering Neville, so neat and exact, felt the nebulosity of my own life blurred with all these phrases. He then boasted, because he was ashamed of one room and one person and his own success. Louis and Rhoda, the conspirators, the spies at table, who take notes, felt, "After all, Bernard can make the waiter fetch us rolls—a contact denied us". We saw for a moment laid out among us the body of the complete human being whom we have failed to be, but at the same time, cannot forget. All that we might have been we saw; all that we had missed, and we grudged for a moment the other's claim, as children when the cake is cut, the one cake, the only cake, watch their slice diminishing.

'However, we had our bottle of wine, and under that seduction lost our enmity, and stopped comparing. And, half-way through dinner, we felt enlarge itself round us the huge blackness of what is outside us, of what we are not. The wind, the rush of wheels became the roar of time, and we rushed—where? And who were we? We were extinguished for a moment, went out like sparks in burnt paper and the blackness roared. Past time, past history we went. For me this lasts but one second. It is ended by my own pugnacity. I strike the table with a spoon. If I could measure things with compasses I would, but since my only measure is a phrase, I make phrases—I forget what, on this occasion. We became six people at a table in Hampton Court. We rose and walked together down the avenue. In the thin, the unreal twilight, fitfully like the echo of voices laughing down some alley, geniality returned to me and flesh. Against the gateway, against some cedar tree I saw blaze bright, Neville, Jinny, Rhoda, Louis, Susan, and myself, our life, our identity. Still King William seemed an unreal monarch and his crown mere tinsel. But we—against the brick, against the branches, we six, out of how many million millions, for one moment out of what measureless abundance of past time and time to come, burnt there triumphant. The moment was all; the moment was enough. And then Neville, Jinny, Susan and I, as a wave breaks, burst asunder, surrendered—to the next leaf, to the precise bird, to a child with a hoop, to a prancing dog, to the warmth that is hoarded in woods after a hot day, to the lights twisted like white ribbon on rippled waters. We drew apart; we were consumed in the darkness of the trees, leaving Rhoda and Louis to stand on the terrace by the urn.

'When we returned from that immersion—how sweet, how deep!— and came to the surface and saw the conspirators still standing there it was with some compunction. We had lost what they had kept. We interrupted. But we were tired, and whether it had been good or bad, accomplished or left undone, the dusky veil was falling upon our endeavours; the lights were sinking as we paused for a moment upon the terrace that overlooks the river. The steamers were landing their trippers on the bank; there was a distant cheering, the sound of singing, as if people waved their hats and joined in some last song. The sound of the chorus came across the water and I felt leap up that old impulse, which has moved me all my life, to be thrown up and down on the roar of other people's voices, singing the same song; to be tossed up and down on the roar of almost senseless merriment, sentiment, triumph, desire. But not now. No! I could not collect myself; I could not distinguish myself; I could not help letting fall the things that had made me a minute ago eager, amused, jealous, vigilant, and hosts of other things, into the water. I could not recover myself from that endless throwing away, dissipation, flooding forth without our willing it and rushing soundlessly away out there under the arches of the bridge, round some clump of trees or an island, out where sea-birds sit on stakes, over the roughened water to become waves in the sea—I could not recover myself from that dissipation. So we parted.

'Was this, then, this streaming away mixed with Susan, Jinny, Neville, Rhoda, Louis, a sort of death? A new assembly of elements? Some hint of what was to come? The note was scribbled, the book shut, for I am an intermittent student. I do not say my lessons by any means at the stated hour. Later, walking down Fleet Street at the rush hour, I recalled that moment; I continued it. "Must I for ever," I said, "beat my spoon on the table-cloth? Shall I not, too, consent?" The omnibuses were clogged; one came up behind another and stopped with a click, like a link added to a stone chain. People passed.

'Multitudinous, carrying attaché-cases, dodging with incredible celerity in and out, they went past like a river in spate. They went past roaring like a train in a tunnel. Seizing my chance I crossed; dived down a dark passage and entered the shop where they cut my hair. I leant my head back and was swathed in a sheet. Looking-glasses confronted me in which I could see my pinioned body and people passing; stopping, looking, and going on indifferent. The hairdresser began to move his scissors to and fro. I felt myself powerless to stop the oscillations of the cold steel. So we are cut and laid in swaths, I said; so we lie side by side on the damp meadows, withered branches and flowering. We have no more to expose ourselves on the bare hedges to the wind and snow; no more to carry ourselves erect when the gale sweeps, to bear our burden upheld; or stay, unmurmuring, on those pallid noondays when the bird creeps close to the bough and the damp whitens the leaf. We are cut, we are fallen. We are become part of that unfeeling universe that sleeps when we are at our quickest and burns red when we lie asleep. We have renounced our station and lie now flat, withered and how soon forgotten! Upon which I saw an expression in the tail of the eye of the hairdresser as if something interested him in the street.

'What interested the hairdresser? What did the hairdresser see in the street? It is thus that I am recalled. (For I am no mystic; something always plucks at me—curiosity, envy, admiration, interest in hairdressers and the like bring me to the surface.) While he brushed the fluff from my coat I took pains to assure myself of his identity, and then, swinging my stick, I went into the Strand, and evoked to serve as opposite to myself the figure of Rhoda, always so furtive, always with fear in her eyes, always seeking some pillar in the desert, to find which she had gone; she had killed herself. "Wait", I said, putting my arm in imagination (thus we consort with our friends) through her arm. "Wait until these omnibuses have gone by. Do not cross so dangerously. These men are your brothers." In persuading her I was also persuading my own soul. For this is not one life; nor do I always know if I am man or woman, Bernard or Neville, Louis, Susan, Jinny, or Rhoda—so strange is the contact of one with another.

'Swinging my stick, with my hair newly cut and the nape of my neck tingling, I went past all those trays of penny toys imported from Germany that men hold out in the street by St Paul's—St Paul's, the brooding hen with spread wings from whose shelter run omnibuses and streams of men and women at the rush hour. I thought how Louis would mount those steps in his neat suit with his cane in his hand and his angular, rather detached gait. With his Australian accent ("My father, a banker at Brisbane") he would come, I thought, with greater respect to these old ceremonies than I do, who have heard the same lullabies for a thousand years. I am always impressed, as I enter, by the rubbed noses; the polished brasses; the flapping and the chanting, while one boy's voice wails round the dome like some lost and wandering dove. The recumbency and the peace of the dead impress me—warriors at rest under their old banners. Then I scoff at the floridity and absurdity of some scrolloping tomb; and the trumpets and the victories and the coats of arms and the certainty, so sonorously repeated, of resurrection, of eternal life. My wandering and inquisitive eye then shows me an awe-stricken child; a shuffling pensioner; or the obeisances of tired shop-girls burdened with heaven knows what strife in their poor thin breasts come to solace themselves in the rush hour. I stray and look and wonder, and sometimes, rather furtively, try to rise on the shaft of somebody else's prayer into the dome, out, beyond, wherever they go. But then like the lost and wailing dove, I find myself failing, fluttering, descending and perching upon some curious gargoyle, some battered nose or absurd tombstone, with humour, with wonder, and so again watch the sightseers with their Baedekers shuffling past, while the boy's voice soars in the dome and the organ now and then indulges in a moment of elephantine triumph. How then, I asked, would Louis roof us all in? How would he confine us, make us one, with his red ink, with his very fine nib? The voice petered out in the dome, wailing.

'So into the street again, swinging my stick, looking at wire trays in stationers' shop-windows, at baskets of fruit grown in the colonies, murmuring Pillicock sat on Pillicock's hill, or Hark, hark, the dogs do bark, or The World's great age begins anew, or Come away, come away, death—mingling nonsense and poetry, floating in the stream. Something always has to be done next. Tuesday follows Monday: Wednesday, Tuesday. Each spreads the same ripple. The being grows rings, like a tree. Like a tree, leaves fall.

'For one day as I leant over a gate that led into a field, the rhythm stopped; the rhymes and the hummings, the nonsense and the poetry. A space was cleared in my mind. I saw through the thick leaves of habit. Leaning over the gate I regretted so much litter, so much unaccomplishment and separation, for one cannot cross London to see a friend, life being so full of engagements; nor take ship to India and see a naked man spearing fish in blue water. I said life had been imperfect, an unfinishing phrase. It had been impossible for me, taking snuff as I do from any bagman met in a train, to keep coherency—that sense of the generations, of women carrying red pitchers to the Nile, of the nightingale who sings among conquests and migrations. It had been too vast an undertaking, I said, and how can I go on lifting my foot perpetually to climb the stair? I addressed myself as one would speak to a companion with whom one is voyaging to the North Pole.

'I spoke to that self who had been with me in many tremendous adventures; the faithful man who sits over the fire when everybody has gone to bed, stirring the cinders with a poker; the man who has been so mysteriously and with sudden accretions of being built up, in a beech wood, sitting by a willow tree on a bank, leaning over a parapet at Hampton Court; the man who has collected himself in moments of emergency and banged his spoon on the table, saying, "I will not consent".

'This self now as I leant over the gate looking down over fields rolling in waves of colour beneath me made no answer. He threw up no opposition. He attempted no phrase. His fist did not form. I waited. I listened. Nothing came, nothing, I cried then with a sudden conviction of complete desertion, Now there is nothing. No fin breaks the waste of this immeasurable sea. Life has destroyed me. No echo comes when I speak, no varied words. This is more truly death than the death of friends, than the death of youth. I am the swathed figure in the hairdresser's shop taking up only so much space.

'The scene beneath me withered. It was like the eclipse when the sun went out and left the earth, flourishing in full summer foliage, withered, brittle, false. Also I saw on a winding road in a dust dance the groups we had made, how they came together, how they ate together, how they met in this room or that. I saw my own indefatigable busyness—how I had rushed from one to the other, fetched and carried, travelled and returned, joined this group and that, here kissed, here withdrawn; always kept hard at it by some extraordinary purpose, with my nose to the ground like a dog on the scent; with an occasional toss of the head, an occasional cry of amazement, despair and then back again with my nose to the scent. What a litter—what a confusion; with here birth, here death; succulence and sweetness; effort and anguish; and myself always running hither and thither. Now it was done with. I had no more appetites to glut; no more stings in me with which to poison people; no more sharp teeth and clutching hands or desire to feel the pear and the grape and the sun beating down from the orchard wall.

'The woods had vanished; the earth was a waste of shadow. No sound broke the silence of the wintry landscape. No cock crowed; no smoke rose; no train moved. A man without a self, I said. A heavy body leaning on a gate. A dead man. With dispassionate despair, with entire disillusionment, I surveyed the dust dance; my life, my friends' lives, and those fabulous presences, men with brooms, women writing, the willow tree by the river—clouds and phantoms made of dust too, of dust that changed, as clouds lose and gain and take gold or red and lose their summits and billow this way and that, mutable, vain. I, carrying a notebook, making phrases, had recorded mere changes; a shadow, I had been sedulous to take note of shadows. How can I proceed now, I said, without a self, weightless and visionless, through a world weightless, without illusion?

'The heaviness of my despondency thrust open the gate I leant on and pushed me, an elderly man, a heavy man with grey hair, through the colourless field, the empty field. No more to hear echoes, no more to see phantoms, to conjure up no opposition, but to walk always unshadowed, making no impress upon the dead earth. If even there had been sheep munching, pushing one foot after another, or a bird, or a man driving a spade into the earth, had there been a bramble to trip me, or a ditch, damp with soaked leaves, into which to fall—but no, the melancholy path led along the level, to more wintriness and pallor and the equal and uninteresting view of the same landscape.

'How then does light return to the world after the eclipse of the sun? Miraculously. Frailly. In thin stripes. It hangs like a glass cage. It is a hoop to be fractured by a tiny jar. There is a spark there. Next moment a flush of dun. Then a vapour as if earth were breathing in and out, once, twice, for the first time. Then under the dullness someone walks with a green light. Then off twists a white wraith. The woods throb blue and green, and gradually the fields drink in red, gold, brown. Suddenly a river snatches a blue light. The earth absorbs colour like a sponge slowly drinking water. It puts on weight; rounds itself; hangs pendent; settles and swings beneath our feet.

'So the landscape returned to me; so I saw the fields rolling in waves of colour beneath me, but now with this difference; I saw but was not seen. I walked unshadowed; I came unheralded. From me had dropped the old cloak, the old response; the hollowed hand that beats back sounds. Thin as a ghost, leaving no trace where I trod, perceiving merely, I walked alone in a new world, never trodden; brushing new flowers, unable to speak save in a child's words of one syllable; without shelter from phrases—I who have made so many; unattended, I who have always gone with my kind; solitary, I who have always had someone to share the empty grate, or the cupboard with its hanging loop of gold.

'But how describe the world seen without a self? There are no words. Blue, red—even they distract, even they hide with thickness instead of letting the light through. How describe or say anything in articulate words again?—save that it fades, save that it undergoes a gradual transformation, becomes, even in the course of one short walk, habitual—this scene also. Blindness returns as one moves and one leaf repeats another. Loveliness returns as one looks, with all its train of phantom phrases. One breathes in and out substantial breath; down in the valley the train draws across the fields lop-eared with smoke.

'But for a moment I had sat on the turf somewhere high above the flow of the sea and the sound of the woods, had seen the house, the garden, and the waves breaking. The old nurse who turns the pages of the picture-book had stopped and had said, "Look. This is the truth."

'So I was thinking as I came along Shaftesbury Avenue tonight. I was thinking of that page in the picture-book. And when I met you in the place where one goes to hang up one's coat I said to myself, "It does not matter whom I meet. All this little affair of 'being' is over. Who this is I do not know; nor care; we will dine together." So I hung up my coat, tapped you on the shoulder, and said, "Sit with me".

'Now the meal is finished; we are surrounded by peelings and breadcrumbs. I have tried to break off this bunch and hand it to you; but whether there is substance or truth in it I do not know. Nor do I know exactly where we are. What city does that stretch of sky look down upon? Is it Paris, is it London where we sit, or some southern city of pink-washed houses lying under cypresses, under high mountains, where eagles soar? I do not at this moment feel certain.

'I begin now to forget; I begin to doubt the fixity of tables, the reality of here and now, to tap my knuckles smartly upon the edges of apparently solid objects and say, "Are you hard?" I have seen so many different things, have made so many different sentences. I have lost in the process of eating and drinking and rubbing my eyes along surfaces that thin, hard shell which cases the soul, which, in youth, shuts one in—hence the fierceness, and the tap, tap, tap of the remorseless beaks of the young. And now I ask, "Who am I?" I have been talking of Bernard, Neville, Jinny, Susan, Rhoda and Louis. Am I all of them? Am I one and distinct? I do not know. We sat here together. But now Percival is dead, and Rhoda is dead; we are divided; we are not here. Yet I cannot find any obstacle separating us. There is no division between me and them. As I talked I felt, "I am you". This difference we make so much of, this identity we so feverishly cherish, was overcome. Yes, ever since old Mrs Constable lifted her sponge and pouring warm water over me covered me with flesh I have been sensitive, percipient. Here on my brow is the blow I got when Percival fell. Here on the nape of my neck is the kiss Jinny gave Louis. My eyes fill with Susan's tears. I see far away, quivering like a gold thread, the pillar Rhoda saw, and feel the rush of the wind of her flight when she leapt.

'Thus when I come to shape here at this table between my hands the story of my life and set it before you as a complete thing, I have to recall things gone far, gone deep, sunk into this life or that and become part of it; dreams, too, things surrounding me, and the inmates, those old half-articulate ghosts who keep up their hauntings by day and night; who turn over in their sleep, who utter their confused cries, who put out their phantom fingers and clutch at me as I try to escape—shadows of people one might have been; unborn selves. There is the old brute, too, the savage, the hairy man who dabbles his fingers in ropes of entrails; and gobbles and belches; whose speech is guttural, visceral—well, he is here. He squats in me. Tonight he has been feasted on quails, salad, and sweetbread. He now holds a glass of fine old brandy in his paw. He brindles, purrs and shoots warm thrills all down my spine as I sip. It is true, he washes his hands before dinner, but they are still hairy. He buttons on trousers and waistcoats, but they contain the same organs. He jibs if I keep him waiting for dinner. He mops and mows perpetually, pointing with his half-idiot gestures of greed and covetousness at what he desires. I assure you, I have great difficulty sometimes in controlling him. That man, the hairy, the ape-like, has contributed his part to my life. He has given a greener glow to green things, has held his torch with its red flames, its thick and smarting smoke, behind every leaf. He has lit up the cool garden even. He has brandished his torch in murky by-streets where girls suddenly seem to shine with a red and intoxicating translucency. Oh, he has tossed his torch high! He has led me wild dances!

'But no more. Now tonight, my body rises tier upon tier like some cool temple whose floor is strewn with carpets and murmurs rise and the altars stand smoking; but up above, here in my serene head, come only fine gusts of melody, waves of incense, while the lost dove wails, and the banners tremble above tombs, and the dark airs of midnight shake trees outside the open windows. When I look down from this transcendency, how beautiful are even the crumbled relics of bread! What shapely spirals the peelings of pears make—how thin, and mottled like some sea-bird's egg. Even the forks laid straight side by side appear lucid, logical, exact; and the horns of the rolls which we have left are glazed, yellow-plated, hard. I could worship my hand even, with its fan of bones laced by blue mysterious veins and its astonishing look of aptness, suppleness and ability to curl softly or suddenly crush—its infinite sensibility.

'Immeasurably receptive, holding everything, trembling with fullness, yet clear, contained—so my being seems, now that desire urges it no more out and away; now that curiosity no longer dyes it a thousand colours. It lies deep, tideless, immune, now that he is dead, the man I called "Bernard", the man who kept a book in his pocket in which he made notes—phrases for the moon, notes of features; how people looked, turned, dropped their cigarette ends; under B, butterfly powder, under D, ways of naming death. But now let the door open, the glass door that is for ever turning on its hinges. Let a woman come, let a young man in evening-dress with a moustache sit down: is there anything that they can tell me? No! I know all that, too. And if she suddenly gets up and goes, "My dear", I say, "you no longer make me look after you". The shock of the falling wave which has sounded all my life, which woke me so that I saw the gold loop on the cupboard, no longer makes quiver what I hold.

'So now, taking upon me the mystery of things, I could go like a spy without leaving this place, without stirring from my chair. I can visit the remote verges of the desert lands where the savage sits by the camp-fire. Day rises; the girl lifts the watery fire-heated jewels to her brow; the sun levels his beams straight at the sleeping-house; the waves deepen their bars; they fling themselves on shore; back blows the spray; sweeping their waters they surround the boat and the sea-holly. The birds sing in chorus; deep tunnels run between the stalks of flowers; the house is whitened; the sleeper stretches; gradually all is astir. Light floods the room and drives shadow beyond shadow to where they hang

in folds inscrutable. What does the central shadow hold? Something?
Nothing? I do not know.

'Oh, but there is your face. I catch your eye. I, who had been thinking
myself so vast, a temple, a church, a whole universe, unconfined and
capable of being everywhere on the verge of things and here too, am
now nothing but what you see—an elderly man, rather heavy, grey
above the ears, who (I see myself in the glass) leans one elbow on the
table, and holds in his left hand a glass of old brandy. That is the blow
you have dealt me. I have walked bang into the pillar-box. I reel from
side to side. I put my hands to my head. My hat is off—I have dropped
my stick. I have made an awful ass of myself and am justly laughed at
by any passer-by.

'Lord, how unutterably disgusting life is! What dirty tricks it plays
us, one moment free; the next, this. Here we are among the breadcrumbs
and the stained napkins again. That knife is already congealing with
grease. Disorder, sordidity and corruption surround us. We have been
taking into our mouths the bodies of dead birds. It is with these greasy
crumbs, slobbered over napkins, and little corpses that we have to build.
Always it begins again; always there is the enemy; eyes meeting ours;
fingers twitching ours; the effort waiting. Call the waiter. Pay the bill.
We must pull ourselves up out of our chairs. We must find our coats.
We must go. Must, must, must—detestable word. Once more, I who
had thought myself immune, who had said, "Now I am rid of all that",
find that the wave has tumbled me over, head over heels, scattering my
possessions, leaving me to collect, to assemble, to heap together,
summon my forces, rise and confront the enemy.

'It is strange that we, who are capable of so much suffering, should
inflict so much suffering. Strange that the face of a person whom I
scarcely know save that I think we met once on the gangway of a ship
bound for Africa—a mere adumbration of eyes, cheeks, nostrils—should
have power to inflict this insult. You look, eat, smile, are bored, pleased,
annoyed—that is all I know. Yet this shadow which has sat by me for
an hour or two, this mask from which peep two eyes, has power to drive
me back, to pinion me down among all those other faces, to shut me in
a hot room; to send me dashing like a moth from candle to candle.

'But wait. While they add up the bill behind the screen, wait one
moment. Now that I have reviled you for the blow that sent me
staggering among peelings and crumblings and old scraps of meat, I
will record in words of one syllable how also under your gaze with that
compulsion on me I begin to perceive this, that and the other. The clock
ticks; the woman sneezes; the waiter comes—there is a gradual coming
together, running into one, acceleration and unification. Listen: a whistle
sounds, wheels rush, the door creaks on its hinges. I regain the sense of

the complexity and the reality and the struggle, for which I thank you. And with some pity, some envy and much good will, take your hand and bid you good-night.

'Heaven be praised for solitude! I am alone now. That almost unknown person has gone, to catch some train, to take some cab, to go to some place or person whom I do not know. The face looking at me has gone. The pressure is removed. Here are empty coffee-cups. Here are chairs turned but nobody sits on them. Here are empty tables and nobody any more coming to dine at them tonight.

'Let me now raise my song of glory. Heaven be praised for solitude. Let me be alone. Let me cast and throw away this veil of being, this cloud that changes with the least breath, night and day, and all night and all day. While I sat here I have been changing. I have watched the sky change. I have seen clouds cover the stars, then free the stars, then cover the stars again. Now I look at their changing no more. Now no one sees me and I change no more. Heaven be praised for solitude that has removed the pressure of the eye, the solicitation of the body, and all need of lies and phrases.

'My book, stuffed with phrases, has dropped to the floor. It lies under the table, to be swept up by the charwoman when she comes wearily at dawn looking for scraps of paper, old tram tickets, and here and there a note screwed into a ball and left with the litter to be swept up. What is the phrase for the moon? And the phrase for love? By what name are we to call death? I do not know. I need a little language such as lovers use, words of one syllable such as children speak when they come into the room and find their mother sewing and pick up some scrap of bright wool, a feather, or a shred of chintz. I need a howl; a cry. When the storm crosses the marsh and sweeps over me where I lie in the ditch unregarded I need no words. Nothing neat. Nothing that comes down with all its feet on the floor. None of those resonances and lovely echoes that break and chime from nerve to nerve in our breasts, making wild music, false phrases. I have done with phrases.

'How much better is silence; the coffee-cup, the table. How much better to sit by myself like the solitary sea-bird that opens its wings on the stake. Let me sit here for ever with bare things, this coffee-cup, this knife, this fork, things in themselves, myself being myself. Do not come and worry me with your hints that it is time to shut the shop and be gone. I would willingly give all my money that you should not disturb me but let me sit on and on, silent, alone.

'But now the head waiter, who has finished his own meal, appears and frowns; he takes his muffler from his pocket and ostentatiously makes ready to go. They must go; must put up the shutters, must fold the table-cloths, and give one brush with a wet mop under the tables.

'Curse you then. However beat and done with it all I am, I must haul myself up, and find the particular coat that belongs to me; must push my arms into the sleeves; must muffle myself up against the night air and be off. I, I, I, tired as I am, spent as I am, and almost worn out with all this rubbing of my nose along the surfaces of things, even I, an elderly man who is getting rather heavy and dislikes exertion, must take myself off and catch some last train.

'Again I see before me the usual street. The canopy of civilization is burnt out. The sky is dark as polished whale-bone. But there is a kindling in the sky whether of lamplight or of dawn. There is a stir of some sort—sparrows on plane tree somewhere chirping. There is a sense of the break of day. I will not call it dawn. What is dawn in the city to an elderly man standing in the street looking up rather dizzily at the sky? Dawn is some sort of whitening of the sky; some sort of renewal. Another day; another Friday; another twentieth of March, January, or September. Another general awakening. The stars draw back and are extinguished. The bars deepen themselves between the waves. The film of mist thickens on the fields. A redness gathers on the roses, even on the pale rose that hangs by the bedroom window. A bird chirps. Cottagers light their early candles. Yes, this is the eternal renewal, the incessant rise and fall and fall and rise again.

'And in me too the wave rises. It swells; it arches its back. I am aware once more of a new desire, something rising beneath me like the proud horse whose rider first spurs and then pulls him back. What enemy do we now perceive advancing against us, you whom I ride now, as we stand pawing this stretch of pavement? It is death. Death is the enemy. It is death against whom I ride with my spear couched and my hair flying back like a young man's, like Percival's, when he galloped in India. I strike spurs into my horse. Against you I will fling myself, unvanquished and unyielding, O Death!'

The waves broke on the shore.

THE END

OXFORD

MORE OXFORD PAPERBACKS

This book is just one of nearly 1000 Oxford Paperbacks currently in print. If you would like details of other Oxford Paperbacks, including titles in the World's Classics, Oxford Reference, Oxford Books, OPUS, Past Masters, Oxford Authors, and Oxford Shakespeare series, please write to:

UK and Europe: Oxford Paperbacks Publicity Manager, Arts and Reference Publicity Department, Oxford University Press, Walton Street, Oxford OX2 6DP.

Customers in UK and Europe will find Oxford Paperbacks available in all good bookshops. But in case of difficulty please send orders to the Cash-with-Order Department, Oxford University Press Distribution Services, Saxon Way West, Corby, Northants NN18 9ES. Tel: 01536 741519; Fax: 01536 746337. Please send a cheque for the total cost of the books, plus £1.75 postage and packing for orders under £20; £2.75 for orders over £20. Customers outside the UK should add 10% of the cost of the books for postage and packing.

USA: Oxford Paperbacks Marketing Manager, Oxford University Press, Inc., 200 Madison Avenue, New York, N.Y. 10016.

Canada: Trade Department, Oxford University Press, 70 Wynford Drive, Don Mills, Ontario M3C 1J9.

Australia: Trade Marketing Manager, Oxford University Press, G.P.O. Box 2784Y, Melbourne 3001, Victoria.

South Africa: Oxford University Press, P.O. Box 1141, Cape Town 8000.

ANTHONY TROLLOPE IN THE
WORLD'S CLASSICS

THE THREE CLERKS

Anthony Trollope

**Edited with an Introduction by
Graham Handley**

The Three Clerks is Trollope's first important and
incisive commentary on the contemporary scene.
Set in the 1850s, it satirizes the recently instituted
Civil Service examinations and financial corruption
in dealings on the stock market.

The story of the three clerks and the three sisters
who become their wives shows Trollope probing
and exposing relationships with natural sympathy
and insight before the fuller triumphs of Barchester,
the political novels, and *The Way We Live* Now.
The novel is imbued with autobiographical warmth
and immediacy, the ironic appraisal of politics and
society deftly balanced by romantic and domestic
pathos and tribulation. The unscrupulous wheeling
and dealing of Undy Scott is colourfully offset by the
first appearance in Trollope's fiction of the bullying,
eccentric, and compelling lawyer Mr Chaffanbrass.

The text is that of the single-volume edition of
1859, and an appendix gives the most important
cuts that Trollope made for that edition.

OXFORD POETS
A PORTER SELECTED
Peter Porter

This selection of about one hundred of Porter's best poems is chosen from all his works to date, including his latest book, *Possible Worlds*, and *The Automatic Oracle*, which won the 1988 Whitbread Prize for Poetry.

What the critics have said about Peter Porter:

'I can't think of any contemporary poet who is so consistently entertaining over such a variety of material.' John Lucas, *New Statesman*

'an immensely fertile, lively, informed, honest and penetrating mind.' Stephen Spender, *Observer*

'He writes vigorously, with savage erudition and wonderful expansiveness . . . No one now writing matches Porter's profoundly moral and cultured overview.' Douglas Dunn, *Punch*

PHILOSOPHY IN OXFORD PAPERBACKS
THE GREAT PHILOSOPHERS
Bryan Magee

Beginning with the death of Socrates in 399, and following the story through the centuries to recent figures such as Bertrand Russell and Wittgenstein, Bryan Magee and fifteen contemporary writers and philosophers provide an accessible and exciting introduction to Western philosophy and its greatest thinkers.

Bryan Magee in conversation with:

A. J. Ayer	John Passmore
Michael Ayers	Anthony Quinton
Miles Burnyeat	John Searle
Frederick Copleston	Peter Singer
Hubert Dreyfus	J. P. Stern
Anthony Kenny	Geoffrey Warnock
Sidney Morgenbesser	Bernard Williams
Martha Nussbaum	

'Magee is to be congratulated . . . anyone who sees the programmes or reads the book will be left in no danger of believing philosophical thinking is un-practical and uninteresting.' Ronald Hayman, *Times Educational Supplement*

'one of the liveliest, fast-paced introductions to philosophy, ancient and modern that one could wish for' *Universe*

WORLD'S CLASSICS SHAKESPEARE

'*not simply a better text but a new conception of Shakespeare. This is a major achievement of twentieth-century scholarship.*' Times Literary Supplement

Hamlet

Macbeth

The Merchant of Venice

As You Like It

Henry IV Part I

Henry V

Measure for Measure

The Tempest

Much Ado About Nothing

All's Well that Ends Well

Love's Labours Lost

The Merry Wives of Windsor

The Taming of the Shrew

Titus Andronicus

Troilus & Cressida

The Two Noble Kinsmen

King John

Julius Caesar

Coriolanus

Anthony & Cleopatra

OXFORD POPULAR FICTION
THE ORIGINAL MILLION SELLERS!

This series boasts some of the most talked-about works of British and US fiction of the last 150 years—books that helped define the literary styles and genres of crime, historical fiction, romance, adventure, and social comedy, which modern readers enjoy.

Riders of the Purple Sage	Zane Grey
The Four Just Men	Edgar Wallace
Trilby	George Du Maurier
Trent's Last Case	E C Bentley
The Riddle of the Sands	Erskine Childers
Under Two Flags	Ouida
The Lost World	Arthur Conan Doyle
The Woman Who Did	Grant Allen

Forthcoming in October:

Olive	Dinah Craik
The Diary of a Nobody	George and Weedon Grossmith
The Lodger	Belloc Lowndes
The Wrong Box	Robert Louis Stevenson

ILLUSTRATED HISTORIES IN
OXFORD PAPERBACKS

THE OXFORD ILLUSTRATED HISTORY
OF ENGLISH LITERATURE

Edited by Pat Rogers

Britain possesses a literary heritage which is almost unrivalled in the Western world. In this volume, the richness, diversity, and continuity of that tradition are explored by a group of Britain's foremost literary scholars.

Chapter by chapter the authors trace the history of English literature, from its first stirrings in Anglo-Saxon poetry to the present day. At its heart towers the figure of Shakespeare, who is accorded a special chapter to himself. Other major figures such as Chaucer, Milton, Donne, Wordsworth, Dickens, Eliot, and Auden are treated in depth, and the story is brought up to date with discussion of living authors such as Seamus Heaney and Edward Bond.

'[a] lovely volume . . . put in your thumb and pull out plums' Michael Foot

'scholarly and enthusiastic people have written inspiring essays that induce an eagerness in their readers to return to the writers they admire' *Economist*

OXFORD REFERENCE
THE CONCISE OXFORD COMPANION TO ENGLISH LITERATURE

Edited by Margaret Drabble and Jenny Stringer

Based on the immensely popular fifth edition of the *Oxford Companion to English Literature* this is an indispensable, compact guide to the central matter of English literature.

There are more than 5,000 entries on the lives and works of authors, poets, playwrights, essayists, philosophers, and historians; plot summaries of novels and plays; literary movements; fictional characters; legends; theatres; periodicals; and much more.

The book's sharpened focus on the English literature of the British Isles makes it especially convenient to use, but there is still generous coverage of the literature of other countries and of other disciplines which have influenced or been influenced by English literature.

From reviews of *The Oxford Companion to English Literature*:

'a book which one turns to with constant pleasure . . . a book with much style and little prejudice' Iain Gilchrist, *TLS*

'it is quite difficult to imagine, in this genre, a more useful publication' Frank Kermode, *London Review of Books*

'incarnates a living sense of tradition . . . sensitive not to fashion merely but to the spirit of the age' Christopher Ricks, *Sunday Times*